Kate Elliott lives in Pennsylvania with her husband and three children. In addition to the Crown of Stars epic fantasy series, she has collaborated with Melanie Rawn and Jennifer Roberson on *The Golden Key*.

By Kate Elliott

CROWN OF STARS
King's Dragon
Prince of Dogs
The Burning Stone
Child of Flame

CHILD OF FLAME

Volume Four of
CROWN OF STARS

Kate Elliott

orbit

An *Orbit* Book

First published in Great Britain by Orbit 2000
This edition published by Orbit 2001

Copyright © 2000 by Katrina Elliott

The moral right of the author has been asserted.

*All characters in this publication are fictitious and any resemblance
to real persons, living or dead, is purely coincidental.*

A CIP catalogue record for this book
is available from the British Library.

ISBN 1 84149 039 3

Typeset in Garamond by M Rules
Printed and bound in Great Britain by
Mackays of Chatham plc, Chatham, Kent

Orbit
A Division of
Little, Brown and Company (UK)
Brettenham House
Lancaster Place
London WC2E 7EN

AUTHOR'S NOTE

The material that makes up the *Crown of Stars* series was originally intended to be a trilogy with a sequel trilogy to follow. As so often happens in writing, it didn't turn out quite the way I had planned, since once I got started I discovered that I had more plot than I had at first realized.

Some of the material I hoped to use I simply cut and set aside for another time, including one entire subplot that takes place among the Quman tribes.

The rest comprises a single series now made up of five (or six) volumes which turned out to be the best way to organize the volumes so that I could maintain the quality of the writing as well as keep the publication dates relatively close together. The final volume in the *Crown of Stars* series will be titled "Crown of Stars."

I do, of course, leave open the possibility of returning to the *Crown of Stars* world for a later saga. Some day I hope to tell the story of Kereka, the Quman chieftain's daughter who wants to be a man.

ACKNOWLEDGMENTS

A bad bout of tendinitis caused an unfortunate amount of delay as I worked on this manuscript.

I would like to thank my publishers for their patience, M. J. Kramer for not just once but twice on short notice typing in my hand-scrawled revisions when I could not, and especially my agent Russ Galen for his exceptional support.

As usual, I must thank Jay Silverstein for input and feedback, as well as the usual suspects: Jeanne Reames Zimmerman, Sherwood Smith, M. J. Kramer, Katharine Kerr, Constance Ash, and my editor, Sheila Gilbert. I spent many wonderful and enlightening hours in the National Museum in Copenhagen, Denmark, and you will, I think, see the stamp of those hours in this book. If Adica has any progenitor beyond that of my imagination, it is the Egtved girl.

To my readers: thank you for waiting.

Dedicated to the memory of Arnold Bodtker, 1904–2000.

"It does make a difference as to what we know and believe, and how we live with what we know and believe."

MAP LEGEND

1. Heart's Rest
2. Lavas
3. Autun
4. Gent
5. Osterburg
6. Walburg
7. Darre
8. Handelburg
9. Queens' Grave
10. Cackling Skerries
11. Hefenfelthe
12. Sliesby
13. Novomo
14. Machteburg
    A. Veser River
    B. Oder River
    C. Nysa River
    D. Rhowne River

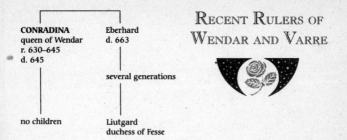

RECENT RULERS OF WENDAR AND VARRE

CONRADINA
queen of Wendar
r. 630–645
d. 645

Eberhard
d. 663

no children

several generations

Liutgard
duchess of Fesse

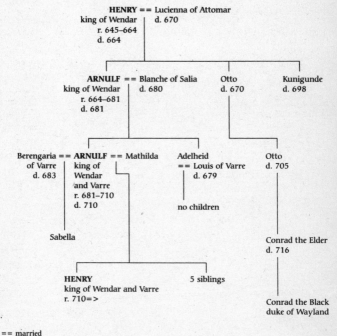

HENRY == Lucienna of Attomar
king of Wendar   d. 670
r. 645–664
d. 664

ARNULF == Blanche of Salia
king of Wendar   d. 680
r. 664–681
d. 681

Otto
d. 670

Kunigunde
d. 698

Berengaria == **ARNULF** == Mathilda
of Varre   king of
d. 683   Wendar
and Varre
r. 681–710
d. 710

Adelheid
== Louis of Varre
d. 679

no children

Otto
d. 705

Sabella

Conrad the Elder
d. 716

HENRY
king of Wendar and Varre
r. 710=>

5 siblings

Conrad the Black
duke of Wayland

== married
r. reigned
d. died

CONTENTS

PROLOGUE

OFF to the southeast, thunder rolled on and on. But in the broad ditch where three youths and two gravely injured soldiers had taken refuge from the battle, the rain had, mercifully, slackened. A wind out of the north blew the clouds away, revealing the waxy light of a full moon.

Ivar listened to the sounds of battle carried by the breeze. They'd scrambled down into the ditch from an embankment above, hoping to escape the notice of their enemies. They hadn't found safety, only a moment's respite, caught as they were behind the enemy's line. The Quman warriors would sweep down from the earthen dike and slaughter them, then cut off their heads to use as belt ornaments. Or, at least, that's what Baldwin seemed to think as he babbled confusedly about Quman soldiers searching the huge tumulus and its twisting embankments, lighting their way with torches.

From his place down in the slippery mud at the bottom of the ditch, Ivar didn't see torches. There was a lambent glow emanating from the crown of the hill, but it didn't look like any torchlight he had ever seen.

Sometimes, when a situation was really bad and there was nothing you could do about it, it was just better not to know.

"Careful," whispered Ermanrich. "This whole end is filled with water. God's mercy! It's like ice."

"Come on, Dedi, come on, lad," coaxed the older of the two wounded Lions to his young companion, but the other man didn't rouse. Probably he was already dead.

Ivar found the water's edge, cupped his hands, and drank. The cold cleared his head for the first time since he had lost his fingers, and finally he could sit back and survey just how bad their predicament was.

Moonlight cast a glamour over the scene. The pool of water had formed up against a steep precipice, the face of the hillside. Over the course of uncounted years a trickling cataract had worn away the cliff face to expose two boulders capped by a lintel stone. Starlight caught and glimmered in one of the stones, revealing a carving half concealed behind tendrils of moss. Ivar negotiated the pool's edge so as not to get his feet wet—not that he wasn't already slopping filthy with mud—and traced the ancient lines: they formed a human figure wearing the antlers of a stag.

"Look!" Baldwin pushed aside the thick curtain of moss draping down over the stones to unveil a tunnel that cut into the hillside.

Their side had lost the battle anyway, and they were cut off from Prince Bayan's retreating army and all their comrades, those who had survived. How could an ancient tumulus be worse than the Quman? Ivar squeezed past the opening, wading in. Cold water poured down into his boots, soaking his leggings and making his toes throb painfully. He couldn't see a thing.

A body brushed against him. "Ivar! Is that you, Ivar?"

"Of course it's me! I heard a rumor that the Quman fear water. Maybe we can hide here, unless this pool gets too deep." The ground seemed firm enough, and the water wasn't deeper than his knees. Plunging his arm into the freezing water, he groped for and found a stone, tossed it. The plop rang hollow. Water dripped steadily ahead of them.

Something living scuffled, deep in the heart of the tumulus.

"What was that?" hissed Baldwin, grabbing Ivar's arm.

"Ow! You're pinching me!"

It was too late. Their voices had already woken the restless dead. A wordless groan echoed through the pitch-black tunnel.

"Oh, God." Ivar clutched at Baldwin's arm. "It's a barrow. We've walked into a burial pit and now we'll be cursed."

But the voice made words they recognized, however distorted they might be by the stone and the drip of water. "Iss i–it you? Iss i–it Ermanrich'ss friendss?"

"L–Lady Hathumod?" stammered Baldwin.

"Ai, t–thank the Lady!" Her relief was evident despite the blurs and echoes. "Poor Ssigfrid wass wounded in the arm and we got losst, and—and I prayed to God to show me a ssign. And then we fell in here. But it'ss dry here where we are, and I think the tunnel goess farther into the hill, but I wass too afraid to go on by ourselvess."

"Now what do we do?" whined Baldwin softly.

"Let's get the others and we'll go as deep as we can into the hill. The Quman will never dare follow us through this water. After a day or two they'll go away, and we can come out."

"Just like that?" demanded Baldwin.

"Just like that. You'll see."

They trudged back to the mossy entrance, where they found Ermanrich shuddering and coughing as he clawed at the moss.

"Ai, God! There you are! I thought you'd been swallowed." He heaved a ragged sigh, then went on in a low voice, making a joke of his fear and relief. "Maybe even the hills think Baldwin is handsome enough to eat, but I don't know what they'd be wanting with an ugly redheaded sot like you, Ivar."

"Dirt is blind, otherwise you'd never get inside. Come on." Ivar waded over to the conscious Lion. "Friend, can you walk?"

"So I can, a bit, lad. But Dedi, here——" The old Lion got suddenly hoarse.

"We'll carry him," said Ivar hastily. "But let's get him out of that mail first. Ermanrich, give me a hand, will you? Baldwin, you help the Lion in, and keep ahead of him in case there's any pits."

"Pits? What if I fall into a bottomless hole?"

"Baldwin, we haven't got time! Here." He found the unconscious Lion's sword sheath. "Take this sword and use it to feel your way forward."

Amazingly, Baldwin obeyed without further objection. He helped the old Lion to his feet and steadied the soldier as he hobbled to the tunnel.

It wasn't easy to get mail off an unconscious man.

"I think he's already dead," Ermanrich whispered several times, but in the end they wrestled him out of his armor.

Nor was it easy to haul him in through the tunnel even without his armor. He was a big man, well muscled, so badly injured that he was a complete dead weight. Luckily, the water did not rise past their thighs before an upward slope brought them shivering out of the water onto dry ground. The weight of the hill pressed above them. Dirt stung Ivar's nostrils, and his mutilated hand burned with pain.

"Thank God," said Baldwin out of the darkness.

Ivar and Ermanrich set down the unconscious soldier, none too gently, and Ivar straightened up so quickly that he banged his head hard against the stone ceiling. The pain made tears flow, and in a way he did want just to sit down and cry because everything had been such a disaster. He really had thought they'd win the battle. Prince Bayan's and Princess Sapientia's troops had looked so magnificent arrayed against the Quman army, and even the dreaded Margrave Judith had ridden out with such a strong host that it seemed impossible that everything had fallen apart, including their line. Prince Ekkehard had vanished in the maelstrom, his companions were scattered or dead, and they were all that was left. Probably they were the last remnant of Bayan's army left on this side of the river: two badly injured soldiers, four novice monks, and one lost nun.

The battle had started very late in the afternoon, and now night settled over them. Two hours at the most separated them from that glorious place where they'd waited at the front of the right flank, ready to sweep into battle. It just didn't seem possible everything had gone wrong so fast.

But meanwhile, someone had to go back to make sure that the Quman hadn't followed them under the hill. Cold, wet, and shivering, Ivar braced himself for the shock of wading back into the water that drowned the lower reaches of the tunnel. His leggings already clung to him like icy leeches, and his toes had gone numb from cold.

A hand snaked out of the darkness to grab at his sleeve. "Are you sure you don't want me to come with you?" Baldwin asked in a hoarse whisper.

"Nay. It's better if I go alone. If something happens to me, it'll take you and Ermanrich and Lady Hathumod to carry the injured Lion."

Baldwin leaned closer. Despite the long weeks of travel in harsh conditions, the terror of a losing battle waged as afternoon gave way to dusk, and the desperation of their scramble over the ancient earthworks, Baldwin's breath was still as sweet as that of a lord sitting in pleasant splendor in his rose garden, drinking a posset of mead flavored with mint. "I'd rather be dead than go on without you."

"We'll all be dead if the Quman find that armor and figure out that we're hiding in this tunnel. Just stay here, Baldwin, I beg you."

Behind, in the stygian blackness, Sigfrid's gentle voice fell and rose in a melismatic prayer. Somehow, the darkness warped time. Hadn't it just been moments ago that they had stumbled upon that hidden opening? It seemed like hours.

Beneath Sigfrid's quiet prayer Ivar heard Hathumod murmuring words he couldn't quite make out. She was answered, in turns, by monosyllabic grunts from the old Lion and whispered questions from Ermanrich. He could not see, not even Baldwin, who stood right next to him. He felt them, though, huddled together like frightened rats under the weight of earth and rock.

He took the unconscious Lion's sword from Baldwin and tested the grip with his good hand, squeezed and relaxed until the leather grip gave enough to fit the curve of his hand. With gritted teeth, he surged forward into the water and shuddered all over again as the tunnel floor plunged down and the icy water enveloped his legs.

With the sword drawn tightly against his left leg, Ivar approached the entrance in relative silence. He smelled the distant stench of the battlefield. Night crows cried far away, alerting their cousins to the banquet. A pebble rolled under his boot, and he grunted softly, balancing himself. The wound on his right hand scraped stone. He caught back a gasp of pain as a hot trickle of blood bled free. Pain stabbed up his hand, and he stumbled forward. The stumps of his missing fingers, shorn off right at the second knuckle, jabbed into a moist tapestry of moss. Tears streamed from his eyes and made salty runnels over his lips. After a while, the pain subsided enough for him to think.

He had reached the entrance. Cautiously, with his good hand, he fingered the tendrils of moss which streaked the crumbling entrance. Behind this curtain he waited, listening. He couldn't see anything, not even the sky. It seemed as dark beyond the curtain concealing the tomb's entrance as it had deep within. The heavy scent of damp and earth and wet moss shrouded his world.

But he could hear the distant murmur of a host moving, hooves, shouts, one poor soul screaming, the detritus of movement that betrays two armies unwinding one from the other as the battle ebbs and dies.

From close by, he heard a grunt, a low breathing mutter.

The sword shifted in his hand before he was aware he had changed his stance. The Lion's discarded armor spoke with that voice granted to all things born of metal: when hands disturbed it, it replied in a chiming voice.

Just as he had feared: a Quman soldier *had* found the discarded armor.

He lunged through the curtain. The Quman soldier had wings curling up above his back where he bent over the mail and helmet. Ivar ducked down to get under the wooden contraption. Just as the other man spun, he thrust. The short sword caught the winged soldier just under his leather-scaled shirt. With his wounded arm he reached out and wrapped his forearm around the man's head and with all his weight pulled him in through the entrance. Wood frames snapped against the lintel as Ivar fell into the water with the Quman landing face first in his lap. The sword drove to the hilt between the enemy's ribs.

Water licked Ivar's lips as he pressed the man down, holding him under. The man twisted one way and then the other, trying to raise his head out of the water, but Ivar countered each movement with a sideways push on the hilt of the sword. Steel grated against bone, causing the warrior to convulse and lose whatever advantage he had gained. His black hair floated like tendrils of moss. Ivar tasted blood in the water. All at once, the Quman went limp.

Ivar shoved the dead man deeper into the pool and staggered to his feet. His body ached from the cold. He dipped a hand in the water to scrub at his face, to wash the taint of blood away, but all around him the pool seemed polluted by the life that had drained into it. He carefully slipped past the moss and found clear water outside.

Lightning streaked the sky, followed by a sharp thunderclap. A voice called out a query. On the earthworks beyond, a man's shape, distorted by wings, reared up against the night sky, questing: another Quman soldier, looking for his comrade. Ivar's position at the base of the ditch, within the shadow of the lintel, veiled him. A moment later the shadow moved on, dropping out of sight behind the earthworks.

A drizzle of rain wet Ivar's cheeks. With a swelling roar, the river raged in the distance like a multitude of voices raised all

at once, but he couldn't see it, nor could he see stars above. A
bead of rain wound down his nose and, suspended from its tip,
hung there for the longest time just as he was suspended,
unwilling to move for fear of giving himself away.

Finally he set down his sword, rolled up the mail shirt,
wrapping it tight with a belt, and looped the helmet strap
over his shoulder. With the sword in his good hand and his
injured hand throbbing badly enough to give him a headache,
he felt his way back under the lintel. Gruesome wings brushed
his nose, one splintered wooden frame scraping his cheek as
feathers tickled his lips. Outside, rain started to fall in earnest.
Thunder muttered in the west. If they were lucky, rain would
obscure the signs of their passage and leave them safe for a day
or two, until the Quman moved on. Then they could sneak out
and make their way northwest, on the trail of Prince Bayan's
and Princess Sapientia's retreating army.

In his heart, he knew it was a foolish hope. The Quman had
scouts and trackers. There was no way a ragged band of seven,
four of them wounded and most of them unable to fight, could
get through the Quman lines. But they had to believe they
could. Otherwise they might as well lie down and die.

Why would they have been granted the vision of the
phoenix if God had meant for them to die in such a pointless
manner?

Baldwin was waiting for him where the tunnel floor sloped
upward and out of the water.

"Come see," said Baldwin sharply. "Gerulf got a fire going."

"Gerulf?"

"That's the old Lion." Baldwin tugged him onward, steadying him when he stumbled. Weariness settled over Ivar's
shoulders. He shivered convulsively, soaked through. He
wanted nothing more than to drop right where he stood and
sleep until death, or the phoenix, came for him. Or maybe one
would bring the other, it was hard to think with the walls
wavering around him.

Strange sigils had been carved into the pale stone, broad

rocks set upright and incised with the symbols of demons and ancient gods who plagued the people of elder days: four-sided lozenges, spirals that had neither beginning nor end, broad expanses of hatching cut into the rock as though straw had been pressed crisscross into the stone.

Yet how could he see at all, deep in the heart of a tomb?

With Baldwin's help, he staggered forward until the tunnel opened into a smoky chamber lit by fire. He stared past his companions, who were huddled around a torch. The chamber was a black pit made eerie by flickering light. He could not see the ceiling, and the walls were lost to shadow. He sneezed.

Just beyond the smoking torch, a stone slab marked the center of the chamber. A queen had been laid to rest here long ago: there lay her bones, a pale skeleton asleep in the torch-light, its hollow-eyed frame woven with strands of rotting fabric and gleaming with precious gold that had fallen around the skull and into the ribs. Gold antlers sprang into sight as Gerulf shifted the torch to better investigate his comrade's wound.

"You shouldn't have lit a fire in a barrow!" cried Ivar, horri-fied. "Everyone knows a fire will wake the unholy dead!"

Frail Sigfrid sat at the unconscious Lion's head, nearest to the burial altar. He looked up with the calm eyes of one who has felt God's miraculous hands heal his body. "Don't fear, Ivar." The voice itself, restored to him by a miracle, was a reproof to Ivar's fear. "God will protect us. This poor dead woman bears us no ill will." He indicated the half-uncovered skeleton, then bent forward as the old Lion spoke to him in a low voice.

But how could Sigfrid tell? Ivar had grown up in the north, where the old gods still swarmed, jealous that the faith of the Unities had stolen so many ripe souls from their grasp. There was no telling what malice lay asleep here, or when it might wake.

Ermanrich and Hathumod sat together, hands clasped in a cousinly embrace. Both had lost a great deal of flesh. How long ago it seemed when the four youths and Hathumod had served together as novices at Quedlinhame, yet truly it wasn't more than a year ago that they had all been cast out of the convent for committing the unforgivable sin of heresy.

Baldwin circled the stone altar and its dead queen, crouching to grasp one of the gold antlers. The light touch jostled the skeleton. Precious amber beads scattered down among the bones, falling in a rush.

"Don't disturb the dead!" hissed Ivar. But Baldwin, eyes wide, reached right in to where strands of desiccated wool rope, whose ends were banded with small greenish-metal rods, curled around the pelvis. His hand closed over a small object, a glint of blue.

"Look!" he cried, with his other hand lifting a stone mirror out of the basin made by her pelvic bones. The polished black surface still gleamed. As Ivar took a panicked step forward to stop Baldwin from further desecration, he saw his movement reflected in that mirror.

"Ai, God, I fear my poor nephew is dead," murmured Gerulf. "I swore to my sister I'd bring him home safely."

Other shadows moved in the depths of the mirror, figures obscured by darkness. They walked out of the alcoves, ancient queens whose eyes had the glint of knives. The first was young, robed in a splendor as bright as burning arrows, but her mouth was cut in a cruel smile. The second had a matron's girth, the generous bulk of a noble lady who never wants for food, and in her arms she carried a basket spilling over with fruit. The third wore her silver hair braided with bones, and the wrinkles in her aged face seemed as deep as clefts in a mountainside. Her raised hands had the texture of cobwebs. Her gaze caught him as in a vise. He could not speak to warn the others, who saw nothing and felt no danger.

Hathumod gasped. "What lies there?" Her words sent ripples through the ghosts as a hand clears away algae from an overgrown pond.

Ivar found his voice. "Baldwin! Put that down, you idiot!"

As Baldwin lowered the mirror in confusion, Hathumod crawled forward. Her hand came to rest on a bundle so clotted with dirt and mold that her hand came away green, and flakes fell everywhere, spinning away to meld with the smoke from the torch. Like Baldwin, she was either a fool or insensible. She groped at the bundle, found a faded leather pouch that actually crumbled to dust in her hands, leaving nothing in her cupped fingers except, strangely, a nail marked by rusting stains.

She began to weep just as Gerulf shook loose the rotting garments: a rusted mail shirt that half fell apart in his hands, a knife, a decaying leather belt, a plain under-tunic, and a tabard marked with the remains of a black lion. "Some poor comrade of mine must have crawled in here to die many years ago," said the old Lion.

"Who's there?" demanded Sigfrid, throwing his head back as if he'd heard something. Baldwin, still gripping the obsidian mirror, screamed and crumpled forward. On the ground, Gerulf's dead nephew jerked as though a demon had poured itself into him.

The chamber flared with blue light.

Ivar cried out, but he could not hear his own voice. His throat muscles strained as he forced out air. Blue fire blinded him. The ground wrenched under his feet, throwing him sideways, and he tumbled to his knees, but no earth met his outstretched hands. He fell, endlessly, hands grasping at empty air, as the young queen with the knife-edged smile walked toward him over a carpet of brilliant fire with her arms extended as if in welcome. He reached for her, grasping for any lifeline.

Touched her hands.

And knew nothing more.

PART ONE

THE FLOWER
TRAIL

I

THE HALLOWED ONE

1

AT sunset, Adica left the village. The elders bowed respect-fully, but from a safe distance, as she passed. Fathers pulled their children out of her way. Women carrying in sheaves of grain from ripening fields turned their backs on her, so that her gaze might not wither the newly-harvested emmer out of which they would make bread. Even pregnant Weiwara, once her beloved friend, stepped back through the threshold of her family's house in order to shelter her hugely pregnant belly from Adica's sight.

The villagers looked at her differently now. In truth, they no longer looked at her at all, never directly in the face, now that the Holy One had proclaimed Adica's duty, and her doom.

Even the dogs slunk away when she walked by.

She passed through the open stockade gate and negotiated the plank bridge thrown over the ditch that ringed the village. The sun's light washed the clouds with a pale purplish pink as delicate as flax in flower. Fields flowered gold along the river plain, dotted here and there with the tumbled forms of the grandmothers' old houses, now abandoned for the safety of the new village. The grandmothers had not lived in constant fear as people did these days.

When she reached the outer ditch, she raised her staff three times and said a blessing over the village. Then she walked on.

By the river three men bent over the weir. One straightened, seeing her, and she recognized Beor's broad shoulders and the distinctive way he had of tilting up his chin when he was angry.

How Beor had protested and complained when the elders had decreed that they two could no longer live together as mates! Yet his company had never been restful. He had won the right to claim her as his mate on the day the elders had agreed to name him as war captain for the village because of his conspicuous bravery in the war against the Cursed Ones. But had the law governing her as Hallowed One of the village granted her the right to claim a mate of her own choice, he was not the one she would have picked. In a way, it was a relief to be rid of him.

Yet, as days and months passed, she missed the warmth of his body at night.

Beor made a movement as if to walk over to catch her, but his companion stopped him by placing a hand on his chest. Adica continued down the path alone.

She climbed the massive tumulus alone, following the path up through the labyrinthine earthworks. As the Hallowed One who protected the village, she had walked here many times but never in as great a solitude as that she felt now.

Nothing grew yet on the freshly raised ramparts except young sow-thistles, leaves still tender enough to eat. Far below, tall grass and unharvested grain rippled like the river, stirred by a breeze lifting off the sun as it sank into the land of the dead.

The ground ramped up under her feet, still smooth from the passage of so many logs used as rollers to get the stones up to the sacred circle at the height of the hill. She passed up a narrow causeway between two huge ramparts of earth and came out onto the level field that marked the highest ground. Here stood the circle of seven stones, raised during the life of Adica's teacher. Here, to the east of the stone circle, three old foundations marked an ancient settlement. According to her teacher, these fallen stone foundations marked the halls of the long-dead queens, Arrow Bright, Golden Sow, and Toothless, whose magic had raised the great womb of this tumulus and whose bones and treasures lay hidden in the swelling belly of the earth below.

Midway between the earthen gates and the stone loom, where the westering sun could draw its last light across the threshold, Adica had erected a shelter out of hides and poles. In such primitive shelter all humankind had lived long ago before the days when the great queens and their hallowed women had stolen the magic of seed, clay, and bronze from the southerners, before the Cursed Ones had come to take them as slaves and as sacrifices.

She made her prayers, so familiar that she could speak them without thinking, and sprinkled the last of her ale to the four directions: north, east, south, and west. After leaning her staff against the lintel of slender birch poles, she clapped her wrists together three times. The copper bracelets that marked her status as a Hallowed One chimed softly, the final ring of prayer, calling down the night. The sun slid below the horizon. She crawled in across the threshold. Inside the tent she untied her string skirt, slipped off her bodice, and lay them inside the stout cedar chest where she stored all her belongings. Finally, she wrapped herself in the furs that were now her only company at night.

Once she had lived like the rest of her people, in a house in the village, breathing in the community of a life lived together. Of course, her house in the village had been ringed with charms, and no one but her mate or those of her womb kin might enter it for fear of the powers that lay coiled in the shadows and in the eaves, but she had still been able to hear the cattle lowing in their byres in the evening and the delighted cries of the children leaping up to play at dawn. Any village where a Hallowed One lived always had good luck and good harvests.

But ever since the Holy One's proclamation, she could no longer sleep in the village for fear her dreaming self might entice reckless or evil spirits in among the houses. Spirits could smell death; everyone knew that. They could smell death on her. They swarmed where fate lay heaviest.

Death's shadow had touched her, so the villagers feared that any person she touched might be poisoned by death's kiss as well.

She said the night prayer to the Pale Hunter and lay still until sleep called her, but sleep brought no respite. Tossing and turning, she dreamed of standing alone and small in a blinding wind as death came for her.

Could the great weaving possibly succeed? Or would it all be for naught, despite everything?

She woke, twisted in her sleeping furs, thinking of Beor, whom she had once called husband. She had dreamed the same dream for seven nights running. Yet it wasn't the death in the dream that scared her, that made her wake up sweating.

She rested her forehead on fisted hands. "I pray to you, Fat One, who is merciful to her children, let there be a companion for me. I do not fear death as long as I do not have to walk the long road into darkness all by myself."

A wind came up. The charms tied to the poles holding up the shelter rang with their gentle voices. More distantly, she heard the bronze leaves of the sacred cauldron ting and clack where the breeze ran through them. Then the wind died. It was so quiet that she thought perhaps she could hear the respiration of stars as they breathed.

She slipped outside. Cool night air pooled over her skin. Above, the stars shone in splendor. The waxing horned moon had already set. The Serpent's Eye and the Dragon's Eye blazed overhead, harbingers of power. The Grindstone was setting.

Was it a sign? The setting constellation called The Grindstone would lead her to Falling-down's home and, when evening came, the rising Grindstone, with the aid of the Bounteous One, the wandering daughter of the Fat One, could pull her home again. The Fat One often spoke in riddles or by misdirection, and perhaps this was one of those times. There was one man she often thought of, one man who might be brave enough to walk beside her.

Ducking back inside her shelter, she rummaged through the cedar chest in search of a gift for Falling-down. She settled on an ingot of copper and a pair of elk antlers. Last, she found the amber necklace she had once given to Beor, to seal their agreement, but of course he had been forced by the elders to return it to her. Then she dressed, wrapping her skirt twice around her hips, tugging on her bodice, and hanging her mirror from a loop on her skirt. Setting the gifts in a small basket together with a string of bone beads for a friendship offering to the head-woman of Falling-down's village, she crawled outside. She slung the basket over one shoulder with a rope and hoisted her staff.

A path wound forward between grass to the stone loom. The circle of stones sat in expectant silence, waiting for her to wake them.

She stopped on the calling ground outside the stones, a patch of dust shaded white with a layer of chalk that gleamed under starlight. Here, she set her feet.

Lifting the mirror, she began the prayers to waken the stones:

> *"Heed me, that which opens in the east.*
> *Heed me, that which opens in the west.*
> *I pray to you, Fat One, let me spread the warp of your*
> *heavenly weaving so that I can walk through the passage*
> *made by its breath."*

She shifted the mirror until the light of the stars that made up the Grindstone caught in its polished surface. Reflected by the mirror, the terrible power of the stars would not burn her. With her staff she threaded that reflected light into the loom of the stones and wove herself a living passageway out of starlight and stone. Through the soles of her feet she felt the keening of the ancient queens, who had divined in the vast loom of the stars a secret of magic that not even the Cursed Ones had knowledge of. Threads of starlight caught in the stones and tangled, an architecture formed of insubstantial light woven into a bright gateway. She stepped through into rain. Her feet squished on sodden ground, streaking the grass with the last traces of chalk. The air steamed with moisture, hot and heavy. Rain poured down. She bumped up against a standing stone, her shoulder cushioned by a dense growth of moss grown up along the stone.

It was, obviously, impossible to see any stars. Nor could she see the path. But Falling-down had built a shelter nearby, and she stumbled around in darkness until she bumped up against its thatched roof. A hummock of straw that stank of mold made a damp seat. While she waited, she worked her part of the pattern of the great working in her mind's eye over again. She could never practice enough the precise unfolding of the ritual that would, after generations of war, allow those who suffered under the plague of the Cursed Ones to strike back.

As the day rose, the rain slackened. She walked down the hillock on a trail so wet that her feet got soaked while her shoulders remained dry. Fens stretched out around her, glum sheets of standing water separated by small islands and dense patches of reeds.

Falling-down's people had built a track across the fens, hazel shoots cut, split, and woven together to make a springy panel on which people could walk above the marshy ground. As she walked along the track, the clouds began to break up, and the sun came out. On a distant hummock, a silhouette appeared. A person called out a "halloo" to her, and she lifted a hand in reply but did not pause. It was easily a morning's walk to the hills at the edge of the fens, where Falling-down and his tribe made their home.

Birds sang. She paused once to eat the curds she had brought with her; once she waded off the track to pick berries. Grebes and ducks paddled through shallow waters. A flock of swans glided majestically past. A heron waited in solitary splendor, queenly and proud. It stirred suddenly and took wing with great, slow flaps. A moment later she heard a distant trumpeting call, and she hunkered down on the track and watched silently as a huge winged shape passed along the horizon far to the south and then vanished: a guivre on the hunt.

At last the track gave out onto dry land that sloped upward to become hills. Abandoned fields overgrown with weeds gave way to fields ripe with barley and emmer. Women and men labored with flint sickles harvesting one long strip of emmer. A few noticed her and called to the others, and they all stopped to watch her. A man blew into a small horn, alerting the village above.

Soon she had an escort of children, all of them jabbering in their incomprehensible language, as she walked up to the scatter of houses that marked the village. On the slopes above lay more fields and then forest.

It was still hot and humid, the fever days of late summer. Sweat trickled down her back as she came among the houses. Two women coiled clay into pots while a third smoothed the coils into a flat surface on which she spread a fine paste of paler clay. A finished pot, still unfired, sat beside her, stamped with the imprint of a braided cord. Four men scraped hides. Two half-grown boys toiled up the slope carrying water in bark buckets.

The headwoman of the village emerged from her house. Adica offered her the bead necklace from the north country, a proper meeting gift that would not disgrace her tribe, and in return the headwoman had a girl bring warm potage flavored with coriander and a thick honey mead. Then she was given leave, by means of certain familiar gestures, to continue on up the slope to the house of Falling-down, the tribe's conjuring man.

As she had hoped, he was not alone.

Falling-down was so old that all his hair was white. He claimed to have celebrated the Festival of the Sun sixty-two times, but Adica could not really believe that he could have seen that many festivals, much less counted them all. He sat cross-legged, carving a fishing spear out of bone. Because he was a conjuring man, the Hallowed One of his tribe, he put magic into the spear by carving ospreys and long-necked herons along the blade to give the tool a bird's success in hunting fish. He whistled under his breath as he worked, a spell that wound itself into the making.

Dorren sat at Falling-down's right hand. He taught a counting game to a handful of children hunkered down around the pebbles he tossed with his good hand out of a leather cup. Adica paused just behind the ragged half circle of children and watched Dorren.

Dorren looked up at once, sensing her. He smiled, sent the children away, and got to his feet, holding out his good hand in the greeting of cousins. She reached for him, then hesitated, and dropped her hand without touching him. His withered hand stirred, as if he meant to move it, but he smiled sadly and gestured toward Falling-down, who remained intent on his carving.

"None thought to see you here," Dorren said, stepping aside so that Falling-down wouldn't be distracted from his spell by their conversation.

Faced with Dorren, she didn't know what to say. Her cheeks felt hot. She was a fool, truly. But he was glad to see her, wasn't he? Dorren was a White Deer man from Old Fort who had been chosen as a Walking One of the White Deer tribe, those who traveled the stone looms to learn the speech of their allies. As Walking One, he received certain protections against magic.

"I heard that Beor made trouble for you in your village," he said finally while she played nervously with one of her copper bracelets. "You endured him a long time. It isn't easy for a woman and a man to live together when they don't have temperaments to match."

He had such gentle eyes. With the withered hand, he had never been able to hunt and swim like other children, but he had grown up healthy and strong and was valued for his cleverness and patience. That was why he had been chosen as Walking One. He had so many qualities that Beor so brazenly lacked.

"Some seem better suited than others," he went on. Surely he guessed that she had watched him from afar for a long time.

Her heart pounded erratically. Remarkably, his steady gaze, on her, did not waver, although he must have heard by now about the doom pronounced over her and the other six Hallowed Ones. Seeing his courage, she knew the Fat One had guided her well.

He began anew, stammered to a halt, then spoke. "It must seem to you that the days pass swiftly. I have meant to tell you—" He broke off, blushing, as he glanced at the path which led to the village. A few children loitering at the head of the path scattered into the woodland, shrieking and giggling.

"There's a woman here," he said finally, in a rush, cheeks pink with emotion. "Her name is Wren, daughter of Red Belly and Laughing. She's like running water to me, always a blessing. Now she says that I had the man's part in the making of the child she's growing in her belly. The tribe elders agreed that if I work seven seasons of labor for them, then I can be named as the child's father and share a house in the village with her."

She couldn't imagine what he saw in her expression, but he went on quickly, leaping from what he knew to what he thought. Each word made her more sick at heart and more humiliated.

"You needn't think I'll shirk my duties as Walking One. I know what's due to my people. But there's no reason I can't do both. I can still walk the looms *and* labor here, for she's a good woman, is Wren, and I love her."

Horribly, she began to cry, silent tears washing down her face although she wanted anything but to be seen crying.

"Adica! Yours is the most generous of hearts, and the bravest! I knew you would be happy for me despite your own sorrow!" Glancing toward Falling-down, he frowned in the way of someone thinking through a decision that's been troubling him. "Now, listen, for you know how dear to me you are in my heart, Adica. I know it's ill luck to speak of it, that it's tempting the spirits, but I wanted you to know that if the child is born a girl and she lives and is healthy, we'll call her after you. Your name will live on, not just in the songs of the tribe but in my child."

"I am happy for your good fortune," said Adica hoarsely through her tears.

"Adica!" Falling-down spoke her name sharply as he looked up from the fishing spear, his attention caught by her lie.

She fled.

Falling-down could see into her secret heart because of the link that bound them when they worked the weaving together, and anyway, she hadn't truly come to see him. She had hoped a wild and irresponsible hope, she'd turned the night wind into a false riddle, and now she'd spent her magic and her time on a fool's journey, a selfish detour. She was ashamed.

She ran down through the woodland, not wanting to be seen in the village. Dorren yelled after her, but she ignored him. She came down to the shore of the fens and splashed out through the cranberry bog. Berries shone deeply red along the water, almost ripe. She got wet to the thighs but managed to get out to the track without meeting anyone except a boy trolling for fish with hook and line. Farther out on the track, two women hauling a net out of the water called to her, but she couldn't understand their words. It seemed to her that all of human intercourse was slowly receding from her, one link severed, another warm hand torn from her grasp, one by one, until she would face the great working alone except for the other six, Falling-down, Two Fingers, Shu-Sha, Spits-last, Horn, and Brightness-Hears-Me. They were a tribe unto themselves now: the ones severed from the rest of humankind. They were the sacrifice through which the human tribes would be freed from fear.

The clouds broke up, and by the time she reached the island of the stone loom, she had only a short while to wait for sunset. Whatever Falling-down might have thought of her behavior, he was too old to walk out here on a whim. He would not follow and importune her with embarrassing questions. Would Dorren follow her? Did she want him to now that she knew he would find happiness with someone else while she remained alone? Not that she begrudged him happiness, not at all. She had hoped, in the end, for a little for herself as well.

But twilight came, and she remained alone. As always, the working had slipped the course of days around her. By the position of the Bounteous One in the sky, she guessed that she had lost two days in the last passage, although it had seemed like only one instant to her.

That was the price those who walked the looms paid: that days and sometimes months were ripped from them when they stepped onto the passageways that led between the looms. But perhaps it was better to lose a day or three of loneliness.

The stone loom, seven stones set in an oblique circle, awaited her as darkness fell and the first stars appeared in the sky. She lifted her mirror and caught the light of the Bounteous One, the nimble-fingered Lady of Grain and Jars, and wove herself a passageway back to her own place. Stepping through, her feet touched familiar ground, firm and dry, untouched by recent rain. She walked slowly to her shelter and put away the gifts she had not given to Falling-down.

From the village below she heard voices raised in song. It took her a moment to recall that Mother Orla's eldest grand-daughter had recently crossed the threshold that brought her

to the women's mysteries and would by now be emerging
from the women's house, ready to take her place as an adult in
the village.

She stood on the ramparts listening to their laughter and
the old familiar melodies. Before, the villagers would have
wanted her there to hallow the celebration, but now her presence would only make them uncomfortable. What if evil
spirits wiggled in, in her wake, and poisoned the new young
woman's happiness just as such spirits sometimes poisoned
sweet wells or fresh meat? The villagers' fear outweighed their
affection.

Why had the gods let the Cursed Ones afflict humankind?
Couldn't they have chosen a different way for humankind to
rid themselves of their enemy? Was it so impossible that she
be allowed some happiness as mate with a man like Dorren,
with his withered hand and gentle heart? Why was it the
Hallowed Ones who had to make the sacrifice?

But she shook her head, impatient with such thoughts,
borne to her on the night wind by mischievous spirits. With
a little spell, spoken out loud, then sealed by the touch of
pungent mint to her lips, she chased them away.

Only the Hallowed Ones possessed the magic to do what
was necessary. So it had fallen to her, and to the others.

She had been called down this path as a child. She had never
known nor wanted any other life than that of Hallowed One.
She had just never expected that her duty would be so harsh.

Sleeping, that night, she did not dream.

2

SHE woke abruptly, hearing the call of an owl. By the smell
of dew and the distant song of birds in the woodland, she recognized the twilight before dawn when the sun lies in wait
like a golden-eared bear ready to lumber over the horizon.

The owl called again, a deep *to-whit to-whoo*.

She scrambled up. After dressing, she opened the cedar chest to get out her sacred regalia. A hammered bronze waistband incised with spirals fit around her midriff. She slipped on the amber necklace she had hoped to give to Dorren: amber held power from the ancient days, and her teacher had told her always to emphasize her tribe's power and success when it came time to meet with their allies. She set her hematite mirror on her knees before carefully unwrapping the gold headdress from its linen shroud. The headring molded easily over her hair. Its antlers brushed the curved ceiling before she ducked down in a reflexive prayer.

"Let your power walk with me, Pale Hunter, you who are Queen of the Wild."

Tucking the mirror into her midriff, she crawled backward out of the tent on her hands and knees. Outside, she straightened to stand as tall as a stag, antlers gleaming, the gold so bright she almost thought she could see its outlines echoed against the sky. Clothed in power, she walked the path that led into the stones.

At the center of the stone loom lay the step stone, as broad across as her outflung arms but no higher than her knee. The sacred cauldron rested on the slab, as it had since her teacher's youth. Here, years ago, Adica had knelt to receive the kiss of power from the woman who had taught her almost everything she knew. She wept a little as she said a prayer in memory of the dead. Afterward, she touched the holy birds engraved on the cauldron's mellow bronze surface and named them: Father Heron, Mother Crane, Grandmother Raven, and Uncle Duck. She kissed each precious bronze leaf, and with one hand skimmed a mouthful of water out of the cauldron and sipped at it, then spoke a blessing over what remained in her palm and tossed it into the air, to seed the wind.

Kneeling before the cauldron, she waited with eyes closed as she breathed in the smell of dawn and heard its sounds: the distant roll of the lazy harvest river, the disgruntled baaing of goats, the many voices of the morning birds calling out their greetings to the waiting sun.

She heard the flutter of wings and felt the owl settle on the rim of the cauldron, but she dared not look up, for the Holy One's messenger was a powerful creature full of so much magical force that even a glimpse of it could be fatal. A moment later hooves rang down a distant path of stone, then struck on a needle-strewn path, and finally the waist-high flax rustled as a large body passed through it. The warm breath of the Holy One brushed the hairs on the back of her neck. Her gold antlers stirred in the sweet wind of the Holy One's presence.

"You have been crying, Adica." Her voice was like the melody of the river, high and low at the same time. "I can smell the salt of your tears."

Hadn't they dried over the night? Yet surely it was impossible to hide anything from a shaman of the Horse people. "I have been lonely, Holy One. The road I walk is a solitary one."

"Haven't you a husband? I remember that you were not pleased when the elders of your village decreed that you should marry him."

"They have taken him away, Holy One. Because death has lain its shadow over me, they fear that any person I touch will be touched by death as well."

"Truly, there is wisdom in what they say."

There was silence except for the wind and the throaty coo of a wood pigeon.

She glanced up to see the land opening up before her as the sun burned the mist off the river. Swifts dived and dipped along the slow current. People already worked out in the fields, harvesting barley and emmer. A girl drove goats past the fields toward the woodland.

The words slipped from her before she knew she meant to say them. "If only I had a companion, Holy One, then the task wouldn't seem so hard. Of course I will not falter, but—I'll be alone for so long, waiting for the end." She bit back the other words that threatened to wash free, borne up on a tide of loneliness and fear. "I beg you, Holy One, forgive my rash words. I know my duty."

"Alas, daughter, your duty is a hard one. Yet there must be seven who will stand when the time comes. Thus are you chosen."

"Yes, Holy One," she whispered.

Unlike the villagers she watched over, Adica had seen and spoken with people from distant lands. She knew that the land was broad and people few, and true humans fewer still. In the west lay fecund towns of fully fifty or more houses. The gray northern seas were icy and windswept, cold enough to drain the life from any human who tried to swim in them, yet in those icy waters lived sea people with hair composed of eels and teeth as sharp as obsidian. She had seen, far to the east, the forests of grass where lived the Holy One's tribe, cousins to humankind and yet utterly different. She had even glimpsed the endless deserts of the southern tribes, where the people spoke as if they rolled stones in their mouths. She had seen the Cursed Ones' fabled cities. She had seen their wondrous ships and barely escaped to tell of it. She had seen the Cursed Ones enslave villages and innocent tribes only to make their captives bow low before their bloodthirsty gods. She had seen what had happened to her teacher, who had joined the fight against the Cursed Ones only to be sacrificed on their altars.

"We are all slaves of the Cursed Ones, as long as the war they wage against us never ends." The Holy One shifted, hooves changing weight as she backed up and then came forward again, the unseen weight of her massive body looming behind Adica. Once, when she was a child, Adica had seen the Holy One's people catch up to and trample the last remnants of a scouting party of the Cursed Ones, and she had never lost that simple child's awe of their size and power. As much as she feared the Cursed Ones' magic, she was glad to be an ally of the Horse people, the ones who had been born out of the mating of a mare and a human man.

"Yet perhaps—" The Holy One hesitated. In that pause, hope whispered in Adica's heart, but she was afraid to listen. "Perhaps there is a way to find one already touched by the hand of death who might be your companion. That way you would not be alone, and he would not be poisoned by your fate. You are youngest of the chosen ones, Adica. The others have lived long lives. You were meant to follow after your teacher, not to stand in her place at the great weaving. It is not surprising that you find it harder to walk toward the gate that leads to the Other Side." Did a hand touch her, however briefly, brushing the nape of her neck? "Such a promise should not be beyond my powers."

Hope battered her chest like a bird beating at the bars of its cage. "Can you really do such a thing, Holy One?"

"We shall see." It was painful to hope. In a way, it was a relief when the Holy One changed the subject. "Have you seen any child among the White Deer people who can follow after you, Adica?"

"I have not," she murmured, even as the words thrust as a knife would, into her gut. "Nor would I have time to teach an apprentice everything she would need to know."

"Do not despair, Child. I will not abandon your people." A sharp hiss of surprise sounded, followed by the distant hoot of an owl. "I am called," the Holy One said suddenly, sounding surprised. That quickly, her presence vanished.

Had the Holy One actually traveled through the gateway of the stones? Had she stood behind Adica in her own self? Or had she merely walked the path of visions and visited Adica in her spirit form? The Holy One was so powerful that Adica could never tell. Nor dared she ask.

Truly, humans had the smallest share of power on this earth. Yet if that were so, why did the Cursed Ones make war against them so unremittingly? Why did the Cursed Ones hate humankind so?

Wind clacked the bronze leaves of the cauldron. She thought, for an instant, that she could actually hear flowers unfurling as the sun rose.

A horn call blared: the alarm from the village.

With more haste than care, she hurried back to her tent, took off her holy garments, and ran down through the earthworks. She got to the gate of the village just as a slender girl with strong legs and a wiry guard dog in faithful attendance loped up. The girl threw message beads at the feet of Mother Orla, who had come to the gate in response to the summons.

Mother Orla's hands were so gnarled that she could barely count off the message beads as she deciphered their meaning. She moved aside to allow Adica to stand beside her. At her great age, Orla did not fear evil spirits or death; they teased her already.

"A skirmish," she said to those who assembled from all the houses of the villages. "The Cursed Ones have raided. From what village did you come, Swift?"

A child brought mead so strongly flavored with meadowsweet flowers that the smell of it made Adica's mouth water. The Swift sipped at it carefully as she caught her breath. "I came from Two Streams, and from Pine Top, Muddy Walk, and Old Fort before that. The Cursed Ones attacked a settlement just beyond Four Houses. There were three people killed and two children carried away by the raiders."

"Did any of Four Houses' people go after them?" demanded Beor, shouldering up to the front. He'd been up early, hunting. He carried his sling in one hand. Two grouse, a partridge, and three ducks dangled from a string on the other. The guard dog nosed the dead birds, but the Swift batted it away until another child ran up with a nice meaty bone for the animal. It lay down and set to chomping.

"Nay," said the Swift, "none of the Four Houses people pursued the Cursed Ones, for those killed were Red Deer people. There were two families of them moved in close by Four Houses two winters ago. They come out of west country."

"What does it matter to the Cursed Ones whether they kill

Red Deer folk or White Deer folk?" Beor had a good anger
about him now, the kind that stirred others to action. "We're
all the same to the Cursed Ones, and once they've killed and
captured Red Deer folk, who's to say they won't come after
White Deer folk next? I say we must fight together, or we'll
all fall to their arrows one by one."

People muttered in agreement. Young men looked nervous
or eager by turns.

"What does the Hallowed One say?" asked Orla with decep-
tive softness.

Everyone fell silent as Adica considered. The Swift finished
the mead and gratefully started in on a bowl of porridge
brought to her by one of the boys she'd beaten at the races the
summer before. He eyed her enviously, her lean legs and the
loose breechclout that gave her room to run. He looked as if he
wanted to touch the amber necklace and copper armbands the
girl wore to signify her status. At the Festival of the Sun last
year, when all the villages of the tribe met at the henge to
barter and court and settle grievances, this girl had won the
races and with that victory the right to the name "Swift," one
of the favored youths who carried messages between the villages of the White Deer people.

"Already the Hallowed Ones of the human tribes work in
concert, and we count as our allies the Horse people. Yet the
Horse people are less human than our Red Deer cousins, and
we accept their alliance gladly." Adica paused, hearing their
restlessness.

The Swift finished off the porridge and hopefully held out
the bowl, in case she could get another portion.

"In this next sun's year is the time of greatest danger. If the
Cursed Ones suspect that we mean to act against them, then
they will send their armies to attack us. We need every ally we
can find, whether Red Deer, or White Deer, or Black Deer. No
matter how strange other tribes may seem to us, we need their
help. If you are still alive after the next year's dark of the sun,
you will no longer have to fear."

Orla made the sign to avert evil spirits and spat on the ground, and many did likewise, although not Beor. The younger ones withdrew to get on with their work or to check their bows and axes. As the villagers dispersed to their tasks, only the elders and the war captain remained.

"I will go with the war party," Adica said.

They had no choice but to agree.

She went to her old house to gather healing herbs and her basket of charms. Inside, the small house lay musty, abandoned. She ran her fingers along the eaves. One of the rafters still leaked a little pitch, and she touched it to her lips, breathing in its essence.

Outside, Beor waited with a party of nine adults whom he trusted to stand and fight, should it come to that. They walked armed with bows, carrying spare arrows tipped with obsidian points, and axes of flint or copper. Agda had a stone ax, and Beor himself carried the prize of the village: a halberd with a real bronze blade fixed at right angles to the shaft. He had taken it off the body of a dead enemy.

As they set out, the Swift loped past them with her dog at her heels, but she took the turning that would lead her on to Spring Water: Dorren's village.

No need to think of Dorren now. Adica could enjoy, surely, this transitory peace, walking under the bright sun and reveling in the wind on her back. It wasn't as hot as it had been on Falling-down's island home. She walked at the back of the band, keeping an eye out for useful plants. When she spotted a patch of mustard and stepped off the path to investigate, Beor dropped back to wait for her. The others paused a short way down the path, out of earshot but within range in case of attack.

She ignored Beor as best she could while she harvested as much mustard as she could tie around with a tall grass stem and set into her traveling basket. He fell in beside her as soon as she started on down the path. She did not look at him, and it seemed to her, by the way he swung the shaft of his halberd out before him, that he did not look at her. Yet it was still comforting to walk beside another person, companions on the long march. Ahead, the rest of the band set out, keeping a bit of distance between them.

"The elders spoke to me yesterday." His voice was a little hoarse, the way it got when he was aroused, or irritated. "They said that the reason we never made a child between us was because your magic has leached all the fertility from you. They said that if I don't give up thinking of you that evil spirits will drain me, too, and I'll never be able to make a child with another woman."

Her feet fell, one step and another and another. She couldn't make any thoughts come clear. The sun was bright. The path wound through woodland where a fresh breeze hissed through leaves.

"I never wanted any woman like I wanted you. But that has to be done with now. So be it. The elders say that Mother Nahumia's eldest daughter over at Old Fort just last moon set her man's hunting bag outside the door and made him leave. She'll be looking for a new man, then, won't she?"

"You'd have to go to Old Fort," said Adica, since he seemed to expect her to say something. "You'd have to live there."

"That's true. But I've a mind to leave. I've even thought of walking farther east, to hunt for a season with my Black Deer cousins."

"That's a long way," said Adica, and heard her own voice trembling, not able to speak the words without betraying the fear in her own heart.

"So it is," he agreed, and he waited again, wanting her sympathy or regret, perhaps, or an attempt to talk him out of this rash course of action. But she couldn't give him more. She had already offered her life to her people, and the magic hadn't even left her a child to keep her name alive among them.

"You're a good war captain, Beor," she said. "The village needs you. Will you at least wait until my work is done before you go? Then maybe it won't matter that they lose you—" Here she faltered. It was forbidden to speak aloud of the great weaving, because words were power, not to be carelessly cast to the four winds in case the Cursed Ones overheard them. "At least wait until then."

He grunted but made no other answer, and after a bit picked up their pace so that they fell in with the others. Since the others feared speaking to her, and would not look at her, she might as well have been walking alone.

The sun had risen halfway to noon by the time they reached Four Houses, a scatter of a dozen sheds, huts, pit houses, and four respectable compounds, each one boasting a round house at each corner with a thatched roof and a rock wall built into storage sheds between. A half-dozen adults labored at a ditch, digging with antlers and hauling away the dirt in bark buckets.

The war captain of Four Houses was a stout woman with two scars who went by the name Ulfrega and who wore the string skirt that marked her as a woman old enough to choose a marriage partner. By the evidence of the pale birth threads that decorated Ulfrega's belly above the band of her low-slung skirt, she had survived several pregnancies.

Ulfrega led them down past the river, through woodland rife with pigs, and along a deer trail that led to the Red Deer settlement. Two round houses and six storage pits lay quiet under the summer sun. Strangely, one of the round houses was entirely burned down to the stone half wall while the other stood as fresh and whole as if it had been built a month ago and lived in only yesterday. There was also a stone corral and a hayrick and a very neatly laid out vegetable garden, lush with ripening vegetables. Flies buzzed. A crow flapped lazily away as they approached. Even the village dogs had fled the carnage. The village lay empty except for a single abandoned corpse.

The Red Deer settlers had begun digging a ditch, too, and had gotten a rampart and ditch halfway around the settlement.

"Too little, too late," said Ulfrega, gesturing toward the half-dug ditch and the fallen and partially burned rampart. Debris from the fight lay everywhere: arrowheads; a shattered spear shaft; and one of the Cursed Ones' swords, a flat length of wood edged with obsidian, although most of that obsidian was broken or fallen off. Ulfrega picked up an arrow shaft and fingered the obsidian point quickly before tucking it away into the leather satchel she wore slung over one shoulder.

"You're late to build a ditch as well," said Beor.

She shrugged, looking irritated. "The other raids always came over by Three Oaks and Spring Water."

"It's not so far to travel between them, not for the Cursed Ones."

"Hei!" She spat in the direction of the corpse. "In open country they may move quickly, but they're slower when they bring their horses into the woodland. There's a lot of dense growth between Three Oaks and here."

"That didn't save these people."

The rest of Beor's people fanned out to scavenge for obsidian points and whatever was ripening in the garden. They avoided the corpse.

"I'll chase the spirit away," said Adica. No doubt the Four Houses people had been waiting for her to settle the matter. Both Beor and Ulfrega made the gesture to avert evil spirits and delicately stepped away from her. She rummaged in her basket and got out the precious copper bowl, just large enough to fit in her cupped hands, that she used for such workings. At the outdoor hearth she struck sparks with flint and touched it to a dried scrap of mushroom to raise a fire, then poured blessing water from her waterskin into the bowl and set it on a makeshift tripod over the flames to heat. The others vanished into the woodland to seek out the trail of their enemy—or to hide while she worked magic.

While the water heated, she stared in silence at the corpse.

His fall had torn his wooden lynx's mask from his face. He had proud features and a complexion the color of copper. His black hair had been coiled into a topknot, as was customary for his kind, and all down his arms various magical symbols had been painted with blue woad and red ocher, one twined into the next. Yet truly his sex mattered little: it was an adult, and therefore dangerous, because it could breed and it could fight.

No animal scavengers had touched the body. The Cursed Ones protected their spirits with powerful spells, so she would have to be cautious. Luckily, none of the Four Houses people had tried to strip the corpse, although he wore riches. A sheet of molded bronze protected his chest, so beautifully incised with figures of animals that she could not help but admire the artistry. Across the breastplate a vulture-headed woman paced majestically toward a burnished sun while two dragons faced each other, dueling with fire. It was hard to reconcile the creatures who stalked and terrorized humankind with ones who could fashion so many beautiful things. His bronze helmet, crested with horsehair, had rolled just slightly off his head, lying askew in the dirt. Someone had trampled the crest during the fight, the crease still stamped into the ground.

A leather belt fastened with a copper buckle held tight his knee-length skirt, all sewn of a piece. The cloth lay so smooth and soft over the body that she could not help but touch her own roughly woven bodice and the string skirt. With such riches as they had, why did the Cursed Ones bother to attack humankind at all?

But didn't they look upon humans as they did upon their own cattle? Maybe it was true that, before the time of the great queens, humankind had roamed like animals, eating and drinking and hunting and rutting, no different than the beasts. But that wasn't true now.

Hanging a sachet of juniper around her neck for protection, she picked out four dried leaves of lavender, then walked to the north and crumbled one between her fingers. Its dust spilled on the ground. To the east, south, and west, she did the same, forming a ring of protection. Standing to the west, she crouched and cupped her hands over her nose to inhale the

fading lavender scent, strong and pure. She murmured words
of power and protection into her hands.

The water boiled. With bone tongs she lifted the copper
bowl off the heat and brought it over to her basket. She
dropped old thistle into the water and waited, hands raised,
palms out.

The spirit manifested in her palms as a tiny vortex. Then
she saw it rising from the body, slippery and white. It quested
to the four corners but could not break free, bound by the spell
of lavender. As it spun like a whirlwind, its plaintive voice first
growled then mewled then whined, and suddenly the cloud of
the spirit, like a swarm of indistinct gnats, sprang heavenward,
running up the tunnel made by the four directional wards. She
jumped forward to sprinkle lavender dust on the corpse's eyes
and dab lavender into the corpse's ears and nostrils and over its
lips. Pulling up the skirt, she wiped paste of lavender over its
man part, then rolled the corpse over so she could seal it completely.

Far above, she heard a howl of despair. She clapped her
hands three times, stamped her feet, and the sensation of a
vortex swirling in her palms vanished. The spirit had fled to
the higher world, up the world axis made by the wards.

Yet it had left a treasure behind: under the corpse lay a
bronze sword.

Cautiously, she ran her hands over the metal blade. It, too,
had a spirit, fierce and implacable. This blade had bitten many
lives in half, and sent many spirits screaming from their
bodies. Yet who should carry such a dangerous and powerful
being? No one in the White Deer tribe, not in all the nine villages that made up the people, had a sword like this.

She found vervain in her basket, rolling it between her
hands and letting it fall onto the sword, to placate that venge-
ful spirit and to temporarily mute its lust for blood.

In addition to the bronze breastplate, the helmet, the sword,
the belt, and the loose linen tunic, the dead one had carried a
knife, and also a pouch containing four common river pebbles,

a sachet of herbs, a conch shell, and a small wooden cube engraved with magical symbols.

After stripping the corpse, she dragged it into the burned house and covered it with firewood. She marked the ruined threshold with hexes and threw the dead man's sacred pouch and his warrior's mask in after. As she shoveled hot coals onto the fallen thatch, the pyre began to burn.

Seeing smoke, Ulfrega led the others out of the wood. "No one will settle here again," observed Ulfrega before she hurried after Beor to examine the treasure.

"Do not touch it," said Adica quickly. Smoke boiled up from the funeral pyre. "The Cursed One's magic lives in those things."

"But I use this halberd, and *it* was taken from the Cursed Ones." Beor eyed the bronze sword with naked hunger.

The vision hit her so hard that she couldn't breathe.

Beor runs with the sword in his hand, leading a crowd of wild-eyed young people, running east to fight their own kind, humankind, burning their homes and stealing their cattle and goats.

This was the madness that the Cursed Ones had brought into their hearts!

Gasping, she found herself braced on her hands and knees. Everyone had stepped away from her. She was sweating, although a cloud covered the sun.

Unbidden, she wept, torn by grief. What would the White Deer people become, after she was gone? Were none of them strong enough to resist the implacable spirit that lived in the sword? Was this what the vision promised her, that her people would be consumed by its anger and lust? Were they fated to be poisoned by this legacy of the Cursed Ones, called war?

The rank smell of burning flesh washed over her, and she floated on that smoke into a more complicated vision, one without beginning or end.

There would be peace and war, kindness and cruelty. There would be honor, and shame.

All this would come to humankind.

It was already here.

Perhaps it was even true that the grandmothers had lived in a peace and loving-kindness unknown to the White Deer tribe now. Or perhaps the ancestors had fought their own battles, as simple as anger between friends or as complex as old enmities between tribes.

What would come, would come. She could only do her duty, here and now. So had the Holy One spoken. So had she agreed, knowing that it was the only way she had to protect her people.

The vision faded. Trembling, she got to her feet to find that the others had retreated to hunker down by the intact roundhouse and chew on stalks of dried meat, waiting for her to come out of her trance. She never had to explain herself. She went down to the nearby stream and cut reeds with her stone knife, then braided them into rope strong enough to bind and carry the dead one's treasure. With this bundle hoisted over her shoulders and her basket tapping at her hip, she walked back to Four Houses. The others followed at a safe distance, keeping their voices low.

They feared her, because she had magic and they had none, because she saw what they could not see. That was how the gods chose, giving sight to some and leaving the rest blind.

Sometimes, she knew, it was more merciful to be blind.

3

THEY sheltered that night at Four Houses. The people hustled out of her way when she approached. Fathers pulled their children in through the gates that barred off the family compounds, where her glance could not scar or cripple any of these most precious young ones. No one invited her inside, and Beor was wise enough—or fearful enough of what she might do if she were angered—that he and his party sat outside, too, taking the meal that the Four Houses adults shared with them.

They ate well: fresh venison and swan; a malty beer almost thick enough to scoop up with her fingers; cheese; and late season greens, rather toothy and fibrous. The Four Houses people kept their dogs tied up so that they could eat in peace without the constant begging menace.

That night she slept outside, alone, in the shadow of one of the hayricks. Yet she could not help stroking the smooth cloth once worn by the dead Cursed One. She could not help crushing its soft weave against her cheek. It didn't comfort her.

In the morning, they walked back to their village. Everyone wanted to see the bronze sword, but she kept it hidden. Its spirit still wept for its former master; it was still angry. She carried the treasure up the hill and wove a warding out of herbs and charms into an old cowhide. In this hide she wrapped sword and armor. A shallow hole just outside the stone loom made a convenient temporary grave.

She knelt by that hole for a long time, but no visions came. Finally, she walked down to the river and washed the linen shirt until no taint of the Cursed One lingered in it. Returning up the hill, she found a platter of food left by her shelter, a pottage now cold and congealed, a mug of ale dusted with a scattering of vegetal matter blown in by the wind. After she hung the linen cloth over the shelter to dry, she ate. No one ever turned down food. No one else ever had to eat alone.

It was a warm summer evening, golden and endless with promise, but she clutched only emptiness at her heart.

Binding on her hallowing clothes, she walked the familiar path to the stones as night fell. Stars bloomed above like the campfires of the dead. Was there a new star among their number, the spirit of the Cursed One she had banished from the Earth yesterday? She could not tell.

With certain gestures of ritual respect, she walked into the stone loom. The great stones seemed to watch her. Kneeling before the cauldron, she sipped at the water before flinging a handful into the air to seed the wind with its holiness. With arms folded across on her chest, she breathed herself into the trance necessary to the working, walked each step of the great weaving so that she would make no mistake when the time came and thus sever the threads. When she had walked it through in her mind's eye without mistake, she walked it again.

But she could only remain deep in the working trance for so long. After a while, she eased herself free of it. She was tired, but not sleepy. Bowing her head, she waited.

Maybe she was only waiting for hope, or release. Maybe she was only waiting for the wind. Or for death.

It was a long night.

Mist crept up into the stones and wreathed her, cold and soft. The stars breathed in and out, souls sighing for their lost home. A nightingale sang.

An owl hooted.

She started up out of a doze. Her knees ached, her left foot was asleep, and as she shifted to banish the needles of evil spirits, come to plague her while she napped, she saw the owl glide in noiselessly on its great wings and settle on the cauldron. Swiftly, she covered her eyes with a hand.

Dawn lightened the eastern horizon. The mist retreated, like a creature withdrawing its claws, until its coils wrapped only the westernmost stones. A blue-white light flared before her eyes. The breath of the Holy One tickled her neck, smelling of grass. Hooves tapped the ground as the Holy One danced away.

The ground shuddered beneath her knees, throwing her back. Some force reached into her guts and yanked them one way while she was jerked in the other direction. The movement tore her in half and yet she was entire, whole and panting with exertion and fright. Her tongue had swollen, and her head spun with a myriad dizzy tumbles, as though she were rolling bodily down a steep hill even as she knelt unmoving beside the cauldron.

Something deep in the cosmos had come undone. The world murmured around her, unsettled and curious, and she heard birds coming awake in the forest and the distant howling of wolves. The breath of the stars grazed her neck, burning her with their fierce heat, as implacable as the souls of swords. She heard a gasp, and then all was silent except for the movements of the Holy One, murmuring quiet words.

Except for another voice, low and confused.

Except for the rank scent of blood, and an unknown smell that smothered her until she understood what it was: wet dog.

Startled, she looked up to see two huge black dogs, as large as half-grown calves, standing alert on the other side of the step stone. She rose cautiously, but the dogs made no move against her, nor did they growl or bark.

A naked man lay on the ground on the other side of the cauldron. He had the lean male body of one who is no longer a youth and yet has not been a man for many years.

The Holy One waited, unmoving, a spear's length away from the prostrate body. A litter of bloody garments lay heaped on the ground before her.

Adica circled the cauldron cautiously, murmuring words of protection. Was this a conjuring man, walking abroad with his spirit guides?

The dogs nosed the body as though smelling for life before settling down contentedly on either side of the prone man. They did not try to bite her as she slid in between them to touch the man on the shoulder. His skin was as soft as a rose petal, marvelously smooth. He was much less hairy than the men of the Deer clans, but he hadn't the bronze complexion that marked the Cursed Ones. Pale and straight, he was like no person she had seen before. She traced the line of his shoulder blade, his skin warm under her hand. He breathed softly and slowly.

"Here is the husband I have promised you, Adica," said the Holy One. "He comes from the world beyond."

His scent was as sweet as wild roses. His ear, the one she could see, had a whorl as delicate as that of a precious seashell, brought in trade from the north, and his lips had a delicate elder-violet tinge, as if he had recently been very cold.

She spoke softly, afraid to disturb him. "Did he come from the land of the dead?" Because of the way he was lying, it was hard to make out the shape of his face.

"Truly it was to the land of the dead that he was walking. But now he is here."

Her hand rested on the curve of his shoulder. He had a young man's thighs and buttocks, but she could not quite bring herself to accept that he was truly a male. Yet her heart pounded loudly. Wind sighed through the stones, scattering the mist as the sun's hard face rose higher in the sky.

It was hard to speak when hope battered so harshly against her fears. Her voice broke on the words she finally forced out. "Will he stay with me until my death, Holy One?"

"He will stay with you until your death."

The calm words hit her like grief. She wept, sitting back on her heels to steady herself, and didn't notice that he stirred until he heaved himself up onto his forearms to look at her. He looked no less startled than she did, yet he also seemed as dazed as if he had taken a blow to the head. His skin had the pallor of one who has been ill. A small red blemish in the shape of a rose marked his left cheek, like the brands the Horse people used to mark their livestock. Despite the blemish and his paleness, he had a pleasing face, expressive and bright.

Before she understood what he meant to do, he brushed a finger gently along the scar that fire had left on her cheek, lifting a tear off her skin. The moisture surprised him so much that he exclaimed out loud and, reflexively, touched tongue to finger, tasting for salt.

"Who are you?" she asked. "What is your name, if you can share it?"

His eyes widened with surprise. He replied, but the words that came out of his mouth sounded like no language she had ever heard. Perhaps this was the language spoken in the land of the dead, incomprehensible to those who walked in the middle world known by the living.

He pushed unsteadily up to hands and knees, sat back on his thighs, and suddenly realized that he was naked. He grabbed for the tangled cloth lying an arm's length away, but when his fingers closed on a patch still wet with blood, he recoiled with a cry and scrambled backward, looking around as if to seek the aid of the Holy One.

No trace of the Holy One remained within the stone loom. Her owl, too, had vanished.

"Come," she said, extending her hands with palms up and open in the sign of peace. "Nothing will harm you here."

The dogs had not moved, so he settled down cross-legged, hands cupped modestly over his lap. To show that she was a human woman, she took off the golden antlers and unbound the bronze waistband, setting them to one side. He watched her with a wary respect but without the fear that dogged every glance thrown her way by the villagers she had grown up with and lived beside for the whole of her life. Either he was still confused, or he was simply not afraid. Yet if he had walked the path that leads into the land of the dead, then perhaps he no longer feared any fate that might overtake him in the land of the living.

The smell of blood hung heavily in the air. The garments that lay in a jumble in the grass were stained with bright-red heart's blood, just now beginning to dry and darken. The dogs showed no sign of injury, and although he bore a fresh pink scar under his ribs, quite a nasty wound, it was cleanly healed and wasn't weeping.

Where had the blood come from?

"Do these belong to you?" she asked, cautiously reaching out to touch the closest garment. The wool shone with a brilliant madder gold, and when she shook it out, she recognized under the bloody stain the image of a spirit fixed to the gold garment: a lean and powerful lion woven of black threads set into the gold.

He jerked away from the sight. His face was so expressive, as if his soul permeated all of his physical being from the core to the surface rather than being lodged in some deep recess, as was true for most people. Perhaps he wasn't a person at all but the actual soul, manifest on the physical plane, of the warrior who had once worn these garments and who had died in them. Perhaps he had killed the man who had worn them, and now recoiled from the memory of violence.

She examined a second garment of undyed wool, bloodier even than the lion cloth, that lay crumpled to one side. Beneath it lay a leather belt incised with smaller lions, fastened by a bronze buckle also fashioned in the image of a lion's snarling face. Foot coverings cunningly molded out of soft leather lay in a heap with lengths of cloth and strips of leather that were, she realized, fine leggings.

Where had his people learned such craft? Why had they not joined the alliance of humankind against the Cursed Ones?

Beneath the clothing lay a garment woven of tiny metal rings, pale in color, yet not silver, or tin, or bronze, or copper. It was heavy. The rings sang in a thousand voices as she lifted them. They had a hard and unforgiving smell. Like the lion coat, the garment had holes that would accommodate a head and arms, and it was long enough to fall to the knees. Perhaps it was not metal at all, but a magical spell of protection made physical, curled and dense, to protect the body. Her shoulders ached from the strain of holding it as she set it down and picked up the knife that lay hidden underneath.

Not stone, not copper, not bronze: the metallic substance of this knife had none of the implacable fire of the bronze sword she had taken from the corpse of the Cursed One. It was blind, with a heartless soul as cold as the winter snows, as ruthless as the great serpents who writhed in the depths of the sea and swallowed whole the curraghs in which the fisherfolk plied their trade: having hunger, it feasted, and then settled back in quiet satiation to wait until it hungered again.

Magic was the blood of these garments. Was it any surprise that blood stained them all?

She looked back at him, hoping, even fearing, to find an answer in his expression. But in the way of any young woman who has gone too long without pleasure, she only noticed his body.

He was quite obviously not a child, to run naked in the summer.

"Wait here," she said, making gestures to show him that she meant to go and return.

As she rose, her string skirt slid revealingly around her thighs, and he blushed, everywhere, easy to see on his fair skin. She looked away quickly, to hide her hope. Did he find her attractive? Had the Holy One truly brought her a mate? She gathered up her regalia and hurried away to her shelter, storing antlers and waistband in the chest and returning to him with the linen shirt draped over her arms.

He still sat cross-legged but with his head bowed and resting on his cupped hands. Hearing her, he lifted his head. Tears ran down his face. Truly, then, he wasn't actually dead, because the dead could not weep.

She set the garment on the ground in front of him and took a few steps away, turning her back so that if he had any secret rituals he had to perform, crossing the threshold of nakedness into civilization, she would not disturb him. There was silence, except for the wind and the rustle and scrape of his movements. Then he coughed, clearing his throat, and she turned around.

The tunic draped loosely over his chest, falling to just above his knees. Amazingly, he stood as tall as Beor. The southern tribes, and the Cursed Ones, commonly stood shorter than the people of the Deer clans. Only the Horse people, with their bodies made half of human form and half of horse, stood taller.

Through a complicated and awkward ritual of gesturing, he indicated himself and spoke a word. She tried it one way on her tongue and then another, and he laughed suddenly, very sweetly, and she looked into his eyes and smiled at him, but she was first to look away. Fire flared in her cheeks; her heart burned in her. He was not precisely handsome. He looked very different than the men she knew. His features were rather narrowed, his forehead a little flatter, his cheek was marked with the blemish, and his hair was almost as dark as that of the Cursed Ones, but as fine as spun flax.

He spoke his name again, more slowly, and one of the big dogs barked as if to answer him.

"Halahn," she said.

"Alain," he agreed good-naturedly.

"I am named Adica," she said. "Ah-dee-cah."

Her name was easier for him to say than his had been for her. When she smiled at him, this time he was the one who blushed and looked away.

"What must we do with the treasure you brought with you?" She gestured toward the heap of garments. A small leather pouch lay off to one side, its thong broken. Underneath it rested a peg no longer than a finger that resembled one of the wooden pins used to fasten together joints at the corners of houses. The peg had been fashioned by magic out of the same heartless metal that made up the coat of rings.

The rusty red of old blood stained the tiny nail. Like the knife, it, too, had a soul, crabbed and devious and even a little whiny in the way of a spoiled child.

He choked out a sound as he staggered backward and dropped to his knees. Did he fear the nail's soul, or had it felled him with an invisible malignance? She quickly concealed it in the pouch. With an effort he got up, but only to retreat to the edge of the loom, bracing himself on one of the guardian stones, shoulders bowed as under the weight of a powerful emotion.

She gathered together the garments and hid them in the shallow grave next to the bronze sword and armor she had taken from the Cursed One. Finally, she returned to him. "Come."

He and his dogs followed obediently behind her. Now and again he spoke to the dogs in a gentle voice. He halted beside the shelter to examine the superstructure of saplings and branches, the hide walls, the pegs and leather thongs that held everything in place.

"This is where I sleep," she said.

He smiled so disarmingly that she had to glance away. Had the Holy One seen right into her heart? Impulsively, she leaned into him and touched her cheek to his. He smelled faintly of blood but far more of roses freshly blooming. His scant beard was as soft as petals.

Startled, he leaped back. His cheeks were so red and she was so overcome by her own rudeness, and the speed of her attraction to him, that she hurriedly climbed the nearest rampart to look out over the village and the fields, the river and the woodland and beyond these the distant ancient forest, home to beasts and spirits and every manner of wolf and wild thing.

The dogs barked. She looked back to see them biting at Alain's heels, driving him after her. He slapped at their muzzles, unafraid of their huge jaws, but he followed her, pausing halfway up to examine the slope of the rampart and exposed soil, and to study the layout of the hill and the span of earthworks that ringed it. Then he halted beside her to survey the village below, ringed by the low stockade, the people working the fields, the lazy river, and a distant flock at the edge of the woodlands that would either be young Urta with her goats or Deyilo, who shepherded his family's sheep.

He spoke a rush of words, but she understood nothing except his excitement as he pointed toward the village and started down, half sliding in the dirt in his haste. She watched him at first, the way he moved, the way he balanced himself, sure and graceful. He wasn't brawny like Beor, all power and no grace, the bull rampaging in the corral, yet neither had he Dorren's reticent movements, made humble by lacking all the parts necessary to an adult's labor. He was young and whole, and she wanted him because he wasn't afraid of her, because he was pleasingly formed, because she was lonely, and because there was something more about him, that scent of roses, that she couldn't explain even to herself.

Hastily, she followed, and he had the good manners to wait, or perhaps he had seen by her regalia that she was the Hallowed One of this tribe and therefore due respect. No adult carelessly insulted a hallowed adult of any tribe.

Everyone came running to see. He stared at them no less astounded, at their faces, their clothing, and their questions, which ran off him like water. Adults left their fields to come and watch. Children crowded around, so amazed that they even jostled Adica in their haste to peer upon the man. After their initial caution toward the huge dogs, they swarmed over them as well. Remarkably, the huge dogs merely settled down as patiently as oxen, with expressions of wounded dignity.

Into this chaos ran a naked girl, Getsi, one of the grand-daughters of Orla.

"Hallowed One! Come quickly. Mother Orla calls you to the birthing house!"

Cold fear gripped Adica's heart. Only one woman in the village was close to her birthing time: her age mate and friend, Weiwara. She found her cousin Urtan in the crowd. "This man is a friend to our tribe. Treat him with the hospitality due to a stranger."

"Of course, Hallowed One."

She left, running with Getsi. The cords of her string skirt flapped around her, bouncing, the bronze sleeves that capped the ends chiming like discordant voices calling out the alarm. As she ran, she prayed to the Fat One, words muttered on gasps of air:

"Let her not die, Fat One. Let it not be my doom which brings doom onto the village in this way."

The birthing house lay outside of the village, upstream on high ground beside the river. A fence ringed it, to keep out foraging pigs, obdurate goats, and children. Men knew better than to pass beyond the fence. An offering of unsplit wood lay outside the gate. Looking back toward the village, Adica saw Weiwara's husband coming, attended by his brothers.

She closed the gate behind her and stamped three times with each foot just outside the birthing house. Then she shook the rattle tied to the door and crossed the threshold, stepping right across the wood frame so as not to touch it with any part of her foot. Only the door and the smoke hole gave light inside. Weiwara sat in the birthing stool, deep in the birth trance, eyes half closed as she puffed and grunted, half on the edge of hysteria despite Mother Orla's soothing chanting. Weiwara had birthed her first child three summers ago, and as every person knew, the first two birthings were the most dangerous: if you survived them, then it was likely that the gods had given their blessing upon you and your strength.

Adica knelt by the cleansing bowl set just inside the threshold and washed her hands and face in water scented with lavender oil. Standing, she traced a circular path to each of the corners of the birthing house in turn, saying a blessing at each corner and brushing it with a cleansing branch of juniper as Weiwara's panting and blowing continued and Mother Orla chanted in her reedy voice. Orla's eldest daughter, Agda, coated her hands in grease also scented with lavender, to keep away evil spirits. Agda beckoned to Adica with the proper respect, and Adica crept forward on her knees to kneel beside the other woman. Getsi began the entering rituals, so that she, too, could observe and become midwife when her age mates became women.

Agda spoke in a low voice. A light coating of blood and spume intermingled with grease on her hands. "I thank you for coming, Hallowed One." She did not look directly at Adica, but she glanced toward Weiwara to make sure the laboring woman did not hear her. "When I examined her two days ago, I felt the head of the child down by her hip. But just now when I felt up her passageway, I touched feet coming down. She is early to her time. And the child's limbs did not feel right to me." She bent her head, considered her hands, and glanced up, daringly, at Adica's face. The light streaming down through the smoke hole made a mask of her expression.

"I think the child is already dead." Agda spat at once, so the words wouldn't stay in her mouth. "I hope you can bind its spirit so Weiwara will not be dragged into the Other Side along with it."

Weiwara labored in shadow, unbound hair like a cloak along her shoulders. She moaned a little. Orla's chanting got louder.

"It's time," gasped Weiwara.

Agda settled back between Weiwara's knees and gestured to her mother, who gripped Weiwara's shoulders and changed the pattern of her chant so that the laboring woman could pant, and push, and pant again. Agda gently probed up the birth canal while Getsi watched from behind her, standing like a stork, on one foot, a birthing cloth draped over her right shoulder.

Adica rose and backed up to the threshold, careful not to turn her back on the laboring woman. A willow basket hung from the eaves, bound around with charms. Because the birthing house was itself a passageway between the other worlds and this world, it always had to be protected with charms and rituals. Now, lifting the basket down from its hook, Adica found the things she needed.

From outdoors, she heard the rhythmic chop of an ax start up as Weiwara's husband spun what men's magic he could, splitting wood in the hope that it would cleave child from mother in a clean break.

Weiwara began grunting frantically, and Agda spoke sternly. "You must hold in your breath and push, and then breathe again. Follow Orla's count."

Adica found a tiny pot of ocher, and with a brush made of pig bristle she painted spirals on her own palms. She slid over beside Agda. "Give me your hands."

Agda hesitated, but Orla nodded. Weiwara's eyes were rolled almost completely up in her head, and she whimpered in between held breaths. Adica swiftly brushed onto Agda's

palms the mark of the moon horns of the Fat One, symboliz-
ing birth, and the bow of the Queen of the Wild, who lets all
things loose. She marked her own forehead with the Old Hag's
stick, to attract death to her instead of to those fated to live.

With a sprig of rowan she traced sigils of power at each
corner of the house. Pausing at the threshold, she twitched up
a corner of the hide door mantle to peek outside. Weiwara's
husband split wood beyond the gate, his broad shoulders
gleaming in the sun. Sweat poured down his back as he
worked, arms supple, stomach taut.

Somewhat behind him, looking puzzled, stood Alain.

Adica was jolted right out of her trance at the sight of him,
all clean and pale and rather slender compared to the men of
her village, who had thicker faces, burlier shoulders, and skin
baked brown from summer's work. Her cousin, Urtan, had a
hand on Alain's elbow, as if he were restraining him, but Alain
started forward just as his two black dogs nosed up beside
him, thrusting Urtan away simply by shoving him aside with
their weight. They were so big that they had no need to growl
or show their teeth.

"Aih!" cried Weiwara, the cry so loud that her husband faltered in his chopping, and every man there glanced toward the
forbidden house, and away.

Adica stepped back in horror as Alain passed the gate. As
the hide slithered down to cover the door, an outcry broke
from the crowd waiting beyond the fence.

"It is born!" said Orla.

"Yet more!" cried Weiwara, her words more a sob of anguish
than of relief.

Agda said: "Fat One preserve us! There comes another one!
Hallowed One! I pray you, take this one. It has no life."

Adica took the baby into her arms and pressed its cold lips
to her own lips. No soul stirred within. The baby had no
pulse. No heart threaded life through its body. Yet she barely
had time to think about what she must do next, find the dead
child's spirit and show it the path that led to the Other Side,

when a glistening head pressed out from between Weiwara's legs. The sight startled her so profoundly that she skipped back and collided with Alain as he stepped into the birthing house. He steadied her with a hand on her back. Only Getsi saw him. The girl stared wide-eyed, too shocked to speak.

What ruin had Adica brought onto the village by bringing him here? The baby in her arms was blue as cornflowers, sickly and wrong. Dead and lost.

The twin slipped from the birth passage as easily as a fish through wet hands. Agda caught it, and it squalled at once with strong lungs. Weiwara began to weep with exhaustion.

Orla took her hands from Weiwara's shoulders and, at that moment, noticed the figure standing behind Adica. She hissed in a breath between her teeth. "What is this creature who haunts us?"

Weiwara shrieked, shuddering all over as if taken with a fit.

Agda sat back on her heels and gave a loud cry, drowning out the baby's wailing. "What curse has he brought down on us?"

Oblivious to their words, Alain gently took the dead baby out of Adica's arms and lifted it to touch its chest to his ear. He listened intently, then said something in a low voice, whether to her, to the dead child, or to himself she could not know. All the women watched in horror and the twin cried, as if in protest, as he knelt on the packed earth floor of the birthing house to chafe the limbs of the dead baby between his hands.

"What is this creature?" demanded Orla again. Adica choked on her reply, sick with dread. She had selfishly wanted company in her last days and now, having it, wrought havoc on the village.

"Look!" whispered Weiwara.

The dead baby stirred and mewled. Color swept its tiny body. Blue faded to red as life coursed back into it. Alain regarded the newborn with a thoughtful frown before lifting the baby girl to give her into Weiwara's arms. Weiwara had the stunned expression of an ewe brought to the slaughter. Living twins were a powerful sign of the Fat One's favor.

"Aih!" she grunted as the last of the pains hit her. Without thinking, she gave the baby back into Alain's arms before gripping the stool one more time. Getsi expertly swaddled the other newborn in the birthing cloth.

When the afterbirth slid free and Agda cut off a corner of it for Weiwara to swallow, all the women turned to regard Alain. He waited quietly. Adica braced herself.

Yet no flood of recrimination poured from Orla. Agda sat silent. The afterbirth lay in glistening splendor in the birth platter at her feet, ready for cooking.

No one scolded him. No one made the ritual signs to protect themselves against the pollution he had brought in with him, the one who had walked into a place forbidden to males. Though it was wrong to let him stay, Adica hadn't the strength or the heart to send him out. He had brought light in with him, even if it was only by the lifting of the flap of hide tied across the threshold, because the flap had caught on the basket hook, halfway up the frame, and hung askew. The rose blemish on his cheek seemed especially vivid now, almost gleaming.

"What manner of creature is this?" murmured Mother Orla a second time.

"The child was dead," said Agda. "I know what death feels like under my hands." She, too, could not look away from him, as if he were a poisonous snake, or a being of great power. "What manner of creature is he, that can bring life out of death?"

But of course that made it obvious, once it was stated so clearly. "He is a man," explained Adica, watching him as he watched her. He seemed confused and a little embarrassed, half turned away from Weiwara as Getsi cleaned her with water and a sponge of bound rushes. "He was walking to the land of the dead when the Holy One brought him to me to be my companion."

Weiwara was still too dazed by the birth to respond, or perhaps even to have heard, but Agda and Orla merely nodded their heads and pulled on their ears to make sure no evil spirits had entered into them in the wake of such a provocative statement.

"So be it," said Orla. "If the Holy One has brought him to you, then she must not be afraid that he will bring any bad thing onto the village."

"If he was walking to the land of the dead," said Agda, "then truly he might have found this child's soul wandering lost along the path, and he might have carried it with him back to us."

Orla nodded in agreement. "It takes powerful magic to call a person off the path that leads to the Other Side. Maybe he has already seen the Other Side. Speaks he of it?"

"He cannot speak in any language I know, Mother Orla," admitted Adica.

"Nay, nay," retorted Agda. "None who have glimpsed the Other Side can speak in the tongue of living people anymore. Everyone knows that! Is he to be your husband, Adica?" She hesitated before going on. "Will he follow you where your fate leads?"

"That is what the Holy One promised me."

"Perhaps," said Orla, consideringly, "a person who can see and capture wandering spirits, like that of this child, ought to stay in the village during this time of trouble. Then he can see any evil spirits coming, and chase them away. Then they won't be able to afflict us."

"What are you saying, Mother?" Agda glanced toward Alain suspiciously.

"I will speak to the elders."

"Let me take him outside," said Adica quickly. "Then I will purify the birthing house so that Weiwara can stay here for her moon's rest." The new mother's bed lay ready, situated along one wall: a wooden pallet padded with rushes, a sheepskin, and the special wool padding bound with sprigs of rowan that brought a new mother ease and protection. Cautiously, Adica touched Alain on the elbow. His gaze, still fixed on the newborn in Weiwara's arms, darted to her.

"Come." She indicated the door.

Obediently, he followed her outside. It seemed in that short space of time that the whole village had heard of the adult male who had walked into the birthing house. Now every person in the village crowded outside the fence, waiting to see what would happen.

Beor shouldered his way to the front. He took the ax from Weiwara's husband and fingered the ax head threateningly as he watched them emerge. Like bulls and rams, men always recognized a rival by means not given to women to understand.

"I will take care of this intruder," said Beor roughly as Adica approached the gate.

"He is under my protection." The dogs pushed through the crowd toward their master. Their size and fearsome aspect made people step away quickly. "And under the protection of spirit guides as well, it seems."

One of the big dogs, the male, nudged Beor's thigh and growled softly: a threat, but not an attack. Alain spoke sharply to the dog, and it sat down, stubbornly sticking to its place, while Alain waited on the other side of the fence, measuring Beor's broad shoulders and the heft of the ax. Under the sunlight, the rose blemish that had flared so starkly on the tumulus and inside the birthing house faded to a mere spot of red on his cheek, nothing out of the ordinary.

Urtan hurried up and spoke in an undertone to Beor, urging him to step aside. Beor hesitated. Adica could see the war waged within him: his jealousy, his sharp temper, his pride and self-satisfaction battling with the basic decency common to the White Deer people, who knew that in living together one had to cooperate to survive.

"No use causing trouble," said Urtan in a louder voice.

"I'm not the one causing trouble," said Beor with a bitter

look for Adica. "Who is this stranger, dressed like a Cursed One? He's brought trouble to the village already!"

"Go aside, Beor!" Mother Orla emerged from the birthing house. "Let there be no fighting on a day when living twins were given to this village out of the bounty of the Fat One."

Not even Beor was pigheaded enough to go against Mother Orla's command or to draw blood on a day favored by the Fat One. Still gripping the ax as if he wished to split Alain's head open, Beor retreated with his brother and cousins while the villagers murmured together, staring at the foreign man who had come into their midst.

Alain swung a leg over the fence and in this way crossed out of forbidden ground so casually that it was obvious that he did not understand there was any distinction. He could not feel it down to his bones the way Adica could, the way she knew whether any hand's span of earth was gods-touched, or hallowed, or forbidden, or merely common and ordinary, a place in which life bloomed and death ate. The crowd stepped aside nervously to make a pathway for him.

"You must wait here, Hallowed One," said Mother Orla once they reached the village gates. "I ask this of you, do not enter the village until the elders have made their decision." She called the elders to the council house, and the meeting pole, carved with the faces of the ancestors, was raised from the centerpost.

Adica had learned how to sit quietly as an apprentice to the Hallowed One who had come before her, the one who had been her teacher, but she was surprised to see how patiently Alain waited, sitting at her side. His dogs lay on the ground behind him, tongues lolling out, quiescent but alert, while he studied the village. The adults went back to their work and the children lingered to stare, the older children careful to keep the less cautious young ones from approaching too close.

In the end, it did not take long. The meeting pole wobbled and was drawn down through the smoke hole. Mother Orla emerged with the other elders walking deferentially behind her. Villagers hurried over to the gates to hear her pronouncement, all but Beor, who had stalked into the forest with his hunting spear. The dogs pricked up their ears.

"The elders have decided," announced Mother Orla. "If Adica binds this man to her and lets him live in her house, she can reside again in the village until that comes which must come."

"So be it," murmured Adica, although her heart sang.

The villagers spoke the ritual words of acquiescence, and it was done, sealed, accepted. The Holy One had brought it to pass, as she had promised.

Adica had her own duties. She had to purify her old house, which had sat empty for two courses of the moon, and she had to purify the birthing house, since a male had set foot in it. Women who had borne living children passed in and out of the birthing house while she worked. They brought presents, food, and drink to Weiwara as they would every day until a full course of the moon had waned and waxed, at which time the new mother could resume her everyday life.

But afterward she was free to watch Alain, although she was careful to do so from a distance, pretending not to. She expected him to wait for her at the village gates, shy and aloof as strangers usually were upon first coming to a new place, but he allowed children to drag him from the well to the stockade, from the freshly dug outer ditch to the pit house where the village stored grain. He crouched beside the adults making pottery and the girls weaving baskets, and examined a copper dagger recently traded from Old Fort, where a conjuring man lived who knew the magic of metalworking. He coaxed in a limping dog so that he could pull a thorn from its paw, and scolded a child for throwing a stone at it, although surely the child understood no word of what he said. He fingered loom weights stacked in a pile outside the house of Mother Orla and her daughters, and combed through the debris beside Pur the stoneworker's platform. He spent a remarkably long time investigating the village's two wooden ards. Adica remembered her grandfather speaking wonderingly of helping, as a young man, to plow fields for the first time with such magnificent tools; all his childhood the villagers had dug furrows with sharpened antlers.

Alain's curiosity never flagged. It was almost as if he'd never seen such things before. Perhaps he was born into a tribe of savages, who still lived in skin shelters and carried sharpened sticks for weapons. Why then, though, would he have carried such skillfully made garments with him?

Although she watched, she was afraid to show too much interest in him. She was afraid that she would frighten him away if he noticed her following after him. She feared the strength of her own feelings, so sudden and powerful. He was a stranger, and yet in some way she could not explain she felt she had always known him. He was a still pool of calm in the swift current that was life in the village. He stood outside it, and yet his presence had the solidity of those things which lie awake and aware in the world, cutting both into what is holy and what is ordinary, blending them in the same way a river blends water from many streams.

So it went, that afternoon, as Alain explored the village, followed by a pack of curious children whom he never snapped at, although they often pestered him.

So it went, that evening, when people brought food to her door, as if to apologize for their neglect from the months before, as if to acknowledge her new household and mate. They still would not look her in the eye, but the children sat easily beside Alain, and he showed them how to play a game made by lines drawn in the dirt and populated by moving stones, a clever way of capturing territory and retreating. Urtan made a flamboyant show of sitting next to him as though they had been comrades for ages, like two who handled the ard together at plowing time or spent a lazy afternoon supervising children at play in the river shallows. Beor still had not returned from his solitary hunt, but the other men were curious enough, and respectful enough of Urtan's standing, that they came, too, and learned to play the game of lines and stones. Alain accepted their presence graciously. He seemed at ease with everyone.

Except that night, when she tried to coax him into her house and showed him that he could sleep on the bed with her. At once he looked agitated and spoke words more passionate than reasoned. She had offended him. Flushed and grim, he made a bed for himself with straw just outside the threshold, and there he lay himself down with a dog on either side, his guardians. In this way, for she checked several times, he appeared to sleep peacefully while she lay awake and restless.

An owl hooted, a presence gliding through the night. One of the dogs whined in its sleep and turned over. A child cried out, then stilled. The village slumbered. In their distant cities, the Cursed Ones plotted and planned, but at this moment their enmity seemed remote compared to the soft breathing of the man who slept outside her door.

At dawn, Urtan took Alain to the weir with his young cousins Kel and Tosti. He went, all of them laughing in a friendly way at his attempts to learn new words. The dogs trailed behind. It was remarkable how good-natured he seemed. She wanted to see how he managed at the weir, but she had her own duties.

Going to renew the charms in the birthing house, she found Weiwara nursing one infant and rocking the other with a foot where it lay asleep in a woven cradle. The new mother examined the sleeping twin with a look compounded mostly of surprise, as though she had opened a door to admit a tame bear. "Is it true that the stranger brought the firstborn back to life?"

"So it seemed to my eyes." Adica crouched beside the sleeping infant but was careful not to touch it. "I held this baby in my arms. Like Agda, I listened, but I heard no spirit stirring inside it. He called the spirit back."

"Is he a conjurer, do you think?"

"No, I do not think so." The woven cradle creaked as it rocked back and forth. The other twin suckled silently. A bead of clear liquid welled up from a nipple and beaded there before slipping down Weiwara's skin.

"I hear he is to be your new husband," added Weiwara. "Is he handsome? I didn't truly see him."

"No," said Adica quickly. "He's not really handsome. He doesn't look like a Deer man."

"But." Weiwara laughed. "I hear a 'but.' I hear that you're thinking of him right now."

Adica blushed. "I am thinking of him now."

"You never thought of Beor when you weren't with him. I think you'd better bind hands with this man, so he'll understand your intentions. If he came from far away, he might not wish to offend anyone. He surely doesn't know what is forbidden here, and what is not. How else could he have walked into the birthing house like he did? You'd better ask Mother Orla to witness the ceremony, so he'll know he's not forbidden to you."

"So I must. I'll have to show him what is permitted."

She walked slowly back to the village, reached the gate in time to see Alain and Urtan and Urtan's cousins carrying a basket slippery with fish up from the river, a catch worthy of a feasting day. Alain was laughing. He had let the cloth slip from his shoulders, to leave his chest bare. His shoulders had gone pink from the sun. He was lean through the waist, and remarkably smooth on chest and back, so different than the Deer men.

"Never did I think to see the Hallowed One at another's mercy," said Mother Orla, shuffling up beside her. She walked with a limp, supporting herself on a broken pole that had once served as the shaft for a halberd.

"Mother Orla! You startled me!"

"So I did. For you truly were not standing with yourself." They had to step aside to make room for the four men and their heavy basket to cross the plank bridge that led over the ditch and into the village. Alain saw Adica, and he smiled. She was not quite sure how she responded, for at that moment Mother Orla pinched her hard on the forearm. "There, now, daughter!"

She had not been touched in so long—except when Alain had brushed tears from her cheeks to see if she were real—that she yelped in surprise, and then was embarrassed that she had done so. But the men had already passed, hauling the big basket up to the council house where it would be divided up between the village families.

Mother Orla coughed. "A stranger who sleeps in a woman's house without her promise and her binding is not the kind of adult a village can trust as one of its own."

"I was hasty, Mother Orla. Do not think it his doing. I invited him into the house without waiting for the proper ceremony."

"He did not enter," retorted Mother Orla approvingly. "Or so I hear."

"I hope you will advise me in this matter," Adica murmured humbly. "I have no experience. You know how things went with Beor."

"That was not a wise match." Mother Orla spat, to free herself of any bad luck from mentioning such an ill-fated decision. "Nevertheless, it is done with. Beor will see that his jealousy has no place in this village."

"So easily?"

"If he cannot stomach a new man in the village, then he can go to his Black Deer cousins, or marry Mother Nahumia's daughter and move to Old Fort."

"I believe it would be better to have a strong fighter like Beor stay here until—until the war is over, Mother Orla."

"That may be. But we've no need of pride and anger tearing down our community in times like these. There will be no more spoken on this matter."

"As you wish." In a way, it was a relief to be spoken to as if from aunt to niece. It was hard to act as an elder all the time when she was really still young.

"Let the stranger sleep at the men's house," continued Mother Orla. "After all, would you want a man for husband who had so little self-respect that he didn't expect courtship?"

Adica laughed, because the comment was so unexpected and so charged with a gratifying anticipation. At first she did not see Alain up by the council house, but she soon caught sight of him among the others because of the dogs who faithfully followed after him. A vision shivered through her, brief but dazzling: she saw, not Alain, but a phoenix, fiery and hot, shining beyond the ordinary with such intensity that she had to look away.

"Truly," Mother Orla continued in the voice of one who has seen nothing unusual, "the Holy One chose wisely."

II
MANY MEETINGS

1

AT night, the stars blazed with a brightness unlike that of any stars Liath had ever seen. They seemed alive, souls writhing and shifting, speaking in a language born out of fire rather than words. Sometimes she thought she could understand them, but then the sensation would fade. Sometimes she thought she could touch them, but the heavens rose as far above her here in this country as they ever had in the land of her birth.

So much lay beyond her grasp, especially her own past.

Right now, she lay on her back with her hands folded behind her head on a pallet made of leaves and grass. "Are the stars living souls?"

"The stars are fire." The old sorcerer often sat late with her, silent or talkative depending on his mood. "If they have souls and consciousness, I do not know."

"What of the creatures who brought me here?"

Here in the country of the Aoi, there was never a moon, but the stars shone with such brilliance that she could see him shake his head. "These spirits you speak of burn in the air with wings of flame and eyes as brilliant as knives. They move on the winds of aether, and now and again their gaze falls like the strike of lightning to the Earth below. There, it sears anything it touches, for they cannot comprehend the frailty of Earthly life."

"If they aren't the souls of stars, then what are they?"

"They are an elder race. Their bodies are not bodies as we know them but rather the conjoining of fire and wind. In their bodies it is as if the breath of the fiery Sun coalesces into mind and will."

"Why did they call me *child,* then?"

He was always making rope, or baskets, always weaving strands into something new. Even in the darkness, he twined plant fiber into rope against one thigh. "The elder races partake of nothing earthly but only of the pure elements. We are their children in as much as some portion of what we are made of is derived from those pure elements."

"So any creature born on Earth is in some way their child."

"That may be," he said, laughing dryly. "Yet there is more to you than your human form. That we speak each to the other right now is a mystery I cannot explain, because the languages of humankind are unknown to me, and you say that the language of my people is not known to you. But we met through the gateway of fire, and it may be that the binding of magic lies heavier over us than any language made only of words."

"It seems to me that with you I speak the language known to my people as Dariyan."

"And to me, it is as if we speak in my own tongue. But I cannot believe that these two are the same. The count of years that separates my people from your land must span many generations of humankind. Few among humankind spoke the language of my people when we dwelt on Earth. How then can it be that you have remembered my people's language all this time?"

It was a good question, and deserved a thoughtful answer. "Long before I was born, an empire rose whose rulers claimed to be your descendants, born out of the mating of your kind and humankind. Perhaps they preserved your language as their speech, and that is why we can speak together now. But truly, I don't know. The empresses and emperors of the old Dariyan Empire were half-breeds, so they claimed. There aren't any Aoi on Earth any longer. They exist there only as ghosts, more like shades than living creatures. Some say there never were true Aoi on Earth, that they're only tales from the dawn time of humankind."

"Truly, tales have a way of changing shape to suit the teller. If you wish to know what the spirits meant when they addressed you as 'child,' then you must ask them yourself."

The stars scintillated so vividly that they seemed to pulse. Strangely, she could find not one familiar constellation. She felt as if she had been flung into a different plane of existence, yet the dirt under her feet smelled like plain, good dirt, and many of the plants were ones she remembered from her childhood, when she and Da had traveled in the lands whose southern boundary was the great middle sea: silver pine and white oak, olive and carob, prickly juniper and rosemary and myrtle. She sighed, taking in the scent of rosemary, oddly comforting, like a favorite childhood story retold.

"I would ask them, if I could reach them."

"To reach them, you must learn to walk the spheres."

The arrow came without warning. Pale as ivory, it buried its head in the trunk of a pine. Grabbing her quiver, Liath rolled off her pallet and into the cover of a low-lying holm oak. The old sorcerer remained calmly sitting in his place, still rolling flax into rope against his leg. He hadn't even flinched. Behind him, the arrow quivered and stilled, a stark length of white against drought-blighted pine bark.

"What is that?" she demanded, still breathing hard. In the four days since she had come to this land, she had seen no sign of any other people except herself and her teacher.

"It's a summons. When light comes, I must attend council."

"What will happen to you, and to me, if your people know I'm here?"

"That remains to be seen."

She slept restlessly that night, waking up at intervals to find that he sat in trancelike silence beside her, completely still but with his eyes open. Sometimes when she woke, half muddled from an unremembered and anxious dream, she would see the stars and for an instant would recognize the familiar shapes of the constellations Da had taught her; but always, in the next instant, they would shift in their place, leaving her to stare upward at an alien sky. She could not even see the River of Heaven, which spanned the sky in her own land. In that river, the souls of the dead swam toward the Chamber of Light, and some among them looked down upon the Earth below to watch over their loved ones, now left behind. Was Da lost to her? Did his spirit gaze down upon Earth and wonder where she had gone?

Yet was she any different than he was, wondering what had become of those left behind? Da hadn't meant to die, after all. *She* had left behind those she loved of her own free will.

At night, she often wondered if she had made the right decision. Sometimes she wondered if she really loved them.

If she'd really loved them, it shouldn't have been so easy to let them go.

Twilight had little hold on this place. Day came suddenly, without the intervening solace of dawn. Liath woke when light brushed her face, and she watched as the old sorcerer's expression passed from trance to waking in a transition so smooth that it was imperceptible. He rose and stretched the stiffness out of his limbs as she sat up, checking to see that her bow was ready and arrows laid out. Her sword lay within easy reach, and she always slept with her knife tucked in its sheath at her belt.

"Go to the stream," he said. "Follow the flower trail to the watchtower. Do not come out unless you hear me call to you, nor should you wander, lest others come upon you. Remember to take care, and do nothing to cut yourself or let any blood fall." He began to walk away, paused, and called to her over his shoulder. "Make good use of the time! You have not yet mastered the tasks I set you."

That these tasks were tedious beyond measure was evidently part of the training. She belted on her sword and fastened her quiver over her shoulders. She had become accustomed to fasting for a good while after she woke; it helped stave off hunger. She took the water jug with her, slung over her shoulder by a rope tied to its handles.

As she walked down the path, she noted as always how parched the ground was. The needles on the pine trees were dry, and perhaps a quarter were turning brown, dying. Few other trees were hardy enough to survive here: white oak, olive, and, increasingly, silver pine. Where dead trees had fallen, carob grew up, shadowing buckthorn, clematis, and spiny grass. She never saw any rodents. Despite the isolation of their living circumstances, she had seen no deer, aurochs, wolves, or bears—none of the great beasts that roamed plentifully through the ancient forests of Earth. Only rarely did she hear birds or see their fluttering flight in the withered branches.

The land was dying.

"I am dying," she whispered into the silence.

How else could she explain the calm, the sense of relief, she'd fallen into since she had arrived in the country of the Aoi? Maybe it was only numbness. It was easier not to feel than to confront all the events that had led her to this place. Was her heart as stony as Anne's, who had said: *"We cannot let affection cloud our judgment"?*

With these words, Anne had justified the murder of her husband. No faceless enemy had summoned and commanded the spirit of air that had killed Bernard. His own wife, the mother of his child, had done so.

Anne had betrayed Da, and she had betrayed Liath not just by killing Da without a scrap of remorse but by making it clear that she expected Liath to behave in exactly the same way.

And hadn't Liath abandoned her own husband and child? She had not crossed through the burning stone of her own volition, but once here, in the land of the Aoi, she had had a choice: to stay and learn with the old sorcerer, or to return to Sanglant and Blessing.

Hadn't she also let judgment override affection? Hadn't she chosen knowledge over love? Hadn't it been easy to do so?

"I'm no use to Sanglant or to anyone until I master my own power," she muttered. "I can't avenge Da until I know what I am."

Her words fled on the silent air and vanished like ghosts into the eerie silence of the drought-stricken land. Even the rage she'd nurtured toward Anne since the moment she'd discovered the truth about Da's death felt cold and lifeless now, like a clay statue clumsily formed.

With a sigh, she walked on.

The stream had once been a small river. She picked her way over river rocks coated with a white rime of dried scum, until she reached the narrow channel that was all that remained of the watercourse. Water trickled over rocks, sluicing down from highlands glimpsed beyond the sparse forest cover. She knelt to fill the pot, stoppered it carefully. In this land, water was more precious than gold.

Holding the full vessel hard against one hip, she leaped from stone to stone over the stream to its other side. Algae lay exposed in intricate patterns like green paint flaking off the river stones. Grass had invaded the old riverbed, but even it was turning brown. Climbing the steep bank, she found herself at a fork in the path. To the right the path cut through a thicket of chestnut that hugged the shore before, beyond the chestnut grove, beginning a precipitous climb to higher ground. To the left lay a remarkable trail through a low-lying meadow lush with the most astoundingly beautiful flowers: lavender, yellow rue, blood-red poppies, delicate gillyvor, fat peonies, pale dog roses, vivid marigolds, banks of irises like earthbound rainbows, all intermixed with a scattering of urgently blue cornflowers.

This flowery trail wound up away from the river like a dream, unheralded, unexpected, and unspeakably splendid in a land so faded to browns and leached-out golds. It was difficult not to linger in this oasis of color, and she did for a while, but eventually she had to move on.

The meadow came to an abrupt end where a finger of pine woods thrust out along the hillside. The drought had taken its toll here as well, and the wood quickly degraded into a grassy heath. At the height of the hill stood a tumble of worked stone that had once been a lookout station. She climbed to the highest safe point, where she crouched on a ledge, bracing herself against what remained of the rock wall, and looked out over the land.

The hillside fell away precipitously, as if the watchtower had once looked over a valley, but in fact there was nothing to be seen below except fog.

According to the old sorcerer, this was the outer limit of the land. Nothing lay beyond the mist. She stared at it for a long time. Above, the sky shaded from the merciless blue of drought-stricken country into an oddly vacant white, more void than cloud.

The silence oppressed her. Out here, at the edge of the world, she didn't even hear birds, nothing except a solitary cricket. It was as if the land were slowly emptying out, as if the heart and soul of it were leaching away into the void. Like her own heart.

Setting quiver and sword aside, she settled down cross-legged. She clapped once, a sound to split away the ordinary world from the world where magic lived, or so the old sorcerer had taught her. With patterns he had shown her, she stilled her mind so that, below the clutter of everyday thoughts, she could listen into the heart of the world: the purl of air at her neck, the slow shifting of stone, the distant babble of water, and beneath all those, the nascent stirring, like a flower about to bloom, of vast power held in check by its own peculiar architecture.

"Humankind was crippled by their hands," the old sorcerer had said. "They came to believe that the forces of the world could only succumb to manipulation. But the universe exists at a level invisible to our eyes and untouchable by our hands, but comprehensible by our minds and hearts. That is the essence of magic, which seeks neither to harm nor to control but only to preserve and transform."

In every object, all the pure elements mix in various proportions. If she could calm her own breathing, draw her concentration to such a narrow point that it blossomed into an infinite vista, then she could illuminate the heart of any object and draw out from it those elements which might be of use to her in her spells.

In this way, the daimones who had enfolded her within their wings had called fire even from stone, even from the very mountains. This was the magic known to the Aoi.

But she had a long way to go to master it.

At last she ascended through levels of awareness and clapped her hands four times, a sharp sound that brought her squarely back to the ordinary world. One of her feet had fallen asleep. She scratched the back of her neck, tickled by a withered leaf, and blinked a mote of dust out of one eye. Slinging her quiver over her shoulder, she clambered back down, testing each stone as she went, bypassing those that rattled or shifted under her probing foot.

In the shade at the base of the tower, she drank sparingly and finally allowed herself to eat: some desiccated berries, a coarse flat bread made palatable by being fried in olive oil, the sugary, withered carob pods she gathered every day, and today's delicacy, a paste of fish-meal and crushed parsnip flavored with onion and pulped juniper berries. There was something so desperate about each meal here that she had quickly learned that the old sorcerer would neither watch her eat nor let her watch him.

After she had licked every crumb off her fingers, she turned to her coil of rope. Twisting fiber into rope was the most tedious of the tasks the old sorcerer had set her but one he insisted she master. She had amassed a fair length of rope. She measured it out against an outstretched arm: forty cubits worth. It would have to be enough.

Tying one end around her waist, she cinched it tight and, with her weapons slung about her, walked to the edge of the fog. She tied the other end of the rope to the trunk of a pine tree, tugging to test the knot, before she swept her gaze along the hillside. Nothing stirred. A bug crawled through the dry grass at her feet, startling because it was the only sign of movement except for the swaying of trees in a delicate wind.

She walked cautiously into the fog. In five steps she was blind. She could not even see where the rope left the fog. She could not see her hands held out in front of her face, although blue flashed from her finger: the lapis lazuli ring given to her by Alain which, he had promised her, would protect her from evil.

She wasn't sure what to expect: the edge of an abyss? A barricade? A dead land drowned in cloying mist?

In another five steps, she walked out onto a ridgeline. At her back drifted the wall of fog. Right in front of her grew a dense tangle of thorny shrubs. As she jerked sideways to avoid them, her trailing hand brushed a thorn. A line of red welled up on her skin. She stuck the scrape to her mouth and sucked. A serpent hissed at her from the shelter of the thornbush and she sidled away slowly as superstitious dread clutched at her heart.

"Even a single drop of your blood on the parched earth will waken things better left sleeping," the old sorcerer had said, *"and every soul left in this land will know that you are here."*

The bleeding subsided, the serpent slithered away deeper into the thorns, but her thoughts continued to scatter and drop.

He meant to keep her a secret. But whether he thought she was a threat to his people, or they to her, she could not tell. As the salty tang of blood mixed with saliva on her tongue, she wondered what would happen when her monthly courses came in another hand's span of days, or if they even would, without the influence of the moon upon her body.

Wind stirred the rope hanging loose behind her. The sun beat down, hot and heavy, on her back. The fog had led her not to the end of the world but simply to an unknown place not markedly different from the highland forest.

She stood at the edge of a plunging hillside. A broad valley ringed by highlands opened before her. On the far side of the valley's bowl rose a saw-toothed mountain range. High peaks, denuded of snow, towered above the wide valley. A road ran along the valley floor below her, leading into a magnificent city that spanned a dried-up lakebed. It was the largest conglomeration of buildings she had ever seen, greater even than the imperial city of Darre. From this vantage point, and through air so clear that she could see the ridgelines in each of the distant peaks, she traced the city's layout as though it were an architect's study rolled out on a table.

Plazas, pyramids, and platforms, great courtyards flanked by marketplaces, houses arranged like flowers around rectangular pools, all of these were linked together by sludge-ridden waterways that had once, perhaps, been canals. Tiered stone gardens and islets lay desolate, furrowed by untended fields. Bridges spanned inlets and narrow straits that divided the island city into districts. Three causeways stretched across the dead lakebed, marking roads into the city.

Bleached like bone, the buildings had been laid out in an arrangement so harmonious that she wondered whether the city had been built to conform to the lake's shallows and bays, or the lake dug and shaped to enhance the city. From this distance the city appeared deserted, empty buildings set in a vast wasteland of drained, cracking ground.

At that moment, she became aware of a solitary figure moving slowly along the road below her. It halted, suddenly, and turned as if it had felt her breath on its neck, although she stood far beyond any normal range of hearing. Its hand raised, beckoning to her, or gesturing with a curse.

The ground lurched under her feet. Stumbling backward, she pulled the rope in tight as she forged back into the fog. White swam around her, static and empty. Her foot hit a rock, and she reeled sideways, found herself up to her thighs in water. Salt spray stung her lips. Waves soughed on a pebbly shoreline, sucking and sighing over the rocks. Grassy dunes humped up beyond the beach. A gull screamed. Turning, she tugged hard on the rope and reeled herself in, one fist at a time, through the blinding fog.

When she staggered out onto the hillside, the watchtower rose before her and she fell to her knees in relief, gasping hard. Water puddled out from her soaked leggings, absorbed quickly into the parched soil.

"You are a fool, Eldest Uncle," said a woman's harsh voice. "You know the stories. They cannot help themselves. Already she has broken the small limits you set upon her. Already she gathers intelligence for her own kind, which they will use against us."

The old sorcerer had a curt laugh. Although he was not a cynic, certainly he was not patient with anything he considered nonsense; this much she had learned about him in their short time together. "How can they use the knowledge of the borders against us, White Feather? There is but one human standing here among us. None but she has crossed through the gateways in all this time. Why do you suppose others intend to? Nay, she is alone, as I have told you. She is an outcast from her own kind."

"So she would have you believe."

"You are too suspicious."

"Should I not be suspicious of humankind? You are too trusting, Eldest Uncle. It was those of our people who trusted humankind who laid down the path that brought us here. Had we not taught human magicians our secrets, they would not have gained the power to strike against us as they did."

"Nay." Liath saw them now, standing on her favorite ledge halfway up the ruined watchtower, looking down upon her like nobles passing judgment on their followers. "It was the *shana-ret'zeri* who corrupted humankind, not us."

"They would have overwhelmed us no matter what we had done," agreed the woman. She wore a plain linen cloak, yellowed with age, that draped over her right shoulder and lapped her knees. Underneath, she wore a shift patterned with red lozenges and dots. A strap bound her brow; at the back, where her hair fell freely down her back, the strap had been ornamented with a small shield of white feathers. A heavy jade ring pierced her nose. "Humankind breeds offspring like to the mice, and disease in the manner of flies. We cannot trust them. You must bring her along to the council ground. The council will pass judgment."

With that, she vanished from Liath's view, climbing back down the ruined watchtower. The old sorcerer clambered down as well, appearing at the base of the tower, although White Feather was not with him. Liath rose to shake water out of her soaked leggings.

"She doesn't trust me," Liath said, surprised at the intensity of the woman's emotions. "I don't think she liked me either. Is that the kind of judgment the council will pass? I see no point in standing before them if they're just going to condemn me."

"Not even I, who am eldest here, the only one left who remembers the great cataclysm, knows what judgment the council will pass."

"How can you remember the great cataclysm? If the calculations of the Seven Sleepers are correct, then that cataclysm took place over two thousand and seven hundred years ago, as humankind measures time. No one can be that old."

"Nor am I that old, as humankind measures years. The measure of days and years moves differently here than there. I know what I lived through. What has passed in the world of my birth in the intervening time I have seen only in glimpses. I know only that humankind has overrun all of the land, as we feared they would."

None of this made much sense to Liath. "What of the

burning stone, then?" She would not make the same mistake she had made with the Seven Sleepers, to wait with resigned patience as they taught her in spirals that never quite got to the heart of what she needed to learn. "If it's a gateway between my world and this one, can you call it at will? Might it be better for me to escape back to Earth rather than stand before the council?"

He considered her words gravely before replying. "The burning stone is not ours to call. It appears at intervals dictated by those fluxes that disturb the fabric of the universe. It is the remnant of the great spell worked on us by your ancestors, although I do not suppose that they meant it to appear. But a few among us have learned how to manipulate it when it does appear."

"How might I do so?"

"Learn to call the power of the stars, and the power that lies in the heart of every object. The first you have some knowledge of, I think. The second is not a discipline known to humankind." He paused to smile wryly. He had faint scars around his mouth and others on the lobes of his ears, on his hands, and even a few marking his heels with old white scar lines. "You must not fear the power of blood, which binds all things. You must learn to use it, even when it causes pain. I do not think you should retreat. It is rarely wise to run."

That Anne considered this ancient sorcerer and all his kind the sworn enemy of humankind, and of her own cause, inclined Liath to take their part. But in the end it was his words that swayed her. How different he sounded from Da, who had always found it prudent to run. Who had taught her to run.

"I'll go with you to the council," she said finally.

"Heh." The grunt folded into that curt laugh which seemed to encompass all he knew of amusement. "So you will. Do not think I am unaware of the honor you give to me by granting me your trust. It has been a long time since any of your kind have trusted mine."

"Or your kind, mine," she retorted. The tart answer pleased him. He liked a challenge, and didn't mind sharp questions.

"Get what you need, then."

"I've everything I came with."

He waited while she coiled the rope.

"It's well made." The praise warmed her, but she only smiled. He had little enough on his own person for their journey. She had finally gotten used to his clothing, the beaded loincloth, the decorated arm and leg sheaths, and the topknot made of his black hair, ornamented by feathers. He was more wiry than skinny, although he did not look one bit well fed. He took the coiled rope from her and slung it over a shoulder before fishing out an arrow from her quiver. As always, he fondled the iron point for a moment, his expression distant.

"I fear what your kinfolk have become," he said at random, "to make arms such as this arrow, and that sword." But he only offered her the fletched end of the arrow to hold. "Grasp this. Do not let go as we walk into the borderlands."

"Shouldn't we tie ourselves to the tree? What if we fall off the edge? You said yourself that this fog marks the edge of your lands."

He chuckled. "A worthy idea, and a cautious plan that speaks well of you. But there is no danger in the borderlands. We are prisoners in our own land, because all the borders fold back on themselves."

"Except through the burning stone."

"Even so." He led her into the fog.

"Where are we going?" she called, but the mist deadened all sound. She could not even see him, a step ahead of her, only knew he was there by the pull of the arrow's shaft against her palm.

He knew where he was going. In six steps she stumbled onto a stone step, bruising her shin. She stood on a staircase lined by monsters' heads, each one carved so that it seemed to be emerging from a stone flower that bore twelve petals. The monster was the head of a snake, or that of a big, sleek cat with a toothy yawn, or some melding of the two: she couldn't tell which. Some had been painted red and white while others had golden-brown dapplings and succulent green tongues, lacy black curling ears or gold-petaled flowers rayed out from their circular eyes. On either side of the staircase lay the broad expanse of a vast pyramidal structure, too steep to climb, that had simply been painted a blinding white, as stark as the fog. Here and there, paint had chipped away to reveal gray stone beneath.

She followed the old sorcerer up the steps. Despite everything, this staircase up which they toiled nagged at her. It seemed familiar, like a whispered name calling from her memory.

They walked up out of the fog on a steep incline, surrounded by those ghastly, powerful faces. The stair steps went on, and on, and on, until she had to stop to catch her breath. She unsealed the water jug and sipped, cooling her parched throat, but when she offered the jug to the old sorcerer, he declined. He waited patiently for her to finally get up and go again. At last, they came to the top of the pyramid.

At her back, below and beyond, lay the dense bank of fog. Before her lay another city, somewhat smaller than the magnificent city by the lake but no less impressive for its courtyards and platforms laid out in tidy harmony. An avenue lined by buildings marched out from the plaza that lay at the base of the huge pyramid they now stood on. Every stone surface was painted with bright murals: giant spotted yellow cats, black eagles, golden phoenix, burning arrows clutched in the jaws of red snakes crowned by feathered headdresses. The city lay alive with color and yet was so quiet that she expected ghosts to skirl down its broad avenues, weeping and moaning.

Wind brushed her. Clouds boiled over the hills that marked the distant outskirts of the city, and she saw lightning. Thunder boomed, but no rain fell. She couldn't even smell rain, only dust on the wind and a creeping shiver on her skin. Her hair rose on the nape of her neck.

"It's not safe so high where lightning might strike," remarked the old sorcerer.

He descended at once down stair steps so steep that she only dared follow him by turning around and going down backward. Behind, the fog simply sliced off that portion of the city that lay beyond the great pyramid, a line as abrupt as a knife's cut.

Thunder clapped and rolled. Lightning struck the top of the pyramid, right where they'd been standing. Her tongue buzzed with the sting of its passing. Her foot touched earth finally, dry and cool.

She knew where she was.

Long ago, when she was a child, when she and Da had fled from the burning villa, he had brought her through an ancient city. In that city, the wind had muttered through the open shells of buildings. Vast ruins had lain around them, the skeleton of a city that had once claimed the land. Along the avenues, she had seen the faded remnants of old murals that had once adorned those long walls. Wind and rain and time had worn the paint from those surfaces, leaving only the tired grain of ancient stone blocks and a few scraps of surviving murals, faded and barely visible.

The ruins had ended at the shoreline of the sea as abruptly as if a knife had sheared them off.

Da had muttered words, an ancient spell, and for an instant she had seen the shadow form of the old city mingling with the waves, the memory of what once had been, not drowned by the sea but utterly *gone*. Wonder bloomed in her heart, just as it had on that long-ago day.

"This is that city," she said aloud.

The old sorcerer had begun to walk on, but he paused.

"I've seen the other part of this city," she explained. "The part that would have lain there——" She pointed toward the wall of fog. "But the ruins were so old. Far older than the cities built by the Dariyans. That was the strangest thing."

"That they were old?"

"Nay, nay." Her thoughts had already leaped on. "That the ruins ended so abruptly. As if the land was cut away from the Earth."

He smiled sadly. "No memory remains among humankind of the events of those days?"

She could only shake her head, perplexed by his words.

"Come," he said.

At the far end of the avenue rose a second monumental structure, linked to the great pyramid by the roadway. Platforms rose at intervals on either side. It was hard to fathom what kind of engineering, or magic, had built this city. The emptiness disturbed her. She could imagine ancient assemblies crowding the avenue, brightly-clothed women and men gathered to watch spectacles staged on the platforms or to pray as their holy caretakers offered praise to their gods from the perilous height of the great pyramid. Yet such a crowd had left no trace of its passage, not even ghosts.

It was a long walk and an increasingly hot one as the storm rolled past and dissolved into the wall of fog. Not one drop of rain fell. She had to stop twice to drink, although the old sorcerer refused a portion both times.

The other temple was also a four-sided pyramid, sloped in stair steps and chopped off short. At the top loomed the visage of a huge stone serpent. An opening gaped where the serpent's mouth ought to have been, framed by two triangular stacks of pale stone.

Flutes and whistles pierced the silence. Had the ghosts of the city come to haunt her? Color flashed in the distance and resolved into a procession of people dressed in feathered cloaks and beaded garments, colors and textures so bright that they would have been gaudy against any background, although the vast backdrop of the city and the fierce blue of the sky almost swallowed them. At the head of the procession bobbed a round standard on a pole, a circular sheet of gold trimmed with iridescent green plumes as broad across as a man's arms outstretched. It spun like a turning wheel. Its brilliance staggered her.

The procession wound its way in through the serpent's mouth, vanishing into the temple.

They came to the stairs, where Eldest Uncle paused while she caught her breath and checked each of her weapons: her knife, her good friend Lucian's sword, and Seeker of Hearts, her bow. A wash of voices issued out through the serpent's mouth like the voices of the dead seeping up from the under-world.

"They will not be friendly," he said. "Be warned: speak calmly. In truth, young one, I took you on because I fear that only you and I can spare both our peoples a greater destruction than that which we are already doomed to suffer."

His words—delivered in the same cool matter-of-fact tone he might have used if he were commenting on an interesting architectural feature—chilled her. The long avenue behind her lay wreathed in a heat haze. Wind raised dust. The great pyramid shone in uncanny and massive splendor.

"I faced down Hugh," she said at last. "I can face down anyone."

They climbed the steps toward the serpent's head. Coming up before it, Liath found herself face-to-face with those two flanking little pyramids of stone, except they weren't stone at all.

They were stacks of grinning skulls.

"What are those?" she demanded, heart racing in shock as vacant eyes stared back at her.

"The fallen." A half-dozen bows and quivers lay on a flat stone placed in front of the serpent's mouth, and a dozen or more spears rested against the stone. All of the weapons had stone tips. The only metal she saw came from three knives, forged of copper or bronze.

"Set your weapons here on the peace stone."

"And walk in there unarmed?"

"No weapons are allowed on the council grounds. That is the custom. That way no blood may be shed in the heart of the city."

She hesitated, but the sight of so many other weapons made it easier to acquiesce. She did not know their powers, but she knew how to call fire, if necessary. She set down her weapons, yet he stopped her before she passed the threshold.

"Water, too, has been forbidden. Even a sip might be used as a bribe. Let us drink deep now. It may be many hours before we emerge from the tomb of the ancient mothers."

The water was brackish by now, warmed by the sun's heat. But it was water and therefore miraculous beyond words to one who is thirsty.

Taking the half-empty jug, he hid it among the skulls. Their dry, grinning faces had lost their horror. They weren't even ghosts, just the memory of folk who had once lived and bled as she did. What fate had led them to this end?

"Come." The old sorcerer gestured toward the serpent's maw.

It seemed very dark inside. Even the whispering of distant voices had stilled, as if in expectation of their arrival.

She *had* faced down Hugh, she *had* learned courage, but she still murmured a prayer under her breath. "Lord, watch over me now, I pray you. Lady, lend me your strength."

Somewhere, in another place, Sanglant surely wondered what had become of her, and maybe Blessing cried, fretting in unfamiliar arms. It seemed to her, as she stepped into the dark opening as though into a serpent's mouth, that she had a long way to go to get back to them.

2

NORTH of the Alfar Mountains the ground fell precipitously into a jumble of foothills and river valleys. At this time of year, that place where late summer slumbered into early autumn, the roads were as good as they'd ever be and the weather remained pleasant except for the occasional drenching thunder-shower. They kept up a brisk pace, traveling as many as six leagues in a day. There were just enough day laborers on the road looking for the last bits of harvest work that their little group didn't seem too conspicuous, as long as they didn't draw attention to themselves.

It was a silent journey for the most part.

When they passed folk coming from the north, Sanglant asked questions, but the local folk, when he could understand their accent, claimed to have no knowledge of the movements of the king. Nor was there any reason they should have. But he heard one day from a trio of passing fraters that the king and his entourage had been expected in Wertburg, so at the cross-roads just past the ferry crossing over the eastern arm of the Vierwald Lake, they took the northeast fork that led through the lush fields of upper Wayland toward the Malnin River valley. In such rich countryside, more people were to be found on the roads, going about their business.

Still, it was with some surprise that, about twelve days after the conflagration at Verna and less than seven days' travel past the lake crossing, they met outriders at midday where forest gave way to a well-tended orchard.

"Halt!"

A zealous young fellow seated on a swaybacked mare rode forward to block the road. He held a spear in one hand as he looked them over. No doubt they appeared a strange sight: a tall, broad-shouldered man outfitted like a common man-at-arms and carrying a swaddled baby on his back but riding a noble gelding whose lines and tackle were fit for a prince, and a woman whose exotic features might make any soldier pause. The pony and the goat, at least, were unremarkable. Luckily, the young man couldn't see Jerna, who had darted away to conceal herself in the boughs of an apple tree.

He stared for a bit, mostly at the woman, then found his voice. "Have you wanderers come to petition the king?"

"So we have," said Sanglant, keeping his voice calm although his heart hammered alarmingly. "Is the king nearby?"

"The court's in residence at Angenheim, but it's a long wait for petitioners. Many have come—"

"Here, now, Matto, what are these two?" The sergeant in charge rode up. His shield bore the sigil of Wendar at its center, Lion, Eagle, and Dragon, marking him as a member of the king's personal retinue. He had the look of a terrier about him: ready to worry any stray rat to pieces.

"They come up the road like any others," protested Matto.

"So might the devil. They might be the Enemy's cousins, by the look of their faces. As foreign as you please, I'll thank you to notice, lad. I'd like to know how they come by that fine nobleman's horse. We're looking for bandits, Matto. You've got to stay alert."

"Trouble, Sergeant?" asked another soldier, riding over.

There were half a dozen men-at-arms in sight, scattered along the road. None were soldiers Sanglant recognized. New recruits, maybe, given sentry duty. They looked bored.

Boredom always spelled trouble, and it wasn't only these men-at-arms who were bored. Sanglant glanced at his mother. Even after twelve days in her company, he still found her disconcerting. She gazed at young Matto with the look of a panther considering its next meal, and she even licked her lips thoughtfully, as though the air brought her a taste of his sweet flesh.

Sanglant knew how to make quick decisions. If he didn't recognize these men, then it was likely they'd come to court after he and Liath had left so precipitously over a year ago and so wouldn't recognize him in their turn. He turned to the sergeant. "Take me to Captain Fulk, and I promise you'll be well rewarded."

"Huh!" grunted the sergeant, taken aback. "How'd you know Captain Fulk returned to the king's progress just a fortnight ago?"

"We were separated." Sanglant leaned sideways so that the man could see Blessing's sweet little face peeping from the swaddling bound to his back.

"Ah." The sergeant's gaze was drawn to Sanglant's mother, but he looked away as quickly, as though something in her expression unsettled him. As well it might. "This is your wife, then?"

Sanglant laughed sharply, not without anger. "Nay. This woman is—" He could not bring himself to speak a title she had not earned. "This woman is a relative to me, a companion on the road. She's a foreigner, as you see. My father is Wendish."

"What happened to your wife, then?"

Grief still chafed him as bitterly as any chains. "My wife— is gone."

The sergeant softened, looking back at the infant. "May the Lord and Lady watch over you, friend. Need you an escort? There's another sentry post some ways up the road, nearer to the palace, and then the palace fortifications to talk your way through. I'll send a soldier to vouch for you."

"I'll take one with thanks. If you'll give me your name, I'll see that it's brought to the king's attention."

The sergeant chuckled while his men looked at each other in disbelief. "You're as sure of yourself as the rooster that crows at dawn, eh? Well, then, when you take supper with the king, tell him that Sergeant Cobbo of Longbrook did you a favor." He slapped his thigh, amused at his joke. "Go on, then. Matto, be sure you escort them all the way to Captain Fulk, and give him over to none other. The captain will know what to do with them if they've lied to us."

Matto was a talkative soul. Sanglant found it easy to draw him out. They rode on through the orchard and passed into another tangle of forest, where Jerna took advantage of the dappled light to drop down from the trees and coil around Blessing's swaddling bands. He could sense her cool touch on his neck and even see the pale shimmer of her movement out of the corner of his eye, but Matto, like most of humankind, seemed oblivious to her. He chattered on as Sanglant fed him questions. His mother was a steward at a royal estate. His father had died in the wars many years ago, and his mother had married another man. Matto seemed young because he was young. He and his stepfather hadn't gotten along, and he'd left for the king's service as soon as he turned fifteen.

"I've been with the king's court for fully six months now," he confided. "They put me to work as a stable hand at first, but even Sergeant Cobbo says I've got a knack for weapons, so I was promoted to sentry duty three months ago." He glanced back toward Sanglant's mother, perhaps hoping she'd be impressed by his quick rise, but nothing about humankind interested her, as Sanglant had discovered.

"You've got a hankering to see battle, haven't you, lad?" Sanglant felt immeasurably ancient riding alongside this enthusiastic youth, although in truth he wasn't even old enough to be the lad's father.

Matto sized him up. "You've seen battle, haven't you?"

"So I have."

"I guess you were part of the group that went south to Aosta with Princess Theophanu. It was a miracle that Captain Fulk kept as much of his company together as he did, wasn't it? What a disaster!"

"Truly." Sanglant changed the subject before Matto discovered that he hadn't the least idea what disaster had befallen Theophanu's expedition in Aosta. "Why so wide a sentry net?"

Matto puffed up considerably, proud to know something his companion did not. "The court attracts petitioners, and petitioners attract bandits."

"Aren't these Duke Conrad's lands? I'd have thought he'd have put a stop to banditry."

"So he might, if he were here. He hasn't even come to the king's feast and celebration! The Eagle sent to his fortress at Bederbor said he wasn't in residence. No one knows where he's gone!"

What was Conrad up to? No doubt the duke was capable of almost anything. But he could hardly ask this lad that kind of question. They came to a stream and slowed for their mounts to pick their way across. Where a beech tree swept low over pooling water, he let Resuelto drink while he waited for his mother. Although she had the pony for a mount, she refused to ride. Still, she caught up quickly enough; she was the strongest walker he'd ever met. The goat balked at the water's edge, and his mother dragged it across the rocky shallows impatiently. She had formidable arms, tightly muscled. With the sleeves of Liath's tunic rolled up, the tattooed red snake that ran from the back of her hands up her arms seemed to stretch and shudder as she hauled the goat up the far bank. Matto stared at her. Sanglant couldn't tell if the boy had been afflicted with the infatuation that strikes youth as suddenly as lightning, or if he had suddenly realized how truly *strange* she was.

"What's your name?" Matto blurted suddenly.

She looked up at him, and he blanched and stammered an apology, although it wasn't clear what he was apologizing for. Her reply was cool and clear. "You will call me 'Alia.'"

Sanglant laughed curtly before reining Resuelto around and starting down the road again. 'Alia' meant 'other' in Dariyan.

Alia walked up beside him. The goat had decided to cooperate and now followed meekly behind the pony, with Matto bringing up the rear. "Why are you not telling those soldiers who you are," she asked in a low voice, her accent heavy and her words a little halting, "and demanding a full escort and the honor you deserve?"

"Since they don't know me, they would never believe I am a prince of the realm. In truth, without a retinue, I'm not really a nobleman at all, am I? Just a landless and kinless wanderer, come to petition the king." He hadn't realized how bitter he was, nor did he know who he was angriest at: fate, his father, or the woman walking beside him who had abandoned him years ago. Blessing stirred on his back and cooed, babbling meaningless syllables, attuned to his tone. "Hush, sweetheart," he murmured. Resuelto snorted.

"Look!" cried Matto. The road was wide enough that he trotted past them easily. He had a hand at his belt, where hung a knife, a leather pouch, and a small polished ram's horn.

Up ahead where the ground dipped into a shrubby hollow, the stream looped back and crossed the road again. In the middle of the ford stood a hag, bent over a staff. Strips of shredded cloth concealed her head and shoulders. The ragged ends of her threadbare robe floated in the current, wrapping around her calves.

"A coin or crust of bread for an old woman whose husband and son fight in the east with Her Royal Highness Princess Sapientia?" she croaked.

Matto had already begun to dismount, fumbling at the pouch he wore at his belt. Perhaps he was a kindhearted lad, or perhaps he was only eager to impress Alia.

But despite its high-pitched tone, the hag's voice was certainly not that of a woman. This was one thing in which Sanglant considered himself an expert. He reined in. A moment later, from the dense thicket that grew up from the opposite bank, he heard rustling.

The arrow hit Sanglant in the shoulder, rocking him back. The point embedded in his chain mail just as a second arrow followed the first from a shadowed thicket. He jerked sideways as Jerna uncoiled and with her aery being blew the arrow off course. It fluttered harmlessly into the branches of a tree.

Alia already had her bow free and an arrow notched. She hissed, then shot, and there came a yelp of pain from the thicket.

The hag hooked Matto's leg and dumped the youth backward into the water. The quick motion revealed the burly shoulders of a man hidden beneath the rags. With a loud cry, the robber brought the staff down on Matto's unprotected head and pummeled him. The boy could only cower with arms raised to fend off blows.

More arrows flew. Jerna became wind, and two arrows stopped dead in midair before Resuelto's neck even as Sanglant spurred the gelding forward. The horse went eagerly into battle. He knew what to expect and, like his master, had been trained for this life. Leaping the brook, Sanglant struck to his left, severing the hand of the first bandit before the man could let another blow fall on Matto. Alia's second arrow took the "hag" in the back as he turned to run.

Men screamed the alert from their hiding place, but Sanglant had already plunged forward into the thicket, crashing through the foliage into a clear hollow where a knot of men, armed variously with staves, knives, an ax, and a single bow, stood ready. Easily his sword cleaved through branch, haft, and flesh. The bowman drew for a final shot as Sanglant closed on him.

Jerna leaped forward as on a gust. The arrow rocked sideways just as the bowman let it fly. The bow, too, spun from the bandit's grasp, and he grabbed for it frantically, caught the arrow point on his foot, and stumbled backward into a thick growth of sedge and fern.

Was that a voice, thin and weak, crying for mercy? Surely it was only the whine of a gnat. Sanglant brought his sword down, and the man fell, his skull split like a melon.

From the road he heard another shriek of pain, followed by a frantic rustling, growing ever more distant, that told of one—nay, two—survivors who would be running for some time.

A horn blatted weakly, nearby, and after a pause sounded again with more strength.

Blessing whimpered. Her voice brought him crashing back to himself. Amazed, he stared at the corpses: six men as ragged as paupers and as poorly armed as common laborers in want of a hire. He hadn't realized there were so many. He hadn't thought at all, just killed. One man still thrashed and moaned, but his wound was deep, having been cut through shoulder and lung, and blood bubbled up on his lips. After dismounting, Sanglant mercifully cut his throat.

Matto hobbled through the gap in the thicket made by

Resuelto's passage and staggered to a stop, staring. "By our Lord!" he swore. The horn dangled from its strap around one wrist.

"Your arm is broken," said Sanglant. He left the corpses and led Resuelto out to the road. The pony stood with legs splayed to resist the tugging of the tethered goat, who was trying to get to water. Alia had vanished. He heard her whistling tunelessly and saw the flash of her movement on the other side of the road, where another group of the bandits had been hiding behind a shield of slender beech trees. Her shadowed figure bent over a sprawled body. She tugged and with a grunt hopped backward with arrow in hand. To her left, another archer had been hiding right up against the trunk of a tree. His body was actually pinned to the tree by an arrow embedded in his throat. Blood had spilled down the trunk. That was the uncanniest sight of all: The obsidian point of the arrow was sticking out from the back of the man's neck, while the fletchings were embedded in the tree itself, as if a hole had opened in the tree to allow the arrow to pass through and then closed back up around the shaft at the instant the point found its mark.

Matto stumbled back to the path, still cradling his broken arm in his other hand. He was trying valiantly not to sob out loud.

"Let me see that," said Sanglant.

The youth came as trusting as a lamb. He sat down where Sanglant indicated, braced against a log, while the prince undid the boy's belt and gathered the other things he'd need: moss, a pair of stout sticks. He crouched beside the boy and fingered around the red lump swelling halfway along the forearm while Matto hissed hard through his teeth and tears started up in his eyes. It seemed to be a clean fracture, nothing shattered or snapped. The arm lay straight, and no bone had broken through the skin.

"No shame in crying, lad. You'll get worse if you stay with Henry's army."

"I want to stay with you, if you'll let me serve you," whispered the lad with that awful glow of admiration in his eyes, augmented by the glistening tears. "I want to learn to fight the way you do."

Perhaps he tightened his hand too hard on the injured arm. Matto cried out, reeling. Alia appeared suddenly and gripped the lad's shoulders to keep him still as Sanglant cradled the lump with moss and used the belt to bind the sticks along the forearm and hand. When he finished, he got the boy to drink, then rose and walked to the middle of the road where he threw back his head, listening. The bandits were all dead, or fled. A jay shrieked. The first carrion crow settled on a branch a stone's throw away. In the distance, he heard the ring of harness as horsemen approached.

Alia came up beside him. "Who's that coming? Do we leave the boy?"

"Nay, it'll be his company, the ones we just passed. The horn alerted them. We'll wait." He undid the sling that bound his daughter to his back, and swung her around to hold to his chest, careful that her cheeks took no harm from the mail. Jerna played in the breeze above the baby's head, carefree now that danger was past. Blessing babbled sweetly, smiling as soon as she saw her father's face.

"Da da," she said. "Da da."

Ai, God, she was growing so swiftly. No more than five months of age, she looked as big as a yearling and just yesterday at the fireside she had taken a few tottering steps on her own.

"How did that arrow go through the tree?" he asked casually as he smiled into his daughter's blue-fire eyes.

His mother shrugged. "Trees are not solid, Son. Nothing is. We are all lattices made up of the elements of air and fire and wind and water as well as earth. I blew a spell down the wind with the arrow, to part the lattices within the tree, so that the arrow might strike where least expected."

She walked over to the tree and leaned against it. She seemed to whisper to it, as to a lover. His vision got a little hazy then, like looking through water. With a jerk, Alia pulled the arrow free of the wood. The body sagged to the ground. Blood gushed and pooled on fern. The crow cawed jubilantly, and two more flapped down beside it on the branch.

Sergeant Cobbo arrived with his men. They exclaimed over the carnage and congratulated Sanglant heartily as Matto stammered out an incoherent account of the skirmish.

"I can see Captain Fulk was sorry to have left you behind," said the sergeant with a great deal more respect than he'd shown before.

But Sanglant could only regard the dead men with distaste and pity. In truth, he despised berserkers, the ones who let the beast of blood-fury consume them in battle. He prided himself on his calm and steadiness. He had always kept his wits about him, instead of throwing them to the winds. It was one of the reasons his soldiers respected, admired, and followed him: Even in the worst situations, and there had been many, he had never lost control of himself in battle.

But Bloodheart and Gent had left their mark on him. He thought he had freed himself of Bloodheart's chains, but the ghost of them lingered, a second self that had settled down inside him and twisted into another form. He was so angry sometimes that he felt the beast gnawing down there, but whether it was anger that woke and troubled the beast, or the beast that fed his anger, he didn't know. Fate had betrayed him: his own mother had used and discarded him, his father had cherished him but only as long as it served his purpose. He had sworn enemies he'd never heard tell of, who hated him because of his blood and who would have watched his beloved daughter starve to death without lifting a finger to help. Liath had been torn from him, and despite Alia's explanation that the creatures who had kidnapped her had been daimones, fire elementals, he didn't actually know what had happened to her or whether she was alive or dead.

Still cradling Blessing, he watched as Sergeant Cobbo's men stripped the bandits of their belongings and clothes, such as

they were, and dug a shallow grave. They came to the bowman
finally, and he heard their exclamations over the power of the
blow that had smashed the dead man's head in. They glanced
his way at intervals with a kind of sunstruck awe, although
thank the Lord they had not been stricken with the babbling
reverence with which Matto now regarded him.

They hadn't heard the bowman begging for mercy as he had
scrambled away. He hadn't heard it either, not really. He
hadn't been listening because he'd simply been furious enough
to kill anything that stood in his path or threatened Blessing.
It was only afterward that he realized what he'd heard. And
now it was too late.

Maybe the pity he felt wasn't truly for these poor, dead
wretches. They would have killed him, after all. The Lord and
Lady alone knew what they would have done to Blessing, had
she fallen into their hands. Maybe the pity he felt was for that
weak, unheeded voice in his own soul, the one that, before,
might have listened and might have heard. The one that
might have stayed his hand and let mercy, not rage, rule him.

With a grunt of displeasure, he acknowledged the men's
fawning comments as they came back to the road. Alia was
ready to leave. The sergeant helped Matto onto his mare while
Sanglant kissed Blessing and settled her on his back again.

"I think that'll have taken care of the bandits," said Sergeant
Cobbo with a smirk. He had taken the severed hand of the
ringleader, the one who'd dressed as a hag, to bring as proof of
the victory. "Don't you want anything? You have first choice of
the booty."

"No." Perhaps it was his expression, or his tone, but in any
case although they all fell in as escort around him, not one, not
even Matto, addressed a single question to him as they rode
on. The silence suited him very well.

The next line of sentries lay within sight of Angenheim
Palace. Sergeant Cobbo did all the talking and got them
through the sentry ring quickly enough. Two of the soldiers on

this sentry duty recognized him: He could tell by their startled expressions, like men who've seen a bear walk in dressed in a man's clothing. But their company rode on before either soldier could say anything.

So many petitioners had come in the hope of being brought before the king or one of his stewards that the fields around Angenheim swarmed with them. The fetid odor of sweat, excrement, and rotting food hung heavily over the fields. Common folk hurriedly got out of the way as Cobbo pressed his detachment through the crowd of onlookers.

Like most of the royal palaces, Angenheim had fortifications, although it wasn't as well situated as the palace at Werlida had been, placed as it was on a bluff above a river's bend. Angenheim boasted earthen ramparts and a double ring of wooden palisades surrounding the low hill on which the palace complex lay.

The court spilled out beyond the fortifications and into the fields where the petitioners had set up tents and shelters. Pasture had been ground into dirt and mud. Fires burned. Peddlers called out their wares; beggars coughed as they held out their begging bowls. Pit houses, dug out in a previous generation, had been cleaned out and inhabited by various wagoners and other servants who needed a place to stay while the king remained in residence. A small monastic estate lay beyond the fortified palace, but it, too, seemed to have been swamped by the influx of visitors. Sanglant had a moment to pity the brothers who were no doubt overwhelmed by the burden of providing hospitality to the king and his massive court. Then the party came to the final gate.

As luck would have it, Captain Fulk himself had been given gate duty this late afternoon. He stepped forward and called Cobbo to a halt, exchanged a few jocular complaints with him, and, in mid-sentence, saw Sanglant.

His face paled. He dropped to his knees, as though felled. In the wake of that movement, the five soldiers with him knelt as well. All of them were men who had pledged loyalty to

Sanglant on that fateful night fourteen months ago when he and Liath had fled the king's progress.

"You've returned to us, Your Highness." Fulk began to weep with joy.

Sanglant dismounted and indicated that the soldiers should stand. "I have not forgotten your loyalty to me, Captain Fulk." He could remember as clearly as yesterday the name and home village of each of the men kneeling before him, which they had confided to him on that dark night: Anshelm, Everwin, Wracwulf, Sibold, and Malbert. He offered Resuelto's reins to Fulk. "I would ask you now to see to my horse. The lad there needs tending by a healer."

"Of course, Your Highness!" They leaped up eagerly while Sergeant Cobbo and his men gaped, and Matto looked ready to fall off his horse either from pain or exhilaration. Cobbo asked a question of someone in the gathering crowd, and a serving-woman said scornfully, "Don't you know who that is, Cobbo? For shame!"

"Where is my father?" Sanglant asked his captain, ignoring the spate of talk his arrival had unleashed.

"Why, at the wedding feast, of course, Your Highness. Let me take you there, I beg you." Fulk gave the reins to Sibold and only then saw Alia and, a moment later, the baby strapped to Sanglant's back.

"I thank you." Sanglant was suddenly apprehensive, but he had to go on. "I wish to see him right away."

It took a moment for Fulk to shake free of amazement and curiosity. With a self-conscious cough and a good soldier's obedience, he led Sanglant to the great hall which lay in the center of the palace complex. A steady stream of servants laden with trays of meat and flagons of wine hurried in and out of the hall, passing through the throng of hangers-on and hopeful entertainers and petitioners who crowded around the doors.

They parted like soft butter under a knife at the sight of Fulk, Sanglant, and Alia. For some reason, Alia was still leading the pony and goat. If she was as nervous as Sanglant had suddenly become, she betrayed nothing of it in her expression or posture. If anything, she looked remarkably grim. Her cold expression emphasized the inhumanity of her features.

He strode in through the doors into the shadow of the hall, hot with feasting and overflowing with a lively and boisterous crowd. The hall stank of humanity. He had spent more of his life on campaign than in court, out in the open air, and he had forgotten what five hundred bodies pressed together and all eating and farting and belching and pissing smelled like.

Angenheim's hall had the breadth and height of a cathedral. Unshuttered windows set into the upper walls at the far end allowed light to spill over the king's table, where Henry, laughing at the antics of a trio of jugglers, shared a cup of wine with a pretty young woman who looked a few years younger than Sanglant. She wore a crown. A banner hung on the wall beside that of Wendar: the sun of Aosta.

"Whose wedding feast?" he demanded of Fulk, but he could not be heard above the noise of the feasting.

He strode forward through the ranks of trestle tables with Fulk at his back. Whippets slunk away from him. Servants leaped aside, and then cried out, seeing Alia behind him. Ladies and lords, seated at table, were struck dumb at his passage, or perhaps Alia had cast a spell on them that stole their voices. What couldn't she do, who could cause an arrow to pierce the wood of a tree?

Silence spread in their wake.

An open space had been cleared in front of the king's table to give the entertainers room to perform their tricks as well as a space where those petitioners lucky enough to have gotten this far could kneel while they waited for the king's notice. The petitioners crouching along the edge of that empty space did not notice him because they were so intent on the king. Sanglant got a good look at the king for the first time, his view blocked only by the antics of the jugglers. Henry looked remarkably hearty, even a little flushed, as the young noblewoman laughed while gold and silver balls flashed in the air between the three jugglers. Sanglant used his boots to discreetly nudge a raggedly-dressed man out of his way. The man glanced up, startled, and scuttled to one side, causing a cascade as all the petitioners scrambled for new places. Princess Theophanu, seated at the king's right hand, noticed the movement and tracked it back to its source. Her expression did not change, although it may have whitened a little, and her hands tightened on the cup she was in the act of lifting to her lips. The cleric standing behind her chair staggered backward, as if he had been kicked in the back of the knees.

A path opened through the throng, blocked only by the jugglers, who remained intent on the balls tossed between them. Sanglant ducked under the flying path of one shiny ball, caught another in his right hand, and was through their net just as Fulk swore under his breath. A ball hit the captain on the shoulder, fell, and shattered on a circle of ground swept clean of rushes that the jugglers had marked out for their tricks. The pony, hauled in this far and perhaps lulled by the stink and the carpet of rushes and tansy laid down on the floor into thinking it had come into a stable, chose this moment to urinate, loud and long.

Henry rose with easy grace. At that moment, as Henry looked him over, Sanglant realized that his father had noticed him as soon as he had entered the hall. As might a captain laying a counter ambush against bandits hiding in the forest, the king had simply chosen to pretend otherwise.

"Prince Sanglant," he said with a cool formality that tore at Sanglant's heart. "You have not yet met my wife, Queen Adelheid."

Obviously, Henry was still furious at his disobedient son, since this was the very woman whom his father had so desperately wanted him to marry. She was pretty, certainly, but more importantly she had that energy about her that is common to women who find pleasure in the bed. No doubt that, together with the Aostan crown she wore, accounted for the becoming blush in his father's cheeks and the smile that hovered on his lips as he regarded his disgraced son, come limping back scarcely better than a beggar.

Who was laying an ambush for whom?

Adelheid had the audacity, and the rank, to look him over as she would a stallion. "Handsome enough," she said clearly, as if he had caught them in the middle of a conversation, "but I have no reason to regret my choice. You've proved your fitness as regnant many times over, Henry."

Henry laughed. Made bold by the king's reaction, some among the audience felt free to chuckle nervously or snicker in response, by which time certain men had made their way through the crowd to throw themselves at Sanglant's feet.

"Your Highness!"

"Prince Sanglant!"

He recognized Fulk's men, who had evidently been serving at table or standing guard throughout the hall. Heribert arrived, pressing through the knot of petitioners who were crowded closest to the king's table, and knelt before him, grasping Sanglant's hand and kissing it.

"Sanglant!" he said triumphantly, as out of breath as if he'd been running. "My lord prince! I feared—"

"Nay, friend," said Sanglant, "never fear. I pray you, rise and stand beside me."

"So I will," said the young cleric, though he wobbled a little as he got to his feet.

"Who are these, who have come forward?" asked Henry. "Does Brother Heribert not serve Theophanu?"

Theophanu still clutched her cup. Old Helmut Villam, seated beside her, leaned to whisper to her, but she was obviously not listening to him. She merely nodded, once, curtly, to Sanglant, before setting down the wine cup.

"This is my retinue, Your Majesty," said Sanglant at last. "These are men who have pledged loyalty to me."

"Don't I feed them?" asked Henry sweetly. "I didn't know you had the lands and wherewithal to maintain a retinue, Son. Certainly you scorned those that I meant to honor you with. I don't even see a gold torque at your throat to mark you as my son."

But Sanglant had his own weapons, and he knew how to counterattack. He stepped aside to reveal his mother.

She stood in a spray of light cast from the high windows. The light made bronze of her hair, burnished and finely-woven into a tight braid as thick as her wrist. She had rolled down the sleeves of Liath's tunic and belted it in the usual manner around her hips, although even with a length of material caught up under the belt the embroidered hem still lapped her ankles. Yet despite the unexceptionable appearance of the clothing, she blazed with strangeness, as alien as a sleek leopard glimpsed running with thundering aurochs.

She said nothing. She didn't have to.

"Alia!" Henry paled noticeably, but he had been king for too many years not to know when to retreat. The mask of stone crashed down over his expression, freezing the merriment in the hall as thoroughly as any magic could have. The goat baaed, followed by complete silence. No one seemed to notice the flutter of wind moving through the robes and cloaks of the seated nobles as Jerna explored the hall.

Finally, Alia spoke. "I come back, Henri," she said, pronouncing his name in the Salian way, "but I am not believing that you cared for the child as you promised to me you would."

III
TWISTING THE BELT

1

THE seeds of conflict bloomed at such odd times that it was often easy to forget that they had been sown long before, not risen spontaneously out of fallow ground. Rosvita of North Mark had been a cleric and adviser at court for twenty years. She knew when to step back and let matters take their course, and when to intervene before a crisis got out of hand.

Although King Henry now stood, the rest of the assembly still sat in astonished, or anticipatory, silence, staring at the confrontation unfolding before them. Even wily old Helmut Villam, seated to her left at the king's table, seemed stunned into immobility, mouth parted and fingers tightly gripping the stem of the wine cup he shared with Princess Theophanu, which the princess had just set down.

Rosvita gestured to Brother Fortunatus to pull back her chair so that she, too, could rise. He hurried forward at once. Although like everyone else in the hall he could scarcely keep his gaze from the father, mother, and child whose battle was about to play out on this public stage, he had also been trained by Rosvita herself. There were many traits she could tolerate in

the clerics who served her, but to be unobservant was not one
of them.

"This is the woman we've heard so much about!" he murmured in her ear as she rose. "God preserve us!"

His gaze had fastened on the Aoi woman. He was not the
only person in the hall ogling her. Her features were striking
but not beautiful, and although admittedly her hair had the
glamour of polished bronze, she wore it caught back in a complicated knot that made her look peculiar rather than regal.
Her gaze was fierce and commanding, even combative. She
was not afraid to look Henry in the eye, and her proud carriage
suggested that she considered herself the regnant and Henry
her subject.

"I come back, Henri," she said, pronouncing his name in the
Salian way with an unvoiced "h" and a garbled "ri," "but I am
not believing that you cared for the child as you promised to
me you would."

"I pray you, Your Majesty," said Rosvita smoothly into the
shocked silence that followed this outrageous accusation, "let
chairs be brought so that our visitors may sit and eat. Truly,
they must have a long journey behind them. Food and drink
are always a welcome sight to the traveler. Indeed, let Prince
Sanglant's mother abide in my own chair, and I will serve
her."

Henry stared so fixedly at the foreign woman he had once
called "beloved," and whom it was popularly believed he
would have married had he been permitted to, that finally
Queen Adelheid rose with cool aplomb and indicated Rosvita's
seat to the right of Helmut Villam. It was not actually
Adelheid's prerogative, but Adelheid was neither a fool nor a
quitter.

"Let a chair be brought for Prince Sanglant so that he may
be seated beside me," she said in her high, clear voice. "Let his
lady mother be honored as is her right and our obligation, for
it was her gift of this child to my husband which sealed his
right to rule as regnant in Wendar and Varre."

Sanglant stepped forward. "I have a child." His voice had a hoarse scrape to it, as though he were afflicted with pain, but his voice always sounded like that. Years ago he had taken a wound to the throat in battle.

He untied a bundle from his back, uncoiled linen cloth, and a moment later held in his arms a yearling child, as sweet a babe as Rosvita had ever seen, with plump cheeks, a dark complexion, and bright blue eyes. "Da da!" she said in the ringing tones of imperious babyhood. He set her on the ground and she took a few tottering steps toward the king, swayed, lost her balance, and sat down on her rump. Lifting a hand, she pointed toward Henry and said, with despotic glee, "Ba! Ba!"

Sanglant swept her up, strode forward and, by leaning over the feasting table, deposited her in Henry's arms. The king did not even resist. Many yearling babies would have shrieked in rage or fear, but the tiny child merely reached up, got a bit of the king's beard between her fingers, and tugged.

"Ba!" she exclaimed, delighted.

"Jugglers!" said Henry hoarsely. He sat and downed the contents of his wine cup in one gulp while the baby tried to climb up to his shoulder to get hold of the gleaming coronet of gold he wore on his brow—not the king's crown of state, too heavy and formal to wear at a feast, but his lesser crown, a slender band of gold worn when circumstances called for a lesser degree of formality.

Prince Sanglant's smile was sharp. Turning, he tossed the silver ball to the nearest juggler. The poor man jerked, startled, but his hand acted without his mind's measure and he caught the ball. The hall came alive then, as dawn unfolds: people recalled the food on their platters; the jugglers returned to their show of skill and daring; the soldiers who had come forward to publicly and thus irrevocably mark their allegiance to Prince Sanglant rose and waited for his command. Sanglant spoke quietly to Captain Fulk, after which the good captain dispersed his men efficiently, obtained the lead lines of the

pony and the goat, and, leading the two animals, retreated
from the hall while Sanglant came forward to take his place at
Adelheid's left. The young cleric, Heribert, who had appeared
so mysteriously in the Alfar Mountains, stuck close by
Sanglant's side. It was he who took over serving the prince,
although before he had served Theophanu. The princess'
expression remained as blank as stone. She rose and went to
kiss Sanglant, once on either cheek, and he caught her closer
and whispered something which, amazingly, brought a whisper of a smile to her face, seen and gone as swiftly as the flutter
of a swallow's wing.

"Go to Princess Theophanu," Rosvita said to Fortunatus in
an undertone. He hastened away to stand behind the princess'
chair so that she would have a person of fitting rank to serve
her now that Brother Heribert had, evidently, defected to her
half brother.

Sanglant turned his attention to charming Adelheid while
Henry had his hands full of clambering, enthusiastic baby.
Something fundamental had changed in the prince in the fourteen months he had been gone from the king's progress.
Rosvita had seen battle joined on the field, and she had seen
skirmishes played out in the subtler fields of court, but never
before had she seen Sanglant maneuvering, as he obviously
was now, in the political arena. Of course, before he hadn't had
a child and a wife.

Where was Liath?

"You I will be thanking, woman," said the one known as
Alia, who came up beside her. "You are one of the god-women,
are you not?"

It took Rosvita a moment to translate the strange phrase.
"Yes, I am a cleric. My service is devoted to God and to King
Henry. I pray you, Lady, sit here, if you please. Let me pour
you some wine."

But the foreign woman remained standing, examining
Rosvita with a stare that made her feel rather like what she
supposed an insect felt before the hand of fate slapped down

upon it. She was shorter than Rosvita and powerfully built, with the same kind of leashed energy common to warriors forced into momentary stillness. Alia did not smile, but abruptly the tenor of her expression changed. "You spoke in the way of an elder," she said abruptly, "when you rose to offer guesting rights. For this short time, there will be no fighting between Henri and his son."

"So I hope," agreed Rosvita, but in truth the observation surprised her. She did not know what to expect from the Aoi woman. She did not know anything, really, about the Aoi except for legends half buried in ancient manuscripts and tales told around hearths at night in the long halls of the common people. Like many, she had begun to believe the Aoi were only a story, a dream fostered by old memories of the ancient Dariyan Empire, but it was impossible to deny the evidence of her own eyes. "Sit, I pray you." At times like this, one fell back on basic formality. "Let me pour you wine, if you will, Lady."

"To you," said Alia without making any movement toward the chair, "I will give my spoken name, because you are wise enough to use it prudently. I am known among my people as *Uapeani-kazonkansi-a-lari*, but if that is too much for your tongue, then Kansi-a-lari is enough."

Rosvita smiled politely. "With your permission, then, Lady, I will address you as Kansi-a-lari. Is there a title that suits you as well? I am unaccustomed to the customs of your people."

"Kansi-a-lari *is* my title, as you call it." With that, she sat, moving into the confines of the chair with the cautious grace of a leopard slinking into a box that might prove to be a cage.

The feast ground on, lurching a little, like a wagon pulled over rough ground, but entertainers took their turns, platters of beef, venison, and pork were brought hot from the outdoor cookhouses, and wine flowed freely. Petitioners shuffled forward in waves and were sent on their way with a judgment or a coin or a scrap from the king's platter for their pains. A poet trained in the court chapel of the Salian king sang from a

lengthy poem celebrating the virtues and fame of the great
emperor, Taillefer, he who had risen from the kingship of Salia
to the imperial crown of Darre. Emperor Taillefer stood alone
in the ranks of the great princes, for no regnant from any land
in the one hundred years since his death had gained enough
power to duplicate his achievement. None until Henry, who
had now, through marriage to Adelheid, allied his kingdom of
Wendar and Varre with the country of Aosta, within whose
borders lay the holy city of Darre. Of course the poet meant to
praise the dead Emperor Taillefer while flattering the living
king, Henry, whose ambition to take upon himself the title
"Holy Dariyan Emperor" was no secret to his court.

> *"Look! The sun shines no more brightly than the emperor,
> who illuminates the earth with his boundless love and great
> wisdom. For although the sun knows twelve hours of darkness,
> our regnant, like a star, shines eternally."*

The entrance of Prince Sanglant and his mother, while never
forgotten, was subsumed into the familiar conviviality of the
feast. And anyway, it gave everyone there something to gossip
about as the banquet, and the poet, wore on.

> *"He enters first among the company, and he clears the way
> so that all may follow. With heavy chains he binds the unjust
> and with a stiff yoke he constrains the proud."*

After all, it was the fifth day of feasting, and even the hearti-
est of revelers might be forgiven for growing restless after
endless hours of merriment and gluttony. In an odd way,
Rosvita was grateful to serve rather than sit. She attended to
Alia as unobtrusively as possible, so as not to startle her or give
her any reason to feel spied upon or threatened.

> *"He is the fount of grace and honor. His achievements have
> made him famous throughout the four quarters of the earth."*

The Aoi woman did not invite conversation. Young Lord Fridebraht, seated to her right, was certainly too much in dread of her strange appearance and fierce gaze to speak one single word to her. Even old Villam, who had known Alia those many years ago in her brief time at court and who certainly had never before lacked the spirit or courage to flatter an attractive woman, attempted only a few comments before, in the face of her disinterest, he gave up. Alia watched the king, the court, and occasionally her son. She ate and drank sparingly. In this way, the feast continued without further incident.

The poet finished his panegyric at last, and a cleric came forward to give a pleasing rendition of "The Best of Songs," the wedding song taken from the ancient Essit holy book.

> *"My beloved is mine, and I am his.*
> *Let me be a seal upon your heart,*
> *like the seal upon your hand."*

The king's favored Eagle, Hathui, beckoned to Rosvita. "His Majesty will take his leave of the hall now."

"What make you of this turn of events?" asked Rosvita. Although Hathui was only a common-born woman, she had a keen eye and the king's confidence.

"It is unexpected." Hathui laughed at the absurdity of her own statement. Henry had gotten the baby settled on his knee and was now feeding her the choicest bits, mashed into a por-ridgelike consistency, from the platter he shared with his queen. "I believe the king would be better served if he sorts it out in the king's chambers, in some manner of privacy, away from the assembly."

Almost as if he had overheard the Eagle's statement, Sanglant rose to toast the newly married couple. Despite his common clothing, he had the carriage of a prince and the proud face of a man who expects loyalty and obedience in those who follow him. He knew how to pitch his voice to carry over the buzzing throng.

"Let many blessings attend this union," he said to cheers. When the hurrahs tailed off, he went on. "But let me call before you one blessing, in particular, that is held by our blessed regnant and my beloved father, King Henry."

The hall quieted. The guards at the doors strained forward to hear. Even the servants paused in their tasks.

At the sound of her father's voice, the baby stood up in Henry's lap and sang out, "Da! Da!" in a voice surely meant someday to ring out above the clash of battle. Henry laughed as many in the assembly chuckled appreciatively or murmured to each other, wondering what the prince was about. Bastards siring children was nothing unknown, alas, but it wasn't customary to bring such a left-handed lineage to the attention of the entire court.

A fly buzzed annoyingly by Rosvita's ear. As she slapped it away, Sanglant continued.

"King Henry holds in his arms my daughter, whom I have named Blessing, as was my right as her father."

"And a blessing she truly is, Son," replied Henry. Despite the shock of Sanglant's and Alia's arrival, Henry had mellowed under the influence of the child. Or so it seemed. He was a subtle campaigner, and in such circumstances it was easy to forget that his wrath, once kindled, was slow to burn out. "In your place, with such responsibilities, it is wise for you to come seeking forgiveness of me. You cannot hope to feed and clothe a retinue in this guise you have taken, garbed something like a common soldier and without even the gold badge of your royal lineage about your neck. Surely your daughter deserves more than this journeyer's life."

Adelheid's smile sharpened as she looked at Sanglant to see how he would respond to this thrust.

The prince downed his cup of wine in a single gulp and, with a flush staining his bronze-dark cheeks, replied with an edge in his voice. "I ask for nothing for myself, Your Majesty. I thought I made that plain when I returned to you the belt of honor which you yourself fastened on me when I was fifteen.

What I wear now I have earned through my own efforts. Nay, I return to court not for my own benefit."

They were like two dogs, growling before they bit.

"If you do not come seeking my forgiveness, then why are you here?" demanded Henry.

"I come on behalf of my daughter, Blessing. I ask only for what is due her as the last legitimate descendant of the Emperor Taillefer."

Taillefer. Dead these hundred years and his lineage died with him, for no child sired by his loins had reigned after him and his empire had fallen apart soon after his death.

Rosvita understood, then, everything that hadn't been plain to her before: the puzzle of the pregnant Queen Radegundis, who had fled to the convent after her husband Taillefer's death; the mystery of Mother Obligatia and the cryptic words of Brother Fidelis; and most of all, the inexplicable luster that made Liath appear to be far more than the simple king's messenger she supposedly was.

"So many show such an interest in a common Eagle," the king had said once, over a year ago, when she had been brought before him to face his judgment. But a child born of Taillefer's line would surely retain some of Taillefer's legendary glory, the corona of power that cloaked him at all times.

Henry stared at his son. "Do you mean to suggest that the Eagle you ran off with is descended from Taillefer?"

Sanglant's answer was pitched not to carry to his father but rather to the entire assembly of nobles and serving-folk. "Who here will witness that I made a legitimate and binding union of marriage with the woman called Liathano?"

Soldiers stepped forward from their stations beside the door. "I will witness, Your Highness!" one called, and a second, and a third and fourth, echoed him. As their shouts died away, Captain Fulk came forward. His steadiness was well known, and he had gained renown for his service to Theophanu on the disastrous expedition to Aosta in the course of which they had, despite everything, rescued Adelheid from the clutches of Lord John Ironhead.

"I witness, Your Highness," he cried, "that you freely stated your intention before God and freeborn witnesses to bind yourself in marriage to the woman Liathano."

"Then there is no impediment," said Sanglant triumphantly. "Liathano is the great granddaughter of Taillefer and Radegundis, born out of legitimate unions and therefore herself legitimate, not a bastard. That is why she now wears the gold torque that I once wore at my throat. In this way, I honored her royal lineage and her right to claim descent from Taillefer." He looked neither at his mother or father as he said this, only at the crowd. Some of the assembly had stood, trying to see better, and that had caused others at the back to stand on their benches or even on the tables. The air in the hall and the very attitude of the crowd snapped with the reverberant energy that precedes a thunderstorm.

Queen Adelheid's smile had gained a fixed look, and for an instant she looked really angry.

"This is unbelievable," said Henry. "Taillefer died without a legitimately born son to succeed him, as was the custom in those days in Salia. He has no descendants."

"Queen Radegundis was pregnant when Taillefer died." Sanglant gestured toward the hapless poet who had entertained the feasting multitude with Taillefer's exploits and noble qualities. "Is that not so, poet?" The poor man could only nod as Sanglant threw back into the hall lines that Rosvita had once read from her precious *Vita* of St. Radegundis, which she had received from the hands of Brother Fidelis. "'Still heavy with child, Radegundis clothed herself and her companion Clothilde in the garb of poor women. She chose exile over the torments of power.' And took refuge in the convent at Poiterri. What became of the child Radegundis carried, Your Majesty?"

"No one knows," said Hathui suddenly, speaking for the king. "No one knows what became of the child."

"I know." Rosvita stepped forward. Was it disloyal to speak? Yet she could not lie or conceal when so much was at stake. She owed the truth for the sake of Brother Fidelis' memory, if nothing else. "I know what became of the child born to Radegundis and Taillefer, for I spoke to him in the hour of his death in the hills above Herford Monastery. He was called Brother Fidelis, and except for a single year when he lapsed from his vows for the sake of the love of a young woman, he spent his life as a monk in the service of God. Fidelis wrote these words in his *Life* of St. Radegundis: 'The world divides those whom no space parted once.'"

She paused to make sure that every person there had time to contemplate the hidden meaning in his words. "Truly, can it not be said that before a baby is born, it and its mother are of one body, of a single piece? What God divides in childbirth can be split asunder by the world's intrigues as well."

When their murmuring died away, she went on. "I spoke as well to the woman whom he married and who bore a child conceived with his seed. She is an old woman now, and she lives in hiding out of fear of those who seek her because of the secret she carries with her. I believe that her story is true, that she was briefly married to Fidelis—the son of Taillefer and Radegundis—and that her union with Fidelis produced a daughter. It is possible that the daughter lived, and survived, and in her turn bore a child."

"She lived and she survived," said Sanglant in a grim voice. "A daughter was born to her, gotten in legitimate marriage with a disgraced frater who had studied the lore of the mathematici. He named the child Liathano. The rest you know."

"Where, then, is Liath?" Henry gestured toward the hall as if he expected her to step forward from a place of concealment. "Why have you returned to me, with this astounding claim, without her?"

It fell away, then, the pride and the anger and the confidence. Sanglant began to weep silently, a few tears that slid down his cheeks. He made no effort to wipe them away. Weeping, after all, was a man's right and obligation.

"Dead, or alive, I cannot say," he whispered hoarsely. "She was stolen from me. I do not know where she is now."

2

AS Liath descended the staircase the light faded quickly, yet where it grew dimmest she could still distinguish walls and steps with her salamander eyes. The old sorcerer matched her step for step even though she stood half a head taller. It grew markedly cool. At intervals, the murmuring of voices swept up the staircase like a wind out of the Abyss.

They walked down for a long time. At some point she stopped feeling the regular seams of worked stone and touched only the seamlessly rough walls of excavated earth. Eventually the staircase leveled out, and they walked down a short tunnel so round that a rod might have punched it out to make a circle within the rock. The tunnel opened into a broad chamber whose walls were illuminated by a small opening far above them. Plants had grown through the opening; roots dangled into empty air and twined along the ceiling, trying to gain purchase against the rock. Dust motes danced along the roof before they swirled into shadows.

The smooth floor descended down two high steps to an oval hollow that marked the meeting place, where the council members had congregated. They wore a bewildering variety of strange clothing: shifts stamped with colored patterns, feathers adorning their hair, sheaths studded with beads and colored stones bound around forearms and calves. Most of them wore some kind of cloak, pinned at one shoulder and draping down to mid-thigh. Each of the women wore a heavy jade ring piercing her nose, all except one.

They had exotic faces, broad across the cheekbones, reddish

or bronze in their complexions. They looked nothing like the Wendish, but she could see Sanglant's heritage in every face there. There were not more than thirty, waiting for her in a chamber obviously large enough to command an audience of hundreds, yet somehow the chamber felt crowded, as if the shades of those who had stood here in the past and who would stand here in the future filled the empty spaces.

Silence reigned.

She stood beneath the wings of an eagle whose semblance had been carved out of the stone archway above the tunnel. Every person seated or standing within the chamber examined her. Yet when she compared their stern and even hostile expressions to Hugh's poisonous gaze, she could not fall into helpless terror. She had walked through the fire and survived.

Eldest Uncle shifted behind her, coughing gently.

In the center of the oval, seated on an eagle literally carved out of the stone floor, sat a very pregnant woman with a gloriously feathered cloak draped around her shoulders. Her hair was pulled back in a topknot. Alone of all the women, she wore no jade ring in her nose. Behind her stood the golden wheel, no longer turning because in this stone womb there was no wind. The emerald feathers trimming the wheel glowed with a light of their own. Feather Cloak lifted a hand and beckoned Liath to come forward.

"I am here," Liath said in response to that languid gesture. She took a big step down, and then the second, to stand at the same level as the others. Lifting her hands, she opened them to show her palms out, empty. "I come unarmed, as is your custom. Eldest Uncle comes with me, to show that I mean no harm to your people. In the language of my people, I am called Liathano, and I seek knowledge—"

That brought them to life.

"Let her be cast out!" shouted White Feather, the woman who had come to see Eldest Uncle. "How dares she bring the name of our ancient enemy into this chamber?" The distinctive shield of white feathers bound into her hair shook as if in response to her anger, and her words unleashed the others, a chorus of discordant views, too rapid an exchange for Liath to see immediately which one spoke what words.

"It's treachery! Kill her at once!"

"Nay, I would hear her speak!"

"We cannot trust any child born of humankind—"

"We are few, and they are many. If we do not seek understanding now, then we will surely all perish."

"I want to know what Eldest Uncle means by bringing her here without the permission of the council. The human woman is nothing to us, however evil her name. It is Eldest Uncle who must stand before our judgment."

One stepped forward belligerently, hard to ignore because he was a strikingly attractive man clothed only in a cunningly-tied loincloth and a plain hip-length cloak and adorned by nothing more than a wooden mask carved into the shape of a snarling cat pushed back on top of his cropped hair. He had a powerful baritone. "I say this to you, sisters and brothers: Let her blood be the first we spill. Let it, and the memory of the one who helped to ruin us, be used to strengthen us as we prepare to fight to take back what was once ours."

"Silence." They fell silent at once. Feather Cloak did not rise from her stone seat. Her crossed legs cradled her huge belly, which was half concealed by the stone eagle's head thrusting up from the floor. The feather cloak pooled over the wings of the bird, giving the woman the appearance of a creature both humanlike and avian. Under her light shift, her breasts were swollen in the way of pregnant women, round and full, and Liath was struck by such a sharp jab of envy that she had to blink back tears.

Where was Blessing now? Who was caring for her?

Feather Cloak curved a hand around her belly. "Remember that this child will be the first born on Earth since our exile. Shall it be born to know only war, or to know peace as well?"

"You have taken the Impatient One's counsel to heart!" snarled Cat Mask. "She threw away her loyalty to her own people to go walking among humankind. You know what she did there!"

"You are only angry that she tossed your spear out of her house!" cried another young man, laughing unkindly after he spoke. He wore a mask carved in the shape of a lizard's head, elaborated with a curly snout. "Very proud you are of that spear, and it galls you to think that another man—not just another man but a human man—might have been allowed to bring his spear into her house!"

This insult triggered a flurry of mocking laughter among some of the others and a clash, like rams locking horns, between the two men that was only halted when a stout older man stepped between them.

Dressed more conservatively than the other men, with his chest covered by a tunic in the manner of the women, he made for an unsettling sight with a necklace of mandibles hanging at his chest and earrings fashioned to resemble tiny skulls dangling from either ear. "The Impatient One chose negotiation over war." With a single finger on the chest of each of the young men, he pushed them apart as though they weighed no more than a child.

"We cannot negotiate with humankind," objected White Feather.

"What do you mean us to do?" asked an elderly woman in a deceptively sweet voice. "We have dwindled. How many children are left to us, and how many among us remain capable even of bearing or siring a child? Where once our tribes filled cities, now we eke out a living in the hills, on the dying fields. If there is one left where ten stood before, then I am counting generously. We will be weak when we stand on Earth once more. We must seek accommodation."

Cat Mask gave a barking laugh of disgust. "Accommodation is for fools! We have enough power to defeat them, even if we are few and they are many."

"So speaks the Impulsive One," retorted the old woman. She had a scar on her left cheek, very like a wound taken in battle.

Her short tunic ended at her waist and below that she wore a ragged skirt, much repaired, striped with rows of green beads. Little white masks, all of them grinning skull faces, hung from her belt. "I ask you, The-One-Who-Sits-In-The-Eagle-Seat, let the human woman walk forward and speak to us. I, for one, would hear what she has to say."

"Come forward," said Feather Cloak.

Liath walked forward cautiously. The council members moved as she walked, shifting position so that they stood neither too close nor too far, yet always able to see her face.

"Stand before me." Feather Cloak looked serious but not antagonistic. Liath felt it safe to obey her, under the circumstances. "Closer. There." Closing her eyes, Feather Cloak rested a hand on Liath's hip. The touch was probing without being intrusive. Even through her tunic, Liath felt the cool smoothness of her hand, almost as if it melted into her.

And she was thrown, abruptly, into the trance she had learned from Eldest Uncle. She slid into it without warning, into that place where the architecture of existence dissolves into view. Dust motes dance, surrounded by empty space, yet those motes are arranged in perfect order, a latticework of being that in its parts makes up all of her and yet, because it is invisible to the naked eye, seems to be nothing of what she actually is. In her mind's eye, the city of memory bloomed into view, on the hill, on the lake, and at its core burned the blue-white fire that consumes mountains—

Feather Cloak jerked back with a gasp as her eyelids snapped open. "She is not what she seems! More than one essence weaves itself within her." Her gaze flashed past Liath to Eldest Uncle. "There is even something of you in her, Eldest Uncle. How can this be so?"

He merely shrugged.

"So often you refuse to answer me!" But Feather Cloak's frown seemed born as much of resigned amusement as irritation. Given the advanced stage of her pregnancy, Liath could well imagine that the Aoi woman might simply be exhausted.

She spoke again to Liath. "So, then, You-Who-Have-More-Than-One-Seeming, why have you come here?"

Liath displayed her empty palms. "I hold no secrets here. I came to learn what I am."

"What are you?"

"In my own land, I am known as the child of mathematici, sorcerers who bind and weave the light of the stars—"

Nothing, not even their reaction to her name, could have prepared her for the uproar that greeted these words.

"Daughter of the ones who exiled us!"

"Heir to the shana-ret'zeri, cursed may they be."

"Kill her!"

"Silence!" roared Feather Cloak. For an instant she seemed actually to expand in size and to take on the features of the eagle, so that as her person swelled and her features sharpened it seemed she might transform into a creature that would fill the entire chamber and swallow those who disobeyed it.

Silence swept down like wings. Liath blinked. In the next instant Feather Cloak appeared to be nothing more than a very pregnant woman with lines of exhaustion around her mouth and the habit of command in her voice. "What do you say to these accusations?"

"In truth, honored one, the story of your people is lost to me. None among humankind knows it now. Our legends say that your kind lived on Earth once, but that you left because of your war with humankind. It is said that you left Earth in order to hoard your power, so that when you returned, you could defeat humankind and make them your slaves." Hastily she gestured to show that she had not yet done, because Cat Mask, for one, seemed eager to throw speech back at her, like a spear. "These are the stories and legends told by my people. I do not know how much truth there is in them. It happened so long ago that all memory of the truth is lost to us."

"But not to us!" cried Cat Mask. "We recall it bitterly enough!"

"Let her speak," shouted Lizard Mask. Like a lizard, he threw his breath into his chest, all puffed out. Little white scars, like lines marking the phases of the moon, scored his dark skin. All at once, she realized why the men seemed so like Sanglant: not one of them had a beard.

"How can none remember it?" asked elderly Green Skirt. "My mother and aunts suffered through the cataclysm, and I can recite their stories of that time as easily as I breathe. How can it be forgotten? We were at war with the shana-ret'zeri and their human allies for generations. It cannot have passed so easily even from human memory."

Others murmured in agreement.

"No," said Liath. "If the measure of days and years moves differently here than there, then more time has passed for those living on Earth than for you, here in this country. According to the calculations I know, your tribe has not walked on Earth for almost two thousand and seven hundred years. That is over a hundred generations, as measured by human lives. All we have left from those days are ancient memories shrouded in tales that make little sense to us now, as well as the remains of what the ancient people built. Yet fallen buildings cannot speak."

"One hundred generations!" Even the hostile White Feather seemed struck by this fact. "My mother's mother died in the Sundering. I had the story from my aunt and my mother's brother. No more time than this has passed, here."

"Then I pray you, tell me the story," said Liath. "Tell me what happened in those days and how you came to this country."

"Beware how much you tell her," murmured Skull Earrings.

"Aren't you the one who advises accommodation with the human tribes?" retorted Cat Mask gleefully.

"Accommodation, but not surrender! That is why some among us agreed when the Impatient One told us her plan. If we tell this one too much, and it can be used against us—"

"I will speak." Feather Cloak's words, as always, silenced the others. "How can the truth harm us? I can only recount the deeds of that time as they were given to me by my aunt, who wore the serpent skirt and danced below the altar of She-Who-Will-Not-Have-A-Husband. Alone among us all, Eldest Uncle remains. He witnessed. Perhaps he will again tell us the tale."

He was hesitant. "It is nothing I desire to remember." He looked at Liath as he said the words. "Yet worse will come if we do not remember."

The council members, even those who had spoken in the most hostile way before, moved back respectfully as he descended to the council ground. Behind the standard, raised on a squat column of stone and concealed up to this moment from Liath's sight by the arrangement of the standing councillors, lay a carving rather like that of the eagle on which Feather Cloak sat. This one resembled a huge cat, lionlike but scarred with lines that seemed to indicate dapplings or lesions upon its stone coat. Its head, tail, and paws thrust up from the stone as if it had been caught in the instant before it fully emerged out of the rock. Eldest Uncle clambered up on this high seat and settled himself cross-legged on the curving back.

When all were quiet and at rest, he began to speak.

"Hu-ah. Hu-ah. Let my words be pleasing to She-Who-Creates. In those days, we called ourselves The-Ones-Who-Have-Understanding. Our people became alive in the place known as Gold-Is-Everywhere. We were the children of the Fourth Sun, which was born after the waters flooded the world and destroyed the Third Sun. In that place known as Gold-Is-Everywhere, we built cities and gave offerings to the gods. But He-Who-Burns became angry with our people. He sent forth his sons and they burned the cities with their fire. After this, there was no peace among the tribes.

"Thirteen of the clans built ships and sailed boldly west over the great water. The moon three times hid her face before land was sighted. Here they found many goats and the pale ones who looked like people but acted like dogs.

"'This is not a good country,' said The-One-Who-Counts. The council listened to her words, and they left that place.

"After much wandering, the thirteen clans came to the middle sea. Here, also, the pale ones lived, but these pale ones acted like people, not beasts. The council met, and The-One-Who-Counts said to them: 'This is a better country.'

"They made a harbor there and built cities in the place known after that as Abundance-Is-Ours-If-The-Gods-Do-Not-Change-Their-Minds. Into this land the clans settled and made new homes. None of the offerings were forgotten, and in this way rain fell at the proper time and sun shone at the proper time. There were many children. In this land, the people called themselves The-Ones-Who-Have-Made-A-New-Home.

"Some of the pale ones, who called themselves humankind, came as friends to our people. Others came from the south, who had skin as black as charcoal, and some from the east, who were the color of clay. Some among humankind walked together with our people and painted the clan marks on their bodies. In this way, they became part of the clans, and their blood and our blood mixed.

"Many Long Years passed. The counting-women walked on the temples and counted the rising and setting of the stars. At the end of every four Long Years, which marks a Great Year, they ascended the Hill of the Star and watched to see if the Six-Women-Who-Live-Upriver would pass the zenith. In this way, the counting-women would know that the movements of the heavens had not ceased and that the world would not come to an end.

"Hu-ah. Hu-ah. Let She-Who-Creates be pleased as my story continues.

"The time of four omens began in the year of 1-Mountain. In the season of Dry Light, the people saw a strange wonder. A column of flame appeared in the sky. Like a great wound, it bled fire onto the earth, drop by drop. The people cried out all together in wonder and in dread, and as was the custom, they clapped their hands against their mouths. They asked the counting-women what it could mean, the counting-women answered that the stars spoke of a great cataclysm, the rising of the Fifth Sun, under which the whole world would suffer. That year, there were many offerings to the gods.

"In the year of 12-Sky fire ran like a river through the sky at daybreak. It split into three parts and the three parts became wind. One part of wind rose up to the Hill of the Stars and smashed the House of Authority. The other two parts lashed the waters of the Lake of Gold until the waters boiled. Half of the houses of the city fell into the boiling waves. Then the waters sank back to their rightful place.

"In the year of 9-Sky, a whirlwind of dust rose from the earth until it touched the sky. Out of the whirlwind came the voice of the crying woman, and she cried, 'We are lost! Let us flee the city.' After that, the sky inhaled the whirlwind, but the crying woman was left behind, and she would often be heard in the middle of the night.

"The-One-Who-Sits-In-The-Eagle-Seat sent out the most gifted seers and sorcerers to see what was happening, but everywhere they went their human neighbors greeted them with stones and spears, violence and battle. The men who speak for peace went out among humankind, but they were killed.

"The shana-ret'zeri were on the move, and they had allied with the human tribes. Even those whom we had taught and taken into our own towns turned against us. The long enmity between our peoples could not be healed. At this time the year 2-Sky came to an end, and the counting-women tallied the beginning of the year 1-Sky with offerings. Thirteen times had the full count of Great Years run to completion, which meant that the Long Count had come full circle. This was the time of greatest danger, for at the end of each Long Count, the gods gained the power to destroy the sun.

"It came to pass that on the two hundredth day of 1-Sky, two of the fisherfolk captured a heron in the waters of the lake. The bird was so marvelous and strange that none of them could describe it, so they took it to The-One-Who-Sits-In-The-Eagle-Seat. She had gone already to the Hall of Night to celebrate the evening banquet.

"A crown of stars was set on the head of the bird. The-One-Who-Sits-In-The-Eagle-Seat said, 'Within the crown I see a mirror, and the mirror shows me the heavens and the night sky. In the mirror, I see the stars we call the Six-Women-Who-Live-Upriver, but they are burning.' Now she was very afraid, because it seemed to her that this was not only strange and wondrous, but a particularly bad omen.

"She looked a second time into the mirror. She saw the human sorcerers standing within their stone looms and weaving a spell greater than any spell known before on Earth. Then the seers and the counting-women of my people understood the intent of the shana-ret'zeri and their human allies.

"Too late had we discovered the danger. Our enemies had already woven the net to catch us."

Abruptly, the old sorcerer could not go on. He faded as the sun fades beneath the hills, losing all power, and his body bent over his crossed knees as though he had fainted.

"I will not speak of the suffering," he said in a whisper that nevertheless penetrated the entire chamber, "or of the ones we lost. Only this. By means of the spell woven by the human sorcerers and their allies, our land was torn away from Earth. Here in exile we have lingered. The land dies around us as all plants die in time, when they are uprooted. We have dwindled. We would die were we to remain in this exile forever."

He straightened up. The fire of anger flashed in his gaze again, the stubbornness of a man who has seen a sight worse than death but means to survive longer than his enemies. He looked directly at Liath. "But what is born out of Earth returns to Earth. This truth our enemies did not comprehend. They thought to rid themselves of us forever, but they only exiled us for a time."

"How can that be?" demanded Liath. "If they flung you and your homeland away from Earth, then surely it must be your own sorcerers who are bringing your land back to Earth."

"Give me your belt."

She undid her leather belt and walked forward with her tunic lapping her calves. The council members had fallen into a profound silence, whether out of respect for Eldest Uncle and his memories, or out of sorrow for what had been lost, she could not know.

He took the belt and held it by the buckle so that the other end dangled loose toward the floor. Grasping the other end, he brought it up to touch the buckle.

"Here is a circle." He placed a finger on the buckle. "If I were to walk on the surface of this belt, where would I end up?" He let her draw her finger from the buckle around the outside flat of the belt, until she returned to where she had started.

"So," he agreed, because she was nodding, "think of the buckle of this belt as Earth. When the human sorcerers wove their spell, they meant to throw my people and the land in which we dwelt off of Earth, to a different place, *so*—" He moved her finger from the buckle to the underside of the buckle. "Now the one is separate from the other. Even if I walk on this side of the belt, I will not come back to Earth. Do so." She ran her finger along the inside flat of the belt and, truly, although she remained close to the other side of the belt, although she passed underneath the buckle that represented Earth, she never returned to it. The two sides were eternally separate, having no point of connection.

He let the end of the belt dangle loose again, holding only the buckle. "But it seems they overlooked a quality inherent in the nature of the universe." Taking the end of the belt, he gave it a half twist and then brought it up to the buckle.

"Now, you see, if I walk the belt, I pass one time around and circle underneath the buckle but I remain on the same surface and continue once more around the belt until I return to the buckle itself."

"Ah," said Liath, fascinated at once. She traced the surface of the belt all the way around twice without lifting her finger from the leather, and the second time she came back to the buckle, where she had started.

"I never thought of that!" she cried, amazed and intrigued. "The universe has a fold in it."

"So you see," said Eldest Uncle approvingly. "Although our land was flung away from Earth, the fold in the universe is bringing us back to where we started."

He rose unsteadily, as if his knees hurt him. Extending an arm, he addressed the council. "On Earth, the measure of days and years moves differently than it does here. Soon, the full count of Great Years will have again run to completion thirteen times on Earth. The ending point will becoming the starting point, and we will come home."

Cat Mask seemed about to blurt out a comment, but Eldest Uncle's gaze stilled the words on his tongue. Ponderously, Feather Cloak pushed up to her feet. No one moved to help her, until Liath finally stepped toward her but was brought up short by Skull Earrings. The elderly man raised a hand, palm out, to show that she must not aid the pregnant woman who sat in the Eagle Seat.

Panting a little, Feather Cloak steadied herself and surveyed the council. Standing, she looked even more enormously pregnant, so huge that it seemed impossible she hadn't burst. "We will come home," she agreed. "Yet there remains a danger to us. We will come home unless the human sorcerers now on Earth use their magic to weave a second spell like the first. Then they could fling us back into the aether, and we would surely all perish, together with our land."

Pain cut into Liath's belly. She tucked, bending slightly, reflexively, but the pain vanished as swiftly as it had come—it was only the memory of her labor pains the day her mother had told her the story of the Great Sundering, and the threat of the Aoi return.

"The only one who can stop them is you," Anne had said.

Had Da known all along? Was this the fate he had tried to hide her from—serving as Anne's tool? Pain stabbed again, but this time it was anger. Da hadn't helped her at all by hiding the truth from her. He'd only made it harder. Ignorance hadn't spared her, it had only made her weak and fearful.

"To use magic in such a way seems like the act of a monster," she said at last, measuring her words, aware of the anger burning in the pit of her stomach. "But I have heard of a story told by my people of a time known as the Great Sundering, when the Aoi—"

"Call us not by that name!" cried Cat Mask. "If you come in peace, as you claim, why do you keep insulting us?"

"I do not intend to insult you!" she retorted, stung. "That is the name my people call you."

"Don't you know what it means?" asked Green Skirt.

"No."

Cat Mask spat the words. "'Cursed Ones.'"

"What do you call yourselves, then?"

They all broke out talking at once.

Feather Cloak lifted a hand for silence. "In our most ancient home, we called ourselves The-Ones-Who-Have-Understanding. After our ancestors left that place and came over the sea, we called ourselves The Ones-Who-Have-Made-A-New-Home. Now we call ourselves The-Ones-In-Exile, Ashioi, which also means, The-Ones-Who-Have-Been-Cursed."

"Ashioi," murmured Liath, hearing the word she knew—"Aoi"—embedded within it. Was that how ancient knowledge survived, only in fragments like the florilegia Da had compiled over the years? Surely Da had understood the true purpose of the Seven Sleepers. What had he been looking for in these notes and scraps of magical knowledge? Had he wondered how a spell as powerful as the Great Sundering could come to be? She had to work it through in order to understand the whole. "Wouldn't it also be true that if such a huge region of land fell to Earth again, it would make a terrible cataclysm?"

"Maybe so," said Eldest Uncle, "yet if this land approaches close by Earth and is flung away again by a spell woven by human sorcerers, that act, too, will cause manifold destruction. The tides of the universe spare no object, for even when bodies do not touch, they influence each other. If you are trained in the craft of the stars, then you understand this principle. No part of the shore is safe from a high tide, or an ebb tide. Either way, Earth will suffer."

Twilight came suddenly; the gap in the ceiling darkened so quickly that spinning dust motes caught in shafts of light simply vanished as shadow spread. For a moment, it was too dark for even Liath to see. Then the Eagle Seat and the Jaguar Seat began to glow, illuminating the two figures who stood on their backs: Feather Cloak and Eldest Uncle. In that gleam, the shells and beads decorating their cloaks and arm sheaths took on new colors, roots of scarlet and viridian that shuddered deep within.

His final words, like an arrow, were aimed at her heart. "The only choice is whether my people perish utterly, or whether we will be given a chance to live."

In her mind's eye she saw the ruined city that ended at a shoreline so sharp and straight that a knife might have shorn it off. A knife—or a vast spell whose power beggared the imagination and left her a little stunned—might have sheared off the land so, cutting it cleanly as one slices away a piece of meat from the haunch.

To contemplate the power of such a spell, such a sundering, left her sick to her stomach and profoundly dizzy. She went hot all over. Her blood pounded in her limbs, and the hot taste of fire burned on her lips as a wind roared in her ears.

Who would perish, and who would live? Who had earned the right to make that choice?

The room blazed with heat. The council members cried out as fire blossomed at the heart of the Eagle Seat, engulfing Feather Cloak entirely. Liath staggered at its brilliance, yet within the archway of leaping flames shadows writhed.

Hanna riding in the train of a battered army across a grassy landscape mottled with trees and low hills.

Hugh seated at a feast in the place of honor next to a laughing man who wears a crown of iron, yet as she takes in her breath sharply, horrified to see Hugh's beautiful face, he looks up, startled, just as if he has heard her. He turns to speak intently to the veiled woman seated at his right hand.

Wolfhere walking with bowed shoulders down a forest path. She forms his name on her lips, and abruptly he glances up and speaks, audibly: "Liath?"

Lamps burn in a chamber made rich by the lush tapestries hanging on its walls. People have gathered around King Henry—she recognizes him at once—but as though a lodestone drags her, her vision pulls past him to that which she most seeks:

Ai, God, it is Blessing! The baby is crying, struggling in Heribert's arms as she reaches out for her mother.

"Ma! Ma!" the infant cries.

Blessing can see her!

"Blessing!" she cries. Then she sees him, emerging out of a shadowed corner. Maybe her heart will break, because she misses him so much. "Sanglant!"

He leaps forward. "Liath!" But a figure jerks him back.

They were gone.

"Look!" shouted Cat Mask.

Through the fading blaze, Liath saw a sleeping man. His head was turned away from her, but two black hounds lay on either side of him, like guardians. He stirred in his sleep. That fast, fire and vision vanished, and the flames settled like falling wings to reveal Feather Cloak standing unharmed.

Liath sank down to the floor, shaking so hard she could not stand.

"Let this be a sign," said Feather Cloak sternly. "Who

among you saw the Impatient One and the man who must be
her son, who partakes both of our blood and of human blood?"

But the others had not seen the vision made of fire, and
Liath was too shaken to speak.

"She must leave," said Feather Cloak to Eldest Uncle. "She
bears an ill-omened name. Her power is too great, and like all
of humankind, she does not understand it. I have spoken."

"So be it," said Eldest Uncle.

Cat Mask jumped forward. "Let her blood be taken to give
us strength!"

They all began arguing at once as Liath leaped to her feet.
"Is this what you call justice?" she cried.

"Silence," said Feather Cloak in a voice so soft that it seemed
more like an exhaled breath, and yet silence fell. A wind blew
outside, making the roots at the ceiling tick quietly against
each other in its eddy. "She must leave unmolested. I will not
risk her blood spilled while we are still so weak."

"Yet I would have her walk the spheres before she goes,"
said Eldest Uncle as congenially as if he wished to offer an
honored guest a final mug of ale before departure.

White Feather hissed. Skull Earrings made a sharp protest,
echoed by others. Only Cat Mask laughed.

Feather Cloak regarded Liath coolly. She had eyes as dark as
obsidian and a gaze as sharp as a knife. "Few can walk the
spheres. None return unchanged from that path."

"This I have seen," said Eldest Uncle, "that if we would live,
we must help her discover what she is."

The glow illuminating the Eagle Seat dimmed until it had
the delicate luminescence of a seashell. With dimness came a
sharpening of smell: dry earth, sour sweat, the faint and distracting scent of water, and the cutting flavor of ginger on her
tongue. Liath felt suddenly weary, cut to the heart by that
glimpse of Sanglant and Blessing, as if her shell of numbness
had been torn loose, exposing raw skin.

"Let her return here no more," said Feather Cloak, "but if
she can mount the path to the spheres, I will not interfere.

When one day and one night have passed, I will send Cat Mask and his warriors in search of her. If they find her in our country, then I will look the other way if they choose to kill her. I have spoken."

"So be it," murmured Eldest Uncle, and the others echoed him as Cat Mask grinned.

IV
JUDGEMENT IN HASTE

1

"SHE isn't at all what I remember."

King Henry stood with his granddaughter in his arms at an unshuttered window in the royal chambers, attended only by Rosvita, Hathui, four stewards, six guards, and Helmut Villam. Princess Theophanu and four of her ladies sat in the adjoining chamber, playing chess, embroidering, and discussing the tractate *Concerning Male Chastity,* written by St. Sotheris, which had only recently been translated by the nuns at Korvei Convent from the original Arethousan into Dariyan. Their voices rang out merrily, seemingly immune from care.

Queen Adelheid had escorted Alia and Sanglant outside to show them the royal garden, with its rose beds, diverse herbs, and the aviary that the palace at Angenheim was famous for. Standing beside Henry at the window, with her fingers clamped tight on the sill, Rosvita saw Adelheid's bright gown among the roses. A moment later, she saw Sanglant on his knees by one of the herb plots, fingering petals of comfrey. Brother Heribert knelt beside him and they spoke together, two heads bent in convivial conversation. The contrast between the two men could not have been bolder: Sanglant had the bulk and vitality of a man accustomed to armor and horseback and a life lived outdoors, while Heribert, in his cleric's robes, had a slender frame and narrow shoulders. Yet his hands, too, bore the marks of manual labor. How had they met? What did Heribert know that he had not told them?

"She isn't anything like what I remember." Henry's expression grew pensive. "It's as if that time was a dream I fashioned in my own mind." Blessing had fallen asleep on his shoulder.

"Perhaps it was," observed Rosvita. "Youth is prey to fancy. We are adept at building palaces where none exist."

"I was very young," he agreed. "In truth, Sister, I find it disturbing. I recall my passion so clearly, but when I look at her now, I fear I made a mistake."

A stiff breeze stirred the leaves in the herb bed next to the prince. Laughing, Sanglant stood as Heribert leaped up, startled. The outside air and Heribert's presence had restored the prince to good spirits, yet now he glanced back toward the open window where his father stood. Had he heard them? Surely they stood too far away for their conversation to be overheard.

"Was it a mistake, Your Majesty?" She nodded toward the prince.

"Nay, of course not. Perhaps I am only a little surprised that memory has not served me as well as you have." He smiled with the craft of a regnant who knows when to flatter his advisers, but Rosvita sensed tension beneath the light words.

"You were very young, Your Majesty. God grant us all the privilege of change and growth, if we only use it. You are a wiser man now than you were then, or so I have heard."

He smiled, this time with genuine pleasure. The baby stirred, coming awake. She yawned, looked around, and said, quite clearly: "Da!" After this unequivocal statement, she frowned up at Henry. She had a clever little face, quite charming, and mobile expressions. "Ba!" she exclaimed. She seemed to have no other mode of speech than the imperious.

"The months do not count out correctly," said Henry. "Nine

months for a woman to come to her time, and even if she deliver early, no child will survive before the seventh month. Sanglant and the Eagle left fourteen months ago, yet this child is surely a yearling or even older. But her coloring is like that of the Eagle's, if I am remembering correctly."

"Do not doubt your memory on this account. I also believe the child resembles its mother in some ways. Look at the blue of her eyes! But you are right, Your Majesty. Even if she were a seven months' child, born early, she could therefore be only seven months of age now."

"Come." Henry carried the baby out to the garden, heading for his son, but as soon as he stepped outside the beauty of the autumn foliage and late flowers distracted the child. Rosvita watched as the king surrendered to her imperial commands: each time Blessing pointed to something that caught her eye, he obediently hauled her to that place, and then to another, lowering her down to touch a flower, prying her fingers from a thorny stem, stopping her from eating a withered oak leaf blown over the wall, lifting her up again to point at a flock of geese passing overhead.

He was besotted.

Sanglant had wandered to the garden by the wall where he spoke privately to Brother Heribert. What intrigue might he be stirring up? Yet had Sanglant ever been one for intrigue? He had always been the most straightforward of men.

Still, he made no move to interfere with the capture of his father: Blessing worked her will without obstacle. Queen Adelheid had gone into the aviary. Rosvita had to admire the young queen: either she was determined to turn Alia into an ally, or else she intended to divert all suspicion while she concocted a plan to rid herself of her rival. It was hard to tell, and even after months of sharing the most difficult of circumstances in Adelheid's company, Rosvita didn't know her well enough to know which was more likely.

But as Rosvita watched Henry dandle the child, her heart grew troubled.

Twilight finally drove them back inside. Adelheid and her attendants came from the mews, Sanglant and Heribert from the garden. Alia lingered outside, alone, to smell the last roses. No one disturbed her. By custom, the feast would continue into the night, but neither Henry nor any in his party seemed inclined to return to the great hall. Too much remained unspoken.

Blessing went to Sanglant at once. She had begun to fuss with hunger. A spirited discussion ensued among the attendants on the efficacy of goat's milk over cow's milk to feed a motherless child. He took her outside.

Rosvita went to the window. A cool autumn breeze, woken by dusk, made her shiver. Sanglant avoided his mother and settled down out of her sight on the far side of the old walnut tree.

Adelheid came to stand beside Rosvita. The queen smelled faintly of the mews and more strongly of the rose water she habitually washed in. She had such a wonderful, vividly alive profile that even in the half light of gathering dusk her expressions seemed more potent than anything around them, as bright as the waxing moon now rising over wall and treetops.

"You have acted most graciously, Your Majesty," said Rosvita.

"Have I? Do you think I am jealous of the passion he once felt for her? That was many years ago. Truly, she looks marvelously young for one as old as she must be, but until she explains her purpose here, it is not obvious to me that she possesses anything he now desires or lacks." The young queen's tone had a scrape in it, as at anger rubbing away inside.

"And you do?"

"So I did," she replied bitterly. "As you yourself know, Sister Rosvita, for you came with my cousin Theophanu to seek me out in Vennaci. Yet did you not just see Henry holding in his arms the living heir to Taillefer's great empire? If it is true, what need has Henry for a queen of my line?"

"What manner of talk is this, Your Majesty? Your family's claim to the Aostan throne is without rival."

Adelheid smiled faintly, ironically. "It is true that no noble *Aostan* family holds a better claim. Certainly the skopos will support me if she can, since she is my aunt. Yet how did my lineage help me after the death of my mother and my first husband, may God have mercy on them? Which of the nobles of Aosta came to my aid when I was besieged? My countryfolk abandoned me to Lord John's tender mercies. I would have become his prisoner, and no doubt his unwilling wife, had you and Princess Theophanu not arrived when you did. What would have happened if Mother Obligatia had not taken us in despite the hardship it placed upon her and the nuns in her care? What if she hadn't allowed Father Hugh to use sorcery to aid our escape?"

"What do you mean?" But trouble, like a swift, may stay aloft for a very long time once it has lifted onto the wind.

"I had no rivals before. Now I do."

"Henry has legitimate children, it is true."

"None of whom can claim descent from Emperor Taillefer. Nay, it is clear that Henry favors Sanglant, Sister Rosvita. Henry would have seen me married to Prince Sanglant, had he been given his way a year ago."

Since it was true, Rosvita saw no reason to reply beyond a nod.

"If that was his plan, then he must have hoped that by marrying me, Sanglant would be crowned as king of Aosta. It is understood, I believe, that only a regnant strong enough to claim the regnancy of Aosta can hope to claim the imperial title of Holy Dariyan Emperor as well. Henry hoped to give Sanglant that title. Or so I assume."

"Henry has never hidden his ambitions. He hopes to take that title for himself."

"Certainly he is now entitled to be crowned king of Aosta because he is my husband. But Ironhead still reigns in Darre. Do you not see my position?"

Rosvita sighed. Adelheid was young but not one bit naive. Yet Rosvita could not bring herself to speak one word that might seem unfaithful to Henry. "You are troubled, Your Majesty," she said instead, temporizing, hoping that Adelheid would not go on. But the one trait of youth Adelheid had not yet reined in was impetuousness.

"Let us imagine that it is true that this child is the legitimately born heir to Taillefer, his granddaughter two generations removed. I brought Henry the crowns of Aosta. But her claim to Aosta's throne, and to the Crown of Stars Taillefer wore as Holy Dariyan Emperor, is far greater than anything I can confer."

Rosvita glanced back into the room. Two stewards stood by the door, looking bored as they guarded the wine. Various tapestries depicting the life of St. Thecla hung from the whitewashed walls: witnessing the Ekstasis; debating before the empress; writing one of her famous epistles to far-flung communities; accepting the staff that marked her as skopos, holy mother over the church; the stations of her martyrdom.

Henry had gone with Villam into the adjoining chamber to oversee the chess playing, Hathui sticking close to him rather like a falcon on a jess. Villam leaned with a hand on the back of the chair inhabited by one of Theophanu's favorites, the robust Leoba. Even at his age, he was not above flirting. Indeed, he was currently unmarried and despite his age still an excellent match. Leoba let him move a chess piece for her, Castle takes Eagle.

The game brought Rosvita back to the moves being enacted here and now. "Surely, Your Majesty, you do not believe that King Henry would put you aside on such slender evidence?"

Adelheid had the grace to blush. "Nay, Sister, do not think me selfish. In truth, I have no fear for myself. I am fond of Henry, and I believe he is fond of me. He is well known for being pious and obedient to the church's law. He will not break a contract now that it has been sealed. But if God are willing and grant us Their blessing, I will have children with him. What is to become of them?"

Now, finally, she saw the battle lines being drawn. "How can I answer such a question, Your Majesty? At best, I may hope that the king hears my voice, and my counsel. I do not speak for him."

"You saved my life and my crown, Sister. I trust you to do what is right, not what is expedient. I know you serve with an honest heart, and that you care only for what benefits your regnant, not for what benefits yourself. That is why I ask you to consider carefully when you advise the king. Think of my position, I pray you, and that of the children I hope to have." She smiled most sweetly and moved away to meet Alia by the door. Beckoning to the stewards, she had a cup of wine brought for the Aoi woman.

"Was that a plea, or a warning?"

Rosvita jumped, scraping a finger on the wooden sill. "You startled me, Brother. I did not see you come up beside us."

"Nor did the queen," observed Fortunatus. "But she has observed a great deal else. Henry already has grown children who will be rivals to whatever children she bears. Yet she does not fear them as she fears Sanglant."

Rosvita set her hands back on the sill, then winced at the pain in her finger.

"You've caught a splinter," said Fortunatus, taking her hand into his. He had a delicate touch, honed by years of calligraphy.

As he bent over her hand, working the splinter loose, she lowered her voice. "Do you think she fears Sanglant?"

"Would you not?" he asked amiably. "Ah! There it comes." He flicked the offending splinter away and released her hand. She sucked briefly at the wound as he went on. "He is the master of the battlefield. All acknowledge that. He returns rested and fit, with soldiers already kneeling before him, although only God know when they pledged loyalty to him, who has nothing."

"Nothing but the child."

"Nothing but the child," Fortunatus agreed. The privations of their journey over the mountains to Aosta and their subsequent flight from Ironhead had pared much flesh from Fortunatus' frame. Leanness emphasized his sharp eyes and clever mouth, making him look more dour than congenial, when in fact he was a man who preferred wit and laughter to dry pronouncements. In the last few weeks on the king's progress he had been able to eat heartily, as was his preference, and he was putting on weight. It suited him. "I would say he is the more dangerous for having nothing but the child. He isn't a man who desires things for himself."

"He desired the young Eagle against his father's wishes."

"I pray God's forgiveness for saying so, Sister, but surely he desired her more like a dog lusts after a bitch in heat."

"It's true it is the child who has changed him, not the marriage. You are right when you say he desires no thing for himself, for his own advancement. But what he desires for his child is a different matter."

"Do you think it will come to a battle between him and Queen Adelheid?"

She frowned as she gazed out into the foliage. Wind whipped the branches of the walnut tree under which Sanglant sheltered with Blessing, although no wind stirred the rest of the garden. It seemed strange to her, seeing its restlessness contrasted so starkly with the autumnal calm that lay elsewhere. The prince rose abruptly. Heribert, beside him, asked for the baby and, with reluctance evident in the stiffness of his shoulders, Sanglant handed her over. She was splayed out with that absolute limpness characteristic of a sleeping child. The prince and the frater stood together under the writhing branches, talking together while the baby slept peacefully. Finally, Sanglant looked up and seemed to address a comment to the heavens. Surely by coincidence, at that very instant, the breeze caught in the branches of the walnut tree ceased.

"What does Prince Sanglant know but war? Did Henry not fight against his own sister? Why should we expect otherwise in the next generation?"

"Unless good counsel and wiser heads prevail," murmured Fortunatus.

Behind them, voices raised as the company who had been seated in the adjoining chamber flooded into the one in which Rosvita and Fortunatus still stood. Rosvita moved away from the window just as Hathui came up to her.

"I pray you, Sister Rosvita," said the Eagle, "the king wishes you to attend him, if you will."

"I would speak with you in private council," Alia was saying to Henry as she looked around the chamber.

Henry merely gestured to the small group of courtiers and nobles and servants attending him, no more than twenty-five people in all. "My dear companions and counselors Margrave Villam and Sister Rosvita are privy to all my most private councils." Deliberately, he extended a hand to invite Adelheid forward. She came forward to stand beside him with a high flush in her cheeks and a pleased smile, quickly suppressed, on her lips. "Queen Adelheid and my daughter, Theophanu, of course will remain with me." He glanced up then, looking around the room. He marked Hathui with his gaze. She needed no introduction nor any excuse; she simply stood solidly a few paces behind him, as always. The others slid back to the walls, making themselves inconspicuous, and he ignored them. "If Sanglant chooses to hear your words, I am sure he will come in from outside."

"You have changed, Henri," Alia replied, not with rancor but as a statement of fact. "You have become the ruler I thought you might become in time. I am not sorry that I chose you instead of one of the others."

He rocked back on his heels as at a blow. Adelheid's small but firm hand tightened on his. "What do you mean? Chose me instead of one of the others? What others?"

She seemed surprised by his outburst. "Is it not customary

among humankind to be making alliances based on lineage, fertility, and possessions? Is this not what you yourself are doing, Henri?" She indicated Adelheid. "When first I am coming back to this world, many of your years ago, I go seeking the one whose name is known even to my people. That is the man you call Emperor Taillefer. But he is dead by the time I am walking on Earth, and he has left no male descendants. I cannot be making an alliance with a dead man. It is to the living I must look. I am walking far in search of the living. Of all the princes in these lands it is in the Wendish lineage I am seeing the most strength. Therefore I am thinking then that your lineage is the one I seek."

Henry had color in his cheeks, the mark of anger, but his voice betrayed nothing of the irritation that sparked as he narrowed his eyes. "I seem to have misunderstood our liaison. I had thought it was one of mutual passion, and that you were gracious enough to swear that the child you and I got together was of my making as well as yours. So that the child would seal my right to rule as regnant after my father. Do I understand you instead to say that you had another purpose in mind? That you actively sought me—or any young prince of a noble line—and chose me over the others because of the strength of the kingdom I was meant to rule?"

"Is it different among you, when you contract alliances?" Alia seemed genuinely puzzled. "For an undertaking of great importance, are you not sealing bargains and binding allies who will be bringing the most benefit to your own cause?"

Henry laughed sharply. "Had you some undertaking in mind, Alia, when first you put yourself in my way in Darre? How well I recall that night!"

She gestured toward the garden, dark now except for the light of moon and stars. Inside, the stewards had gotten all the lamps lit. St. Thecla's many figures on the tapestries shimmered in the golden light; her saint's crowns had been woven with silver threads, and the lamplight made them glimmer like moonglow.

"What other undertaking than the making of the child? Was this not our understanding?"

"Truly, it was my understanding. I understood why I needed to get a child, even if the getting of the child came second to my passion for you. But never did I understand that you wanted a child as well." He spoke bitterly. "You abandoned the two of us easily enough. What could you have wanted a child for if you were willing to walk away from him when he was still a suckling babe?"

She walked forward full into the light from the four dragon-headed lamps that hung from hooks in the ceiling to illuminate the center of the chamber. Despite her tunic, she could not look anything but outlandish, foreign, and wildly unlike humankind. "In him, my people and your people become one."

"Become one?"

"If there is one standing between us who carries both my blood and yours, then there can be hope for peace."

Fortunatus stirred beside Rosvita, and she pressed a hand to his wrist, willing him to remain silent while, around them, Henry's attendants whispered to each other, puzzling over her words.

How could Alia's people seek peace when they no longer lived on Earth, and perhaps no longer lived at all? Of all their fabled kind, Alia alone had walked among them once, some twenty-five years ago, and then vanished utterly, only to reappear now looking no older for the intervening years.

But the years had not left Henry unscarred. He pulled out a rust-colored scrap of cloth and displayed it with angry triumph. Alia recoiled with a pained look on her face, as if the sight of the scrap physically hurt her.

"I held this close to my heart for all these years as a reminder of the love I bore for you!" In those words Rosvita heard the young Henry who, coming into his power, had not always known what to do with it, and not the mature Henry of these days who never lost control. "You never loved me at all, did you?"

"No." His outburst might have been foam flung against a sea wall for all the impact it had. "I made a vow before the council of my own people that I would sacrifice myself for this duty, to make a child who would be born with the blood of both our peoples."

Finally, as if his voice had at last reached his ears, he schooled his expression to the haughty dignity worthy of the regnant. "For what purpose?"

"For an alliance. A child born of two peoples has the hope to live in both their tribes. We are hoping that the boy will be the bridge who will be bringing your people into an alliance with mine. We knew you would not be trusting us. That is why I left him with you, so that you and your people would come to love him. I was thinking he would be raised to be the ruler after you, in the fashion of humankind. In this way our task would be made easy. Now I return and I find him as an exile. Why were you not treating him as you promised to me?"

"I raised him as my own!" cried Henry indignantly. "No man treated a son better! But he was a bastard. His birth gave me the right to the crown, but it granted him nothing save the honor of being trained as a captain for war. I did everything I could, Alia. I would have made him king after me, though everyone stood against me. But he threw it back in my face, all that I offered him, for the sake of that woman!" He was really angry now, remembering his son's disobedience.

Sanglant walked in from the garden. Folk parted quickly to let him through their ranks. He came to rest, standing quietly between the king and the Aoi woman, and all at once the resemblance showed starkly: his father's forehead and chin and height, his mother's high cheekbones and coloring and broad shoulders: two kinds blended seamlessly into one body. But he had nothing of Alia's inhuman posture and cold, harsh nature. In speech and gesture he was entirely his father's child.

"Liath is the great granddaughter of the Emperor Taillefer." Without shouting, Sanglant pitched his voice to carry strongly throughout the long chamber. "Now, truly, my father's people, my mother's people, and the lineage of Emperor Taillefer, the greatest ruler humankind has known, are joined in one person. In my daughter, Blessing." He indicated Brother Heribert, who had come in behind him carrying Blessing. "Is that not so?"

Henry lifted a hand, a slight movement, and his Eagle stepped forward to answer the prince. "What proof have you that the child is born of Taillefer's lineage?" Hathui asked.

"Do you accuse me of lying, Eagle?" he asked softly.

"Nay, Your Highness," she replied blandly. "But you may have been misled. Sister Rosvita believes that a daughter was born to Taillefer's missing son. Any woman might then claim to be the lost grandchild of Taillefer."

"Who would know to claim such a thing?" He shook his head impatiently. "This is an argument that matters little. If proof you will have, then I will get proof for you, and after that no person will doubt Blessing's claim."

"Son." How strange to hear Alia's voice speaking that word. It made Sanglant seem a stranger standing among them, rather than a beloved kinsman. "It is true that I was hoping when first I crossed through the gateway into this country to make a child with a descendant of Taillefer. But it was not to be. That you have done so—" She had a fatalistic way of shrugging, as if to say that her gods had worked their will without consulting her. "So be it. I bow to the will of She-Who-Creates. Let proof be brought and given if humankind have no other way of discerning the truth. But proof will be mattering little if all of you are dead because of the great cataclysm that will fall upon you."

Most of Henry's retinue still seemed to be staring at Blessing, who had stirred in Heribert's arms, yawning mightily and twisting her little mouth up as she made a sleepy face and subsided again.

But Henry was listening. "What cataclysm do you mean?" He regarded her intently.

"You are knowing an ancient prophecy made by a holy woman among your people, are you not? In it is she not speaking of a great calamity?"

Rosvita spoke, unbidden, as words came entire to her mind. "'There will come to you a great calamity, a cataclysm such as you have never known before. The waters will boil and the heavens weep blood, the rivers will run uphill and the winds will become as a whirlpool. The mountains shall become the sea and the sea shall become the mountains, and the children shall cry out in terror for they will have no ground on which to stand. And they shall call that time the Great Sundering.'"

"Are you threatening my kingdom?" asked Henry gently.

"By no means," retorted Alia with a rare flick of anger. "Your people exiled mine ages ago as you know time, and now my people are returning. But the spell woven by your sorcerers will rebound against you threefold. What a cataclysm befell Earth in the long ago days is nothing to what will strike you five years hence, when what was thrown far returns to its starting point."

"Like the arrow Liath shot into the heavens," said Sanglant in a soft voice. He seemed to be speaking to himself, mulling over a memory no one else shared. "Shot into the sky, but it fell back to earth. Any fool would have known it would do that."

"What mean you by this tale?" demanded Henry. "What do you intend by standing before me now, Alia?"

Alia indicated her own face, its bronze complexion and alien lineaments. "Some among my people are still angry, because the memory of our exile lies heavily on us. After we have returned to Earth, they mean to fight humankind. But some among us seek peace. That is why I came." She stepped forward to rest a hand on Sanglant's elbow. "This child is my peace offering, Henri."

Henry laughed. "How can I believe these wild prophecies? Any madwoman can rave in like manner, speaking of the end times. If such a story were true, then why do none of my studious clerics know of it? Sister Rosvita?"

His outflung hand had the force of a spear, pinning her under his regard. "I do not know, Your Majesty," she said haltingly. "I have seen strange things and heard strange tales. I cannot be sure."

Theophanu spoke up at last. "Do you mean to say, Sister Rosvita, that you believe this wild story of cataclysms? That you think the legendary Aoi were sent into a sorcerous exile?"

"I recall paintings on the wall at St. Ekatarina's Convent. Do you not remember them, Your Highness?"

"I saw no wall paintings at St. Ekatarina's save for the one in the chapel where we worshiped," replied Theophanu with cool disdain. "It depicted the good saint herself, crowned in glory."

"I believe the story," said Sanglant, "and there are others who believe it as well. Biscop Tallia, the daughter of Emperor Taillefer, spent her life preparing for what she knew would come."

"She was censored by the church at the Council of Narvone," pointed out Theophanu.

"Don't be stubborn, Theo," retorted Sanglant. "When have I ever lied to you?" The barb caught her, but she recovered quickly, smoothing her face into a passionless mask as Sanglant went on. "Biscop Tallia instructed the woman who raised Taillefer's granddaughter and trained her as a mathematici. Taillefer's granddaughter gave birth to Liath. She already works to drive away the Lost Ones again, and to destroy them."

Henry spread his hands wide. "How can it be that Taillefer's granddaughter has not made herself known to the great princes of these realms? How can she live in such obscurity that we have never heard any least rumor of her existence?"

"She is a mathematici," Sanglant observed. "The church condemned such sorcery at the Council of Narvone. Why should she reveal herself if it would only bring her condemnation?" He nodded at Theophanu.

"Where is this woman now?" continued Henry relentlessly. "Where is your wife, Sanglant?"

"Ai, God!" swore Sanglant. "To tell the whole—!"

"How can I believe such a story if I do not hear the whole?" asked Henry reasonably. "Wine!" He beckoned, and a steward brought twin chairs, one for Henry and one for Adelheid. "I will listen patiently for as long as it takes you to tell your tale, Son. That is all I can promise."

2

THERE was to be no more feasting that night, although servants brought delicacies from the kitchen and folk ate as Prince Sanglant told his story haltingly, backtracking at times to cover a point he had missed. He was more disturbed than angry, impatient in the way of a man who is accustomed to his commands being obeyed instantly. A wind had got into the chamber, eddying around the lamps so that they rocked. Shadows juddered on the walls and over the tapestries like boats bobbing on water.

The silence and the jittery shadows made Sanglant's tale spin away into fable. A woman calling herself Anne had approached Liath at Werlida, claiming to be her mother. He and Liath had left with Anne. They had traveled by diverse means and in the company of servants who had no physical substance, no earthly body, to a place called Verna, hidden away in the heart of the Alfar Mountains. There, Liath had studied the arts of the mathematici.

"Condemned sorcery," said Henry, his only comment so far.

"It is her birthright," retorted Sanglant. "You cannot imagine her power—" He broke off, seeing their faces. Too late, he remembered, but Henry had not forgotten. Henry still had not forgiven Liath for stealing his son.

"The Council at Autun, presided over by my sister Constance, excommunicated one Liathano, formerly an Eagle in my service, and outlawed her for the practice of sorcery," said Henry in his quietest and therefore most dangerous voice. "For all I know, she has bewitched you and sent you back to me with this tale of Taillefer's lost granddaughter to tempt me into giving her daughter a privilege and honor the child does not deserve." He did not look at the sleeping Blessing as he said this.

"What of me?" asked Alia, who had listened without apparent interest. "I am no ally of this Liathano, whom I do not meet or know. I am no ally of these womans who are sorcerers, who mean to do my people harm. That is why I come to you, Henri, to ally against them."

Henry drained his cup of wine and called for another. Beside him, Adelheid sat with the composure of stone. Only her hair moved, tickled by a breeze that wound among the lamps hung from the ceiling. "If I send an embassy to your people, then we can open negotiations."

Alia's jaw tightened as she regarded him with displeasure. "None among your kind can pass through the gateway that leads to our country."

"So you say. But you are here."

She opened her left hand, palm out, to display an old scar cut raggedly across the palm. "I am what you call in your words a sorcerer, Henri."

"Do we not already harbor mathematici among us? They might travel as you did. We are not powerless."

"Father!" protested Theophanu, although she glanced toward Adelheid, "you would not allow condemned magic to be worked for your advantage—?"

Henry lifted a hand to stop her. She broke off, looked at Rosvita, then folded her hands in her lap and regarded the opposite wall—and the tapestry depicting St. Thecla's draught of the holy cup of waters—with a fixed gaze.

"You do not understand the structure of the universe, Henri. I was born in exile, and for that reason I can travel in the aether. I have walked the spheres. None among you would survive such a journey."

Sanglant's lips moved, saying a word, but he made no sound.

Henry shook his head. "How can I believe such a fantastic story? It might as well be a fable sung by a poet in the feast hall. I and my good Wendish army are marching south to Aosta to restore Queen Adelheid to her throne. You may march with us, if you will. A place at my table is always reserved for you, Alia." He turned to regard Sanglant, who stood with hands fisted and expression pulled down with impatience. Hereby lay the danger in giving a man command for all his young life; soon he began to expect that no person would gainsay him, even his father. "You, Son, may march with my army as well, if you will only ask for my forgiveness for your disobedience. I will show every honor due to a grandchild of my lineage to your daughter, as she deserves. There is a place for you in my army. If you ask for it."

"You believe none of it," said Sanglant softly.

Henry sipped at his wine, then spun the empty cup in his fingers as he contemplated his son in the same manner he might a rebellious young lord. "How can I believe such an outrageous story? I am regnant. We had this discussion before. If you wish my forgiveness, you must ask for it. But you know what obligations your duty to me entails."

"Then I will look elsewhere for support."

The words struck the assembly like lightning.

Villam stepped forward. "Prince Sanglant, I beg of you, do not speak rash words—"

"I do not speak rashly," said Sanglant harshly. "You have not seen what I have seen. You do not understand Anne's power nor her ruthlessness."

"What do you mean, brother?" asked Theophanu. She had distanced herself so completely from Rosvita after the escape from St. Ekatarina's that Rosvita could no longer even guess what might be going on in her mind. "If your words and the words of your mother are true, then it would appear to me that this woman, Anne, seeks to protect Earth from the Aoi. Why, then, would you act against her unless you have thrown in your lot with your mother's people? This might all be a diversion to aid them."

Blessing woke up crying. She struggled in Heribert's arms, but she wasn't reaching for her father. She was reaching for the middle of the room, tiny arms pumping and face screwed up with frustration.

"Ma! Ma!" she cried, wriggling and reaching so that Heribert could barely keep hold of her as she squirmed.

The air took on form.

Mist congealed at the center of the chamber, in the space ringed by the hanging lamps. Like a window being unshuttered, pale tendrils of mist acted as a frame. Rosvita staggered, made dizzy by this abrupt displacement of what she knew and understood while all around her the people in the room leaped backward or fled into the other chamber, sobbing in fright. Adelheid rose to her feet. Henry remained seated, but his hand tightened on one of the dragon heads carved into the armrests of his chair.

"Ma!" cried the baby.

There came a voice in answer, faint and so far off that it might have been a dream.

"Blessing!" Changing, made hoarser by pain or sorrow, that disembodied voice spoke again. "Sanglant!"

Sanglant leaped forward. "Liath!" he cried.

Alia grabbed him by the elbow and jerked him back, hard. Her strength was amazing: Sanglant, who stood a good head and a half taller than her, actually staggered backward.

Blessing twisted out of Heribert's arms. Henry cried out a warning as she fell, and Sanglant flung himself toward the baby, but he was too far away to catch her.

But some *thing* was already under her.

Blessing sank into folds of air that took on a womanlike form, a female with a sensuous mouth, sharp cheekbones, a regal nose, a broad and intelligent forehead, and a thick fall of hair. She was not a human woman but a woman formed out of air, as fluid as water, made of no earthly substance. A veil of mist concealed her womanly parts, but she was otherwise unclothed, and she had the ample breasts of a nursing woman. In her arms, Blessing calmed immediately, and she turned her head to nurse at that unworldly breast.

Henry's face whitened in shock as he rose. "What obscenity is this? What manner of creature nurses the child?"

Sanglant stationed himself protectively in front of the creature. "Liath was too ill to nurse her after the birth. Blessing wouldn't even take goat's milk. She would have died if it had not been for Jerna."

"What is it?" murmured Theophanu. Her ladies, clustered behind her, looked frightened and disgusted, but Theophanu merely regarded the scene with narrowed eyes and a fierce frown.

Everyone backed away except Heribert. Adelheid's hands twitched, and she leaned forward, quite in contrast to Theophanu's disapproving reserve, to stare at the nursing aetherical with lips parted. Hathui remained stoically behind Henry's chair.

"It is a daimone, I believe," said Rosvita. Fortunatus, at her back, whistled under his breath. He had not deserted her. "One of the elementals who exists in the aether, in the upper spheres."

"Do such creatures have souls?" asked Adelheid.

"The ancient writers believed they did not," murmured Rosvita reflexively. A collective gasp burst from the people pressed back against the far walls. No one spoke. The baby suckled noisily as everyone stared. Ai, Lady! What manner of nourishment did it imbibe from a soulless daimone?

"It is true, then." The mask of stone crashed down to conceal Henry's true feelings. "You have been bewitched, Sanglant, as Judith and her son said. You are not master of your own thoughts or actions. Lavastine was laid under a spell by Biscop Antonia. Now you are a pawn in the hands of the sorcerer who stole you from me. Where is Liathano? What does she want?"

"I pray you, Your Majesty," cried Rosvita, stepping forward. She knew where such accusations would lead. "Let us make no judgment in haste! Let a council be convened, so that those best educated in these matters can consider the situation with cool heads and wise hearts."

"As they did in Autun?" replied Sanglant with a bitter grimace. He eased Blessing out of the grip of the daimone. The baby protested vigorously, got hold of one of his fingers, and proceeded to suck on it while she stared up at his face. The daimone uncurled herself; Rosvita knew no other way to explain it—the creature simply uncurled into the air and vanished from sight. Just like that.

With a deep breath to steady himself, Henry took a step back and sat. "I will call a council when we reach Darre. Let the skopos herself preside over this matter."

"You expect me to bide quietly at your side?" demanded Sanglant.

"Once you would have done what I asked, Son."

"But I am not what I was. You no longer understand what I have become. Nor do you trust me. I have never abandoned this kingdom, nor will I now. I know what needs to be done, and if you will not support me, then I will find those who will act before it is too late."

"Is this rebellion, Sanglant?"

"I pray you," began Rosvita, stepping forward to place herself between the two men, because she could see the cataclysm coming, the irresistible force dashing itself against the immovable object.

"Nay, Sister," said Henry, "do not come between us." She had no choice but to fall silent. She saw in the king certain signs of helplessness before the son he had loved above all his other children, the way his lips quirked unbidden, the tightness of his left hand on the throne's armrest, his right foot tapping on the ground in a rapid staccato. "Let him answer the question."

Sanglant had never been a man to let words get in the way of actions. "Heribert!" He gathered his daughter more tightly against him and strode to the door with Heribert following obediently at his heels. At the door, he turned to regard his sister. "Theo?"

She shook her head. "Nay, Sanglant. You do not know what I have witnessed. I will not follow you."

"You will in the end," he said softly, "because I know what is coming." His gaze flicked over the others, resting briefly on Rosvita, but to her he only gave a swift and gentle smile. "Counsel wisely, Sister," he said in a low voice. He bowed toward Adelheid, and left.

The lamps swayed. One of the lamps blew out abruptly, with a mocking *hwa* of air, like a blown breath, and an instant later a second flame shuddered and then was extinguished. All was still.

If not quiet. Everyone began whispering at once.

"I pray you," said Henry in a voice so stretched that it seemed ready to break.

They gave him silence.

"You do not go with him," observed Henry to Alia. She stood by the door that led into the gardens.

She smiled, not a reassuring expression. Lifting a hand, she murmured something under her breath and gestured. At once, the two doused lamps caught flame. As the folk in the room started nervously at this display of magic, she smiled again in that collected way a cat preens itself after catching a particularly fat and juicy mouse.

"He is young and hot-tempered. What I am not understanding is why you are not listening to me, Henri. Is so much knowledge lost to humankind that you refuse to believe me? Do you truly not remember what happened in the long-ago days? I come as—what would you say?—walking as an emissary, from my people to yours. To tell you that many of us are wanting peace, and not wanting war."

"Where are your people? Where have they been hiding?"

She gave a sharp exhalation of disappointment. "I am offering you an alliance now, when you are in a position of strength. Many among our council argued against this, but because I gave of my essence to make the child, I was choosing to come now and they could not be stopping me. I was choosing to give you this chance." She walked to the door and paused by the threshold. "But when I appear before you next, Henri, you will be weak."

She walked out of the chamber. No one tried to stop her.

There came then a long silence. Fortunatus brushed a hand against Rosvita's elbow. From somewhere beyond the garden, she heard a woman's laugh, incongruous because of its careless pleasure. The lamplit glow made the chamber like the work of an ancient sculptor, every statue wrought in wood or ivory at the artisan's pleasure:

There sat the regnant with his dark eyes raging in a face as still as untouched water. There stood the queen whose high color could be seen in the golden light of burning lamps. The old lord rubs habitually at the empty sleeve of his tunic, as though at any moment a breath of sorcery will fill it again with his lost arm. The princess has turned away, ivory face in profile, jewels glittering at her neck, and a hand on the shoulder of one of her ladies, caught in the act of whispering a confidence.

The King's Eagle had folded her arms across her chest and she seemed thoughtful more than shocked, as was every other soul. As were they all, all but Henry, whose anger had congealed into the cold fury of a winter's storm. St. Thecla went her rounds on the tapestries, caught forever in the cycle of her life and martyrdom, an ever-present reminder of the glory of the Word. Villam coughed.

The king rose. He glanced at his Eagle and made a small but significant gesture. The Eagle nodded as easily as if he had spoken out loud, then left the chamber on an unknown errand.

"I will to my bed." Henry took two strides toward one of the inner doors before he paused and turned back toward

Adelheid, but the young queen did not move immediately to
follow him.

"Do you believe it to be an impossible story, Sister Rosvita?"
she asked.

At first, Rosvita thought she had forgotten how to talk.
Her thoughts scattered wildly before she herded them in. "I
would need more evidence. Truly, it is hard to believe."

"That does not mean it cannot be true." Adelheid glanced
toward the garden. The cool wind of an autumn night curled
into the room, making Rosvita shudder. What if it brought
another daimone? "We have seen strange sights, Sister Rosvita.
How is this any stranger than what we have ourselves witnessed?" She beckoned to her ladies and followed Henry into
the far chamber.

"You have won Queen Adelheid's loyalty," said Theophanu
to Rosvita. "But at what cost? And for what purpose?"

"Your Highness!"

Theophanu did not answer. She retreated with her ladies
into the chamber where they had been playing chess, and
where beds and pallets were now being set up for their comfort.

How had it come to this?

"Do not trouble yourself, Sister," whispered Fortunatus at
her back. "I do not think Princess Theophanu's anger at you
will last forever. She suffers from the worm of jealousy. It has
always gnawed at her."

"What do you mean, Brother?"

"Do you not think so?" he replied, surprised at her reaction.
"Nay, perhaps I am wrong. Certainly you are wiser than I am,
Sister."

Servants and guards dispersed to their places, but Villam
lingered and, at last, came forward, indicating that he wished
to speak to Rosvita in complete privacy. Fortunatus moved
away discreetly to oversee the night's preparations.

"Do you believe their story?" Villam asked her. The lamplight scoured the wrinkles from his face so that he resembled

more than ever his younger self, hale and vigorous and handsome enough to attract a woman's gaze for more reason than
his title and his estates. Hadn't she looked at him so, when she
had been a very young woman come to court for the first time
and dazzled by its splendors? In her life, few men had tempted
her in this manner, for God had always kept a steadying hand
on her passions, and Villam respected God, and the church,
and a firm 'No.' They had shared a mutual respect for many
years.

"I cannot dismiss it out of hand, Villam. Yet it seems too
impossible to believe outright."

"You are not one to take fancies lightly, Sister, nor do you
succumb to any least rumor. What will you advise the king?"

"I will advise the king not to act rashly," she said with a
bitter laugh. "Villam, is it possible you can go now and speak
to Prince Sanglant?"

"I will try." He left.

The king's particular circle of clerics, stewards, and serv-
ingfolk had the right to sleep in his chambers, and Rosvita
herself had a pallet at her disposal. Despite this comfortable
bed, she spent a restless night troubled by dreams.

A pregnant woman wearing a cloak of feathers and the features of an Aoi queen sat on a stone seat carved in the likeness
of an eagle. Behind her, a golden wheel thrummed, spinning
her into a cavern whose walls dripped with ice. Villam's lost
son Berthold slept in a cradle of jewels, surrounded by six
attendants whose youthful faces bore the peaceful expression
known to those angels who have at last seen God. But the
golden calm draped over their repose was shattered when a
ragged band of soldiers blundered into their resting hall, calling out in fear and wonder. Ai, God, did one of those
frightened men have Ivar's face? Or was it Amabilia, after all,
come to visit her again?

Amabilia was dead. Yet how could it be that she could still
hear her voice?

"Sister, I pray you, wake up."

Fortunatus bent over her. A faint light limned the unshuttered window and open door that led out into the garden. Birds trilled their morning song.

Soldiers had come to wake the king. Henry emerged from his bedchamber with a sleepy expression. He was barefoot. A servingman fussed behind him, offering him a belt for his hastily thrown on tunic.

"Your Majesty! Prince Sanglant just rode out of the palace grounds with more than fifty men-at-arms and servants in attendance. He took the road toward Bederbor, Duke Conrad's fortress."

Henry blinked, then glanced at Helmut Villam, who at that moment walked into the room. "Did no one make any effort to stop him?"

The sergeant merely shrugged helplessly, but Villam stepped forward. "I spoke to him."

"And?"

Villam shook his head. "I advise you to let it rest for now."

"Bring me my horse," said Henry.

Before the others could rouse, he was off. Rosvita made haste to follow him, and she reached the stables just in time to commandeer a mule and ride after him. Besides a guard of a dozen soldiers, he rode alone except for Hathui, whom he engaged in a private conversation. When Rosvita caught up with the group, he glanced her way but let her accompany him without comment.

At first, she thought he meant to pursue his son, but once past the palace gates they took a different track, one that led past the monastery and into the forest, down a narrow track still lush with summer's growth.

The path wound through the forest. Alder wood spread around them, leaves turning to silver as the autumn nights chilled them. A network of streams punctuated the thick vegetation, low-lying willow and prickly dewberry amid tussocks of woundwort and grassy sedge. A rabbit bounded away under the cover of dogwood half shed of its leaves. The hooves of the horses made a muffled sound on the loamy track. Through a gap in the branches, she saw a buzzard circling above the tree-tops.

The track gave out abruptly in a meadow marked by a low rise where a solemn parade of hewn stones lay at odd angles, listing right or left depending on the density of the soil. One had fallen over, but the main group remained more or less intact.

"Here?" asked Henry.

"This far." Hathui indicated the stone circle. "She went in. She did not come out, nor have I seen any evidence she walked through the stones and on into the forest beyond. There isn't a path, nothing but a deer track that's mostly overgrown."

He beckoned to Rosvita. "Your company passed through one of these gateways, Sister. Could it not be that the Aoi have hidden themselves in some distant corner of Earth, biding their time?"

"It could be, Your Majesty. But with what manner of sorcery I cannot know."

"Yet there remain mathematici among us," he mused, "who may serve us as one did Adelheid."

She shuddered, drawing in a breath to warn him against sorcery, but he turned away, so she did not speak. Light spread slowly over the meadow, waking its shadows to the day, and these rays crept up and over the king until he was wholly illuminated. The sun crowned him with its glory as he stared at the silent circle of ancient stones. A breeze stirred his hair, and his horse stamped once, tossed its head, and flicked an ear at a bothersome fly. He waited there, silent and watchful, while Hathui made a final circuit of the stones.

"What news of the mountains?" he asked as the Eagle came up beside him at last.

"Most reports agree that the passes are still clear. It's been unseasonably warm, and there is little snow on the peaks. If God will it, we will have another month of fair weather. Enough to get through the mountains."

On the ride back he sang, inviting the soldiers to join in. Afterward, he spoke to them of their families and their last campaign. At the stables, a steward was waiting to direct him to the chapel where Adelheid, Theophanu, and their retinues knelt at prayer.

Henry strode in like fire, and Adelheid rose to greet him with an answering strength of will. Theophanu waited to one side with inscrutable patience as the king made a show of greeting his fair, young queen. But he did not neglect his daughter. He kissed her on either cheek and drew her forward so that every person, and by now quite a few had crowded into the chapel, would note her standing at his right side.

"Theophanu, you will remain in the north as my representative." He spoke with the king's public voice, carrying easily over the throng. The news carried in murmurs out the door and into the palace courtyard, where people gathered to see how Henry would react to the news of Sanglant's departure.

What Theophanu's expression concealed Rosvita could no longer guess. Was she glad of the opportunity or angry to be left behind again? She only nodded, eyes half shuttered. "As you wish, Father."

Henry extended an arm and took Adelheid's hand in his, drawing her forward to stand by his left side, as he would any honored ally. "Tomorrow," he said, addressing the court with a sharp smile, "we continue our march south, to Aosta."

3

LIGHT lay in such a hard, brilliant sheen over the abandoned city that Liath had to shade her eyes as she and Eldest Uncle emerged out of the cave into heat and sunlight. The stone edifices spread out before her, as silent as ghosts, color splashed across them where walls and square columns had been painted with bright murals. She retrieved her weapons from the peace stone and the water jar from the pyramid of skulls. Her hands were still unsteady, her entire soul shaken.

She and Da had run for so many years, hunted and, in the end, caught. She had been exiled from the king's court, yet had not found peace within her mother's embrace. Now this place, too, was closed to her. Was there any place she would ever be welcome? Could she ever find a home where she would not be hounded, hunted, and threatened with death?

Not today.

The huge carved serpent's mouth lay empty, although she heard the incomprehensible sound of the councillors' distant conversation, muted by the labyrinthine turnings of the passageway, each one like a twist of intrigue in the king's court, muffling words and intent.

"I have been given a day and a night," she said to the old sorcerer. She had learned to keep going by reverting to practical matters. "Can I walk the spheres in that length of time?"

"Child, the span of days as they are measured on Earth has no meaning up among the spheres. You must either return to Earth, or walk the spheres."

"Or wait here and die."

He chuckled. "Truly, even with such meager powers of foretelling as I possess, I do not predict that is the fate which awaits you."

"What fate awaits me, then?"

He shrugged. Together they walked back across the city toward the bank of mist. "You are new to your power," he said finally. "The path that leads to the spheres may not open for you."

"And the burning stone may remain hidden. What then? Will Cat Mask choose to hunt me down?"

"He surely will. Given the chance."

"Then I must make sure he is not given the chance." The silence hanging over the abandoned city made her voice sound like nothing more than the scratch of a mouse's claws on the stone paving of a vast cathedral. "I could return to Earth."

"So you could," he replied agreeably. He whistled, under his breath, a tune that sounded like the wandering wind caught among a maze of reed pipes.

"Then I would be reunited with my husband and child."

"Indeed you would, in that case."

"My daughter is growing. How many days are passing while we speak here together? How many months will pass before I see her again?" Her voice rose in anger. "How can I wait here, how can I even consider a longer journey, when I know that Sister Anne and her companions are preparing for what lies ahead?"

"These are difficult questions to answer."

His calm soothed her. "Of course, if this land does not return to its place, there might be other unseen consequences, ones that aren't as obvious as a great cataclysm but that are equally terrible."

"So there might."

"But, in fact, no one knows what will happen."

"No one ever knows what will happen," he replied, "not even those who can divine the future."

She glanced at him, but could not read anything in his countenance except peace. He had a mole below one eye, as though a black tear had frozen there. "You're determined to agree with me."

"Am I? Perhaps it is only that you've said nothing yet that I can disagree with."

They walked a while more in silence. She pulled one corner of her cloak up over her head to shade her eyes. The somber ranks of stairs, the platforms faced with skull-like heads and gaping mouths or with processions of women wearing elaborate robes and complicated headdresses, the glaring eye of the sun, all these wore away at her until she had an ache that throbbed along her forehead. The beat of her heart pulsed annoyingly in her throat. When they came to the great pyramid, she sank down at its foot, bracing herself against one of the monstrous heads. She set a hand on a smooth snout, a serpent's cunning face extruding from a petaled stone flower. Sweat trickled down her back. Heat sucked anger out of her. She would have taken off her cloak, but she needed it to keep her head shaded. The old sorcerer crouched at the base of the huge staircase, rolling his spear between his hands.

"Did you use magic to build this city?" she asked suddenly.

His aged face betrayed nothing. "Is the willingness to perform backbreaking labor a form of magic? Are the calculations of priests trained in geometry and astronomy more sorcery than skill? Perhaps so. What is possible for many may seem like magic when only a few contemplate the same amount of work."

"I'm tired," said Liath, and so she was. She shut her eyes, but under that shroud of quiet she could not feel at peace. She saw Sanglant and Blessing as she had seen them through the vision made out of fire: the child—grown so large!—squirming toward her and Sanglant crying out her name. "I'm so tired. How can I do everything that is asked of me?"

"Always we are tied to the earth out of which we came whether we will it or not. What you might have become had you the ability to push all other considerations from your heart and mind is not the same thing that you will become because you can never escape your ties to those for whom you feel love and responsibility."

"What I am cannot be separated from who I am joined to in my heart."

He grunted. She opened her eyes just as he gripped the haft of his spear and hoisted himself up to his feet. A man ran toward them along the broad avenue with the lithe and powerful lope of a predator. As he neared, she felt a momentary shiver of terror: dressed in the decorated loincloth and short cloak ubiquitous among the Aoi males, he had not a human face but an animal one. An instant later she recognized Cat Mask. He had pulled his mask down to conceal his face. In his right hand he held a small, round, white shield and in his left a wooden sword ridged with obsidian blades.

She leaped up and onto the stairs, grabbed her bow, slipped an arrow free, and drew, sighting on Cat Mask. Eldest Uncle said nothing, made no movement, but he whistled softly under his breath. Oddly enough, she felt the wind shift and tangle around her like so many little fingers clutching and prying.

Cat Mask slowed and, with the grace of a cat pretending it meant to turn away from the mouse that has escaped it, halted a cautious distance away. "I am forbidden to harm you this day!" he cried. The mask muffled his words.

"Is that meant to make me trust you?" She didn't change her stance.

After a moment he wedged the shield between arm and torso and used his free hand to lift his mask so that she could see his face. He examined her with the startled expression of a man who has abruptly realized that the woman standing before him has that blend of form and allurement that makes her attractive. She didn't lower her bow. Wind teased her arrow point up and down, so she couldn't hold it steady. With an angry exclamation she sought fire in the iron tip and let it free. The arrow's point burst into flame. Cat Mask leaped backward quite dramatically.

Eldest Uncle laughed outright, hoisting his spear. The bells tied to its tip jangled merrily. "So am I answered!" he cried. He frowned at Cat Mask. "Why have you followed us, Sour One?"

"To make you see reason, Old Man. Give her over to me now and I will make sure that she receives the fate she deserves. Humankind are not fit for an alliance with us. They will never trust us, nor any person tainted by kinship to us."

"Harsh words," mused Eldest Uncle as Liath kept Cat Mask fixed in her sight while the arrow's point burned cheerfully. "Is it better to waste away here? Do you believe that your plans and plots will succeed even if nothing hinders our return? Have we numbers enough to defeat humankind and their allies, now that they are many and we are few?"

"They fight among themselves. As long as they remain divided, we can defeat them."

"Will they still quarrel among themselves when faced with our armies? Do not forget how much they hated us before."

"They will always hate us!" But even as he said those words, he glanced again at Liath. She knew the expression of men who felt desire; she had seen it often enough to recognize it here. Cat Mask struggled with unspoken words, or maybe with disgust at his own susceptibility. Like Sanglant, he had the look of a man who knows how to fight and will do so. He was barely as tall as Liath but easily as broad across the shoulders as Sanglant, giving him a powerful, impressive posture. "And we will always hate them!"

His expression caught in her heart, in that place where Hugh still presided with his beautiful face and implacable grip.

"Hate makes you weak." Her words startled him enough that he met her gaze squarely for the first time. "Hate is like a whirlpool, because in the end it drags you under." With each word, she saw more clearly the knots that bound her to Hugh, fastened first by him, certainly, but pulled tighter by her. "That which you allow yourself to hate has power over you. How can you be sure that all humankind hates your people still? How can you be sure that an envoy offering peace won't be listened to?"

He snarled. "You can never understand what we suffered."

The flame at the tip of the arrow flickered down and snapped out, leaving the iron point glowing with heat. With deliberate slowness, to make it a challenge, she lowered the bow. "You don't know what I can or cannot understand. You are not the only one who has suffered."

"Ask those who are dead if they want peace with humankind. How can we trust the ones who did this to us?"

"The ones who did this to you died so long ago that most people believe you are only a story told to children at bedtime."

He laughed, not kindly, and took a step forward. "You are clever with words, Bright One. But I will still have your blood to make my people strong."

Resolve made her bold and maybe reckless as she gestured toward the heavens with Seeker of Hearts. "Catch me if you can, Cat Mask. Will you walk the spheres at my heels, or do you prefer to face me after I have returned from the halls of power, having learned the secret language of the stars?"

Cat Mask hissed in surprise, or disapproval. Or maybe even fear.

Eldest Uncle set down his spear with a thump. "So be it." He raised the spear and shook it so the bells rattled, as though to close the circle and end the conversation. "Go," he said to Cat Mask. It was a measure of the respect granted him as the last survivor, the only Ashioi who had seen the great cataclysm personally, that when he spoke a single command, a warrior as bold as Cat Mask obeyed instantly.

They watched him jog away down the length of the avenue. When he was distant enough that he posed no immediate threat, Eldest Uncle set foot on the stairs. Liath followed, using her bow to steady herself as they climbed higher on those frighteningly narrow steps. She caught her breath at the broad platform that defined its height before they descended the other side and passed into the mist, traversing the borderlands quickly and emerging at the lonely tower.

The unnatural silence of the sparse grassland, with its thorny shrubs and low-lying pale grasses, tore at her heart. Like a mute, the land could no longer speak in the many small voices common to Earth. The stillness oppressed her. Light made gold of the hillside as they walked up and over the height, bypassing the watchtower. She was grateful to come in under the scant shade afforded by the pines. Even the wind had died. Heat drenched them. A swipe of her hand along the back of her neck came away dripping.

She halted at the forest's edge, such as it was, breaking from pine forest into scrub and giving way precipitously to the hallucinatory splendor of the flowering meadow.

Under the shadow of the pines she slid her bow back into its case and let the spray of color ease her eyes. Eldest Uncle stood beside her without speaking or moving, beyond the thin whistle blown under his breath and an occasional tinkle of bells as he shifted the haft of his spear on the needle-strewn ground.

"How do I walk the spheres?" she asked finally, when Eldest Uncle seemed disinclined to move onward or to say anything at all. "Where do I find the path that will lead me there?"

"You have already walked it." He gestured toward the flower trail that led down to the river. "Why do you think I bide here, out of all the places in our land? This place is like a spring, the last known to us, where water wells up from hidden roots. Here the land draws life from the universe beyond, because the River of Light that spans the heavens touches our Earth at this place."

Wind stirred the flowers. Cornflowers bobbed on their high stalks, and irises nodded. The breeze murmured through crooked rows of lavender that cut a swathe of purple through tangles of dog roses and dense clusters of bright peonies. Marigolds edged the trail, so richly gold that sunlight might have been poured into them to give them color.

The view humbled her. "I thought you camped here because of the burning stone." She gestured toward the river, and the clearing that lay beyond it, where she had first crossed into this land.

"There are many places within our land where a gateway may open at intervals we cannot predict. It is true that the clearing in which I wait and meditate is one of those. But it is this place that I guard."

"Guard against what?"

"Go forward. You have walked this trail many times in these last days."

Wind cooled the sweat on her forehead and made the flowers dance and sway in a delirious mob of colors. Why hesitate?

Reflexively, she checked her gear, all that she had brought with her, everything and the only things she now possessed: cloak and boots, tunic and leggings; a leather belt, small leather pouch, and sheathed eating knife; her good friend Lucian's sword; the gold torque that lay heavily at her throat; the gold feather that Eldest Uncle had once given to her, now bound to an arrow's haft; the griffin quiver full of strong iron-pointed arrows and her bow, Seeker of Hearts; the lapis lazuli ring through which Alain had offered her his protection. The water jar did not belong to her, so she set it down on the path. When she stepped forward, crossing from shadow into sun, the blast of the sun hit her so hard she staggered back, raising a hand to shield herself.

Something wasn't right. Hadn't she learned more than this, even in her short time here in the country of the Aoi? Every spell, drawn out of an interaction with the hidden architecture of the universe, must be entered into correctly and departed from correctly, just as all things have a proper beginning and a proper ending.

By what means did a sorcerer ascend into the spheres? How could any person ascend into the heavens in bodily form, because the heavens were made up of aether, light, wind, and fire? Mortal substance was not meant to walk there.

Would she have to study many days and weeks and even months more, before she could walk the spheres and seek out her true power? Even if she ought to, she could not wait.

On Earth, days and weeks passed with each breath she exhaled here in this country. In the world beyond, her child grew and her husband waited, Anne schemed and Hugh flourished and Hanna rode long distances at the mercy of forces greater than herself. What of the Lions who had befriended her? What of Alain, whom she had last seen staggering, half dead, through the ruins of a battlefield? Where was he now? How could she leave them struggling alone? How much longer would she make them wait for her?

In one day and one night, as measured in this country, Cat Mask and his warriors would come hunting her.

It was time for her to go.

Yet how did one reach the heavens?

With a ladder.

She shut her eyes. Wind curled in her hair like the brush of Da's fingers, stroking her to sleep. Ai, God, Da had taught her exactly what she needed, if she had only believed in him.

She knelt to set her palm against the earth. As she rested there for the space of seven breaths, she let her mind empty, as Eldest Uncle had taught her. Dirt lay gritty against her skin. When she let her awareness empty far enough, she actually felt the pulse of the land through her hand, thin and fragile, worn to a thread. But it was still there. The land was still, barely, alive.

With a finger, she traced the Rose of Healing into the dirt, brushing aside dried-up needles and desiccated splinters of pine bark so that the outline made a bold mark on the path. Heat rose from that outline, and she stood quickly to step over it and into the sunlight.

At first her voice sounded hesitant and weak, a frail reed against the ocean of silence that lay over the land.

"By this ladder the mage ascends: First to the Rose, whose touch is healing." She took two more steps before bending to trace the next sigil into the dirt. "Then to the Sword, which grants us strength."

Three steps she forged forward now, and either perhaps the heat had increased or maybe only the strong hammer of the sun was making her light-headed, because some strange disturbance had altered the air around her so that the air resisted her passage as porridge might, poured down from the sky.

She crouched, and drew. "Third comes the Cup of Boundless Waters."

When she straightened, the flowers flowing out from either side of the trail had taken on a shimmering, unearthly cast, as though they bloomed with something other than material substance. Poppies flared with impossible scarlet richness. Lilacs lay a tender violet blush over swaying green stalks, shading into the complicated aftertones seen at sunset, although the sun still rode high above her.

She pressed forward four steps as a hazy glamour rose off the path like mist. Through this soft fog she reached, searching for the ground at her feet. It was hard now to see the path beneath her, but the dirt felt the same. Into the cool soil she traced the next pattern.

"Fourth lies the blacksmith's Ring of Fire."

Fog billowed up along the path, swirling around her knees as she took five steps forward. Ahead, through the hazy shimmer that now lay over the meadow, she saw the river. A figure stood on the far bank, caught in a moment of indecision among the rocks at the ford. Even from this distance, Liath recognized the stocky body and distinctive face of one of the Ashioi, but the woman was dressed so strangely, in human clothing, with human gear. She looked utterly out of place and yet entirely familiar as she gazed at the scene unfolding before her.

The fragrance of roses surrounded Liath, so dense it made her woozy.

Was it dizziness? Or was that Ashioi woman actually wearing Liath's other tunic, the one she had folded away into the saddlebags thrown over Resuelto's back just before she and Sanglant and the baby had tried to make their escape from Verna?

It was too late to stop now. She couldn't pause to find out the answer. She had to go on.

She knelt, and drew. Rising, she spoke as she walked. "The Throne of Virtue follows fifth."

The field of flowers expanded around her as though the clearing had breached the bounds holding it to the earth and had begun to spread up actually into the sky. Cornflowers burned with a pale blue-fire luminescence, blazing lanterns, each one like a shard of the burning stone cracked and shattered and strewn among the other flowers. Through this dizzying terrain she took six steps. It was both hard to keep to the path and yet somehow impossible to step off of it.

"Wisdom's Scepter marks the sixth."

She was almost to the river. Ahead, the flower trail melded and became one with the river itself, but the river no longer resembled an earthly river, bound by its rock bed. Like the River of Heaven, it streamed up into the sky, a deep current pouring upward, all blue and silver. Vaguely, beyond it, or below it, she saw the shadows of those things that still stood on the land: a pale figure more shade than substance, algae-covered rocks whose chaotic patterns nevertheless seemed to conceal unspoken secrets, withered trees so dark that they seemed lifeless.

She must not pause to look back. Her feet touched the water, yet it was not water that swirled around her calves as she took seven steps forward. She waded into a streaming river of aether that flowed upward to its natural home. When she thrust her hand into its depths, the currents pooled around her, swift and hot.

She traced the outlines of the final sigil, the crown of stars. Where her hand drew, the blue-silver effluence surged away with sparks of gold fire.

"At the highest rung seek the Crown of Stars, the song of power revealed."

She climbed the River of Light.

The path opened before her, the great river spoken of by so many of the ancient writers. Was it the seam that bound together the two hemispheres of the celestial sphere, as Theophrastus wrote? Or was the theory of Posidonos the correct one, that by its journey through the heavens it brought heat to the cold reaches of the universe?

Or was it only the ladder linking the spheres? She toiled upward, the current pushing her on from behind. Beneath her feet the land dropped away into darkness. Above, stars shone and yet began to fade into a new luminescence, one with a steely white light like that of a great, shining wall, the boundary that marked the limit of the lowest sphere. Low, like the delicate thrumming of plucked harp strings, she heard an eerie music more pulse than melody.

Rivulets sprang away from the main stream, so that the river itself became a labyrinth winding upward. On the currents of aether, insubstantial figures shaped in a vaguely humanlike form but composed of no mortal element danced in the fields of air through which these rivulets ran. The daimones of the lower sphere, those that lived below the Moon. If they saw her, they gave no sign. Their dance enraptured them, caught in the music of the spheres.

The thin arch of a gateway manifested in the shining wall that marked the limit of the sky. With a shock like the sight of a beloved kinsman thought dead but standing alive before her, she recognized this place. She had known it all along. Da had trained her in its passages, in the spiraling path that led ever upward. Although the way seemed obscure and veiled before her, she had a feeling very like that of homecoming as she ascended to the first gate, the gate she knew so well from the city of memory in whose architecture Da had trained her.

Had he known that the city of memory reflected, like a hazy image in a pond, the true structure of the universe? Or had he merely taught her what others had taught him, and by this means passed on to her what had remained hidden to generations of magi before him?

No matter.

She knew where she was going now. Each gate was part of the crossroads that linked the worlds.

As though her thought itself had the power of making, an archway built of aether and light flowed into existence against the shining wall. Before it stood a guardian, a daimone formed out of the substance of air and armed with a glittering spear as pale as ice.

"To what place do you seek entrance?" Its voice was as soft as the flow of water through a grassy side channel.

"I mean to cross into the sphere of the Moon," she replied, determined not to quail before this heavenly creature.

"Who are you, to demand entrance?"

She knew well the power of names. "I have been called Bright One."

It stepped back from her, as though the words had struck it like a blow, but kept its spear fixed across the gateway. "Child of Flame," it whispered, "you have too much mortal substance. You are too heavy to cross. What can you give me to lighten your load?"

Even as it spoke, she felt the truth of its words. Her belongings dragged on her and, in another instant, she would plunge back to earth—or into the Abyss, falling forever. She had no wings.

Swiftly, she tugged off her boots and unpinned her cloak. As they fell away, she rose. A breath of aether picked her up bodily, and the guardian faded until she saw it only as a spire of ice sparkling by the gateway.

The way lay open.

She did not look back as she stepped over the threshold.

PART TWO

QUEENS' GRAVE

V

IN THE AFTERLIFE

1

PROBABLY he was dead.

But when the fish twisted and slipped out of his hands to escape back into the river, it acted like a living fish. The men who laughed uproariously around him sounded lively enough, and the stocky man who had yesterday threatened him with an ax had certainly looked alarmingly alive.

He knew what death felt like. Just yesterday he had held a newborn infant in his hands that was blue with death, but he'd learned the trick from Aunt Bel that sometimes newly reborn souls needed chafing to startle them into remembering life. Just yesternight he'd stumbled through a battlefield with his own life leaking from him in flowering streams of blood.

It was hard to believe that he was alive now, even standing up to his hips in the cold river as the tug of the current tried to drag him downstream. It was easier to believe that he was dead, even if the fish in the baskets up on the shore churned and slithered, bright sunlight flashing on their scales. His companion, Urtan, clapped him on the shoulder and spoke words, none of which meant anything but which sounded cheerful enough. Maybe death wouldn't prove onerous as long as God granted him such good company.

The other men, Tosti and Kel, had started splashing each other as soon as the last weir had been hauled into the shallows and emptied of its bounty. Now Kel stoppered up the weir with a plug of sodden wood and flung it back into the river, and they swam a little, laughing and talking and with gestures making him welcome to join them.

He let the current jostle him off his feet as he lay back into its pull. Didn't death claim its victims in exactly this manner? Perhaps he was only streaming upward on the River of Heaven, making his way toward the Chamber of Light through a series of way stations. But as the water closed over his face, he heard the hounds barking. Just as he heaved himself over and stood, Sorrow bounded out into the river, paddling madly, while Rage yipped anxiously from the shore.

"Nay, nay, friend," he said, hauling Sorrow by his forelegs back to the shallows, "I'll bide here in this place for a while yet, if God so will it." His companions swam closer, unsure of his intent. They smiled cautiously as he shook out his wet hair, then laughed when Sorrow let fly a spray of mist as the hound shook himself off.

The village lay just beyond the river. Towering behind sod-and-timber houses rose the huge tumulus with its freshly raised earthworks and the gaunt circle of giant stones at the flat summit. In many ways, the tumulus reminded him of the battlefield where he had fallen, but the river had run on a different course there, and the forest hadn't grown as thickly to the north and west, and the tumulus itself had been so very ancient. Nor had there been a village lying in its shadow. This couldn't be the same place where he had died.

"But it's a good place," he assured Sorrow, who regarded him reprovingly. Rage padded over for a pat and a scratch. "Yet doesn't it seem strange to you that there should be no iron in the afterlife? They carry daggers of flint, and their ploughs are nothing but the stout fork of a tree shaped so that one length of it can turn the soil. It seems strange to me that God would punish common folk by making their day-to-day work harder in the other world."

So Aunt Bel would have said. But of course, she wasn't his aunt any longer; he had no family, orphaned child of a dead whore.

"Alain." Urtan gestured toward the baskets, which needed two men each to hoist.

Perhaps he had no family, but in this land they needed him, even if only for as humble a task as carrying a basket of fish up to the village. Hadn't he given everything else to the centaur woman? Maybe at this way station of the journey toward the Chamber of Light, he had to learn to forget the life he had once lived.

They hauled the baskets up the slope. Children shrieked and exclaimed over the fish, and after much good-natured jesting he realized that it wasn't so hard after all to learn a few words: "fish," "basket," "knife," and a word that meant "child," applied equally to boys and girls.

It was a good idea to learn as much as he could, since he didn't know how long he would bide here, or where he would end up next.

By the gates he saw Adica. Without the gold antlers and spiral waistband that had made her presence awe-inspiring up among the stones, she looked like any young woman, except for the lurid burn scar on her cheek. She watched them as they hauled the baskets through the gate, and he smiled, unaccountably pleased to see her, but the spark of pleasure reminded him of last night, when she had gestured toward the bed in her house. Her movement as she smiled in response made her corded skirt sway, revealing the length of her bare thighs.

He flushed and looked away. He had made vows to Tallia, hadn't he? If he must abjure them, if he must admit that he and Tallia were no longer husband and wife, then hadn't he long before that been promised to the church? He ought not to be admiring any woman.

Yet as they came to the big house that stood at the center of
the village, he glanced back toward the gates, lying below
them. Adica still stood there beside the elderly headwoman,
called Orla. Hadn't he given up all the vows and the promises,
the lies and the secrets? Hadn't the centaur woman taken his
old life and left him as naked as a newborn child in a new
world?

Perhaps, like the infant yesterday, he needed to learn how to
breathe again. Perhaps that was the secret of the journey, that
each way station taught you a new lesson before you were
swept again downstream toward the obliterating light of God.

At the big house, children of varying ages swarmed up and,
by some pattern he couldn't quite discern, Urtan doled out the
fish until a small portion was left for Tosti and Kel.

"Come, come," said Kel, who had evidently been stung at
birth by the bee of impatience. He and Tosti were close in age,
very alike except in temperament. They led Alain through
the village to the only other big house. It had a stone foundation, wood pillars and beams, a thatched roof, and pungent
stables attached at one end, now empty except for the lingering aroma of cattle. Inside, Kel showed him a variety of furs
and sleeping mats woven of reeds rolled up on wooden platforms ranged under the sloping walls. The young man showed
him a place, mimed sleeping, and made Alain repeat five times
the word which perhaps meant "sleep" or else "bed." Satisfied,
he led Alain outside. Setting the guts aside for the stew pot,
they lay the cleaned fish out to dry on a platform plaited out
of willow branches. It took Alain a few tries to get the hang of
using a flint knife, but he persevered, and Tosti, at least, was
patient enough to leave him alone to get the hang of it.

There were other chores to be done. As Aunt Bel used to say,
"work never ceases, only our brief lives do." Work helped him
forget. He set to willingly, whether it was gutting fish or, as
today, felling trees for a palisade. He learned to use a stone ax,
which didn't cut nearly as well as the iron he was used to and,
after a number of false starts, got the hang of using a flint adze.

Could it be that God wished humankind to recall that war had no place in the Chamber of Light? War sprang from iron, out of which weapons were made. After all, it was with an iron sword that the Lady of Battles had dealt the killing blow.

Yet if these people didn't know war, then why were they fortifying their village?

Kel got impatient with the speed at which Alain trimmed bark from the fallen tree, and by gestures showed him that he should go back to felling trees while Kel did the trimming. Tosti scolded Kel, but Alain good-naturedly exchanged adze for ax. He and Urtan examined a goodly stand of young beech and marked four particularly strong, straight trees for felling.

Alain measured falling distance and angle, and started chopping. His first swing got off wrong, and he merely nicked the tree and had to skip back to avoid hitting his own legs. A man appeared suddenly from behind and with a curse gave a hard strike to the tree. Chips flew and the ax sank deep.

Startled, Alain hesitated. The man turned, looking him over with an expression of disgust and challenge. It was the man who had threatened him yesterday, who went by the name Beor. He was as tall as Alain and half again as broad, with the kind of hands that looked able to crush rocks.

The men around grew quiet; two more, whose faces he recognized, had appeared from out of the forest. Everyone waited and watched. No one moved to interfere. Once, with senses sharpened by his blood link to Fifth Son, who had taken the name Stronghand, he would have heard each least crease of loam crushed under Beor's weight as the other man shifted, readying to strike, and he would have tasted Beor's anger and envy as though it were an actual flavor. But now he could not feel Stronghand's presence woven into his thoughts; the lack of it made his heart feel strangely empty, distended, and limp. Had he given that blood link to the centaur sorcerer, too, or had he only lost the link to Stronghand because blood could not in fact transcend death?

Yet envy and anger are easy enough to read in a man's stance and in his expression. Rage padded forward to sit beside Alain. She growled softly.

Alain stepped forward and jerked the ax out of the tree. He offered it to Beor who, after a moment's hesitation, took it roughly out of his hands. "You've great skill with that ax," Alain said with defiant congeniality, "and I've little enough with a tool I'm unaccustomed to, but I mean to fell this tree, so I will do so and thank you to stand aside."

He deliberately turned his back on the man. The weight of the other workers' stares made his first strokes clumsy, but he stubbornly kept on even when Beor began to make what were obviously insulting comments about his lack of skill with the ax. Why did Beor hate him?

Behind him, the other men moved away to their own tasks. Beor's presence remained, massive and hostile. With one blow, he could strike Alain down from behind, smash his head in, or cripple him with a well-placed chop to the back.

It didn't matter. Alain just kept on, fell into the pattern of it finally as the wedge widened and the tree, at last, creaked, groaned, and fell. Beor had been so intent on glowering that he had to leap back, and Urtan made a tart comment, but no one laughed. They were either too afraid or too respectful of Beor to laugh at him.

It was well to know the measure of one's opponents. That was why he had lost Lavas county to Geoffrey: he hadn't understood the depth of Geoffrey's envy and hatred. Could he have kept the county and won over Tallia if he had acted differently?

Yet what use in rubbing the wound raw instead of giving it a chance to heal? Lavas county belonged to Geoffrey's daughter now. Tallia had left him of her own free will. He had to let it go.

Kel began trimming the newly fallen beech, and Alain started in on the next tree. Eventually, Beor faded back to work elsewhere, although at intervals Alain felt his glance like a poisoned arrow glancing off his back. But he never dignified Beor's jealousy with an answer. He just kept working.

In the late afternoon, they hitched up oxen to drag the trimmed and finished poles back toward the village. Sweat dried on his back as he walked. The other men wore simple breechclouts, fashioned of cloth or leather. The tunic Adica had given him looked nothing like their clothing. It had a finer weave and a shaped form that was easy to work and move in, even when he dropped it off his shoulders and tied it at his hips with a belt of bast rope. The men of the village had stocky bodies, well muscled and quite hairy. They had keen, bright faces and were quick to laughter, mostly, but they didn't really resemble any of the people he knew or had ever seen, as if here in the afterlife God had chosen to shape humankind a little differently.

Unlike his kinsman Kel, Urtan had the gift of patience, and he fell back to walk beside Alain to teach him new words: the names of trees, the parts of the body, the different tools and the type of stone they were made of. Beor strode at the front with various companions walking beside him. Now and again he shot an irate glance back toward Alain. But unlike an arrow, a glance could not prick unless you let it. Beor might hurt and even kill in a fit of jealous rage, but he could never do any other harm because he hadn't any subtlety.

The village feasted that evening on fish, venison, and a potage of barley mush flavored with herbs and leaves from the forest, sweetened by berries. Urtan ate with his family, his wife Abidi and his children Urta and a toddler who didn't seem to have an intelligible name, leaving Alain to eat with the unmarried men, all of them except Beor little more than youths. Adica ate by herself, off to one side, without companionship, but when Alain made to get up to go over to her, Kel grabbed him and jerked him back, gesturing that it wasn't permitted. Adica had been watching him, and now she smiled slightly and looked away. The burn scar along her cheek looked rather like a congealed spider's web, running from her

right ear down around the curve of the jawline to fade almost
at her throat. The tip of her right ear was missing, so cleanly
healed that it merely looked misshapen.

Beor rose abruptly and began declaiming as twilight fell.
Like a man telling a war story, he went on at length. Was he
boasting? Kel and Tosti started to yawn, and Adica rose suddenly in the middle of the story and walked right out, away into
the village. Alain wanted to follow her, but he wasn't sure if such
a thing was permitted. At last, Beor finished his tale. It was time
for bed. Alain's friends had given him a place to sleep beside
them but at the opposite end of the men's house from Beor. He
was tired enough to welcome sleep, but when he rolled himself
up in the furs allotted him, stones pressed into his side. He
groped and found the offending pebbles, but they weren't stones
at all but some kind of necklace. It hadn't been there earlier.

At dawn, when he woke, he hurried outside to get enough
light to see: someone had given him a necklace of amber. Kel,
stumbling out sleepily behind him, whistled in admiration for
the handsome gift, and called out to the others, and they
teased Alain cheerfully, all but Beor, who stalked off.

Down by the village gates, Adica was already up, performing the ritual she made every day at the gateway, perhaps a
charm of protection. As if she heard their laughter, she glanced
up. He couldn't see her face clearly, but her stance spoke to
him, the way she straightened her back self-consciously, the
curve of her breasts under her bodice, the swaying of her string
skirt as she walked from the gates over the plank bridge. It
was difficult not to be distracted by the movement of her hips
under the revealing skirt.

Kel and Tosti laughed outright and clapped him on the
shoulder. He could imagine what their words meant: gifts and
women and longing looks. Some things didn't change, even in
the afterlife.

He had come a long way. He no longer wore the ring that
marked him as heir to the Count of Lavas. He no longer had to
honor the vows pledged between him and Tallia. He no longer

served the Lady of Battles. With a smile, he put on the amber necklace, although the gesture made his friends whoop and laugh.

That day they hoisted the poles they'd cut the day before into place in the new palisade. Once, Beor neglected to brace while Alain was filling in dirt around a newly upright pole, and the resultant tumble caused two poles to come down. Luckily no one was hurt, but Beor got a scolding from one of the older men.

Alain went down with Kel and Tosti to the river afterward to wash. "Come!" shouted Kel just before he dove under the water. "Good!" he added, when he came up for air. "Good water. Water is good."

Alain was distracted by the sight of the tumulus. Here, upstream from the village, the river cut so close below the earthworks that the ramparts rose right out of the water except for a thin strand of pebbly beach from which the men swam. He couldn't see the stone circle from this angle, but something glinted from the height above nevertheless, a wink like gold. The twisting angle of the earthworks reminded him of the battle where he had fallen. He heard Thiadbold's cries as if a ghost whispered in his ear. The past haunted him. Did the bones of their enemies lie up there? Two days ago, he had wandered off the height in a daze, following Adica. He hadn't really looked.

Stung by curiosity and foreboding, he began to climb. His companions shouted after him, good-humoredly at first, then disapprovingly and, finally, as he got over the first earthwork and headed for the next, with real apprehension. But no one followed him. At the top a wind was rising and he heard the hoot of an owl, although the sun hadn't yet set. Where it sank in the west, clouds gathered, diffusing its light. The stones gleamed. He ran, with the hounds beside him, sure he would see his comrades, the Lions, fallen beside their Quman enemies, whose wings would be scattered and molting, melting away under wind and sun.

As soon as he crossed into the stone circle, mist boiled up, drowning him, and he floundered forward. Was that the ring of battle in the distance? If he walked far enough, would he stumble back to the place he'd come from?

Did he want to?

He struck full against the altar stone, banging his thighs, and held himself up against the cold stone. The ringing had a gentle voice, not weapons at all but the click of leaves on the bronze cauldron.

"Why come you to the gateway?" said a voice he recognized from his dream.

He looked up but could see only a shape moving in the mist and the spark of blue fire, quickly extinguished.

"Why am I here? Where am I?"

"You have not traveled far as humankind measures each stride of the foot," she answered. "I brought you off the path that leads to the Other Side. Has it not been told to you that you are to be the new husband of the Hallowed One of this tribe?"

He touched the amber necklace at his neck, remembering the way Adica had invited him to sleep beside her. He had been angry, then, because he felt his desire was shameful. "None here speak in a language I understand, nor can they understand me. How is it that we can speak together, you and I, while I speak as a foreigner would with the others? You aren't even human."

"By my nature I am bound to what was, what is, and what will be, and so my understanding is alive in the time to come as well as the time that is and the time that was." Abruptly her tone changed, as though she were speaking to someone else. "Listen!" Her voice became faint. He heard the soft percussion of her hooves on the ground, moving away. "I am called. Adica comes looking." Fainter still: "Beware. Guard the looms. The Cursed Ones walk!"

"Can't you give me the gift of speech?" he called, but she ~~~dy gone.

"Alain!"

The mist receded as suddenly as it had come. Adica hurried to meet him as twilight settled over the stones. He sat down, worn out by labor and by strangeness.

Adica stopped before him and looked him over, both alarmed and concerned and, maybe, just a little irritated. She was handsome rather than pretty, with a wickedly sharp gaze and a firm mouth. This close, he had the leisure to study her body: she had the pleasing curves of a woman who usually gets enough to eat, but she had a second quality about her, an intangible strength like the glow off a hidden fire. In a funny way, she reminded him of Liath, as if magic threw a cloak over its wielders, seen as a nimbus of power.

Her next words reproved him, although he couldn't be sure for what. Abruptly, she saw the line of the amber necklace where it lay concealed under his linen tunic.

Reproof vanished. She brushed a finger along the ridge the string of amber made under the soft fabric, then flushed.

"You gave this to me, didn't you?" he asked, lifting it on his fingers to display it.

She smiled and replied in a tone half caressing and half flirtatious.

"Ai, God, I wish I could understand you," he exclaimed, frustrated. "Is it true I'm to be your husband? Are we to come to the marriage knowing so little of each other? Yet I knew nothing of Tallia on the day we were taken to the wedding bed. Ai, Lady, so little did I know of her!" He could still feel the nail in his hand, proof of her willingness to deceive.

Mistaking his cry, or responding to it, Adica took hold of his hand and pulled him to his feet. For an instant, he thought she would kiss him, but she did not. In silence, she led him back to the village. The clasp of her hand made his thoughts swim dizzyingly until they drifted up at last to the centaur shaman's last words. Who were the Cursed Ones? What were the looms? And how could he tell Adica, when they had no language in common?

2

"COME, up, to morning sun!" Kel prodded Alain awake. "To work!" He made an expansive gesture that included himself, Tosti, and Alain. "We go to work."

Three more days had passed in the village. It was a prosperous place, twelve houses and perhaps a hundred people in all. They had about a fourth of the outer palisade raised and today headed back to the forest to fell trees. Work made the day pass swiftly.

During one leisurely break, Kel finished carving a stout staff out of oak, ornamenting each end with the face of a snarling dog. When next Beor hoisted his ax near Alain with a surly and threatening grimace, Kel made a great show of presenting the newly carved staff to Alain and even got Tosti to stand in for a demonstration of how the snarling dogs could "nip" at a man's most delicate parts.

The men's laughter came at the expense of Beor this time, and he grunted and bore it, since to stalk off into the forest would have made him look even more ridiculous. Grudgingly, he let Alain work in peace as the afternoon wore on.

But that evening they returned home to a somber scene. During the day, a child had died. By the stoic look on the faces of the dead child's relative, they'd known it was coming. Alain watched as women wrapped the tiny body in a roughly-woven blanket, then handed the limp corpse to the father. He laid it in a log split in half and gouged out to make a coffin. After the mother placed a few trinkets, beads, feathers, and a carved wooden spoon beside its tattooed wrist, other adults sealed the lid. Together, they chanted a singsong verse that sounded like prayer.

A strange half-human creature emerged from Adica's house, clothed in power, with gold antlers and a gleaming torso. It took two breaths to recognize Adica, dressed in the garments of had been wearing when he had first arrived.

She blessed the coffin with a sprinkling of scented water and a complicated series of gestures and chants. Four men carried it out of the village as Adica sealed their path, behind them, with more charms and chants. The entire village walked in silent procession to the graveyard, a rugged field marked by small mounds of earth, some fresh, some overgrown with nettles and hops. Male relatives laid the coffin in a hole. The mother cut off her braid and threw it on top of the coffin, then scratched her cheeks until blood ran. The wailing of the other women had a kind of ritual sound to it, expected, practiced; the mother did not weep, only sighed. She looked drained and yet, in a way, relieved.

Maybe the child had been sick a long time. Certainly Alain had never seen this one among the children who ran and played and did chores in the village all day.

The grave was filled in and the steady work of piling and shaping a mound over the dead child commenced. In pairs and trios, people returned to the village, which lay out of sight beyond a bend in the river. Alain remained because Adica had not yet left. Sorrow and Rage flopped down, resigned to a long wait.

Twilight lay heavily over them. Even in the five days he had been here, he noticed how it got darker earlier every night as the sun swept away from midsummer and toward its midwinter sleep. By the harvest and the weather, he guessed it was late summer or early autumn.

A few men worked steadily, bringing sod in a wheelbarrow shaped all of wood, axle, wheel, supports, and plank base. He pitched in to help them while Adica stood by, arms raised, silently watching the heavens or praying in supplication. In her hallowing garb she seemed as much alarming as wondrous, a spirit risen out of the earth to bring help, or harm, to her petitioners.

Dusk blurred the landscape to gray. Other men brought torches and set them up on stout poles so the work could continue, as it did steadily as night fell and the moon rose, full and splendid. Adica shone under its rays, a woman half deer and half human, a shape changer who might at any moment spring away four-footed into the dark forest and run him a merry chase.

He saw them, suddenly, as starlight pricked holes in the blindness that protects mortal kind: he saw the ghosts and the fey spirits, half-seen apparitions clustering around the living people who sought to inter the dead. Was that the child's soul, clamoring for release, or return? Sobbing for its mother, or screaming that it had been betrayed into death?

Yet the spirits could not touch the living, because Adica in her garb of power had thrown up a net, as fine as spider's silk, to keep them away. It shone under the moonlight as though touched with dew fallen from the fiery stars. No hungry spirit could pass through that net. Inside its invisible protection, the men labored on, a little nervous in the darkness in the grave-yard, but trusting. They understood her power, and no doubt they feared her for it.

Sorrow whined.

That fast, the vision faded, but her lips continued to move as she chanted her spells. The moon rose higher and began to sink. Very late the mound was finished, a little thing, lone-some and forlorn in the deathly-still night. The father wiped his eyes. They gathered their tools and headed back toward the village, not without apprehensive looks behind them.

But Alain lingered, waiting. Adica paced an oval around the tiny mound. Her golden antlers cut the heavens as she strode. Now and again she tapped her spiraling bronze waistband with her copper bracelets. The sound sang into the night like the flight of angels.

Yet what could Adica know of angels? None here wore the Circle of Unity. He had seen their altars and offerings, remind-ing him of customs done away with by the fraters and deacons but which certain stubborn souls still clung to. Her rituals did not seem like the work of the Enemy, although perhaps he ought to believe they were.

She fell silent as she came to a halt on the west side of the fresh mound. That quickly, she was simply Adica, with her frightfully scarred cheek, the woman whom he had heard in a dream ask the centaur shaman if Alain was to be her husband. She had spoken the words with such an honest heart, with such simple longing.

"Alain!" She looked surprised to see him. With practiced movements she took off her sorcerer's garb and wrapped them up with staff and mirror into a leather skin, not neglecting certain charms and a prayer as if to seal in their magical power.

Slinging the bundle over her back, she began walking back to the village. He fell in beside her, finding room on the path as the hounds ambled along behind. His staff measured out the ground as they walked. The moon marked their way straight and bright.

They passed through a narrow belt of forest and emerged west of the village. The moon's light made silver of the river. Beyond the village rose the tumulus. Nearer, the sentry's watch fire burned red by the village gates. Closer still lay the birthing house, and from within its confines he heard a baby cry fretfully. A nightingale sang, and ceased. The thin glow heralding dawn rimmed the eastern sky as the moon sank toward the horizon in the west. Birds woke, trilling, and a flock of ducks settled in a rush in the shallows of the river. In the distance, a wolf howled.

Adica took his hand. She leaned into him, and kissed him. Her lips were sweet and moist. Where her body pressed against his, his own body woke hungrily. His hand tangled in the strings of her skirt, and beneath the wool cording he touched her skin.

A small voice woke in the back of his head. Hadn't he made vows? Hadn't he promised celibacy to Tallia, to honor God? Oughtn't he to remember his foster father's promise that he would cleave to the church and its strictures?

He let the oak staff fall to the ground as he tightened his arms around Adica. Her warmth and eagerness enveloped him.

He'd given all that away when he had come into this country. Now he could do as he pleased, and what he pleased right now was to embrace this woman who desired him.

Once, perhaps, in those long ago days when he had been joined to Stronghand in his dreams, Alain would have heard the shouting first. Now, because he was lost in the urgency of her embrace, the blat of a horn startled him so badly he jumped. Sorrow and Rage began barking. Adica pulled away and threw back her head to listen.

The sun hadn't yet risen, but light glinted at the height of the tumulus, lying to the east. Distant thunder rolled and faded.

She exclaimed out loud, words he could not understand. As she bent to grab her leather bundle off the ground, an arrow passed over her back, right where she had just been standing up straight. He dove and knocked her down. A flight of arrows whistled harmlessly past, pale shafts skittering to a halt on the ground beyond.

Figures sprang out of the forest. The horn sounded again, and a third time, shrill and urgent.

The masked attackers who rushed out of the forest swarmed toward the birthing house, where Weiwara sheltered with her infant twins. Adica was already up, staff in hand, leaving her bundle behind. Sorrow and Rage bolted forward in her wake, and Alain, fumbling, got hold of his staff and raced after her.

But no matter how fast they ran, the bandits got to the birthing house first even as he heard Adica scream out Weiwara's name. Too late.

Weiwara shouted from the house. There came a shriek of anger, followed by the solid thunk of a heavy weight hitting wood. Two figures darted from the house, each carrying a small bundle. Adica got near enough to strike at one with her staff, hitting him forcefully enough at the knees so he stumbled. The other raced on, back to the forest, as the first turned and, with the child tucked under one arm, thrust out his

sword. Dawn made fire of the metal as he cut. Adica danced
aside. The rising light played over the man's face, since he,
unlike the other two, wasn't masked. Nor was he human: he
had a dark complexion, with black hair and striking features
that reminded Alain of Prince Sanglant.

Another Aoi warrior emerged from the birthing hut, this
one a young woman clad, like the others, in a bronze breastplate fitted over a short tunic. The feathers woven into her hair
gave her a startling crest, and her mask had been carved into
a peregrine's hooked beak. She carried a small round shield and
a short spear.

Alain struck with his staff. She barely had time to parry.
Her companion, hampered by the infant, contented himself
with thrusting again, but Adica's reflexes were too good.
She sprang back and swung her staff hard around, aiming for
the woman instead of the man, and caught the Aoi warrior a
glancing blow to the jaw. Blood dribbled out from the
young warrior's neck as she bit back a yelp of pain. Alain circled right to close the two against the wall of the birthing
house. He heard shouts from behind, Kel's voice, and suddenly Kel and his brother came running with their spears
ready.

The Aoi man dropped the infant and bolted for the trees,
following his companion; Alain clipped the woman as she
tried to follow, and she fell heavily. Adica stepped back. Kel
and Tosti shrieked with glee as the Aoi woman rolled over,
lifting her shield to protect herself.

"No!" cried Alain, for truly, she was helpless before them,
and it would be more merciful to take her captive. But they
hated her kind too much. He winced as they pinned her to the
ground with angry spear thrusts. Her blood ran over the dirt.

The baby wailed.

"Weiwara!" cried Adica, dashing inside.

He looked away from the dying warrior thrashing on the
ground. Tosti had run inside after Adica. Kel wrenched his
spear free and grabbed Alain by the shoulder.

He shouted a word, indicating the woman. Beyond, fire
sparked and caught in the thatched roof of one of the village
houses.

"Come! Come!" Kel stooped to pick up the screaming baby.

About ten Aoi warriors fitted in bronze armor and wielding
weapons forged of metal emerged from the last bend in the
earthworks.

"Come!" cried Kel with more urgency, gesturing toward
the village and its closed gates. A man lay prone by the
outer ditch. Farther out, five of the enemy clustered behind
the shield of a ruined hut. From this shelter they shot flaming arrows toward the village, an easy target over the low
stockade.

Adica and Tosti appeared at the door with Weiwara's limp
body between them. Blood ran down the side of her face, and
a nasty bruise discolored her left cheek, but she breathed.

"The other baby!" cried Alain. He pointed to the shrieking
infant and then to the forest.

"No!" said Adica, indicating the threat to the village.

The horn rang out again. Armed adults sallied out from the
village, yelling defiantly. Beor led them; Alain recognized him
by his height and his shoulders, and by the bronze spear he
carried. A half dozen split off from the main group to hurry
toward the birthing house, among them Weiwara's husband
and Urtan.

"Go!" said Alain, because it was a word he knew, and
because help was coming. "I go get baby."

Kel shrieked with glee and shoved the infant into Tosti's
arms. He grabbed the dead woman's bronze spear from the
ground. "I go!" He struck his own chest with a closed fist, and
then Alain's. "We go!"

There wasn't time to argue. The ones they sought had
already gotten a head start, and Alain wasn't going to let that
baby be stolen, not when God had welcomed him to this village by granting it the blessing of living twins on the day he
had arrived.

He grabbed the shield off the corpse and ran for the forest as the sun split the horizon behind them. Adica called after him, but the clamor of battle drowned out her voice. They hit the shadow of the trees, and he raised a hand for silence as he and Kel and the hounds came to a halt. They heard the headlong flight of the other two as cracks and rustles in the forest ahead. Rage bounded away, so they followed her trail as she pelted through the trees.

Alain saw the two Aoi when he burst out of the woods at the border of the burial field. Sorrow and Rage loped after them, big bodies closing the gap. They hit the man limping behind without losing momentum and he tumbled to the ground beneath them. Kel reached him first. Before Alain could shout for mercy, Kel stuck him through the back. As the bronze leaf-blade parted the man's skin, Kel screamed in triumph.

The sound shook Alain to his bones, made bile rise in his throat. He had known for a long time that he couldn't serve the Lady of Battles by killing. But he could save the child.

The hounds matched him stride for stride as he ran after the third warrior, the one who carried the crying infant under his arm. The warrior cut left, and then right, as if expecting to dodge arrows. Glancing over his shoulder, he saw Alain and the hounds and that made him run harder, although he seemed to be grinning like a madman, caught in an ecstasy of flight and fury. But Alain knew fury, too, rising in his heart, goaded by the memory of a tiny body coming to life beneath his hands.

By now they had moved well away from the river, but a stream cut down from a hill on the eastern side of the burial field. When the other man tried to head up the stream, he found himself boxed in by the hillside and by a cliff down which a cataract fell, not more than twice a man's height but too rugged to climb without both hands.

The warrior was no fool. He kept hold of the baby and brandished his spear threateningly as he sprang back to put the rock wall behind him. The baby hiccupped in infant despair, exhausted by its own screaming, and fell silent. Far behind, Kel shouted Alain's name.

He threw down shield and staff as Sorrow and Rage stalked forward on either side of him. "Give me the child, or strike me down, I care not which you choose."

The warrior's eyes widened in fear or anger, flaring white, all that could be seen of his face behind the grinning dog mask he wore.

Alain took another step forward, showing his empty hands but keeping his gaze fixed on his opponent. "Just give me back the child. I want nothing else from you."

The warrior shied nervously, keeping his spear raised, and he made a testing thrust toward Alain, who did not step back but instead came forward once again.

"As you see, I do not fear dying, because I am already dead. Nothing you can do to me frightens me. I pray you, give me the child."

Maybe it was Kel, shouting as he came up from behind. Maybe it was the silent hounds. Maybe the warrior had simply had enough.

He set down the child, turned, and scrambled as well as he could up the cliff face. Alain sprang forward to grab the infant just as the warrior lost hold of his spear and it sailed down to land in the cataract with a splash. The haft spun, rode the cascade, and lodged up between two rocks as water roared over it. With an oath, the man vanished over the lip. Pebbles spattered down the cliff face, then all trace of him ceased.

Kel whooped as he came up behind Alain. The baby whimpered, more a croak than a cry. Kel waded out to fetch the spear and offered it to Alain.

"Nay, I won't take it!" Alain snapped. Kel flinched back, looking shaken. "Here," said Alain more gently, giving him the man's shield. With a hand free again, he took up his oak staff.

They went swiftly back, but cautiously, skirting the corpse

sprawled in the burial field and taking a deer trail through the forest, not knowing what they might find at the village or if they would need to fight when they got there. Luckily, the newborn fell into an exhausted sleep.

Easing out from the forest cover, they saw the village with the first slant of morning sun streaming across it and figures moving like ants, in haste, scurrying here and there. As they watched, trying to understand what they saw, a cloud covered the sun and the light changed. Thunder rumbled softly. Rain shaded the southeastern hills.

"Beor!" said Kel softly, pointing.

Alain saw Beor walking down through the earthworks with a spear in his hand, his posture taut with battle anger. At least fifteen adults accompanied him, all armed, some limping. Smoke striped the sky, rising from the village, but it had the cloudy vigor of a newly doused fire. A few corpses lay evident, some clad in bronze and one, alas, the body of a villager. It seemed strange that these people would strike with such determined ferocity and swiftness only to retreat again, like a thunderstorm opening up overhead with fury and noise that, as suddenly, blows through to leave fresh puddles and cracked or fallen branches in its wake.

Halfway between the river path and the birthing house, Alain saw a lump on the ground. Fear caught in his throat. He ran, only to find, as he feared, Adica's leather bundle bulging open on the ground right where she'd dropped it when she first ran for Weiwara's house. It seemed wrong that rain should fall on the gold antlers. As he wrapped up the bundle, he found her polished mirror lying beneath.

Adica never went anywhere without her mirror. At that moment, the same choking helplessness gripped him that had strangled hope on the night when Lavastine had been trapped by Bloodheart's revenge behind a locked door.

Voices called from the village. He slung the bundle over his shoulder and rose just as Kel hurried up with a scared look on his face.

"No. No," he repeated, over and over, pointing to the bundle. Alain ignored him and hurried on. He had to find Adica.

Weiwara had been taken to the council house and settled upon furs there together with the other wounded folk, not more than six, although six was too many. When Alain gave the lost infant into her arms, she burst into tears. Both Urtan and Tosti were among the wounded. Urtan had taken a blow to the head and he lay unconscious, with his young daughter Urta moistening his mouth with a damp cloth. Tosti drifted in and out of awareness, moaning; he had two nasty wounds in his right shoulder and left hip. Kel dropped down beside him, keening, scratching his chest until it bled.

Mother Orla shuffled in, leaning heavily on her walking stick as she surveyed the injured. She called for her daughter, Agda, who brought potions and poultices. Exhaustion swept Alain, but as he tried to make his way to the door, to find Adica, Mother Orla stopped him, her expression grim. He heard voices outside, but it was Beor who entered, not Adica.

The moment Beor saw Alain, he spat on the floor. It took Mother Orla herself, raising her walking stick, to restrain him from charging through the crowd and attacking. The hounds, waiting outside, barked threateningly.

Although Beor was almost beside himself with a warrior's hot anger, he contented himself with a hard glance at Alain before launching into an involved and desperate tale. Certainly something far more serious than a man's jealousy had afflicted the village this day. As Beor spoke, Mother Orla's stern features showed not one sign of weakness even as those around her and the ones who crowded outside set up a moan in response to his words.

Thunder cracked and rolled, bringing a moment's silence in its wake. It began to rain.

"Where be Adica?" Alain demanded, swinging down the

bundle containing her holy garments so that they all could see that he had recovered it for her.

Beor roared like a wounded bear, overcome by fury. The others wailed and cried out. Although they had few words in common, it didn't take Alain long to understand.

Adica was gone, stolen by the raiders.

VI
A COMPANY
OF THISTLES

1

ON the roads traveling north from the Alfar Mountains, following the trail of the prince, Zacharias found it easy enough to ask innocuous questions when opportunity arose and to make himself inconspicuous when necessary. After an unfortunate detour to escape a pack of hungry wolves, in the course of which he lost one of his two goats and picked up a nagging infection in his left eye, he found himself among a trickle of petitioners and pilgrims walking north to see the king. Some of these humble souls had heard tell of a noble fighter who had single-handedly vanquished a pack of bloodthirsty bandits.

"Truly, he must have been a prince among men," he said more than once to the folk he met, trying to keep the sarcasm from his voice. At last one fellow agreed that he had heard from a steward riding south that indeed Prince Sanglant had returned to the king's progress.

When he came to the palace complex at Angenheim and found the court in the throes of making ready to leave, he hoped to press forward among the many plaintiffs come to beg alms or healing or justice from the king. He didn't look that different from the filthy beggars and poor farmers camped out in the fields and woodland outside of the palace fortifications. Most people liked to gossip. Surely no one would take any special notice of a few innocent questions put to the guards.

But after seven years as a slave among the Quman nomads and a year traveling as an outcast through the lands of his own people, Zacharias had forgotten that his ragged clothing, disreputable appearance, and easterner's accent might cause people to distrust rather than simply dismiss him.

In this way, he found himself hauled up past the impressive fortifications and into the palace grounds themselves. Once they had taken away his goat and searched his battered leather pack for weapons, guards marched him through the handsomely carved doors of one of the noble residences. By prodding him with the butts of their spears, they tried to make him kneel before an elderly lord seated on a bench with a cup of wine in one hand and a robust and handsome young woman next to him.

The old lord handed the cup to her and looked Zacharias over with a frown as he tapped his fingers on a knee. "He refuses to kneel." He had a touch of the east about his voice, blurred by the hard stops and starts characteristic of the central duchies.

"I mean no offense, my lord," said Zacharias quickly. "I am a frater and sworn to kneel before none but God."

"Are you, then?" As the lord sat back, a slender, middle-aged servant circled around to whisper in his ear. When the guardsman had finished, the lord shifted forward. "Do you know who I am?"

"Nay, I do not, my lord, but I can hear by your speech that you've spent time in the east."

The lord laughed, although not as loudly as his young companion, who gestured toward the embroidered banner hung on the wall behind a table laden with gold and silver platters and bowls. The profusion of food made Zacharias' mouth water—apples, pears, bread, cheese, leeks, and parsley—but the sigil on the banner made his blood run cold and his mouth go dry with fear. It was only then that he noticed that the lord had only one arm; one sleeve had been pinned back so that it wouldn't get in his way.

"The silver tree is the sign of the house of Villam, my lord," he said, cursing himself silently. That had been his mistake among the Pechanek tribe: he had let those in power notice him, because in those days he had still believed in the God of the Unities and thought it his duty to bring their worship to the benighted, those who dwelt in the darkness of ignorance. "Can it be that you are Margrave Villam? I crave your pardon, my lord, for truly he was an old man in my youth, so it was said, and I thought the old margrave must be dead by now and the margraviate gone to his heirs."

"I pray to God you are not dead yet," said the woman boldly. "I trust you have enough youth in you to play your part on our wedding night."

Villam had an honest smile. "They say a horse may die if ridden too hard."

She was, thank God, not a giggler, but she laughed in a way that made Zacharias uncomfortable because it reminded him of what Bulkezu had cut from him. "I hope I have not chosen a mount that will founder easily."

"Nay, fear not on my account, for I'm not in my dotage yet." He took the cup of wine from her and gestured to a servant to refill it. "I pray you, beloved, let me speak to this man alone."

"Is this intrigue? Do you fear I will carry tales to Theophanu?"

If her youthful teasing irritated him, he did not show it. "I do not wish the king disturbed on any account, since he means to leave in the morning. If I am the only man to hear this tale, then I can assure myself that it will go no farther than me."

She did not retreat easily from the field. "This frater—as he calls himself—may carry tales farther than I ever would, Helmut. He has a tongue."

The horrible fear that they, who had the power, would take from him the one thing he prized above all else caught

Zacharias like a vise. His legs gave out and he sank to his knees. It was hard not to start begging for mercy.

"So have we all a tongue, Leoba," replied Villam patiently. "But I will have solitude in which to interview him."

Although clearly a woman of noble station, Leoba was young enough to be Villam's granddaughter and therefore, whatever equality in their stations in life, had to bow to the authority that age granted him. She rose graciously enough, kissed him modestly on the cheek, and left. The old man watched her go. Zacharias recognized the gleam in his eyes. The sin of concupiscence, a weakness for the pleasures of the flesh, afflicted high- and lowborn alike.

Once she was gone, the old margrave returned immediately to the matter at hand. "I do not wish to know your name, but it has been brought to my attention that you have been asking questions of the guards regarding the whereabouts of Prince Sanglant."

"You seem to me a reasonable man, my lord. Now that I am thrown into the lion's den, I may as well make no secret of my quest. I seek Prince Sanglant. Is he here?"

"Nay, he is not. He has as good as declared open revolt against King Henry's authority. I feel sure that a man of your learning understands what a serious offense that is."

"Ah," said Zacharias, for a moment at a loss for words. But he had always had a glib tongue, and he knew how to phrase a question to protect himself while, perhaps, gaining information. "Yet a man, even a prince, cannot revolt alone."

"Truly, he cannot." Villam knew this ploy as well. "Do you mean to join his retinue, such as it is?"

"Nay, my lord. I have not followed him with any such intention, nor have I at any time known of any plan to revolt. My interests lie not in earthly struggles but with the composition of the heavens and the glory of creation. In truth, my lord, I have never spoken with the prince."

"Then why did you come to Angenheim asking about his whereabouts?"

"I merely come to ask a boon of him."

Villam laughed delightedly. "I am smothered in words. Yet you trouble me, frater, with your talk of the heavens. Do you know what manner of man Prince Sanglant is?"

"What do you mean, my lord?"

"I pray you, do not play the innocent with me. You look rather less artless and more disreputable, and you speak with a cunning tongue. Prince Sanglant is no man at all but a half blood, born of a human father and an Aoi mother. What manner of aid might you wish to ask from such a creature?"

This struck Zacharias as dangerous ground. Nor had Villam betrayed any knowledge of Kansi-a-lari's whereabouts, even though Zacharias knew she had walked north with her son.

"Very well," he said after a long silence. "I shall tell you the truth. I walked east to bring the word of God to the Quman tribes, but instead they made me a slave. I dwelt among them for seven years and at long last escaped. This is the tale I bring to you: the Quman are massing an army under the leadership of the Pechanek begh, Bulkezu, and they mean to strike deep into Wendish territory. Already raiding parties burn villages and murder and mutilate our countryfolk. You know how the Quman treat their victims. I have seen many a corpse without a head. Your own lands in the east are at risk, my lord."

"Princess Sapientia was sent east with an army together with that of her new husband, Prince Bayan of Ungria."

"That I had not heard, my lord."

"Yet we've had no news from them, so perhaps it goes ill with their campaign, although I pray that is not the case. This chieftain, Bulkezu, has plagued Wendish lands before. Yet why seek Prince Sanglant? Here is the king and his court. Surely your plea is best voiced before the king."

"Truly, it is," said Zacharias, thinking fast. "But I have heard much talk during my travels about the king's ambitions in Aosta. The king cannot march both south and east. At the same time, I have heard many stories about Prince Sanglant's prowess in battle. Is the regnant's bastard firstborn not raised to be captain of the King's Dragons? If the king himself cannot take the field against the Quman, then it would take such an army, commanded by a man second only to the king in courage and reputation, to defeat them."

"A fine tale. It is true that you speak with the accent of the eastern border, and certainly you look as if you've walked a long way with nothing more than the clothes on your back and, so I hear, a goat. But a fine tale may be nothing more than a brightly woven tapestry thrown up on the wall to conceal an ugly scar which lies hidden behind it. The Quman brand their slaves with a mark."

Shaking, Zacharias stood. He turned, pulling the torn shoulder of the robe down to reveal his right shoulder blade and the brand, healed badly enough that skin still puckered around it, marking him as slave of the Pechanek begh. Releasing the cloth, he turned back to confront the margrave. "So stands the mark of the snow leopard's claw, my lord."

"A desperate man can have himself cut to lend credence to his story," remarked Villam pleasantly.

"Would a man cut himself in this manner, merely to lend credence to his tale?" Zacharias demanded, boldly lifting his robe.

At the sight of Zacharias' mutilated genitals, Villam actually gasped out loud, lost color, and groped for his wine cup. He gulped it down, and then signaled to his steward, the slender man who had stationed himself at the door. "Bring wine for this man, if you please. He must be desperately thirsty."

Zacharias drank deeply. The wine was very good, and he saw no reason to waste it. Perhaps the shock of his mutilation would throw Villam off the scent.

But the margrave was too old and too crafty, he had played the game for too long, to be thrown off his attack even by such a vicious strike. Once he had taken a second cup of wine, he gestured to his servant. "Humbert, bring me the man's pack."

Resigned, Zacharias watched as Villam emptied the pouch

and, of course, picked up the one thing that would condemn any man. He displayed, for Zacharias' edification, the parchment scrap covered with Liath's writing, the scribblings of a mathematici.

Zacharias drained the last of his wine, wondering what he would get to drink when he languished in the skopos' prison damned as a heretic. "You're holding it upside down, my lord," he observed after Villam said nothing.

Villam turned the scrap over and studied it again. "It means even less to me this way." He looked up with the sharp gaze of a man who has seen a great deal of grief and laughter and trouble in his time. He was getting impatient. "Are you a sorcerer?"

No such interrogation could end happily, but Zacharias refused to collapse in fear as long as his tongue seemed safe. "Nay, my lord, I am not."

"Truly, you do not resemble one, for I have always heard it said that a sorcerer has such magnificent powers that she will always appear sleek and prosperous, and you, my friend, do not appear to be either. Why are you seeking the prince?"

"To find out where that parchment came from, my lord. I have reason to believe that he knows who made those marks on that parchment. That person must know some portion of the secret language of the stars. I have no wish to be a sorcerer, my lord. But I was vouchsafed a vision of the cosmos." He could not keep his voice from trembling. The memory of what he had seen in the palace of coils still tormented him; he dreamed at night of that billowing cosmos, rent by clouds of dust and illuminated by resplendent stars so bright that, like angels, they had halos. His loss of faith in the God of Unities no longer troubled his sleep, because the desire to understand the workings of the universe, a dazzling spiral wheel of stars hanging suspended in the midst of a vast emptiness, had engulfed his spirit and consumed his mind. "That is all that I fear now, my lord: that I might die before I understand the architecture of the universe."

That I might die before I see another dragon. But that thought
he dared not voice out loud.

Villam stared at him for a long time. Zacharias could not
interpret his expression, and he began to fidget nervously,
waiting for the margrave's reply. He had told the truth at last.
He had no further to retreat except to reveal the one thing
which would damn him most: that he had traveled as a servant
with the Aoi sorcerer and witnessed her humbling and frightening power. Once they discovered that, they would not care
that she had, in the end, discarded him as thoughtlessly as she
would a walking stick she had no further use for.

"I am at your mercy, my lord margrave," he said finally,
when he could bear the silence no longer.

"So we come to her again," murmured Villam. "Can it be
true, what the prince said of her ancestry? Is it not said of the
Emperor Taillefer that 'God revealed to him the secrets of the
universe?' The virtues of the parent often pass to the child."

"I do not understand you, my lord," he stammered, temporizing. Villam would mention Kansi-a-lari's name in the next
sentence, and the trap would be sprung.

"Do you not?" asked Villam, looking honestly surprised.
"Did Prince Sanglant not marry the woman named Liathano?"

Relief hit like a fist to his gut. "I do not know her, my lord."

Villam smiled wryly. "Had you seen her, you would not so
easily forget her."

"That one! Was she young and beautiful, my lord, not in
the common way of beauty but like a foreign woman with skin
of a creamy dark shade? Had she a child in her or newly born?"

"That one." Villam sighed, considered his wine cup, and
took a hank of bread to chew on. "What became of her?"

"You do not know? Angels took her up into the heavens."

"Angels?"

"We might also call them daimones, my lord."

"I do not know what to make of these tidings," said Villam
thoughtfully, looking troubled. "Is she an agent of the Enemy,
or that of God? Is she of humble origins, or of the noblest

birth? Did she bewitch the prince, or is her favor, bestowed upon him, a mark of his fitness to rule?"

"My lord margrave," said the servant Humbert so sharply that Villam blinked, thrown out of his reverie by those words. "The King's Eagle waits outside. She bears a message for you."

Villam said nothing for a while, although as he mused he drew his fingers caressingly over the curve of an apple. "I will need a rider to carry a message to my daughter," he said at last, "a trustworthy and loyal man, one from the home estates. Waldhar, perhaps. His father and uncle served me well against the Rederii, and his mother is a good steward of the Arvi holdings. Let him make ready to leave and then come to me."

The servant nodded. He had a tidy manner, efficient and brisk. "Will you need a cleric, my lord margrave, to set the message down on parchment?"

"Nay. It is to go to my daughter's ears alone. Give him an escort of three riders as well."

"I would recommend six, my lord margrave, given the news of Quman raids."

"Yes." Villam had been margrave for many years, with the habit of command and the expectation that his servants would run to do his bidding at once, and effectively. "See that this frater is given food and drink and then send him on his way. Best that it be done quietly."

"So will it be done, my lord margrave." Humbert looked Zacharias over with a look compounded half of curiosity and half of disdain. "Would you prefer that those who serve him are like to gossip or to remain silent about which direction the prince rode out in three days ago?"

"Alas, people are so wont to chatter. That is why I keep a discreet man like yourself as my steward, Humbert."

"Yes, my lord margrave." Humbert gestured to Zacharias. He did not have a kindly face, but he looked fair. "Come, Brother. You will not want to linger long here at the king's court, for it will go hard with you, I am sure, should your quest become generally known."

"I thank you for your hospitality, my lord," said Zacharias, but Villam had already forgotten him as the doors opened and a woman strode in. She wore fine clothing and, over it, a cloak trimmed with red and pinned at one shoulder with a brass brooch shaped as an eagle.

Zacharias knew her at once, that familiar, fierce expression, her hawk's nose, and the way she had of sauntering with a little hitch in her stride, noticeable only because he knew to look for it, that she had developed after falling from an apple tree when she was a child.

He hurriedly stepped sideways into shadow, hoping his hood would obscure his face. She had the habit of a good messenger, looking around swiftly to mark the chamber and its inhabitants. When she saw him, she faltered, puzzling over his shadowed face. He knew her well enough to interpret her expression, for it was one she'd worn as a child: seeing something that she knew was familiar but could not quite put her finger on.

Annoyance and curiosity tightened her mouth, and she seemed about to speak when Villam spoke instead.

"Eagle, you bring me a message from the king?"

"Yes, Margrave Villam," said Hathui, her well-loved voice deepened by maturity and altered by a woman's confidence and pride. At once, she turned her attention to the margrave.

How different their fates had turned out to be, the admired elder brother and the doting young sister. She had become a respected Eagle, standing beside the king's chair, while he had been marked forever as a slave, hunted and desperate.

He slipped out the doors before her attention drifted back to him. He was so ashamed. He didn't want her to recognize him, to see what a poor wretch he had become, no longer a man at all, used and discarded many times over. He remembered the pride shining in her face on that day years ago when he had left their village to walk as a missionary into the east. She must never know what had really happened to him. Better that she believe he was dead.

He took the food and drink offered to him, took his goat and his worn pack and left the palace complex as quickly as he could in case she should come looking, to assuage her curiosity. West, Humbert told him, the road toward Bederbor.

So he walked, alone, nursing his despair. What he had seen, what had been done to him, what he had himself acquiesced to, had opened a chasm between him and his family that could never be bridged. All that was left him was the secret language of the stars, the clouds of black dust and the brilliant lights, the silver-gold ribbon that twisted through the heavenly spheres, the beauty of an ineffable cosmos in whose heart, perhaps, he could lose himself if only he could come to understand its mysteries.

Determined and despondent, he trudged west on the trail of the prince.

2

USING a stout stick as his sword, Sanglant beheaded thistles one by one, an entire company hewn down by savage whacks.

"You're in a foul mood," observed Heribert. The slender cleric sat on a fallen log whittling the finishing touches into the butt of a staff. He had carved the tip into the likeness of a fortress tower surmounted by a Circle of Unity. Behind them, half concealed by a copse of alder, Captain Fulk supervised the setup of a makeshift camp among the stones of an ancient Dariyan fort long since fallen into ruin.

"The king was right." Sanglant kept decapitating thistles as he spoke. He could not bear to sit still, not now, with frustration burning through him. He felt as helpless as the thistles that fell beneath his sharp strokes. "How can I support a retinue without lands of my own?"

"Duke Conrad's chatelaine made no protest. She put us up in the hall at Bederbor for a full five days."

"And Conrad did not return, nor would she tell us where he had gone or when she expected him back. Thus leaving us to go on our way. We're dependent on the generosity of other nobles. Or on their fear."

"Or their respect for your reputation, my lord prince," said Heribert quietly.

Sanglant lifted his free hand in a gesture of dismissal. He did not stop whacking. The thistles made good enemies, plentiful and easy to defeat. "Nevertheless, my reputation cannot feed my retinue forever. Nor will my cousins and peers feed me forever, knowing it may bring my father's wrath down upon them. He could accuse them of harboring a rebel and call them to account for disloyalty."

"Then it will only bring his anger down on them twofold if they listen to your words. What are you speaking if not of rebellion, my friend?"

These words brought his hand to a halt. Battered thistles swayed and stilled. What, indeed? He turned to consider Heribert.

"What is it you want?" Heribert continued. "What is it you intend? You know I will follow you no matter where your path leads you, but it seems to me that you had better know in your own mind where you are going before you walk any farther down this road."

Just in this way, a wineskin full to bursting could be emptied with a single precise hole stabbed into its side. He sank down onto the log beside Heribert. "Thus am I reminded of the burdens of ruling," he remarked bitterly as Heribert continued his carving. "It was easier to do what I was told, back when I was captain of the Dragons."

"It's always easier just to do what you're told," murmured Heribert. His hands stilled as he lifted his eyes to regard the distant trees, looking at a scene hidden to everyone but himself.

Sanglant hadn't the patience to wallow in self-pity. It made him too restless. He jumped up and began pacing. "If Eagles came with a report of a great invasion, and my father did not believe them, it would be left to me to counter that invasion, would it not?"

Heribert's gaze shifted abruptly back to the prince. "Would it? If you could find safety for yourself and your people—"

Sanglant beheaded seven thistles with one blow. Then he laughed. "Nay, friend, you know me better than that. How can I rest if Wendar is in danger? I swore to guard the realm and every soul who lives under my family's rule."

Heribert's smile was soft, but he did not reply.

"But I also have a duty to my mother's people. My mother claims the Aoi who were exiled will all die if they do not return to Earth. Yet Sister Anne wants to deny them their rightful return."

"Sister Anne claimed that the Aoi would bring in their wake a great cataclysm."

"Sister Anne claimed many things, but she also would have let Blessing starve to death. She spent years hunting down her own husband, and in the end she killed him because she wanted to get her daughter back. No one has ever explained to my satisfaction why a man like Bernard would run away with Liath in the first place, or hide her so desperately. What if he knew something we do not? Nay, Sister Anne may say many things, and twist the truth to serve her own purposes, and in the end we cannot know what is truth and what is falsehood, only that she is heartless when it comes to those she would use to advance her own objectives."

"You'll hear no argument from me on that score," murmured Heribert. "I built her a fine hall, yet I do not doubt that she would have disposed of me without a second thought once I was of no further use to her." He sighed suddenly and sheathed his knife. Running his fingers over the finely carved tower which now crowned his oak staff, a crenellation, arrow slits, a suggestion of stonework etched into the wood, and the Circle of Unity rising from the center, he spoke softly, his voice shifting in tone. "All ruined, so you said."

"Everything. The hall burned like kindling." He lowered

his stick and set a companionable hand on Heribert's shoulder. "You can't imagine their power."

"The power of Anne and her sorcerers?"

"Nay, although truly Sister Anne commands powers greater than anything I can understand or have ever seen before. I spoke of the fire daimones who stole Liath away. Everything their gaze touched burst into flame. Even the mountains burned." Just as his anger burned, deep in his heart, fueled by helplessness and frustration. The words came unbidden. "I could do nothing to stop them." Grief made his voice hoarse, but then, after the wound to the throat he'd taken in battle five years ago, his voice always sounded like that.

A breeze had come up in the trees. He listened but could not make words out of their rustling: they were not spirits of air, such as Anne had commanded, but only the wind. Yet that sound of wind through autumn leaves reminded him that he still had hope. In the palace at Angenheim, he had seen a gateway opening onto a place veiled by power and distance and the mysteries hidden in the architecture of the universe— as Liath would have said. He had heard Liath's voice. "She's still alive," he whispered.

"It is amazing anyone survived."

Sanglant hefted the stick in his hand, weighed it, eyed the ragged thistles and, choosing mercy, lowered the stick again. "I know Sister Anne survived the maelstrom. How many of her companions did as well, I don't know."

"Sister Venia survived," said Heribert grimly.

"How can you know?"

"She's the type who does survive, no matter what."

"You would know that better than I. She was your mother, and the one who raised you."

"Like a dog on a leash," muttered Heribert. Sanglant watched with interest as that smooth cleric's amiability peeled off to reveal an ancient resentment, nurtured secretly for many years. But, like a dog, the young cleric shook himself after a moment and put the veil back on. His expression cleared, and he glanced up at Sanglant with a cool smile. "Where might such sorcerers go, burned out of their home? Would they try to rebuild at Verna?"

"I wouldn't stay there, not after daimones of such power had come calling. There's a mystery here, Heribert. Those daimones were looking for Liath. Bernard fled from Anne and her company because he feared that the Seven Sleepers might twist Liath to their purpose. But maybe he also feared the daimones. Nay, there is much I cannot explain. What I know is this: Anne will not rest. She will look for Liath, and even if she cannot find her, she will still try to stop the exiles from returning. She hoped that Liath would prevent the Aoi from returning, but just because Liath is gone, Anne won't give up. I have to stop Sister Anne and her companions. I have to make sure the exiles can return."

"Well," said Heribert, gesturing toward the camp rising among the ruins. "You, and a cleric under ban, and seventy men, and a baby, and one aery sprite. That's a weak army to take against a sorcerer as powerful as Sister Anne."

"So it is." He bent to pick up one of the thistle heads, cut off raggedly just below the crown. It prickled and stung his palm, but at least pain muted the anger and bitterness swelling in his heart. "I suppose this is how a loyal hound must feel when its mistress abandons it at the side of the road. I actually thought my mother—" He cursed, shaking off the thistle as his skin pulsed from its bite. "I actually thought—"

He could not go on and had to just stand there, struggling to control himself, while Heribert watched compassionately. Distantly he heard the *baa* of the goat, and then a goatish reply in a higher pitch. The voices in the trees seemed to mock him, even if it was only the wind.

"The more fool I. Did she ever treat me any differently than she did the pony who carried her pack?"

Heribert seemed about to object but thought better of it.

"Once I was of no more use to her, she abandoned me again, just as she did when I was an infant."

"Nay, Sanglant, don't judge her harshly yet. Perhaps the king detained her."

"The king could not detain a sorcerer with her powers. She could have followed us if she had chosen to. But she did not. I no longer serve any useful purpose in her plotting, now that I am, as you say, as good as a rebel against my father's authority. That was all she cared for."

"Nay, friend, I am sure there is a greater part for you to play—if these prophecies come true."

"But will I play the part they wish me to play? I'm not captain of the King's Dragons anymore, a piece to be moved about in their chess game." He frowned abruptly, shading his eyes as he stared westward at the camp. A commotion had arisen. He heard voices but couldn't quite make out the words. Was that two goats complaining, when they only had one? Yet Captain Fulk could deal with it. He had other battles to fight.

Resolve came swiftly, and with all its sweet savor. Knowing that he knew what had to be done and that he was the one to do it cleared his mind of doubts and despairs. A man who doubted fared poorly in battle, so he had long ago trained himself not to doubt.

"The Seven Sleepers must be stopped, Heribert. If my father won't believe me, and won't act, then I must act." He knew he was right, just as he knew in battle when it was time to turn a flank or call the charge. He'd only been wrong once, defeated by Bloodheart's illusions. He didn't intend to be wrong again. "Consider what my mother did, and why I am here at all. She never cared for Henry. She didn't become his lover out of lust or passion or love. She did so in order to give birth to me, so that I would be a bridge between his people and hers. We walked for twelve days together, fleeing Verna, and during that time when she spoke at all she told me about the Aoi council and how it is broken into factions. Some of them hate humankind still and hope to conquer all human realms, while some seek compromise and alliance."

"Alas, not even the fabled Aoi are immune from intrigue."

"Even animals mark their territories and who comes first and who last in their herds. If that faction of the Aoi who still hate humankind comes to power after the return, then some prince born of human blood must prepare for war. If my father will not do so, then I must."

Heribert coughed lightly. "My lord prince. My good friend. If you did not trouble Anne, and let her work her sorcery, then the Aoi would not return at all. And Wendar would remain at peace."

Sanglant looked away. "And all my kin would be dead. Nay. I cannot. I can't turn my back on my mother's people. I will not let them all die."

"Will you instead be the unwitting tool by which they conquer humankind? You said yourself that they showed little enough interest in you. In truth, Sanglant, you might be better served to ask your father's forgiveness and help him restore the Aostan throne to Queen Adelheid. With Aosta in his grasp, he has power enough to be crowned Holy Dariyan Emperor, like Taillefer before him. Such power would give him the strength to meet any Aoi threat, should the events you speak of come to pass."

The image of Bloodheart's chains rose in his mind's eye. Those chains still weighed on him. They always would. "I won't ask for my father's forgiveness because I did nothing wrong except marry against his wishes."

"Had you married Queen Adelheid, as your father wished you to, you would have been king in Aosta and heir to your father. Then you would have had the strength to do what needed to be done."

Sanglant turned, stung into fury, only to see Heribert jump to his feet, half laughing, in the way of folk who seek to appease an armed man whom they have inadvertently insulted. He knew the look well enough. The cleric held his staff out before him, as if to protect himself, although he hadn't any skill with arms.

"I only speak the truth, Sanglant. I would offer you nothing less."

Sanglant swore vigorously. But following the strong words came a harsh laugh. "So you do, and so you do well to remind me. But I won't seek my father's forgiveness."

"So be it," agreed Heribert, lowering the staff. "I know what it is to be unable to forgive. But it is well to understand the road you walk on, and what brought you to it."

"Hush." Sanglant lifted a hand, hearing his name spoken in the camp. "Come." Heribert hastened to follow him as he strode toward the ruins. He had gotten about halfway when the youth Matto came jogging toward them.

"You see there, Heribert, a lesson to you. I need counselors who are not blinded by their admiration for my many fine qualities."

Heribert laughed. "You mean by your ability to fight. Forgive him, my lord, for he is young."

"I fear that if he persists in following me, he will not get much older."

"Do not say so, may God forgive you!" scolded Heribert. "We cannot know the future."

Sanglant did not reply because the youth ran up then. His broken arm still hung in a sling, but it didn't pain him much anymore. His cheeks were flushed now with excitement, and he still seemed likely to cast himself on the ground at Sanglant's feet, hoping for a chance to kiss his boots. Luckily, he had learned from the example of Fulk and his soldiers. Drawing himself up smartly, he announced his message as proudly as if he were a royal Eagle.

"Your Highness! Captain Fulk begs you to come at once. A frater's come into camp seeking you."

Entering camp, Sanglant sought out Blessing first; she was safely asleep in a sling tied between an old stone pillar and a fresh wooden post, rocking gently in a breeze made by Jerna. As the baby took more and more solid food and less of the dai-mone's milk, Jerna's substance had thinned as well. He could barely make out her womanly shape as a watery shimmer where the late afternoon sun splashed light over the pillar. Just as well. Those womanly curves increasingly bothered him in his dreams, or when he woke at night, or when he had any reason to pause and let his mind wander. Better that he not be able to see her at all than be tempted in this unseemly way.

It was a relief to have distraction. He turned his attention to the stranger. It took him a moment to recognize the ragged man dressed in robes that had once, perhaps, been those of a frater. The man came attended by a fractious goat which was at this moment trying to crowd the other goat out of a particularly lush patch of thistles. A dozen of Fulk's men, as well as Fulk himself, watched over him, not standing too close.

"You're the man who traveled with my mother," said Sanglant, looking the man up and down. He was an unprepossessing sight, dirty, with an infected eye. He stank impressively. "She said you were dead."

"Perhaps she thought I was," said the man.

"Address Prince Sanglant properly," said Captain Fulk sharply. "Your Highness, he is to you. He's a prince of the realm, son of King Henry."

"Your Highness," said the ragged frater ironically. "I am called Brother Zacharias." He glanced at the prince's entourage, the soldiers now come to stand around and watch since there was nothing of greater interest this fine evening to attract their attention. What he thought of this makeshift retinue he did not say, nor could Sanglant make sense of his expression. Finally, the man met his gaze again. He had a stubborn stare, tempered with weariness. "I followed you, Your Highness."

"Which is more than my mother did," said Sanglant in an undertone, glancing at Heribert before gesturing to the frater. "So you did, Brother. Is there something you want of me?"

Zacharias drew a smudged roll of parchment out of a battered cook pot that dangled from his belt, held there by a well-worn string of leather. He unrolled the battered parchment tenderly, with the greatest solicitude, to reveal a torn scrap marked with numbers and ciphers and diagrams, eccentricities, epicycles, and equant points, and pinpricks representing stars.

Sanglant recognized that impatient scrawl at once. He took the paper from the frater without asking permission, nor did the man protest with more than a mild blurt of surprise, quickly cut off as he eyed the soldiers surrounding him.

"Liath." Sanglant pressed the scrap to his cheek as if some essence of her might reside in those hastily scrawled numbers and circles, a lingering tincture of her soul and heart that he could absorb through his skin.

"Know you who wrote these calculations, Your Highness?" asked the frater, with rising excitement. His cheeks flushed, and he blinked his infected eye so rapidly that tears oozed along the swollen lids.

After a long silence, Sanglant lowered the parchment. They were only markings, after all. He knew the names she had called them, but he didn't really know what they meant. "My wife."

"Then she *is* the one I seek!" cried the frater triumphantly. He extended a hand, trembling a little, wanting the scrap back.

With some reluctance, Sanglant handed it over. "You saw what became of her, surely. She was stolen by fire daimones."

The soldiers had heard the story before, but they murmured among themselves, hearing the words spoken so baldly. At times, it amazed Sanglant that they rode with him despite his defiance of his father and regnant, despite the reputation of his wife, who had been excommunicated by a church council for the crime of sorcery and had vanished under mysterious circumstances from Earth itself. Despite the inhuman daimone who attended him as nursemaid to his daughter.

"Ah." Zacharias considered the goats, who had resolved their dispute by pulling to the limits of their ropes where they had found satisfaction in a bramble. His profile seemed vaguely familiar to Sanglant, but he couldn't place him. Had he seen him before? He did not think so, yet something about the man rang a resonance in his heart. The frater had a bold nose, a hawk's nose, as some would have been wont to say, and a vaguely womanlike jawline, more full than sharp. He had the thinness of a man who has eaten poorly for a long time, and a shock of dark hair tied back at his neck. Like a good churchman, he had no beard. But his gaze was clear and unafraid. "Do you believe she is lost to you, Your Highness?"

"I will find her."

Zacharias considered the words, and the tone, and finally nodded. "May I travel with you, then, my lord?"

Oddly, the question irritated Sanglant. "Why do you seek her?"

"So that she may explain to me these calculations. She, too, seeks an understanding of the architecture of the universe, just as I do. She must know something of the secret language of the stars—"

"Enough." The man spoke so like Liath that Sanglant could not bear to hear more of it. Ai, God, it reminded him of the conversation he had overheard between Liath and Sister Venia: Hugh could read, could navigate the night sky, could plot the course of the moon; Hugh had a passion for knowledge, and Sanglant did not. Would Liath like Zacharias' company better than his? She lived at times so much in her mind that he wondered if she ever noticed that with each step her feet touched the ground. Maybe her feet no longer touched Earth at all, not now. Perhaps all the secrets of the stars had been revealed to her on some distant sphere, and she need never return to the Earth he understood and lived on.

Heribert coughed slightly, and Sanglant realized that every man there was waiting for him. "You may travel with us, Brother, as long as you abide by my orders and make no trouble."

"I have a wretched tongue, Your Highness," said the frater, "and it has gotten me into trouble before." He spoke bitterly, and made a kind of gesture with his hand, toward his hips, quickly cut off, as though he hadn't meant to make any such gesture at all.

"A little honest gossip is common to men accustomed to the soldiering life, Brother, but I don't tolerate lies or betrayal. Nor do I punish men for speaking the truth."

"Then you are an unusual prince, my lord."

"So he is," interposed Fulk. The good captain regarded the dirty frater with suspicion. "You'll do your share of the camp work, I trust?"

"I'm humbly born, Captain," retorted the frater tartly. "I do not fear hard work, and have done my share, and more than my share, in the past. I survived seven years as a slave among the Quman."

The soldiers murmured on hearing this boast.

"Is that so?" demanded Sanglant. "What tribe took you as a slave, and what was their chieftain's name?"

The frater's grin had the beauty of a hawk's flight, swiftly seen and swiftly vanished. "I walked into the east to bring the light of God to their lost souls. But the Kirakit tribe, whose mark is the curve of an antelope's horn, scorned me. They traded me to the Pechanek tribe as part of a marriage agreement. You can see it on my back, if you will: the rake of a snow leopard's claw, to mark me as the slave of their begh Bulkezu."

"Bulkezu," echoed Sanglant.

Zacharias shuddered. Even spoken so softly, and at such a distance, names had power.

Sanglant touched his throat, felt the scar of the wound that ought to have killed him, but had not. "I fought against him once, and neither of us won in that encounter." He smiled grimly. "I will take you gladly, Brother, for it seems to me that a man who can survive seven years as a slave of the Quman will not falter easily."

"Nor will I," agreed the frater, "although I was hoping for a wash."

"Who's on water duty, Captain?"

Fulk had been regarding the frater with surprised admiration. Now he turned to the prince. "I had meant to bring the matter to your attention, Your Highness. The ruins make a good defense, but there is no nearby water source. I've got the men carrying in buckets, enough for the night. Brother Zacharias may go down to the stream, if he wishes." ·

"Nay, wait a moment, Captain." Heribert stepped forward. "This is a Dariyan fort, is it not?" He surveyed the ruins with the eye of a man familiar with ancient buildings.

Sanglant had camped in old Dariyan forts before. Well built, they had usually weathered time and war so well that their walls still provided a good defensive position, and Sanglant had fought for too many years to pitch camp even in peaceful territory without an eye to defense. This fort, like all the others, had square walls and two avenues, one crossing the other, that split the cramped interior into four quarters, with four gates. Fulk had posted sentries along the outer walls and had placed the camp in the central square, itself ringed by a low wall. Heribert crossed to that inner wall and began a circuit, bending now and again to brush accumulated dust from the reliefs of eagle-headed soldiers and women with the muzzles of jackals that adorned the walls, a parade etched into stone that ringed the entire square.

Abruptly, Heribert struck at the ground with his staff, then called over a soldier. With a spear's haft and a shovel, they dug and levered and, that suddenly, got a stone lifted. A cloud of moisture billowed up.

"Sorcery!" murmured one of the soldiers.

"A miracle!" said a second.

Heribert returned in time to hear this comment. "Nay, there's no sorcery or miracles involved," he said, somewhat disgustedly. "All Dariyan forts were built to the same plan. One cistern always lies in the central square, marked by a woman dressed in a skirt hung all around with lightning bolts and carrying a water lily. Usually, in forts that were inhabited for a lengthy period, an entire network of rain spouts and channels leads rainwater into that central cistern, and—"

Because he seemed ready to go on indefinitely, caught up by his passion, Sanglant interrupted him. "Let me taste the water first."

A rope and bucket were found. When a soldier brought him the half-full bucket, Sanglant dipped a hand in the cool water, sipped, and let the taste of it wash over him. No taint of poison or foulness burned him. The water smelled fresh, and had been covered for so long and so tightly that no animal had fallen in to poison it. "I judge it safe to use, Captain."

"Truly, that will save us labor, Brother," said Fulk, eyeing Heribert with new respect. Captain and cleric went aside, and Heribert began pointing out to him certain features of the fort. Zacharias left camp to wash himself in privacy. Blessing stirred and woke from her nap, and Sanglant unwound her from the sling as the soldiers built up a good fire and brought out their equipment for mending torn cloaks and tunics. The cooks roasted the six deer they'd shot in the course of their march that day.

In this manner, they settled down for the night. Sanglant fed Blessing a paste made of pulses and goat's milk, sweetened with honey that the soldier Sibold had stolen from a bee's nest two days ago, although the poor man still had swollen fingers, the price he'd paid for this prize.

"Da da!" Blessing said in her emphatic way. "Da ma ba! Wa! Ge! Ge!" She wriggled out of his lap and grabbed his fingers, wanting to walk. In the past ten days she'd gotten so steady on her legs that she could now run, and did, whenever he wasn't holding on to her or she wasn't in her sling. She was so used to the soldiers that she would run, screaming with excitement, to any one of them, as her father chased her, and hide behind their legs. This had become part of the nightly ritual of the war band. Once she had exhausted them in this way, she presided, from her father's lap, over the singing that followed dinner. Every man there knew a dozen tunes or twenty or a hundred. Blessing babbled along enthusiastically, and although she couldn't quite clap her hands together to keep time, she waved them vigorously.

When she finally slumped into her father's chest, eyes half closed, he called Brother Zacharias over to him and questioned him closely about Bulkezu and the Quman. The frater had managed to wash the worst of the dirt off him, although his clothing still stank. He had the accent of a man born and bred in the east among the free farmers, those who had settled in the marchlands in exchange for land of their own and the protection of the king. Of the Quman, Zacharias had a slave's knowledge, incomplete and sketchy, but he noticed details and he knew how to talk.

"Maybe it's best we ride east," said Sanglant finally as Fulk and Heribert listened. "Sapientia will not like this news of our father's marriage to Queen Adelheid."

"It's a long road to the east," observed Heribert.

"All roads are long roads." Blessing had fallen asleep on his chest. He bundled her up in the sling, off the ground so no crawling creature could bite her. The others rolled themselves up in their blankets. From farther off he heard sentries pacing on their rounds, their footfalls light on packed earth. He could not sleep. His hand still smarted from the prick of the thistle.

Jerna's aetherical form fluttered down beside him, rippling like water. She curled herself as a veil of protection around the sleeping bundle that was Blessing. Perhaps, like an amulet, she did protect the baby. Blessing had not taken sick for even one day since Jerna began suckling her, nor was the baby troubled by fly or mosquito bites like the rest of them. Hot sun did not make her dusky skin break out in a rash, nor did she seem to mind the cold. She was growing so fast that every man there knew it was uncanny and abnormal, although none spoke a word out loud.

Maybe he was a fool for letting an abomination nurse her. Perhaps it wasn't wise. But what else could he have done? He had made the only choice open to him.

So be it.

3

AS King Henry's army lurched and toiled up the pass, Rosvita found herself for the fifth time that day at a standstill behind a wagon. This one had gotten stuck where its wheels had broken through an icy crust to bog down in mud beneath.

Fortunatus reined his mule up beside hers, and sighed. "Do you think it was wise of King Henry to cross the mountains this late in the year?"

"Speak no ill of the king, I pray you, Brother. He marches at God's bidding. You see, the sun still shines."

So it did, however bleak and wan its light seemed against a backdrop of dark clouds, cold mountainside, and a cutting wind. Soldiers and servants hurried forward with planks and sticks to coax the wagon out of its mire. Soon a dozen of them had gathered around the stricken wagon, arguing with each other in the tone of men who have had their endurance tested to the limit.

"Shall I speak to them, Sister?"

"Nay, let them be unless it comes to a fistfight. But you may take the reins of my mule, if you please." As she had done the other times they had halted in this manner, she dismounted from her mule to give a few words of comfort to a wagon's load of soldiers so stricken with the flux that they were too weak to walk.

"Let us pray, friends," she said as she approached the wagon, although in truth most of the soldiers were too delirious with fever to hear her words. The wagon stank of their illness, for these were the poor souls who no longer had the strength to hoist themselves off the wagon and stagger off the path before voiding their bowels.

It took her perhaps four steps to walk from her mule to the wagon. Only for that long did she turn her back to the pass up which the army struggled.

The wagon driver had a cloth tied over most of his face to mask the stench of sickness, but even so, she saw his eyes widen in terror as he looked past her. She heard it first as a rumble, a crackling thrumming roar that obliterated distant shrieks and warning calls.

"Sister!" cried Fortunatus. "Ai, God, we are overtaken!"

She turned back. She hadn't turned away for longer than it would take to count to ten, but in that brief span the sun had vanished under a curtain of white descending off the mountains. For an instant, the sight so disoriented her that she imagined them overwhelmed by a deluge of white flower petals.

The blizzard hit without warning. She had time only to grab at the wagon's side, to brace herself. Fortunatus flung himself down from his mount and yanked on the reins of her mule. Then the storm swallowed him, and smashed into her.

She could not even hear the moans of the ill soldiers. Wind lashed her and snow blasted her. Pebbles caught up by the wind peppered her back as though a giant was hurling them against its enemies. She groped her way along the wagon until she shouldered up against the protecting bulk of the oxen. Luckily, she wore gloves, but even so her fingers stiffened where they clutched at wood and harness. She had to keep her back to the wind in order to breathe.

For an endless time, as the warmth ebbed out of her, she just held on.

By the time the wind slackened enough that she dared look up, snow drifted knee-deep around her legs and her feet had gone numb. Through the furious snow she could barely make out shapes staggering along the road. They were no longer

marching south, up the pass toward Aosta. Now they fled
north, down the pass, back the way they had come.

"Ai, God!" swore the driver, shouting to be heard above the
screaming wind. "I've got to turn around now or the wheels'll
be stuck in the snow!"

She waved down a trio of soldiers retreating with their backs
to the storm. With their help they wrenched the wagon
around, although it was a tricky business on the narrow road,
with the land falling away steeply on one side and rising precipitously on the other. There was nothing she could do to
help the wagon ahead of them, still stuck in the mud.

"Sister!" Fortunatus had miraculously kept hold of both
mules, although he had been forced very close to the edge. He
laboriously tied the reins of the mules to the back of the
wagon, his fingers clumsy with cold. By walking beside and
clinging onto their mules, they followed the wagon back down
the pass.

The storm made white of the world. Shapes stumbled past
them, and sometimes they passed knots of soldiers stopped to
help a fallen comrade. The wagon ground down the old road
with fresh snow squeaking under its wheels. The wind pressed
them along as though it were glad to be rid of them. She
stumbled on rocks and found she'd drifted off the road.
Fortunatus hauled her back, and with her lips set tight and her
energy flagging, she hung onto her stirrup and concentrated
on taking one step at a time.

Faintly, above the howl of the wind, horns signaled the passage of the king.

Soon enough, the king's party overtook them. Henry had by
sheer strength of will managed to stay mounted on his sturdy
warhorse. Queen Adelheid rode bravely beside him, swathed
in a fur cloak coated with so much snow that she looked
dusted with ice. As he passed, he shouted encouragement to
the soldiers staggering along.

Despite the storm, he recognized Rosvita and hailed her.
"Sister Rosvita! Need you a wagon?"

"Nay, Your Majesty. These ill soldiers need it more than I."

He nodded. "We'll come soon enough to the hostel where we quartered last night."

He moved on, vanishing quickly into the streaming snow. After an interminable while in which she only knew she was walking because her legs moved, they came to a thrusting ridge that cut off the worst of the wind. Snow still swirled all around them, soft and abundant as it blanketed the ground.

The hostel had a main hall, crudely built but adequate enough for a sizable party of merchants, stables enough for some forty beasts, and a half dozen outbuildings and sheds. But it couldn't house a king's army. Last night they had staked out their camp under the open sky in balmy autumn weather, with not a finger of snow on the ground, confident that the weather would hold for the five days it would take them to pass over the summit and begin their descent into Aosta.

The wagon driver was barely able to maneuver his team in beside a dozen others, crowded together just off the road. Hunching his shoulders against the cold, he swung down from the seat. A Lion hurried up and helped him cover the oxen's backs with a blanket. Then, with some of his fellows, he hunkered down in the lee of the wagon. There was nowhere else for the servants to go. Soldiers and clerics moved among the sick, helping those who could still walk into the stables. Of the dozen men languishing in the back of the wagon, three were already dead. She murmured a brief prayer over them through lips stiff with cold.

"Alas," murmured Fortunatus where he huddled beside her. "I fear none of these sick men can survive the cold."

"If God will it, these poor souls will survive. If not, they'll gain a just reward."

"Truly, so shall it be," echoed Fortunatus.

When all was said and done, there was nothing she could do. "Come," she said to Fortunatus. "Let us attend the king."

Henry and his nobles had taken refuge in the hall. The press of bodies made the place warm, although there were

only two fires going in the hearths built into either end of the
structure. Smoke raked her throat raw. So many people had
crushed into the hall to escape from the storm that it was difficult to make her way to the king.

Henry had given pride of place in front of each of the
hearths to certain captains and nobles who had taken sick with
the flux and to a few common soldiers known to him, Lions or
members of his personal guard. With a ring of advisers he
stood in the center of the hall holding court, discussing their
desperate situation together with the wizened nun who was
mother of the order who ran the hostel. As he drank ale
straight out of a pitcher, he listened to the old woman, whose
words were translated by a second nun.

"Nay, Your Majesty, when a storm comes sudden-like this
time of year, it's not likely it'll clear up soon. When it does in
a day or three, you'll find the snow too deep to cross."

Helmut Villam stood beside the king. He looked exhausted,
worn through by the struggle to get out of the storm. Just a
week ago he had shone with youth at the betrothal feast celebrated for him and his bride, young Leoba. Now he looked as
old as he was, a full sixty years, as though the youthful vigor
that had always before animated him had been sucked out of
him by the bitter cold.

"But there was so little snow here this morning," he
protested. "Surely if we wait this out, we can make one more
attempt to cross the pass before winter descends in earnest."

"That you may," agreed the nun. "That you may. But I've
served in these parts for well on thirty years, my lord. I know
these storms. You'll not get across now until late spring. If you
try, it'll go hard on your army, Your Majesty."

Henry took another quaff of ale as he considered these tidings. Abruptly Rosvita's feet began to hurt so horribly, as
though a thousand tiny knives were cutting into her soles, that
she staggered and would have fallen had Fortunatus not
caught her.

Henry saw her. He sent one of his Lions to open up a stool

for her to sit on. Ale was brought, and she drank gratefully. For a while, as the murmur and flow of disparate conversations swirled around her as thickly as the snow had done outside, she sat with her head bowed, catching her breath and gritting her teeth as pain flared and subsided in her feet.

After a while, a servant unwrapped her leggings and uncovered her feet. Her toes felt frozen through. Fortunatus knelt before her and chafed her feet between his hands until tears ran down her cheeks.

Through the haze of pain, she heard Henry speaking.

"Nay, we can't risk it. The season is late. To be defeated by the mountains is no dishonor to us. We can't stay here since there isn't shelter enough for everyone. We must retreat to Bederbor and live off Conrad's bounty for the winter."

"He'll give that grudgingly," remarked Villam.

"So he will," agreed Henry. "We'll make good use of his hospitality to remind him of the loyalty that is due to his regnant. But this way we can keep the army strong. When the passes clear next year, we'll march south and catch Ironhead unawares. Yet surely, Helmut, you'll be glad of one more winter in the north. We'll send for your bride, and she can keep your bed warm!"

Laughter followed this sally, and the mood in the hall lightened considerably. Such was the king's power.

Her feet prickled mightily, as though stung by a hundred bees. "I pray you, Brother, that is enough!"

Fortunatus regarded her with a grim smile. "Better than losing your toes, Sister, is it not? Can you ride?"

She flexed her feet and found that although they still hurt, she could move them and even set her weight upon them without undue pain.

"This is ill news," she said to him, "that we must wait until next year to march to Aosta. Where is the queen?"

Henry had moved away toward the door to direct his captains to start an orderly retreat toward Bederbor. Rosvita got to her feet and tested them gingerly, but found them sound enough. Through the milling crowd she caught sight of Adelheid in a corner, sitting on one of the beds built in under the rafters. She was vomiting into a basin held by a serving-woman.

"Your Majesty!" Rosvita hastened forward, alarmed. Just in this way did the flux first afflict its victims. But as she reached Adelheid's side, the young queen straightened up with a wan smile and allowed a servant to wipe her face.

"Nay, it's nothing dangerous." The queen reached out to grasp Rosvita's hands. Adelheid's hands were warm despite the cruel storm raging outside which she had so recently escaped. Her grip had unusual strength, and her eyes held a gleam of triumph as she glanced past Rosvita toward her husband, whose head could be seen above the others in the crowd. "I believe that I am pregnant."

4

ONE ruined Dariyan fort looked much like any other. Sanglant led his men north through Wayland following the ancient trail of the Dariyan invasion, laid down hundreds of years ago. The forts had lasted far longer than the empire.

This night, as every night, after he made sure Blessing slept, he walked the perimeter to greet each soldier standing sentry on first watch. A jest exchanged with Sibold, a comment on the weather by Everwin, an astute observation about the land-scape from Wracwulf, and he moved on. By the time he returned to the campfire, both Zacharias and Heribert were asleep, rolled up tightly in their cloaks under cover of a half fallen roof. Heribert had shoved aside broken tiles to make space for Sanglant, but the prince was, as usual, too restless to sleep. He sat brooding by the fire.

A quiet wind brushed all the clouds away. Under the clear sky cold crept in, chasing away the dregs of summer. The bitter stars reminded him of Liath, for she would have loved a night such as this, so clear and cold that the stars seemed twice as bright and a hundred times more numerous than usual. The three jewels, Diamond, Citrine, and Sapphire, burned overhead as the Queen drove the Guivre down into the western horizon. The River of Souls streamed across the zenith. Did Liath walk there now? Could she see him? But when he spoke her name softly onto the breeze, he heard no answer.

They kept their secrets well.

After a while the waning moon rose to wash the sky with silver light. He heard them before the sentries did: a muffled yip, softly signaling, and the brush of fur against dry leaves, perhaps a tail dragged along a bush. He jumped up to his feet just as Jerna unwound herself from Blessing's sling and shot away into the air. With sword in hand, he followed the aery daimones' form, a shimmering streak against the night sky, to the fort's wall, which stood chest-high. Wracwulf greeted him briefly, alert enough to notice how Sanglant's gaze ranged over the forest cover. The soldier, too, turned to survey the woodland.

Three wolves emerged from the undergrowth in that silence known only to wild things. The sentry hissed, but Sanglant laid a stilling hand on the soldier's arm. A fourth wolf ghosted out of the trees a stone's throw to the left. They came no closer, only watched. Their amber eyes gleamed in moonlight.

Wracwulf raised his spear. A bowstring creaked from farther down the wall, where Sibold stood watch.

"Don't shoot!" cried Sanglant.

Shouts and the alarm broke out in camp. The wolves vanished into the trees. Sanglant spun and, drawing his sword, sprinted back to camp to find the soldiers risen in agitation, whispering like troubled bees. They had gathered near Blessing's sling, but the commotion had not troubled her; she slept soundly.

"Your Highness!" Captain Fulk leveled his spear at a dark figure which stood next to the sleeping baby.

"Who's this?" demanded Sanglant, really angry now, because fear always fueled anger.

The man stepped out of the shadows. His hair had the same silvery tone as the moonlight that bathed him in its soft light. "When I realized it was you, Prince Sanglant, I had to see the child."

"Wolfhere!"

The old Eagle looked tired, and he walked with a pronounced limp. His cloak and clothing were neat enough, but his boots were scuffed and dirty. An overstuffed pack lay on its side on the ground behind him.

"Your Highness." He examined the soldiers surrounding him with a smile so thin that Sanglant could not tell whether he were amused or on the point of collapse. "I feel as welcome as if I'd jumped into a bed of thistles."

Fulk did not lower his spear. The point hovered restlessly near the Eagle's unprotected belly. "This man is under the regnant's ban."

"Is that so?" asked Sanglant amiably.

"Alas, so it is," Wolfhere admitted cheerfully enough. "I left court without the king's permission. When my horse went lame, I was unable to commandeer another."

"Sit down." Now that any immediate danger to Blessing was past, Sanglant could enjoy the irony of the situation. "I would be pleased to hear your tale. In any case it seems you are now in my custody. It is well for you, I suppose, that I do not currently rest in the king's favor either."

"Nay, so you do not. That much gossip, at least, I heard on the road here." Wolfhere's mask of sage detachment vanished as he spoke again, a remarkable blend of anxiety and agitation flowering on that usually closed face. "Where is Liath?"

"Captain Fulk," said Sanglant, "have a fire built over by the well. I would speak with the Eagle alone. Set a double guard over my daughter."

Most of the soldiers went back to their rest. The prince led Wolfhere over to a freshly built fire, snapping brightly in a niche laid into the stone wall that had once, perhaps, held an idol, or weapons set ready for battle.

Wolfhere sighed sharply as he sat down, grateful for a cup of ale and a hunk of bread. "I'm not accustomed to walking," he said, to no one in particular. "My feet hurt."

As Sanglant settled down on a fallen stone, opposite Wolfhere, Heribert hurried up, rubbing his eyes. Wolfhere glanced at him, seeing only the robe, and then looked again, a broad double take that would have been comical had he not leaped up with an oath and tipped over the precious ale.

"How came he here?" he demanded.

"He's my counselor, and my friend." Sanglant gestured to Heribert to sit beside him. Because Wolfhere did not sit, Heribert did not either, hovering beside Sanglant rather like a nervous bird about to flap away.

"You're aware of what manner of man this is?" Wolfhere asked.

"Very much so. I would trust him with my life. And with my daughter's life, for that matter."

"Condemned by a church council for complicity in acts of black sorcery! The bastard son of Biscop Antonia!"

"Then, truly, I would be first to condemn him, being a bastard myself." Sanglant grinned sharply but, glancing at Heribert, he saw that the cleric had gone as stiff as a man who expects in the next instant to receive a mortal blow. "That argument holds no water for me, Wolfhere. Heribert has long since honored me with the truth about his birth and upbringing, although I admit that he's never known who his father was." Wolfhere began to speak, but Sanglant lifted a hand. "Don't try to turn me against him. I know far more of Heribert's inner heart and loyalties than I do of yours!"

Wolfhere's usually calm facade cracked even further to reveal indignation and a glimpse of wrenching pain. "Is it true that Biscop Antonia has gone to Anne and been taken into the Seven Sleepers?"

"So I swear by Our Lady and Lord," murmured Heribert, "for I was with Biscop Antonia when we escaped your custody, Eagle, as you well remember. When we came to Verna by various complicated paths, Anne took my mother's pledge to serve as—" He broke off to stifle a giggle as a child might when it came to laughing over a much-hated adult's discomfiture. "—as seventh and least of her order."

Distantly, a wolf howled. Jerna whispered above the prince, sluicing down on the breeze to curl protectively around his shoulders. Her touch was soft and cool. Two sentries bantered over by the outer wall as they changed watch.

At that moment, Sanglant understood the whole. As if sensing his growing anger, Jerna slipped away into the air. He rose slowly, using his height to intimidate. "You know them, then, Anne and the others." He didn't need to make it a question. "You've been one of them all along, and never loyal to my father, or to his father before him. Never loyal to your Eagle's oath."

This was too much for Wolfhere. "Don't mock what you don't understand, my lord prince! King Arnulf trusted me, and I served him until the day he died. I never betrayed Wendar." Agitated, he continued in a choked voice as he sank down onto the stone block with the weariness of a man who has walked many leagues only to find his beloved home burned to the ground. "Ai, Lady! That it should come to this! That Anne should be willing to use evil tools in a good cause. Have I misjudged her all this time?"

"Does this surprise you?" demanded Sanglant. "Liath and I were her prisoners for many months. It does not surprise *me.*"

"You were not her prisoners! Liath was—" Here Wolfhere halted, breaking off with an anguished grimace.

Sanglant finished for him. "Her tool. Even her daughter was only a tool to her. Did Anne ever love her?"

Wolfhere covered his eyes with a hand. The pain in his voice was easy to hear. "Nay, Anne never loved her. Bernard was the one who loved her."

"Anne killed him in order to get Liath back."

"Bernard took what wasn't his to have! It may even be possible he meant well, but he was horribly and dangerously misguided and full of himself, never listening to any voice but his own. He damaged Liath by hiding her from those who understood what she is and the power that is her birthright. We had no choice but to do what we did to get her back!"

Hands in fists, he rose and paced to the fire, staring into it as though he could see memories within the flames. At last he looked up. "Liath isn't here, is she?" The old Eagle seemed ready to strangle on the words. "Verna lay abandoned when I reached it, everything in ruins, and Anne had left already with the survivors."

"You did not follow her?"

"Crossing the mountains on foot at this time of year? I haven't the skills to travel as Anne may, walking the stones. God's mercy, Prince Sanglant, where is Liath?"

Sanglant had to close his eyes to shut away the memory. He could not speak of it; the pain still burned too deep and if he spoke he knew he would break down into sobs.

Heribert touched him, briefly, on the arm before stepping forward. "I had already left," he said softly, "so I did not witness the conflagration myself, but my lord prince has told me that unearthly creatures with wings of flame walked into the valley through the stone circle and took Liath away with them."

"Even the stone burned," whispered Sanglant hoarsely. The sight of the mountains washed in flame had stamped itself into his mind, so that even with his eyes shut he gained no respite. Splendid and terrible, the creatures had destroyed Verna without seeming even to notice that it was there.

"Ai, God." Wolfhere's sigh cut the silence. He simply collapsed like a puppet whose strings have gone lax, folding down to sit cross-legged on the dirt with the fire casting shadow and light over his lined face and pale hair.

Sanglant waited a long time, but Wolfhere still did not

speak. After a bit, the prince called to Matto and had the boy fill the empty cup with ale. Wolfhere took the cup gratefully and drained it before devouring a second wedge of bread and a corner of cheese. After Matto retreated, Heribert finally sat down. His movement released the words that Wolfhere had clearly been holding back.

"All those years, Anne and I, raised together in the service of a common goal. I was taken from my parents as a child of six to serve her. I thought I knew her better than any other could, even Sister Clothilde, who was never privy to all of Anne's youthful dreams and wishes, not like I was. Anne was always more pure and exalted than the rest of us. I never thought she would league herself with a *maleficus* like Antonia, who raised *galla* out of the stones with the blood of innocents, fed living men to a guivre, and did not scruple to sacrifice her own loyal clerics to further her selfish aims." Heribert winced at these words but said nothing, and Wolfhere—who wasn't looking at him—went on. "We were not raised to use such means and to league ourselves with the minions of the Enemy! How can Anne have taken such a person into her confidence, and given her even greater powers?"

"Such are the chains binding those who rule," retorted Sanglant. "The great princes use whatever sword comes to hand. Isn't this merely quibbling? If your plan succeeds, then all of the Aoi will die anyway. What matters it what tools you use, when killing is your goal?"

"It matters that the cause be just. It matters that our enemies are wicked. It matters that our efforts be honorable and that our hearts do not turn away from holiness."

"Drowning an infant is honorable and holy? You've never denied that you tried to murder me when I was just a suckling baby."

"I did what I thought was right at the time."

Sanglant laughed angrily. "It gladdens my heart to hear you say so! Why, then, do you suppose that I will let you dwell even one night near my daughter, whom you might feel called upon to attempt to murder in her turn! Anne would have let her starve to death. How are you any better than that? You are welcome to leave, and return to Anne who, I am sure, will be glad enough to see you."

The moonlight washed Wolfhere's face to a striking pallor. "It was easy enough to drown an infant before I knew what it was to love one. You must believe me, my lord prince. I cared for Liath as much as I was allowed to, when she was a child. But Anne did not think it right that we love her, that we weaken ourselves or her in such a manner. Only Bernard did not heed her. Bernard never heeded her." He turned his head sharply to one side as though he had just been slapped. "I gave Anne everything, my life, my loyalty. I never married or sired children. I never saw my family again. What did faithless Bernard care for all that? He stole everything I loved."

Examining Wolfhere's face, Sanglant simply could not tell whether he was acting, like a poet declaiming a role, or sincere. Did the outer seeming match the inner heart?

"This is a touching confession, but I am neither cleric nor frater to grant you absolution." Sanglant let the irony linger in his voice as Wolfhere regarded him, calmer now that the flood of words had abated but still agitated. "Many things have been said of you, but I have never heard it said that you are gullible, or naive."

"Nay, I was most gullible of all. It troubled me that Anne made no effort to love the child, but I refused to let myself think on what it might mean about her heart. But now I fear my doubts were justified. Anne is not the person I thought she was."

The prince lifted both hands in disgust, crying surrender as he began to laugh. "I am defenseless against these thrusts. Either you are the most shameless liar I've ever encountered or you have come to your senses at last and can see that Anne cannot be trusted. What she plans is wrong. She is the wicked one. How can you or I know what the Lost Ones intend? Do

they want peace, or war? Have they plotted long years to get
their revenge, or were they the victims of human sorcery long
ago, as my mother claimed? Anne intends some spell to defeat
them. Tell me what she means to do."

For a long time Wolfhere regarded the moon. Its light
bathed the wall behind them until the stone shone like
marble, revealing flecks of paint, red, blue, and gold, and the
malformed figures common to old Dariyan forts: creatures
with the bodies of women and the heads of hawks or snakes or
lions. A wolf howled in the distance, as a companion might
call out advice to one in need. "I cannot. My gifts are few. Nor
have I ever been privy to the deepest councils, or understood
the full measure of the mathematici's art. I am not nobly born
as you are, my lord prince." Was that sarcasm, or only the cutting blade of truth? "I was raised to serve, not to rule."

"Then why follow me instead of Anne, after you saw what
transpired at Verna? What do you want from me?"

Wolfhere considered the question in silence. It was a mark
of his sagacity that he could not be hurried, although by now
Sanglant felt the urge to pace itch up and down his legs.
Finally he gave in to it, taking two strides to the wall and tracing the attractive curve of a woman's carven body with a
finger. He had reached such a pitch of excitement that each
grain of stone seemed alive under his touch. He noticed what
he was doing, that his fingers rested on the bulge of a breast,
and quickly pulled back his hand and trapped it under his
other arm.

At last, Wolfhere shook himself as a wolf might, emerging
from water. "I don't know. I want to find Liath, my lord
prince."

"As do I. But what do you mean to do with her, should you
find her? Take her back to Anne? Is that what Anne commanded you to do?"

"Nay. I was meant to follow Anne and the others from
Verna, but I could not bring myself to, not after what I had
seen there. So much destruction! The monks at the hostel had

seen a man fitting your description walking north. It was easy
enough to follow you and your mother, although not so easy to
avoid the notice of the king's soldiers as King Henry and his
army marched south."

"Where did Anne go?"

Wolfhere hesitated.

The prince took a half step forward. An arm's length was all
that separated the two men now: the old Eagle, and the young
prince who had once been a Dragon. "Tell me the truth,
Wolfhere, and I'll let you travel with me if that's your wish. I'll
let you help me look for Liath, for you must know that there
is nothing I want more than to find her."

Wolfhere examined him. The firelight played over his
expression, brushing light and dark across his features as if one
never quite overpowered the other. "How do you mean to look
for Liath, my lord prince, when it took eight years for Anne
and me to find her before? With what magic do you intend to
seek out a woman stolen away by unearthly creatures who fly
on wings of flame?"

"If she loves me and the child," said Sanglant grimly, "she'll
find a way back to us. Won't she? Isn't that the test of love and
loyalty?"

"Perhaps. But what do you intend to do meanwhile? You
didn't ride south with your father's army. Had you done so,
you would discover soon enough that Anne and the others
traveled south to Darre."

"Ah! Is that why Anne sent you? To spy on me? Very well.
I'll take up her challenge, because I mean to defeat her now
that I understand what she is and what she means to do to my
mother's kin." As usual, now that Sanglant knew what his
objective was, a plan unfolded before him. "I'll need griffin
feathers and sorcerers to combat her magic. And an army."

"All of which will be useless, my lord prince." Wolfhere was
far too old and wily to be won over by the excitement of such
a bold plan; no doubt he expected a full-grown eagle, not just
a fledgling. "You do not understand her power. She is

Taillefer's granddaughter, and a mathematicus of unequaled strength and mastery."

"I respect her power. But you forget that I am married to her daughter, and that her granddaughter bides in my care. Blessing is half of my making. I am not without rank and power in my own right."

"You no longer wear the gold torque that marks your royal lineage."

"Liath wears the torque that once was mine, as is her right. My daughter wears one."

"But will you wear one again? Or have you turned your back on what Henry gave you, as was his right as your father?"

The cool words irritated him. "I will take what I need and deserve when I am ready, not before! My father does not own me." But irritation could be turned into something useful, just as anger makes splitting wood go faster. "Help me restore Taillefer's line to its rightful place, Wolfhere, in preparation for the return of the Aoi, so that we can face them from a position of strength. Help me find Liath. Help me defeat Anne. In truth, your experience would prove valuable to me."

"You would risk your precious daughter so near to me, my lord prince?" Yet was there a glimmer of vulnerability in the old Eagle's expression as he leaned forward to stir the fire with a stick? Sparks drifted lazily up into the night, flicking out abruptly where they brushed against the stone.

"I can't trust you, it's true. This might all be a ruse on your part. But my daughter is well guarded by a creature that never sleeps, and who will soon know what manner of threat you pose. And it seems to me, my friend, that when we first met this night you had snuck into my camp without being seen. You were close enough to my daughter to kill her, had that been your intent. A knife in the dark offers a quick death. Yet she lives, despite my carelessness."

Was that a tear on Wolfhere's cheek? Hard to tell, and the heat of the fire wicked away all moisture.

Sanglant smiled softly and glanced at Heribert, who only shrugged to show that, in this case, he had no advice to offer. "Travel with me and my company of thistles, Wolfhere. What better option do you have? You don't trust Anne. King Henry has pronounced you under ban. At least I can protect you from the king's wrath."

Wolfhere smiled mockingly. "It isn't the king's wrath I fear," he said, but he raised no further objection.

VII
A DEATH SENTENCE

1

STRONGHAND had seen in his dreams that it was the habit of humankind to make their festivals an interlude of excess and self-gratification. They let fermented drink addle their minds. They ate too much. Often they became noisy, contentious, and undisciplined, and they spent their resources extravagantly and as though their cup of plenty ran bottomless.

Even the chieftains of his own kind had grown into the habit of celebration after each victory. They might command their warriors to parade treasure before them, or they might lay bets on fights staged between slaves and beasts. By such means, and in the company of their rivals, they boasted of their power.

He had no need of such displays. The ships of his dead rivals lay beached on his shores and now swelled the numbers of his fleet. Weapons he hoarded in plenty, and the ironsmiths of twenty or more tribes hammered and forged at his order. The chieftains of twenty tribes had come to Rikin Fjord at his command to lay their staffs of authority at his feet. They had accepted him—some willingly—as ruler over all the tribes:

first among equals, as the humans styled the regnant who reigned over those who called themselves princes and lords. He had named himself Stronghand, by the right of naming given by the OldMother of his tribe. He was, after all, the first chieftain to unite all the tribes of the RockChildren under one hand.

But he felt no thrill of triumph, no ecstacy of power. He had no wish to celebrate. He nursed in his heart and mind only the chill knife of ambition and the cold emptiness that marked the absence of the one whom he had known as a brother in his heart: Alain, son of Henri, now vanished utterly from mortal lands.

Stronghand no longer dreamed. This lack was a nagging source of bitterness and sorrow.

But dreams were not all of his life. He did not need his dreams. He had thought through his desires with all due calculation. Not even the loss of his heart would divert him from his purpose. After all, ambition and will serve best the one who is heartless.

From his chair, staff in hand, he surveyed the assembly gathered before him: a host of RockChildren spread out on the gently sloping land that descended toward the strand that marked the water's edge. Twenty-two staffs lay at his feet, and the chieftains who had surrendered their staffs to his authority stood at a respectful distance. The warriors of Rikin tribe stood behind them, intermingling with those warriors who had sailed to Rikin with their war leaders. Beached on the strand and anchored farther up and down the fjord lay at least eighty ships, each one manned with no less than fifty warriors. Yet even this large assembly represented only a portion of the army he could call on now.

They were many, and more waited in the fjords that were home to the other tribes. But the humans still had greater numbers in their own country than all of the RockChildren leagued together.

That was what Bloodheart and the old chieftains had always

failed to understand. The humans might be weaker in body, but they had the implacable strength of numbers.

The assembly waited. Distantly, wind sang down from the fjall, where the WiseMothers conferred in the silence that is the privilege of stone. Behind, the SwiftDaughters shifted restlessly. They did not have the patience of their mothers and grandmothers. Not for them the slow measure of eternity. Like their brothers and cousins, they would tread the Earth for no more than forty or so winters before dissolving under the press of time.

Rikin's OldMother stood at the entrance to her hall, witnessing, as was her right and obligation. He felt her respiration on his neck, although she neither spoke nor made any sign.

This was his day. After all, even when she relinquished the knife of authority to the YoungMother and began her slow trek up to the fjall, she would live far longer than any of her children. His great endeavor must seem to her like the sport of young ones, briefly fought and briefly won.

Yet he intended to make of it as much as he could.

Hakonin's chief came forward, last of all, and laid his staff atop the careful pile, last to come because Hakonin's OldMother had been first to understand the scope of Stronghand's ambition and to offer alliance. Then Hakonin's chief, too, stepped back to wait at the fore of the assembly, beside Tenth Son of the Fifth Litter, Stronghand's helmsman and captain, his own litter mate.

Stronghand rose. First, he cut into the haft of each staff the doubled circle that signified his rule. He stained these cuts with ocher to make each incision clearly visible. None spoke as he confirmed his authority in this manner: the staffs of these chieftains would be permanently marked with the sigil of Stronghand's overlordship.

When he had finished, after each chieftain had come forward to receive his staff, he stared out over the fjord. The waters ran cold and still. Nothing broke that calm surface.

Nothing broke the hush cast over the assembly.

Let them wonder at his lack of expression. Let them fear him because he did not howl in triumph, as any of them would have. What need had he for howling and shrieking, yammering and outcry? Let those he struck against cry and wail. Silence was his ally, not his enemy.

While they watched, he walked through their ranks down to the shoreline. From the water's edge, he threw a stone into the water. The stone, like any action, created ripples. What his allies did not know was that he had prearranged this signal.

They burst from the quiet waters all at once, more than he could count. Arching upward, thrust there by the pumping strength of their hindquarters, the merfolk twisted in the air and spun down. Those waiting up by the hall saw only silvery bodies, a brief glimpse of fearsome heads and hair that slithered and twined in the air, then the massive splash as the heavy bodies of the merfolk hit the water. With a resounding slap of their tails, the merfolk vanished. Water churned, stilled, and lay as calm as a mirror again. On that surface he saw the reflection of trees and a single, circling hawk. A thread of smoke streaked the sky: the watchfire set on the bluff that guarded the mouth of Rikin Fjord.

A murmur swept the ranks of the assembly, and died away. They all knew how his last enemy, the powerful Nokvi, had met his end. After losing his hands and his victory, he was thrown into the sea to be devoured by the merfolk. It was not a glorious death.

Stronghand walked back to his chair and hoisted his staff. He had no need to shout: let the wind carry his words as far as it was able and let those in the back strain to hear him.

"Hear my words. Now we will act. Already my ships hunt down those of our kind who refuse to stand with us. Yet none of us can rest while others do this work. We must build and make ready."

Along the high slopes of the valley, scars in the forest cover marked where his human slaves had opened up new land for farming. Not much, truly, but enough to give plots to each one of the slave families that were part of his original slave-holding. He had plans for them as well. War was not the only way to create an empire.

Tenth Son of the Fifth Litter called out the necessary question. "For what do we make ready?"

"Can it be that we will turn our backs on the tree sorcerers of Alba, who thought to make one of our own chieftains into their puppet and slave?" Stronghand let his gaze span the crowd. "They made a fool and a corpse of the one who called himself Nokvi. Are we to let these tree sorcerers believe that we are no better than Nokvi and his followers? Or will we take revenge for the insult?"

They roared out their answer in a thousand voices. He let it die away until silence reigned again. At his back, the steady presence of Rikin's OldMother weighed on his shoulders.

"Go home to your valleys. During this autumn and winter, fit out your ships and forge your weapons. When the winter storms have blown out their fury, we will strike at the island of Alba. In the summer to come, I ask this of you: strike hard and strike often. Hit where you can. Take what you want. One sixth of your plunder deliver to me, and bring me word when you meet the tree sorcerers. I will find them and root them out, and when that time comes, the island of Alba and its riches will belong to our people. This is how it begins."

They hailed him loudly and enthusiastically, with the howls and shouts appropriate to a ready and dangerous host. Best of all, they dispersed swiftly and with an efficiency brought about by anticipation and forethought. Already they moved less like a bestial horde intent on momentary satisfaction and more like thinking beings who could plan, act, and triumph.

He turned, to approach the OldMother, but she had gone back inside her hall. Her door was shut. She had no need to interfere, after all. She had already made her pronouncement on the day she had allowed him to take a name: *"Stronghand will rise or fall by his own efforts."*

He gestured, and Tenth Son came forward. "When our allies have all left the fjord, let the ones assigned as reavers go forth to harry in Moerin's lands. Let them make sure that none of those who once gave allegiance to Nokvi still live. But let a few skiffs patrol the coast, and let some of our brothers, the quiet and wily ones, travel where they can. They must listen. It may even be that some who claim to be our allies now will talk against us. I must know who they are."

"It will be done." Tenth Son beckoned, and certain of his trusted lieutenants hurried forward to carry away Stronghand's chair. "Are there any you trust less than the others?"

Stronghand considered. "Isa. Ardaneka's chief, because he came only when he saw that all the others had allied with me. A Moerin pup will need to be found, to groom as chieftain over what remains of that tribe. But send on this expedition those who can walk with their eyes open." A thought occurred, and he turned it over and around, examining it, before he spoke it out loud. "Let them take slaves with them, ones who are both strong and clever. There may be much that can be discovered from among the slaves of the other tribes."

Of all his people, only Tenth Son had ceased being surprised when Stronghand made use of his slaves in unexpected ways. Tenth Son canted his head to one side, in the way of a dog listening, and looked thoughtful. "It will be done," he agreed. "There is another way to look for the tree sorcerers. News of them must surely come to the merchants who sail from port to port. Although Bloodheart lost the city of Hundse—" What the humans called Gent. "—much treasure still came to our tribe by his efforts. Some of these treasures we could trade, and the ones who trade could listen and seek news in that way."

The words afflicted him as mightily as would the sun's brightness, shorn of cloud cover. He had not expected his brother to think so cleverly. "I must consider what you say."

The SwiftDaughters moved away about their own errands, those things that mattered most: the continuation of the life of the tribe. No wonder that they left him to work alone, unremarked. In their eyes, such enterprises as raiding and plunder, fighting and conquest, were insignificant and trivial. In a thousand winters the rock would remain much as it always had, while his bones, and his efforts, would have long since been ground into dust.

With chieftain's staff in hand, he took the long walk up to the fjall. Long halls gave way to abandoned slave pens, empty except for a few ragged slaves too stupid to leave their confines. Always, as he passed, he would first smell and then see a half dozen or more scraping mindlessly at the dirt or rocking from side to side in the ruins of their old shelters. The decrepit lean-to barracks in which the slaves had once wintered had been torn down and the wood and stone reused to build decent halls. Deacon Ursuline and her people had been industrious in the weeks since he had taken the chieftainship of Rikin.

Fields spread everywhere along the lower slopes, fenced in by low rock walls. The human slaves once owned by his vanquished brothers had been given a measure of freedom under the strict supervision of his own warriors and those of his slaves whom he trusted. Now they toiled to grow crops where crops were suited to the soil and drainage. Higher up, half-grown children shepherded flocks of sheep and goats and the herds of cattle on which the RockChildren depended. Slaves at work in field and pasture noticed him pass, but none were foolish enough to stop working or to stare.

Fields gave way to meadow and meadowlands to a sparse forest of spruce, pine, and birch. As the path banked higher, the forest opened up, shedding the other trees until only birch grew with a scattering of scrub and heather shorn flat by wind. The last of the stunted trees fell away as he emerged onto the high fjall, the land of rock and moss and scouring wind. The wind whipped at his staff, making the bones and iron rods tied to the crosspiece clack alarmingly. His braided hair rustled and twined along one shoulder, as if it retained a memory of the living hair grown by the merfolk.

A rime of frost covered the ground. The youngest WiseMother had made some progress on the trail since he had last come this way. He brought her an offering, as he always did: this day, a dried portion of the afterbirth from a slave. Let it serve as a symbol of life's transience, and his impatience. He did not stay to speak with her, since even a brief exchange might take hours. Instead, he walked on along the trail toward the ring of WiseMothers. At first they appeared like stout pillars but as he closed in, careful to avoid stepping on the snaking lines of silvery sand that marked the trails made by the deadly ice wyrms, the WiseMothers' shapes came into focus. Although they had all but stiffened entirely into stone, the curve of limbs and heads remained apparent, a vestige of their time among the mobile.

The WiseMothers congregated in a circle at the rim of the nesting grounds. Here he paused, checking the stones gathered into his pouch, watching the smooth hollow of sand that lay before him. Only the WiseMothers knew what they were incubating under that expanse of silver sand.

One stone at a time, he made his careful way out to the hummock that bulged up in the center of the hollow. The smooth, rounded dome radiated warmth and smelled faintly of sulfur, but once he was standing on it, he was safe from the ice wyrms that inhabited the glimmering hollow around which the WiseMothers gathered. There, in the solitude afforded him by the perilousness of his surroundings, he contemplated the path he had walked so far, the place he stood now, and the journey that still lay before him.

A stray leaf fluttered over the hollow and came to rest, so lightly, on the sand. A gleaming, translucent claw thrust up from beneath the sands, hooked the leaf, and yanked it under. All was still again. The wind sighed around his body. He heard a distant rockfall as a low rumble, so far away that it might have been a dream. But when he closed his eyes to slide into the resting trance, the same blank emptiness met him, dull and gray.

Alain was still gone, their link shattered.

He was utterly alone.

Night fell. Standing as still as any ancient stone lost under the canopy of stars, he heard the WiseMothers speaking.

Move. South. Press. East. Shift. The. Fire. River's. Flow. Westward. Ten. Lengths.

The. Sea. Waters. Will. Rise.

Listen.

Earth. Cries. For. Earth.

What. Was. Torn. Asunder. Returns.

Make. Room.

His were not the only new ideas. Others among his people were learning to think. The words of Tenth Son rose in his memory: "We could trade. We could seek news in the ports of humankind."

In the old days, before the rise of the warring chieftains in the time of Bloodheart's own sire, the RockChildren had traded with the human tribes and, of course, with the fisherfolk. The wars for supremacy had changed all that. The rich harvest brought by slaving, the ease of plunder, and the joy of raiding had altered the old ways. What need to trade for what you could take for nothing?

Yet every stone thrown into calm water casts ripples. Just as tribes that warred incessantly among themselves could never truly grow strong, no clan which built its power solely on plunder had any hope of long-lasting success. The store of riches Bloodheart had amassed would serve Stronghand, but by themselves these treasures were just objects. They had only what worth others set on them. Of course that was a kind of worth he could exploit. War had its uses, yet it alone could not achieve all things.

He stood in the center of the nesting grounds and listened to the waking "awks" of gulls. The horizon paled toward dawn. Any one life span mattered little in the long unwinding of the world's life, whose span was measured by the conversations of the WiseMothers and not the transitory and quickly forgotten struggles, as brief as those of the mayflies, of mortal creatures. That he thought and planned did not make him any more consequential than the least of Earth's creatures. But maybe it gave him more freedom to act.

A ruler who controls trade controls the passage of goods, controls taxes laid upon those goods, controls who gets what and what goes where. There was more than one way to stretch the hand of rulership over the ruled.

With dawn, the WiseMothers settled into their daylight stupor. One stone at a time, he made his way back across the sands of the nesting grounds. The day, shortening as autumn overtook them, was half gone by the time he reached the safety of solid ground. He retrieved his staff from its hiding place in the crack of a towering rock and started down the path that led off the fjall and into the valley. Passing the youngest WiseMother, he laid a sprig of moss in her rough grasp, and walked on.

An arrow of honking geese passed overhead. A kestrel skimmed a distant rise. Stronghand crossed from fjall to birch forest and down into the denser pine and spruce woodlands. In the distance ax blows rang to a steady rhythm. The chopping ceased, and a man called a warning. The sound of a tree cracking and falling splintered the air. The thud of its impact shuddered along the wind, and that same voice shouted orders.

Curious, he took the side path that led to the upper meadows. In a clearing, his slaves were building their church.

It was rising fast. One among them had devised a cunning way of working with northern trees, many of which were too slender to be split into planks. Log-built, the structure had a squat, ungainly look. A few half-grown slaves, lackwits by the look of them, hung around at the clearing's edge and stared, jabbering in bestial cries. These weak-minded beasts even got in the way of the laborers trimming branches from downed trees or scraping off bark or planing logs with stone adzes and axes.

Deacon Ursuline saw him and hurried over, followed by the male who acted as chieftain among the slaves, although he only called himself Papa Otto. A gull circled above the clearing, no doubt searching for scraps of food. Its "awk" was harsh and nagging, and soon a second gull coasted into view, hanging back along the tree line.

"My lord." Ursuline used terms familiar to humankind, and he accepted them from her. Even though she was only human and therefore very like to the beasts, she was still owed some measure of the authority and respect granted to OldMother. Because she alone of all his slaves was no longer afraid of him, she spoke frankly. "You have treated fairly with us, my lord, as we both know. Although God enjoin that none should be held as slaves, both you and I know that slaves exist both among the Eika and among humankind. Because of that, we who were made captive still live captive to your will. But let me ask you this: Was it your will that some among us were taken away this morning with Rikin war parties?"

"So it was." Although Alain no longer inhabited his dreams, he retained the fluent speech he had learned in that dreaming. "A few of your kind who are strong and clever have been taken to act as spies. They will travel with my own warriors to see if any of my new allies speak with a different voice when I do not stand before them. Those of your kind can speak with the human slaves among the other tribes, for it may be that the slaves—those who have wit—will have heard things that would otherwise remain concealed from us."

"Why should the slaves of other tribes tell the truth?" demanded Papa Otto.

"Surely in this way word will spread," observed Stronghand. "They will have hope of gaining such freedom as you have earned, as long as the Eika remain under my rule."

"There is truth in what you say," said Ursuline. She glanced at Otto, and an unspoken message—unreadable to any creature except another human—passed between them.

"Who are these working here?" Stronghand indicated the

folk who, having paused in their labors to stare when he entered the clearing, had now self-consciously gone back to work.

"Have you any complaints of our labor?" asked Ursuline gently. "Has any task been left undone that you or your captains have requested? Is any animal untended? Are any fields left to the wild? Is there not firewood enough for the winter, and charcoal for the forges?"

"You are bold," said Stronghand, but he admired her for it.

She smiled, as if she knew his thoughts. "You have no complaint, because we have worked harder now that you have fulfilled your share of the bargain laid between you and me."

"Yet I am still troubled by these among you who roam as do the animals and yet provide neither work nor meat. They are only a burden. With the hardships of winter coming on, they must be disposed of."

"How are we to choose among them, my lord?" asked Papa Otto.

"Kill the ones who remain animals. I see them here and there about the valley, no better than pigs roaming in the forest and quite a bit filthier. They are vermin. They are of no possible use to me, nor to you."

"None of them are animals, my lord," retorted Otto. He was a strong chief for the human slaves, but weak because he feared killing. "It is only that they have been treated as animals, and bred and raised as animals by your people. They have forgotten the ways of humankind."

"That makes them useless to us, does it not?"

"Nay, my lord," said Ursuline quickly. She laid a hand on Otto's arm, a gesture which served to stop the words in his mouth. "It may be true that those of the slaves born and raised in the slave pens for many generations without benefit of the church's teaching will never be able to work and speak as we do. But they are still of use to you."

"In what way?"

"They can breed. Their children can be raised by those of us who were not crippled by the slave pens, and those children will serve you as well as any of us do. As long as you treat them as you do us. Perhaps those children will serve you better than we can, for they will only know loyalty and service to you. They will not recall another life, as we do."

Truly, she was a clever person. He knew that she used words to coax and cozen. In his dreams—when he had had dreams—he had seen that lying and cheating ran rife among humankind. A knife is a knife, after all, a tool used for cutting or killing. No need to give it pretty words to pretend that it was something other than what it was. Yet perhaps they could not help themselves. Perhaps, like cattle chewing their cud, they twisted words and flattered and deceived because it was part of their nature.

"What you say may even be true. Yet it seems to me that there are many from the slave pens who will not breed and who can never learn. I have no use for tools that are broken. In two months my men will cull the herds for the winter. At that time any among the slaves who cannot speak true words to me will be culled along with the rest of the animals."

"Two months is not very long," objected Otto. "Even in our own lands a child will not speak for two years or even three, and truly five or six years must pass before any child can speak like to an adult." Otto had fire in him, a passion for life and what humankind called justice. That was what had brought him to Stronghand's attention in the first place. "Surely if we must teach them to speak as we do, as well as to obey the simple commands they already know, we need as much time as it would take to teach a child of our own people to speak."

"I weary of this debate. Now you will listen to what I command." He stretched his claws, letting them ease out of their sheaths, sharp tips grazing the air. "Rikin tribe will not carry useless burdens. We have far to go, and everything we carry must be useful. I will allow no argument on this matter."

He paused, but neither of them replied. Otto's age lay heavily on him. Deep lines scored his face. The harsh winter wind

and bright summer sun had weathered his skin. Even his hair
had turned color, washing brown to white, so that in a way he
seemed to be mimicking the coloring of his Eika masters,
even though Stronghand understood that this happened to be
the way age marked humankind. Deacon Ursuline simply listened, face composed and silent.

"In two months, the herds will be culled. If you cannot or
do not choose among the slaves, then I will. My choice will fall
heavier than yours would, so accept now the responsibility or
give it back to me and abide by my decision."

Ursuline was as persistent as she was patient. "Let me ask
one boon of you, then, my lord."

He was tired of bargaining. He was tired of the sight of
mewling, whimpering, dirty slaves, who were of less use to
him than the scrawniest of his goats and cattle because their
flesh was too sour to eat. He cut off her words with a sharp
gesture. Turning, he lifted a foot to walk away—

*Confined within white walls, it pushes restlessly against its prison,
but it is too weak to do more than nudge up against its prison wall
before the bath of warm liquid in which it floats soothes it back into
lassitude. Awareness flickers dimly. Hunger smolders. Shapes, or
thoughts, spin and twirl in its mind before dissolving. It remembers
ancient fire, and a great burning. Is it not the child of flame, that all
creatures fear? Voices whisper, but it cannot understand the meaning
behind such sounds, and within moments it has forgotten what a
voice is. Memory dies. The waters of forgetfulness rock beneath it. It
sleeps.*

Stronghand's foot hit the ground, jolting him back to himself. He had to blink, because the weak autumn sun seemed so
strong that his eyes could not adjust. Stark terror flooded him,
surging like a tide through his body. In the spawning pools of
every tribe, the nests of the RockChildren ripened. Once he,
too, had been a mindless embryo bathed in the waters of forgetfulness, seeking nothing more than his next meal. In the
nesting pools, those hatchlings lived who devoured their nest
brothers rather than being devoured themselves. Those that

ate matured into men, and those that simply survived instead of being eaten remained dogs.

Yet before Alain freed him from Lavastine's cage, he had been, like his brothers, a slave to the single-minded lust for killing and war and plunder that still afflicted most of his kind. How close had he come to being a dog instead of a thinking man? How close was any creature to unthinking savagery, forgetting what it was?

With effort, he forced the fear back. He had not bathed too long in those waters. He had clawed his way free. Alain had freed him from his cage, and he meant to remain the way he was. He would not let memory sleep, and instinct rule.

Slowly, the world came clear around him and he could see again. He tightened his grip on his staff. Deacon Ursuline and Papa Otto had averted their eyes, careful not to be seen noticing his weakness. But even so, they looked startled, utterly amazed.

Let them not believe he had changed, or faltered.

"This is my decision. It is true that these half-wits are your family just as the dogs who swarm around our halls are my brothers. If you can take care of these half-wits, and if it does not interfere with your labors, then I will not touch them. But I lay the same obligations on you that I did when we agreed to the bargain over your god's house. As long as their presence among you does not interfere with the tasks set for you by your masters, then you may deal with them as you see fit. If I am dissatisfied, then I will act swiftly."

"We cannot ask for more than that," said Deacon Ursuline, quick to seal the bargain.

"No, he agreed, "you cannot."

Before he could make any more rash bargains, he walked away, still shaken. Yet because of his keen hearing, he heard them as they spoke to each other in low voices.

"These slaves served the Eika for many years in such tasks as cleaning out the privies. We ought not to waste the labor of those who are clever on that kind of mindless work when they could be doing other things like tanning or building. Surely we can find a place for each person to do some task, even the ones who act little better than dogs."

Deacon Ursuline did not reply right away. He heard her suck in her breath, as at a blow to the stomach. Where the path knifed into the forest, he paused to listen. Her words drifted to him as faintly as a sigh.

"I served a lord in Saony who was less just than this one."

Papa Otto made no reply.

Silently, Stronghand followed the path into the forest. There was wisdom in what Papa Otto said, of course. By releasing the strong from tasks that could be as easily done by the weak, all would prosper.

He had acted too hastily in this matter of the half-witted slaves. A wise leader gives enough rope to those clever enough to use it well, as he would need to pay out rope to Tenth Son. Do not keep the loyal ones lashed up too tightly; their obedience is bought by trust, not by fear.

His slaves had not failed him yet, even if they thought, now and again, of rebellion and of freedom. He had no need to say more, or to act other than he had just done. They knew what the consequences would be if they failed him, and they knew what would happen to them if his rule over Rikin Fjord ended.

It was in their interest to keep him strong.

2

"IT'S uncanny, it is," said Ingo that night at the campfire in the tone of a man who has said the same thing the day before and expects to repeat himself tomorrow. "Rain behind but never before. At least my feet are dry."

"It's that weather witch," said Folquin impulsively. "She's making it rain on the Quman army and not on us." His comrades shushed him violently, glancing around as though they feared the wind itself might carry their words to the powerful woman about whom he spoke.

Hanna cupped her hands around a mug in a desperate attempt to keep them warm, for although it was dry, the wind out of the northwest stung like ice. "Have a care, Folquin. Prince Bayan's mother has an eye for good-looking young men to be her slave bearers, and she might take a liking to you if you come to her attention."

Ingo, Leo, and Stephen laughed at her jest, but perhaps because Folquin wasn't the kind of young man girls flocked around, her words stung him. "The way Prince Bayan has an eye for you, Eagle?"

"Hush, now, lad," scolded Ingo. "It isn't any fault of Hanna's that the Ungrians think her light hair a sign of good luck."

"No matter," said Hanna quickly as Folquin seemed ready to fall all over himself apologizing for his wretched tongue. "Mind you, Prince Bayan's a good man—"

"And no doubt would be a better one if he could only keep his hands to himself," said Folquin with an appeasing grin.

"If a roving eye is the worst of his faults, then God know, he's better than the rest of us," replied Ingo. "I've no complaints about his leadership in battle. We'd all be heads dangling from Quman belts if it weren't for his steely nerves at the old high mound last month."

"If it had been Prince Sanglant leading us," said taciturn Leo suddenly, "we'd have won, or we'd not have engaged at all, seeing that the odds were against us."

"Ai, God, man!" exclaimed Ingo with the sneer of a soldier who has seen twice as much battle as his opinionated comrade, "who was to know that Margrave Judith would fall dead like that, and her whole line collapse? She had a third of our heavy cavalry. With her Austrans routing we hadn't a chance. Prince Bayan made the best of a bad situation."

"It could have been much worse," agreed Stephen, but since

he was accounted a novice, having survived only one major battle, his opinion was passed over in silence.

The fire popped. Ashy branches settled, gleaming briefly before Leo set another stick on the fire. All around them other campfires sparked and smoked as far as Hanna could see up along the cart track that the army followed as it retreated toward Handelburg. But the sight of so many fires did not make her feel any safer. She sipped at the hot cider, wishing it would warm the chill that constantly ate away at her heart.

Ivar was missing. She'd searched up and down through Bayan's retreating army and not found a trace of him. She hadn't even found anyone who remembered seeing him on the day of the battle except the injured prince, Ekkehard, who was so vexed at having lost his favorite, Baldwin, that he couldn't be bothered to recall where and when he'd last seen Ivar.

"Only God can know the outcome of battles in advance," she said at last, with a sigh. "It's no use worrying over what's already happened."

"Have you any milk to spill?" asked Ingo with a laugh, but he sobered, seeing her grief-stricken expression. "Here, have more cider. You look cold, lass. What's the news from the prince's camp?"

"Princess Sapientia has taken a liking to Lord Wichman, now that he's recovering from his wounds, and you know how Prince Bayan humors her in everything. But that Wichman and his lordly friends——" She hesitated, but she could see by their expressions that her comments would shock no one here. "Truly, I'd as soon run with a pack of wormy dogs. Sometimes I think the princess—well, may God bless her and I'll say no more on that score. But she'd be better served in attending to her poor brother."

"He still can't use his spear arm?" asked Ingo.

"For all I know he'll never regain use of it, for he was sorely wounded. Lord Wichman is insufferable precisely on that account, for he was the one who rescued Prince Ekkehard from the Quman prince who was about to cut him down."

"I tell you truly," said Folquin in a low voice, "and not meaning to speak ill of the princess, may God bless her, but I wonder does she know what Prince Ekkehard does in the evening here in camp?"

"What do you mean?" demanded Hanna.

Folquin hesitated.

"You'd better show her," said Ingo. "There's been some fights about it already, in the ranks, and an army in our position can hardly afford to be fighting among itself."

"Come on," said Folquin reluctantly.

Hanna drained her mug and gave it to Ingo. The four Lions had stationed their campfire where wagons had been lined up in a horseshoe curve to form a barrier between the rear guard and the outlying sentries. The wooden cart walls gave some protection against the winged riders who dogged them persistently as they retreated north just ahead of the most astoundingly bad weather. There always seemed to be a rainstorm following at their heels, and as Hanna followed Folquin she could hear it like a storm front breaking in front of her. Wind and rain agitated the woodland behind them, but no rain ever touched Bayan's army. The dry ground they walked on surely was churned to muck behind them, hindering their pursuers so badly that the main mass of the Quman army had never been able to catch up and finish them off.

Such was the power of Prince Bayan's mother, a formidable sorcerer, princess of the dreaded Kerayit people.

But even with her magic to aid them, they had had a miserable month following their defeat by Bulkezu's army at the ancient tumulus. The Ungrians had a saying: a defeated army is like a dying flower whose falling petals leave a trail. Every dawn, when they moved out, the freshly dug graves of a few more soldiers, dead from wounds suffered at the battle, were left behind to mark their path. Only Prince Bayan's steady leadership had kept them more-or-less in one piece.

But even his leadership had not been enough to save Ivar.

The Lions formed the rear guard together with the stoutest

companies of light cavalry left to Bayan, now under the captaincy of Margrave Judith's second daughter and her admired troop of fighters. Lady Bertha was the only one of Judith's Austran and Olsatian commanders who hadn't lost her troops to rout when the margrave had lost her head on the battlefield. A popular and unquenchable rumor had spread throughout the army that Lady Bertha had so disliked her mother that the margrave's death had emboldened rather than disheartened her. It was to the fringe of her bivouac that Folquin now led Hanna.

Six campfires burned merrily to mark out a circle. In their center sat Lady Bertha and her favorites, drinking what was left of the mead they'd commandeered from a Salavii holding two days before. Usually Hanna could hear them singing all the way up in the vanguard, for they were a hard drinking, tough crew, but tonight they sat quietly, if restlessly, and Lady Bertha bade them be still as she listened to Prince Ekkehard.

"It's the same story he's been telling every night," whispered Folquin. A dozen or more Lions had come to stand here as well, positioned out of the smoke that streamed south-east from the fires. Those nearest turned irritably and told him to be quiet so that they could hear.

Prince Ekkehard was an attractive youth, still caught on that twilight cusp between boy and man. With his right arm up in a sling and his hair blown astray by the cold wind, he made an appealing sight. Most importantly, he had a bard's voice, able to make the most unlikely story sound so believable that you might well begin to swear you'd seen it yourself. He had his audience enraptured as he came to the end of his tale.

"The mound of ashes and coals gleamed like a forge, and truly it was a forge for God's miracles. It opened as a flower does, with the dawn. Out of the ashes the phoenix rose. Nay, truly, for I saw it with my own eyes. The phoenix rose into the dawn. Flowers showered down around us. But their petals vanished as soon as they touched the earth. Isn't that how it is with those who refuse to believe? For them, the trail of flowers is illusory rather than real. But I believe, because I saw the phoenix. I, who was injured, was healed utterly by the miracle. For you see, as the phoenix rose, it gave forth a great trumpeting call even as far as the heavens, and we heard it answered. Then we knew what it was."

"What was it?" demanded Lady Bertha, so intent on his story that she hadn't taken a single draught of mead, although she did have a disconcerting habit of stroking her sword hilt as though it were her lover.

Ekkehard smiled sweetly, and Hanna felt a cold shudder in her heart at the single-minded intensity of his gaze as he surveyed his listeners. "It was the sign of the blessed Daisan, who rose from death to become Life for us all."

Many in his audience murmured nervously.

"Ivar's heresy," Hanna muttered.

"Didn't the skopos excommunicate the entire Arethousan nation and all their vassal states for believing in the Redemption?" demanded Lady Bertha. "My mother, God rest her, had a physician who came from Arethousa. Poor fellow lost his balls as a lad in the emperor's palace in Arethousa, for it's well known they like eunuchs there, and he came close to losing his head here in Wendar for professing the Arethousan heresy. It's a pleasing story you tell, Prince Ekkehard, but I've taken a liking to my head and would prefer to keep it on my own shoulders, not decorating a spike outside the biscop's palace in Handelburg."

"To deny what I saw would be worse than lying," said Ekkehard. "Nor is it only those of us who saw the miracle of the phoenix who have had our eyes opened to the truth. Others have heard and understood the true word, if they have courage enough to stand up and bear witness."

"Are there, truly?" Lady Bertha looked ever more interested as she swept her gaze around her circle of intimates. After a moment, she settled on a young lord, one Dietrich. Hanna recalled well how much trouble he'd caused on the early part of their journey east from Autun last summer, when she'd been sent by the king with two cohorts of Lions and a ragtag assortment of other fighters as reinforcements for Sapientia. But at some point on the journey he had changed his ways, a puzzling change of heart that hadn't seemed quite so startling then as it did at this moment.

Slowly, Lord Dietrich rose. For a hulking fighting man he seemed unaccountably diffident. "I have witnessed God's work on this Earth," he said hesitantly, as though he didn't trust his own tongue. "I'm no bard, to speak fine words about it and make it sound pretty and pleasing. I've heard the teaching. I know it's true in my heart for I saw—" Amazingly, he began to weep tears of ecstatic joy. "I saw God's holy light shining here on Earth. I sinned against the one who became my teacher. I was an empty shell, no better than a rotting corpse. Lust had eaten out my heart so I walked mindlessly from one day to the next. But God's light filled me up again. I was given a last chance to choose in which camp I would muster, whether I would chose God or the Enemy. That was when I discovered the truth of the blessed Daisan's sacrifice and redemption—"

Hanna grabbed Folquin's arm and dragged him away. "I've heard enough. That's a wicked heresy."

The light of many fires gave Folquin's expression a fitful inconstancy. "You don't think it might be true? How else can you explain a phoenix? And the miracle, that all their hurts were healed?"

"I'll admit that something happened to change Lord Dietrich's ways, for I remember how you Lions complained of him on the march east this summer. Is it this kind of talk that people are fighting over?"

"Yes. Some go every night to hear Prince Ekkehard. He'll preach to any person, highborn or low. Others say he's speaking with the Enemy's voice. Do you think so, Eagle?"

"I've seen so many strange things—"

The horn call came, as it did every night. Men cried out the alarm. Ekkehard's audience dissolved as soldiers grabbed their weapons, lying ready at their sides. Out beyond the wagon lines, winged riders broke free of the storm to gallop toward the rear guard, but only a few soggy arrows skittered harmlessly into camp before Lord Dietrich and his contingent of cavalry chased them off with spears and a flight of whistling arrows.

By the time Prince Bayan arrived from the vanguard to investigate, all lay quiet again except for the ever-present wind and the hammer of rain off to the southeast. He rode up with a small contingent of his personal house guard, a dozen Ungrian horsemen whose once-bright clothing was streaked with dirt. Foot soldiers lit their way with torches. Bayan had the knack of remaining relatively clean even in such circumstances as this—in the torchlight Hanna could see the intense blue of his tunic—and the contrast made him all the more striking, a robust, intelligent man still in his prime whom adversity could not tarnish.

"Fewer attacked tonight," said Lady Bertha, handing him an arrow once he had dismounted. "It may be that they've fallen back so far they've given up catching us. Or perhaps they mean us to grow complacent, until they attack in force and take us by surprise."

Prince Bayan turned the arrow over in his hands, studying the sodden fletchings. "Perhaps," he echoed skeptically. "I like not these attacks which are coming each night same time."

Lady Bertha had the stocky build and bandy-legged stance of a person who has spent most of her life on a horse, in armor. She looked older than her twenty or so years, weathered by a hard apprenticeship fighting in the borderlands. "I've sent three scouts back to see if Bulkezu's army still follows us, but none have returned."

Bayan nodded, twisting the ends of his long mustache. "To Handelburg we must go. We need rest, repair, food, wine. With good walls around us, then can we wait for—" He turned to his interpreter, Breschius, a middle-aged cleric who was missing his right hand. "What is this word? More troops to come."

"Reinforcements, my lord prince."

"Yes! Reinforcements." He had trouble pronouncing the word and grinned at his stumbling effort.

Lady Bertha did not smile. She was not in any case a woman who smiled often, if at all. "Unless we can't get word out from Handelburg because Bulkezu has used the cover of this storm to move his army so that he surrounds us."

"Not even Quman army can ride all places at one time," replied Bayan just as he caught sight of Hanna loitering in the crowd which had gathered to observe the commanders. "Snow woman!" His face lit with a bold smile. "Your brightness hides here. So dark it has become by my campfire!"

Hanna felt her face flame with embarrassment, but luckily Bayan was distracted by Brother Breschius, who leaned over to speak to the prince in a low voice.

"Ekkehard?" exclaimed Prince Bayan, looking startled.

Hanna glanced over at the ring of campfires, but Prince Ekkehard had vanished. She grabbed Folquin's sleeve and slipped away, eager to be out of Prince Bayan's sight. She had sustained Sapientia's anger more than once and didn't care to suffer it again as long as she had any choice in the matter.

By asking permission of Sapientia to continue searching out news of Ivar, she kept a low profile in the last days of the march until they came to the frontier fortress and town of Handelburg. From the eastern slopes, as they rode down into the valley of the Vitadi River, she could see the walled town, situated on three islands linked by bridges across the channels of the river. West lay the march of the Villams, which stretched all the way to the Oder River. To the east beyond sparsely inhabited borderlands spread the loose confederation of half-civilized tribes known as the kingdom of the Polenie.

The biscop's flag flew from the high tower to show that she had remained in residence in her city despite the danger from

Quman attack. All the gates stood closed, and the few hovels resting along the banks of the river, homes for fisherfolk and poor laborers, sat empty, stripped of every furnishing. Even crude furniture could be used for firewood in a besieged city. Fields had been harvested and the riverbanks stripped of fodder or bedding: reeds, straw, grass, all shorn in preparation for a Quman attack. In a way, the countryside surrounding Handelburg looked as though a swarm of locusts had descended, eaten their fill, and flown on, leaving not even the bones.

A messenger came from the vanguard: the Eagle, representing the king's ear, must ride in the front. With trepidation, Hanna left her good companions among the Lions and rode forward to take her place, as circumspectly as possible, beside Brother Breschius.

"Stay near me," he said in a low voice. "I'll do my best to keep you out of their way."

"I thank you, friend."

The gates were opened and they advanced into the city. The townsfolk greeted Bayan and Sapientia and their ragged army with cheers, but Hanna noted that the streets weren't crowded despite this welcome. She wondered how many had already fled west into the march of the Villams.

Biscop Alberada met them on the steps of the episcopal palace, dressed in the full splendor of her office and wearing at her throat the gold torque that signaled her royal ancestry. A number of noble ladies and lords attended her, including one dashing man who wore the peaked cap common to the Polenie. The biscop waited until Princess Sapientia dismounted, then descended the steps to greet her and Prince Ekkehard. With such precisely measured greetings did the nobles mark out their status and territory. Had it been King Henry riding into Handelburg, the biscop would have met him on the road outside of town. Had it been Margrave Villam, come to pay his respects, Alberada would have remained inside so that he had to come in to her.

Sapientia and Ekkehard kissed her hand, as befit her holy station, and she kissed their cheeks, the mark of kinship between them. It was not easy to see the resemblance. Alberada was older than Henry, fading into the winter of her life. In the year since she had presided over Sapientia's and Bayan's wedding, she had aged noticeably. Her hair had gone stark white. Her shoulders bowed under the weight of her episcopal robes.

She turned from her niece and nephew to greet Bayan and acknowledge the other nobles, those worthy of her immediate notice. Hanna could not tell whether she meant to greet Bayan's mother, hidden away in her wagon, or ignore her, but in any case by some silent communication the wagon was drawn away toward the guest wing.

If Biscop Alberada noticed this slight, she gave no sign. "Come, let us get out of the cold. I wish I had better news to greet you with, but troubles assail us on every side."

"What news?" asked Sapientia eagerly. The long march had made the princess more handsome; what she lacked in wisdom she made up for in enthusiasm and a certain shining light in her face when her interest was engaged.

"Quman armies have attacked the Polenie cities of Mirnik and Girdst. Girdst is burned to the ground. Both the royal fortress and the new church are destroyed."

"This is sore news!" exclaimed Lady Bertha, who stood to Sapientia's left.

"Yet there is worse." It began to rain, a misting drizzle made colder by the cutting wind. "The Polenie king is dead, his wife, Queen Sfildi, is a prisoner of the Quman, and his brother Prince Woloklas has made peace with the Quman to save his own life and lands. This we heard from Duke Boleslas—" She indicated the nobleman standing on the steps above. "—who has taken refuge with his family in my palace."

"Who rule the Polenie folk, if their king is dead?" asked Bayan.

Evidently Duke Boleslas could not speak Wendish well

enough to answer easily, because Alberada replied. "King Sfiatslev's only surviving child, a daughter, has fled east into the lands of the pagan Starviki to seek aid. Shall I go on?"

Bayan laughed. "Only if I have wine to drink to make the news go down easier. Of wine there is none this past month."

"Let us move into the hall!" exclaimed the biscop, looking more shocked by this revelation than by the Polenie defeat. Or perhaps she just wanted to get out of the rain, which began to come down in sheets. Her servants hurried away to finish their preparations. "Of course there is wine."

"Then I fear not to hear your news. The war is not lost if there is wine still to drink."

Biscop Alberada had laid in a feast worthy of her status as a royal bastard. Because of her kinship with the Polenie royal family, she had been allowed to found the biscopry of Handelburg thirty years ago when only a very young woman newly come to the church. One of King Sfiatslev's aunts had been taken prisoner during the wars between Wendar and the Polenie fifty years ago, and this young noblewoman had been given to the adolescent Arnulf the Younger as his first concubine, a royal mistress to assuage his youthful lusts while he waited for his betrothed, Berengaria of Varre, to reach marriageable age. In the thirty years Alberada had overseen the growing fortress town of Handelburg, the noble families of the Polenie had all been thoroughly converted to the Daisanite faith in a right and proper manner.

The biscop reminded them of her successful efforts at conversion as wine was poured and the first course brought. "That is why I fear for Sfiatslev's daughter, Princess Rinka, for the Starviki have been stubborn in holding to their pagan ways. What if they induce her to marry one of their princelings? She might become apostate, or even worse, fall into the error of the Arethousans, for the Starviki are known to trade furs and slaves to the Arethousans in exchange for gold nomias. What news of your father, Sapientia? I trust we expect him in the east soon, for truly we have need of his presence here."

Sapientia glanced toward Hanna, standing back among the servitors. "This Eagle brought the most recent news," she said in a tone which suggested that whatever bad news she had to impart was Hanna's fault. "King Henry means to ride south to Aosta. He sent a paltry contingent of two hundreds of Lions and not more than fifty horsemen even though I pleaded with him that our situation was desperate."

"He seeks the emperor's crown," said Alberada.

"I wonder what use the emperor's crown if the east burns," mused Bayan.

"These are troubled times in more ways than one." Alberada gestured to her steward, who refilled all the cups at the table. "An emperor's crown may bring stability and right order to a realm afflicted by the whisperings of the Enemy. These Quman raids are God's judgment on us for our sinfulness. Daily my clerics bring me more stories of the pit of corruption into which we have fallen——"

After so many days on sparse rations, Hanna was glad enough to be obliged to serve, since it meant she could eat the leavings off the platters. A stew of eels was followed by roasted swan, several sides of beef, and a spicy venison sausage. Despite the biscop's forbidding disquisition on sinfulness, the nobles ate with gusto, and certainly there was enough to spare both for the servants and for the dogs.

Prince Bayan had cleverly turned the topic of conversation to what interested him most: the war. "We must hold here the whole winter."

"Surely winter will put a stop to the Quman raids." Freed from her armor and heavy traveling cloak, Sapientia looked much smaller. She hadn't her father's height or breadth of shoulder, but months riding to war had given her a certain heft that she had lacked before her marriage.

Bayan laughed. "Does my lion queen tire of war?"

"Certainly not!" Sapientia had a habit of preening when Bayan paid lush attention to her. She could never get enough of his praise, and the prince had a knack for knowing when to flatter his wife. "But no one ever fights during the winter."

"Nay, Your Highness," said Breschius as smoothly as if he and Bayan had rehearsed the exchange, "the Quman are famous for attacking during winter, when ice dries out the roads and makes streams into paths. Snow doesn't stop them. Nothing stops them but flowing water. Even then, they have captive engineers in their army who can build bridges for them and show them how to make use of fords and ferries."

"I have prepared for a siege," said Alberada. "Although, truly," she added disapprovingly, "sieges come in many guises." Farther down the table, Lord Wichman was drinking heavily with his cronies. He had been seated beside Lord Dietrich, but despite baiting him with crude jokes and cruder suggestions, Wichman could not get Dietrich either to join him or to lose his temper. Having lost this skirmish, he had turned to harassing any servingwomen who ventured within arm's reach. "If your army winters here, Prince Bayan, then I must have some assurance that they will not disrupt the lives of my townsfolk and servants."

"It's my army, too!" said Sapientia. "I do not tolerate insolence or troublemakers."

"Of course not, niece," replied Alberada with such a soothingly calm expression that Hanna knew she would continue to talk around Sapientia because she, like everyone else, knew who really commanded this army. "I expect you to see that your Wendish forces behave themselves, just as I expect Prince Bayan to keep proper order among his Ungrian countrymen."

Bayan laughed. "My Ungrian brothers do not cause trouble, for otherwise they are to have their swords cut off, at my order."

"I do not approve of such barbarity," said Alberada primly, "but I hope your soldiers keep the peace rather than breaking it."

The stewards brought round a savory condiment of boiled pears mixed with hog's fennel, galingale, and licorice, as an aid to digestion for the noble folk who were by now surely stuffed and surfeited. Yet the feast dragged on well into the autumn night. A Polenie bard from Duke Boleslas' retinue sang, and he had such an expressive voice and so much drama in his gestures that the hall sat rapt, listening, although he sang in an unintelligible language. Hanna's eyes stung from the smoke in the hall. She had been so long marching out-of-doors that she'd forgotten how close air got within walls, even in a great hall as capacious as the one in the biscop's palace.

Despite the biscop's rank and wealth, her palace hadn't the ornamentation common to the older palaces in Wendar proper. This hall had only been finished ten years ago and had about it still an unfinished look, as if its wood hadn't yet been worn down by the use of many hands and feet, the polish of age. The pillars in the hall stared glumly at her, carved in the likeness of dour saints who no doubt disapproved of the gluttony and singing, men stamping their feet as they shouted out a chorus, dogs scrabbling under the tables for scraps, servingwomen deftly pouring out wine while at the same time dodging teasing fingers. In truth, Bayan's Ungrian lords did behave better than their Wendish counterparts; maybe Bayan's jesting threat had not been a jest.

Late, the nobly born went to their resting places while servants like Hanna scrambled for what comfortable pallets they could find. In a hall this large there were plenty of sleeping platforms built in under the eaves, and when Sapientia made no move to call Hanna to attend her to the chamber in which she slept more privately, Hanna found herself a snug place among a crowd of servingwomen. They lay close together, a warm nest of half-naked women covered by furs, and gossiped in the darkness.

"The Ungrians do smell. I told you."

"Not any more than do the Wendish soldiers. Ai, God, did you see how poor Doda had to dodge that Lord Wichman's hands all evening? He's a beast."

"He's son of a duchess, so I'm sure he'll have what he

wants." Nervous giggles followed this pronouncement. A woman shifted. Another sighed.

"Not in the biscop's palace, friend," replied a new voice. "Biscop Alberada's stern but fair, and you'll find no such wild behavior in this hall. Now I'll thank you to hush so that I can sleep!"

But they didn't all hush. Hanna drifted asleep, lulled by their whispering and the strange way they hissed their "p"s and "t"s, just as the folk had in that lonely village east of Machteburg where a Quman scouting party had attacked them. Where she'd seen Ivar again, seen how he'd changed so much from the impulsive, good-natured youth she'd grown up with. He had seen the miracle of the phoenix. Was it actually possible the story was true? Had God worked a miracle of healing and given Ivar and his companions, and Prince Ekkehard, a vision of truth?

She twisted the heavy emerald ring that King Henry had given her. Here, curled up beside the other women, she felt warm and safe in body at least, but her heart remained restless. She knew her duty. First and foremost she was Henry's servant, his messenger, his Eagle, sworn to his service and to uphold whichever church doctrine he recognized, not to question the authority of those he acknowledged as the rightful leaders of the church. Yet what of her grandmother's gods? Hadn't they treated their followers fairly and granted them good harvests, or sometimes turned their faces away to bring bad times? What of the many other people who lived outside the Circle of Light? Were they all damned to fall endlessly in the Abyss because they held to a different faith? How would Brother Breschius, who had survived the wrath of a Kerayit queen, reply to such questions?

She fell away into sleep, and she dreamed.

There comes into the hall as silent as the plague one of the slave men kept by Bayan's mother. His skin is so black that she can hardly see him in the smothering darkness of the hall, now illuminated only by the glowing coals of two banked hearth fires which are watched over

*by dozing servant girls. Yet he can see her where she lies half hidden
among the other women. He beckons. She dares not refuse such a summons, just as she would never defy the will of the king. She recognizes
power when she sees it.*

*She rises, slips her wool tunic over her shift, and pads barefooted
after the slave man. He walks the paneled corridors of the biscop's
palace without a torch, yet manages not to lose his way. The rough
plank floors scrape her soles, and once she picks up a splinter and has
to pause, wincing, catching a gasp in her throat so that she won't wake
the soldiers who sleep in ranks on either side of the broad corridor.*

*The slave bends to take her foot in his warm hands while she bal-
ances herself on his shoulder, all the while aware of the taut strength
of his body and the steady breathing of the sleeping soldiers around
them. He probes, grips, and slips the splinter out. She would thank
him, but she dares not speak out loud, and probably he does not understand her language anyway. They walk on in a silence that hangs as
heavily as fog.*

*At last he opens a door and leads her into a chamber swathed in
silk hangings, so many that she has to push her way through them
until she comes free of their soft luxury and finds herself in the center
of the room. It is cold here. No fire burns on the empty hearth.*

*The wasp sting burns in her heart as she faces the veiled figure that
is Prince Bayan's ancient mother. The old woman's voice rasps with
age and, perhaps, exhaustion brought on by weeks of weaving weather
magic. "Where are you going?"*

*Hanna thinks probably she doesn't mean anything so simple, that
no common answer will do: "to the privies," "west to the king," "back
to my home."*

*"I don't know," she answers truthfully. Cold bites at her hands,
making them ache, and her foot hurts where the splinter pierced her skin.*

*"No woman can serve two queens, just as no man can serve two
masters," remarks the ancient woman. One of her raddled old hand-
maidens hurries forward out of the shadows, bearing a tray. A single
ceramic cup, so finely crafted that its lip looks as thin as a leaf, rests
on the enameled tray. Steam rises delicately from its mouth. "Drink,"
speaks the cricket voice.*

The spicy scent stings Hanna's lips and burns her throat. As she drains the liquid, tilting her head back, she sees a scene engraved onto the bottom of the cup's bowl: a centaur woman suckling a human baby at her breast.

"In the end," continues Bayan's mother, "you will have to choose."

Cautiously, Hanna lowers the cup. Bayan's mother sits sedately in a chair, her gnarled and wrinkled hands, age-spotted yet somehow still supple, resting in her lap. The veil conceals her face. The handmaiden waits patiently, like a statue, holding out the tray. Hanna sees no sign of the slave man who escorted her here. They are alone, the three of them, except for a green-and-gold bird perched in a cage that eyes Hanna warily as she sets the empty cup down on the tray. It lifts one foot, replaces it, then lifts the other in a stately if slightly anxious dance, waiting for her answer.

The handmaiden retreats behind the silk curtains, which rustle, sway, and fall silent. The only light in the chamber comes from a lamp. Shadows ride the walls, shifting as though they have caught the movements of unseen spirits.

"I have nothing to choose between," says Hanna, feeling a little dazed. "I am King Henry's Eagle."

"And Sorgatani's luck."

The words seem ill-omened. Hanna shudders. "Sorgatani lived years ago. She's dead." She chafes her hands nervously, remembering that Brother Breschius lost a hand when the Kerayit princess he loved and served as her slave died all those years ago.

"Souls never die," chides the old woman. "I had a cousin twice removed who is dead now, it is true. That may be the woman you think you speak of, the one who took the Wendish priest as her pura. But a name is like a veil, to be cast off or put on. It can be used again. You are Sorgatani's luck, for so is my niece called. In the end, you will have to choose."

The curtains stir as though in a wind. In those shimmering depths she thinks maybe she can see all the way to the land where the Kerayits roam and live among grass so tall that a man on horseback can't see over it. Here, in her dreams, she has seen griffins. Here, in a distance made hazy by a morning fog rising up from damp ground, she sees the

encampment of the Bwrmen, the dreaded centaur folk. Pale tents shift
in the wind, felt walls belling out, and sagging in, as though they are
themselves living creatures. She smells the tang of molten metal on the
wind. An eagle drifts lazily above the camp, then plummets down, out
of sight. A young woman wanders at the edge of that camp, dressed in
a gown so golden that it might have been torn and shaped out of sun-
light.

Across the distance, Sorgatani speaks, "Come to me, luck. You are
in danger."

Maybe Hanna could step through the silk curtains and find herself
in a far land, in the wilderness, in the hazy morning. But she does not
move. She speaks.

"I haven't found your pura *yet. I have no handsome man to bring*
you."

The sun glints over the mist, riding higher, and its bright light
flashes in Hanna's eyes.

"Liath," she cries, thinking impossibly that she sees Liath above in
the iridescent air, a lustrous play of colors glistening like silk as she
pushes through the curtains, trying to reach Liath, only to find the
slave man standing silently beside an open door. He gestures toward the
door and the corridor filled with sleeping soldiers. With a foreboding
in her heart, as though she had turned a deaf ear to a summons she
ought to have heeded, she follows him back to the hall—

Hanna woke abruptly as a hand groped over her, fondling
her roughly. She smelled the stink of sour breath on her cheek
and felt a man's weight lowering over her. She kicked, hard
and accurately. With an angry oath the shadowed form that
had been molesting her staggered back and slammed into
another figure who had also come calling to the sleeping platform. Women shrieked and cursed. The furs writhed as all at
once every woman came awake. One woman, at the edge of the
platform, choked out gasping cries as she struggled with a
brawny man who had gotten on top of her.

Stewards and servants appeared, some carrying torches, and
a scuffle started. Half a dozen men went down before Prince

Bayan came roaring in, furious at being rousted from his bed. Half a dozen Ungrian soldiers, the men who guarded him night and day, waded into the fray with gleeful curses. By the time the biscop arrived, flanked by stewards carrying handsome ceramic lamps, the battle lines had been drawn: the servingwomen huddled in the pallet, all chattering accusations so loudly that Hanna thought she would go deaf, the steward and servants off to one side, licking their wounds, and Lord Wichman and his pack of wormy dogs—a dozen scarred, cocky, brash young noblemen—standing defiantly by the smoldering hearth.

"Why am I disturbed?" Alberada held a lamp formed into the shape of a griffin. Flame licked from its tongue. At this moment, dignified and enraged, she did not look like a woman Hanna would care to fool with. "Have you the gall, Wichman, to rape my servingwomen in my own hall? Is this how you repay me for my hospitality?"

"I haven't had a woman for days! These women were willing enough." Wichman gestured toward the sleeping platform casually, and for an instant one of his companions looked ready to leap back in. "We can't all be satisfied with sheep, like Eddo is." His comrades snickered. "Anyway, they're only common born. I wouldn't touch your clerics." This set off another round of snickering.

"You are still drunk, and as sensible as beasts." Alberada's stinging rebuke fell on insensible ears. One of Wichman's companions was actually fondling his own crotch, quite overtaken by lust. The sight of his pumping hands made Hanna want to throw up. Meanwhile, various armed servants had hurried up behind the biscop. "Take them to the tower. They'll bide there this night, for I won't allow them to disturb the peace in my hall. In the morning, they will leave to return to Duchess Rotrudis. No doubt your mother will be more merciful than I, Wichman."

At that moment, Hanna realized that Bayan had spotted her among the other women. He looked in that instant ready to leap in himself. He laughed, as at a joke only he understood, and began twisting the ends of his long mustache thoughtfully. He beckoned to Brother Breschius and spoke to him in a low voice.

"I pray you, Your Grace," said Breschius. "Prince Bayan suggests that you punish Lord Wichman as you wish, *after* the war is over."

Alberada's glare was frosty. "In the meantime, how does Prince Bayan suggest I protect my servants from rape and molestation?"

Bayan regarded her quizzically. "Whores live in all city. These I will pay for of my own wealth."

"Repay sin by breeding more sin?"

He shrugged. "To fight Quman, I need soldiers."

"To fight Quman," began Wichman, enjoying himself in the drunken way of young men who think only of themselves, "*I* need—"

"You are young and stupid," snapped Bayan, abruptly shoved to the end of his patience. "But you fight good. So in this season I need you. Otherwise I throw you out to the wolves."

Wichman had a high-pitched, grating laugh. "If you need me so much, my lord prince," he drawled, "then I'll set my own price and expect it to be paid tenfold." He gestured obscenely toward the watching servingwomen.

Bayan moved swiftly for a man just risen from his bed. He grabbed Wichman by his shift and held him hard. Wichman was a little taller, and certainly half Bayan's age, but the Ungrian prince had righteous anger and true authority on his side; he'd commanded entire armies in the field and survived countless battles. It took a tough soldier to live as long as he had, and he knew it. So did Wichman.

"Never challenge me, boy," Bayan said softly. "I rid myself of dogs when they piss on my feet. I know where to find the slave market, who always wants young men. *I* do not fear the anger of your mother."

Wichman turned a rather interesting shade, something like

spoiled bread dough. Any man might have said those words in a boasting way, but when Bayan said them, they burned.

"To the barracks." Bayan released his grip on Wichman. Ungrian guards surrounded Wichman and his cronies.

"I cannot approve," said Alberada. "These men should be punished, and banished."

"I need them," said Bayan. "And so do you and this your city."

"It is in this way that war breeds evil, Prince Bayan, because both good and bad alike profit in evil ways and sow evil seeds and lapse into evil deeds, driven by desperation or what they call necessity."

"To your words I have no answer, Your Holiness. I am only a man, not one of the saints."

"It is quite obvious that none of us are saints," answered Alberada reprovingly. "Were we all saints, there would be no war except against the heathens and the heretics."

"Yet surely war is not the cause of our sins, Your Grace," interposed Breschius. "I would argue that Wichman's evil was brought about not by war but by his own reckless and unrestrained nature. Not every man would behave so. Most of the soldiers come here today did not."

"I'm not the only one sinning," protested Wichman suddenly. He sounded as indignant as if he'd been accused of a crime he hadn't committed. "Why don't you see what my little cousin Ekkehard does at night now that he's lost his favorite catamite?"

Bayan gave a sharp whistle of anger.

Ai, God, Bayan had known all along. Why had Hanna thought that a commander as observant as Bayan hadn't known the whole time what was going on in the ranks of his army? He'd just chosen to overlook it, in the same way he choose to overlook Wichman's assault. All he cared about was defeating the Quman.

Given their current situation, Hanna had to admire his pragmatism.

"What do you mean, Wichman?" Biscop Alberada had a way of tilting her head to one side that made her resemble, however briefly, a vulture considering whether to begin with the soft abdomen, or the gaping throat, of the delectable corpse laid out before it. "What sin has young Ekkehard polluted himself with?"

"Heresy," said Wichman.

3

LIATH walked as if into the interior of a pearl. The glow of the Moon's essence drowned her vision, a milky substance as light as air but so opaque that when she stretched out her hand she could barely see the blue lapis lazuli ring—her guiding light—that Alain had given her so long ago. Her ears served her better. She heard a susurration of movement half glimpsed in the pearlescent aether that engulfed her. The ground, although surely she did not walk on anything resembling earth, seemed firm enough, a sloping path like to a silver ribbon that led her spiraling ever upward.

She had not known what to expect, but truly this nacreous light, this sea of emptiness, seemed—well—disappointing. Shimmers undulated across the distance like insubstantial veils fluttering in an unfelt breeze. Had she crossed the gate only to step right inside the Moon itself?

A shape flitted in front of her, close enough that its passage stirred her hair about her face, strands tickling her mouth. It vanished into the aether. An instant or an eternity later, a second shape, and then a third, flashed past. Suddenly hosts of them, their hazy forms as fluid as water, darted and glided before her like minnows.

They were dancing.

She recognized then what they were: cousins to Jerna, more lustrous, less pale; some among the daimones imprisoned by

Anne at Verna to act as her servants surely had come from the Moon's sphere.

They were so beautiful.

Entranced, delighted, she paused to watch them. Beat and measure throbbed through the aether. Was this the music of the spheres? Swiftly ran the bright tones of Erekes and the lush melody of Somorhas. The Sun's grandeur rang like horns, echoed by the soft harp strings that marked the Moon's busy passage of waxing and waning. Jedu's course struck a bold martial rhythm. Mok gave voice to a stately tune, unhurried and grave, and wise Aturna sounded as a mellow bass rumble underlying the rest.

They turned and they shifted, they rose and descended, spun and fell still. Their movements themselves had beauty just as any thing wrought by a master artisan is a joy to behold.

She could dance, too. They welcomed her into the infinite motion of the universe; if she joined them, the secret language of the stars would unfold before her. In such simplicity did the cosmos manifest itself, a dance echoing the greater dance that, hidden beyond mortal awareness, turned the wheel of the stars, and of fate, and of the impenetrable mystery of existence.

She need only step off the path. Easier to dance, to lose oneself in the universe's cloudy heart.

"Liath!" Hanna's voice jolted her back to herself. Was it an echo, or only her imagination?

She stood poised on the brink of the abyss. One more step, and she would plunge off the path into the aether. Staggering, she stumbled back, almost toppling off the other side, and caught her balance at last, quite out of breath.

The dance went on regardless. In the splendid expanse of the heavens, she was of no account. Her own yearning might bring her to ruin, but nothing would stop her whichever choice she made.

That was the lesson of the rose, which needs tending to reach its full beauty. Its thorns are the thorns of thoughtless

longing, that bite the one who tries to pluck it without looking carefully at what she is doing.

She had come so close to falling.

With a bitter chuckle, she climbed on. At last the path
parted before her, the silver ribbon cutting out to either side
along a pale iron wall that betrayed neither top nor bottom. A
scar cut the wall, a ragged tear through which she saw a featureless plain. Was this the Gate of the Sword, which heralded
the sphere of Erekes, the swift sailing planet once known as the
messenger of the old pagan gods?

As if her thought took wing and brought form boiling up
out of the aether, a figure appeared, a guardian as white as
bleached bone. It did not, precisely, have mouth or eyes but
rather the suggestion of a living face. The delicate structure of
its unfurled wings flared as vividly as if a spider had woven the
threads that bound bone to skin. It barred her path with a
sword so bright it seemed actually to cut the aether with a
hiss.

Its voice rang like iron. "To what place do you seek
entrance?"

"I mean to cross into the sphere of Erekes."

"Who are you, to demand entrance?"

"I have been called Bright One, and Child of Flame."

That fast, as though in answer to her words, it thrust,
attacking her, and she leaped back. Instinctively, she reached
for Lucian's friend, the sword she had borne for so long.
Drawing it, she parried, and where the good, heavy iron of
Lucian's friend met the guardian's bright sword, sparks spit
furiously. It struck again, and she blocked, jumped back,
checked her position on the path, and made a bid to cut past it.

Yet where it had not stood an instant before, it stood now,
sword raised. "You have too much mortal substance to cross
the gate," it cried triumphantly, its voice like the crack of the
blacksmith's hammer on iron.

The breath of hot wind off Erekes' dark plain weighed her
down. She was too heavy to cross.

But she would not be defeated. She would not fall, nor would she turn back now.

"Take this sword, then, if you must have something," she cried, and flung the sword at it.

The iron pierced it. The creature dissolved in a thousand glittering fragments of luminous iron. Unexpectedly, a strong wind caught her, and she tumbled headlong over the threshold into the pitch-black realm of Erekes.

4

THE trial commenced two days later, much to Bayan's evident disgust. Surprisingly, Sapientia refused to hinder her aunt's inquiry, and while Biscop Alberada had shown herself willing, if reluctant, to look the other way when it came to sins of the flesh, she stood firm on matters of heresy.

It continued to rain steadily, making life in the palace environs wet and miserable. The stench of smoke from all the hearth fires became almost unbearable, and a grippe, an aching snot-ridden cold that left its victims wretched, raced through the army crowded into the palace compound and outlying barracks.

So there was a great deal of coughing and snorting and sniffling among the audience when the biscop's council met in the great hall. Alberada presided from the biscop's chair, flanked by Bayan and Sapientia to her left and a dozen scribbling clerics seated at a table to her right. Heresy was such a grave charge that Alberada's clerics wrote down a record of the trial as well as of her judgment, to be delivered to the skopos so that Mother Clementia might remain aware of the corruption that had infiltrated her earthly flock.

Normally Alberada would have called for at least two other biscops to be present, to lend full authority to the proceedings. Given the season and the desperate situation, with Quman patrols sighted daily from the city walls, she contented herself with the local abbot and abbess from their respective establishments ensconced within the safety of Handelburg's walls. They were complaisant, unworldly folk, unlikely to challenge the biscop no matter what she said.

As the King's Eagle, Hanna had to stand in attendance on the entire dreary proceeding so that she could report in detail to the king about the sins of his son and the righteous inquiry made by the biscop, Henry's elder and bastard half sister.

Ekkehard was given a chair facing his accusers. The rest of the accused heretics had to stand behind him, according to their rank, while witnesses were brought forward and, after several tedious hours of testimony, Alberada laid out her judgment:

A prince of the realm had used his rank and influence to infect hapless innocents with the plague of heresy. And while some of his victims, faced with the wrath of a royal biscop, recanted quickly, others remained stubbornly loyal to his impious teachings.

Ekkehard sat through it all swollen with the most magnificent indignation that a youth not yet sixteen years of age could muster out of his own terror, uncertainty, and fanatic resolve. Perhaps he was too young and self-important to be truly afraid. Six of his intimate companions had survived the battle at the ancient tumulus. Biscop Alberada showed her respect for the loyalty necessary between a noble and his retinue by making no attempt to force them to repudiate their lord. For them to abandon him, as it were, in the heat of battle would have been a worse offense even than their spiritual error. Let them be punished along with him. That was fitting.

The intransigence of Lord Dietrich, his retainers, and about twenty assorted folk of various stations and purpose troubled her more.

"What minion of the Enemy has fastened its claws inside you?" she demanded after Lord Dietrich refused for the third time to disavow the doctrine of the sacrifice and redemption. "The Mother and Father of Life, who are God in Unity, brought forth the universe. Into this creation they placed the four pure elements, light, wind, fire, and water. Above creation rests the Chamber of Light, and below lies the Enemy, which we also call darkness. Yet as the elements drifted in harmony, they came into contact with the darkness, which had risen out of the depths. Together, they mingled. The universe cried out in distress at this pollution, and God therefore sent the Word of Thought, which we also call Logos, to be its salvation. God made this world through the Word of Thought, yet there remains darkness in it. That is why there is evil and confusion in the world."

"The blessed Daisan redeemed us," said Ekkehard stubbornly, interrupting her. Lord Dietrich had the sense to remain silent.

"Of course he did! The blessed Daisan brought the Word of Thought to us all. He prayed for seven days and seven nights seeking redemption for all who would follow the faith of the Unities and be brought into the Light. And at the end of that time, angels conveyed him to heaven in a light so blinding that St. Thecla herself, who witnessed his Ekstasis, could not see for seven times seven days afterward."

"He was sacrificed! He was flayed by the order of the Empress Thaissania, but his blood became roses, and he lived again! *He rose from the dead.*"

"Silence!" Alberada struck the floor with the butt of her crosier. The sharp knock silenced him as well as all those whispering excitedly in the hall at his outspoken words. Even the cleric whispering a translation into Duke Boleslas' ear clamped his mouth shut. "You are guilty of heresy, Prince Ekkehard. The penalty for heresy is excommunication and exile, or death."

"I am willing to die," said Lord Dietrich calmly, not without triumph. He coughed, and blew his nose into a handful of straw.

"You can't punish me," exclaimed Ekkehard manfully. "I'm the king's son, born out of legitimate marriage!"

"I am the church, here in Handelburg," replied Alberada, ignoring the reference to her own illegitimate birth. "I do not punish you, Prince Ekkehard. It is the church which punishes you and all those who follow your heretical teachings. But it is true that you represent a special case. You will have to be sent to the king's court."

"To my father?" Ekkehard abruptly looked much younger, a boy caught in mischief who has just realized he'll get in trouble for it.

Bayan let out an explosive grunt of anger. "How many soldiers must I send in escort to him? How fewer many then will stand on the walls, when Quman attack us?"

"Can't you just put Ekkehard in the monastery until the Quman are defeated?" Sapientia placed a hand on Bayan's arm as though to soothe the savage beast. "He's abbot of St. Perpetua's in Gent, after all."

"And expose the holy monks to this plague of heresy? Bad enough that I receive reports every week of this pollution spreading in the countryside! Nay, he must go to the king, or remain here in prison, without recourse to the sacraments, until the Quman are defeated and he can travel safely and with a large escort. A guard will be placed in the tower to assure that he does not communicate with any sympathizers—"

"Ach!" Bayan threw up his hands in exasperation. With a foul glare at a dog which had draped itself over his feet, he kicked it free, grabbed his cup, and downed a full goblet of wine. A servant hurried to refill it. "I need guards to walls, to sentry. To fight the Quman. Not to sit on our own country-folk."

"You do not appreciate the gravity of our situation, Prince Bayan, which I fear I must attribute to some deficiency in your understanding as a recent convert. I cannot allow the Enemy to triumph. I cannot allow the Arethousan pollution to defile the kingdom and the holy church. I cannot turn aside and look the other way when Prince Ekkehard's errors threaten us all."

"To my thinking," said Bayan, "it is the Quman who threaten us all."

"Better we be dead than heretics!"

Bayan twisted the ends of his mustaches irritably, but he did not reply. As at the ancient tumulus, he recognized the point where one chose a strategic retreat over wholesale disaster.

"I choose death," said Lord Dietrich. "Let my martyrdom prove who speaks the truth."

Alberada looked surprised and discomfited. "I am not accustomed to presiding over executions, Lord Dietrich."

"If you fear to do so, Your Grace, you must acknowledge that I am right. I do not fear death because the blessed Daisan embraced it in order to redeem humankind from our sins."

"Neither do I!" exclaimed Ekkehard, not wanting to look less courageous than a mere lord. Since he had not been afflicted by the grippe, his voice had a clear and robust ring, free of doubts or phlegmatic listlessness. "I will embrace martyrdom, too!"

"I think an execution would be bad for morale," said Sapientia wisely. Oddly, she looked not at all nervous at the thought of her younger brother's potential demise. After two days in the biscop's palace, she had a sleek satisfaction clinging to her in the same way a sour smell clings to a dying person. It was almost as if she hoped to be rid of him.

"King Henry must be told," began Alberada, temporizing. "A prince of the royal line, who wears the gold torque, cannot be treated as though he were a common-born troublemaker."

"Then send my Eagle," replied Sapientia, with a wickedly complacent smile. "She has made the journey twice before from the east. She'll take the news to the king."

Was this the blow that Hanna had feared for days, landing at last? Did Sapientia mean to rid herself of her supposed rival by any means necessary?

Bayan said nothing. Brother Breschius, standing behind his chair, leaned down to whisper in his ear, but the Ungrian prince merely shook his head impatiently as if, after his last outburst, he had resolved to stay out of the fray no matter what.

Abandoned on every side, Hanna waited for doom to fall. Thunder clapped in the distance. She heard rain clearly, and then it subsided again, as though a door had been opened and closed. Reprieve came from an unlikely source.

"Send an Eagle alone through the marchlands while the Quman ride where they will and we hide here behind our walls?" Alberada surveyed her heretics with distaste. "That is in itself a death sentence, Sapientia."

"Make way!" A messenger hurried in, sopping wet. Her dripping cloak left a drunken line of water drops the length of the hall, and her feet, wrapped only in sodden leather shoes laced up with a cord, made a trail of mud on the carpets. Servants scurried forward to wipe the dirt away while it was still moist.

"Your Grace!" The messenger dropped to her knees. She looked relieved to be kneeling rather than walking or riding, secure in a safe haven. "Is this Princess Sapientia and Prince Bayan? Thank God, Your Highness. I bring terrible news. Machteburg is besieged by the Quman. The town of Dirden is burned, and those who weren't killed have been dragged away into slavery."

Bayan rose, looking grim. "We are answered." He raised a fist as though it were a club. "Bulkezu mocks me." His good nature had vanished, and Hanna thought she saw the ghost of his dead son in his expression, ceaselessly goading him toward vengeance. She shivered, remembering how he had chopped off the fingers of a Quman prisoner. It was hard to reconcile a man so often pragmatic and cheerful with the harsh, merciless soldier who sometimes took his place. "Your Grace, this is not time to prison good soldiers. Every person who can fight, must fight."

"The Quman are not our only enemies, Prince Bayan. Once we let the minions of the Enemy into our hearts, they will destroy us. What they will bring is worse than death."

She would not be moved. She called her stewards to her and spoke to them in an urgent undertone. As soon as they had hurried away to make whatever preparations she had ordered, her palace guards led Ekkehard, Dietrich, their retinues, and the dozen or so other heretics to the church. At Alberada's command, the rest of the assembly followed.

Like the great hall and the palace rooms, the biscop's cathedral—if one could dignify it with that word—had a raw newness about it. There were still artisans working on the ornamentation inside and out. Here in the marchlands, wood was easier to come by than stone, and even a biscop's cathedral might appear humble compared to the old imperial structures still standing in the west.

Here, too, dour saints surveyed the multitude—some hundred souls—who crowded uneasily into the nave. These statues carved of oak and walnut looked so remarkably displeased that Hanna expected them to begin scolding the sinners gathering below them. Four remained unfinished, all angle and suggestion, a hand emerging from wood, the curve of a forehead half hewn from dark wood, a frowning mouth in an eyeless face.

Tapestries relieved the monotony of the oak walls, but they had been woven in such dark colors that Hanna couldn't make out their subject because so few windows cut the gloom. The largest window, behind the altar, faced east. Segments of old Dariyan glass had been pieced together to formed a mosaic, an image of the Circle of Unity, but because it was afternoon, most of the light filtered into the nave through the open doors. Cold air licked in from outside, stirring cloaks. From her station in the front, Hanna felt the merest breath of it on her lips, cool and soothing. A hot, oppressive atmosphere weighted down the crowded chamber, a scent of fear, anticipation, and righteous wrath as thick as curdled cheese.

Every noble in Bayan's army attended, because not to attend

might place them under suspicion. From her position close to
the altar, Hanna scanned the crowd, but she hadn't enough
height to see anyone except the top of Captain Thiadbold's
head, recognizable because of his red hair, far to the back. The
biscop had commanded the highest ranking Lions to witness
as well, so they could report the proceedings to the soldiers
under their command. No spiritual charge was graver than
heresy. It was, truly, akin to treason against the regnant.

But all Hanna could think about was losing her head to a
Quman patrol. Maybe she would have been better off letting
magic carry her east. Maybe she'd been meant to choose
Sorgatani over that glimpse of Liath. Yet hadn't that been
only a dream? Couldn't she be excommunicated if Biscop
Alberada knew the extent of her involvement with sorcery?
Sometimes it was better to keep quiet. In a way, that puzzled
her most about Ekkehard, Lord Dietrich, and lost Ivar. Why
did they have to be so obstreperous about their beliefs? Why
did they have to keep rattling the chain?

But that was her mother, Mistress Birta, talking. "Why
make a date to meet trouble," she would say, "when trouble
won't go out of its way to avoid you should you happen on it
in the road?" Like Prince Bayan, Mistress Birta saw the world
in practical terms. Probably that was one reason Hanna
respected Bayan, despite his annoying admiration of her—
scarcely possible to call it a flirtation, given the chasm between
their stations—that might well send her to her death. Of
course, Birta had never cut off anyone's fingers, but there was
no saying she wouldn't do so, if she thought it necessary.

A morose hymn came to its close. Hanna used her elbow to
get room, nudging aside one of Sapientia's stewards so she
could see better. Clerics walked forward in ranks. Each carried
a lit candle to signify the Circle of Unity, the Light of Truth.
These they set in a circle around Ekkehard, Dietrich, and the
others, who had been herded into a clump at the front of the
nave. Their light burned hotly, making Hanna blink. The
bright light threw the expressions on the carved saints into

relief, a lip drawn down in pity, a hand lifted with two fingers extended to show justice, a glowering frown under heavy-cut eyebrows, twin to that emerging on its unfinished companion. They watched, and they judged.

Biscop Alberada mounted steps to the biscop's platform. She raised her hands for silence.

"Let unsweetened vinegar be brought forward, so that the accused may taste the bitterness of heresy."

Her servants brought cups forward, each distinguished according to the rank of its recipient: for Ekkehard a gold cup, and a silver one for his noble companions; for Lord Dietrich a silver cup as well, and one of brass for his stubborn retinue. The common-born heretics had to make do with a wooden cup passed between them. One man refused to drink and was whipped, three times, until he did so. All of them choked and gasped, coughing, from the bite, all but Lord Dietrich, who drained his cup as though it were honey mead and did not flinch as his defiant gaze remained fixed on the biscop.

"Let any who wear the Circle be stripped of it, for they no longer rest within the protecting ring of its light and truth. Let their hair be cut, to be a badge of their shame."

One of Ekkehard's youths was vain of his blond hair, and he began to weep while Ekkehard stood at a loss to aid him as clerics moved among them with knives, chopping off their hair in ragged bunches. Only when Lord Dietrich moved to comfort the lad and speak to him softly did the young man stiffen, clench his hands, and lift his chin with tremulous pride as a sour-faced cleric hacked off his beautiful hair.

"Let them see in truth that the light of truth no longer burns in their hearts." Descending from her pulpit, she paced the circle, extinguishing the candles one by one by capping them. Smoke drifted up in wispy ribbons. "Thus are you severed from the church. Thus are you become excommunicate. Thus are you forbidden the holy sacraments. Thus are you cut off forever from the society of all Daisanites."

Light died. Afternoon dwindled to twilight. Colors faded into grays.

"Let any woman or man who aids them be also excommunicated. They no longer stand in the Circle of Light. God no longer see them."

Ekkehard staggered as if he'd been struck. One of his companions fainted. Others sobbed.

"I do not fear," said Lord Dietrich. "Let God make Her will known. I am only Her willing vessel."

There was silence. Alberada seemed to be waiting for a sign. Back in the crowd, a man coughed.

Lord Dietrich gave a sudden violent jerk that spun him out of the circle. Three candles went rolling as he fell hard to the floor. He twitched once, twice, and thrashed wildly, struck by a fit of apoplexy.

"So you see," cried Alberada triumphantly. "The Enemy reveals its presence. An evil spirit has taken control of this man. This is the fate that awaits those who profess heresy."

The bravest of Lord Dietrich's noble companions knelt beside the afflicted man and got hold of his limbs, holding him down until he went unaccountably still. Foamy spittle dribbled from his lips. A single bubble of blood beaded at one nostril, popped, and ran down his lax cheek. He shuddered once, and then the floor darkened and a stink rose where he had voided his bowels.

"He's dead," said Ekkehard in a choked voice, shrinking away from the distorted corpse.

In the shocked silence, Biscop Alberada's voice rang as clearly as a call to battle. "Take the excommunicates to their prison. None shall speak to them, for any who do so will be excommunicated in their turn. The Enemy dwells deep within. Tomorrow we will scourge those who remain, so that we may drive the Enemy out of their bodies."

No one objected. They had just seen the Enemy at work.

The church cleared quickly. Alberada left with a phalanx of clerics at her back. Guards carried away the corpse, and servants stayed behind to clean up the mess. Hanna waited, because Sapientia did not move away immediately. The princess waited because Bayan knelt at the altar, as if praying. Somehow, Brother Breschius had gotten hold of one of the silver cups, and when the church was empty except for Bayan, Sapientia, and several of their most loyal servants, he offered it to Bayan.

Bayan wiped his finger along the lip of the cup, touched it to his tongue, and spat, making a face. "Poison," he said softly.

There was a long silence while Hanna willed herself invisible, hoping they would not notice she had witnessed this horrible revelation. If it were even true.

"Will she poison Ekkehard?" asked Sapientia. "Should we try to stop her if we think she might?"

They had their backs to Hanna still, examining the silver cup and the sooty smudge left on the floor by the overturned candles. She edged sideways into the shadows.

"Ekkehard is not threat to us," said Bayan heavily.

"Not now. He's still young. But he might become a threat. And what of the church? Surely my aunt knows what she is doing if this heresy is so terrible. We must support her."

Bayan shook his head just as Hanna touched the border of one of the tapestries. "If we not defeat Bulkezu, then are we dead or slave. This war must we finish first. Let the church argue heresy after. Eagle."

They all leaped, all but Breschius, looking as surprised and anxious as conspirators as they turned round to see her. The tapestry could not hide her now. Bayan had known she was there all along.

"Eagle," he repeated, now that he had her attention. "At dawn you ride to King Henry."

"Yes, Your Highness," she said, barely able to get the words out. She had a sickly vision of her shrunken, blackened head dangling from the belt of a Quman warrior. Was Bayan sacrificing her because of what she'd heard? Or was this only a sop to his wife's jealousy while they hatched their plans for the succession?

"Wife." He rose to take Sapientia's hand. The princess hadn't moved. One of her stewards held a ceramic lamp, a rooster crowing a lick of flame, and the light softened her expression and made her black hair glisten like fine silk. "To you, this task. Ekkehard must ride at dawn with the Eagle."

"Is this wise?" demanded Sapientia.

"He and other prisoners must ride. We need no—what is this, Breschius, nothing to make our minds fall away from the war."

"No distractions, Your Highness."

"Yes, none of this thing which I cannot pronounce. Consider, how matters are desperate. The biscop is a godly woman, I know this. But she believes God come before war. Bulkezu waits not for God." He indicated the altar and the wreath of candles burning there, the light of the Unities.

"But where do we send Ekkehard?"

"Let him go to the march of the Villams. There he can fight. There he will die or live, as God will it. He and his retinue can escort the Eagle so far, out of danger. She must to Henry go, and speak our trouble. But Ekkehard will I not have in Handelburg. That he is prisoner here makes strife in our camp. We have very bad of a situation. If King Henry send no reinforcements, if he not march east himself, then Bulkezu will burn all these lands. This is a hard truth. Maybe we can hold here for a while. *If* we have no strife in our army. If we have no dis—ah! No *distraction*."

"It's a good plan," said Sapientia slowly as she considered his words. That was the great change Bayan had wrought in her; she had learned to think things over. "Ekkehard might still die, fighting the Quman, but that would be a better death for him than being executed for heresy. As a prisoner, his presence can only make things more difficult for us. Some will surely sympathize with his plight. He may still whisper his wicked words to the guards, and maybe there are some in the army who still believe him but lied about it at the trial because they did not want to get punished."

Bayan nodded.

"But how will I free him from my aunt's tower? She will excommunicate me for aiding him."

Brother Breschius stepped forward. "You are the heir, Your Highness. You have already proved your fitness to rule. Think of this as a test of your regnancy. Biscop Alberada would not contest King Henry, were he to tell her that Prince Ekkehard must be sent to the Villam fortress for safekeeping, with or without a large escort, for surely in such times of trouble we cannot afford to lose a large number of men to guard duty. Nor should she contest you, who are destined to rule after your father, may God will that he be blessed with a long life."

Sapientia twisted the fine embroidered border of her tunic in her hands, crushing roundels between her fingers. The gesture made her look a little like a goose girl about to scold her lover. Yet even a humble goose girl might develop the habit of command.

For an instant, Hanna remembered what Hathui used to say: God make the sun rise on noblewoman and commoner alike, for all folk are equal before God. What truly separated Hanna from Sapientia?

Sapientia lowered her hands. She had a queen's bearing; in that moment, in the gloomy church with the silent saints staring down at them from on high, one could see the luck of the regnant in her face. "I will speak to my aunt. Ekkehard will ride out at dawn, to escort the Eagle until it is safe for her to ride on alone."

Hanna laughed softly to herself. *At* herself. God had long since separated the lowborn from the high, no matter what Hathui said. A few words exchanged, and Hanna's fate was sealed.

"Eagle." Bayan rose. His gaze on her was steady, a little admiring still, but quite final, as though he knew he had said farewell to her for the last time. "By no means turn south until you have come west of the Oder River. Even then, be cautious. The Quman range far."

"Yes, Your Highness."

"Ekkehard is young and foolish, snow woman," he added. "Take care of him."

"Come, we should go," said Sapientia sharply. Bayan went obediently. He did not even glance back. His husky, authoritative figure faded into the gloom alongside that of the princess. Hanna heard them continue talking although she could not make out their words.

Breschius lingered. He took her hand and drew her forward to stand before the altar. "Trust in God, friend Hanna." He made the sign of a blessing over her.

"I thank you, Brother. In truth, I feel afraid."

He walked with her to the entryway, still holding her hand. His grasp felt comfortable, like a lifeline. Once they stood on the porch, beyond the most holy precincts, he bent his head to speak softly into her ear. "Never forget that a Kerayit princess has marked you as her luck."

The silence, and the secrecy, and the strange tone in his voice, like doom, made her shudder. Death had brushed her with its cold, callous hand.

They left in the cold light of dawn, Hanna, Prince Ekkehard, his six noble companions, and the twenty other heretics, excommunicates all. Sixteen of them marched, since Bayan did not care to lose so many horses.

Frost made the ground icy, a thin crust that hooves and boots crushed easily. As they crossed the western bridge, Hanna looked back to see Lord Dietrich's head stuck on a pike above the gate. After that, she could not bring herself to look back again. Ivar was probably dead anyway. Looking back would not bring him to life. She kept her gaze fixed on Ekkehard's banner, fluttering weakly in a lazy wind. The rain that had followed them for so long had passed. They rode out in cold, hard weather with the sun glaring down and not a feather's weight of warmth in it.

Hanna had not even been given leave to say farewell to her

friends among the Lions. Ekkehard's escape had an unsavory air about it, tainted by Lord Dietrich's ghastly death and the threat of excommunication.

They saw no sign of Quman scouts.

It seemed an inauspicious way to ride out.

VIII
UNKNOWN COUNTRY

1

ALAIN pushed through the crowd now arguing and lamenting in the council house. Once outside, he whistled the hounds to him and ran to the small house, marked by various charms, chimes, and wreaths, that belonged to Adica. She never went in, or out, without making certain gestures at the threshold, and certainly he had not seen a single person from the village enter this hut. But if their gods, or their council, meant to strike him down, they could do it later.

Inside, he stowed the leather bundle with her precious items inside a wooden chest for safekeeping. He grabbed one of her sleeping furs and hurried outside, where the hounds waited.

Sorrow and Rage weren't alone. Half the village had followed him, although they hadn't come inside; the other half waited uneasily outside the council house.

As the hounds sniffed the fur, Kel stepped forward as if to speak, but Beor thrust him aside and set his spear against Alain's chest. The bronze blade gleamed wickedly. Alain grasped the haft of Beor's spear. The other man was stronger, with a bear's muscular bulk, but Alain was on fire.

"Move aside," he said in his own language, staring him down. "If we go quickly, we may still be able to follow their trail and get Adica back. If they meant to kill her at once, they'd have done so, but if they took her, it means we have a little time at least. For the sake of God, do not hinder me."

A strange expression passed across Beor's face. Behind him, villagers murmured to each other. Beor stepped back hesitantly.

"I go," said Alain, groping for words. "I find Adica."

Mother Orla spoke. Instantly, several folk ran off into the village.

Kel jumped forward, carrying now a bronze knife in addition to the bronze spear he had taken off the corpse of the dead invader. "I go!" he cried triumphantly.

"I go," said Beor abruptly.

Belatedly, a dozen other adults volunteered, but a large party could not move in haste and secrecy. "Kel." Alain paused, then nodded sharply. "Beor. We go."

Quickly, they made ready. Alain wished keenly for his knife and sword, but he didn't know where Adica had hidden them, and there wasn't time to look. Instead, he accepted a bronze knife. Mother Orla's errand runners brought rope, waterskins full of mead, a wooden tube lined with fired ceramic and filled with hot coals, and a pungent supply of dried fish, wayfarer's bread, and a bundle of leeks. Both Beor and Kel had wood frames to sling on their backs, fitted with a leather sack for carrying these provisions. Even this took precious time.

Alain led the hounds down to the birthing house. Urtan's daughter, following, showed him the scuffed ground where the altercation had taken place; by means of signs and mime, she showed him what she had seen from the watchtower at the gate. Urtan and his companions had run up to Adica and Tosti moments before a group of at least twenty raiders had come running down from the tumulus. They had split into two groups, one to harry the village and one to capture the Hallowed One, Adica.

The hound sniffed the ground and, at a command from Alain, trotted away toward the tumulus, following a trail only they could perceive. Alain followed at a jog, with Kel and Beor at his heels. The villagers gathered like mourners at the gate, watching them go. Then, prudently, the gate was swung shut. The half-finished outer palisade looked flimsy from this height. He saw a scrap of color fallen in the ditch: a corpse.

Who were the raiders who had struck? Why did they look like relatives of Prince Sanglant? Everyone knew that no Aoi roamed the Earth any longer—not unless they were shades, caught in a purgatory between substance and shadow. Why did they want Adica?

Beor and Kel could probably answer these questions, but he had no words to ask. He could only pursue.

He expected the hounds to lead them to the stone circle, but they cut away at the highest ring of earthworks and padded along in the shadow of the twisting serpent of earth until, at the eastern edge, they scrambled downslope.

There, most of the way down the eastern slope, stood a stone lintel, the threshold of a passageway that led into the great hill. Kel moaned with fear as the hounds sniffed at the opening. A long-dead craftswoman had carved into the left-hand pillar a humanlike figure wearing the skin and antlers of a stag. Beside the yawning opening lay an offering of flowers, wilted now, scuffed by the passage of animals and wind. A deer had left droppings where it had paused to investigate the flower wreath, and the hounds became enamored with this fascinating reminder of its passage.

Beor knelt. When he rose, he displayed a scale of bronze that might have fallen from armor. Alain searched to make sure they hadn't missed any other sign of the raiders' passage. A stone had fallen from the hillside and now rested among faded cornflower blossoms. Tansy had found a foothold in a hollow off to one side, where water collected. That was all.

Sorrow barked and vanished into the passage. Kel had gone quite pale, as though painted with chalk. Beor only grunted, but he had a fierce grin on his face as he looked toward Alain as if to see if the other man were brave enough to continue on.

No matter.

A half-dozen torches lay ready, stacked neatly inside the threshold. Alain caught a spark in the pitch-smothered head. Flame blazed up. With his staff skimming the ground ahead to test for obstacles and a second unlit torch thrust between his belt and tunic, he followed Sorrow into the passage.

Beor and Kel exchanged words, soon muffled by stone. Alain had to crouch to move forward. Ahead, he heard Sorrow snuffling and panting. The torch bled smoke onto the corbeled ceiling. Hazy light revealed carvings pecked into the stones that lined the passageway: mostly lozenges and spirals, but here and there curious sticklike hands which reached toward four lines cut above them. Such symbols of power betrayed the presence of the old gods, but he wasn't afraid of them. They had no power over those who trusted to the Lady and Lord.

The ceiling sloped up, and the thick stone walls rose higher and higher until he walked, unexpectedly, into a great chamber. A stone slab lay on the ground in the center of this chamber. Sorrow sniffed impatiently around it, as though he smelled a rat.

Alain held up the torch as Beor cautiously stepped into the chamber behind him, spear held ready for battle. Rage padded in his wake. There was no sign of Kel.

The high corbeled ceiling arched up into a darkness the hazy torchlight could not reach. Opposite Alain, and to either side, lay niches, each alcove carved with the representation of an ancient queen.

Here, deep in the womb of stone and earth, not even the wind could be heard. But someone was watching them.

"Where is she?" Alain demanded of that unseen presence.

The torch whuffed out as though a gust of wind had extinguished it. One moment, it hissed and threw smoky light all around them. The next, it was too black to see, and he smelled the scent of burning pitch curl and die away until all he smelled was earth and damp and cold, and the comforting aroma of dog. Beor swore under his breath, more prayer than oath.

Then even those sensations were gone, and Alain could no longer feel or hear anything, not the breathing of the hounds, not the stone itself beneath his feet. He was alone except for a shuddering, wheezing sigh that breathed in and out around him, as though the hill itself was a living creature, half asleep and half aware.

"Where is she?" he called again.

The vision hit like a blast of light, searing his eyes.

Three queens stand before him, one to the north, one to the south, one to the west.

"Who are you, to make demands of us?" cries the youngest. She holds in her hand a bow whose length runs writhing with gold salamanders, burning like fire. Her tomb is carved with two sphinxes. Their clever faces, as much feline as woman, gleam as though touched by phosphorus.

"Who are you, holy one?" She is no saint known to the blessed Daisan, but he can respect her nevertheless, for she is a woman of power even if she is dead.

Her voice rings through him with the fierce clamor of a thunderstorm. "I am the one called Arrow Bright. Have you not heard of me? Was I not fostered by the lion women of the desert, who taught me the secret ways known only to the Pale Hunter?"

"There is much I do not know," he admits.

"What do you want?" asks the second queen, standing to the south. Her tomb glows with gold beaten into the shape of a sow, and she has herself the ample outlines of a prosperous woman, sleek and radiant.

"What do you want?" Only a rash man states his true purpose before he knows what he is facing.

She laughs. "I am Golden Sow. It was my magic that made all the women of my tribe fertile, and all their children healthy. Is this not what all people want?"

"How is it that death has marked you, and yet you stand living?" asks the third queen. Her voice has a rasp that makes his skin crawl. Her cairn stands to the west, opposite the passageway. More primitive than the others, it consists of a simple mound of discolored stones like so many worn teeth that once belonged to a creature so vast that each tooth was as big as an adult's head. She is ancient, and toothless, but her eyes are as brilliant as stars.

"How do you know I am living?" he retorts.

"Only living things suffer desire," retorts Toothless in kind. "What can you give us in return for an answer?"

He laughs. "I have nothing to give you, for I came naked to this place."

"Do not say you have nothing," scolds Golden Sow. "You have youth and vitality. You have life."

"You are untouched, still whole," says Arrow Bright. "You are a virgin, as are all those sworn to the Pale Hunter's service."

"It is not the Pale Hunter I serve," he says, as respectfully as he can, for it would not do to insult queens of such power, especially since they are dead.

"You serve the Lady, as do we all." Toothless moves a step closer. The scent of the grave wafts from her as her cape, woven of grass, stirs in an unfelt wind. "The Lady commands both life and death."

"Then I am in Her hands." He bows his head under the weight of a greater presence looming beyond, an effortless stillness that pervades the chamber and, swelling, expands to fill the entire universe.

Toothless laughs. "Let it be witnessed."

"I know where she went," says Arrow Bright suddenly, "but it is the way of this place that no thing can be given without an offering pledged in return."

He will give them anything, if only it brings Adica back to her village. He has lost so many; he will not lose her, too. "What do I have that you want? I came naked—"

He knows at once what they want from him, and he blushes furiously, heat spreading along his body.

"Pledge to us that which you have held to yourself for so long. If you find her, bring her here, and here, fulfill your pledge."

"So be it," he murmurs.

Sorrow barked. Alain staggered as though the ground had dropped out from under him. Beor caught the torch before it fell. He seemed about to speak, but they heard a ghostly whimper and both turned, weapons raised, just as Kel stumbled into the chamber, sweating with fear but with a grimace of determination on his young face.

Rage began digging furiously by the stone altar. Dirt flew, stinging the walls, and a moment later the deepening hole revealed a small plank door laid flat against the ground. Straining, Beor tugged it up. An ancient stairway cut down into the rock. At once, Sorrow descended cautiously. Kel muttered imprecations under his breath, but when Alain started down after the hound, he felt Kel head down behind him. Light flared; Beor had lit a second torch to bring up the rear.

The stairs were as smooth as if they'd been polished, and they descended in a curving sweep for long enough that they might have sung Nocturns and seen the sun rise at Prime. Instead of counting the steps, Alain focused his attention past Sorrow so they wouldn't be ambushed out of the dark. Once he stopped so abruptly, hearing a noise, that Kel bumped into his back. The entire party came to a halt.

The noise came again. And again. It was only water, dripping into an unseen pool.

Beor handed round the waterskin and a corner of wayfarer's bread, enough to slake thirst and hunger.

Torchlight flickered on featureless walls. The ceiling lay so low that he could easily touch it with the flat of his palm. By lifting his arms, he could tap the walls with his elbows. Truly, the rock had them closed in. Better not to think about it. Better not to dwell on a force of armed warriors skulking ahead of him, with spears leveled to pierce his gut. Better to be grateful that the rock remained dry instead of dripping clammy water all over them. It was always wise to thank God for small mercies. He smiled grimly as Sorrow headed down into darkness again. What need had he to fear, when he had already suffered the worst that could happen to any mortal?

They kept going until the stairs gave out abruptly in a landing just large enough to contain the two hounds and the three men. Beor lifted his spear to tap the rock ceiling, now out of arm's reach. Two tunnels opened before them. A breath of air teased Alain's face as though the rock itself had exhaled. Then all was still.

They each took a sip of water to wet their dry throats. The air had changed, stung with a sharp scent. The rock had changed as well; it didn't precisely look like rock any more but had a smooth, polished gleam to it, shuddering under torchlight.

Kel spoke in a frightened whisper, something about a hill, or something under the hill. Nay, a *people* who lived under the hill, or so it seemed, for he used the word *skrolin-sisi* several times, enough that Alain was able to pick it out from the others. Was there a tribe who lived deep in the earth? Someone had carved these tunnels.

Beor answered in his big man's rumble. If he, too, were afraid, it was impossible for Alain to tell.

Rage snuffled around the two black openings and chose the one to the right. They went on, but soon the tunnel split into two again and two more. If not for the hounds, they would have lost themselves, for they had stumbled into a labyrinth that went on and on for what seemed forever. Yet the stone walls remained dry and unmarked, oddly warm to the touch, unnaturally smooth. Whatever hand had built this place had not chosen to adorn it with any form of ornamentation. That made it easy for Alain to paint a sooty mark on the right-hand side of each new turning they took, so that they could, he devoutly hoped, find their way back.

The torch, burning low, began to sputter. They paused to take water with a bite of dried fish. The pitchy smoke steamed past Alain's head, making him cough. His eyes streamed.

Fighting for air, he inhaled but took in a lungful of the noxious smoke instead. Head spinning, he caught himself on the wall, leaning with his head pressed against the cool stone, trying to get steady. From deep in the rock noise shuddered up to drown out the pounding of his heart: a grinding rumble kicked at rhythmic intervals with a decisive clang, like the stroke of a gigantic blacksmith's hammer.

He shut his eyes to stop the dizziness. For an instant he hallucinated: his cheek, pressed against the wall, lay against iron, as though he had fallen asleep on his sword.

He slid a hand up the wall as understanding struck him. The walls were not stone at all. Iron had been forged and shaped to form a cloak for the walls in the same way that soft leather was formed into a glove to fit a person's fingers.

The torch died in his hand. He groped for the spare one tucked in his belt, but a big hand closed over his, to stop him. Beor's hostile presence hulked beside him. Nothing could stop Beor from killing him right here and right now. The hounds did not growl.

In the silence, he heard what Beor and Kel were straining to hear: the distant clash of a melee echoing weirdly down the labyrinth of iron halls. Beor pushed past Alain to take the lead, but he had gone no farther than ten steps, past two branching tunnels, before he faltered. Some trick of the labyrinth made the sound fade. For a moment, the hiss of Beor's torch drowned out the battle. The big man turned back to try one of the other tunnels, but the hounds surged past him, Alain in their wake, and continued on in the same direction. As the passage twisted, the clamor of arms would sound close, then far, and although they went quickly, still Alain was careful to mark each turning so that they could return.

His sight had adjusted to the dimness. With Beor's torch flaring fitfully behind him, painting shadows and streaks of light over the uncannily regular curve of the tunnel's ceiling, he had no trouble marking his footing. The hounds did not falter. Kel brought up the rear.

He had no trouble marking his footing until he stumbled, slipped where the ground banked sharply down, and half slid into a chamber lit by sorcery, a flaring yellow-white light that blinded him because it was so bright.

One of the hounds barreled into him. He staggered back into the shadowed archway of the tunnel, fell to his knees, and flung up his staff, thinking he would be struck down while he was helpless. No blow came.

Not four steps in front lay an abyss, into which he had almost stumbled. From this angle, he couldn't see its bottom.

The clash of arms echoed all around the chamber, making it hard to tell where it was coming from. Strangest of all, he heard no voices, as if the melee were being conducted in silence. The hounds did not bark or cry out a warning. Kel whispered a word: *skrolin!* Beor gave a sharp hiss to keep Kel quiet.

Bright light flared again and immediately dimmed to a mellow glow as suddenly as if a giant's breath had blown out a rack of ten torches, leaving only one burning. By this light, Alain saw a melee strung out on the other side of the chasm. About a dozen of the masked warriors struggled against slender, small creatures, who looked like half-grown children whose skin had been polished until it had the muted gleam of pewter. The feathers ornamenting the warriors' helmets and armor convulsed with their movements. Many had pushed their masks down for better sight in the dimness. Their bronze spears rang on the round shields held by the little people, shields incised with strange geometric patterns too peculiar to recognize. In their left hands these small fighters held slender clubs with knobby heads that seemed inadequate to the task of war.

All at once, Alain saw Adica, caught in the mob, her hands bound. A man with a helmet crested entirely with snow-white feathers shoved her forward into the hands of his foremost soldiers, trying to move her toward a far archway that gave into a larger passage: their escape route.

Beor nudged Alain, pointing.

A bridge spanned the chasm.

"Ashioi," Beor continued in a low voice. "Fe skrolin d'Ashioiket."

Alain set two fingers to his lips for silence and crept forward.

The narrow bridge was cunningly spun out of massive iron rope. He crossed swiftly, crouched low, with the hounds at his heels and the two men following. The bridge swayed beneath his tread. No one on the other side had seen them; they were too intent on keeping alive as the battle swayed back and forth, voices grunting, coughing, and once a shriek of pain, quickly cut off.

The light changed again, brightening with a flash. The skrolin leaped forward in unison to grapple with their enemies. Now Alain could see that the skrolin weapon was more vicious than it appeared: protruding from the club were two moist spikes, serpent fangs with drops of venom that sparkled in the sorcerous light. They used it to strike at the legs of their taller opponents, bringing them down. One masked warrior, forced to her knees, came eye-to-eye with the small warrior whose club was now pinned under her weight. The skrolin punched its shield into her beautiful hawk's mask, splintering wood, but as the skrolin drew back for another strike, the kneeling warrior wrapped the haft of her spear behind the neck of the skrolin to force it against its own shield, choking it until its eyes bulged and its head began to loll as it fought for air. Its helmet fell free, rolling along the edge with a rhythmic tinkling sound before plummeting into the black pit.

Alain leaped from the bridge to the firm rock below. Swinging his staff in a full arc, he caught the warrior on the side of the head to knock her flat. The skrolin struggled, squirmed, and rolled away. The fallen woman's eyelids fluttered. Her mouth, visible through the shattered mask, sighed open as in death. Had he killed her? But she moaned again and tried to rise before falling back, still stunned.

The nearest masked warrior slammed his shield against the skrolin facing him, before thrusting hard at Alain's head. Alain gave a sharp parry and stepped inside his range to bring the butt end of his staff hard up into the gut of the warrior, then whipped the staff back down onto the man's shoulder, forcing him to the ground.

Beor and the two hounds charged past Alain. The white-crested captain stepped forward to counter this new threat. Rage and Sorrow leaped to the attack but were met by a mist of gnats. Sorrow yelped and collapsed to the ground, scratching violently at his head, as Rage bit the haft of a spear. With jaws clenched tight over the wood, she shook the spear back and forth, worrying it free of the captain's grasp. Beor quickly took advantage of White Feather's helplessness with a thrust at the man's unprotected back, but the white-crested warrior let go of the spear, dropped, and rolled to evade the thrust. In an eye blink, he leaped to his feet and drew his bronze sword. Beor had no shield to counter its thrusting tip. With a berserker's fury or perhaps only an experienced warrior's quick calculation of the odds, Beor dropped his spear, dodged the thrust, and grappled hand to hand with the captain.

Kel had joined Alain and together they parried blows from the other warriors, trying to sow confusion. Trying to stay alive. Rage leaped into the fray and Alain quickly lost sight of her. Sorrow had rolled out of harm's way, still frantically clawing at his muzzle.

Kel had courage but little experience. His hesitations were costly, and only the presence of the skrolin kept the enemy from overwhelming them. But many of the skrolin had already fallen. Alain could mark each one—who was wounded, who was dead. That awareness swelled to encompass the entire field marked by the skirmish as he fought to keep alive, to keep his companions alive, and to drive a path through their ranks to Adica. The Lady of Battles did not attend him here. He had no desire to kill; the thought of killing revolted him. But as he parried and struck, spared Kel a glancing blow and shoved a fallen skrolin out of harm's way, the melee gained sharpness and clarity, an uncanny predictability, a slowing down of time and motion as though all the other participants had been caught in a spell.

The openings became obvious, the blows struck at him easy to counter. As a child he had so loved and dreamed about the frescoes that adorned the church walls:

The fall of the ancient city of Dariya to savage horsemen. The fateful battle of Auxelles, where Taillefer's nephew and his men lost their lives but saved the empire. The glorious victory of the first King Henry against Quman invaders along the River Eldar, where his bastard grandson Conrad the Dragon charged his troop of cavalry straight into the midst of the terrible host of Quman riders, breaking their line and sending them scattering back to their own lands.

The field of battle became itself like one of those tapestries, not an undecipherable chaos but a painting in which each fighter was as transparent to him as if he had opened a window into that mind. He knew who was scared and who was hesitant, who new to war, who dangerous through experience or because she was cold-blooded. He knew who was ready to run and who was prepared to die.

The warrior before him did not wish to fight; she wanted nothing to do with humans and had all along thought it unwise to trespass below ground. The other warrior, facing Kel, was young, ready to prove himself valiant, and fearful enough of humans that he had the advantage over Kel. Alain stepped in to knock away a spear thrust that Kel, attention caught by Beor's tumbling on the ground, wasn't prepared to meet. At the same time the experienced warrior swung her haft toward his head, but he caught the blow on his staff. He pushed the lower tip of his staff behind the leg of the younger one, and with a twist tripped the young one while striking the elder in the forehead. Both fell.

Kel exclaimed aloud. The enemy line was breaking. Freed of her guard, Adica ducked low and dashed away along the cavern wall, into shadow.

The woman below Alain struggled to get up. Alain placed the heel of his hand on the center of her chest to pin her to the ground. Her eyes widened: they flashed green, like jade, bright and penetrating. Sanglant had such eyes, startling with their gemlike intensity. He stared at her and she at him, he in wonder at her beauty and fierce heart, she in a puzzlement that expanded into surprise and respect. Without a word, Alain granted her passage to leave. She sprang up and retreated, dragging the stumbling youth with her. Rage tumbled, unhurt, out of the melee to take up her position beside Alain.

Beor hadn't as much luck. White Feather struck him hard in the shoulder, rocking him back, and jumped to his feet, calling out in a voice that reverberated through the chamber. His warriors, some still struggling and some in retreat, formed up into a stout line with their wounded at the rear.

Where was Adica?

The skrolin, many of them leaking a greenish-tinged blood, waited in an eerie silence, as though they would not, or could not, speak. Alain sensed, then, that they were biding their time, delaying their enemy. Waiting—but for what?

Beor got to his feet, slipped on his own blood, and staggered back to stand beside Kel. Adica broke free seemingly from out of nowhere and tumbled over corpses to reach their side.

With angry cries, the masked warriors charged the four humans and the remaining half-dozen skrolin. That quickly, the skirmish dissolved into confusion again. With bound hands Adica grabbed for, and dropped, a spear fallen to the ground. A second time she got her fingers around it and lifted it just in time to clumsily parry a blow. A sword stroke hit Kel's back as he turned in the wrong direction in confusion, but the wood frame of the pack protected him. The leather sacking sagged, sliced open by the blow, and provisions spilled out. One warrior slipped on dried fish, falling hard. But the rest pressed forward under White Feather's command, seeking Adica. Kel fell back, unable to hold his own, and slammed into Adica, who stumbled. Half bent over, Beor set about himself, still a threat despite his wound.

Where had that clarity gone, that had made of the battle a brightly woven tapestry? It had seemed so easy before, for those brief moments drawn out like thread into an unbroken present. Now Alain was barely able to block a blow thrown at Adica's head by the white-crested warrior as the captain's sword cut into and hung up in his oak staff. Sorrow was missing, and Rage had dashed out of his sight again. Claws scraped at his calves. Maybe it was possible to die twice. The thought struck him more with astonishment than fear.

Then the world came apart.

Light failed between one breath and the next, drowning them in blinding darkness. The ground buckled and heaved beneath him. Kel shouted out in fear. Sound cracked like thunder in his ears. The earth splintered between his left foot and his right. He grabbed for Adica and dragged her backward but felt himself sliding forward on his knees toward a new chasm. Heat blasted up from black depths, unseen but felt as a narrow gulf of empty air blasted by a blistering wind. When he opened his mouth to shout a warning, the air scalded his tongue. He couldn't hear his voice above the scream of the wind.

Teeth grabbed him. A jaw closed on his right foot. The hounds were trying to stop his slide. Adica scrabbled for purchase. A spear slid past him. Its cool length brushed past his calf and then tumbled away, and away, and away—it never hit bottom. It seemed an eternity he slid inexorably toward the chasm with Adica struggling upward beside him. His straining hand, trying to brace against the slick stone, scraped on the edge, and he was falling forward as his spare torch slid out of his belt, bumped back against him because of the force of that wind, and tumbled away.

A small hand caught his linen tunic, then his rope belt. A hundred hands swarmed him, poking and pinching everywhere as they hauled him back. He was helpless in their grip, his back scraping on the ground.

The hands released him, all but one, which searched his torso with wickedly sharp jabs. Its breath, made pungent by a sulfurous tang, tickled his face. Those claws scrabbled up his right arm and gave it a hard pinch, twisting the skin so he yelped. Blood welled where a claw had scraped through the skin. A cool pressure twisted onto his arm. At once, the hounds were all over him, licking and nosing him. The creature assaulting him had vanished.

"Adica?" His throat hurt, and his back ached. Utter darkness hemmed him in. He couldn't hear anything except for the wind.

A lamp flared.

Adica lay beside him, looking half stunned.

Their enemy glared at them from the other side of the chasm, a dreadful fissure out of whose depths boiled that searing wind, which shot straight up toward the cavern's hidden ceiling. The flame trembled and steadied as the captain sheltered it with a hand. Of the dozen warriors still able to fight, six had bows, which they had readied and nocked with arrows during the blackness. White Feather barked a command. Alain threw himself over Adica's prone body. They shot.

None of the arrows made it across the fissure. The blast tore them away, spinning them up toward the ceiling, lost to sight.

"Hei! Hei!" shouted Kel, a call for help.

Alain jumped up, wiping the sting of the wind from his eyes. Beor and Kel clung to the edge of the fissure. Alain dragged them up. In a strange way, the blasting wind helped him. Beor had lost his torches, and his injured shoulder still bled, but he could walk. Kel's slashed pack dangled dangerously. They hadn't any weapons, but on the flat plateau between them and the bridge a few spears lay scattered. Kel hurried, limping, to gather them up as Alain knelt beside Adica, cutting the rope that bound her hands. Shaking her head and wincing, she got to her feet.

The fissure had split the ground in such a way that they could no longer reach the larger passageway toward which they had originally been heading. Instead, only a single, smaller tunnel opening offered escape from their section of the cavern.

White Feather shouted something very much resembling curses, but there was nothing he and his men could do. His proud face twisted with thwarted anger; a livid cut ran from lip to chin, and a bruise mottled his left cheek. Blood dripped from one ear, dribbling down to stain the leather armor that protected his shoulders. He wore a breastplate of beaten bronze incised with a vulture-headed woman, fierce and commanding. With a snarl, he turned his back on his enemies.

One archer masked with a boar's face loosed a second arrow, but the wind caught the arrow and lifted it high until it was lost in the cavern's murky heights as wind roared. They couldn't leap the fissure, and the chasm had fractured like a trident into three crevasses, slitting the cavern's floor into tiny islands surrounded by gulfs of wind. The most youthful of the warriors made as if to cast his spear, but a companion restrained him. After a brief conference, they walked cautiously across the length of floor left them, hauling with them three comrades too injured to walk, and crossed into a small tunnel so low that most had to duck as they entered.

Kel swore furiously. As the lamplight faded, Alain looked to see that the bridge over the first abyss had split down the middle, each half dangling down the face of the chasm.

They were trapped in the middle, caught on a narrow ridge poised between two crevasses.

White Feather vanished down the small tunnel, and his light with him. Blackness descended again. From out of the fissure boomed a throbbing like a giant's reverberant footfalls, each one as loud as a thunderclap. The wind ceased in the next instant.

Rage barked as if surprised, and then all was still and utterly dark.

2

HER hands smarted as blood rushed back into them. She flexed them as she took steadying breaths in the darkness. Free, but not yet safe. Still, it was better than being trussed up as a captive of the Cursed Ones.

"Hallowed One, can you speak?"

"Beor, how came you to follow me? What happened at the village? Who else was taken?"

He stood to the right of her, panting in the way of a fighter trying to overcome the pain of his injuries. "One of Weiwara's infants was stolen, but the foreigner won it back. Nay, Hallowed One, no others were taken. Only you. It was all a feint."

"To get me."

He grunted to show his agreement.

"We're trapped." Kel's voice cracked, hitting a boy's pitch before sliding down again.

"Adica."

She couldn't see Alain, but she felt him as she would have felt a roaring bonfire. He stood about an arm's length from her. Instead of answering, she extended her hand into the blackness and, searching, found his arm. He squeezed her hand. That was all. The darkness in the cavern was so absolute that she could not even see his face.

Or was it?

Light rose gently, with the gleam of magic in it. At first she couldn't see where it was coming from. Kel swore.

Alain was glowing.

Nay. An instant later she saw an armband the color of bronze, wound three times around Alain's upper arm. This object glowed. By his expression, Alain was as surprised as she was. He fingered the armband cautiously, twisted it, and grimaced in pain when it would not come off.

"There's an old story told by the grandmothers," said Beor

in an odd tone, "that the Wise Ones give precious gifts to those who aid them."

Alain turned away, hiding his face as he examined the strange armband. The breeze blowing up from the fissure, light and cool now, stirred his linen tunic. From the back, with his fine black hair and his slender build, he might have been a cousin of the Cursed Ones—but he was not. He had felt human enough to her, by the birthing house in those moments before the Cursed Ones' raid, when she held him close and kissed him.

"Rope," said Kel. She looked over at the sound of the youth's voice and saw him beside the fallen bridge, staring down into the gaping chasm with his expression painted with overflowing youthful frustration. He held salvaged rope from his pack. With his gaze he measured the distance between the posts on either side of the chasm. Beor limped over to test the strength of one of the bridge posts. She crossed to him at once and made him sit so she could examine his wounds. He had several, chiefly cuts in both legs and a deeper injury to his left shoulder. Someone had thought to put a compress and a length of loosely woven cloth for wound-binding into Beor's pack. She used herbs from her own pouch to make a small charm, and bound it in with the compress and the cloth.

He grunted his thanks, no more.

Kel had a funny lopsided smile that betrayed his fear, although he wanted to look brave. "Will the Wise Ones kill us for trespassing in their territory?"

"Surely they could have killed us by now," said Beor, "if they meant to. How did it come about that they fought with the party who kidnapped you, Hallowed One?"

"I do not know. At first I thought the white-feathered one, he who was the leader, meant to take us to the loom."

Both Kel and Beor looked shocked. "Surely the Cursed Ones do not know the magic of the looms," said Kel, voicing what Beor knew better than to speak aloud. "Isn't that the only power we have that keeps us free of their dominion?"

"So I have always believed," murmured Adica. "In any case

another party ran up to the stones, perhaps as a decoy. White Feather and his soldiers dragged me into the queens' grave, and there, as you found, was a tunnel built by the Wise Ones who live under the hills."

Beor coughed judiciously, as might a person who meant to step from hiding out behind an armed adult. "I never heard tell stories of a passageway leading beyond the graves of the holy queens."

"Truly, neither did I. It may be that the Wise Ones attacked White Feather and his party simply because they trespassed. The Wise Ones are not our allies, to come to our aid."

Kel said nervously, "I wasn't sure they really existed."

At once, Adica drew a complicated spell in the air to ward off bad luck. "Do not speak so! Just because you have not seen something does not mean it cannot exist! Have you seen the ocean, as I have? Nay, you have not. Have you seen your mother's mother, may her soul be at rest on the Other Side? Does that mean she did not exist, to give birth to your mother, who in turn gave birth to you? The elders were not fools, to tell stories idly. Listen to their words, and do not close your ears to what they have to say!"

He bent forward, touching his forehead to the ground in apology, fearful of the spirits that always eddied around her, smelling death. "I beg your pardon, Hallowed One. Do not curse me!" He was almost weeping.

She felt immeasurably ancient, watching his young face, even though they had been born in the same season, the same year. He wasn't even old enough to grow a proper beard, although fuzz shadowed his jawline. "I won't curse you, Kel. You were brave to rescue me."

"Nay, it wasn't my idea," he said, and added defiantly, "nor even Beor's. It was Alain. We only followed him."

Alain gave up fiddling with the armband and, turning, paused when he realized that they were studying him. The grandmothers told many stories about ancient times. Adica had always supposed that some were true and some were not, and yet now Alain faced her wearing an armband woven of magical substance. She had always known that the Wise Ones who live under the hills existed, but she—who had seen so much!—had never seen them nor had she believed the tales about the potency of their magic. She had witnessed their magic today: light without flame and the ability to split the very rock. Truly, what she had seen awed her, for she did not understand the root of their power.

Yet here also stood Alain, wearing an armband forged and shaped by the Wise Ones. She had seen him fighting, when she had had time to look. Nothing had touched him. He hadn't hesitated. Nor did he seem afraid now, watching them with a puzzled expression on his face, as if he expected them to ask him a question. The armband's light cast strange shadows on his face, but somehow it only made his eyes seem brighter and more sweet.

Maybe she understood then that he was not quite like other people. Some unnameable quality separated him from the rest of humankind, perhaps because he had walked on the path that leads to the land of the dead. Except he had stepped off of it. He had come back to the land of the living. He had been touched by a power outside any she understood.

She loved him.

One of the dogs brushed up against her legs and leaned into her so heavily that she staggered sideways, half laughing because her heart was beating so hard already. The other dog, standing at the edge of the light, whined softly and padded a few steps away into the blackness, down the ridge toward the far wall of the cavern, made invisible by darkness.

"I think we must follow the spirit guide." Her fingers still hurt as she collected three spears and two arrows from the floor. It was hard to really get a good grasp on anything, but her legs worked well enough.

As Alain moved, the light shifted, and together they walked cautiously along the ridge of stone, a crevasse gaping on either side.

The dogs had found an opening. This tunnel lay low to the ground, an easy height for the Wise Ones or for dogs, but Alain had to bend almost double to follow the dogs inside.

"I don't want to go in there," said Kel.

"Come." Alain's voice echoed weirdly out of the stone passageway.

Kel smiled weakly, and went after him.

"Go," said Adica to Beor. "You're wounded. Carry what you can. I'll bring up the rear."

Beor had many flaws, but arguing when he was wounded and their party possibly trapped was not one of them. They crept forward through the low passageway with the dogs in the lead.

The passage struck straight, only a few smaller tunnels branching off. In time, the ceiling lifted and they could walk upright, although never more than single file. After some time Beor tired, and they rested, sharing drink and food. They walked again, and rested again. The loss of Kel's provisions hurt them; they only had enough to gnaw off the edge of their hunger, not to satisfy it.

They spoke little. Beor had enough to do to keep going, and the silence and darkness frightened Kel too much to break it with words. Now and again Alain whistled softly under his breath. At intervals he would call lightly ahead to the dogs but otherwise he, too, remained silent.

Adica worried. Would the Cursed Ones stumble upon them, here in the dark? If they knew who and what she was, then had they kidnapped her six comrades as well? If there were not seven to cast the spell, then the spell would fail and the Cursed Ones would spread their empire of blood and sacrifice and slavery across all human lands.

Worst of all, did they understand what the human sorcerers meant to do? Had they learned the secret of the looms? Humankind could never triumph if they lost the power of the looms.

These troubled thoughts distracted her. She didn't hear the

scrabbling behind her until it was too late. An object, then a second, fell heavily at her heels, knocking her forward. She cried out just as Alain exclaimed out loud ahead of her. A dog barked, and Alain's light vanished.

She whirled with her spear raised to face the threat from behind, but nothing stirred in the black tunnel. Finally, hearing Beor question her, she knelt. Feeling along the floor, she discovered their lost torches, the ones that had fallen into the crevasse. A moment later she realized she could see her hand as a pale blur.

"Hallowed One! We've found a way out!" Kel called from up ahead. She gathered up the torches and followed the sound of his voice. He was helping Beor up a rugged slope of rock. At its top, light bled through tree roots. By getting purchase with one foot on the rocks and grasping the stout tree roots in a hand, she was able to drag herself up into a dense copse. The light hurt her eyes despite the protection of leaves. By the position of the sun she judged it around midday, but they had been so long underground that she supposed an entire day and night had passed since the raid. She gulped down cool, fresh air.

With some difficulty, they got the hounds out and helped Beor climb out as well. Finally, they all lay on a hillside in the cover of the trees, panting. She wanted to laugh, out of relief, but dared not. Their enemies might be lurking nearby. Kel took a spear and went scouting, and after some time returned triumphantly with an escort of six astonished White Deer tribespeople.

"We're nearby to Four Houses!" Kel exclaimed, and with Ulfrega and her companions as an escort, they walked to the safety of the other village. A healer tended to Beor. A Swift was sent to Queens' Grave to deliver the message that Adica had been found. The Four Houses folk knew how to lay out a good feast: freshly killed boar and venison, pears and apples stewed into a potage, bread, and barley porridge sweetened with honey. Beer flowed freely, and the tale was told at length,

and then a second time when the most experienced of the Four
Houses warriors asked for more details.

What weapons did the Cursed Ones use? What of these
clubs borne by the Wise Ones? Did the under hill people have
eyes, or were they blind? Was it true they could not speak?
Had the foreigner been enchanted by the Wise Ones, or was he
simply a sorcerer himself, hoarding great power? Could Four
Houses take one of the bronze spears in exchange for the hospitality they had shown to the Hallowed One this day?

In return, Beor scolded them for their unfinished palisade,
and Kel gained a circle of admiring youths who wanted to hear
all about his heroic efforts. Alain sat quietly. He was too
strange a figure to be fawned over, nor did he seem to care that
he was left alone to attend to his food. Certainly he had
become accustomed to being stared at. Now and again Adica
caught him looking at her, and each time her heart beat a
little harder for thinking of what might yet come to pass. For
her own part, she waited with mounting impatience for the
return of the Swift. The youth returned in the late afternoon:
a large escort would come from Queens' Grave tomorrow to
escort the Hallowed One back to her own village. The
Walking One known as Dorren waited for her there; he had
brought a message from Falling-down.

She passed a fretful night and in the morning paced
restively while Kel and Alain helped the Four Houses villagers raise the log walls of their palisade and Beor rested. At
last the escort came, overjoyed to see her and flush with the
news that none of the injured people at Queens' Grave had
died in the attack or caught a festering infection in their
wounds. The march back to the village passed swiftly, and in
the village itself, still marked by the recent battle, roasting
and baking went on at a great rate in preparation for a cele-
bratory feast on the morrow.

Dorren waited on the bench in the council house, sipping at
beer. How eagerly he greeted her!

"Hallowed One!" He could not touch her. Standing beside

the table, he contented himself with turning his mug around, and around again, with his good hand. "I bring a message from Falling-down, but I feared I came too late when I arrived here and heard the news of the attack." He glanced past her and flushed, eyes widening with surprise, as Alain entered the council house. "This is the foreigner. Just as Falling-down predicted. He saw this one in a dream."

"Did he?" A knot curled in her gut. Falling-down had the gift of prophetic dreaming, and if he spoke against Alain's presence, then even Mother Orla might go back on her agreement.

"He saw a foreign man stumble weeping through a gateway of blue fire, with two hounds at his side. There was a creature beside him, with flaming wings, one of the gods' servants."

"He came here through the loom. The Holy One brought him."

"Truly, Falling-down did not know whether he had had a vision of the past, or of the future. He said I must journey here to look at this foreign man myself, and to bring you a message."

Adica did not look again at Alain. She did not need to. She knew exactly where he stood in relation to her; she felt him take the mug of beer offered to him by Mother Orla's granddaughter, Getsi, and thought perhaps she could taste the bite of it on his lips as he drank. "What message?"

Dorren composed himself, going still as he brought the words to his tongue. She saw, in his face, the qualities that had attracted her to him, gentleness, intelligence, and wit, but somehow he seemed, not diminished, but set in shadow, now that she had seen Alain. When Dorren spoke, he did so in the singsong voice used by most Walking Ones to deliver their memorized messages. His good hand wove little pantomimes as he spoke, each one helping him to recall.

"Falling-down of the Fen tribe speaks these words to Adica of the White Deer people. Shu-Sha of the Copper people sends this warning to her sisters and brothers." His hand fluttered like a crane, which flies easily and which because of its alert disposition cannot easily be surprised. "The Cursed Ones have discovered that we are leagued against them. They may strike at any time, from any direction. Be vigilant." He made the sign for a hawk, striking unexpectedly. "Horn believes the Cursed Ones know the secret of the loom and hoard it until they will strike all at once against each one of us, but Brightness-Hears-Me speaks these words in disagreement: a man may see holy blood come forth from a woman, but that does not mean he can make it come forth from his own body. Two Fingers has seen disturbances in the deep places. Beware above ground and below, for the Cursed Ones have the power to strike from any place. Fortify your dwelling places, and make fast your houses. Retire to the wilderness, or ring your encampment with charms. Do not walk the looms except in dire need. If the Cursed Ones have unraveled the secret of the looms, then no person who walks the looms will be safe from them. Send the Walking Ones if there is need for a message. Be like the griffins, who watch their eggs carefully against the lion: Guard yourself well until the day that is coming, when we will act."

She gave him peace to drink after he finished speaking, but she could not stop from shifting restlessly from one foot to the other, waiting for him to down the mug of beer. When he had recovered, she spoke. "Yet the Cursed Ones struck here. If they had wanted slaves, they would have carried off many, yet they only took me."

"Then what Shu-Sha fears is already coming to pass," said Dorren. "We had heard no report of any disturbances when I left the fens, but by the moon I would say that three days passed while I stepped through the looms."

"You must return quickly to see if anything has befallen Falling-down. Tell him what happened here, and let the Walking Ones take this story to my sisters and brothers, so they can know the danger that awaits us."

"Those words I will carry back to Falling-down. What of our allies, the Horse people?"

"The Holy One sometimes visits this place at the full moon. I wait for her then." Dorren nodded. She looked back, wondering at the silence behind her, to see Alain listening intently. His expression burned with frustration as he shook his head and, with a grimace, set down his cup.

"Let me sit with him until it's time for me to leave," said Dorren. "I can teach him some of our language. The Walking Ones who taught me gave me certain secrets to help me learn the languages of our allies more quickly."

"Truly, do so, and I will be grateful."

He glanced at her oddly. "Is it true that the Holy One sent him to be your husband?"

She had to look away. Dried fish and herbs hung from the beams; smoke had gathered in the rafters. "I bow to the Holy One's will." Would they think it unseemly if they knew how quickly she had fallen under Alain's spell? Would they suspect that the Holy One had used magic to bind her to the stranger? Not everyone trusted the Horse people and their powerful shaman, but she did. No magic had influenced her. Sometimes passion took people so: like a hawk, striking unexpectedly.

Dorren examined the council house thoughtfully before addressing Mother Orla with respect. "Where is my apprentice, Dagfa? She does not attend the Hallowed One as she should."

"Her mother stopped breathing just as the barley harvest came in. She had to go back to Muddy Walk to help lay the path that will lead her mother's spirit to the Other Side. Your old teacher is too crippled to walk all the way from Old Fort, and his other apprentice has gone to learn the language of the Black Deer people."

"A strange time to do so when one is needed here with the Hallowed One at all times," said Dorren with a frown. "Send a Swift to fetch Dagfa back. Her sister can draw the final spiral herself. When I am gone, Dagfa can teach the foreigner, so he can learn to speak. Falling-down would not have dreamed of him if he were not important. What if he brings a message

from the Other Side? What if the gods have chosen to speak
through him, but we cannot understand him?"

"So be it," said Mother Orla, acknowledging the truth of his
argument.

Yet Alain could communicate, even if not always in words.
That evening when Adica led Dorren up to the loom Alain
came with her, although no common villager dared witness
sorcery for fear of the winds and eddies of fate called up by
magic.

She had spent the afternoon with Pur the stone knapper,
repairing her mirror. He promised to make her a new one, but
meanwhile he had glue stewed from the hooves of aurochs by
which he could make the mirror whole again, good enough to
weave the loom this night.

When she met Dorren and Alain again before sunset, Alain
greeted her very prettily, although it was clearly easier for him
to parrot the words Dorren had taught him than to understand
her reply. They left the village and walked up through the
embankments to the tumulus.

"I remember my father toiling on these embankments,"
said Dorren. "He believed that such fortifications would protect all the White Deer people from the incursions of the
Cursed Ones, yet how can they if the Cursed Ones have
learned how to walk the looms?"

They paused to look back at the village below, the houses
with their long sides facing south to get the most warmth
from the winter sun, the garden plots denuded except for
the last leafy turnips going to seed, a restless mob of sheep
huddled together for the night. Adults swarmed around the
outer palisade, raising logs. "Each village must protect itself,"
said Adica softly, "until that day we are rid of the Cursed
Ones."

Dorren looked away from her quickly, remembering the
fate laid on her.

Beside her, Alain knelt to dig a hand into the soil. "This is called 'earth,'" he said, sounding each word meticulously, although he couldn't reproduce the sounds precisely. He gestured toward the nearest curve of the embankment. "This is called 'wall of earth.'"

Dorren chuckled. "You will learn quickly with a good teacher."

"A good teacher," echoed Alain, wiping his hand off on grass.

They reached the loom as night fell. The circle of stones stood in silence, as they always did. She set her feet on the calling ground. Dorren knew to stand to her right side and, after a moment, she got Alain stationed to her left, although he seemed as likely to wander right into the loom itself.

Clouds covered part of the sky, which made the weaving more complicated. Since the Grindstone lay concealed by clouds, she would have to weave a gateway by means of the Adze and the Aurochs, whose hulking shoulders she could use as a weight to throw the gate open to the west.

Lifting her mirror, she began the prayer to waken the stones: *"Heed me, that which opens in the east. Heed me, that which opens in the west."*

Alain did not tremble or run, as many would have, faced with sorcery such as she wove now out of starlight and stone. The hill woke beneath her. The awareness of the ancient queens gripped her heart, as though their hands reached through stone and earth and death itself to take hold of their living heir, to seize her for their own purposes.

Starlight caught in the stones and she wove them into a gateway of light. She scarcely heard Dorren's murmured "fare you well" before he swiftly left her side, stepped into the gate—and vanished from her sight.

Alain took two steps forward to follow him. Adica pulled him back. "No. Do not follow him." He moved no farther, yet his expression as he stared into the gateway of light had a blankness in it, as though his thoughts, his soul, his heart had left to cross into unknown country, where she could never follow. Unbidden, unexpectedly, her voice broke. "I would not have you leave me, Alain."

The light faded, the gateway splintered and fell apart, and all at once she began to weep.

One of the dogs whined. Its jaws closed, gently but firmly, on her hand, drawing no blood but tugging firmly. Alain took her mirror out of her hands and looped it at her belt. He scolded the dog softly, and it released her, but Alain clasped her hand instead.

"Come," he said, gently but firmly. "I give to the not-breathing ones. To the—the queens." He struggled to recall the words Dorren had taught him. "To the queens I give an offering."

To the queens. They still resided in her. The echo of their presence throbbed in tune to the beating of her heart. The queens demanded an offering only from those who begged for their help. Yet once that bargain was struck, no matter how bitterly the price weighed on the one who had braved holy ground to petition them, it had to be fulfilled. Even she, especially she, could not escape promises made to the holy dead.

Like a stick thrown in a river, she went where the current pulled her. Alain led her down the eastern slope of the tumulus to the stone lintel that marked the sacred entrance to the queens' grave, the holy place for which the village was named. There lay the threshold of the passageway that led into the secret womb where the ancient queens rested. Clouds crept up over the heavens, veiling stars one by one.

Alain groped for and found a torch. She struck flint and lit it. The torch bled smoke onto the corbeled ceiling, revealing the symbols of power carved into the stones: ships drawing the sun down to the underworld, the spiral path leading the dead to the Other Side, the hands of the Holy Ones who had gone before, reaching for the four staffs of knowledge. Crouching at first, they were able to straighten up as the ceiling sloped upward, so that they walked upright into the low chamber where the queens rested in three stone tombs, each in her own niche.

The tombs bore carvings representative of each of the queens. The tomb of Arrow Bright, lying to the west, was carved with two sphinxes: the lion women of the desert from whom she had learned the secret ways of the Huntress. In the southern niche, Golden Sow's tomb gleamed with gold melted from phoenix feathers and beaten into the shape of a sacred sow, the spirit guide of the queen whose magic had made all the women of her tribe fertile and their children healthy. Last, in the niche that faced north, lay Toothless' cairn, more primitive than the others, for she had reigned in the days when the magic of metalworking was not known among humankind.

Here, deep in the womb of stone and earth, not even the wind could be heard.

She stepped forward to offer a prayer, but Alain pressed her back and stepped forward in her place. He stood straight and proud, bright and fearless, as he spoke words in his own language, which she could not understand.

What was he telling them? She knew they were listening, because the dead are always listening.

The torch blew out, leaving her caught in their vast silence. She couldn't even feel Alain's comforting presence nor hear the panting of the dogs.

The vision hit like a blast of light, searing her eyes.

Alain, dressed in clothing unlike any garb she has seen before, stands beside a stone tomb so remarkably carved into the shape of a supine man that she believes that in a moment the stone will come to life and the man will sit up. Stone dogs lie with him, one at his head and one at his feet. Alain weeps silently, tears streaming down his face. A company of women enters the house behind him, only it is no house but a high hall of cunning and astounding design, lofting impossibly toward the sky. Alain turns to the one who walks foremost among them, a queen so thin and wasted that she is ugly; truly, the Fat One gave none of her blessing here. In the heart of this queen lies thwarted spring, knotted coils twisted and bent around a withered spirit stained with fear. But Alain loves her. The young queen offers him nothing, and yet he loves her anyway.

Adica weeps, bitterly, and her tears wash the vision away until she floats on the vast waters. Foam licks around her as she is caught in the wake of an animal as sleek as a dragon and as swift as a serpent, driving through the sea. At first she thinks it is a living creature, lean and long, but then she sees it is a ship. It is utterly unlike the low-bellied, hide-built curraghs in which the coastal tribes scour the shoreline for fish and fowl. A dragon's head carved out of wood adorns its stem. A creature like a man yet not one of humankind stands at the stem, searching as mist closes in around him. What manner of creature is he? What is he looking for?

But she knows as soon as she wonders, for within the vision she can see into the pumping mass of flesh veined with stone that serves him as a heart. He, too, is looking for Alain.

Mist sweeps in like a wave, blinding her. The tendrils that coil around her burn as brightly as if they are formed out of particles of fire. She sees into them and beyond them.

There are spirits burning in the air with wings of flame and eyes as brilliant as knives. Yet one among them sinks, weighted with mortality. This one falls, blazing, into a threshold composed of twisting blue fire, the passageway between worlds. Through the gate this falling woman sees onto the middle world, the world known to humankind: there in the middle world, a huge tumulus ringed by half-ruined ramparts rests in silence. Dead warriors lie scattered along the rampart walls and curves. A killing wind has blown them every which way. Like leaves the dead lie tumbled up against a ring of fallen stones, some shattered, some cracked in half, that stands in ruins at the height of the hill.

Adica prays for the protection of the Fat One and the courage of the Queen of the Wild, though no words pass her lips—or if they do, she cannot hear them. She knows this hill and these ramparts, now worn away, crumbling under the hand of an immeasurable force she cannot name. She recognizes the ring of fallen stones, covered by lichen and drowned by age. It is Queens' Grave, but it is not the Queens' Grave she knows, with freshly dug ramparts ringing the queens' hill and a stone loom newly set in place on the summit in the time of her own parents.

It is Queens' Grave garbed as the Toothless One, the hag of old age. Its youth and maturity have long since been worn away by the bite of the seasons and the winds and the cold rain. It is like glimpsing herself as an aged woman, old and ruined and forgotten.

Yet one stone still stands within the stone loom. Clothed in blue-white fire, it shelters a dying warrior. Clothed in metal rings, slumped against the burning stone, he waits for death attended by two spirits clothed in the forms of dogs. The falling woman cloaked with blazing wings of aetherial fire whirls past Adica's sight. She reaches for the dying warrior, and as she grasps him and pulls him after her, Adica recognizes Alain. But the blazing woman's grip tears away, off his shoulders, and he is lost, torn off the path that leads to the land of the dead so that he walks neither in the world where he lived or on the path that should take him to the Other Side. He is lost, with his spirit guides crowded at his feet, for the space of a breath and a heartbeat, until the Holy One's magic, the binding power known to the Horse people, nets him and drags him in. He lands, bleeding, dying, and lost, on the great womb of the queens.

She gasped into awareness at the same moment his hand found her shoulder and closed there. He said her name and dropped down onto his knees behind her, his face wet against her neck.

"Alain," she whispered. She turned to face him, together on their knees, and he clung to her, or she to him; it was hard to tell and perhaps they clung to each other, flotsam washed in a vast wave off the sea.

It seemed to her then that they knelt not on stone but on a bed of grass, under the stars on a night made for mysteries. Trees surrounded them. Nearby a waterfall spilled softly onto moss-covered rocks. How they had come to this place she did not know, only that the wind breathed into her ears with certain subtle and alluring whispers. He held her tightly, and as she shifted, moving her arms on his back, his hands found other places to wander as well. He murmured under his breath, but though his words remained a mystery to her, the language of the body needed no words to convey its message.

He spoke in other, wordless ways: I ought not, but I want to. I am unsure, disquieted, yet my desire is strong.

This was the offering. Yet still he hesitated.

She had not become Hallowed One because she thought sluggishly. She groped for and found the rope that bound his linen tunic tight at his waist, and when he kissed her, she unbound this crude belt so that the linen fell askew. She slipped her fingers down through his, twining their hands together, and with her free hand bound the rope around their clasped hands, once, twice, and a third time. She knew the words well enough:

With this binding, we will hold fast together.

May the Fat One bless our union.

May the Green Man bring us happiness and all good things.

May the Queen of the Wild reveal what it means to walk together.

Like coals stored within a hollow log, he burned hot and shy. But in the end, the queens had their way. No doubt in their silent graves they still dreamed of that congress which is as sweet as the meadow flowers. She felt them inhabiting her body just as she knew their power blazed in her for this while, caught in an unnatural enchantment of their devising. Truly, in this place, what man could resist her?

Not he.

PART THREE

THE VALE OF ICE

IX
A SLICE OF APPLE

1

WINTER laid in its usual store of bitter weather. For three days a viciously cold wind blew down from the north to turn the shores and shallows of the Veser River to ice. Every puddle that graced the streets of Gent had frozen through, and in some ways, Anna reflected, that was a good thing. It meant the stink froze, rainwater, sludge, and sewage in crackling sheets that little Helen liked to stomp on so she could hear them snap and splinter. At times like this Anna remembered the months she had hidden in the tanneries with her brother Matthias: the city had been cleaner when the Eika inhabited it, but perhaps that was only because it had been mostly deserted then.

Not anymore. Even in the dead of winter folk walked the frozen avenue alongside the freshly whitewashed wall marking the mayor's palace. Walled compounds faced the avenue on the other side. Well-to-do artisans and merchant families lived and worked in these compounds. A peddler trundled his cart up to one of the gates and called out, hoping for admittance. A servant boy emerged and, after looking the peddler over and examining the condition of his heavy winter tunic and cloth boots stuffed with straw, let him inside. At times, these signs of prosperity still amazed her. It had been less than two years since refugees and newcomers had flooded back to Gent after the Eika defeat.

Anna had learned to amuse herself with such thoughts when she took Helen along on errands because inevitably she did a great deal of waiting. With her arms full of wool cloth, she couldn't just grab hold of Helen's arm and drag her along. The little girl didn't understand any need for haste, nor did she seem to feel the cold even as Anna's fingers grew numb, through her wool gloves. Helen warbled like a bird, phrases that leaped up and slid down with lovely precision, as she stamped on a particularly fine landscape of thin puddles, creamy with frozen shells that made a satisfyingly sharp crack when they shattered.

"Here, now, little one, this is no weather for a child to be playing outside." The voice came from behind them. Helen continued her singing and stomping without pause.

Anna turned to see Prior Humilicus walking down the street with several attendants. The cathedral tower loomed behind him, marking the town square that lay just past the northwest corner of the mayor's palace. The prior of the new monastery dedicated to St. Perpetua was a familiar sight in town these days, especially in the months since the abbot, Prince Ekkehard, had ridden off with Lord Wichman to fight in the east. Humilicus visited the biscop every day no matter the weather.

"Ah," he said, seeing Anna's face and her burden. "You're the weaver's niece." Like all noble folk, he had the habit of touching without asking. He stripped off his sheepskin mittens and fingered a bolt of cloth admiringly. "Very fine, indeed. A rich scarlet. Did Mistress Suzanne dye this wool herself?"

Anna nodded. Helen had come to the last of the string of frozen puddles and was crushing the grainy ice that made a lacework of its miniature shoreline.

The prior's lean face tightened and his lips pressed together. "You're the mute one, are you not? God have surely afflicted your family twice over." Anna didn't like the way he examined Helen. From a filthy, abandoned, half-starved toddler, she had grown into an angelically pretty little girl, some four or six years of age. "She has a remarkably true voice," he mused. "I wonder if she can be trained to sing hymns."

His gaze shifted past Helen. The long wall of the mayor's palace had once been painted with vivid scenes of the death and life of the blessed Daisan but had been painted over for the third time three days ago. Humilicus picked up a rose encrusted in hoarfrost, examining the wilted flower with the kind of scrutiny most folk reserved for maggots crawling on rotten meat. "I thought all these leavings were picked up last week."

"They were, Prior," said the eldest of the monks, whose thin nose was blue with cold. A gust of wind shook the banners set atop the palace wall and set Anna's teeth chattering. "The biscop's clerics go around every week collecting such offerings. They brought in two wreaths, one carving, and four candles yesterday."

Helen darted forward to pluck the rose out of Prior Humilicus' fingers, then scurried away to hide behind Anna.

"Here, now!" scolded the thin-nosed man.

"Nay, let her go," said Prior Humilicus. "A whitewash won't erase memory. If the common folk still lay offerings here after all this time, then chastising one witless girl won't have any effect on the stain that's crept into them. It was that stout lad who let the pollution in, he and his tongueless accomplice." Despite his grim looks, he had a mild if somewhat sardonic disposition. He paused to examine the wall with an ironic smile. "A clever and well-spoken lad was Brother Ermanrich. It passes my understanding that God should have allowed the Enemy's work to enter such a fitting vessel."

"God's ways are a mystery, Prior," agreed his companion. "It is a good thing those young monks rode away with Prince Ekkehard."

Humilicus bowed his head as if in submission to the unfathomable mind of God. The procession of monks moved away down the street.

Anna stamped twice, sharply, to get Helen's attention. The little girl followed happily, skipping and singing, as they walked down to the waterfront gate, to the fullers' yard. The mistress allowed them to sit on their cloaks by the hearth while she inspected each finger of cloth with an eye to flaws, but Anna didn't mind waiting, since it was warm. She carried distaff and spindle with her, and began spinning fiber to yarn. Helen pried all the thorns from the rose and tucked it behind her ear, like an ornament. Sleepy, she yawned so widely that her mouth looked ready to split. A few girls their ages sat or stood in the hall, spinning, although most of the activity at this time of day took place out in the yard or in the tenters' field situated below the city walls.

"That'll do," said the fuller, who usually hadn't a kind word to say about anyone. That she couldn't find any flaws in the weaver's work was high praise. "I don't want anyone saying we'd damaged the goods in the fulling or tenting." An assistant hurriedly took the cloth away to the yard. "I've twelve lengths done for you to be taking back to your aunt, although I see you've an errand to run before you go home." She indicated the scarlet cloak, already fulled and finished, that Anna had set on the bench behind her. The fuller fingered the cloth in the same avaricious way Prior Humilicus had. "Not many can get such a good scarlet color. Did Mistress Suzanne get the wool already dyed?"

Anna allowed herself a vapid smile. She hated being mute. The lack of a voice was like lacking hands, most noticeable when you weren't thinking about it and reached instinctively to tighten your belt or take a slice of apple, but occasionally it had advantages.

"Well, you've nothing to say! And no wonder. Your aunt has

made much of herself in Gent since the Eika were driven out. If I didn't know you were mute, I'd suppose you were simply too proud to talk to such as me!" The fuller had the kind of face easily creased by smiles, round and full, but she hadn't any smiles in her gaze, only envy. "Still, you're old enough to be betrothed, and you look as though you're likely to be moving to the women's benches come St. Oya's Day. Has Mistress Suzanne found a husband for you yet?"

Anna shook her head. She didn't mind that her body was changing; that was part of the natural order. But she didn't like the way people tried to tempt her with marriage offers. After all, no one actually cared about *her*.

"You've a funny color of skin, it's true, but you're healthy enough and it would be a good alliance with a prosperous family, and advantageous for both our households to be allied one with the other. I've a likely nephew. He's a good lad, almost nineteen—" The fuller seemed ready to go on at length, but shrieks erupted from the yard, followed by angry voices. She rose with a grunt of anger. "Gutta, give the weaver's niece the cloth that's done." To Anna's relief, she strode out to the yard, where Anna heard her voice raised in a blistering scolding.

A girl no older than Anna transferred the fulled and dried cloth into Anna's keeping as soon as Anna tucked distaff and spindle into her belt. She layered the good scarlet cloak in between the other cloth, for protection, and stamped twice to attract Helen's attention. She held a dozen folded lengths of cloth that Mistress Suzanne would either trade to tailors' row or finish herself into cloaks and winter clothing. With a sigh of satisfaction, she left the fullers' yard behind.

As usual, she had saved the best delivery for last.

She loved visiting the mayor's palace. The guards at the gate recognized her and let her and Helen inside without any trouble, although one of them, a lad not more than twenty years of age, bent down to speak to her.

"I beg you, sister, say a good word for me to the lovely

Frederun. I know she favors you for the handsome cloth you
bring."

The other guard snorted. "This girl's mute, Ernust. She
can't say anything to the lovely Frederun, not that it would
mean much to you if she did! She hasn't taken a man to her
bed since Lord Wichman went away. Get on with you, then,
child, and leave us out here in the cold. Maybe poor Ernust's
nether parts will cool off a little!"

The palace compound had a neat layout, easy to get around.
The stables and storerooms lay to one side, the palace on the
other, and the kitchens at the far end of the central courtyard
so that any fire that might break out wouldn't spread to the
other buildings. Despite the Eika occupation, the palace had
survived more-or-less intact. One wing of the stables still lay
in ruins, and three of the storerooms had burned to the
ground and lay in various stages of repair. The eastern gate
had fallen in completely to make a great heap of stone, but it
had taken all this time to make the palace interior habitable
and only this winter had his lordship sent to Kassel and
Autun to find engineers who could direct the rebuilding of
the gate.

The palace itself had a great hall and several wings, one of
them fully three stories tall, added on over many years. Anna
made her way around to the carters' entrance and was admitted to the servants' hall, a goodly chamber busy with women
sewing up rents in linens, mixing cordials, binding up sachets
of aromatic herbs to relieve the smell in the closed-up winter
rooms, and polishing the mayor's silver plate, salvaged in the
headlong retreat from Gent.

Frederun had become chief of the servingwomen of the
palace mostly because Lord Wichman had quickly singled her
out when he'd taken over the lordship of Gent after the great
victory over Bloodheart and the Eika. She had a chair set at the
largest table, the seat of her authority, and when she saw Anna,
she beckoned her forward and took the cloak from her.
Standing, she shook it out. Work in the hall came to a halt.

"Truly," said Frederun, "Mistress Suzanne has outdone herself this time!" The cloak had a rich scarlet hue, fur lining, and a beautifully sewn trim in a fanciful design of elegant dragons outlined in gold-dyed thread.

"Surely that's not for you, Frederun?" demanded an older woman whose face bore an unsightly scar, the mark of an Eika ax.

"Nay, it's for Lord Hrodik. Now that Lord Wichman is gone, he fancies himself the proud defender of the city. It's to go over his armor."

The women laughed.

"His sister's armor, you mean," continued the scarred woman. "He'll never be half the fighter Lady Amalia was, may God bless her name."

All the women there drew the Circle of Unity at their breasts and murmured a prayer for peace. Many of them remembered the noble lady who had died of her wounds after the battle for Gent that Count Lavastine and King Henry had won.

"No sense in calling the poor young man names, for all his faults," scolded Frederun. "The rats have fled the nest, and the mouse that's left us is a kinder master than they ever were."

"True-spoken words," agreed the scarred woman, resting a hand on Frederun's shoulder. "You took the brunt of it, friend. We've none of us forgotten that."

Frederun traced the outlines of dragons embroidered along the edge of the rich fabric. She had dreamy eyes of a limpid brown, the kind one imagined gazing into a lover's ardent gaze, set off by light hair caught back and covered by a shawl tied so loosely that curling strands of hair had escaped to frame her pretty face. She was, everyone agreed, the second handsomest woman in Gent.

"Come, now," she said, shaking off her reverie impatiently without responding to her companion's comment, "here's these two lasses who must be cold from walking outside in that wind just so Lord Hrodik can have his cloak the instant he desires it! Here, child, let you and your sister come in and have a bit of hot cider to drink for it's that cold out, isn't it now? Sit by the hearth." She addressed one of the younger servants. "Give them a slice of apple, and be sure they have a bit of cake from the lord's table as well." She clapped her hands sharply twice. "Back to work! Let's have no sleeping in the hall. We've little enough light these months as it is. Fastrada!" The scarred woman had taken the cloak from her to fold it up. "I pray you, will you see that the cloak is delivered to Lord Hrodik?"

"Truly, Frederun, you know how he will complain if you're not the one to deliver it to him."

Frederun exclaimed sharply on a gusty sigh, but she reached for the cloak and finished folding it with practiced ease. She had strong hands from years of hard work, although certainly she couldn't have been more than twenty years of age. "Why must he believe he is owed what Wichman took?"

No one else appeared to be listening, perhaps only because of the boring familiarity of the situation. "Can you not speak to Biscop Suplicia?" asked Fastrada.

"She is kin by way of certain cousins to Lord Hrodik's family. Why should she feel any compassion for a bond servant like me? Do I not owe service to their noble house?"

"I thought you served at the mayor's palace, not in the lord's bed."

"You know as well as I that Mayor Werner was the last of his family. Nay, the noble lords have hold of Gent now, and they won't give it up."

The older woman frowned sourly. "Very well. I'll take the cloak up to him, and let him bleat as he may."

Frederun cast down her gaze, as though in exhaustion. "I thank you." She straightened one of her sleeves and wiped a fleck of ash, floating out from the hearth, out of an eye. "He has grown worse—"

"Since the weather keeps him locked inside instead of out hunting. Truly, he has more cock than sense!"

"Isn't that true of most men!" interposed one of the younger women. She had a pretty mouth, bright eyes, and pox marks on her cheeks. "Here, Fastrada, I'll take the cloak up to his lordship. He fancies me, and I want some of that honey he hoards, for my family to trade for cloth for my sister's dowry."

"Take care, Uota, that you don't walk into a fire so hot that it burns you," replied Frederun quietly.

"I hadn't heard you were so shy," retorted Uota with a flash of anger, "in the days before Lord Wichman took to beating you for his pleasure. It's said you gave yourself freely enough if the lord was of *princely* disposition."

"Hush, Uota!" cried Fastrada, although Frederun made no reply except to sink down on the bench beside Anna. "You're a latecomer here. You can't know what any of us suffered—"

Uota took the cloak and flounced out.

"Here, now," began Fastrada as the other servants turned away to give the illusion of privacy, although truly there were no secrets in the servants' hall. "Frederun—"

The younger woman raised a hand to forestall further comment, and after a moment Fastrada moved away to supervise three women polishing the silver plate.

Anna examined Frederun with interest and pity. It seemed to her that they shared something in common, she and the servingwoman: they had survived the worst kind of hardship and found themselves in a decent and even prosperous life, with a warm bed and two ample meals every day, yet she recognized in Frederun's expression a discontent like her own, bothersome and mysterious. Why couldn't she just be satisfied, as Matthias was?

Little Helen looked up suddenly, slid the rose from behind her ear, and presented it to Frederun.

"Ai, thank you, child!" Tears welled up in Frederun's eyes. She brought the rose to her face and sniffed at it, smiling ruefully. "All the scent's gone. Where did you find such a lovely treasure?"

Anna signed as well as she could, and unlike many people, Frederun watched her hands carefully, intent on what she was trying to communicate. "By the city wall? Nay, here, the palace wall. Ah, of course! It's one of the offerings folk leave." Her face shuttered, growing still and thoughtful, as she touched the wooden Circle that hung from her neck. "Some things are hard to forget," she muttered, stroking the rose's withered petals before collecting herself with a shake of the head. "Will your aunt make a wedding cloak as fine for her betrothed, the tanner she's to marry in the spring?"

Anna smiled and nodded, but what flashed across Frederun's expression was difficult to understand: Pain? Longing? Envy?

"She's done well, has your aunt. None knows better than I what she suffered in Steleshame at the hands of Lord Wichman. I remember pitying her there. How could I have known it was to come to me in my time?" She straightened up sharply with a frown. "No sense in sorrowing over what's past, is there, little sister? You've suffered more than I, poor child, not able to speak a word." She wiped a smear of soot off Helen's delicate face. "And this poor creature, what will become of her with such a pretty face to plague her all her years?"

Helen smiled beatifically up at Frederun, for she was always the happiest of creatures as long as she was fed and clean. A pang gripped Anna's heart, hearing truth in Frederun's words. Probably Helen would never be quite right in the head, and her child's beauty, if it held as she grew, would only bring her grief.

"Come now," added Frederun briskly, "you finish that up and get you home or Mistress Suzanne will be fearing for you and the little one with dusk coming on."

Standing, she had just turned to call to one of her women when the door slammed open, helped by a gust of wind, and two of the mayor's guardsmen came in, beards tipped with ice, slapping their hands together to warm them.

"Ho, Mistress Frederun!" cried one in a voice too loud for the hall, pitched to carry over the wind. "There's a great party of soldiers and their noble lord ridden in, come to beg hospitality of Lord Hrodik."

"And to grant themselves first pickings at the armory," added his comrade irritably.

Frederun froze, as might a rabbit when the shadow of an owl skimmed across it. "Who might it be? Is it Wichman, returned?"

"Nay. They come from the west. They're riding east to fight the Quman. I saw no banner, nor did I speak to the outriders. You'll have to go into the hall to see who it might be."

Frederun hadn't time to answer before a trio of flustered servingmen hurried into the hall through another door, calling out Lord Hrodik's orders.

Anna grabbed a last bit of cake and wolfed it down before getting her arms around her load of cloth and hustling Helen out of the way. The winter wind hit hard as they came out into the courtyard. Men called to each other in the stables, and the yard had the look of a hive of bees stirred into action. Two outriders stood chatting with the stable master, but they wore no device to indicate to which noble kin they owed allegiance. No one paid any mind as she and Helen left by the western gate, nor did she see any war party on the streets as they cut through the town square, past the cathedral, and came back around to the other side of the mayor's palace. The eastern gate here was a tumble of stone. More than one child had broken a leg or an arm climbing these ruins. Beyond the marketplace, quiet in winter except for a flurry of activity around the butchers' stalls, lay a number of workshops: smaller compounds made up of a house, workshops, and outbuildings surrounded by a wall.

With Helen tagging at her heels, Anna crossed the marketplace to the open gate that let her into the place she now called home, the workshop taken over by the woman everyone called her aunt, Suzanne. Once known to all of Steleshame as Mistress Gisela's niece, Suzanne was now known in the city of Gent simply as *the* weaver, although of course in a city as large as Gent, crammed with fully five thousand people so the biscop claimed, there were other weavers. None of them were asked to supply fine cloaks and tunics to the lord who resided in the mayor's palace.

Out in the courtyard, by the trough, a donkey stood patiently, one leg cocked slightly as its ear twitched at each shudder of wind. Raimar was sawing a log into planks, his pale hair caught back with a leather thong. He had stripped down to his summer tunic. The light fabric showed off the breadth of his shoulders. Flecks of sawdust flew from the wood, scattering like pale gold dust around his feet on the hard packed earth.

Young Autgar held the other end of the saw. He was singing in an off-key voice about the pain roasting his heart because it had been three days since he'd caught sight of the beautiful shepherd girl, which was after all a strange song for Autgar to be singing since he'd been married two years before in Steleshame to one of Suzanne's weavers and had two children already.

Raimar whistled sharply, and they laid up the saw. He turned to grin at the two girls. "Take those into the wool room, Anna. Suzanne was just asking after you. I see you still have some crumbs on your face. I told her you'd be dining at your ease at the mayor's palace!"

Anna smiled back at him, and Helen ran over to watch the bubbling dye pot, this day stewing yarn to a strong tansy yellow.

Anna left Helen outside and went into the workshop, a long, low room hazy with smoke. Four looms stood in the workshop, and Suzanne's three assistants worked, each with a girl at her side learning the trade. A toddler raced around the room, shrieking with delight, while an infant slept in a cradle set rocking by one of the girls.

Anna crossed through the side door that led into the darker chamber, shuttered in, where fleeces, raw and scoured wool, and spun wool stored in skeins as well as unsold cloth were stored. The weighty scent of all that wool comforted her, dense and pungent. Suzanne was standing at the table, haggling with a farmer out of West Farms over the skeins of yarn he'd brought her.

"This just isn't as good quality as the last lot. I can't give you as much for it."

Anna set down her cloth on the table and got out her spindle so that she could spin while she waited for the negotiations to end. In time the farmer took away cloth as payment for his yarn.

"You've crumbs on your face, Anna," said Suzanne as she sorted through the yarn, setting some on one shelf and some on another, according to its quality and fineness. "I hope they fed you well at the palace, for we're fasting tonight. Raimar brings news from the tannery." She examined Anna with a smile. That smile, no doubt, had gotten her into trouble before, just because of the way it made her face turn rosy and sweet. "Nay, I'll let Matthias tell you himself! Come, give me a hand with this yarn. Move what's at the back of the shelf forward. That lot. Prior Humilicus came by. They're bringing in a dozen novices on St. Eusebe's Day and he wants enough cloth for a dozen robes by summer. Did you know that Hano the saddler's daughter is to marry next autumn? To a young man all the way from Osterburg, if you can believe that!"

She chatted on in this companionable way as they tidied up the wool room. It was her way of making Anna comfortable. After they got everything in order, Suzanne returned to her loom while Anna picked up the baby, who had woken and begun to fuss, so that her mother could finish off a line before nursing.

In the afternoon, with winter twilight sighing down outside, Matthias came in with Raimar and Autgar. He was taller than Suzanne now, filled out enormously from a combination of steady meals and hard work. He stank of the tannery, and as he washed the worst of the stink off his hands, he broke his

news. "Anna! I'm to be taken in as a journeyman at the tanning works!"

His words left her cold, although she managed to hug him.
They all expected her to be happy for him. He continued to
speak as he stepped back from Anna, exchanging a look with
his betrothed, the youngest of the weavers who had fled
Steleshame with Suzanne. She was a girl about his age who had
round cheeks and clever hands. "I'll live at the tannery now,
and I'll have every other Hefensday off."

They all fell to talking as they made ready to attend the
Hefensday Eve service, washing their hands, tidying their
clothing, the women retying their hair scarves. Because Anna
couldn't join in the talk, she waited by the door like a lost
child peeking in at a feast of camaraderie she could never share
in. Matthias would move on with his life. After everything
they'd survived together, he was leaving her behind. She could
never be more than an afterthought in his new life. She wasn't
more than an afterthought in any of their lives, not really, no
matter how kindly they treated her.

Reflexively, she drew her finger in a circle around her
wooden Circle of Unity, the remembered gesture that her
mother had habitually repeated in moments of fear or sadness
or worry. What had become of the Eika prince who, when
they had crept to the door of the crypt in the cathedral, had
watched them silently and let them go? He had drawn his
finger, just so, around the Circle of Unity he wore at his chest,
although she still could not fathom why a savage Eika would
wear a Circle, symbol of the faith of the Unities.

Tears filled her eyes suddenly, bringing with them the bitter
memory of the young lord who had knelt before her at
Steleshame and spoken gently to her. She hadn't answered
him, and ever after that moment, she had lost her voice, as
though God were punishing her for her silence.

"Here, now, Anna," said Suzanne, "it's a fine day for
Matthias, is it not?" With a smile, she tugged Anna along
with her, gesturing to the others to follow. "You look well

enough, lass. You won't disgrace us when we process like a fine and wealthy family into church, will you?"

Helen was wiggling in Raimar's arms, and he was laughing good-naturedly as he tried to wipe a sooty stain gotten God knew where off her cheek. The rest of the household trailed behind Suzanne like so many sheep, and in this cheerful fashion they made their way down the dusky streets to the cathedral.

On Lordsday many folk crowded into the cathedral for the evening services, for tomorrow would be Hefensday, seventh and therefore highest of the days of the week. The service had already started as they entered, making their way down the nave to the spot under a window painted with a scene of the blessed Daisan teaching his disciples. An ugly scar still marred the painted robe of the blessed Daisan, where an Eika weapon had mauled the paint. Most of the pillars had sustained damage during the Eika occupation. Stone angels, gargoyles, and eagles carved into the pilasters bore rake marks, as though they had been repeatedly clawed by a creature powerful enough to gouge stone. The paved floor had been scrubbed often enough that only a few traces of the fires that had burned here remained. The shattered windows had been restored first, although one was still boarded over.

At the altar, a cleric led the congregation in the seventh-day hymn. "'Happy that person who finds refuge in God!'"

The altar had been cleaned and polished to a gleam, a holy cup of gold placed upon it, together with the ivory-bound book containing the Holy Verses out of the which the clerics and the biscop dictated the service. Only one object lent a discordant note to the apse: a heavy chain fastened to the base of the altar, hammered in with an iron spike.

Anna remembered the daimone whom Bloodheart had chained to the altar in misery. Suzanne noticed her shuddering, and put an arm around her to comfort her. But nothing could ever drive out that recollection, flashes of recognition that always assaulted her when they came to services.

"In the crypt lies the path you seek," the daimone had said in its

unformed, hoarse voice. By that path she and Matthias had
escaped Gent.

Yet it was the Eika who had stood by silently to let them
escape. Matthias had forgotten that, but she never would.

The toddler had fallen asleep, but the baby was wakeful,
now and again smacking its lips and taking a quick nurse at its
mother's breast as the clerics sang the opening hymns.

"Where do you think Lord Hrodik is?" Raimar said to
Suzanne. He caught Anna looking at him, and smiled at her.
He always treated her and Matthias well. He had lost his
family to the Eika, a young bride, his parents, and three brothers, and like Suzanne he was determined to make a good life for
himself out of the wreckage. For that reason, as well as mutual
respect, they had come to an agreement a few months ago and
announced their betrothal, to be consummated in the spring.

Suzanne craned her neck to see the front of the congregation. The Lord's place near the altar stood empty. "He hasn't
missed a Hefensday Eve service once since Lord Wichman quit
the city. That must be fully eight months ago."

"Nay, love, he missed services that one time when he was
caught out in a storm and broke his nose."

Suzanne stifled a giggle. In Steleshame she hadn't laughed
much. No one had smiled much in Steleshame, but after being
thrown to the dogs by her Aunt Gisela, Suzanne had had less
reason to smile than most. Yet, in time, prosperity had cured
her ills. She seemed content enough.

Anna only wished she felt content as well, but every night
she dreamed of the young lord, Count Lavastine's heir. She
couldn't remember his name. It seemed to her that he was
weeping and lost, torn between sorrow and rage at the indignities and pain suffered by those he had loved.

Surely she could have helped him, if she had only spoken
up. That must be the reason God were punishing her.

The clerics led the congregation in a hymn as the biscop
entered from the side porch and took her place in her high seat
behind the altar.

> *"Like a dry and thirsty land that has no water,*
> *so do I seek God.*
> *With my body wasted with longing,*
> *I come before God in the sanctuary.*
> *As I lift my hands in prayer*
> *I am satisfied as with a feast,*
> *and in the watches of the night*
> *I trust in the love which shelters me."*

The cleric leading the singing faltered, face washing pale, and a hush poured forward like a wave from the great doors at the entrance to the cathedral. Everyone turned to look.

A nobleman stood in the entryway. He seemed frozen, hesitant, as if he could not make his feet move him forward into the nave. Tall and broad-shouldered, he had a sharply foreign look about him: a bronze-complexioned face, high cheekbones, and night-black hair cut to hang loose at his shoulders. His features struck Anna with a disquiet that made her mouth go dry. He seemed familiar, but she couldn't place him. Lord Hrodik waited awkwardly behind him, staring at the big man in awe.

Suzanne staggered, and Raimar steadied her on his arm. "Prince Sanglant," she whispered.

The nobleman's gaze swept the congregation. For an uncanny instant, Anna actually thought he found and fastened on Suzanne, alone of the throng. Suzanne made a noise in her throat—whether a protest or a prayer was hard to tell—and hid her face against Raimar's shoulder.

As if that muffled sound goaded him forward, he strode up the aisle without looking to his left or to his right. The altar brought him up short. He stared at the chain lying at rest in a heap at the stone base, nostrils flaring like those of a spooked horse. The biscop hurried forward from her seat, but he dropped down to a crouch without greeting her and reached to touch the chain as though it were a poisonous snake.

"God save us." Matthias grasped Anna's arm so tightly that his grip pinched her skin. "It's the daimone!"

Anna shook her head numbly. The daimone trapped here by Bloodheart had not been human; it had only taken on human form when it had been forced down out of the heavens and into its painful imprisonment within the bounds of earth.

"It wasn't a daimone at all," Matthias went on breathlessly, "but a noble man, that same prince they spoke of. By what miracle did he survive?"

Sweating now and shaking, the prince settled to his knees before the altar and looked unlikely to budge. Lord Hrodik hurried forward as if to remonstrate with him, but a slender cleric placed himself between the two men and with an outstretched hand waved to the young lord to move away.

Biscop Suplicia was not easily startled, although for an instant her lips parted in astonishment. She gestured to her clerics to step back, resumed chanting the service alone in a resonant soprano. Slowly, in stuttering gasps, her clerics joined in, although many of them could not stop staring at the man in his rich tunic and finely-embossed belt who had fallen to his knees right there before the altar. It was hard to tell if he were remarkably pious, stricken by God's mercy, or simply striving not to fall apart altogether, for his hands clutched at that chain until his knuckles whitened and a trickle of blood ran from one scraped finger.

In this way, the congregation, led by an anxious Lord Hrodik, dutifully followed the service to completion. The prince spoke not one word throughout, and when the biscop lifted her hands to heaven at the close of the final prayer, he bolted up as though he'd been nipped. That fast, like a wind from heaven, he fled down the aisle toward the entryway, then suddenly cut through the crowd, who parted fearfully before him.

Anna darted away, using her elbows to make a path for herself through the crowd, which was by now in a furious state of excitement, everyone talking at once. The prince ducked under the doorway that led down to the crypt, and the folk following in his wake hesitated. The crypt below Gent had become a charnel house during the Eika occupation, and few dared walk there.

But Anna had to find him, to see if it were truly the same creature. Perhaps he was only masquerading as a man, or perhaps he had been a man all along, cast out of a mold different than that from which most folk were formed.

She hurried down the steep curve of the steps, remembering the way the darkness hit abruptly. The noise of the congregation washed away with unexpected suddenness, and she barely recalled the jarring end to the steps as she stumbled down the last one.

She was blind.

He said, out of the darkness, "Liath?" The voice drifted to her, scarcely more than a whisper, but memory flooded back as she swayed, made dizzy by fear and the pounding of her heart. She would never forget that voice, the hoarse scrape to it, as though it hadn't formed quite right.

Of course, she did not reply.

His boots scuffed the floor. An unvoiced curse came off his lips in a hiss. A hand brushed her shoulder. Then he grabbed her arm. "Who are you?"

She could not answer.

He touched her face, exploring it with his free hand, grunted, gave up in disgust, and released her.

A soft glow penetrated the gloom, advancing steadily. Torchlight made her blink. The slender cleric who had stood beside the prince at the altar moved hesitantly off the last step and ventured into the vaults.

"Sanglant?" He extended the torch first this way and then that, pausing in surprise when he caught Anna in its smoky light. Beyond, the prince stood mostly in shadow, at the edge of the light, staring fixedly into the depths of the crypt, an impenetrable gloom beyond the torch's smoky flare.

"Do you know this girl?" demanded the prince. "She seems familiar to me, but I can't recall her."

She wanted to tell him, but she could not speak.

"Who are you, girl?" asked the cleric in a kind voice, examining her. She could only shake her head, and abruptly he moved past her, following the prince on into the vault, past the gravestones of the holy dead, those who were once biscops and deacons. Anna trailed after them, torn by curiosity and longing. Anyway, she didn't want to be left alone in the dark.

"She brought them here," said the prince to his companion. "Liath led the refugees into this crypt. There was a passage, so they say. That's how the children were saved from the ruin of Gent."

They wandered farther in, vaults lost in the darkness that spread everywhere outside the torch's light. Anna was too terrified to leave them. At every step she expected her feet to crunch on the bones of the dead soldiers who had lain here, decaying, when she and Matthias had passed through, but she saw no trace of them now, not even a finger bone, not even a forgotten knife. The miraculous light carried by St. Kristine had led the two children through the vault to the secret passage, but she could not now recall what path they had taken nor recognize any landmarks.

The prince halted beside one newly carved stone, an effigy of a lady fitted in armor. Her carved face lay in repose, peaceful and, perhaps, a little stubborn even in death. "This must be the grave of Lord Hrodik's sister, Lady Amalia. She died when they took back the city."

"Come, my friend," said the cleric sadly, "let us climb out of this place." He glanced at Anna, aware that she followed them. "Can you speak, child? Know you the passage of which Prince Sanglant speaks?"

She dared only to shake her head. She knew she would never find it again.

"It's closed to such as me," said the prince bitterly. "Ai, God, Heribert, my heart is torn out of me. Five months have passed. Was it only a vision I saw at Angenheim? Liath must be dead."

"Nay, do not say so. How can we know? There are so many mysteries we do not comprehend."

The prince threw back his head and howled like a dog. The horrible sound reverberated through the crypt, echoing and whispering down the vaults and through the many chambers. The cleric stumbled back in surprise, bumping into Anna, and almost dropped the torch.

The prince shuddered all over, pressing a palm to his head. Light shivered over him, steadying as Heribert got a good grip on the torch.

"Your Highness?" the cleric asked softly.

Prince Sanglant dropped his hand. His expression was grim and angry, but his gaze was quite sane. "Nay, I beg your pardon, my friend. Liath stood here with me once, that day Bloodheart breached the walls." He caught in a breath, then went on. "Lord help me. I never thought I'd have the courage to touch those chains."

"Come," said Heribert, "you've had courage enough for one day. Lord Hrodik promises to entertain us with the best wine in Saony."

"That's not the worst thirst I'm suffering." He walked to the edge of the flickering light thrown off by the torch and surveyed the gloom. With his back to her, Anna could not see his expression. "I heard it told that my Dragons were thrown down here to rot, but I see no sign of them." He stood there for a while in silence. The torch snapped and popped. Smoke tickled her nose. She sniffed hard and sneezed.

"Come," said the prince, as if the sound spurred him out of his reverie. He took the torch from the cleric and led them back up into the light.

"Why did you go down into the crypt?" Suzanne demanded later, when they had escaped the crowd and gotten home to a still-burning hearth, just enough warmth that they could take off their cloaks and sit sipping cider to warm their stomachs. A servant girl, left behind to tend to the house, served them, bringing mugs to pass around before taking a drink herself from the ladle. "It's dark down there. You might have gotten hurt."

Anna said nothing.

Suzanne sipped at her cider but could not leave the question alone.

"What did he say to you?" Her fingers asked another question, playing self-consciously with her hair. She glanced at Raimar, who regarded her with thoughtful concern and a flicker of distress in his expression. "Why did you follow the prince down into the crypt?"

Anna couldn't answer, not even with such signs as she had learned to communicate with. She couldn't answer because she didn't know.

There were so many mysteries that humankind simply could not comprehend.

2

TO his surprise, Zacharias had come to admire the prince in the months they had journeyed eastward from one noble estate to the next. Prince Sanglant was frank, fair, honest, and a resolute leader, and he never asked anyone to do anything he wasn't willing to do himself.

"Nay, I never expected willingly to follow along in a noble lord's retinue," Zacharias said to Heribert as they shared a platter in the great hall of the mayor's palace in Gent, where wine flowed freely and a young apprentice poet mangled a hymn celebrating the encounter between the aged Herodia of Jeshuvi and the blessed Daisan in which the future saint had prophesied that the young Daisan would bring light to a benighted world.

"In truth, I never thought I would sit down to eat with a common man," replied Heribert thoughtfully. Sanglant sat at the high table, drinking heavily and speaking little as young Lord Hrodik boasted about a recent boar hunt in which he'd broken his nose.

"It was to escape men such as you that I became a frater rather than a monastic, for in a monastery I'd have had to bow down to a master born of noble kinfolk. My grandmother despised nobles as thieves and louts. She said they lived off the labor of honest farmers, and forced their foreign God of Unities onto those who preferred to worship in the old ways."

"She was a heathen?"

"Truly, she was. She worshiped the old gods. They repaid her faithfulness with a long life and prosperity and many grandchildren."

Heribert sighed. The young cleric had a lean, clever face, almost delicate, and the most aristocratic manners of any nobly born person Zacharias had ever come into contact with, although in all honesty he had not rubbed shoulders with noble folk much in his life. He had spent more of his adult life among the barbaric Quman tribes, to his sorrow.

"What fate befell your grandmother is long since settled. It is your soul I fear for, Zacharias. You do not pray with us."

"Yet I pray in my own way, and not to my grandmother's gods. Let us not have this conversation again, I beg you, for nothing you say will change my mind. I saw a vision—"

"Who is to say that it was not the Enemy who cast dust into your eyes?"

"Peace, friend. I know what I saw."

Heribert lifted a hand in capitulation.

Zacharias chuckled. "I will not pollute your ears with another description of the vision granted me. You are safe from that, at least."

"Safer from that than from this poet's wailing."

Zacharias snorted, for indeed the poet was not as skilled as he ought to have been—or else he was drunk. "Better the poet's song than Lord Hrodik's boasting. Is there a male servant among those serving at the high table? All of them women, as if to boast that he's bedding one or all of them each night." He had never shaken his grandmother's distaste for thralldom, and could not keep the disgust from his voice. "I suppose they're bonded servants, and cannot leave his service even if they wished to."

Heribert looked at him in surprise. "We are all of us dependents in one manner or another. Regnant and skopos, too, are vassals of God. How is this different?"

"Does God force regnant and skopos to be whores against their will?"

Chief among the servants and the one who stood somewhat removed from the others, directing the flow of food and drink into the hall, was a remarkably pretty young woman whose handsome features were marred only by a scar along her lower lip, as if she'd been bitten hard enough to draw blood. Lord Hrodik seemed determined to make an ass of himself by continually calling her over and making much of her presence, although any idiot could see that the poor woman had fallen completely under the spell of Prince Sanglant's charisma. Trying not to stare at the prince, she made it all the more obvious that she was trying not to stare at him.

"Ai, Lord," said Heribert with a rueful smile, "there is one woman who has caught Sanglant's eye."

"How can you tell? It seems to me he looks at her no differently nor more often than he does the others."

Heribert chuckled softly. "Does it seem so to you? Yet I think it seems otherwise to her. She's both shapely and handsome, and I fear me that our prince is particularly susceptible to women like her."

"Pretty enough," agreed Zacharias, who did not object to admiring handsome women and in years past—before his mutilation—had fallen short of his vows a handful of times. "Perhaps it's your own chastity you must watch over, friend, rather than the prince's."

Heribert blushed slightly. "Nay, friend, the charms of women hold no power over me. Pity poor Lord Hrodik. He fades quickly when seated beside Sanglant, and the more so because of his incessant bragging."

"Truly, he wouldn't have lasted a day among the Quman tribes. For all that they were savages, no man among them dared boast of his exploits unless he were truly a warrior and hunter."

"Lord Hrodik's retinue is agreed that he shot a buck last month, so perhaps he can be accounted a hunter."

Zacharias laughed, unaccustomed to hearing the fastidious cleric resort to sarcasm.

Prince Sanglant's head came up at the sound, and he stood abruptly. The poet broke off in confusion, staring around wildly as if he thought an armed party might thunder into the hall.

"I pray you, Brother Zacharias," said the prince, turning to address him across the length of two tables, "if you can recite the hymn to St. Herodia, then do so. You know it perfectly, do you not?"

Zacharias rose, handing the wine cup to Heribert. "I can recite it, Your Highness, if it pleases you."

"It would please me greatly." Sanglant left the high table and came to sit beside Heribert, throwing himself into Zacharias' seat and gulping down what was left of the wine in his cup, leaving only dregs. "Ai, God," he said in a low voice, "I have no more patience for that pup's tail wagging nor for that truckler who claims to be a poet." He looked around desperately, lifting his cup, and the handsome servingwoman rushed forward to fill it, pouring the wine through a silver sieve that filtered out most of the dregs. Sanglant stared at her frankly, and she did not lower her eyes, so that this time it was the prince who looked away first, coloring somewhat, although a blush was hard to see against his bronze complexion. Lord Hrodik called to her sharply, and she hurried away to attend to him.

"Ai, Lord," muttered the prince. "I am not fit to be a monk."

"Our lord prince needs distraction," murmured Heribert to Zacharias.

When young, Zacharias had devised a way of memorizing the hymns and verses he loved so much by thinking of them as beasts tied up in a stable, each one in a separate stall and each stall marked by a bird or plant to remind him of its first unique word or phrase, something to launch him into the words. Walking down that stall in his mind's eye, he found a figure of a vulture, known as the prophet among birds, carrying a stalk of barley, called *hordeum* in Dariyan and sharing enough sounds with "Herodia" that it was easy to recall the second out of the first. It took him as much time as it took the prince to drain another cup of wine to gather the first words onto his tongue.

> *"Let us praise the first prophet, called Herodia,*
> *Who walked among the streets and temples of Jeshuvi*
> *And did not turn her eye away from mortal weakness,*
> *Nor did she fear to speak harshly to those who transgressed*
> *God's law."*

Once he had begun, the words flowed freely, one linking itself to the next in an unbroken chain. It was the genius, so his grandmother had said, that the gods had granted to him. The frater who had brought the word of the Unities to their frontier village had praised him, telling him that he had been named well, for truly the angel of memory, Zachriel, had visited a holy gift upon him.

> *"So let the holy St. Herodia speak her blessings upon*
> *Us all,*
> *For her word is the word of truth."*

As he finished, he heard the prince mutter an exclamation just as Lord Hrodik jumped to his feet.

"Look here, cousin!" cried the young lord as a dozen townsfolk entered the hall, looking nervously about themselves.

Unfortunately, the young woman standing at the head of the party with the scarf signifying her status as a respectable householder tied over her hair was even prettier than the servingwoman. Sanglant rose with cup in hand and his familiar, captivating smile on his face.

"Come, Mistress Suzanne," exclaimed Hrodik impatiently as she and her kinfolk hesitated. "I have called you to attend me here in order to honor you, not to eat you." He giggled at his own joke. Certain of his attendants made laughing noises as well, glancing over at the prince to see if he found the comment as funny as Hrodik did. But the prince had not taken his gaze from Mistress Suzanne's person since she'd entered the hall. Hrodik made a great show of leaving his place at the high table and moving out to the center of the hall, his feet half smothered in rushes, where he must become the center of attention simply by virtue of his position.

"You must not fear to stand before Prince Sanglant, for truly he is a noble prince and no harm will come to you. Come forward, for I mean to show Prince Sanglant what help we can be to him, here in Gent. His soldiers aren't properly outfitted for this winter weather. I mean to convince him to abide a while here while we provide him with such cloaks and armor as is fitting to his magnificence." He almost fell over himself with eagerness as he beckoned to the pretty servingwoman, who appeared at a side door. "Come, now, Frederun. Do you now bring forward those gifts which I mean to present to the prince, so that he may later boast of the fine hospitality he met in my hall!"

Sanglant still hadn't taken his gaze from Mistress Suzanne, but she had not looked at him at all, except for one shuttered glance. The man beside her kept his hand on her arm.

"Well," Heribert murmured as Zacharias sidled over to stand behind his chair, "there's one who's as handsome as Liath."

Sanglant glanced down at Heribert with a sharp smile composed more of irritation than amusement. "I am not my father, Heribert."

"Nay," agreed Heribert companionably, "for King Henry was famous for never walking down the path of debauchery, even after his wife died."

"How can sinless congress, when a woman and a man of their own free will join together for mutual pleasure, be counted debauchery? The Lord and Lady conceived the Holy Word between them, Brother, is that not so? Is not the universe and Earth their creation, brought about by desire?"

"By joining together in *lawful* congress."

Sanglant laughed, and every soul in the hall turned to look at him. "Truly, Heribert, it does me no good to dispute church doctrine with you." He sat down abruptly and lowered his voice. "But I swear to you, friend, I do not think I can remain virtuous much longer."

Lord Hrodik bustled forward to meet the servant Frederun, who held a fine scarlet cloak in her arms. Behind her, a young servingman carried an object draped with a sheet of linen. Hrodik grabbed the cloak out of her arms and shook it free to well-deserved exclamations of delight and amazement from the feasting crowd. The cloak was masterfully woven out of thread dyed a rich scarlet hue and trimmed by an accomplished hand with an embroidered edge of golden dragons twined each about the next.

"This is the work of Mistress Suzanne, whom I bring to your attention, Your Highness. Let me present it to you as a gift, for truly it is worthy of your eminence." Hrodik had gotten quite breathless with excitement as he draped the cloak over Sanglant's arms. His thin, pimply face shone with pride as he beckoned the young weaver forward, although she came reluctantly.

"Fine work, truly," said the prince in a tone that suggested that he praised the woman as much as the cloak. She still did not look at him.

"How many cloaks do you need for your soldiers?" demanded Hrodik. "Truly, you have full sixty soldiers in your retinue."

"Seventy-one," said Sanglant.

The weaver paled. "My lord, I can't supply you with so much cloth in so short a time!"

"Nay," cried Lord Hrodik expansively, "it need not be a short time. They can't ride east in this cold, nor with the spring thaws coming. I see no reason they can't abide with us for two months or more!"

The poor weaver looked ready to faint, but Zacharias had a strong hunch that it was not the order for cloth that made her anxious but the presence of the prince, who was still watching her as he ran a finger lightly around a tracery of dragon outlined in fine golden thread.

Lord Hrodik was clearly almost beside himself in his desperation to please the prince, and now he noticed Sanglant's fascination with the dragon embroidery. He leaped forward to take the linen-shrouded object out of the servant's arms, whipping the cloth off to reveal a stunningly beautiful helmet, glorious iron trimmed with gold to suggest the fierce visage of a dragon.

Prince Sanglant jumped up so fast that his chair fell over backward, hitting the rushes with a resounding thud. He thrust the cloak into Heribert's arms, had to brace himself against the table as if he feared his legs would give out.

"Where did you get that?"

Hrodik looked startled and not a little scared by the prince's vehemence. "It came from the crypt, Your Highness. We recovered a great deal of armor there, after the king and Count Lavastine returned Gent to human sovereignty. Lord Wichman had this piece restored and polished, but he allowed no man to wear it. Nor did he take it with him when he rode east to fight the Quman."

Slowly, Sanglant straightened. "What of the rest of the armor found there?" The casual words could not disguise a blossoming of pain in his voice, although truly his voice always sounded hoarse.

"Wichman's companions commandeered most of it,"

Hrodik said, "and his mother Duchess Rotrudis sent stewards to carry off the rest. Nothing as rich as this piece, of course, but all of it well made and—" He broke off, a look of horror on his face. Stammering nonsense, he set the helmet on the table between a platter of chicken eaten down to the bones and a bowl of fish stewed in broth.

"I pray, grant me your pardon, Your Highness." His hands were actually shaking. "I mistook myself. I cannot gift this to you, for it was yours once, was it not? When you were captain of the King's Dragons."

Sanglant hesitated, then touched the helmet as though it were an adder. After a moment, he slipped his fingers through the eye slots and lifted it to examine it more closely, turning it to study the dragon inlay, the raised wings wrapping around the helmet's curve, the gleaming face staring down its foe. Zacharias could not interpret the expression on his face, deep emotions surging beneath a taut control. Without a word, he tucked the helmet under his arm in a gesture obviously remembered more by his body than by his mind and strode from the hall without looking at anyone or making any polite excuses. He simply walked out, such a stark look on his face as might be seen on a man who had watched his beloved comrades fall one by one before him, without hope of saving even one.

So he had, hadn't he? Zacharias had heard the story of Gent from Fulk's soldiers, but it was a story they only told when out of the prince's hearing.

Yet wasn't that why soldiers followed him with their whole hearts? Because he gave his heart to them in turn? Prince Sanglant knew the name and history of every man in his retinue. Not one among them doubted that their prince would lead them bravely, fight with them until the end, grieve over any of the fallen, and pay fair restitution to the families of those who, if God so willed it, did not survive.

"Come with me," said Heribert in a low voice.

Zacharias didn't need to be told twice, but at the door he

paused to look back just as Lord Hrodik, waking as though from a stupor, spoke in an almost apoplectic voice.

"Go now, Mistress, come with me. We must go to his chambers and discuss what manner of outfitting his soldiers need."

The weaver had a pleasant voice, low and melodic, although it shook a little. "I beg you, Lord Hrodik, it seems to me that the prince is in no humor to be plagued by a lowly common woman such as myself. I and the other weavers in Gent can provide what you wish, if you will only allow us to——"

"Nay! Nay! I will have him satisfied exactly as he wishes! I am still lord over this town. You will abide by my command!"

"I pray you, Brother." The whisper came from the corridor. Zacharias turned to see the servingwoman, Frederun, standing in the shadow where door met wall. Heribert had already vanished down the hall. With all the windows along the outside wall of the corridor shuttered, it was too dark for him to make out her face. "Does the prince know *that* woman? The weaver?"

"I have not been with the prince more than five months. I know little of his past. Yet I must counsel you, sister, do not let lust overmaster you. I do not know what binds you to this place, but surely you realize that the prince will ride on, and you will remain behind."

"I am bound as a servant here, Brother. Will you counsel me now to accept meekly what God have ordained for such as me? Is all happiness to be denied me?"

"Nay, sister, I am not what you think I am," he said, stung by her tone. "My kinsfolk walked east to the marchlands rather than suffer under the yoke of servitude to any noble. Yet carnal desire furthers no ends but its own. Truly, you must care for yourself before you surrender to carnal urges. What if you get with child?"

"I was forced to be Lord Wichman's whore for six months," she said bitterly, "and yet no child fastened itself to my womb. Ai, God." Her voice came as a sigh, ragged and desperate.

"Did you see the way he looked at her?" Abruptly, she hurried away down the corridor.

With a frown, Zacharias returned to the chambers allotted to the prince, but the sight that greeted him there gave his heart no peace. Prince Sanglant stood in the center of the room, his tall, broad-shouldered form made daunting by the magnificent dragon helmet he now wore. He turned at the sound of Zacharias' footsteps, pulling the helmet off as though he didn't want anyone to see him wearing it.

"I fear you are about to be visited by Lord Hrodik, Your Highness," said Zacharias.

"Lord preserve me," muttered the prince, cocking his head to one side to listen. He held the helmet, two fingers crooked into the eye slot, as though it were a comfortable weight. "*She's* with him."

"Who is *she?*" asked Heribert softly from his station beside the table. He watched Sanglant closely, a compassionate half smile on his face.

"Mistress Gisela of Steleshame had a handsome niece, whose name was Suzanne. She was a fine weaver. She wove cloaks for the King's Eagles, among other things. My Dragons and I spent a week's worth of nights at Steleshame getting refitted by the Steleshame armorer, when we rode to Gent." He swore then, half laughing, and tossed the helmet to the boy, Matto, who had been left in the chamber to sit in attendance on the sleeping Blessing, her slack toddler body bundled all cozy in the middle of the big bed where Sanglant took his rest.

Matto caught the helmet, grunting at its weight, and ran his hands over the gold fittings in astonished awe. "Lord bless me. I've never seen aught like this in the whole of my days. Not even the king has a helm so grand as this!"

"Hush, Matto," said Sanglant, not unkindly. "Do not speak disrespectfully of King Henry, to whom God have granted Their favor."

"No, Your Highness," said the youth obediently.

By now, they could all hear Lord Hrodik as he approached

down the hall, calling orders to one of his stewards in his wheedling, ill-tempered voice. "Go, therefore, and let the prince know we attend him at his pleasure."

Sanglant sat down in the chamber's only chair, a richly carved seat set on a thick Arethousan carpet woven with flowers and vines. He gestured to Matto to stand by the door. The youth scarcely had time to position himself there before a flustered steward made a great show of announcing Lord Hrodik.

By sitting down, Sanglant made the gulf between his authority and the authority of the young lord quite plain. He knew how to use his presence and his size to intimidate, and he did so now by leaning forward to brace his hands on his knees. Hrodik simpered and stammered and finally moved aside to let the young weaver step forward. She had such a high blush in her cheeks that she looked feverish. Still she would not meet Prince Sanglant's gaze.

"Well met," he said without any seeming irony. "It seems you are a renowned weaver in this town, Mistress."

"Yes, Your Highness." Boldly, she lifted her gaze to look at him, before sweeping it around the chamber, marking Heribert, Zacharias, the youth Matto by the door, the three young hounds panting under the table, who had been given to the prince as a gift by the monks of St. Gall, and finally at the bed. Now she was startled, eyes widening as she recoiled slightly. "Is this your child, Your Highness?"

"So it is," he agreed, still watching her. "That is my daughter, Blessing."

Mistress Suzanne found the carpet a fascinating sight, compared, at least, to the child on the bed. Such currents ran between the man and the woman that Zacharias thought that probably he could trace them, had he only the ability to see emotion as light. "A handsome and well-grown child, Your Highness. Any child must be accounted a blessing." She faltered as though brought up short by the snap of a whip. Her flush washed pale, but her voice remained strong. "Yet not every child is conceived in blessed circumstances. Some of us

become pawns, Your Highness, to those whose worldly power
is greater than their fear of God." She glanced for the first time
back at her little retinue, her eager household, who stood clustered behind her staring at the prince in awe and trepidation.
The man standing at the fore nodded reassuringly to her in the
way of a good companion tied by bonds of trust and affection.
Nothing like as handsome as the prince, he had the broad
shoulders and thick forearms of a laborer, and a certain grim
fatalism lay on his shoulders as he eyed the prince.

His rival, thought Zacharias, knowing the thought for truth
as soon as it surfaced.

Mistress Suzanne continued to speak, and as each word fell
it seemed to make the next one easier. "After the fall of Gent
I was given against my will to Lord Wichman, while he lived
with his retinue at Steleshame and harried the Eika. After the
Eika were driven out, I left my aunt and Steleshame and came
to Gent to begin anew, and to escape Lord Wichman. I was
already pregnant. In time I gave birth to his bastard child.
Because he had taken up residence in Gent, as its lord, I feared
letting him know of my presence in Gent because I did not
want him to—" This was too much, and she could not finish
the sentence.

"Knowing my cousin Wichman, as I do," Sanglant said
softly, "I can see that you would not have wished him to know
that you lived close by him."

She sighed gratefully, gathered her resolve, and went on.
"Yet the child must be baptized, Your Highness. In this way,
it came to the attention of Duchess Rotrudis. Before the babe
was six months of age, a cleric came to our house and took the
child away." She remained dry-eyed and confident. "I confess
I was thankful to have that burden taken from me. I am sure
the duchess has given the child a better life than I ever could.
Truly, I could never love it, remembering what I suffered in its
making."

Sanglant could never be fully still, yet even with one foot
tapping quietly on the carpet beneath his chair he knew how

to listen with his full attention. His attention became almost a second presence in the chamber, the cloak of power any great prince carries beside her. Even Hrodik dared not speak without permission. But the prince's silence, like assent, gave the weaver leave to go on.

"My household has prospered, Your Highness. Duchess Rotrudis was generous in paying me for the trouble of bearing her a grandchild. I used that restitution to improve my workshop. I had already pledged myself to this man, Raimar. With our newfound prosperity we were able to make our vows of betrothal before the biscop. We will marry in the spring. Raimar was able to leave the tannery, for he was put there as a slave by the Eika in the last weeks of their occupation but had apprenticed before the invasion to a carpenter. With our servingman Autgar, he built two new looms and added on a wool room, as well as shelves and beds for the household, and other small projects."

"Nay, nay," said Sanglant, lifting a hand. She broke off, flushing hotly again. "Truly, you have earned the prosperity you now enjoy. I will not disturb you any longer. If Lord Hrodik can see to it that I am supplied with twenty stout wool cloaks for my company, then I will ask nothing more of you."

"Do not think me ungrateful, Your Highness, I pray you." At last, she lifted her gaze to meet his. With his words, she had allowed herself to relax. The play of lantern light over her face made the curve of her full lips and the quiet brilliance of her eyes most striking, so that even Zacharias felt a stirring of desire. Sanglant gave a sharp sigh. "Do not find me unmindful of the roses of summer," she said, "which can never be reclaimed although we recall their scent and sweetness and beauty with an ardent heart."

"You have my leave to depart," the prince said irritably. "You as well, Hrodik." But as they turned to go, he called out. "Nay, stop a moment. Who is that girl?" He indicated one of Suzanne's party. The girl had nothing of obvious interest about her except an odd burnt butter complexion, as though she had been dipped in a tanning vat. Mostly grown, not quite a woman but no longer a child, she stepped forward fearlessly to confront the prince. The top of her head didn't even come to his shoulder.

"I know you," he said, almost dreamily.

Heribert stepped forward. "She was the child who followed you down into the crypt, my lord prince."

"Nay, true enough, but I know her. *I know her.* What is your name, child?"

"She is mute, Your Highness." Mistress Suzanne stood protectively behind the child, setting a hand on her shoulder. "Her name is Anna. She and her brother Matthias escaped from Gent long after the Eika had taken it. How they survived there for all those months I do not know, but they got free of Gent through the intervention of St. Kristine and came to Steleshame. I brought them with me to Gent as part of my household. Her brother Matthias is betrothed to one of my younger weavers. He's now a journeyman at the tannery."

"You're the daimone," said the girl suddenly in a voice as hoarse as the scrape of sandpaper.

Suzanne shrieked, and her family began talking all at once, crowding forward to touch the girl.

"Ai, God," Suzanne said through tears. "She's not spoken a word for two years."

"Sanglant?" Heribert rushed forward to lay a hand on the prince's arm. Zacharias, too, pressed forward to stand beside the prince, because Sanglant looked utterly stunned, as though an unexpected blow had slammed into his head.

Blessing woke up and began to cry, frightened by all the noise. "Dada! Dada! I want Dada!"

"Ai, God," Sanglant murmured, "it wasn't a dream at all. Those two children, the boy with the knife and the girl with the wooden Circle of Unity hanging at her chest. I thought it was a delusion."

Blessing wailed. She had the lungs for it, a voice to pierce the clamor of battle. The girl, Anna, got to her first, picked her up, and carried her over to her father. Sanglant took her without thinking. Blessing hid her face against his shoulder and, with a few hiccuping cries, lapsed into silence.

"Haven't you a nursemaid for this child?" the girl called Anna demanded, looking around the chamber. Although Zacharias could feel the familiar snap, like the taste of lightning in the air, that he had come to recognize as Jerna's presence, he could not see the aery daimone at all. But he felt the current of wind that marked her trail.

Yet that wind grew stronger, and stronger still, as though someone had opened shutters facing into a storm. An unnatural whirlpool of milky air spun into existence in the center of the room. Jerna flickered into view above it.

In these last months as Blessing grew with unnatural speed and ate porridge and cheese more while nursing less, Jerna had in contrast begun to lose that womanlike mimicry that had made her seem more substantial before. In a way, it seemed as if Blessing's need had helped shape Jerna's human form. Now the daimone only vaguely resembled a pale woman creature with the tone and texture of water.

The pool of light had nothing to do with Jerna. It was something entirely *other,* a sorcerous manifestation right there in the middle of the chamber.

Shrieks and shouts erupted as the gathered people shrank back in fright. Zacharias could not tell what frightened them more: Jerna's wispy form, or the strange whirlpool of light pouring brightness into the chamber. Blessing reared back, clapping her hands over her ears. Hrodik's steward had fallen down to the floor in a faint, and young Matto tried to haul him up to his feet so he wouldn't be trampled.

A sound emerged as a faint murmur, emanating from the whirlpool of light.

"Sanglant."

"Silence!" cried Sanglant in the ringing tones of a man accustomed to shouting orders above the chaos of battle.

Silence fell like a shroud. For an instant it was so quiet that

Zacharias thought he had gone deaf, but then Hrodik giggled nervously.

The whirlpool spoke. "Sanglant. *Blessing?*"

Blessing twisted around in her father's grasp and reached toward the eddying light, opening like an unshuttered window onto a place lying far beyond the walls of this world. "Mama! Mama come!"

"Ai, God!" Sanglant's voice sounded ragged with hope, and pain. "Liath?" He took a step forward. "I can't see you. Where are you?"

Zacharias saw nothing through that window of light but a hard glare, like staring into a vale of ice when the cold winter sun dazzles you. Was this truly the woman he sought? Where was she?

The voice spoke again. "Sanglant, if you can hear me, know that I am living, but I am on a long journey and I do not know how long it will take me."

"Come back to us, Liath!" cried Sanglant desperately.

"Wait for me, I beg you. Help me if you can, for I'm lost here. I need a guide. Is Jerna there?" A dark shape moved through the icy gleam, one arm outstretched and the other thrown up before its eyes. A blue light winked and dazzled on the outstretched hand, and on the figure's back hung a bow, visible because of fiery fire-red salamanders sliding up and down the inner curve of the bow. The figure reached. For an instant it seemed she would pass right through the curtain of light. Zacharias gasped and leaped back, slamming into Heribert, as Sanglant jumped forward to grab for her.

"Take my hand, Liath!" His hand swiped through empty air.

She said, "Yes! I see you!" just as Jerna's silvery form spun down from the ceiling to wrap protectively around Blessing's body. "Come if you will, Jerna. Return to your home. The way is open."

The daimone spilled like water all down Blessing's body, soaking her in light and in the aetherical substance of her aery form. Blessing cried out in surprise and delight; a moment later, Jerna coiled into a slender reed, twisted, and vanished through the window of light.

The whirlpool collapsed as Sanglant leaped after her. He landed hard in the middle of the carpet, looking, if truth be told, a little foolish. Blessing laughed and clapped her hands, as though it had all been a trick for her amusement, but her father was white at the mouth, almost rigid. Blessing sobered, looking frightened by the man holding her with such a look of wretched anger on his face.

Heribert pushed past Zacharias and grabbed the whimpering child out of her father's arm. As though that movement freed him, Sanglant whirled around, grabbed the chair, and hoisted it.

He smashed it against the floor.

Splintered wood flew everywhere. Mistress Suzanne and her household fled the chamber. Even Lord Hrodik stumbled out in their wake.

Zacharias took a step forward to calm the prince, but Heribert stopped him with a gesture.

"But not for me!" cried Sanglant. "The way is open, but not for me! Do I mean nothing to her that she should call someone else in my place?" He hoisted what remained of the heavy chair in his right hand, making ready to smash it again, when the girl, Anna, stepped right out in front of him. She hadn't fled with the others, nor did she show any fear.

"Are you truly a daimone from the heavens?" she asked in that scrape of a voice. "Is that why you want to return there?"

The wrath of King Henry was famous throughout the land. Nobles feared the king's anger for good reason, although Henry was said to use it sparingly. Surely Prince Sanglant was the most easygoing of noblemen, or so Zacharias had come to believe. For the first time, he saw the regnant's anger full in the prince's face, forbidding and intimidating, and it made him step back beside Heribert, who spoke soothingly to the sniveling Blessing. She had never seen her father so angry before.

Anna just stood there, waiting.

Sanglant opened his hand and with a shuddering breath let the chair drop. It hit the carpet with a thud, clattering on the shards of its broken legs.

It was suddenly very quiet. The coals in the brazier shifted, ash spilled, and the fire made a wheezing sound, quickly stifled. The torches blazed back up, as if Sanglant had sucked the flame out of them to fuel his anger, but probably it was only the backwash from the aetherical wind that had driven into the chamber and vanished as abruptly. The room looked very ordinary with its two handsomely carved chests, for storage, and the tapestries on the wall depicting the usual noble scenes: a hunt, a feast, an assembly of church women.

Sanglant stepped past the girl and walked to the side table. He poured water from a pitcher into a copper basin, splashed his face until water ran down his chin to drip into the basin, and swiped a hand across his beardless chin. Without thinking, he licked the drops of water off his palm. His back remained stiff with anger, or despair. "Not an hour goes by that I do not think of her," he said to the basin, "yet does she call for me? Does she seek me? She lives, but she journeys elsewhere. Just like my mother."

"Have you a nursemaid for the child?" the girl asked in her funny little voice.

"I had one," he said bitterly, "but my wife took her from me."

"I can care for children."

"We are riding east to war, child. There will be no fine carpets and warm feet with my company. I've no use for camp followers who slow me down, and who run at each least glimpse of danger."

She had a hard stare, like a young hawk's. In a way she reminded Zacharias of Hathui: fearless, sharp, confident, and irritatingly persistent. "I survived a spring and summer in Gent when Bloodheart ruled here. I'm not afraid."

The prince regarded her with a half-forgotten smile on his

face. She stared right back at him. She had her hair pulled back in a braid, and she wore a good wool tunic, neatly woven, with two roses embroidered at the collar for decoration. A wooden Circle of Unity hung at her chest.

At the door, Matto cleared his throat. "My lord prince? Here is the weaver returned to speak to you."

Mistress Suzanne appeared at the threshold, her face drawn and her hands wringing the fabric of her skirt as she sidled into the chamber. "Your Highness, I— Ach, Anna! There you are! I thought we'd lost you."

"I'm going east," said Anna stoutly. "I'm to be the nurse-maid for the young princess."

"But, Anna—!"

"It's a sign, don't you see? Why else would God have given me back my voice now?"

"I pray you, Mistress Suzanne," said Sanglant. "Outfit the girl with what she needs, and return her here in the morning. I'll see that she is well taken care of."

Even a prosperous weaver could not argue with a prince. Subdued but obedient, Mistress Suzanne took the girl and left.

"Want down, want down," insisted Blessing as she squirmed out of Heribert's arms. She rushed over to her father, seeking solace, and he picked her up.

"I pray you, Matto," he said, cuddling his daughter against him, "the helmet needs repadding. Have Captain Fulk see to it. We'll fit it more exactly tomorrow. I'll want more water for washing." Matto nodded and quickly fetched pitcher and helmet before leaving the chamber. "Zacharias."

"Yes, my lord prince."

"We'll need a straw pallet for the girl. Sergeant Cobbo can see to it."

Zacharias glanced at Heribert, but the cleric only gave a puzzled shrug. With a bow, Zacharias left on the errand.

Unaccustomed to palaces, he quickly got lost, but a sympa-thetic servingman directed him to the servants' hall. He passed through the mostly deserted hall and found a door that led outside. The hush of early evening hung over the courtyard. Stars glittered overhead. An unrelenting cold seeped through his clothes to chill his bones. His old scars ached, and he suddenly had to pee. Looking for a private place where no one might accidentally see his mutilation, he finally stumbled up to the door of the cookhouse, meaning to ask for directions to the privies.

Smoke and the odor of burned roast drifted out of the cooking house, together with something tangier, so sharp it made his neck prickle. In the Quman camp he had learned to walk quietly, because Prince Bulkezu had liked his slaves to be silent and had once killed a man for sneezing in the middle of a musician's performance.

Her voice had the breathy quality of air. As he peered into the smoky interior, he saw a woman standing at the big block table, hands hovering over a platter ringed by four candles placed to form a square. An apple fanned into neat slices lay on the wooden platter, so freshly cut that the juice welling up from its moist flesh shone in the candlelight, making his mouth water. No one else was in the cookhouse.

"I adjure you by your name and your powers and the glorious place wherein you dwell, O Prince of Light who drove the Enemy into the Abyss. Let your presence rest upon this apple and let the one who eats of it be filled with desire for me. Let him be seized by a flame of fire as powerful as that fire in which you, Holy One, make your dwelling place. Let him open his door to me, and let him not be content with anything until he has satisfied me—"

Nay, there was someone else there, over by the spit. She emerged from the shadows, a woman of middling years. In the half light, Zacharias saw the wicked scar blazed on her right cheek, puffy and white.

"What madness is this, Frederun?"

The pretty servingwoman broke into tears. "I thought he was dead! I was so happy when I was his lover—"

"Hush!" hissed her companion, laying a hand on the young woman's shoulder. "There's someone in the doorway."

Zacharias slipped away into the shadows. The wind shifted, and he smelled the privies, dug over by the stables. It still hurt to urinate, but he was no longer sure if the pain was actually physical or only an artifact lingering in his mind from those first weeks after Prince Bulkezu had mutilated him.

He found Sergeant Cobbo together with a dozen soldiers standing in the aisle between stalls, watching a chess game. Captain Fulk had set up a board and pieces on a barrel and brought two bales of hay to serve as seats. He had the dragon helm on his knee, with a hand curved possessively over its top. As Zacharias approached, the captain used an Eagle to take a Lion.

"My biscop takes your Eagle," said his opponent, the exiled Eagle known as Wolfhere. He paused, still holding the chess piece, and glanced up past Cobbo and the ring of watchers to catch Zacharias' eye.

"Come you from the prince?" The old man had a piercing intelligence and remained in all circumstances so calm that Zacharias did not trust him.

Zacharias explained his errand, and Cobbo designated a man to accomplish the task in the morning. The soldiers settled back to gossip about this turn of events.

"Will you play, Frater?" asked Fulk. "I can't best him."

"Nay, I've no knowledge of such games. They're meant for nobles and soldiers, not for simple fraters such as myself. I'm not one of those folk who will be moving pieces to and fro in a game of power."

Wolfhere chuckled. "Yet what harm might there be, friend, in learning the rules of the game, if only to protect ourselves?"

"I'm thinking you're not needing any protection, Eagle, beyond that which you already possess."

"Here, now," objected Fulk. "We're at peace in my lord prince's company."

"Nay, I've no quarrel with Wolfhere," said Zacharias. "He's a common man like myself."

"So I am," agreed Wolfhere genially, but his smile was like that of a wolf, sharp and clean. He had once been King Arnulf the Younger's favored counselor, yet now he rode in secrecy in Prince Sanglant's company because he had been interdicted and outlawed by King Henry, accused of sorcery and treason, a friend and boon companion to the very mathematici whose influence Prince Sanglant meant to combat.

Yet it was this man, so the story went, who had freed Liath from servitude at the hands of an unscrupulous and nobly-born frater. This man was a favorite of little Blessing's, and the ones whom Blessing liked the prince favored.

"Prince Sanglant's wife appeared to us in a vision," Zacharias said suddenly, wanting to prod the old man, to see him jump.

Wolfhere's lips tightened, that was all. He rolled the Eagle in his hand, thumb caressing the lift of its carven wings, as he lifted his gaze to regard Zacharias blandly. "This is unexpected news. How did she appear to you?"

"Quite unexpectedly. Truly, Wolfhere, you are a man who plays chess most masterfully. But you must ask Prince Sanglant for particulars. I dare not say more. The church frowns upon all sorcerous acts or even those who witness them."

Wolfhere laughed, setting down the Eagle, but Captain Fulk rose, cradling the dragon helm against a hip.

"Can you not tell us more, Frater? We have seen many strange things traveling with the prince. All of us have seen the daimone that suckles the young princess. We have seen stranger things besides, in Aosta, when we rode with Princess Theophanu. News such as this may be important to all of us. It seems to me that Prince Sanglant has not suffered the absence of his wife well, and I pray that they may be reunited soon."

"Or truly the prince will be united with some other woman," joked one of the soldiers.

"I'll hear no more of that, Sibold!" said Fulk curtly. "Which of you would act differently? It's no business of ours whether the prince chooses to live as a cleric, or as a man."

Wolfhere smiled. "True-spoken, Captain, yet it's true that Prince Sanglant has long been famous for his amorous adventures. Have I ever told you about Margrave Villam's daughter, she who is heir to the margraviate? It's said she was taken by such a passion for the young prince that—"

Zacharias eased out of the gathering and retreated to the yard. His hands, always chilled in the winter, got stiff with cold, but he lingered outside.

That the fault of concupiscence, the seemingly unquenchable desire for the pleasures of the flesh, plagued Prince Sanglant made him no different from most of humankind. Unlike many a noble lord or lady, and entirely unlike the Quman warriors, who took what they wanted at the instant the urge struck them, the prince struggled to keep his cravings under control. For that reason alone, Zacharias had cause to respect him.

Yet it was not the prince he sat in judgment on.

Nay, truly, he recognized the sinful feeling that had crept into his breast: He envied Wolfhere his knowledge. The exiled Eagle kept a cool head and a closed mouth, and despite Zacharias' hints and insinuations over the months of their trip, Wolfhere never admitted to the knowledge that Zacharias knew in his bones the old man kept clutched to himself as a starving man clutches a loaf of precious bread and a handful of beans.

Was Zacharias unworthy? Prince Sanglant had taken Zacharias on in part because of his knowledge of the Quman but mostly because the prince had, underneath his iron constitution and bold resolve, a sentimental heart. He had taken Zacharias into his company because the frater had spoken of his vision of Liath, because Zacharias had brought him a scrap of parchment on which the prince's beloved, and lost, wife had scribbled uninterpretable signs and symbols, themselves a kind of magic, readable only by mathematici.

He touched the pouch at his belt, felt the stiff cylinder cached there: the rolled-up parchment, his only link to the knowledge he sought. Liath had studied the heavens, too. She had asked the same questions he had, and maybe, just maybe, she would listen with astonishment and fascination to his description of the vision of the cosmos that had been vouch-safed to him in the palace of coils.

Maybe she had some answers for him. Maybe she was willing to search.

Standing out under the pitiless winter sky, he prayed that she would be restored to Earth. Because if she wasn't, he had no one else to go to.

Shivering, he made his way back into the servants' hall and, by a minor miracle, found with no trouble the corridor off which lay the chambers reserved for the prince.

Someone had reached the door before him.

He knew her by the curve of her gown along her body, the way her shawl had fallen back to reveal the curling wisps of her light hair. He stepped back, staying in shadow. She hadn't heard him, or maybe she just wasn't paying attention, because she was waiting at the door.

It opened, finally, to reveal the prince.

"My lord prince," she said in a remarkably level voice, "you called for wine and refreshment?"

Sanglant held a candle whose yellow flame revealed the sharp lines of his face and the carefully fanned-out apple, eight slices making a blunt star, two on each side. A silver goblet shone softly in the candlelight beside it.

"Nay, I asked for nothing more," he said, but he didn't close the door, he only stood there. After a moment, she slipped past him to go inside.

With that uncanny sixth sense he had, as exquisite as a dog's, Sanglant looked directly at Zacharias, although surely he ought not to have been able to see him, drowned as the frater was in night's shadow.

"What is it, Zacharias?" he asked softly.

"Nay, nothing, my lord prince." Zacharias took two steps back, paused. "All is as you wish, Your Highness. I'll go now. Wolfhere has promised to teach me to play chess."

As he walked away, he heard the door close and latch behind him.

X
BEYOND THE VEIL

1

IT was too dark to see the landscape of the sphere of Erekes. As soon as the wind loosened its grip, Liath halted to take her bearings. A hot wind blasted her face. She missed her cloak, which she could have used to shield her skin, and more desperately she missed her boots. The surface she stood on scraped the soles of her feet, but when she moved forward to stand on what appeared to be smoother ground, her foot sank into a viscous liquid so cold that her toes went numb.

She jumped back, stumbled, and for a moment couldn't put any weight on that leg. At last sensation returned, but that was worse; her skin burned and blistered. Limping, she fell back to the shelter of a high outcropping whose bulky lee protected her from the worst of the blasting wind. The iron wall, and the gate, had vanished. She leaned against the stone, catching her breath, but the slick cold, as penetrating as melting ice, burned her fingers. She jerked away, and an instant later felt that same ulcerous pain lance up her hand.

She stood there in misery, half out of the wind and with a foot and a hand throbbing, and surveyed the landscape, what she could see of it. Beyond the shoreline, more a suggestion of textural change than an actual visible line, the landscape stretched into the distance as smoothly blank as a sea littered with fragments of lamplight. Darting fingers of brilliance moved upon that sea, illusive daimones bent upon unfathomable errands, but she could not hear the music of the spheres above the whine of that endless hot wind.

Was it the wind off the sun? Yet why then did the sun not shine here?

One question always led to another. She puzzled again over her brief sojourn among the Ashioi. How could time move differently there than on Earth? Why did day dawn and night fall with such an irregular rhythm? Why did no moon rise and set, wax and wane, in the country of the Ashioi?

Did it, too, travel the spheres? Or was there another plane of existence lying within or beside the universe which she did not comprehend? Eldest Uncle had shown her the twisted belt, his crude representation of the path on which he and his people had found themselves, but that didn't explain where they were right now in relation to Liath.

So many mysteries.

And it were better not to linger here, dwelling over them. She might stand here forever, lost in contemplation, except that the wind blew hot in her face and the ground rubbed uncomfortably against her bare feet. Like her heart, her hand and foot were going numb.

Cold crept up her wrist like poison. Wind scalded her eyes. She couldn't feel the coarse sand under one foot, and the lack of feeling disoriented her so much it was hard to keep her balance.

Time to move on.

The path was clearly marked, once you thought to look for it. Those lamplit sparks were stepping stones, each one about an arm's length in diameter, set across the blistering sea. The challenge lay in stepping from one to the next with no staff for balance and feeling in only one foot. She hitched her quiver tightly against her body and set off, cautiously at first, more boldly after she got the knack of compensating for her crippled foot and navigating against the constant pressure of wind blowing so hard into her face that her eyes ran with tears.

The dark shore receded behind her, quickly lost, until only the sea surrounded her, yet she felt the presence of hulking shapes around her, impossible to distinguish. The wind stank of bitter wormwood. Will-o'-the-wisps twinkled and vanished in the distance. Even in darkness, the landscape seemed as desolate as a woman's heart that has been scoured clean.

That fast, just before she took her next step, the wind turned. One instant it blasted her face with heat; the next it buffeted her from behind with an arctic chill. The sudden shift caught her off guard, almost tumbling her off her safe perch on a broad stepping stone. Light washed the landscape.

She stared.

The sphere of Erekes was a vale of ice, a blinding sea of whiteness.

She had always assumed that Erekes, often hidden by the sun's glare, would reflect something of the sun's substance: burned, charred, or at least a desert. But of course, that was the weakness of assumption. Erekes wasn't any of the things she had expected.

Wasn't that the lesson of the sword? If you go into battle thinking you know what to expect, the hand of confusion will always sow chaos and death in your ranks.

Yet how could she have prepared herself for this? Instead of a neat trail of beacons leading her forward, she stared at a confusing scatter of stepping stones sprayed across the icy sea, too many to count. She took an arrow and, reaching, touched the stone directly in front of her. The arrow sank through the illusory stone and, sizzling from the bite of that poisonous seawater, dissolved into ash. Only the iron tip remained, floating on the gelid surface.

Three other stepping stones remained within reach and beyond them, hundreds more, receding to an impossibly near horizon. In daylight, it was impossible to tell which of the stepping stones was real and which illusion. The sea of ice had no limit, none that she could see, and she had only seventeen arrows left. Lucian's friend, her sword, would have come in awfully handy right now, since it appeared that the icy liquid couldn't burn iron. But she had thrown it away.

The knife edge of the wind tore into her back. Her tunic flapped around her knees. Her long braid writhed against her back, distracting her, until she finally flipped it over her shoulder, where it whipped against her jaw. She couldn't feel her left arm from hand to elbow, and her right leg was numb from the knee down.

A pale shape flitted in front of her, careless as a breeze. Had this daimone come to taunt her? Or did it hope to guide her? Could she hope for their aid?

"Are there any here who were made captive at Verna?" she called. "Do you know me? I am Liathano, daughter of Anne and Bernard, wife of Sanglant, mother of Blessing. Can you help me?"

She saw more of them spinning and swooping among the staggeringly bright ice floes. Their movements seemed entirely random, unfixed and purposeless. What did they care if she triumphed, or failed?

The poison filtered up her limbs. She needed a guide quickly, a creature who could survive in the aether. Truly, she only knew where to find one such creature. She had to act fast.

On Earth she had learned to mold fire into a window. It proved no different here. Even in the sphere of Erekes, frozen in ice, fire came to her call.

It flared up with an audible crack, followed by a murmurous clattering like a thousand wings battering against an unbreachable wall. The sound died quickly. In the ice floes nearest her, daimones fled from the heat.

She wrapped fire into an archway, a window to see onto distant Earth.

"Sanglant," she called, because the link to him was the strongest chain she had.

With her poisoned hand raised to shadow her eyes, she kept the living one outstretched toward the archway of fire, bleeding and burning sparks and swirling air onto another vista, pale and blurry as through a veil. Were those vague shadows human forms? The sea hissed around her.

"Sanglant!" she cried again. A small child's body took form beyond the archway, so bright that it shone even into Erekes, casting a shadow. "Blessing?" Her voice caught on the beloved name.

To her shock, she heard an answer.

"Mama! Mama come!"

Ai, Lady! Blessing was so *big,* speaking like a two-year-old. Had so much time passed in the other world already, although she had only lived among the Ashioi for a handful of days? She wanted them so badly, but she hardened her heart. How easy it was to harden her heart.

"Sanglant, if you can hear me, know that I am living, but I am on a long journey and I do not know how long it will take me." *To get back to you.* She faltered. He was only a shadow dimly perceived across an untold distance. Blessing blazed in the realm of shadows, but Liath could not really be sure if anyone else heard her or even was aware of the rift she had opened between Earth and the sphere of Erekes.

"Wait for me, I beg you! Help me if you can, for I'm trapped here. I need Jerna."

Surely if Blessing had grown so large, Liath need not feel guilty about stealing Jerna away. A child of two could thrive on porridge and soft cheese, meat and bread and goat's milk.

A daimone flashed as a silvery form across the shadows, beyond the veil.

"I see you!" She reached out just as Jerna's gleaming, wispy form coiled protectively around Blessing, soaking the child in Jerna's aetherical substance. Blessing cried out in surprise and delight, a sweet sound that cut to Liath's heart. But she could not stop now. No time to savor it. The poison had reached her left shoulder, and her right hip. If she couldn't escape the sea of ice, she would die.

"Come if you will, Jerna. Return to your home. The way is open."

As she reached into the whirlpool of light, wind cut her hand to ribbons. She jerked back, crying out in pain as the archway of fire collapsed into a hundred shards that spun on a whirlwind out into the sea. Reeling back, she remembered too late that she would only fall into the poisonous sea.

But she never plunged into the depths. A cool presence wrapped itself around her, lifting her.

In the aether, Jerna's luminescence dazzled. She had form as much as softness and only the vaguest memory of the human shape she had worn on Earth.

"Come," she said, a murmur made by the flow of her body through the aetherical wind. On Earth, Liath had not understood the speech of the daimones, not as Sanglant had. Here, all language seemed an open book to her. "The blessing needs me no longer. This last act I will grant you, her mother, so I can become free of humankind."

She twisted upward on a trail of gauzy mist that flowered into life as Jerna ascended. Liath's arm and leg throbbed painfully, all pins and needles, where Jerna's substance wrapped them in a healing glow. The pain made her head pound, and the reflection of light off the ice floes and the white sea blinded her until, dizzy, she couldn't tell what was up and what was down and whether earthly directions had any meaning in the heavens.

A rosy glow penetrated the ice-white blaze of Erekes' farthest boundary. Silky daimones clustered along a series of arches that formed not so much a wall as a porous, inviting border, an elaboration of detail so sensuously formed that she wondered if earthly architects saw this place in fevered dreams.

"Now am I come to my home," whispered Jerna.

But as they reached the many-gated border, weight dragged Liath down once again.

"I cannot carry you within," said Jerna. "You still wear too much of Earth about you, Bright One. For the sake of the blessing you allowed me to nurse, I have carried you thus far, but I can hold you no longer."

Liath panicked as she slipped out of Jerna's grasp. Ai, God, she would plunge back into the poisonous sea. Her clumsy fingers found her belt buckle. As she loosened it, the leather slithered down her legs, caught on her foot, and the belt and the items hitched to it—her leather pouch and her sheathed iron eating knife—fell away.

Jerna released her. The many-gated wall passed beneath her, and she tumbled into the sphere of Somorhas, whose warm and rosy light embraced her.

2

THAT first night out of Handelburg, huddled in miserable cold in such shelter as a half-ruined ancient hill fort afforded them, Hanna suggested to the prince that he and his party all shave their heads. That way they could tell any folk they met that they'd battled lice and perhaps no one would suspect they had been excommunicated for heresy. Probably she risked excommunication herself for suggesting it, but it was the most practical thing to do.

She refused to shave her own head. Until that moment, she'd never known, or even considered, that she might be vain of her white-blonde hair. Maybe she hadn't minded Prince Bayan's attentions as much as she had protested to herself and to others. Maybe Princess Sapientia's jealousy had saved her from temptation.

God worked in strange ways.

When a snowstorm stranded the party for a month in a fortified village five days' march west of Handelburg, Ekkehard spoke sternly to his retinue.

"I don't know how long it will be until we can come clear of this village," he said, "but there's to be no preaching."

"But, my lord prince," objected Lord Benedict, always the first to speak when an opinion was asked, "it's a worse sin to remain silent when we can save lives with the truth!"

"That's true, but I made a promise to Prince Bayan that I wouldn't preach until the war is over and Bulkezu is defeated. I'll lose face if I don't keep my promise, and no one will ever respect me. We'll ride to the Villams and fight the Quman alongside them." How he would fight the Quman when his wounded shoulder still hadn't healed was a consideration no one addressed.

"We're not riding to your father, my lord prince?" Lord Frithuric was the biggest of Ekkehard's cronies, a strapping lad somewhat younger than Hanna.

Ekkehard shuddered. "I'll not throw myself on my father's mercy just yet. He's probably still mad at me for stealing Baldwin from Margrave Judith."

Lord Lothar was the eldest of the youths and, in Hanna's opinion, the only one with a feather's weight of sense. "But Margrave Judith is dead, my lord prince. Her daughter, Lady Bertha, didn't care one whit about Lord Baldwin, except for that trouble about the marriage portion."

"True enough," observed Ekkehard thoughtfully. He had so thoroughly absorbed the mannerisms of the better bards who came through the royal progress that the inflections of his stock phrases all sounded as though they were copied from some epic poem, weary pronouncements of doom, wise musings, angry retorts, and noble resolutions. "Remember what Bayan said. We'll have no one to preach to if we lose this war to the Quman savages. God would want us to fight to make Her lands safe for Her true word."

"Very true, my lord prince," they agreed, all six of his noble companions, Lord Dietrich's two cousins, and nineteen miscellaneous others who had survived that five-day ride. One poor man had drowned during a river crossing, and there had been a great deal of discussion whether this meant his faith in the Sacrifice and Redemption hadn't been strong enough to save him. Hanna personally thought that it was because he had slipped, fallen, and panicked because he hadn't known how to swim. No one had been able to reach him in time.

"Let us all remember the phoenix," finished Ekkehard portentously as he ran a hand through the stubble of his hair, scratching it cautiously as though it might at any moment sprout thistles. "The phoenix rises in its own time. We must have faith that we have other tasks to accomplish before the church is ready to embrace the truth."

With a party of twenty-eight visitors in a village populated by no more than sixty souls, half of whom were children, there were indeed plenty of tasks to accomplish. Hanna knew how to make herself useful and did so, figuring their party would be better off building up a store of goodwill considering how much food they were eating. She carded and spun wool, sewed, cooked, ground grain, churned butter, and spent many a pleasant hour combing the hair of her new friends. Luckily, most of the cast-off soldiers also had practical gifts. They helped dig out the village after the first, and worst, snowfall, repaired those portions of the palisade they could reach through the drifts, built benches and tables, dug out two canoes from logs, searched out lost sheep, and otherwise kept themselves busy. Lord Dietrich's two cousins set themselves to caring for the horses, although of course the presence of twelve horses in such a village was a terrible strain on the forage supply. Because of the heavy snow, Ekkehard was able to take his lads hunting only twice, but at least both times they brought back game to supplement the common house table. Hanna hated to think what hunger these villagers would suffer as winter gave way to the privations of early spring, with all their stores eaten up by their unexpected visitors.

Of course it was inevitable that this respite wouldn't last, even though Ekkehard entertained the villagers every night with a princely rendition of one of the many epics he had memorized. Song couldn't substitute for food, once all was said and done. Small irritations multiplied into fistfights. A householder complained that her entire store of apples had been eaten, so Ekkehard gave her a gold armband as restitution to keep the peace. Despite his religious vows, he took up with a village girl, although neither she nor her mother seemed displeased at the prospect of the rings and other little gifts he offered in exchange for her favors.

Lady Fortune smiled upon them. The main road, such as it was, was almost passable the morning Lord Manegold was discovered in the hayloft with the blacksmith's young wife and her younger sister. Murder was averted when the two hot-heads, Thiemo and Welf, were prevented from stabbing the furious blacksmith by the intervention of his adulterous wife, who threw herself bodily over her prone husband. By then it was already clear they were no longer welcome to stay in the village.

Prince Ekkehard was furious when they rode out at midday. "If I'd known she was willing, I wouldn't have settled for Mistress Aabbe's daughter, who isn't half as pretty."

"I would have shared her with you," protested Manegold. He wasn't as handsome as the infamous Baldwin, of course, but nevertheless was an appealing sight to girls who liked pretty, blond young men born into a noble house and unbur-dened by any notion of consequences. His blackening eye only added to his enticing good looks. "But I'd only just discovered myself how very willing she was! And that sister! You wouldn't think a common-born country girl would know how to do all those things!"

The villagers crowded together at the main gate, pitchforks and staves in hand, to make sure the prince and his retinue actually left. Four of the soldiers walked at the front, breaking trail. Lord Welf rode directly behind them, carrying Ekkehard's gold-and-red battle banner. This tattered and much-mended piece of cloth had, like Ekkehard himself, been rescued off the battlefield by the tumulus, so its presence was considered a sign of good luck as well as status, marking the progress of a royal prince. However meager his retinue might be.

"Perhaps, my lord prince," said Hanna reluctantly, "in the future you and your followers might be more cautious in your amorous trysts. In a marchland village such as this, the blacksmith is an honored member of the community and not to be insulted in such a grave way."

"You haven't the right to say that kind of thing to me!" replied Ekkehard indignantly.

"I ride as the king's representative, my lord prince. The villagers were generous with their hospitality. I am sure King Henry would think it unwise to repay their generosity in such a way that they throw us out."

"How will King Henry ever know if there's no one to report to him?" demanded Lord Thiemo, laying a hand on his sword hilt.

"It's treason to kill a King's Eagle," said Lord Dietrich's elder cousin.

"So it is," snapped Ekkehard. "Leave her be."

"How is being a traitor worse than being a heretic?" asked Lothar, genuinely puzzled.

Ekkehard had no answer to such a difficult question. "It doesn't matter anyway. I promised Prince Bayan I'd see the Eagle safely to the seat of the Villams, and so I will. After that, she's on her own to return to the king."

But Hanna noted how Lord Dietrich's cousins fell a little behind, talking intently to each other where the others could not hear them.

A warm sun rapidly turned the snow to heavy slush, and Hanna pitied the men who had to walk at the front to make a way for the horses. The weather remained changeable, freezing at night, sometimes warm and sometimes cold with a froth of snow during the daytime. One horse slipped and broke a leg, and although they ate well of its flesh over the next few days, the poor man who'd been thrown in the accident and hit his head finally lost consciousness completely and died of a seizure. One of the soldiers who did most of the trail breaking lost the use of his feet to frostbite, and when the infection began to stink, he begged them to kill him, but Ekkehard hadn't the guts for it. Instead, they abandoned him in a hamlet in the care of an old woman who claimed to know herbcraft. Hanna smelled the stink of witchcraft in that place, but there was nothing she could do to countermand Ekkehard's orders. She could hear the man's screaming for leagues afterward, long after they had marched out of earshot.

That night, Lord Dietrich's cousins and seven men deserted.

In the morning, Ekkehard would have upbraided the sentries, except it was the very men who'd been on watch who had left. They followed the trail made by the others, bold prints across virgin snow, but as the day wore on, bitterly cold, one of the foot soldiers fell gravely ill and had to be carried by his comrades. They fell farther and farther behind.

Here in the marchlands, forest ranged everywhere, woodland cut frequently by meadows, marsh, and higher heath lands. They took refuge that night within the remains of a deserted village. Most of the buildings had fallen in or been demolished but one had half a roof intact. Thatch scavenged from the outbuildings made decent sleeping pallets, and there was plenty of wood for a fire.

Ekkehard paced impatiently at the limit of the fire's light as the rest of them listened to the sick man struggle to breathe. Lord Lothar, too, was ill; his breath rattled in and out as he huddled miserably by the fire. Hanna stood with one foot up on the ruined foundations, watching the land.

The stars shimmered beyond a veil of night haze, strangely luminous. Snow-shrouded trees lay in perfect stillness. The moon's light etched shadows across the abandoned village and once or twice she thought she saw the shade of one of the lost inhabitants scurrying across the common yard on an errand, but it was first an owl and a second time simply a phantasm glimpsed out of the corner of her eye. The snow lay untouched except where their own feet had churned it. A sentry, stationed in the ruins of a pithouse right on the edge of the forest, coughed. Behind her the horses, crowded in with the men for warmth, stamped restlessly.

She stroked her hands down her braid. A cold suspicion was growing in her that Bayan had sent them all out here knowing they might well die. Was he more ambitious than he seemed? Did he mean to eliminate any possible threat to Sapientia's crown? Was it actually possible that Bayan could flirt as outrageously as he had with her and then send her out on such a dangerous journey? After all, the Quman could be anywhere, although surely they wouldn't ride abroad in this weather. Only a fool would march cross-country at the mercy of winter—a fool, or an Eagle sent about the regnant's business.

But, of course, Bayan hadn't made her an Eagle. She'd accepted the position, knowing its dangers. Any person who rode long distances was at risk, and if anything her Eagle's cloak and badge gave her a measure of security most travelers never knew.

Nay, Bayan wasn't bent on revenge or intrigue. In truth, Prince Ekkehard was a nuisance: young, untried, immature, and reckless. And as big a fool as Ivar to get mixed up in heresy. In Bayan's place, she would probably have done the same thing. Only she wished right now that she was snug in that sleeping platform in Biscop Alberada's hall instead of standing out here in the middle of wilderness with no fortified holding within a day's ride on either side. This was just the kind of place a small party like theirs could be attacked and overwhelmed.

In the distance, a wolf howled, the only sound in the lonely landscape. Whispered talk died by the fire as men paused to listen, but nothing replied to that solitary call. A twig snapped at the fringe of the trees.

Was that a shape, creeping in among the snow-laden branches? Were those pale wings, advancing through the trees?

"Who's there?" demanded the sentry. His voice trembled.

"Hsst!" Ekkehard stepped forward, sword drawn, to stand beside Hanna. "What do you see, Eagle?" he whispered. Behind, his companions drew their swords while the soldiers scrambled to ready spears and shields. Hands shaking, she hoisted her bow and nocked an arrow.

There was nothing there. Snow tumbled from a heavily-laden fir tree, shrouding the imagined wing shape, and all was still. The moon's light cast a drowsy glamour over the silent forest.

"Hai!" cried the sentry, so startled that his spear fell, clattering on stone foundations.

It arrived noiselessly and settled down in the midst of a stretch of untouched snow. Despite its size, it did not break through the hard crust. It was the largest owl she had ever seen, with tufted ears and a coat of mottled feathers, streaked with white at the breast. The owl gazed at her, unblinking, incurious, looking ready to snatch her up as it would a delectable mouse.

"That would make a tasty meal," muttered Ekkehard, elbowing Hanna. "Shoot it."

"Nay, my lord prince," she answered, suddenly afflicted by dread at the thought of shooting this magnificent creature, "for everyone knows that the flesh of an owl is like poison to a human being."

Ekkehard hesitated. In that instant, the owl took flight and was gone.

"Damn it! We've few enough provisions, Eagle. One owl shared between us wouldn't have sickened any one of us more than the rest!" He seemed ready to go on chastising her when Lord Benedict hurried up.

"Your Highness, come quick. The sick man is vomiting blood, and the old sergeant thinks he's going to die. You'd better give him a blessing so his soul will be safe when he passes to the Other Side."

The poor man did die, a little before dawn. Hanna paced all

night, wrapped in her cloak, too cold and nervous to sleep, while the moon set and the forest sank into a deeper slumber. As Ekkehard's company drifted in and out of their fitful sleep, interrupted now and again by Lord Lothar's hacking coughs, she wondered if she would have been better off if the deserters had invited her to join them.

They found their bodies the next day.

They had saddled up their remaining eight horses in the morning and started down the road, following the tracks left by the others. The cold had frozen a crust over the snow heavy enough to take a man's weight for a few moments before he broke through, and while that made the traveling easier for the men, it doubled the effort for the horses. Hanna quickly dismounted to lead her horse, and after a few more struggling steps, the young lords did so as well. They weren't fools about horseflesh. Hanna had long since observed that many noble folk had more concern for their hounds, horses, and hawks than for the common people bound into their service.

"Look here," said Frithuric, who had taken the lead as usual. "There's a set of tracks leading off the path, into the forest. Back toward the abandoned village. Should we follow them? Maybe one of these damned deserters had a change of heart and came back to look for us."

"Nay," said Ekkehard impatiently, "we'll want shelter tonight and I've no intention of wasting time on them, since they're the ones who left us behind."

They went on, breath steaming in the cold air. The exercise made Hanna sweat, but her feet stayed cold and her toes ached incessantly. They had followed the path for less than half a league when Lord Frithuric, still ranging ahead, gave a strangled cry. Hurrying forward, they saw him beside a wayside shelter, chasing away crows.

Lord Dietrich's cousins and their seven fellow deserters had made their final stand at the wayside shelter, vainly attempting to use its walls as protection. Three of the men were missing their heads; the rest were simply dead, stripped of their weapons, any decent armor, and, of course, the three horses. Blood soaked the snow. Fire had scorched the thatch before burning itself out harmlessly. Singed straw lay scattered downwind along the snowy ground as far as Hanna could see. By the evidence of hoofprints, the deserters had been attacked by at least a dozen horsemen. A few stray feathers trampled in the snow or caught beneath the corpses left no doubt that their assailants had been a Quman raiding party.

No one dared speak for fear their voices would carry on the still winter air across the sea of snow and blanketed forest to the waiting Quman. Surely they were still out there.

They hadn't the time or the energy to dig graves in the frozen ground, so they just left them for the wolves, not even building a cairn of rocks over them as they had for the man who'd died during the night. What else could they do?

As the others made ready to go, Hanna grimly followed the tracks of the raiding party a short way, just to get an idea what direction they were heading. That was the eeriest thing of all: the Quman riders had obviously ridden back down the trail toward the abandoned village. One man had been bleeding enough to leave a faint trail of blood in his wake, quickly churned away by the passage of his fellows. It seemed possible, in retrospect, that the solitary hoofprints veering off from the trail a stone's throw from the abandoned village had been those of a Quman scout rather than one of the deserters. Had it only been a dream that she'd seen pale wings moving among the trees last night?

Of course it had. If the Quman had spotted them, they would have attacked. They hadn't spotted them, and they hadn't attacked.

Never argue with Lady Fortune, her mother would say.

Nervous every time a branch creaked or cracked under the weight of snow, she returned to the others. They were eager to be gone from the scene of carnage.

"Didn't they kill even one?" demanded Lord Frithuric. "I thought Lord Dietrich's cousins were strong fighters."

"Maybe they were taken unawares," said Hanna, which shut them up.

Maybe she had ridden under worse conditions in her time as an Eagle, but she couldn't think of any. The silence became excruciating. Little arguments flared up over nothing, tempers goaded into flame by anxiety. They slogged on and on and on along the path that led them deeper into the forest, far past the woodland fringes where they had traveled thus far, on into the old uncut heart, a vast tract of trees and silence. They saw no living creatures except themselves. The path was their only landmark. They waded knee-deep through snow along a narrow track bounded by trees. Except for a detour here and there to cut around an escarpment or dip down to a ford in a stream, the path took a fairly straight course through the old forest. Luckily for their feet, the streams had all frozen over, making every crossing easy.

The worst part of the whole long, cold, nerve-racking, miserable day was that it got dark so early, leaving them caught in twilight deep in the forest without shelter.

Fortunately, the old sergeant, Gotfrid, knew woodcraft. He spotted a dense stand of fir trees off to the right of the path. In their center, under overhanging branches, they discovered a living cathedral blanketed with needles and almost free of snow. The air lay close and quiet underneath the overarching branches. In an odd way, Hanna felt protected here, as though they had stumbled upon an ancient refuge. Eighteen people and the eight horses could all crowd in, as long as two men were posted as sentries at the fringes to peer out into the darkening forest. Clouds hung low, seeming to brush the tops of trees, and snow skirled down, spinning and drifting.

"It's really beautiful," she murmured to old Gotfrid. She had come up beside his sentry post to survey their situation. "Or would be, anyway, if we had a fire and mead."

"And no Quman lurking like wolves to feed on us," he agreed. He was a good man, stable, shrewd, and steady, who had spent most of his adult life as a Lion.

"There's something I don't understand, though, Gotfrid." She glanced back to make sure the others couldn't hear them. Several ranks of trees, each taller and broader than the last, separated them from the hidden center. "Why would a practical man like you throw away everything for a heresy?"

He chuckled, taking no offense at the question, as she'd guessed he wouldn't. He was old enough to have white in his hair and a few age spots on his face. "You're thinking that those young lords might be taking to a heresy just because they're young and rash and fools, aren't you? That's because you're a practical young woman, as I've seen." He spoke the words approvingly, and it was a measure of the respect she'd gained for him on this desperate journey that she smiled, pleased with the compliment. "But it isn't a whim, friend." He faltered, growing suddenly serious.

Snow fell softly throughout the vista beyond, a mantle of white over everything. It was almost too dark to see.

"Have you ever seen a rose?" he asked finally.

"Truly, I have seen one or two in my time. I saw the king's rose garden at Autun."

"Well, then." He hesitated again. She studied him. He wasn't handsome or ugly but rather comfortably in between, with the broad shoulders and thick arms of a soldier. He was, perhaps, the same age as the king but rather more weathered by the hardships of life in the infantry, and if he stumbled with his words it was because he'd had a soldier's education, not a cleric's. "Think of a rose blooming all of a sudden in your heart." He gestured toward the silent forest, all chill and white, a sea of winter. "Think of a rose blooming there, in the snow, where you'd never think to see it. Wouldn't that be a miracle? Wouldn't you know that you'd stumbled upon a little sliver of God's truth?"

"I suppose so."

He spoke so quietly that she almost couldn't hear him. "A holy one walks among us. But we mustn't speak of it, because God hasn't chosen to make Her messenger known yet. But the rose bloomed in my heart, Eagle. I have no better way to explain it, how I knew it was truth when I heard the preaching about the Sacrifice and Redemption. The rose bloomed, and I'd rather die than turn my back now. I'd rather die."

There wasn't a breath of wind.

"Those seem ill-chosen words, friend, considering our situation," said Hanna finally, not unkindly.

"We've had poor luck, haven't we? God is testing us."

"So They are." The cold seeped down into her bones. She chafed her hands to warm them. "But Lord Dietrich was stricken down and died when he professed the heresy."

"I think he was poisoned by the biscop." Gotfrid spoke these words so calmly that Hanna expected the sky to fall, but it did not. All she heard was the muffled noises of their party, hidden among the firs: a low mutter of conversation, the sting of smoke in her nostrils from a fire, the stamp and restless whickering of the horses. Twice she heard Lord Lothar's hacking cough.

"That's a bold charge," she said at last.

"You think so, too," he said grimly, "or else you'd leap to her defense. I think she poisoned him because she saw he wouldn't back down. He was the strongest of us in faith. She hoped to frighten the rest of us into recanting." He leaned toward her, close enough that his breath stirred her hair. "Don't think there weren't others among the crowd who had heard and believed. They hold the truth in their hearts as well."

"But hadn't the courage to step forward."

"Well," he said generously, "not everyone is ready to die, if it comes to that. Someone has to survive to spread the truth, don't they?"

She chuckled, finding it amusing that they could debate matters of heresy while running for their lives through this vale of ice. "I like living, and I wouldn't mind a nice hot cup of spiced wine right now."

"Well, lass, truly, so would we all."

But back in their refuge, there wasn't anything but stale bread. She did manage to sleep curled up in her cloak until one of the soldiers woke her for a turn at watch. Within the shelter of the trees, with so many bodies crowded together, it had actually gotten—not warm, of course, but bearable. As she pushed her way out through the stinging branches, she felt all the warmth sucked away by a raw cold so profound that for a moment she thought it might seize her heart. She came to the edge of the thick stand of trees and at once floundered into a thigh-high drift of new snow, all powdery soft. Snow slipped down her leggings to freeze her ankles and toes. She staggered back into the shelter of the firs and tried to make sense of the scene before her.

She heard it, and felt it, more than saw it, because it was still too dark to see. She tasted that flavor the air has when snow falls thick and fast and the clouds weigh so heavily that one knows a blizzard is on the way. Flakes settled on her nose, and cheeks, and eyelids, and melted away.

Ai, God, if the Quman didn't kill them, then they would freeze to death in the coming storm.

A thread of falling snow, dislodged from a branch just to her right, hissed down past her ear. She went as still as a rabbit who has just sensed the shadow of an owl. *Something was out there.*

Beyond the veil of snow, wraithlike figures darted forward among the trees.

Quman.

Nay, not Quman at all. There was just enough light now, a hint of dawn, that she could make out their outlines: Slender and pale, these creatures walked rather than rode. Dark hoods obscured their faces, and where their feet brushed the snow they did not sink down through the light powder, nor did they leave tracks. They were shadows.

Ghosts.

One flung back its hood. She saw its face clearly: an Aoi face, more shade than substance, with the sharp cheekbones and broad lineaments common to Prince Sanglant's ancestors. Feathers decorated its hair, and the bow it carried in its hands gleamed softly, as if it weren't made of wood but of ensorcelled bone. Its eyes were as cold as the grave as it paused to sniff the air, scenting for prey.

There were some things more frightening than the Quman.

She whistled sharply. The sound gave away her position. Before she could even take a single step back into the protecting tangle of firs, an arrow caught in her sleeve. As delicate as a needle, it had no fletching. It hung from the cloth, point lodged where the fabric creased at her elbow, and dissolved into smoke, simply and utterly *gone*.

Instinct made her duck to the right. A second arrow spit past, just where she'd been standing. A third caught in the dense fir above her, tumbled, and vanished as it fell.

A cry of alarm split the air. Shrieks and shouts erupted from the refuge within the firs.

Hanna scrambled back into the firs. Branches scraped her face, pulled at her cloak, and yanked her hood back from her hair. Her braid caught and tangled in the crook of a branch. As she jerked her head sideways to free it, another spray of needles whistled past, spattering like falling stones down around her before they hissed out of existence. One struck her in the heel, but the needle-thin arrow couldn't penetrate leather. Or so she hoped. Stumbling forward, she didn't have time to check.

She burst into the open space under the tallest trees, as dark as sin except for the fire smoking and sparking where someone had thrown needles over it to kill it. She sucked in a breath to cry a warning but got such a lungful of smoke that she could barely breathe. Hacking, eyes burning, she grabbed for the nearest horse, snagged its reins, and glimpsed Gotfrid. The old Lion had formed up with two of his fellows to make a little wall of shields to defend Prince Ekkehard, much good that it did them.

Someone yelled, "God save us! My arrows go right through them! They're demons—"

The voice cut off. Then a man—maybe the one who had shouted—fell backward right onto the smoking fire, clawing frantically at the arrow stuck in his throat.

Between one breath and the next, Ekkehard and his entire party panicked.

Hanna barely kept hold of the horse as men and horses bumped and careened past her. Smoke filled her eyes, blinding her, and she staggered into the thickest tangle of branches until she fetched up there, face scratched and raw, one glove torn off, hair coming free of her braid. She couldn't go any farther, and she'd lost the horse's reins. She turned around to try to find it, and almost screamed.

Facing her stood a pale figure, more shadow than substance. It had a woman's body but the face of a vulture, and the gleaming bronze armor at its chest was embossed with vulture-headed women bearing spears into battle.

Hanna could actually see the faint outline of the fir trees through its body, or maybe, horribly, actually even piercing its body, as though it weren't really entirely there.

Lowering its bow, it spoke. "I smell the stench of our old enemy upon you, human. That is how we tracked you down." It drew a long, ugly knife.

Stark terror flooded her.

It was going to kill her. With the branches pressed in against her, she couldn't reach her bow. Her fingers found the hilt of her eating knife, but she knew it was hopeless, that cold iron would do nothing more than stick itself in the trunk of the tree behind the phantom, while any least touch from a cursed elven blade or arrow would sicken a mortal unto death.

It was going to kill her.

That was it, her last thought: Ai, God. I'll never see Liath again.

The owl appeared out of nowhere, all beating wings and tearing beak. A moment's reprieve, that was all. A moment was all Hanna needed. She dropped to her knees and crawled like a madwoman, finding room to escape all the way down against the ground under a roof made of the lowest branches. Her bow scraped wood, and an arrow, catching on a branch, snapped as she broke forward. The bed of dry needles gave way to a dusting of snow, and she pushed through low-hanging branches and found herself facing into a drift. She burrowed up between two sprawling branches and floundered forward through the snow.

All she could think about was getting away.

There was enough light to see, now, although everything was still in shades of gray as dawn fought to vanquish night, not an easy task with snow falling heavily and a dense blanket of clouds covering the sky. It was bitterly cold. Through the snow she saw other figures struggling to flee and, there, a lone horse.

With difficulty, she plowed through the snow and got hold of the horse's reins. It reared back, terrified, and she almost lost hold of it.

One of the young lords materialized out of the snow beside her. He grabbed the reins out of her hands and within moments had the horse under control. By the way he favored one arm, she realized it was Prince Ekkehard. He turned to stare at her. He looked pale, scared, and very very young.

"Come on, Eagle. Lothar's dead and Thiemo's lost. We've got to run."

Behind them, a man screamed horribly. She began to turn, to go to his aid, but Ekkehard lurched forward as if the cry had propelled him on, and she didn't want to be left alone, God help her, to face those creatures. Sick at heart, she pressed through the snow in the prince's wake. From this angle, she saw thin red gashes scoring the horse's flanks, the mark of elfshot. Ekkehard's cloak was torn. They hadn't gone more than twenty wallowing steps through the snow when they were hailed.

"My lord p—prince." The voice was ragged and almost incoherent with fear. Four of the young lordlings had taken refuge behind a massive elm, now stripped of foliage. They had three horses between them. As soon as they saw that Ekkehard was safe, they all blundered out into the snowy forest, aiming in no certain direction but only *away* from the refuge where they had so hopefully taken shelter the night before.

Hanna glimpsed a handful of other figures retreating far off to one side. Was that Gotfrid? She couldn't be sure, and she dared not call out to him, and anyway, he was already gone, lost beyond the veil of snow and the ranks of evergreens. Maybe she had only dreamed them. Maybe it was the shadow elves, circling around in order to ambush them somewhere else.

One of the boys was weeping, "Lothar's dead. Lothar's dead."

Ekkehard said, in a breathless voice, "Shut up, Manegold. They'll hear us."

"As if we aren't making the noise of an army," muttered Frithuric.

Lord Welf still had hold of the banner, although the haft had gotten broken off halfway, and the young man was so dispirited that he dragged it through the snow as he stumbled on. Snow fell densely around them, soft and silent, until Hanna thought they would be buried alive.

After a long time, Benedict said in a whisper, "I think we've escaped them."

They all stumbled to a stop, breath billowing white in the cold air. The horses whickered nervously. Frithuric coughed. Ekkehard hissed a warning. They stood there with the trees all around them half invisible through the falling snow. It was utterly silent, except for the delicate shift of snow through branches and the merest whisper of wind through the crowns of trees. Because of the falling snow, Hanna couldn't see more than a stone's toss in any direction, but it all looked the same anyway: snow and trees, trees and snow.

"We're lost," said Lord Benedict finally in a very small, very frightened voice.

"I'm going to barf," said Lord Welf suddenly.

"My foot hurts," said Ekkehard, sounding surprised.

"We're all going to freeze out here," said Hanna sensibly, "if we don't keep moving. We mustn't believe we've escaped those—those shades. Whatever they were."

"They're the ancient ones," whined Manegold, half frantic, almost babbling, "who were cursed for being pagans and foul murderers who cut up babies on their altars. They were cursed to walk as ghosts forever. That's why they hate us. My old nurse told me stories—"

"All the more reason to keep moving," snapped Hanna, hoping a firm hand would get them going.

So it did. She'd learned that trick from her mother when it came time to get drunken men out of the inn and off to their homes late at night.

She grabbed the reins out of the prince's hands and pushed forward. There was no point in caring what direction they went now, except away from where they'd come. She supposed that the shades of the Aoi would have no trouble tracking them down no matter what the weather, but she'd be damned if she'd stand here waiting for them to take her unawares from the back. Let her die if she must, but as she'd said to Gotfrid not that many hours before, she'd really prefer to keep on living even if she wasn't going to get a nice hot cup of spiced wine for her trouble.

Ekkehard and his comrades followed smartly. For all their complaining, they were strong young men, well fed, strengthened by riding and weapons drill, and so scared that none of them wanted to be the one to fall behind.

Hanna's feet felt like ice and her hands were freezing. Flakes of snow stuck to her eyelashes. She flinched at every least crack and hiss from the snow-laden trees around them, but she pressed on determinedly. As long as they were moving, they weren't dead.

That was the only thing she was sure of right now.

The trees looked denser up ahead, although it was hard to

tell anything for sure through the snow. A crowded line of
trees like that, matted with underbrush, usually signaled a settlement or a stream. If it were the former, then they'd have
shelter. If the latter, then they could follow its frozen path
more easily through the forest, hoping it would lead them
eventually to a place of refuge.

She reached the edge of the trees and found a deer trail, still
visible because the snow made a trough where the path cut
through the trees. Was that smoke she smelled? But the smell
was gone quickly, nothing but a wish fled like mist under the
morning sun. It began to snow harder. If they didn't find shelter soon, they would die.

The path cut around a corner. She glimpsed an opening
through a curtain of branches.

"Wait!" cried one of the young lords behind her.

Too late she remembered caution. The shadow elves weren't
the only enemies they were running from. But she had already
taken enough of a step. Her calf caught on a trip wire, and she
flew headlong, hit a slope tumbling, and slid and rolled down
until she came to rest, dizzy and shaken, on her back in the
snow under a cold, hard sky. It had, abruptly, stopped snowing.

The spear point came first, neatly shoved right up to the
bridge of her nose. With an effort, eyes almost crossing, she
focused away from that light but deadly pressure. Someone
was holding that spear, someone big and very solid, not a
shade at all but quite horribly real.

The hideous and most menacing thing about him was that
he had gleaming iron wings and no face, only a flat iron-gray
visor with eyeholes.

With something that sounded suspiciously like a laugh, he
twisted off his helmet without letting slip his grip on the
spear. Glossy black hair spilled over his shoulders like silk.
Still stupefied, Hanna stared up into the face of the handsomest man she'd ever laid eyes on:

A Quman warrior wearing the wings of a griffin.

3

THEY had blundered into the camp of the Quman raiding party.

Of course. Their luck could hardly get any worse.

She didn't dare move, even though the snow was leaking in through her clothing, making her skin sting. Men called out to each other in an incomprehensible language. A horse neighed in challenge.

Was that the sound of a skirmish? Or only the ring of cooking pots clanging together? She listened for Ekkehard's voice but heard nothing.

The warrior lifted his spear point from her face and handed it to someone unseen. He dropped to his knees beside her and, with an expression of astonished delight, reached down to touch her hair. She clenched her jaw, willing herself not to react as he traced a line down to her ear and picked up what remained of her braid, fingering it as if it were the most precious substance he'd ever encountered.

The unexpected beauty of his face, together with the knowledge that she was probably just about to have her throat slit, stunned her. He had a dark complexion, piercingly dark eyes, a scant mustache, and a wisp of a beard, but it was the elegant shape of his face, the dimple in his left cheek, and the brightness of his expression that marked him most. By this time his hair had fallen down over his shoulders, spilling everywhere, so glorious that she had an insane urge to touch it.

Until, that is, her gaze fastened on the gruesome ornament dangling from his belt. The shrunken head swayed gently. Its grisly face, so revolting with those distorted features and blackened skin, swung in and out of her view. There was something nauseatingly familiar about it, maybe only that it was a human face and had once, not long ago, ornamented a living, breathing person rather than a savage's belt. The hair that crowned it had a sickly orange-brown hue, as though the poor

dead man had once had hair as light as her own before it had
been dipped in a noxious dye.

A voice called out. Her captor stood up, attention skipping
so quickly away from her that she risked levering herself up on
an elbow. No one leaped in to slaughter her, so she was able to
watch as the prince—what else could he be, with those griffin
wings and that swagger?—walked across the clearing to
regard his captives.

They had Ekkehard and his four remaining comrades
trussed up like birds being taken to the cooking pot. One of
the Quman soldiers tossed a scrap of cloth to the prince. At
first, the breadth of his wings hid him from Hanna's view.
From this angle she saw clearly the harness attached to his
lamellar armor, curving wood wings fletched by griffin feathers. Breschius had told her about griffin feathers. Only the
greatest Quman heroes wore them, since they had to kill and
pluck the beast themselves.

He turned sideways to shake out the banner, laughing as he
saw Ekkehard's standard embroidered there: a golden harp
and lion salient on a red field. He seemed to find the strangest
things amusing. With a sharp whistle, he summoned to his
side a man of indeterminate years but classic Wendish features.
They spoke together. The Wendish man turned to regard the
five youths with a sour frown.

"Which of you rates this banner, then?"

Ekkehard and company stood stubbornly silent.

The Wendish man spat on the snow. "Oh, for the love of the
blessed Daisan, do you want yer cock cut off or not, for they'll
not be hesitating if you don't give them satisfaction. Don't be
thinking there's any bargaining with His Pompousness here."
As he spoke the insulting name, he bowed with outward
respect to the man with the glorious hair. "Because let me tell
you, you're lucky you're not all lying dead. He wants to know
whose banner it is, and if any of you have the right to it."

As boldly as he could, given the rope binding his wrists, the
condition of his hair and face, and the rips and stains in his

clothing, Prince Ekkehard stepped forward. "I am Ekkehard, son of King Henry, royal prince of the realm of Wendar and Varre. I wear the gold torque to mark my kinship to the royal house. Spare our lives, and I vouch that my father will pay a worthy ransom for us."

The interpreter stopped listening after the words "gold torque," and spoke quickly to his master.

The Quman prince listened intently. He seemed to have forgotten Hanna, or else he was the kind of man who only did one thing at a time. Cautiously, she ventured to sit all the way up.

The Quman camp consisted of one large round tent imperfectly camouflaged by a coating of snow and about a dozen smaller round tents, each one big enough for four men to sleep in. A long and slender standard dangled from the center post of each tent, white cloth marked with three raking stripes. After a moment, she recognized what it must be: the claw's rake, mark of the Pechanek clan. Lady Fortune was surely laughing at Hanna today: she had fallen in with a raiding party from the tribe of Bulkezu himself, leader of the Quman army.

The prince stepped forward to unpin Ekkehard's cloak, pull down the front of his tunic, and run a finger along the twisted gold braids of Ekkehard's torque. For an instant, Hanna expected him to rip the torque right off Ekkehard's neck, because surely that's what savages did in their lust for gold. But he only grunted and stepped back without further molesting Ekkehard. With a grand gesture, he spoke, then waited for the interpreter's translation.

"His Magnificence says these words: 'You escaped my sister's son on the battlefield, but now I have your life in my hands, as I was meant to, Brother.'"

"He's the one you fought?" exclaimed Benedict. "He almost killed you!"

"Nay, it's some other one of them with those damned iron wings who fought me," said Ekkehard, looking increasingly nervous. "He just said so himself. Why does he call me 'Brother'?"

It was just hard to remain calm with all those nasty shrunken heads dangling from every belt. Hanna eased up to her knees. Strange that they had no campfires. How did they mean to cook the three skinned deer strung up on branches? And what was that seen beyond the trees that edged the other side of the clearing? Chalk cliffs? A ridge of snow? She couldn't make it out.

"Princes are brothers, are they not?" replied the translator sarcastically. "Unlike us poor bondsmen, who suffer at the whims of princes and pray only that we may live to see the next sunrise."

"Are you always so insolent?" demanded Frithuric. "Don't you fear your master's anger?"

The interpreter's smile appeared sincere, but he had a way of thrusting his chin forward that betrayed his resentment. "Only a fool wouldn't fear Prince Bulkezu's anger, for he almost never loses his temper, which makes him the worst kind of tyrant." He nattered on, a petty tyrant himself glad of the chance to lord it over folk more helpless than he was, but Hanna reeled and Ekkehard and his comrades swayed fearfully and changed color.

Bulkezu.

Ai, God, this glorious man was Bulkezu? She'd thought their luck couldn't get any worse.

But it had.

"Anyway," the interpreter continued, "none of these miserable Quman understand our tongue, so I can say what I wish. I could tell His Arrogance right now that you've insulted his mother, and then you'd be seeing something you'd rather wished you hadn't, like your guts spilled out on the ground before you're too dead to notice." Gleefully, he turned to Bulkezu and said several sharp sentences.

Ekkehard gasped out loud, but got control of himself as though he'd just remembered that, in the epics, the hero

always died nobly. Straightening up, he composed his face
sternly to meet his doom.

Bulkezu laughed again. He clapped Ekkehard on the shoulder and gestured toward the large tent.

The interpreter spoke mockingly. "Prince Bulkezu wishes to
share wine with his Wendish brother, in token of their kinship."

"Is he going to poison me?" whispered Ekkehard, trying to
look courageous and cool.

"Nay, my lord prince, he's going to do just as he says, share
a cup of wine with you that he's taken off some poor God-fearing decent folk who are now dead and lying unburied, food for
the ravens. I hope you enjoy it."

It seemed to Hanna that not one man there was paying
attention to her. There were no obvious sentries anywhere.
Most of the two dozen men in the small clearing stood around
watching with various expressions of amusement the interplay
between their prince and his prisoners. Off to the right,
beyond the tents, seven men moved among the horses. These
stocky creatures looked awkward compared to the bigger, prettier mounts captured with Ekkehard. One older man with a
tattooed face and wearing a strange costume composed of
dozens of scraps of cloth sewn into a patchwork stood off to
one side, where he fingered the elfshot gashes torn into the
roan's rump. With an absent, almost crazy smile, he smeared
a yellowish paste onto the wounds, letting another man hold
the horse's head so it wouldn't bolt.

She shifted sideways on her knees as Ekkehard made up his
mind to approach the princely tent with as much dignity as
his tied hands allowed. With everyone watching that little
procession, she might have a chance to make a break for it.

But to what end? Would abandoning Ekkehard result in his
execution? Could she really expect to escape when they had
horses and she was on foot? Were the shadow elves still lurking in the forest?

Yet no matter what, no matter the risk or the consequences,

she had to try to reach the king. He had to be made to understand that Quman raiding parties were overrunning the eastern borders of his kingdom.

Hanna got a foot under her, pushed up—

—and saw a needle-thin arrow skate across the snow right in front of her. It dissolved into smoke, melting down into the snow. A cloud of air, puffing out from nose and mouth, shrouded her vision briefly, but the shadow forms of the Lost Ones were unmistakable once you knew them, old enemies returned to haunt her. She sucked in air, and the mist cleared. A dozen bows aimed down at the camp as the shadow elves gathered at the forest's edge

At whose hands would death be worse?

Like firebrands being quenched in water, arrows hissed and smoked through the brittle air. Two struck into the snow, first at one side of her and then, as she rolled away, to the other. Tiny trails of smoke rose where the arrows melted into the snow.

It seemed impossible for such delicate threads to be so deadly.

A scream pierced the quiet clearing. A Quman soldier reeled backward, hands grasping his head. Blood leaked between his gloved fingers as he staggered and fell, although his scream echoed on and on in time to the pounding of her heart.

She scrambled backward. An arrow streaked toward the Quman prince. Whether by luck or calculation, he twisted, catching the dart on his griffin wings. A shower of sparks like a hot iron forge lit up the dawn.

Bulkezu shouted unintelligible orders. Those with horses near turned them to become shields against the shadow foe. A few Quman loosed arrows in reply, but their shots flew wildly, clumsily drawn, and the shadows always faded into bush or tree before Quman arrows could strike a target.

A half-dozen Quman soldiers shoved Prince Ekkehard and his company toward the big pavilion. Lord Welf fell, although

Hanna did not see where he was hit. A burly soldier hooked him under the armpits and dragged him on after the others.

The patch-cloak man let out a sudden whoop, dancing toward the prince, who had slapped his helmet back over his head. The shaman stripped off his cloak to reveal a naked torso, his chest and back covered with fantastic blue-black tattoos. As he babbled and pranced, the designs, wild and magical animals, scenes of battle, celestial forms, began to writhe and come to life.

Hanna shook her head hard, thinking she was seeing things, and found shelter behind a stalwart pony too stupid to be scared. She could not keep her gaze from the dancing man, his stocky, hairless torso, muscular legs, and powerful arms. In each of his ears he wore a chain of three human noses. A golden needle pierced the septum of his nose, with a human ear, dried and withered, skewered on each end. His hands were gloved in skins from human feet and his feet in skins from human hands.

Bulkezu ducked, catching a shower of arrows in his wings again, and took cover behind the captured roan. But the shaman crouched in plain sight and sang. With each phrase he hunkered lower and lower until Hanna thought he meant to dig himself entirely into the snow. A white haze rose around him, like wind blowing the top layer off a snowy field, and his tattoos actually slipped off his body onto the snow and like a thousand wriggling worms climbed up onto Bulkezu, and the horse, spreading and growing until a half-dozen men and then a dozen more were dappled with his tattoos.

Bulkezu mounted the horse and shouted a command. With bows and spears and swords, the Quman charged up the hill. A hail of darts fell among them, but neither Bulkezu nor his soldiers flinched. As the shadow arrows struck, the tattoo beasts and warriors caught and swallowed them, and any harm they might cause. Neither horse nor rider could be wounded. With Bulkezu in the lead, they crested the slope and fell upon the shadow elves.

The battle thrashed away into the trees as the Quman drove

off their attackers. Prince Bulkezu was nowhere in sight, a dozen men scurried to corral the spooked horses, and the shaman, rising from the snow, threw his patchwork cloak back on and with a few assistants got busy tending to the wounded, including poor Lord Welf.

No one was paying attention to Hanna, no one at all.

Lady Fortune had a strange way of showering her favor over the hapless. Hanna got as far as the tree line before, amazingly, she tripped over that same damned trip line that had caught her in the first place. She fell hard, wind knocked out of her. Her head ached, and her hands had gone numb. But by God she was going to get out of here. She forced her elbows under herself and began to push up, just as hands grabbed her ankles.

She swore helplessly as a soldier dragged her back into camp. It was as much as she could do to keep her head up off the ground so she didn't smother in snow. Her captor didn't let go of her until he reached the entrance to the great tent. There, he let go of her ankles and rolled her over the threshold—a ridge of wood that bruised an arm and hip as she was tipped over it—onto a miraculously soft carpet that had no snow on it. She lay there, gasping for breath, as melting granules of snow trickled from all the creases in her clothing to numb her skin under her clothing. She wanted to weep, but she didn't have the luxury.

After a moment, she pushed up to her hands and knees, staggered slightly, and stood, aware that about a dozen men had crowded into the pavilion, eager to watch the final tawdry scene unfold.

Bulkezu sat on a stool at his ease, watching her. He still wore his armor, but his wings and his helmet had been set aside and his skin and clothing bore no sign of the tattoos that had protected him. If the fight had discomposed him at all, she saw no sign of it in his posture or his serene expression. He said a few casual words to the interpreter, who like Hanna was still breathing hard, looking relieved to have escaped death.

"His Imperiousness Prince Bulkezu suggests with all politeness that you not try to escape again. He's quite taken with your blonde hair. If you're lucky, he'll like you well enough to keep you to himself for a bit before he throws you to the wolves."

"I wonder that he can't hear what a bastard you are just from your tone of voice," said Hanna. "I'll thank you, traitor, to let His Most Gracious Prince Bulkezu know that he'd better not touch me, because I'm a King's Eagle, and my person is sacrosanct."

The interpreter merely snorted, then repeated what she hoped were her words. Bulkezu only laughed as he rose and approached her. Miraculously, her cloak hadn't come unpinned despite all the dragging and tumbling about. He grabbed hold of her brass Eagle's brooch and ripped it clean off. Her cloak slid down her body to land in a heap on the carpet, all ridges and rumpled valleys. Her tunic, torn, drooped a little, revealing skin.

Bulkezu sighed, lifting a hand to fondle her hair.

"Sorry to tell you," said the interpreter, who hadn't moved from his place beside the prince's stool. "The Quman believe that blonde hair is good luck. I've seen a man killed fighting to get possession of a light-haired bed-slave."

She was really getting frightened now, knowing how ugly it was probably going to get, and her fear made her angry and reckless. She hated the feel of Bulkezu touching her like she was an animal, or already his bed-slave. Grabbing his wrist, she yanked his hand down from her hair.

He hadn't expected her to defy him, and anyway, she'd worked hard all her life and wasn't a weakling. For the space of two breaths they stood poised there, she holding his wrist away and he gone tense, resisting her. They were almost exactly the same height. This close, she saw a shadow flicker in his eyes, the spark of anger. Something about him changed, his posture, the cant of his head, the tension in his shoulders. The atmosphere in the tent altered completely. The interpreter made a strangled noise in his throat, catching back a gasp of fear.

The ugly scene was upon them.

Bulkezu forced her hand down slowly, slowly. It wasn't easy for him to do it, but in the end he was stronger although she fought him all the way. He just held her arm down by her hip to prove that he had her, that she'd lost, that nothing she could do would change the fact that she was his now, to do with as he willed. He kept his gaze locked on hers, to drive her into utter submission.

She didn't flinch. In this contest, he could kill her if he wished, but he would never win. She refused to be beaten.

Fluttering up from the depths of her memory in that moment before the worst happened, she remembered Brother Breschius.

Without looking away from the Quman prince, Hanna spoke clearly and strongly. "I pray you, traitor, tell your master that he'd rather be dead than touch me because I'm the luck of a Kerayit shaman."

She saw the word "Kerayit" strike Bulkezu as might an arrow, right in the eyes. His grip on her slackened, just for an instant, but hesitation is usually fatal. She twisted her wrist within his fingers and jerked out of his grasp.

The interpreter made a gagging noise in his throat, as though a bone had stuck there. But he spoke words nevertheless. Prince Bulkezu stepped back from her at once, alarmed and surprised. He snapped an order in his own tongue. It seemed like every man there gaped at her, faces white or flushed, as one darted out of the tent. He returned quickly with the man dressed in the patchwork cloak.

The shaman groped in one of his barkskin pouches. He came up with a handful of powder and flung it at her. Coughing, she waved the white powder away as it settled down into her hair and on her shoulders, drifting to the carpet. Its stink ate into her and woke the wasp sting in her heart. The shaman's eyes got very wide. He babbled in a high, anxious voice, made a number of signs that looked like the kind of gestures witches made when casting protection about themselves, and became so agitated, drooling and spitting froth, that most of the men fled the tent. His nose earrings swayed as he shuddered and twitched. Finally, he sank down into a huddle on the floor, exhausted. As well he might be, after fighting off the shadow elves with his magic.

There was silence. Hanna began to wonder where Ekkehard was, or if he was even still alive.

And then, of course, Prince Bulkezu laughed, as if he'd just heard the best joke of his life. That easy laughter was beginning to make her nervous.

Her wrist hurt, and her stomach and breasts ached from the jolting drag across the ground, and her feet especially were freezing with flashes of hot and cold. But she couldn't afford to look weak now.

With an amused smile on his handsome face, Bulkezu sat back down on his camp stool and gave some orders, nothing she could understand. The old shaman unrolled himself from his stupor, rose, and hurried away without any sign he'd had a fit. He returned with a fine copper basin engraved with griffins devouring deer and a copper pitcher filled with hot water. Where on Earth had they come by hot water in this godforsaken wilderness when they had not even one campfire burning to alert enemies to their position?

He gestured toward a curtain while Bulkezu watched her with avid interest. Other men hurried out, sent on errands. Hanna allowed the shaman to show her behind the curtain. Here lay pillows and furs, the plush sleeping quarters of a nomad prince. The shaman ignored them, indicating that she should wash herself.

Why not? She washed her hands and face and cleaned up the worst of the stains on her clothing, then, daringly, took off her boots and bathed her freezing feet in the cooling water. Maybe she had never felt anything so wonderful in her life up to then as that water pooling over her toes. She dug out her wooden comb from her pouch, undid her braid, and untangled her hair before braiding it up again.

The shaman watched her with interest and respect. Strangely, he didn't scare her, despite the gruesome ornaments he wore. He had tended his own people and Lord Welf with equal skill. Nor he did look likely to rape her. And at least he didn't dangle a shrunken head at his belt like the rest of them did. As horrible as the noses and ears were, she could pretend that they were just dried apricots, discolored and withered into peculiar shapes. If anything, he looked a little crazy, but in a mellow way, as if he'd inhaled too much smoke and spoken to the gods once too often.

"Thank you," she said to him when she was finished. She made to wrap her leggings back on, but he indicated that she should hang them up to dry instead. He poked about among the prince's sparse belongings and came up with a gorgeous silk robe. She shook her head, sensing all at once that someone was peering in through a gap in the curtains. "No, I thank you. I'll keep my own clothing on, if you please. I don't want His Gracious Highness Prince Bulkezu to believe for one instant that I am giving in to him or indeed taking anything from him that might lead him to believe I feel myself indebted to him."

The shaman smiled beatifically, nodding his head in time to the rhythm of her words. Obviously he couldn't understand a single thing she'd said. She rose, crossed to the curtain, and pulled it aside to reveal Prince Bulkezu himself, lounging just on the other side. He had gotten out of his armor and now wore a silk robe dyed a lush purple that set off his eyes. His hair had been combed out, and it lay draped over the robe in all its luxuriant beauty. He had that same irritating smile on his face. Had he been peeking, to see if she stripped?

If he laughs, she thought, I'll strangle him.

He merely indicated a neat semicircle of felt-covered pillows set in the center of the pavilion. Prince Ekkehard and his fellows were already seated there, trying to look as comfortable and relaxed as if they dined every day in the tent of their enemy, the man whom Bayan hated above all others in the whole wide world. Even Lord Welf, looking much recovered from his elfshot wound, sat with them, although he was pallid.

"His Mightiness begs that you honor him with your presence, Honored One," said the interpreter to Hanna with considerably more politeness than he'd shown before. "Now that the Cursed Ones have been driven off, there is time to celebrate the victory, and your fortuitous meeting."

"One wonders who it was lucky for," muttered Lord Benedict.

"Those shades would probably have tracked us down and killed us if we hadn't stumbled upon Prince Bulkezu," said Ekkehard crossly to his companion. He glanced back at the interpreter. "Is the Eagle to sit with us as though she's nobly born?"

"If I were you, my sweet prince," said the interpreter insolently, "I'd keep my mouth shut about her."

"Does Prince Bulkezu mean to take her as a concubine? I've seen prettier, but I suppose her hair is striking."

"You're an ignorant young sot, aren't you? Don't you know what she is?"

"She's a damned Eagle, and deserves the respect with which the king has honored her. I recognize the ring on her hand, the mark of my father's favor. I can't believe your savage master hasn't cut that emerald off her finger yet."

"Or that he hasn't cut off your head for your insolence," added Lord Frithuric.

Prince Bulkezu cleared his throat suggestively as he ushered Hanna up to a pillow and, with the manners of a courtier, indicated a wine-colored pillow decorated with clashing eagles. Once she sank down cross-legged, uncomfortable sitting as an equal among Wendish lords, Bulkezu placed himself on the remaining vacant pillow, between Hanna and Ekkehard. He clapped his hands, once, and his soldiers hurried to serve them on perfect wooden trays carved with filigree done to resemble twining vines. The cups were cruder, plain ceramic, but warm to the touch, and she almost laughed out loud when she breathed in the aroma: hot spiced wine.

A pang struck her, clawing at her heart. What had happened to Gotfrid and his fellows? Had they escaped, or did they lie dead in the snow?

But Gotfrid surely wouldn't begrudge her a moment's pleasure after everything they'd been through. Gotfrid would probably be the first to say that it was well worth enjoying what you had while you had it, since you didn't know how quickly it might be taken from you.

As Bayan had said, no war was ever lost if there was still wine to drink.

Bulkezu examined her in the silence as they sipped their wine and nibbled on hard cakes flavored with coriander. Truly, there was a war going on right now in more ways than one, and she didn't suppose it would be over very quickly. After all, despite their fear of the Kerayit, she was still his prisoner.

A soldier entering carrying an odd-looking two-stringed lute. He settled himself to one side and serenaded them in a grating, nasal voice that droned on and on. After a long while, he finished, and they were permitted to go to sleep. Although she was most graciously offered the use of Bulkezu's furs, she took herself to the opposite wall of the tent, near the entrance, and wrapped herself tightly in her cloak. She was so exhausted that she fell asleep at once.

She woke to snoring. Without raising her head or otherwise giving herself away, she studied the dark interior. Prince Ekkehard and his comrades lay sleeping nearby, sprawled in ungainly postures on the floor of the pavilion. Each of the young lords had a partner in sleep, a Quman soldier at rest beside them, so that if their prisoner stirred, they would wake, too. Only Hanna wasn't guarded.

Or maybe she was.

One person wasn't sleeping. In the center of the pavilion, illuminated by the pool of light afforded by a single burning lamp hung from the center pole, Prince Bulkezu still sat on his gold-braided pillow. He had an easy posture, cross-legged, one elbow braced on a knee while the other fiddled with the stem of an elaborate ceramic pipe. Steam bubbled up from its belly. He took a puff from the pipe, exhaling softly. A veil of smoke hazed the air around him as he watched her. Did he know she'd woken?

The strangely-scented smoke filled her lungs and made her consciousness drift on hazy currents out through the smoke hole, lofting above the camp. There lay the prince's pavilion, below her, glowing with a faint golden ring of protection, and the other tents, ranged in a circle around it, seemed marked by yet more magical wards. There stood the horses, restless in the cold night, and their stalwart guard. To one side, unseen before, she noticed a corral and, within that fence, the patchwork cloak of the shaman. He cooked meat over a kettle filled with coals, and abruptly glanced up, as if he sensed her. But her awareness already ranged beyond him, to the sentries in their concealed posts, the glittering trip lines laid high and low, and a pair of hawks perched on a branch, waiting for dawn.

What waited beyond Bulkezu's little camp struck dismay into her heart. As her awareness lifted higher, caught on an aetherical breeze, she saw that Prince Bulkezu's was only one campsite situated among many—more than she could count in the darkness. The tents of the Quman lay scattered through the forest like uncounted pebbles.

This wasn't a raiding party at all. It was the Quman army.

Bulkezu had swung wide around Handelburg. He'd abandoned Bayan and his shattered army, left them holed up and impotent in the east, and now was driving west toward the heart of Wendar itself.

The Quman weren't the only ones waiting in the cold night. Dread creatures stalked the Earth, patient and single-minded. Beyond the trip lines and other protective wards, the shadows of elves waited, arrayed in hunting groups, their thwarted rage like the throb of a lute string in the air. Would she never escape them? Why did they pursue her, she who had never glimpsed such creatures before? How had she angered them, or called attention to herself? Had they, like the hideous *galla*, learned her name?

A breath of cold air brushed her lips, like a kiss, and she came crashing back into her body, heart pounding with fear. But she hadn't moved, nor had anyone touched her. The night wind had teased the entrance flap open. Through the gap she saw outside into the open space between the tents. It had been snowing again. The tracks of the battle lay buried under a fresh blanket of snow, white and pristine.

The owl glided into view and came to rest on the unbroken snow. It blinked once, and she knew then that it was looking right at her.

She had seen this owl before. This was the owl who had appeared at the abandoned village, just two nights ago, before disaster had broken over them. This was the owl Liath had spoken to at the palace of Werlida just as though it could understand her.

She knew now what it was. This was the centaur woman's owl, that Hanna had seen in her dreams.

It waited, golden eyes staring. Silence settled like snow.

Bulkezu laughed. He sucked on his pipe before speaking in comprehensible Wendish. "Nay, dreaded one, I will not harm the woman with the frost-white hair. I fear your power too much. But now she's mine. Get her back if you can."

XI
THE NOISE OF
THEIR WAKING

1

ON the first fine spring day, Adica walked down from the stone loom after a weary afternoon of meditation. The gorgeous weather had not helped her keep her mind focused, not when the song of birds kept distracting her, and primrose and blooming flax painted the ground in pale yellows, blues, and violets. She kept wondering where her husband was, and what he was doing.

As usual, she had no trouble finding him. She had only to follow the sound of laughter, to walk down to the river where it seemed most of the village had gathered, whooping and hollering over some ridiculous male contest. Spring had come, and that of course meant men became infected with the Green Man's mischief.

Alain stood knee-deep in the river shallows, having challenged all comers to a wrestling match. She arrived in time to see him flip poor Kel into the deep water, dunking him. Kel came up shrieking from the shock of the cold water. A half-dozen other men stood shivering and wet on the bank, egging their fellows on.

"Throw him in!"

"It's more than he deserves! Hold him under!"

"Whoo! Ha! That water's so cold it'll be summer before my wife gets any pleasure out of me!"

"Well, then," called his wife from the crowd, "the Black Deer traders come through this time of year. I'll have to please myself with them until you're fit for use." She started a rowdy chorus of "My man can't even walk up the path to his own house," and most of the other women joined in.

Alain was laughing as he helped Kel out of the water. He had stripped down to a simple loincloth; it was the first day warm enough to do so. Even though Adica knew his body intimately by now, she still admired his lean hips and broad shoulders. Usually she combed and braided his hair for him, but it had all come loose around his shoulders. A man's beard had grown in over the winter, thus proving to the last of the skeptics, such as they were, that he had not one drop of the Cursed Ones' blood running in his veins.

Weiwara moved over to stand beside her. She held the elder twin, Blue-bud, in her arms. Adica ached to hold the baby, beautiful and plump as it was, but dared not ask. "You'd think you were married yesterday instead of last autumn the way you ogle him," said Weiwara with a chuckle, shifting the baby to her other hip. "Look, here comes Beor."

Kel, still whimpering, staggered out of the river and grabbed a skin cloak to wrap around himself just as Beor stalked up to the shore and stripped off his knee-length tunic.

"Now you'll see what a real man can do," growled Beor.

The contrast between the two men was striking: Alain lean and smooth, Beor with his broad chest densely matted with curly hair. Alain always seemed to have a smile on his face, the look of a person who no longer has anything to worry about, while Beor suffered from a nagging, irritable discontent. But, in truth, Beor had mellowed over the winter. He didn't argue nearly as much as he had once done. Maybe it was just that it had been a mild winter during which the village hadn't suffered hunger or anything worse than the usual stink of being closed up in their homes for months on end. Maybe they were all just more at peace, despite the ever-present menace of the Cursed Ones, now that Alain lived among them.

"I said I will take on all men, not all bears," said Alain to general laughter.

Beor lifted his hands in imitation of a lumbering bear and, with a mock roar, charged Alain. A child yelped with excitement. Alain sidestepped him, but not fast enough. Beor got hold of a shoulder, they grappled, then Beor twisted Alain back and with brute strength lifted him up and tossed him backward into the current. The big man threw out his arms and let out a scream of triumph that echoed off the tumulus. Adica laughed helplessly along with the rest of the village.

Alain came up thrashing, drenched through.

"Peace!" he cried. "You win."

He extended a hand. When Beor took it, to help him up, Alain yanked so hard that Beor tumbled forward into the freezing water beside him. By this time the two black dogs had begun barking, and as the two men heaved themselves spluttering and laughing up out of the water, the dogs splashed into the shallows and, in their excitement, knocked them both over again.

"My stomach hurts," moaned Weiwara, tears leaking from her eyes as she laughed.

"The village will smell a lot better now," cried Beor's sister, Etora, from the crowd. "Whew! Look how the river has changed color downstream."

Adica found Alain's wool cloak lying on the rocks. After he waded out of the water, she draped it over his shoulders. A winter spent mostly indoors and the immediate effects of the freezing water had made him pale, dimpled with goose bumps.

"Cold," he proclaimed cheerfully as she fastened the cloak at his left shoulder with a bronze pin. He kissed her cheek.

His lips were as cold as death.

She shuddered.

"Adica." Instantly attentive to her moods, he took her hand in his. His skin was as cold as a corpse's. The vision hit like the slap of cold water.

Six figures, made indistinct by darkness, sit huddled in a stone chamber. A seventh rests on the floor, sleeping, injured, or dead, the figure of a lion sewn into the cloth on his heavy tunic. At the fringe of the light cast by a smoking torch lies a stone slab. On this altar a queen has been laid to rest. Her bones have been arranged with care and respect, and the garments and jewelry fitting for a woman of her status have fallen in among the bones, strands of rotting fabric, beads, a lapis lazuli ring, and armbands of gold. One of the figures lifts the torch to see better, and all at once the gold antlers placed at the skeleton's skull spring into view.

Those are the holy antlers she wears, to mark her place as Hallowed One among her people.

"Adica."

She swayed, clutching him. "I saw my dead body," she whispered hoarsely. "I saw my own grave."

He grabbed her, pulling her close. "Speak no evil words! No harm will come to you, beloved. I will not let any bad thing touch you."

"I love you," she murmured into his hair.

"Always you will love me," he said fiercely as the dogs bounded up and thrust their cold noses and damp fur against her hips, trying to squeeze between them, "and always will I love you."

She had never had the courage to tell him the full truth about the task that lay before her. It hurt too much ever to think of leaving him. That was the secret of the Fat One, whose face was twofold, wreathed half in light and shrouded half in shadow. She was the giver of all things, pain and death as well as plenty and pleasure. Was it any wonder that Adica chose pleasure when sorrow and death waited just beyond the threshold?

Meanwhile, villagers had gathered at a respectful distance, waiting for her attention.

"Hallowed One, Getsi has that cough again."

"Hallowed One, my husband's snare out in the south woods is being vexed by evil spirits."

"Hallowed One, we've finished repairing the roof that was damaged in the snow, and it needs your blessing."

Alain laughed. Even in repose, his face had a kind of glow to it, but when he smiled, his expression shone. He had the most luminous eyes of any person she had ever met. "You make the village live, so it is for me to make you live and be happy."

It is easy to find death in the world, but a greater magic by far to bring life. He was a life bringer.

He had come to her in late summer, and in the natural order of things the days and months had passed as the moon waxed and waned and waxed again. Autumn had worked free of summer, winter had cast her white blanket over the world, and in the course of time the Green Man lifted his head from his winter's slumber. So it went, and so it would go on, long after she was gone from the Earth. Even knowing the fate that awaited her as the wheel of the year continued to turn, when the seasons rolled from spring into summer and at last to her final autumn, she was content.

The Holy One had chosen wisely.

Right now, however, the villagers waited.

By late afternoon she finished weaving a protective spell around the snare in the south woods that was being plagued by evil spirits. Returning, she found the village gathered for the last day of feasting in celebration of the new spring. She went into her own house and, with the proper prayers and spells, put on her regalia, the antlers and bronze waistband. With staff in hand, she led the villagers in procession up the tumulus to stand outside the stone loom around the calling ground. Together, they watched the sun set a little to the right of the spring and autumn ridge that marked the equinox. Winter had left them. Now they could plant.

She sang. "I pray to you, Green Man, let the seeds take root." She turned to welcome the full moon, rising in the east.

"I pray to you, Fat One, let the village prosper. Let your fullness be a sign of plenty in the year to come."

Every villager had brought offerings, a posy of violets, a copper armband, flint axes, beads, arrowheads, and daggers. With the moon to light their way, they circled down the tumulus and followed the path that led to the marsh at the eastern limit of the hills. Adica knew the secret trail of firm tussocks that led through the marsh to the sacred island As the oldest uncrippled man in the village, Pur the stone knapper was given the honor of carrying in the offerings in her wake.

A fish jumped. The moon made silver of the water trembling through glittering beds of reeds and around grassy hummocks. The wind brought the scent of the cook fires from the village, and the smell of roasting pig.

The sacred island was itself scarcely bigger than two men laid end to end. An old stone altar carved with cups and spirals had been set up here in the time of the ancient queens. She knelt before it and set her palms into two depressions worn into stone. Pur waited patiently. He knew how to listen, having mastered the art of letting stone speak to him, and so he didn't fear the dark of night as some did. He recognized its familiar noises and understood the magic that lies just beneath the surface of the world. After a while she heard the ancient voice of the stone, more a drone than voiced speech, as wakeful as stone ever could be at the quarters of the year when stars and earth worked in concert. She whispered to it, telling it the hopes and wishes of the villagers as well as the various small signs she had observed over the winter: where the first violets had bloomed, how a forest stream had cut a new channel, how both Weiwara and a ewe had borne living twins, how many flocks of geese had passed overhead last autumn on their way south to their winter nesting grounds. The stone understood the secret language of earth, and it held the life of the village in its impenetrable heart.

When she was done with the prayers, she and Pur cast the

offerings into the marsh, as they did every year at the festival of spring, a sacrifice for a good year.

After that, she was through with being the antlered woman, the crossing-over one who can speak both to humankind and to the gods, to made things and to wild things. Pur moved away so as not to see anything forbidden, and with the prayers and spells she knew best, she became Adica again, putting away her regalia in its leather bag.

As they made their way back, water squelched and sucked beneath her feet on the lowest hummocks, half drowned in the marsh. A water snake glided away over the quiet water. Pond weed edged the marsh. Within the sheltering darkness, she overheard the conversation of those waiting for her return.

"All winter you speak of the war with the Cursed Ones," Alain was saying. "Do you think they attack with the spring?"

"Of course they will attack." Kel always sounded as if he had fire burning under his feet. "They hate us."

"Why? Can there not be trading and talk? Why can there only be hate?"

Alain was always full of questions about things that seemed obvious to everyone else. The wind blew a light stalk of reed against her face, then away. Pur shifted behind her, but she didn't move. Wherever she walked, people marked where she was. Rarely did she have a chance to overhear when people spoke words unshaped by their concern about what she might hear.

Kel snorted. "Never can we trust the Cursed Ones. They sacrifice their human captives by flaying them alive, and then they cut out their hearts and eat them!"

"Have you seen it done, Kel?" asked Alain quietly.

"No! But everyone knows—"

Urtan broke in. "Humankind has always warred against the Cursed Ones, ever since they came over the seas in their white ships. Only now the fight has grown more desperate because the Cursed Ones have brought their metal weapons to the killing field."

"Now we have a chance to defeat the Cursed Ones," exclaimed Kel eagerly. "That's why they tried to kidnap the Hallowed One. They'll try again. We must be on our guard day and night—"

"Hush, now, Kel," said Urtan quietly. "You'll wake the sleeping. That's why we have to wait here for the Hallowed One to return from the offering ground. In the old days, she would have walked to the marsh and returned all alone, but now we can't risk leaving her alone. The Cursed Ones won't give up."

"I'll protect her," said Alain in that stubborn way he had, more sweet than grouchy.

"No one can protect her," said Kel, stung by Urtan's words into speaking unwisely. "She has a doom laid on her—"

Behind her, Pur hissed displeasure.

"What do you mean?" asked Alain.

Adica was suddenly aware of the grass stuck to her fingers. An owl hooted. There came a sudden splash, then silence.

Urtan started in. "If your mother were alive today, she'd be ashamed to hear you talking like a crow, all loud noises and strutting but without two thoughts to rub together. You treat words like pebbles. Grab a handful and throw them to the winds. Maybe you sleep in the men's house now, but that doesn't mean you're a man until you've earned the right to have your counsel listened to."

"Here, now," began Alain.

"Nay, let him go," said Urtan as Kel thrashed away into the brush. "That'll make his ears sizzle. He'll think twice next time he speaks."

"But what did he mean about—?"

Pur coughed loudly.

"Hush," said Urtan. "Here comes the Hallowed One and Pur back again."

Adica made as much noise as possible, coming those last ten

steps before she emerged into the clearing where a dozen adults waited, armed with spears or staffs. "Come, let us go to the feast."

Mother Orla had died at the solstice of a lung fever and been buried with her gold neck ring, one hundred amber beads, a full bark bucket of beer, and a handsome flint dagger. The villagers had held council for over a month—there wasn't much else to do in the winter—and finally chosen a new headwoman for the village, one who would bring them luck and prosperity.

Now, it was young Mother Weiwara who stepped forward to hand Adica a wooden ladle full to the brim with ale brewed of wheat, cranberries, and honey, flavored with bog myrtle. It stung a little, having gone somewhat flat after a winter in storage, but still had a good, strong taste, nothing sour or corrupt.

It was a balmy night, as sweet as a newborn child. They ate roast pig garnished with bistort and nettle tops, flat loaves of barley bread, stewed hedgehog, and greens, and drank enough ale to fill two rivers while Weiwara told the story of how the ancient queen Toothless built the tumulus with magic. Urtan sang of the hunt of the young queen Arrow Bright, who had captured a dragon and then set it free. If, as the night wore on and the moon cast its dazzling spell over the village, some women went off into the dark with men who weren't their husbands, no one minded. The Green Man would have his own way in these matters.

Adica sat beside her husband, content. She had bathed his hair in violet-scented water that morning, and she could still smell it there. He always smelled of flowers.

He knew songs, too, that he sang in the language of the dead, which none of the living could understand. The dead still feasted and loved and fought on the Other Side. Of course they would need songs, like offerings. They sat by the fire for a long time, watching the flames tumble and lick, hearing the red-hot coals pop or sigh. Everyone else had gone. The moon rode high along her path, and Adica didn't ever want the night to end, as if they could be stranded here forever, untouched by fate.

Alain held her close. He stroked her belly and whispered in her ear. "We make a child?"

One of the dogs, lying to his left, growled.

She smoothed a thumb over his cheek, found his lips, kissed him. "No child." She had no more grief to give over to a child who would never be born. Like a loosed arrow, she had to remain fixed and true so that she would hit her mark. The Holy One had given her more than she had hoped for, and she would not let regret stalk her now.

He misunderstood her. "No child lives here yet." His fingers tapped her skin caressingly. "We can make a child, yes?"

She sighed, not wanting to have to make him understand. "No child, beloved."

"I will never let you or a child come to any harm." Suddenly passionate, almost angry, he leaned away from her, still grasping her elbows, so that he could look into her face. "You think I cannot protect you, just like I could not protect—"

Both dogs growled and stood.

"That's the loom! Someone is working the loom." She leaped up and ran to the gate. Alain and the dogs caught up with her there. He had brought a torch but not lit it.

"Do you hear the stones?" She waited for the night watch to open the narrow portal and squeezed through, Alain following after. Crossing the bridge, she turned her face toward the hill. Threads woven out of the loom of the sky, drawn down by magic's shuttle, traced so faint a pattern against the night sky and the glare of the full moon that only an eye trained to magic could discern them. The stones lay out of her sight at the height of the hill.

"Look!" said Alain as both dogs barked. A torch bobbed high up on the ramparts.

Who had come? Was it the Cursed Ones again?

The night watch blew two short calls to alert the village. Alain pulled her back through the portal, barring it behind them. Safe behind the palisade, she climbed the ladder that led to the gate tower. There, she waited as the torchlight approached and as adults of the village gathered outside the common house, ready with weapons.

A woman she had never seen before approached the gate, torch held high to light her path. In her other hand, she held a spear tipped with a flint point. Her hair, braided with bone and shell beads, gleamed under the torchlight, and her skin was mottled with strange markings, perhaps a scabrous disease.

But her voice was clear and strong. "Let there be peace among allies."

"Let those who suffer join hands," called Adica in reply. She signaled to the night watch. As he unbarred the portal, she climbed down from the parapet so that if the messenger brought evil spirits in with her, she would be the only one to take harm from them. The crowd gathered at the common house murmured at her appearance, but none called out. They, too, waited.

The woman had no disease: she bore the tattoos common to Spits-last's people, who called themselves "Akka," the Old Woman's people. She spoke the language of the Deer people with so heavy an accent that it was hard for Adica to understand her.

"I am a Walking One of the Akka people. This message I bring for the sorcerer of the Deer people from the one who falls down when the spirit rides him."

"I am Hallowed One of the White Deer people. Do you bring me a message from Falling-down?"

"This message I bring from the sorcerer who falls down when the spirit rides him: 'Walk with the messenger who brings you this message. Danger time this day and tomorrow. Knife of Cursed Ones cuts our threads. They know who we are. Come to the land of the Akka people, of the north country. Come quick quick. There I wait.'"

The words chilled Adica. "I will come."

Alain had the intent look on his face that meant he was working hard to understand words. At once, she realized how long it would be until she saw him again. This the looms demanded: you could never predict how many days or even months each crossing would take. The loom's burden had never seemed as harsh as it did at this moment. How could she make him understand how bitterly it hurt her to leave him?

He spoke first. "I come with you to keep you safe." He turned at once, not waiting for her answer, and sent Kel off to fetch his staff, dagger, and cloak.

Relief left Adica speechless.

Mother Weiwara came forward. "Winter departs late in the north country where the Akka dwell." She sent villagers for water and travel bread, winter clothing, hide leggings and shirts, fur cloaks fastened with precious copper pins, and a complicated binding of grass and leather to protect feet from bitter cold.

Alain beckoned Beor over. "Put more adults on the night watch. Let all adults walk armed to the fields. If there is danger, if the Cursed Ones are planning an attack, then you must be ready."

Beor turned to Adica. "Give me the bronze sword, the one you hid away. If the Cursed Ones attack us and you are not here to protect against them with your magic, then it will go worse for us. It isn't right that we might have had a weapon in our hands to fight them off."

The memory of her vision flashed in her mind, of the bronze sword in Beor's hand as he wreaked havoc. It was a terrible choice, and perhaps an unfair one, but because she had no time, because the river had caught her in its grasp and swept her forward, she gave in. "Very well. Come with us to the loom. I will give you the sword."

They made a silent procession, walking up through the ramparts girded with staffs, torches, and traveling pouches slung over their shoulders. Beor admired the Akka Walking One; Adica recognized his belligerent way of flirting. The Akka woman did not return his admiration. She paid no attention to him at all. Indeed, she seemed most interested in Alain's black dogs. She had the broad features common to the Akka people and the broad shoulders of a woman who has tackled a lot of reindeer, and it was hard to tell whether she contemplated those dogs with such an avid gaze because they looked fit to serve her, or to be eaten for supper.

Adica made them wait at the base of the highest rampart while she went up alone to dig up the grave of bronze. Six months buried in earth had caused the sword's metal to fur over with green, and its soul to slumber. But where the starlight's gleam stroked the blade she felt it waken under her touch, felt it grope upward in the way a hand brushes aside a spider's web that blocks the entrance to a cave.

War is coming. The sword had a seductive voice. *Free me.*

She had no spells to counter its angry soul, no way to bind it so that it would slumber again. Perhaps Beor was right. If war was coming, then they had to defend themselves. It wouldn't be right to leave the village with anything less than what the Cursed Ones themselves carried. Perhaps the conjuring man of Old Fort could study this bronze sword and learn the secrets of its making. Perhaps he could make more such swords. Then the White Deer people would not always fight at a disadvantage.

It still wasn't easy to give Beor the sword.

"Go," she said to him. "I must weave the passage, and you must go back to the village."

He drew her aside, looking restless. "I was a good husband to you, Hallowed One." He pulled on his right ear, as he often did when he was irritated. "But you never said so."

He went on without waiting for her reply. "Not that I begrudge you the man. I know he's not like us. If the Holy One brought him to you, then I'm not one to say 'nay' to her wishes, but I won't have it said that I wasn't a good husband

to you or that I went without protest when the elders made me
leave your house."

"No, you did not go without protest," she murmured.

That satisfied him enough that he left, halberd and sword
held triumphantly before him. She shuddered. Light flashed
off the tip of the bronze sword, and for an instant she thought
she saw blood. Then she lost sight of him.

"Quick, quick," said the Akka woman.

"Stand there, to that side." Adica stationed herself on the
chalk calling ground and studied the stars. The passageway to
the Akka loom was made most easily when the Ploughing Man's
Eye rose in the east, but there were other, more circuitous routes
to every loom just as there were many ways to pattern cloth. It
was too late in the evening to catch and hold the threads of the
Bounteous One and her swift, shy child, Six Wings. But the
Sisters were rising, and their twin lights could be woven in
with the scatter of stars known as the Shaman's Headdress and
hooked to the Dipping Cup as it dipped into the north.

She raised the obsidian mirror, caught the light of the gold-
haired sister and, by shifting the mirror slightly, the silver hair
of her twin. Light caught in the stones. As she wove it in with
the other stars, threads flowered to life among the flattened
oval of the stones to form a passageway leading to another
loom.

She picked up her sack and, with the others behind her,
crossed through into a snow as light as feathers, spitting from
heavy clouds. They stood on a high plateau composed mostly
of boulders tumbled every which way, covered with lichens
and mosses and a dusting of snow. The rocky land gave way
toward the horizon to heaps of golden stones jutting up like
huge tumuli, untouched by snow. No trees gave shelter
against the cutting wind. Only the circle of stones and the
gleaming hillocks defied the swirling snow. Mountains cut
an edge along the eastern horizon. The light was cloudy and
gray, lightening with dawn, although Adica could not see the
sun.

Their guide trudged away down a path worn into scant earth, more pebbles than soil, and marked out with a trail of chalk that, curiously, was free of snow. Adica hurried after her. Alain took up the rear guard with his dog-headed staff raised and the dogs at his heels. The path cut down through rock that fell by degrees into a steep valley smothered in trees and snow. Winter still lay heavily on this land. After a time, she saw clearings that had been hacked out of the forest. Pigs and deer had made tracks through these snow-drenched clearings. Otherwise they were a featureless white.

Down by the valley's mouth, near the arm of water that bounded the lowest reaches of the valley, rock corrals penned in reindeer. Three boats draped with felt rode high on logs, upturned above the shoreline. A half-dozen smaller, sleeker skiffs lay drawn up on the rocky beach. Ice rimmed the shallows, but the deep waters lay as smooth as glass, unfrozen despite the bone-chilling cold.

Beyond the corrals, torches ringed a longhouse. This hall served the entire tribe as home, storage, and stable. Even Spitslast, their sorcerer, lived cheek by jowl with them, never knowing solitude.

Flakes of snow spun past. Although the wind had cut harshly on the plateau above, the shadow of winter burned more intensely within the valley's heart. The shock of the temperature change made her shudder. She paused once to catch her breath. Alain put an arm around her shoulders to warm her. His expression was grave.

"This country knows me," he said in his stumbling way, "and I know this country. In this country was born fifth son of the fifth litter, who became a strong hand." He shook his head, puzzling out the words."His hand is strong. Hei! I cannot speak the name. There were children of rock here, but I see them not now. Many children of rock lived here when I saw it. They do not live here now."

"I don't understand what you're trying to say."

"Quick!" The Akka guide beckoned impatiently. "Walking

One of Water people dead is, or not dead is. To her you must speak."

People came out of the long hall to stare at them. A boy doused torches as weak daylight rose. It was too cloudy for her to mark the position of the sun's rise against the distant cliffs and ridges. Beyond the hall she saw other structures, pit houses or burial mounds, dug into the ground. She had only visited Spits-last once, in his homeland, and it had been snowing then, too, drowned in winter's darkness.

They stepped into the long hall to be greeted by a powerful reek. The long, low space was lit by three hearth fires and so smoky that the air seemed alive with particles. She smelled cattle and sheep, penned farther down. The taint of rotting crab apples hung in the air, a sweet tinge above the thick perfume of human bodies pressed together. Alain spoke a few words to his dogs, and they sat down, unmolested, on either side of the door. Their Akka guide made a path for them through the people by using her spear's butt to poke and prod everyone aside, but Adica and Alain were not as lucky as the dogs: hands reached forward to pinch her bare skin or fondle the strings of her skirt, until she pulled out of the grasp of one only to find another waiting to handle her. They breathed into her face, gabbled in their hard tongue, and poked and prodded her with their fingers as though to assure themselves that she was a living being.

Beside the second hearth fire, on a pallet, lay Falling-down side by side with a dead woman half-covered with pine needles. His eyes were closed. For an instant Adica thought he, too, was dead. She knelt beside him and touched his hand, and he opened his eyes at once. He had the hazel eyes common to his tribe, rheumy with age but still sharply intelligent.

"Adica!" he said with pleasure in his brittle voice. She helped him up to a sitting position. "I sent the Walking One of Tanioinin's people twelve days ago to fetch you. Alas that the loom brought you here so slow. My cousin is dead now. She died at sunset."

"What happened?"

Alain crouched beside the woman and, without any thought of death's dangers and taboos, brushed aside pine needles and placed a hand around the curve of her throat, listening.

Falling-down watched him with bemusement. "Can this be the man the Holy One brought to be your husband? Where did he come from not to fear death?"

"He was walking the path to the Other Side. I don't know where he came from before that."

Alain sat back on his heels. The people who had crowded up behind him to stare skittered back, as if afraid that he, having touched that which was dead, would infect them. He did not appear to notice them as he looked at Adica.

"Her soul no longer lives in her body."

"So you see," said Adica to Falling-down. "He knows when a spirit still walks in the land of the living. Why are you here, Falling-down? Why did you leave your tribe? Such a long journey is difficult for you. And it is so dangerous now to walk the looms, if the Cursed Ones stalk us."

He lifted a hand for silence. A child brought him a wooden cup filled to the brim with mead. He sipped at it before reciting his tale. The Akka Walking One translated his words to her people, who crowded around to listen.

"The ships of the Cursed Ones landed on the coast of our land. Scouts of our cousins the Reed people saw them. They sent a Running Youth to alert us. Then another Running Youth came. The ships put to land near the nesting ground of guivres. The guivres rose and feasted on them."

Voices murmured in satisfaction at this gruesome and well-deserved fate. The Akka woman spoke sharply, and the people quieted, not without a lot of pinching and protests, so that Falling-down could go on.

"We feel happy, when this news runs to us. Then the loom opens. This one, my cousin, who is a Walking One of our people, falls through. She is wounded. She brings a terrible story with her." As he got caught up in the awful tale, his

words began to slip; past became present, and his careful use of
Adica's language, learned over a lifetime, became sloppier.
"The Cursed Ones attack the people of Horn. All their houses
and all their villages the Cursed Ones burn."

A general moan spread through the crowd, and was hushed,
again, by the Akka woman's terse command.

"Even the children they kill, cut cut." He made a chopping
motion with his hand. Children who had crowded up behind
him to listen leaped back with frightened cries. But no one
laughed. "The people of Horn escape to the hills. Horn is old
woman. She is not strong. She is more weak now. Maybe she
die. But she send this Walking One, who is once my cousin,
through the loom. She send her home, with the warning.
Maybe Horn die already."

"But if Horn dies, then we can't weave the great spell!"
cried Adica, shocked out of her silence. Alain set a hand on her
shoulder to calm her.

"No more news brings this Walking One," said Falling-
down, indicating the dead woman. "She is not yet dead, in the
home of my tribe, but no healer in my people can save her. So
I bring her here. Healer woman of the Akka people is
renowned."

Adica looked around, but she did not see the famous healing woman of the Akka people: a tiny woman who wore a
cloak of eagle feathers. "Even the Akka healing woman could
not save her?"

"No. The Fat One turned her face away. After half a moon's
journey, this Walking One dies. Now, Akka healing woman
and our brother Tanioinin pray to the ancestor, the old mother
of their tribe. But you, Adica. You have strong legs. I am too
old, and Tanioinin cannot walk. Tell me this: Why did the
Cursed Ones attack Horn's people and my people so close
together? Why did they try to steal you?"

"The Holy One warned us. They've learned that we mean to
act against them. They want to kill us so that we cannot work
the great weaving."

"Yes. We must know if Horn lives. We must know if the Cursed Ones attack our comrades also, and if Shu-Sha is safe. Walking Ones are not strong enough alone to do this. You have strong legs and strong magic. You must warn the others."

She gestured toward the eaves. "The sky is cloaked with clouds. We will have to wait until the stars shine again and the weather clears off."

"For that we cannot wait." He spoke so gravely that his words frightened her. She knew that the Holy One had power over the weather, but her magic was ancient and even more frightening, in some ways, than the blood magic of the Cursed Ones. "We wait now in this house for the other Akka sorcerers to come. Tanioinin's brothers and sisters and the cousins of the healing woman, they will come down from their halls north of this place and south of this place. When they come, they will call that thing which can blow the clouds away so you can travel."

"Quick, quick," echoed the Akka woman. She stamped a foot and clapped her hands together. The crowd around them echoed her words, the foreign syllables sounding strangely on their tongues. Someone threw pine needles and a rain of dried herbs and tiny pebbles on the fire. The flames hissed and spit, and a thick cloud of smoke boiled up, drowning Adica. She coughed violently, starting back, and Alain found her by touch and drew her away as the Akka people sang in loud and rather discordant voices a song repeating the same words over and over: "nok nok ay-ee-tay-oo-noo nok nok."

When she had done blinking and could see again, the dead woman, and the pallet on which she had lain, were gone. Had they vanished through magic, or simply been carried off? She did not really care to know. The secrets of her own gods, and her own magic, were perilous enough.

"Come." By some mode of communication unknown to her, Alain found a raised pallet under the eaves and there, after setting down their packs, they lay down together. She was too tired to do anything but rest in his arms.

What if it all came to nothing? What if the Cursed Ones had discovered all their plans? What if the Cursed Ones used their blood magic to kill the human sorcerers who threatened them? Truly, she was willing to sacrifice herself knowing that her death would free her people from fear, but it seemed the gods mocked her now. Without realizing, she had started to cry.

"Hush," said Alain, stroking her arms. "Sleep, lovely one. Do not fear for what is to come. Just sleep."

His quiet voice brought her a measure of peace. With him held tightly alongside her, she slept.

2

ALAIN woke to humming. At first he thought it was Adica, who could be counted on to make all kinds of strange noises in the course of her prayers and spells. He smiled, so blindingly happy that he didn't even want to open his eyes, only soak it in. How strange to think that it was only after he'd lost everything that he gained what mattered most. Tightening his arms around her, he tucked her closer against him. Which was when he realized that the warm body lying alongside him wasn't Adica's but that of a rancid-smelling child.

"Hsst!" A woman clad in oiled sealskins jostled Alain and the child awake and, with an expression of urgency, beckoned to Alain to follow her. He bumped his head on the eaves as he swung out of the bed and stood up too soon; everything was built for shorter people here in the north. The long hall was empty, silent and cool. Winter had sucked the warmth out of the fires. Except for Sorrow and Rage, sitting faithfully by the door, the three of them were the only ones inside. Muttering and rubbing his sore head, he followed woman and child outside.

The humming sounded out here as well, a sound that rang up through the ground to reverberate in his head. Sorrow whined, irritated by the noise, but Rage remained silent. The woman called urgently to him again, gesturing that he should follow, but he hesitated, looking for Adica.

"Ta! Ta!" cried the woman, beckoning. She hustled the child toward the mounds that clustered like a flock of sheep along the valley floor behind the long hall.

Alain hurried after her. Several people ducked down into the entrance of one of the mounds. Coming up behind them, he looked down a low tunnel, a smaller version of the passage that led into the queens' grave at Adica's village. This passage, too, was lined by stones, but it hadn't as sophisticated corbeling. In a crouch, he scuttled down the passage to a chamber that smelled of vegetables stored for a long time in a cool place, slightly spoiled by damp. No light illuminated the chamber, yet it was warmer here beneath the earthen mound than outside. Bodies pressed against him, all smelling slightly of rancid oil.

"Adica?"

She did not answer. She wasn't here. He knew it in the same way he knew he had a hand at end of his arm. The moon had waxed full seven times since that day when he had found himself lying naked by the bronze cauldron up among the stones, but sometimes it seemed as if it had only been seven days, or as long as seven years. But in any case, he wasn't going to hide in here without knowing where she was.

Crawling backward, he ducked out into the fresh air. The cloudy light of afternoon made him blink. The constant throbbing hum continued unabated. Adica wasn't inside any of the eight mounds. The people crowded within seemed nervous, but not panicked. Each time he found his way in to one of the dark chambers, hands pulled him farther in, and when he made to leave, they plucked at him, urging him to stay.

But he had to find Adica.

He ran back to the long hall. It lay empty, and when the

hounds snuffled around, they seemed unable, or unwilling, to find her scent. The hearth fire was burning low. How annoyed Aunt Bel would be to find a fire neglected! He fetched several dried cow pats and laid them on the coals, fanning the flame with a leather-and-wood bellows. The wheeze of the bellows didn't mask Rage's soft growl.

"Quick. Quick!"

He jumped. The Akka woman who had guided them here stood at the entrance to the hall. "Into the houses of dirt you must go. The dragons come."

He whistled to the hounds and came out to stand beside the woman on the flat porch of hewn planks that fronted the hall. Now that it was light, he noticed the brilliant swirl of tattoos mottling her skin, red chevrons, white lines, and small black circles.

She frowned at him, gesturing irritably. "Quick, you go."

"Where is Adica?"

"She goes above with the one who falls down when the spirit rides him and my brother who we call Tanioinin, something this means like the one who spits last. They walk to the high fjall." She gestured toward the path they had walked down that morning, where it wound up the valley and was soon lost among the trees. Mist lay heavily over the high land above, as though a huge creature steamed in its sleep. Then she gestured toward the arm of the sea that lay quiescent below. A dozen skiffs were beached on the icy shore, twice the number that had been there at dawn. "The other sorcerers of my people come when he calls them. Now they will raise the dragons from their sleep to blow the clouds away. Then we walk the loom to the far land of the one whose god shines in her face."

None of this made sense, and he was actually becoming alarmed. He hadn't thought of his old life in months, but as if jolted by a spark of magic, he shuddered, remembering that terrible night when a locked door had blocked him from reaching Lavastine in his hour of need. "Where is Adica?"

The Akka woman made a gesture of frustration. "She go above with the other sorcerers. Now you must go to shelter. Only in shelter is it safe from the wind of the dragons."

"I go above, too."

"Foolish to walk after the sorcerers. You must to shelter go. Yes?"

"No. I will go after Adica."

They regarded each other for the space of five breaths. She flung up her hands, half laughing, half cursing. "Come."

He fetched his pack and, with Sorrow and Rage, headed up the path that led to the fjall. The Akka guide strode beside him, seemingly unperturbed by this change of plan.

"You do not take shelter?" Alain asked her.

The woman had a tart grin, like that of a woman who has played a trick on a companion who tried to cheat her. She shook the necklace of bear claws and yellowing teeth that hung around her neck. "This charm protects me."

Alain began to pant as the path steepened. "I don't know by what name I should call you."

"I am elder sister of Spits-last." She did not break stride as she spoke, nor did she seem winded. Like a good Walking One, she had the stamina of an ox. "In my people's tongue I am called Laoina."

They came clear of the denser growth of spruce and pine whose branches drooped under a heavy load of snow and into a thinning woodland composed mostly of birch trees, combed by the wind. A glow rimmed the eastern horizon, rather like the promise of dawn, but it had an amber gleam, rich and almost solid against the veil of clouds above. No part of the sky was visible, only low-hanging clouds, gray with unshed snow. The humming sounded louder here. The rocks seemed to vibrate with the noise. It was getting dark.

He hadn't realized he'd slept for so long. He ought to have stayed awake and watched over Adica. He hated being away from her for long. He was so afraid that something would happen to her.

"Quick. The dragons wake."

They broke into a jog. Alain puffed and wheezed, more out of anxiety perhaps than from being winded. He had heard stories of dragons, of course, but everyone knew they no longer existed on Earth. They had all been turned into stone a long time ago, like the one at Osna Sound which had become the ridge running between the village and the now-destroyed monastery. But this talk of dragons made him nervous anyway. If they were just a story, then why did people hide away under mounds of earth?

So many things were different here. In seven months, he had not seen a single iron tool. Most of their implements were chipped out of stone. They made buckets out of bark, dug ditches with antlers, and carved canoes out of whole logs. Their ploughs were little better than a smoothed shaft of wood that couldn't turn more than a finger's depth of soil, and they didn't keep any horses, although they knew what they were. Even the grains and food were different: no wheat, no oats, no wine, not even turnips and cabbage, although big game was far more plentiful. He'd never eaten so much aurochs meat in his life.

In the afterlife, if that was what this was, maybe wine had been banished, but dragons still existed.

He tried to imagine them, creatures formed out of earth and fire. Their breath of flame might consume the unwitting traveler, and the unremarked lash of their thick tails might hammer soft flesh into the dirt.

Adica had gone up to the fjall to meet them.

He got a second wind and actually moved out in front of his companion, the nervous hounds lagging behind as though to watch their trail. As they picked their way onto the fjall, they came fully into the teeth of a strangely warm wind, almost seductively pleasant. He saw the stone circle immediately. Upright and in perfect repair, it looked nothing like the old ruined stone crowns he knew. It didn't seem right, somehow, that it should look so . . . *new*.

A dozen human figures stood inside the stones. Eight wore the skins typical of the Akka people, furs and hides sewn into clothing. These eight bore stone mallets, and with those mallets, to a rhythm they all seemed to understand, they beat on the stones.

The stones sang. High and low harmonics rang off the rock, throbbing through the air, as first one mallet, then the next and then a third, swung into a stone and dropped away.

Laoina stopped at the edge of the scree, hunkering down in the shelter of an overhanging boulder. "We wait here."

But the humming of the stones drew him forward to the stone circle. At the center of the circle a woman wearing an eagle-feather cloak stood behind two men. One of them, tattooed like his Akka tribesfolk, sat on a litter. His frail body rocked back and forth in time to the ringing of the mallets on stone. Beside him, an ancient man with white hair and weathered skin had tucked his face into his cupped hands, praying.

Where was Adica?

Crossing the threshold, stepping over the invisible line that demarcated the inside of the circle of stones from the outside, Alain walked from a world filled with a throbbing hum to one of silence except for the murmuring of the two sorcerers, for surely that was what they were. They wore like an invisible mantle an aura of power, just as Adica did: the Hallowed Ones of their tribes chosen for their ability to walk the path of magic.

The old man, then, was Falling-down, whom Adica often spoke of fondly. The other, Tanioinin, seemed not much older than Adica, as far as Alain could tell, but he lived in a broken body. By the evidence of the litter, he could not even walk.

At last Alain saw Adica, curled up into a ball on the other side of Tanioinin. The hounds padded past him and nosed her. She started up, alarmed to see him. He hurried over to crouch beside her.

"I would have sent for you after the danger was over," she whispered.

"I do not leave you," he said stubbornly. "Do not ask me to go, because I will not."

She knew him well enough not to argue when he spoke in that tone.

He indicated Tanioinin and bent closer to murmur in her ear. The singing of the stones concealed his words from anyone except her, who was accustomed to his whispered endearments. "How can this one be a sorcerer? Can he even walk?"

"Spits-last is the most powerful sorcerer born into the human tribes." She regarded Tanioinin with an expression of respect and, perhaps, a little pity. "His people nurtured and raised him because of his exceedingly clever and deep mind. He has served them as sorcerer for many years. But his body is so crippled that he is helpless in the middle world. Others have to take care of him. Only in the spirit world can he truly roam free. That is why he is so strong."

Alain could see by the man's blank expression and the way his eyes had rolled up into his head that he was already gone into the spirit world. He was calling to the dragons . . . wherever they were.

Adica hissed under her breath, caught Alain's wrist, and pointed.

Those golden-stone hummocks arrayed along the eastern horizon like six giant tumuli were not stone at all. They glowed with the rich gleam of amber and the lustrous fire of molten gold. They hummed and, slowly, as he sank down— too stunned to cry out in astonishment—they woke.

They lifted great heads first. Their eyes had the winking fever of the hottest fire. Some had crests along their heads and necks, fans of gold unfolding as they rose. A tail lashed to dislodge boulders which smashed through the landscape, thrown about like pebbles. It was then that he realized how huge they were, and how far away. The noise of their waking rumbled and crashed around him, echoing against the heavens.

First one, and then a second, huffed mightily. Sparks rained from their nostrils. Fires bloomed and faded on rocks and among the mosses and low-lying scrub that lived in the fjall. Alain stared. Rage and Sorrow were whining, although it was hard to hear them above the distant crash and clamor of the waking dragons.

Adica struggled to her feet. She still held his wrist in a crushing grip; perhaps she had forgotten that she still held on to him. Mallets struck stone. The world hummed. As though drawn forward in a dream, Adica let go of Alain's arm and stepped forward, past the two murmuring sorcerers, to stand with arms raised at the threshold of the protective circle of the stone crown just as the first dragon launched itself into the air.

Alain leaped after her, but he did not even reach her. The backwash from the dragon's wings drove him to his knees. The screaming wind pounded him as a second, and then a third, dragon leaped toward the sky and caught the air under their vast wings, wider than houses. Their bellies shone like fire, and their tails lashed the air. Ice billowed off the distant eastern peaks, blown by their passage. A fourth and fifth rose. Battered by the wind of their rising, Alain struggled to stay on his knees. A hot stream of stinging wind passed over his back. His hair singed, and his hands and lips cracked under the sudden blast of heat as all his tears dried away.

He crawled forward. Adica stood framed by the stone lintel, arms still raised. The wind did not batter her down, nor did she bow beneath it. She didn't need his help. She was the Hallowed One of her tribe, as powerful as the dawn, able to face without cowering the great creatures they had woken. All he could do was keep low to the ground and pray.

The dragons rose in glory, as bright as lightning. The wind of their rising stirred the clouds into a rage of movement, swirling in a gale stronger than any storm wind. As the dragons rose, the heavy layer of clouds began to break up, shredding in all directions. Drops of rain sizzled on stone. A single snowflake drifted down, dissolving before Alain's eyes.

As the dragons rose, their brilliant figures dwindling, dusk came. Stars winked free of cloud. A cool wind swept in from

the north. The dragons had driven the clouds away, and now
the sorcerers could weave starlight in the loom.

Shaking, Alain clambered to his feet. His exposed skin hurt
like fire.

Adica turned to examine him. "You should have waited
until we called you." The brush of her fingers stung his raw
skin.

He flinched away. "I can go on," he rasped. "You know I
will never leave you."

Her expression softened. She stepped past him and spoke in
a low voice to Falling-down. Alain swayed, dizzy, still stunned
by what he had seen. He had never imagined creatures of such
vast power and terrible indifference. The life of the middle
world, the fleeting span of human years, was as nothing to
them, who could slumber for a hundred years as though it
were one night. He sank down cross-legged onto the hard
ground. Rage and Sorrow flopped down beside him. The
eagle-cloaked woman bustled up beside him to rub a soothing
ointment onto his stinging skin.

The mallet wielders ceased their hammering. Evidently
their voluminous skin cloaks and hoods had protected them
rather better than his traveling clothes had protected Alain, or
else they, too, wore an invisible mantle of magic. Chattering in
low voices, they lifted Spits-last's litter from the center of the
stone circle and carried him outside to a patch of ground covered with chalk.

Though his crippled body was weak, his spirit was strong.
He was alert, and all at once he looked directly at Alain. His
gaze was no less brilliant than the passage of the dragons.
Alain met his gaze boldly. All Spits-last's strength lay in his
eyes. Even his arms were so withered that they were as thin as
sticks. He had little compassion; perhaps he was too racked by
pain all the time to feel sympathy for those whose pain was
temporary. But he called to Alain with his expression. His
eyes were a fathomless brown, set under thick eyebrows, the
only robust thing about him. Secrets lay veiled in that face. It

seemed to Alain that Spits-last could see all the way through him, all the things Alain had ever done right and all the things he had ever done wrong, a vision that pierced without passing judgment. Because the worst judgment is the one you pass on yourself.

Then Spits-last looked away. Alain sagged forward, all the breath knocked out of him.

With great effort, Spits-last lifted an obsidian mirror. His mirror was narrow, etched with triangles and circles to help guide his sight. He caught the yellowish light of the Guivre's Eye, in the northeast, where she skated above the horizon, always watchful. He drew her gleaming thread across the warp of the stones to the southwest, to weave her in among the threads of the Serpent, who slides across the sands of the desert.

A brilliant portal plaited out of starlight wove into being.

"May fortune walk with you," said Falling-down from far away.

The eagle-cloaked woman thrust a pack into Alain's hand. Staggering, he got to his feet just as Laoina caught hold of his elbow to steady him. Where had she come from?

"Quick!" She dragged him forward until he got his feet under him.

Behind, Falling-down shouted after them. "Beware of the lion queens!"

"Where is Adica?" he gasped.

"I'm here!" she called behind him. The hounds' nails clacked on the pebbly ground. The gateway of light arched before them. He shook free of Laoina's supporting hand and stepped through into a heat as blasting as that of the dragons. The sun hit like a hammer. Everywhere lay desolation, nothing but sand.

The shock of the transition, the weight of uncounted days lost as they passed through the gateway, struck him as hard as the sun did. The world, the light, the heaving and endless hills of sand, all shuddered around him as though someone was shaking them. But perhaps it was only him, stumbling. He hit the ground hard, and where his palms slammed into the sand, he felt fire. Everything burned.

Laoina and Adica stumbled out of the stone circle. The glittering archway flashed, and vanished. Adica fell forward onto the hot sands in a faint. He caught hold of her and with an effort got her slung over his shoulders.

"Where are we?" he gasped. Around them lay desolation, nothing but a wasteland of sand, no sign of life except for the stone circle. Hills of featureless sand rose on all sides.

Laoina used her spear to measure an angle between two stones, seeking a direction. She pointed. "Come now." Grabbing Adica's pack, she started walking.

Alain groaned, but he followed her. It took an eternity to get to the top of the hill while the sun's heat and light hammered them. Thank God the ground was hard-packed rather than drifts of sand. A boulder stood at the top of the rise, and by the time he reached it, sweat was pouring down his back, and his hands, trying to keep hold of Adica's wrists, had gotten slick.

In the distance, down the far side of the hill and beyond a parched flat of cracked ground made hazy by heat, a lush garden of green blossomed out of the sandy wasteland. He smelled water and thought he might die of wanting. His mouth was so dry. He simply could not go one step farther. Sinking down into such shade as the boulder granted them, he eased Adica down to the sands and collapsed beside her, shaking too hard even to get a grip on his water pouch. The ground quivered beneath him, and at first he thought it was just his trembling, but that vibration came from the earth itself, which shuddered as though a huge beast tramped past.

A *huff* of hot wind stirred his hair. The normally imperturbable Laoina cried out. He leaped up and spun around just as Rage and Sorrow erupted in a frenzy of barking.

She stalked the sands like a queen, powerful and swift. The

fluidity and dignity of her movements made her both beautiful and frightening. Four-footed like a lion, her massive paws
splayed over the sand so that they didn't sink in. She resembled a lion in most ways, with a tawny coat and a sleek body
twice the size of a bull, but she also had wings, bristling with
feathers the color of wax, and above her broad shoulders she
wore the head of a woman, more vain than proud, fierce in
aspect and with a silken mane of gold flowing down her massive shoulders.

"*Maoisinu*," whispered Laoina. "The lion queen."

He knew in that moment that he had traveled far from
Osna village, farther than he had ever believed possible. Maybe
this *was* the afterlife. Maybe he had wandered into the realm of
legend. Or maybe he was just in a place so incomprehensible,
without iron, without turnips, without decent ploughs or
ships or even the God of Unities, that he had passed beyond
anything known in the lands of his birth.

XII
DEEP WATERS

1

THE emporium of Sliesby boasted a network of sturdy plank walkways, wrapping the town like stout vines, so that the busy merchants on their way from dock to warehouse would not wet their feet in bad weather. Stronghand admired their industriousness even as the town elders quivered before him. Like a trading network, the walkways linked harbor to town, workshop to storage shed to drinking hall. Even on such a day as today, early in spring with a hard rain blowing down over the town and the streets whipped into muck, merchants could walk unimpeded as long as they had good cloaks to cover themselves.

The rain battered Stronghand's back as he examined the folk huddled before him, most of them coughing and shuddering as the storm broke over the town. They stank of terror. Tenth Son of the Fifth Litter had spearheaded the early season strike, abetted by the fisherfolk, who'd had a dispute with the human community at Sliesby last season over the herring catch.

Out in the lowlands on the landward side of the town's palisade, a levy of disarmed soldiers was digging a mass grave for their fallen comrades. He smelled the distant stench of blood and offal, picked out of the souse of rain. Although the fight had been short, the Sliesby militia hadn't gone down easily.

Behind him lay the bay. Many islets and larger islands crowded the sound, all of them newly brought into the sphere of human cultivation. Rain made a sheet over them, although he saw lighter sky to the south.

According to the tribal history, two generations ago these lands had lain uninhabited by all but the animals and the occasional visit of one of the fisherfolk, seeking rushes or hemp for basketry and netting. Once, deeper inland in a district known for its lakes, the farthest eastern tribe of the RockChildren had built its OldMother's hall. That tribe, called Sviar, had not been heard of since two Sviar ships had been sighted raiding southward in the time of Bloodheart's father's chieftainship. With the recent incursion of human tribes, well armed, vigilant, and only slightly less belligerent than the RockChildren themselves, none among the RockChildren had gone to investigate their absent brethren.

But he might. At last, goaded by the long silence, one woman stepped out from under the porch that gave his prisoners scant shelter and into the beating rain. Unlike most human women, she wore a light veil that concealed her features. Her cloak glistened with raindrops.

"Chieftain," she said in the common language used by all traders, a melange of Wendish, Salian, and old Dariyan, "what is your will with us, who have harmed none but only seek to trade?"

The others shrank back against the wall of the town hall. The gap widened between them and their colleague, as if they hoped to escape the punishment sure to be inflicted upon her for her rash speech.

"What are you called?" asked Stronghand. "What nation among humankind do you call your mother?"

She had expressive hands, spread wide now as she gestured to two darkly-featured and nervous men standing among the crowd who wore peaked hats and ornamented sleeves, whose ends they twisted at this very moment. "We are children of the people called Hessi in the language of the Wendish folk and Essit among ourselves. I am known as Riavka, daughter of Sarenha. I act as Holy Mother to those of my people who live and visit in this port. I come before you as a supplicant, for I know well what stories are told and indignities suffered by those who have fallen under the fierce attack of your people."

He grinned so that his audience could see the many jewels that studded his teeth. She alone did not flinch. "I do not intend to attack, only to safeguard this port. A fair tithe paid to me by every merchant for each shipload will assure that no further disturbances plague you. Does that not seem fair?"

The others murmured among themselves and then, remembering that he could understand them, fell silent. They were as taut as snared rabbits, waiting for the ax to fall. The rain slackened as the storm moved through.

"What tithe will you demand?" Either she had taken his measure and decided that he respected most those who did not cringe before him, or else she simply did not fear death. "This port was founded by those on whom tithes laid heavy in the southern lands. If you lay your hand upon us too harshly, who is to say we won't rise up against you in rebellion?"

"Then you will all die."

Brows were wiped, sweat-drenched despite the cold. Several of the merchants glanced back toward the distant palisade, half concealed by buildings. They knew what grim work went on out of their sight, burying the dead in a mass grave. A portly man staggered forward to the edge of the porch's shelter to whisper into her ear, but she did not respond to him as she continued speaking. "Then who is to say we won't simply abandon this town, sail away come summer, and seek another site from which to trade?"

He regarded her with curiosity. "Are you not afraid that I might kill you for your presumptuousness?"

Her damp fingers flicked the lower edge of her veil, and he caught a glimpse of the hollow of her throat before the veil swayed back into place. "Had you wished to kill us outright or break us down into slave pens, surely those of your soldiers who attacked us yesterday would already have done so. You are meeting with us now because you have another plan in mind."

"What tithe would you consider a fair one, Riavka, daughter of Sarenha?"

She did not hesitate. "One part in ten."

"One in six," he replied as quickly, "and you will create a council among you of six elders to oversee the tithing. A governor of my own people will remain here with a garrison."

"So be it." She inclined her head to show her assent. Behind her, the others hurriedly agreed.

"That is not all," he went on. "I wish to establish another trading port, like this one, along the coast where my own people dwell. I have already chosen a harbor, in Moerin country, in the southern part of my people's lands. It is sheltered, and there is easy passage from there to sea-lanes that lead as far west as Alba, south to Salia, and eastward to these countries. Do any among you care to build such a port under my protection?"

The portly man had found his tongue, and he stammered out a anxious question. "It is a long and sorry voyage at this time of year, my lord. The lands of the Eika are known to us by report as a rugged, inhospitable country. Few will wish to settle there."

"Then, truly, I will pick some from among you." The gathered merchants reacted with such comical expressions of dismay that Stronghand had to suppress an odd urge to laugh, something learned from Alain, who had not been afraid to find pleasure in the foibles of humankind.

Riavka gestured toward the younger of the two Hessi men. "I will send my son and his household." In the same way water builds up behind flotsam jamming a narrow channel and then breaks through, her words released the others from their paralysis. They began speaking at once, a clamor that irritated Stronghand. The sound of a horn rose high over their noise.

He lifted a hand, unsheathing his claws. At once, the elders stuttered and gasped into silence.

The alert rose again over the waters, made gray by misting rain and tendrils of cloud hugging the distant watery isles. A crimson flag whipped into life on one of the outermost ships, waving once, twice.

He paced to the edge of the quay. Water lapped at the wooden pilings, shushing and slurping to the rhythm of unseen waves. Rain spattered the waters and stilled. Wide-bellied knarrs laden with cargo lay along the quay. Farther out on the bay, the sleek outlines of his own warships rested on unquiet waters, wreathed with fingers of mist.

The surface of the bay eddied in a spot where neither ship nor reef had its place, the wake made by an unseen pod of merfolk, come to call.

He turned to Tenth Son. "Had you any warning of this?"

Tenth Son gave a sharp lift of his chin, to signify "no."

A pair of glittering, ridged backs snaked above the water and vanished. Tails slapped down. The townsfolk yelped and skittered back, all but the veiled woman, who, amazingly, took a step closer in order to see better. She made a noise, unintelligible through her veil, and extended a hand, palm out, as if she could taste their essence through her skin.

Without warning, a big body heaved up out of the water not a body's length from him, high out of the water like a whale breaching. The flat face took them in, although what it could actually see with those hard, red eyes he could not be sure. The eels that were its hair writhed wildly, eyeless snouts snapping mindlessly at the empty air. It spun with a half turn backward and hit the water with such weight that water sprayed everywhere, a new shower of rain, salty and tasting of the waste that humans so thoughtlessly dumped into their harbors.

He laughed sharply and shook off the water. The Hessi woman took a startled step backward, hastily brushing herself off, but did not otherwise retreat. Her colleagues spilled backward onto the town walkways in fright. Their voices rose like those of startled crows.

A visage rose from the water, pale and stretched, hoisted by the razor-tipped hands of the merfolk. The object resolved itself into a spar, water-logged, wreathed by vinelike leaves tangled around something that resembled a face. Stronghand leaped backward as, with a final heave, the great spar clattered down onto the wooden quay and came to rest at his feet.

The spar was the remains of the mast of one of the living ships of the tree sorcerers. Caught in its leafy spire rested an object so bloated and pale that at first he did not recognize it.

"Ai, Lord have mercy!" cried the portly merchant, voice cracking. "It's a man's head."

Sea worms writhed in and out of the decaying eye sockets. In places the skin had peeled away to reveal the gleam of skull beneath.

"One of the Alban ships did not escape our allies," observed Tenth Son.

Stronghand stepped over the spar and its rotting centerpiece. The water eddied in cool circles below him. The rain had stopped, and the clouds above the islets lightened perceptibly as the sun tried to beat through.

"This was unexpected. I have not forgotten that Alba awaits." Truly, he did not understand his mysterious allies. At first, he thought they wanted only the flesh of his enemies to sustain them, but there was a greater purpose beneath their movements, something that spoke of intelligence and a slow-moving, cetacean plan, something swallowed into the depths of the sea, shuddering on tides known only in the deep waters.

What did the merfolk want?

Negotiations remained difficult, for they didn't share a common language. Indeed, they seemed to know what he wanted more than he knew what they desired out of this alliance. Yet surely it must be something they thought he alone could help them obtain. He couldn't ask. He dared not show his ignorance, because ignorance signaled weakness.

Stronghand could never betray weakness. Too many knives waited to plunge into his back.

The waters roiled. A dozen tails flicked out of the muddy bay and slapped down, in tribute, in command, in question, or simply in answer. He did not know. Ridged backs cut the water as they sped bayward. With their wake spreading behind them, they vanished beyond the outermost ships, plunging into the deep channel, and were gone.

2

A SINGLE lamp burned in the chapel of St. Thecla the Witnesser, not enough light to illuminate the magnificent frescoes depicting the life of the blessed saint for which the chapel was justly famous. Nor, really, could Antonia see clearly each distinctive pillar, carved with the visage of one of the seven disciplas, that ringed the inner sanctum. The marble columns breathed quietly in shadow. The dim light granted only a glimpse of each carved face: Matthias, Mark, and Johanna to the left, and Lucia, Marian, and Peter to the right. Back by the main door the column depicting St. Thecla herself took the honored place, directly facing the eighth pillar, which stood behind the altar but had no representation carved into it, nothing but a circle of rosettes at the base and the capital.

What need to see the carved faces of the pillars when the lamp did a perfectly good job of lighting the face of the man who knelt before the altar? He had set the ceramic lamp on the marble floor between him and the altar in such a way that the flame gave his face a saintly glow, as if God had touched him with Their holy light.

Did he know that she watched? Did he suspect that during his long hours of prayer people came sometimes to stand in the gallery to look down into the inner sanctum? Where they would see him, as fair as the dawn, as pious as a saint, and sublime in his virtue?

Beautiful Hugh.

I'm too old for this, she thought, irritated at the way her thoughts were tending. Old enough to be his grandmother if she had been married off at fifteen, as her sister and cousins had been, to seal alliances between families. But she had been allowed to enter the church after the husband chosen for her had died quite spectacularly the night before the wedding. She had misjudged the dosage. She hadn't meant to make his death messy, just final, but after all she had only been fourteen.

Her years in the church had gone much more smoothly.

One lapse, that was all, in forty years. One lapse, and a single mistaken assessment, when she had judged that Sabella had the means and support to overthrow King Henry. Now she had lost both her son and her position in the church. She had no more margin for error. There must be no more misjudgments, no more miscalculations. Not one false step.

Below her, Hugh bowed his fair head to rest on folded hands. She knew he wasn't praying. He was studying that mysterious book the others called "Bernard's book," a book of secrets. It never left Hugh's side except to be locked into a chest sealed with several layers of protective wards. Here in the chapel, he had arranged his presbyter's robes to cover it where it lay open in front of his knees. His robes spread out around him in such a way that their drape and fall made a pleasing picture, framing him. An artist could not have done a better job of painting a representation of a dutiful and noble presbyter, intimate counselor to the king, confidant of the Holy Mother herself.

He looked up abruptly, as if he'd heard her breathing in the gallery, but he was only gazing toward the domed span that separated him from the heavens above. His lips moved. He spoke a word, more a sigh than a name.

"Liath."

There was something terrible in the way he said it, like a curtain drawn aside so that one glimpsed what was better left unseen. He bowed his head again, and this time she thought he really was praying, desperately, passionately.

The ardor suggested by his tightly clasped hands, the anguished cant of his shoulders, the intensity of his entire being was itself the flame drawing her. Like the galla whom she could call at need, luring them with fresh blood, she lapped up his suffering, if suffering it was. She had killed strong emotion in herself because it hindered her, but she had never lost her taste for it, even if she had to experience it secondhand.

Poor child. How terrible for him that his brilliance was flawed by this one weakness, this obsession for the one thing he could not have.

And yet, why not? Liath herself had spoken approvingly of Hugh's passion for knowledge. There remained a link between them, one the girl herself had acknowledged reluctantly back in Verna. In a way, Hugh did possess her, because she could never forget or forgive him. Yet in her heart, Liath probably knew that Hugh was a better match for her than Prince Sanglant.

A footstep scuffed the floor. A presbyter dressed simply but richly in robe and long scarlet cloak came forward to stand in the shadow behind Hugh. He made the Circle at his breast, a sign of respect toward the holy altar and the gold cup resting there. As Hugh shifted back and turned to look at him, the man bowed deeply and with obvious reverence before speaking in the hushed tones appropriate to the dignity of their setting.

"Your Honor, the Holy Mother has awakened and is asking for you. You know how your presence does her so much good."

"I thank you, Brother Ismundus. You are kind to disturb your own sleep this night."

"Say not so! I should be praying for God's mercy to heal her, as you are, but—but I haven't your strength."

Hugh winced slightly as he turned his head to gaze at the uncarved pillar, whose smooth marbled surface represented the holy purity of the blessed Daisan. No need to carve a crude rendition of an earthly face when the blessed Daisan had been lifted bodily in a cloud of God's glory and transported directly to the Chamber of Light.

"It isn't strength but sin." Was he aware how exquisitely the lamp limned his profile at this angle? "I beg you, Brother Ismundus, do not grant me virtues I do not possess. I will come at once. Just let me finish my psalms."

"Of course, Your Honor." Ismundus bowed again before he retreated from the chapel. Of course the old man had no obligation to honor another presbyter in this way. He had served thirty years in the skopos' palace and had risen to become steward of the holy bedchamber. In truth, in the common way of things, a young presbyter like Hugh ought to be bowing to *him,* not the other way around.

But these days, as she knew well enough, nothing ran anymore in the common way of things. In recent years the world had been overset by sin and disobedience. If everything she had been taught in the last year were true, it would soon be overset catastrophically by God's hand, or Aoi sorcery.

Out of the coming chaos a strong leader could, and must, arise.

Maybe she had been wrong to believe that leadership could come from Liath and Prince Sanglant. There were leaders besides Sanglant, men with greater power and more sophisticated ambition.

"I know where you are," said Hugh suddenly into the sanctum's holy silence. The lamp flickered as she froze, wondering by what sorcery he had managed to detect her presence up here in the dense shadows of the gallery, spying on him. "I know what you're doing, my treasure. I can see you now, I can call the burning stone to make a window onto your journey, and I swear to you, Liath, I will follow you there."

He bent his head and began to sing.

"Hear my cry for mercy when I call out to you,
when I lift my hands toward your holy sanctuary.
Do not number me with the wicked and the evildoers
who speak sweetly to their fellows
while malice boils in their hearts.
Reward them according to their deeds.
Glorify those who trust in God.
Blessed are They, who listen to my plea for mercy."

He waited a moment in silence after he had done. Was that flickering in the lamp's flame the passage of angels, attracted by the sweetness of his voice? But if he were waiting for something, it did not come. He rose. Closing his book of secrets, he tied it shut with a red ribbon, tucked it under his arm, and walked away, passing under the archway and out through the doors. The lamp burned on. It was so silent she heard the hiss of the wick.

She lingered in the shadows in the gallery that ringed the inner sanctum. No need to risk being seen exiting the gallery so soon after Hugh's departure. Anyway, she liked it here in St. Thecla's Chapel. Emperor Taillefer had modeled the royal chapel at Autun on this very sanctuary, with its eight sides, double-vaulted walls, and domed roof. According to Heribert, St. Thecla's Chapel was more perfectly proportioned than the copy at Autun, but certainly the royal chapel at Autun inspired awe and holy fervor because of its grandeur.

Liath was Taillefer's great granddaughter, heir to his earthly glory and power. Just as she, once known as Biscop Antonia of Mainni but now called Sister Venia, understood the delicate balance of power at play within the skopos' palace as a long and deadly winter turned the corner into the lean weeks of early spring. The Holy Mother Clementia lay dying. Soon, her soul would pass out of her body and ascend through the seven spheres to the Chamber of Light while, below, on Earth, some noblewoman of proper birth, rank, and holy stature would be elected to govern in her place.

"'Our hearts have not gone astray,'" she murmured, "'nor have our feet strayed from Your path.'"

3

LIATH dozed in comfort in the soft embrace of Somorhas. It was like luxuriating in a bath filled with rose petals with the water neither too hot nor too cold. She was so spectacularly comfortable that she simply did not want to move or even open her eyes. Nothing hurt; she had not a single nagging discomfort. No reason to hurry forward. She had been on the road for so long it seemed cruel not to rest here a while.

In the distance she heard faint singing, a vocal accompaniment to the chiming music of the spheres. A person could just lie here forever and bathe in the perfect counterpoint of the music, never ending, always melodious and in faultless harmony.

Wind brushed her face. A touch, as soft as a feather, tickled her lips. A cool rush flowed down her throat as though a breath of wind had insinuated itself into her very body.

"Pass through the horned gate of Somorhas, if you would see your heart's desire."

She opened her eyes, startled by those sweet-toned words, as fluid as water. Who had spoken? It almost sounded like her own voice. Without realizing she meant to, she rose. A featureless plain surrounded her. The pleasant bed on which she had been resting was simply the rosy-colored ground, boiling with a layer of mist. Alabaster towers bristled on the horizon, as numerous as the spears of a vast army. A vast domed building built entirely of marble stood between her and the forest of towers. She knew at once that in this building she would find a library complete with every scroll and book she had ever wished to read. The towers receded into the mist even as the dome rose before her, flanked by avenues of stone lined with oversized statues of every animal known on Earth and in the sky: ravens and peacocks, panthers and bears, ibex and serpents. Where the avenues met in the forecourt, they joined into a broad stair surmounted by an archway, two ivory pillars linked by a curving arbor of dog roses and belladonna.

As her feet led her forward under the arch, a tremor passed through her body rather as a pan of water, shaken, will run with ripples and wavelets and then quiet. She found herself in a vast hall where churchmen ornamented by scarlet cloaks and clerics robed in wine or forest-green silk hurried about on their errands. Tables lit by a profusion of ceramic lamps stood in rows throughout the hall. Here sat scholars bent over ancient scrolls or freshly copied tomes bound into codices. A pair of young clerics, scarcely more than girls, whispered as they searched through some old chronicle.

On a stand at the center of the hall rested a thick book. She crossed between the tables and halted here. No one glanced at her strangely. No one found her presence remarkable, although she wore only tunic and leggings, quiver with arrows and bow, the gold torque given to her by Sanglant, and the lapis lazuli ring. The stone floor remained pleasingly warm to her bare feet.

As at Quedlinhame, the stand held the library's catalog: different scribes at many different periods had added to the list. As she leafed through the catalog, she saw where a square Dariyan script, all capitals, changed abruptly to the rounded Scripta Actuaria favored by the early church mothers and gradually picking up the minuscule letters that marked the ascendancy of Salian clerics under the influence of Taillefer's court schola. These days, the simpler Scripta Gallica held sway, imperial yet elegant.

What riches the catalog laid bare before her eyes! Not only Ptolomaia's *Tetrabiblos* but also her magisterial *Mathematici's Compilation*, Virgilia's *Heleniad* and also her *Dialogues*, various geographies of heaven and Earth by diverse ancient scholars, the *Memoria* of Alisa of Jarrow with its detailed instruction in the art of memory, and more volumes on natural history and astronomy than she had ever seen before in one place. She skipped over the massive inventories of the writings of the church mothers but closely examined those pages marked black for caution. The numerous condemnations and tracts against various heresies held no attraction but, as she had hoped, there were forbidden texts on sorcery, like Chaldeos' *The Acts of the Magicians* and *The Secret Book of Alexandros, Son of Thunder*.

How amazing and odd that a library of this scope should exist in the sphere of Somorhas. But hadn't the voice said that beyond the gateway she would find her heart's desire?

A small voice niggled at her from deep inside, annoying as a thorn. The merest prick of pain throbbed lightly behind her right eye. Hadn't she read somewhere that in Somorhas lay only dreams and delusions?

"It cannot be so," her voice whispered, almost as if she were two people, one watching, one speaking. "In the city of memory a great library stands in the third sphere, where the Cup of Boundless Waters holds sway, the ocean of knowledge available to mortal kind."

That was true, wasn't it? Best to make use of the time while she had it. She found the notation listing the location of St. Peter of Aron's *The Eternal Geometry* in one of the library chambers and, seeing that others waited patiently behind her to use the catalog, hurried away. At every moment, with every footfall, she expected one of the robed clerics to challenge her. What are you doing here? Who are you? Where have you come from?

No one ever did. It wasn't that they didn't see her. Gazes marked her before moving away as easily as if she were someone expected. No one unusual. Not a stranger at all.

The corridor she had thought would lead her to the room of astronomies led her instead, unexpectedly, to a chapel elaborately decorated with gilded lamps hanging from a beamed ceiling and frescoes depicting the life of St. Lucia, guardian of the light of God's wisdom. Her knees bent as if of their own volition, and in this way she knelt behind a pair of clerics robed in white and cloaked with the scarlet, floor-length capes that in the world below distinguished presbyters in the service of the skopos.

Strange how her thoughts scattered every which way. Because she could not calm her mind enough to lift her thoughts to God, she listened. The two clerics kneeling right in front of her evidently did not have calm minds either, because they were gossiping in low voices while, at the front of the chapel, an elderly man led a chorus of sweet-voiced monks in the service of Sext.

"Didn't you hear? He saved poor Brother Sylvestrius a lashing."

"Nay, how can Brother Sylvestrius possibly have given offense? He scarcely speaks a word as it is, and sometimes it seems impossible to me that he even knows the rest of us exist because he's so busy with his books."

"It was nothing he said, but what he wrote in the annals."

"Nothing deliberately disparaging, surely? That's more Biscop Liutprand's style."

"Of course not. Sylvestrius wrote a dispassionate account of the crowning, rather than a flattering one."

"And Ironhead couldn't abide it. He'd rather hear one of those noxious poets singing his praises as though he were the next Taillefer rather than what he really is."

"You know what a rage Ironhead can get into."

"Truly, I do, and have the mark here on my cheek to prove it. Yet how then did Sylvestrius escape the lash? Nay, nay, you need not say. I know *who* must have intervened."

"Truly, Brother, he is the sole gentling influence now that the Holy Mother, may God grant her healing, lies ill. He is the one person who stands between Ironhead's coarseness and barbarity and the lives of so many innocents."

As if this thought struck them hard with a vision of God's mercy, they bent their heads in sincere prayer as the old presbyter in front began the *Gloria*.

Odd to feel that her body was not her own. She rose, quite
unexpectedly, and edged backward, but there must have been
another door into the chapel that she hadn't seen before
because, instead of backing into the corridor she'd just come
down, she found herself in a gloomy, dank passage illuminated by a single flickering torch. The light was bad, but
with her salamander eyes she saw a trio of guards standing at
a heavy wood door exactly like a dozen other such doors set
into the corridor behind her. The stone walls seeped moisture. The floor stank of earth and cold. No fine lofty ceilings
here. No skilled artisans had toiled to make this place a pleasure to look at or walk through.

"Ach, here's the key," said one of the guards. "Poor lads. I
hate to think of their heads being stuck up on the wall just for
stealing a bit of bread because they was too poor to buy none
at market."

"A bit of bread is one thing," objected the second guard,
"but stealing the king's bread is quite another."

"Tchah! King's bread, indeed." The third guard laughed
coarsely. "That basket was headed for the king's whorehouse, if
you please."

"Still, what belongs to the king is meant for the king, not
for beggars like these two."

They got the key turned in the lock and with some effort
shoved the door open. "Come on out, lads," said the third
guard.

Not more than fourteen, the two boys had the weary,
pinched look of children raised in constant hunger, starved
rats. One was weeping. His companion was trying to be brave.

"We was just hungry," whimpered the weeping one, a
familiar refrain which had been sung once too often.

"Nay, give them not the satisfaction," hissed his companion.
"We'll go bravely to our death—"

"Bravely enough, lad," said the third guard. "I'm under
orders to pardon you and turn you loose. Here's a silver *lusira*
for your trouble. Use it wisely, and get you out of the city. My

lord king has a long memory for people who have crossed him, and if he ever recognizes you, he'll cut off your heads right in the street."

The weeper wept copiously at this news of reprieve. The brave lad dropped to his knees, trying to kiss the hands of the third guard while at the same time clutching the precious silver to his breast. "I pray you, friend, how can we thank you? God will bless you for your mercy."

"It's not me you should be thanking. I would have let you hang. But there is one at court who chooses the rose of mercy over the sword of justice."

"Ai, Lord and Lady!" breathed the brave one in the tone of a child who has just recognized the visitation of an angel. "Was it *that one,* who we saw in the square next to the lord king?"

"Truly, *that one.* Don't forget that some walk closer to God than do the rest of us sinners. You can thank him in your prayers." Two of the guards, working together, dragged the door shut. It scraped noisily over the stone floor, the sound grinding and echoing down the corridor.

With a grunt, the first guard led the two boys away. Liath did not move while the others lingered.

"You could have kept the silver and let them hang," whispered the second guard. "How do you dare go against the king's wishes?"

"The king will have forgotten the incident in a week's time. Poor lads, they hadn't any harm in them. I remember being that hungry and desperate once. But don't ever think I'd have kept the silver, boy." The third guard's voice got tight as he chided the other. "Not when you know *who* gave it to me to give to those poor lads. We get two meals a day in the king's service. They've nothing, all the poor wandering in the streets while the king raises taxes in order to buy more soldiers for his army."

"How would *he* have known, the one who gave it to you, if you'd have kept it? You could have let them go and kept it for yourself. That's a month's wages!"

"Tchah! He'd know."

"And he'd punish you?"

"Truly, so it would be punishment, to be called before him and have to look him in the eye who is a better man than any of us. I've no wish to go standing there before him while he forgives me for giving into temptation, not a word of blame from him, who knows how sinful humankind is and how we struggle with the evil inclination. I'd rather not sin than be shamed before him."

"Oho, is that why you've not been to Parisa's brothel in the last month?"

"So it is, lad, and I'll never go again. I'm courting a young woman who's a washerwoman down by the Tigira docks. I mean to marry her and live a Godly life."

"Once this war is over."

"Once this damned war is over. Have you heard the latest rumor?"

Moving from the corridor under a stone archway that led to a staircase, they vanished from her view, carrying the only torch. Their conversation was quickly muffled by stone and distance. Her legs carried her after them, but by the time she reached the staircase she could only follow the receding glow of torchlight. She climbed quickly, chafed by a sudden cold draft of wind. Between one breath and the next, the torch went out, leaving her in pitch-blackness. She climbed the stairway by touch, fingers brushing the dressed stone, feeling the cracks and flaking mortar smoothing away beneath her skin until it seemed to her that she was in a narrow stair with wood walls, wood floors, and a ceiling so low that it brushed her hair. She stumbled up against a latch. Though her fingers touched the latch, they hesitated.

Her jaw had gone tight, clenched hard, and the pain brought a rush of questions. Where was she? Had she unwittingly descended back to Earth?

Quickly vanquished and fled. "Walk through the door," her voice murmured, "and I will be one step closer to my heart's desire." Wasn't it true? Surely it was true. She set her hand on the latch just as she heard muffled sounds of weeping to her right. Startled, she jerked back as the latch twitched, turned from the other side, scraped against wood, and snapped up.

The door was thrown open.

A pretty young woman blinked into the darkness. She had a fresh scar on her upper lip and wore only a shift, the fabric so finely woven that Liath saw the blush of her nipples beneath the cloth. "Oh, thank the Lady," she said, grabbing Liath's wrist and tugging her out into a bright chamber where a rosy light poured in through four unshuttered windows. "You got her safely hidden."

The mellow light pooled over a parquet floor and set into relief a set of frescoes depicting such obscene subjects that Liath blushed. Her new friend pressed past her into the hidden cupboard—for such it was—and helped the weeping woman out from the shadows. She wore the long and rather shapeless wool tunic, dyed a nondescript clay red, worn by common folk, although unlike the Wendish style she wore also a tightly fitted bodice and a brown apron over it. Her hair was bound up in a crown of braids rather than covered by a light shawl, as a respectable Wendish woman's would be. Beneath the streaked tears and the frightened expression, Liath could see that she was remarkably pretty, black-haired with the kind of eyes one could stare into for hours. She shrank away from the sight of the huge bed and its silken canopy.

"I'll not be abused by him without a fight!" she said in a voice made hoarse by screaming. "He may be king, but I'm a Godly married woman and I only come to pray at the cathedral to ask for God's mercy on my poor sick child."

"Hush," hissed the pretty woman. "He's gone now. What did you say your name was?"

"I'm known as Terezia. Ai, Lady!" She began to snivel again, overcome by relief. "I was just there in the Lady Chapel, praying, when in he come and grabbed me right out of there. What was I to say to the king? I never imagined—" She began

to sob again while the pretty woman in the shift gave Liath a
look to show that she'd seen this scene played over many times
before, a shared glance of commiseration and disgust. "—that
he would try to rape me. If it hadn't been for that holy man
who come in and put a stop to it—"

"Yes, friend, if it hadn't been for him."

"I thought the king was like to run him through. Ai, Lady,
how brave he was!" Her eyes shone with remembered admiration. "And so *handsome*."

"And a holy presbyter, sister, not for the likes of us, so go
back to your good husband and your sick child. Hurry, now,
for the king might come back any time." Two doors stood
open, one leading into an opulent hallway and the other to a
narrow servants' corridor. She beckoned toward the servants'
corridor. "Go on. That'll get you down to the servants' hall.
My friend Teuda will get you out of the palace. She'll be waiting at the bottom of the stairs."

"What about you? Aren't you wanting to escape as well?"

The pretty woman laughed lightly. "Nay, we're the king's
whores. We're paid well enough to want to stay."

"But you're so pretty." Terezia looked ready to faint again, and
she hadn't even gotten as far as the door, stopping to lean on the
back of a chair. "Why would he be coming down to the cathedral to abduct God-fearing women who've just come there to
pray when he has lemans as pretty as you to warm his bed?"

"Poor innocent," said the whore with the slightest hint of
contempt. "He does it because he can. Nay, listen. I hear someone coming."

Terezia bolted down the servants' corridor. Before the noise
of her hasty escape had faded, the whore threw herself onto the
bed with a chuckle. Rolling over, she reached for a silver tray,
found a goblet, and raised herself up to sip at the wine contentedly. "Ai, Lady. When I think of those poor women slaving
all day at their washing or cooking or raising a host of brats in
a filthy hovel down by the marsh, I thank God that you and I
lie here in silks."

"Beauty doesn't last forever," said Liath, feeling the headache coming back. What a sight she herself must look in her tunic, fallen loose because she had no belt, with her quiver strapped to her back. Yet the whore smiled as seductively at Liath as if she, too, wore a fine shift to mark her exalted status, as if they had shared other intimacies here in this light-draped chamber while they waited for the king. Liath even took a step forward, as if to go lie down on that bed beside the pretty whore, as if her body meant to do what it willed without consulting her. It was like fighting a stubborn horse, to grab hold of a chair and sit down solidly, with a thump.

"Oh, don't talk to me like that," said her companion now. "I've seen you eyeing him when he comes in with Ironhead." She laughed, not kindly. "Iron head, indeed. He's as elegant as an ax, is the king. Pump and grunt, that's him. Nothing like his presbyter, is he, darling? My Lord, now there's a true man, all bright and handsome, clever and kind, with such a beautiful voice as you can get all lost in, and the hands of a saint. Haven't you ever snuck into St. Thecla's Chapel to watch him praying? I have, and I know you have, too. I just wonder what it would be like to have those hands soliciting me. Haven't you just? Haven't you? All witty and elegant as he is, thoughtful and wise. But I see the look in his eyes. He's all lit inside, God's chosen one." She sighed so passionately, shifted so sensuously on the bed, that Liath felt all on fire, remembering the ecstasies known to the body. "Don't you wish he'd choose you?"

"Yes," she whispered, not sure what question she was answering, except that arousal warred with nausea as her thoughts sharpened for an instant. She had to get out of here. She lurched out of the chair, tipping it over behind her, and fled to the door.

But instead of the safety of the servants' corridor, she stumbled into an anteroom so soft with carpets that her bare feet made no sound as she hurried across the room to the only open door. Out of breath, she leaned against a doorframe

painted with a mural depicting the ancient Emperor
Tianathano driving a chariot pulled by griffins.

In the dim chamber beyond, a man was reading aloud from
the Holy Verses in a voice so beautifully composed and melodious that like a roped lamb she was drawn in past a carved
wooden screen into a vast and subdued bedchamber shrouded
by approaching death.

"'In those days,'" the voice declaimed, "'young Savamial
came into the service of God. One day she was given the task
of sleeping beside the holy curtain that concealed the glory of
God. The lamp burning beside the holy curtain had not yet
gone out, and while Savamial lay sleeping in the temple the
voice of God called out to her, and she answered, "I'm
coming." She ran to the veiled woman and said, "Here I am.
You called me." But the veiled woman replied, "I didn't call
you. Go back to sleep."'"

That harmonious voice made her head throb painfully.

A single lamp hung from a tripod set beside the bed. It illuminated an aged woman, so frail that the hands lying on the
coverlet were seamed with blue veins, as pale and thin as finest
parchment. Her eyes were closed. One could only tell she was
alive because she had the merest brush of color in her cheeks
and, once, an eyelid flickered at the expressive lift of the
reader's voice. Another man stood back in the shadows, looking on with a rapt face. The reader's face was concealed from
Liath because his back was turned, but she saw how his robe
fell in elegant drapery from his shoulders. His hair gleamed
golden in the lamplight as he continued to read.

"'So she went back and lay down again. But God called a
second time, "Savamial!" Savamial got up and ran to the holy
woman and said, "Here I am. You called me."'"

"Hugh," Liath breathed, lips moving although she hadn't
meant to make a sound. A sick, horrible pain clutched in her
guts, and she could not move.

He turned to see who had come in. "Who is there?" he
asked softly. She knew she should run, but her legs moved her

forward into the soft glow of the lamplight. Seeing her, he looked surprised and even a little shy. Was he actually blushing as a youth might faced with the lady for whom he has conceived a sweetly guileless passion? It was hard to tell because the light was behind him.

He carefully closed the book and handed it to his companion, who took it without demur as Hugh rose and came to stand before her. Already the knot in her gut and the aching in her head subsided, subsumed under a flood of new thoughts.

She had actually forgotten how beautiful he was—not a shallow beauty that bloomed quickly and withered with the next season, but something bone-deep, unfathomable because golden hair and a certain arrangement of features cannot by itself create a pleasing face. Why had God seen fit to shower him with that combination of lineaments and expressiveness, charm and intensity, whose sum is beauty?

"Liath! I—" He broke off, confused and flustered. "Where have you come from? Why are you here?" He glanced back at the elderly presbyter, who stood serenely by the bedside of the aged woman, watching the lamplight twist over her pallid face. "Nay, come, let's go outside to talk. I can't understand how it is you've come here."

But they had barely crossed the threshold into the anteroom, and her lips parted to speak, she not even knowing what she meant to say, when a middle-aged presbyter with the stout girth of a person who's eaten well since childhood hurried into view.

"Thank God, Your Honor. I hoped to find you here. How is the Holy Mother?"

"She has not changed, alas, Brother Petrus. May God have mercy. I've been reading to her."

"Yes, yes." The stout presbyter was clearly in a mounting frenzy, hands twitching, shifting his weight from one foot to the other like a child who has to pee. "You must come at once. The king—"

"Of course I'll come." Hugh looked at Liath, opening his

hands as if to say, "what can I do?" "Will you wait?" he asked her in a low voice. "Or perhaps, I don't know, I can't believe— Nay, perhaps you'll not wish to wait."

Perhaps it was curiosity that goaded her, even as it occurred to her that there was nothing about him now at all threatening. "I'll come with you, if I may," her voice said.

His face lit. He smiled sweetly, then looked away as if embarrassed at his own reaction.

"I pray you, Your Honor, I fear there'll be violence if you don't come quickly—"

"Don't fear, Brother Petrus. Let us go."

One lavishly decorated corridor led to the next. She was lost in a maze of staircases and archways, colonnades and court-yards. At last they crossed out of one palace compound and into a second. Here, where the great hall abutted a long wing of princely chambers, they stepped outside into a small court-yard ringed by fig and citron trees. In the center, on a dusty oval of ground, soldiers took arms training. Yet under the rosy light of a cloudy day, so strangely bright that she realized she had no idea what season or hour it was, something in the ring wasn't going right.

One man, wearing a grim iron helm and a heavily padded coat, was in the process of pounding some poor youth into the dirt.

Brother Petrus was so out of breath that he could barely wheeze out an explanation. "You know how it is . . . a woman down at prayers in the cathedral . . . he saw her . . . conceived a lust . . . had her brought to him . . . but then he was called out of his chambers . . . and returned to find her gone. He's in a fury. You know how he hates to be crossed."

Hugh's mouth tightened. He lifted a hand to his face, laying the back of that hand to his cheek as though at a memory unlooked for and unwanted. The iron-helmed man had a blunted sword carved from wood, but by now he was simply laying into his victim as though he'd forgotten everything except that reflexive snap, over and over, of his sword arm. The young man was crying out loud, begging for mercy. Soldiers stood back, uneasily, but no one moved to stop them.

Hugh unbuckled his belt and stripped out of his presbyter's robe to reveal a simple linen tunic and leggings beneath, the kind of thing worn by a noble lady's younger son when he rides off in the retinue of his elder cousin. He was tall, lean, and strong. He gestured. A servant, running, brought him a padded sword.

"Nay, my lord king," he said in a clear, carrying voice as he stepped out onto the oval, "this poor lad's not much of a contest, is he? I'll test you."

The king hesitated between one blow and the next, lifting his head. Liath caught a glimpse of a cruel gaze behind the visor. He spoke with the voice of a man plagued by a surfeit of spleen.

"No doubt it was your doing the woman was taken out of the palace, my precious counselor."

"She was a married woman praying for God to heal her sick child. She has both a father and a husband in the mason's guild, my lord king. How does it benefit you to insult the men who build and repair the city walls?"

"I'd have given her back unharmed!"

Seeing that Hugh had no helmet, the king pulled off his before leaping forward. Hugh was ready for him. He hadn't the breadth of shoulder of a man always in armor, but clearly he had trained for war. And why not? Abbots and churchmen often led contingents to war. Such a man must be ready, even in the midst of prayer, to answer when the regnant called.

The king had far less grace than a bull. He had strength, exasperation, and experience as he thrashed and struck, but there came no physical pleasure in watching him at work. As elegant as an ax, his whore had said of his lovemaking, all pumping and grunting. Watching him fight, Liath could well believe it.

Watching Hugh fight, she saw how Hugh measured his opponent and worked him patiently, saw the grace of his

movements, never too subtle or too bold. Sweat broke first at
the back of his neck. Somehow, she remembered that: how he
would get a sheen of sweat there and down between his shoulder blades. How his hands would get moist. A bead of sweat
trickled down his forehead. His gaze never left his opponent;
like a lover, he had eyes for no one else.

Not even for her.

She found her hands at her own throat, and she was trembling hard, choking, shaking all over. The dance of swordplay
went on regardless, bruises traded, a cut lip, hair gone damp
with sweat. The king had a scar on one cheek that flared
vividly the more he sweated. He had a look about him that
suggested he didn't fight so much for love of fighting but
rather because he wanted to win. Hugh was overmatched,
both in size and in prowess, but since Hugh didn't care about
winning, he could focus all his efforts on defense.

Her hands fell to her side. Strange that she had reacted like
that. She had nothing to fear. Eventually the king stepped
back and, panting, tossed his padded sword aside. He wiped
sweat from his brow as he chuckled.

"Well fought, Counselor. I'll make you a fighting man yet."

"Alas, it cannot be, my lord king, for God has chosen me for
other work. I must go back to attend the Holy Mother."

"And I must go to the barracks to inspect the new troops.
You'll attend me at the feast tonight."

"As you wish, my lord king."

The king called his captains together and they strode off the
field.

Hugh lingered to speak to a steward, making sure that provision had been made for the injured man's care.

The courtyard cleared, leaving Hugh alone with Liath. Two
servants loitered under the colonnade, ready to hurry forward
at his command. He mopped his face with a cloth and joined
her in the shadow of a fig tree.

"You've come to get the book. I'm surprised you came
alone. You have no reason to trust me."

No, I don't, she thought fleetingly, but her voice said, "The book."

He gestured, inviting her to walk with him. "I've found an old scholar here who is familiar with the writing in the central portion."

It had been so many months since he had stolen Da's *Book of Secrets* from her that it took her a moment to understand what he meant. Da's book was actually three books, bound together. The first book, written on parchment, contained a florilegia on the topic of sorcery: quotes and comments copied out of other books by Da over the years. The third book, written in the infidel way on paper, was a copy of al-Haithan's astronomical tract *On the Configuration of the World*. She had never been able to read the middle book. Written on papyrus in a language unknown to her, it remained a mystery. A different hand than the original had penned in a few words in Arethousan as a gloss to the text, and some of these she had puzzled out, because Hugh had taught her a little Arethousan.

Hugh had taught her, in those terrible months when she had been his slave in Heart's Rest.

She stopped dead under the colonnade, shivered convulsively as the memory of that winter night shuddered through her body. Had she gone utterly mad to walk here beside Hugh as though he were an ordinary man? He took two steps more, noticed that she had halted, and turned back quizzically to regard her. Seeing her face, his expression changed.

"I beg your pardon. I have been too bold. One of my servants will show you safely out of the palace. Please believe you have nothing further to fear from me."

"I don't fear you, I hate you," she wanted to say, but her voice said, "What do you mean?"

He looked away diffidently. "It is impossible to believe what I read in that ancient text. Nothing I ever expected, for I admit I had thought, and hoped, that I would find written there an ancient study of sorcery, mastery of knowledge long since hidden from us."

"Did you?" she demanded, unable not to want to know what secrets the ancient text held.

"What I read changed my life. God has shown me how wrong I have been, and how I must change." The shadow gave depth to his expression, his handsome eyes, the curve of his mouth as he frowned. "Nay, but it began before that. First of all it was the woman who took you away from Werlida. She humbled me. She made me think. Change does not come easily."

A mellow wind chased itself through the colonnade archways, stirring the wisteria wound down and around the stone pillars. A faint chiming ring serenaded them, but she couldn't tell where it was coming from, everywhere and nowhere. The two servants waited patiently a stone's toss away, by the archway that led out toward the courtyard linking the two palaces, one secular and one religious, regnant and skopos.

I know where I am. I am in Darre, the holy city, home of the Holy Mother who presided over the church.

She could practically breathe in the ancient stones, the memory of the empire that had risen here centuries ago and then collapsed into ruins, devastated by the raids of the Bwrmen and their savage allies and by its own internal corruption. If she crossed under that archway, she could walk away into the city—except that she could not move.

"Where is the book?" her voice asked.

He glanced up, face lit by the simple question. "If you will." He indicated the passageway. "I have my own suite of chambers in the skopos' palace. All of the presbyters do, of course, except those who travel as ambassadors." He did not stumble over his words. He was far too well educated, too composed, too experienced in a courtier's smooth affability. "There's also the library. Ai, God, Liath! You can't believe the library here! So much that one could never hope to learn it all! Sometimes I just go down and sit there among the books, breathing in the weight of them. I wish I could just press them against my skin and let the voice of each writer melt into my body."

Had it gotten hot suddenly? Fire burned in her cheeks.

"Do you know what I found there?" he asked, letting her precede him down a hall lined with thick curtains long enough to conceal oneself in. But before she could ask and he answer, a presbyter hurried up, a lean man with a cadaverous face. "I pray you, Your Honor. A delegation from the towns-folk has come. There's trouble in the city again. You know how it is with these mercenaries that Ironhead has hired. They will harass the townspeople, but with the Holy Mother so ill there's no one to mediate between them. Ironhead can't be spoken to—"

"I'll come." Hugh turned to Liath. "One of my servants will show you to the library. I'll come there once I'm free." Again, he hesitated. "But only if—well, I'll say no more. If it pleases you."

Her voice answered. "I'll wait for you there."

Soon enough she stood again at the catalog, running her fingers over the vellum, scanning the titles. *Commentary on the Dream of Cornelia* by Eustacia. Artemisia's *Dreams*. A copy of the *Annals of Autun* lay abandoned on the table next to her, a chronicle complete through the end of the reign of Arnulf the Younger and bound together with a full account of the moon's phases and movements through the zodiac over a period of one hundred and sixty-eight years.

Her hands turned the pages idly as her mind tried to concentrate on the words. Taillefer's youngest daughter, Gundara, married off to the Duc de Rossalia . . . but she kept looking toward the doors, wondering if that man walking in was Hugh, wondering if she could find Hugh in whatever hall or official chamber was set aside for such delicate negotiations as he was now conducting, an attempt to keep the peace in a troubled kingdom where conflict would only lead to the death of innocents.

Finally, she just gave in to that stifling grip that teased her mind and eddied through her body. She sat on a bench and let the weight of so many books caress her, breathing them in.

Could all those words, written by so many scribes and scholars, drift through the air and into her pores, melding with her body, becoming one and always a part of her? It is always easier just to let go, to give in.

She dozed.

In her dreams, she walks in a daze through a rose mist, trying to find the path, but she is lost, forever lost, and she has to find the way upward but someone has hold of her, she is chained at the throat with a ribbon of silk that has slid down all the way through her entire body, and she can't get away.

"Liath."

She woke suddenly, heart hammering, flinching away from his hated touch. But as she sat up, feeling the ache in her back from the hard bench and a knot in her hip where the edge of the quiver had jammed into the bone, she saw Hugh, standing an arm's length from her. The great domed chamber had gotten dim, as if the sun had set. Two servants stood behind Hugh carrying a lamp to light his way.

He smiled. "I thought I'd find you reading."

"I fell asleep." Irritation flashed, briefly felt, quickly swaddled and stilled.

"I beg your pardon. The negotiations went longer than I expected. Now I must beg your pardon again, for I'm expected at the feast. The king has a short temper, and it's best if when he's drinking there's someone close by who can, as they say, temper his outbursts. If you're hungry, you can take a meal in a private chamber."

"Nay," the voice said, "I'll come with you."

Did lust glint in his gaze? Desire, surely; he could not disguise that, although he frowned reticently enough. "If you wish for other clothing, something more suitable, I can see that it is provided."

The touch of silk pooled along her skin like the caress of a hand. Memory flashed, sharp and bitter: his fingers in her hair.

"No," she blurted out although another word rose like bile

in her throat: *Yes*. "I'll stay as I am." The quiver settled comfortably against her back as she stood to face him. These paltry things that were hers—tunic and leggings, quiver and bow, the gold torque and lapis lazuli ring. She had to cling to them, although she didn't know why. He nodded thoughtfully, intrigued by something—her paltry belongings, or her stumbling words. He wore his presbyter's robes again, a fall of pale silk, not a stark white but gently shaded with the tone of ivory, like the moon's gleam.

"You're beautiful," she said, the words just popping out. But it was true, after all. Wasn't it? Some things were true whether you wanted them to be or not.

He flushed, turning aside so that she could see only his profile. "Liath," he said, faltering, a man in the grip of strong emotion. What he wanted to say next would not come out. He was ashamed or bashful, startled or modest; impossible to tell. Finally he shook his head as if to shake it off. "The king waits. I must go." He extended a hand to her, thought better of it, and pulled it back as a fist to his body.

They went, walking side by side but an arm's length apart.

The king's feasting hall was twice the size of any she'd seen before. It was built all of stone, and in the ancient Dariyan style, or perhaps it was an ancient hall still in good enough condition to be used for state occasions. Tapestries and curtains covered the walls, making it gold and red, all ablaze, the colors of fire.

She remembered fire. None burned here. Except for the lamps, she had not seen flame at all, not a single fire or hearth. But of course it was warmer in Aosta, all year round. Perhaps they didn't need so many fires. It still seemed strange.

The king sat at the high table, up on a dais, with his best companions surrounding him and Hugh at his right hand. John Ironhead, king of Aosta, had the loudest laugh, and the bluntest voice, and the coarsest eyes, of any man there. He wore an iron crown, perhaps in mockery of his position, knowing as everyone did how he'd come by it—with the sword, not through blood right. Perhaps he wore it to remind people of his power. He had captured Queen Adelheid's treasure, and the one who held the royal treasure had enough gold to do as he wished.

"He'd have preferred to capture Queen Adelheid's other treasure," said the man Liath sat beside at table. He snickered. "But he couldn't lay his hands on her. That's why he wears the iron crown. He doesn't possess the royal crowns or seals. She got away with them."

"How can he rule here, if he possesses none of the seals of regnancy?" asked Liath. Hugh sat at her left, and this Aostan duke to her right.

The Aostan duke snorted. "He has two thousand Arethousan and Nakrian mercenaries in the city, and fifty noble children as hostages." He gestured toward a lower table where children of varying ages sat in anxious silence as they ate the food brought to them. One among them, a light-haired girl no more than thirteen, was brought forward to sit at Ironhead's left hand. The king plied her with wine, fondling her shoulder, and she had a glazed look on her face as she slid helplessly toward hysteria. She was in his power, and she knew it, and he, knowing it as well, savored it.

Liath looked away quickly, only to find Hugh watching her. He offered her wine from his cup. She shook her head numbly and turned back to her other companion.

"The Holy Mother crowned Ironhead, confirmed him as king," added the Aostan duke. "How can we go against her word?"

"Isn't the Holy Mother dying?"

"So she is, may God have mercy upon her. The illness came on suddenly. Some have whispered she's being poisoned."

"What do you think?"

He shrugged uneasily. "Why would Ironhead poison the very one who made his reign possible?"

"What about Hugh of Austra?"

He blinked. For an instant, she thought he hadn't understood her, as if she'd suddenly begun speaking Jinna.

"Presbyter Hugh? That she's survived so long is only due to the care he gives her. She rallied for a time after he became one of her intimate attendants, but in this last week she's gotten very bad."

"She's not young."

"Truly, she is not. God act as They see fit. If They choose to take the Holy Mother back into Their bosom, so be it." A haunch of beef was brought round, but she couldn't bring herself to eat. She wasn't hungry. Ironhead was getting drunker and more aggressive. He interrupted the poets singing his praises, called belligerently for more wine, and practically forced it down the throat of the poor girl beside him, who was beginning to cry. Abruptly the king leaped to his feet.

"I have a thirst no wine can slake!" he bellowed.

A hollow silence fell over the hall. Ironhead yanked the girl to her feet and dragged her out of the hall. Before anyone could react, Hugh was out of his chair and hurrying after them.

"If any person can save that poor girl, it'll be Presbyter Hugh," said the Aostan duke. "Would you care for some wine?"

"Nay, I thank you." She caught the edge of her quiver on the chair's back as she rose too quickly, but by the time she got into the broad passageway that led from the hall down toward the royal suite she saw no sign of the king at all, only Hugh, with the girl sobbing at his feet.

"Bless you, Your Honor. He meant to rape me, and I didn't—I didn't know how—it's that rumor he's heard from the north that my mother the Lady of Novomo was harboring the queen last year. I knew he would punish me to get at her. But you saved me! You're the only one brave enough to stand up to him—"

"Hush, now, child." He helped her up before calling over a servant. "See that she is taken to her chambers and left alone. Keep her out of the king's way, if you please."

"Of course, Your Honor."

"That was nobly done," said Liath as the girl was led away. Strange to hear words meant sardonically but spoken as if in praise.

"It isn't right." There was a lamp here, too, set on a tripod along the wall, a plump ceramic rooster with a flame burning from its crest. Its light gilded his hair and made his robes shimmer. "She was so young, and unwilling."

Anger burned away the chains that fettered her tongue. "And wasn't I, Hugh? Wasn't I?"

He changed color. "To my shame," he murmured hoarsely. That fast, he walked away—from her, from the hall where singing and merriment carried on, oblivious to the absence of the hated king. She hurried after him but somehow could not quite catch up, down carpeted corridors, up stairs whose banisters were carved with sinuous dragons, crossing a high bridge, out into the night air, still rosy from the sunset, that led them over into the holy precincts of the skopos' palace. At last he paused, high on a parapet overlooking the river below and the distant lights of the harbor to the west. They were alone except for a lamp swaying in a soft breeze, flame twisting and flaring as the wind teased it.

He turned on her. "Why do you follow me? Can you forgive me for what I did to you?"

It was like lashing a stubborn mule to drive the words out. "How can you think I would?"

"Then why come here? Why torment me? Although truly if that's how you wish to punish me for the harm I did to you, then you are amply justified."

"How am *I* tormenting *you?*"

"To hear your voice and see your face after so long? To stand so close and not touch you? Isn't that torment enough? Nay." He turned away suddenly to open doors she hadn't seen before. "Let me not speak of torment, who sinned so grievously and caused you so much pain."

Her voice was her own again, but her limbs still worked as though to another's will. She followed him into a simply furnished chamber, a single bed, a table covered with books, a bench, a chest, and a lamp hanging from the ceiling. The curtains softening the walls had no pattern, only a plain gold weave as richly brilliant as his hair, like an echo of the sun. He stood beside the table, not looking at her, profile limned by lamplight. Like the sun in shadow.

It was just too sudden. Words spilled out of her unbidden as her fingers brushed her own neck. "It was just that you had to have your hand on the throat of everything you wanted to possess. And I was one of those things."

Fretfully, he fingered a parchment sheet that lay at the corner of the table, running a hand up the neat lines of its text and then down again, up and then down. "You were all that mattered. From the first day I met you it was as if I had been blinded, a veil cast over my sight. I could see nothing but you." He fell silent, and at last went on. "I know your secret, I know what you are, but I will never betray you."

"What am I?"

He looked up at last, meeting her gaze, and his stare was so intense and so scalding that she wished he hadn't. Better not to see him, scarred and flawed as he was but still as beautiful as the dawn; standing this nakedly before her, his desire for her was plain to see.

"Fire," he said hoarsely. "Ai, God, Liath, go. *Go.* I desire you too much. I can't trust myself with you so close. I've tried to make a decent life here as a presbyter, doing what I can to serve God, and it will be enough."

"I'll go," she said, stumbling over the words as the chains wrapped their silken cord around her again, wanting to say, *"I'll stay."* "But you said that you have Da's book."

"The book." He lifted a hand to conceal his face. He stood so still for a moment, his emotions hidden from her, that she actually had an instant of disorientation, as though the world was spinning wildly beneath her feet and she was about to fall, or was already falling endlessly and forever down through the spheres until she would be lost in the pit and never free.

"The book." He lowered his hand to rustle the parchment. The movement drew her gaze down to the figures neatly inscribed there.

"What is that?" she asked, enticed by the orderly lines and repetitive figures. Fetters drew tighter, binding her again as she moved to stand beside him so that she didn't block the light. "That's a date."

"A date? I've been puzzling this out. I don't know what it means, but there's clearly a pattern. Do you know?"

"Yes, yes," she said with mounting excitement. "Da and I saw a clay tablet with writing like this in the ruins of Kartiako. There was a very old man there, a sage who claimed to have knowledge of the most ancient days of his tribe. Of course I can't read this writing, all sticks and angles, but he said it was a table charting the course of Somorhas. When it appears in the evening sky and when in the morning."

"And the intervals of disappearance?"

"Yes, exactly! But this is a whole page! The other was only fragments. Is there more?"

"This is the only page I have seen. I believe it was copied from a more ancient source, perhaps from one of these clay tablets you mention. Do you see, here," he pointed to a smudge, "how the scribe made a mistake and then corrected it. How does it work?"

"The ancient Babaharshans observed the stars for a thousand years. They recognized that Somorhas is both the evening star and the morning star, and that when she falls into the shadow of the sun that she vanishes for an interval, sometimes about eight days and sometimes about fifty days."

He nodded, caught up in her excitement. "But Somorhas is part of God's creation. Fate guides her movements. Isn't it every eight years that she comes again to the place she was before, relative to the position of the sun?"

"Yes, of course. Look, here. That set of markings is a date, according to the sage at Kartiako. He called it—"

A moment only it took her to shift her attention into her

city of memory. She skipped past the seven gates, the Rose of Healing, the Sword of Strength, the Cup of Boundless Waters, the Ring of Fire, the Throne of Virtue, the Scepter of Wisdom, passing beneath the Crown of Stars itself to the topmost part of the city where lay the astronomer's hall, a circular building ringed with smaller, curving walls. Here in these galleries she had set her memory pictures of the cycles of the wandering stars and the precession of the equinoxes. Here, in an alcove marked with a drifting sand dune and lit by a bright sapphire—no brighter than Hugh's eyes—to signify the sage's complete love of wisdom, she found what she was looking for.

"He called it the month of 'Ishan.' These lines signify numbers, so that would be eleven. I don't know how to read the rest, but this says that on the eleventh day of the month of Ishan, Somorhas would—well, that's the puzzle, isn't it? Her first appearance as morning star for that cycle, perhaps, or her disappearance into the sun's glare." She faltered, remembering how quickly others got bored when she got caught up in cycles and epicycles, conjunctions and precession, the endlessly intriguing wonder of the universe.

"Do you know," he said slowly, absently tracing the pattern of the markings, "there has been debate here among the college of astronomers about Ptolomaia's use of the equant point. Of course many claim that if planets move with varying speeds, then the heavens do not move in a uniform motion, as we know they must. But without the equant point, then truly we cannot account for all the movements of the planets in the heavens."

"Unless Ptolomaia is wrong, and the Earth isn't stationary."

Stunned, he stared at her while the lamp flame hissed and a breeze off the parapet rustled through the papers scattered over the table.

She went on, made rash by the dreamlike quality of their meeting, by his surprise, by a fierce recklessness overtaking her, here where she could speak freely the forbidden words known to the mathematici. "What if the heavens are at rest and it is Earth which revolves from west to east?"

He leaned down, both hands on the table, shutting his eyes as he considered. "West to east," he murmured. "That would create the same effect. Or if both the heavens and the Earth moved, one from east to west and the other from west to east—" He trailed off, too caught up in the puzzle to finish, gripped by the same passion for knowledge that had always held her in thrall.

Had she misjudged him? Had his humiliation at Anne's hands caused him to look into his heart, deep waters indeed, and transform what he found there? How could she have felt that silken touch winding through her body as a chain and fetter, when it was what had brought her here in time to see, and to aid, the change that would make Hugh over into a new person, her heart's desire?

A door thumped gently against the wall as the breeze caught it. The lamp flame flared up boldly, illuminating him. Wind kissed her face. He was so inadvertently close to her, eyes closed, expression almost innocent, if the desire for knowledge can ever be innocent. He smelled faintly of the scent of vineflower and cypress. This close, she felt the heat of his body, no less potent than the yearning in her heart. Was that her heart pounding? Was this what she had been looking for all along? Someone with the same passion, the same questioning, unquiet mind?

Was it her hand lifting to touch his chest, where his heart beat most strongly? Was it she who leaned closer, into him, and brushed his cheek with her lips?

He opened his lips in a soundless sigh. Turning to her, seeking, he kissed her even as she kissed him. In a moment they stood together, so close that like the aetherical daimones who mingle sometimes in ecstasy they seemed to melt one into the other, as if their bodies could actually interpenetrate and become one in truth, a union so complete that no earthly intimacy could rival the depth of their sharing.

"Ai, Liath." He murmured her name as a caress as the lamp blazed behind him, making him shine.

A small voice shunted away into the deepest, dustiest corner of her mind, almost too faint to hear, spoke in her heart.

I'm going to wake up and find myself in Hugh's bed.

At that instant, choking, she felt the writhing worm, an actual presence inside her. The silk ribbon, but a living one, that had insinuated itself into her body and now sank its aetherical touch deep into her flesh, mingling and melting until her arm raised of its own accord, not hers, to caress Hugh, until her body pressed itself against him, seeking his touch, until she would give herself to him of her own free will—

But it was not her.

Lies and deceit. In the sphere of Somorhas dwelt dreams and delusion.

"No, Liath," he said, as if he'd heard her thoughts, as if she'd cried out loud. "This is the truth of your heart's desire. I am with you. I am not a dream. Hate me if you must, but see that we are alike, you and I."

Wasn't it true, after all? No matter what he was now or what had gone before? Didn't she recognize in him a soul like her own, passionate and eager? Ai, Lady, had she always hated him and loved him in equal measure?

Nay, that was the worm speaking.

The daimone was now so thoroughly intermixed with her own being that it was becoming impossible to separate out her own thoughts from those it spoke within her mind, from those it uttered with her voice.

"I am not like you, Hugh," she said, each word a struggle as the daimone tried to form other words on her lips: *"I'll stay with you, I'll love you and only you."*

"If you turn away from me now, Liath, then what choice will I have but to go back to being what I was before? You are fire. You can cleanse me. Your love can purify me. Stay with me, Liath."

Fire.

She reached for that single lamp flame, flickering as the wind rose. His arms tightened around her.

She called fire.

The room exploded in flames.

Hugh was gone, torn away. She stood on a featureless plain, rose-colored mist twining around her body, the fog of lies and deceit that had ensnared her. In that mist, even into and inter-penetrating her own flesh, she saw the pale glamour of a daimone actually *inside* her, part of her body.

Fire raged at the horizon, a wall of flames that marked the gate of the Sun.

It faded as the tower chamber swam back into view, as the daimone infesting her pulled her back into the dream, into the lie.

One step she took, toward the Sun, then a second agonizing step as Hugh winced in pain and she wanted to reach to him, to smooth anguish from his brow, to show him that he truly was her heart's desire. No one else. No one else fit for her.

A third step, like walking on broken glass, and she had crossed the plain. The inferno that was the sphere of the Sun began actually to burn the clothes off her body.

Scour herself clean. She wasn't afraid of fire. She never had been. The fire cut deeper, melting away her flesh, but that was not really her flesh but rather the daimone, writhing as the sun's fire forced it to twist out of her body. It fled down along a gleaming thread, back to Earth.

"Damn." Hugh's voice was almost lost in the crack of flame as the wall of fire rose in a sheet of brilliance in front of her.

Had it all been a lie? Or had she seen truths within herself, far down in those depths, that she could not bear to acknowl-edge? Wasn't it true, after all, that beneath the surface they shared a similar passion? That she had more in common with Hugh than she had ever had with Sanglant?

The truth was too horrible to contemplate. Naked, she flung herself into the blazing furnace of the Sun.

4

NO doubt the old Dariyan Empire had fallen in large part because of the corruption that had ripened within the imperial house and burst at last in a final flowering of putrescence. Ancient images and obscene pagan carvings still fouled old corners and forgotten rooms in the skopos' palace. Not all had been chipped away and replaced by saintly figures more appropriate to a land presided over by the Daisanite church.

Corruption still insinuated its tentacles into the heart of earthly empire, whether spiritual or secular. That much was achingly apparent to Antonia as she sat at the Feast of St. Johanna the Messenger and watched King John, known as Ironhead, publicly molest the daughter of the Lady of Novomo, she who had harbored the fugitive Queen Adelheid last spring. The girl was barely into pubescence, in the first flush of development. Ironhead drank heavily and acted every bit the coarse bastard he in truth was, even fondling the girl's small breasts through her gown. That she wept silently, tears coursing down her face at this humiliation, open for all to see, did not stop him.

But Hugh did.

He called over a steward and whispered instructions into the man's ear. Soon enough, a trio of the king's whores—Ironhead had installed a dozen or more in his chambers—emerged to the sound of lute and drum. They were pretty young things, skilled in the art of lascivious dancing, something not meant to be viewed in such a public arena. Their antics would have made Antonia blush if she were not made of sterner stuff. She understood the attractions of the flesh though she had long ago strangled any such carnal desire in herself. It only got in the way.

Presbyter Hugh was no fool. He understood the weak stuff that Ironhead was made of. Once the king's attention had been caught by the obscene undulations of the dancing girls,

Hugh sent the king's hostage away and substituted another of the king's whores in her place. Ensnared in the grasp of wine and lust, Ironhead either did not notice or in any case soon ceased to care.

The feast dragged on in this manner. Where were the pious readings of the book of St. Johanna, to remind the faithful of her apostolic journey and her noble martyrdom? None stood to sing psalms or to declaim from the Holy Verses. Feast days had always been celebrated with the solemnity they deserved in Mainni, when she had been biscop in that city. But the skopos lay dying and could not control Ironhead's excesses.

In the midst of the merrymaking, Hugh rose quietly and left. Antonia made haste to follow him. He had gone outside to the shelter of the colonnade. Scattered clouds made a patchwork of the night sky. A misting rain fell.

He was not alone. By the heavy scent of lilac, she knew that the womanly form leaning against him, embracing him, was one of the king's whores.

"He'll never notice I'm gone this one night," the young woman said in a breathless voice. "I've wanted you since the first moment I saw you."

He set hands firmly on her shoulders and pushed her away. "I beg your pardon, Daughter. My heart is already given to another."

She hissed, like a cat ready to claw. "What's her name? Where is she?"

"Not walking on this Earth."

The whore began to snivel. "I hate God for stealing you. You ought to be warming women's beds, not praying on cold stone."

"Don't hate God," he said gently. "Pray for healing."

"What do I need healing for? You could heal me, if you'd come to me. Aren't I pretty? Everyone says so. All the other men desire me."

"Beauty doesn't last forever. When men no longer desire

you, you'll be cast onto the street. Which will serve you better, Daughter? Men's lust, or God's love?"

"It's all very well for you to babble piously about God's love! What other profession is open to me? My mother was a whore. There are at least five presbyters smirking like saints in the skopos' palace who might be my father, any one of them! What am I to do, a girl like me, bastard daughter of a whore, except be a whore in my turn? That's the only life I know. What respectable man would want someone like me?"

He didn't flinch under the assault of her scathing fury. "I happen to know," he said quietly, "that there is a certain respectable sergeant of the guards at the skopos' palace who has a brother who is a tailor down in the city. That brother has had cause to visit the sergeant a time or two, and he saw you in the garden more than once. I expect he even makes excuses to come visit his brother in the hopes of catching a glimpse of you. But of course to his way of thinking, what chance has a common tailor like him with little enough to offer compared to the silks and wine given you in the king's suite?"

"His kin would all know I was a whore, and hate me for it," she muttered, but the edge of anger in her voice had muted. She sounded unsure of herself, afraid to hope. "He's probably some ugly, leprous, wizened dwarf anyway, who can't get a decent wife."

"Ah, well. I happen to know he visits his brother every Ladysday and that they attend Mass together in the servants' chapel."

"You lead that Mass," she said, surprised. "Everyone knows you do. All the servants talk about it. But I know that the presbyters don't let whores into the church, the old hypocrites, poking their lemans in the nighttime and calling them nasty sinners during the day."

"When I lead Mass in the servants' chapel, no one is turned away, no matter what they have been in their past. No matter what they have done."

She knelt at his feet abruptly, bowing her head. "I pray you,

Father, forgive me. You know I'd do anything for you in return for your kindness and mercy."

"So be it, Daughter." He touched her on the head, his blessing, and she caught in a sob, jumped up, and hurried away.

It was too dark to see his face. He stood there for so long that Antonia wondered if he was on the verge of turning around and going back into the feasting hall. The bell tolled the end of Compline, and she recalled belatedly that she had other obligations. But she dared not move until he at last shook himself and walked away down the colonnade, returning to the skopos' palace. When she could no longer hear his footfalls, she followed that same path past the great hall and through the monumental court where king and skopos might meet to survey their troops in times of trouble. Her feet thudded quietly on the cobbled stone walkway. Light rain moistened her skin. A servant hurried past toward the hall, carrying a lamp and a basket, and a brace of presbyters hastened from their prayers to the promised joviality of the feast already in progress.

The whore's words stayed with her. Would these pious presbyters spend their nights in carnal pleasure, only to turn around the next day and condemn sinful humankind? Truly, God's creation had slipped to the very edge of the Abyss. It needed a firm hand to guide it back to holy ground.

The skopos' palace was a warren of chambers suitable for intrigue, or so it seemed to Antonia. Heribert might have corrected her; once, after he had spent a year in Darre studying at the palace schola, he had returned with many a boring explanation of how the palace had been built out of the remains of an old Dariyan emperor's residence, then expanded upon, partially destroyed in a fire, and rebuilt, only to be expanded again during the time of Taillefer.

But while Anne might keep secrets, she had not come to the skopos' palace to skulk about like a thief. She had already a suite of chambers suitable to a cleric of the highest rank and a bevy of servants and lesser clerics to serve her. By the time

Antonia reached the innermost chamber of Anne's suite, where the Seven Sleepers met each week to discuss their progress, the others had already all arrived and taken their places. Polished silver cups gleamed under lamplight, and after servants poured wine, they retreated soundlessly and closed the doors, leaving Anne and her four companions alone.

"You are late, Sister Venia," said the Caput Draconis, she who sat first among them. That damnable hound always lying at her feet growled.

"I beg your pardon. I lost my way again."

"So do we all at times, alas. If you will sit, Sister Venia, then we may prepare ourselves."

The hound lifted its head to watch as Antonia sat on the bench next to Brother Marcus. He acknowledged her with a quirk of his lips, nothing more. He wore the presbyter's robe and cloak easily. Except for Anne, he had made the smoothest adjustment when they had fled south from the smoking ruins of Verna. Antonia still found the city of Darre confusing, a labyrinth of ancient ruins and modern timber buildings, courtyards and alleys, pastures and paved squares, and the palace compound a maze of corridors, chambers, and servants' passages in which she often got lost even after all these months. Marcus had grown up here. To him, navigating in the skopos' palace was as natural as breathing.

"I am not sure he is the right person to ask to join us," Severus was saying. "I don't trust him."

Marcus laughed sharply. "Don't trust him because you fear he's ambitious, or because you're jealous of his influence over the Holy Mother and the college of presbyters?"

"I trust no person who uses beauty as a weapon to gain advancement," said Severus sourly. "Nor should you."

"Beauty is not a weapon," said Meriam softly from her couch, "but a gift from God. It would be a sin to shroud that which God have molded."

"Women are always fools when thrown into the company of attractive men, or so I have observed," muttered Severus.

"Even if that is true," said Antonia, amused by the tenor of their conversation and especially by Severus's indignation, "we are but six when we must be seven. Hugh of Austra is born of a noble line, he has Bernard's book, he studies sorcery, and he seems pious. Must we cast away this opportunity to make our number whole again just because you don't trust his handsome face, Brother Severus?"

He grunted irritably. "In my old monastery, we understood that vanity is a mortal sin."

Anne raised a hand for silence. "Time is short, and our need is great." Three lamps burned in this richly furnished chamber, enough to light the table and elaborately carved benches at which they sat. Tapestries softened the walls, but the lamplight barely illuminated the shadowed images of the holy martyrdoms of St. Agnes and St. Asella, youthful girls who, in the early days of the church, had chosen death over marriage to nonbelievers. "I saw last year at Werlida that Hugh had promise. That is why I let him take Bernard's book."

"*You* let him take it?" Severus sat back in outrage. He still bore scars on his face from the conflagration at Verna. Of all of them, except of course for poor dead Zoë, he had sustained the worst injuries. "After all I had done to erase that knowledge so that we alone would possess it?"

"Of course. I could have prevented him from leaving with the book, but I chose not to. Now that I see what he has made of his opportunity to gain in knowledge, I know that I was right to do as I did then. He is clever, and he seems to have tempered his obsession for Liathano, which hindered his ability to learn and wax stronger in knowledge."

Antonia thought better of mentioning that illuminating episode in St. Thecla's Chapel. Secrets, like treasure, were best hoarded until that day when they could be spent most usefully by the one who possessed them.

"The new year is almost upon us," continued Anne, "and the rains will soon cease here in Aosta. Travel will be possible again. We must consider certain errands." The gold torque, signifying her royal lineage, winked at her throat, barely visible beneath the rich wine-colored robes she wore to mark her status as a member of the holy Mother's innermost circle of counselors. It irked Antonia that Anne had simply walked into the skopos' palace early last autumn and by means unknown to Antonia had gotten herself seated at once at the Holy Mother's council table, especially since Antonia herself had been relegated to the schola as a mere cleric. But Anne's power was not to be trifled with, or challenged. Not yet, anyway. "Sister Meriam, you must continue your work with Hugh of Austra."

"So I will," agreed Meriam from her couch. "It is always a pleasure to work with a young man whose manners are elegant and whose understanding is quick rather than dead. It goes slowly because he will not let the book out of his grasp, and he is often busy with other matters in the palace. But in any case, I urge caution." She paused to catch her breath.

"Go on," said Anne after a suitable interval.

"This text Bernard bound into the middle of his book is not proving to be what I expected. If it goes on as it has begun, from what little we have translated so far, then it may prove more dangerous than any of us can know."

"Yet what we seek may still be found there. You must continue, Sister. If we cannot find the key to the Aoi crowns, through which they wove their magic, we will not be able to prevent the Lost Ones from returning."

"I will continue," said Meriam, her frail body almost hidden by shadows. The lamplight did not quite reach her. "What of the other matter? What of the promises made to my son?"

Anne frowned as if she'd forgotten what she was about to say next, but the expression passed quickly. "That must wait until we see what transpires with Ironhead. King Henry's mind is closed to me, and his Eagles shroud him from my sight. Let us see what course events take before we act. Meanwhile, another serious matter must be dealt with. Brother Lupus is missing."

"Do you suppose he is dead?" asked Severus.

"Do you hope he is?" asked Marcus with a smirk. "You've never cared for Brother Lupus."

"A common-born man with no family to recommend him? And no respect for those born of noble kin?"

"I would know if Brother Lupus were dead," said Anne, thus ending the exchange. "He is missing, and I cannot say why, nor can I find him when I seek him through fire or stone. Brother Marcus, you must seek him out. Rescue him if need be."

"Travel again! Sister Venia remains whole and hearty, and knows the northern kingdoms better than I do. My Wendish is a frail thing, easily flustered. She could go."

"Sister Venia remains under ban in the northern kingdoms and might be recognized. It will be you, Brother Marcus."

He sighed. "Very well."

Anne nodded. Her calm expression never altered. Why should it? Her wishes were never refused. "There remains the unfinished business of my mother, Lavrentia, whom I thought long since dead. One among us must go to St. Ekatarina's Convent in Capardia. Without seven to bind a daimone to our will, we haven't the power to do what needs to be done, as we did with Bernard." There it came, the look that none could disobey. "Therefore, it must be you who goes, Sister Venia."

Antonia sighed, an echo of Marcus' displeasure at having to leave the manifold comforts of the skopos' palace. She had eaten well this night at the Feast of St. Johanna the Messenger. But she knew better than to object. "What am I to do there?"

"Gain the confidence of the sisters. Enter the convent as a guest. Discover what you can. When the opportunity arises, kill my mother."

Anne did not keep them much longer. Antonia had only postponed her hunt, not given it up. Once she was sure that the others had gone to their beds, she made her way to the suite of chambers reserved for the use of the skopos.

The carpeted anteroom leading into the skopos' bedchamber muffled her footfalls, so she entered in silence and paused behind the concealing wooden screen. She scented magic at work here, a perfume like that of almonds. She always wore certain amulets to protect herself against the effects of bindings and workings, what she called common magic, as easily learned by an old wisewoman as by a noble cleric. Love spells, sleep spells, invisibility spells: these she had no fear of, and the scent of almond seemed to her like a veil, one that worked as a double-edged sword in her favor. If Hugh used common magics to conceal his intrigues, then he might just be arrogant enough to believe that no person in the skopos' palace was immune to them. Except Anne.

She peered out into the chamber. The presbyter sitting in attendance with Hugh had fallen asleep, snoring softly in a chair set against the far wall. Hugh was alone with the dying woman.

At first, Antonia thought he was actually spinning Mother Clementia's soul out of her wasted body, a pale thread of light that writhed and curled in his hands. But she had lived in Verna long enough to recognize the aetherical form of a daimone. Marcus had been right: Hugh had bound a daimone and used it to control the skopos.

She had to admire his audacity and skill. After all, he was using his power for good. So what did it matter what means he employed?

Mother Clementia sighed in her sleep. The pink color seeped out of her cheeks as Hugh wound the struggling daimone into a red ribbon. The skopos grayed, fading. Dying fast. Only the daimone had kept her alive for so long.

At last Hugh sat back, finished. The red ribbon in his hands twisted and fluttered like a live thing, and perhaps it was now that it contained a daimone. He concealed the ribbon in his sleeve and, to her surprise, slipped his precious book out from under the shelter of the skopos' featherbed. Antonia stepped back into the shelter of the angled screen as Hugh walked past her to the door, so lost in thought that he didn't even scan the shadows to make sure he hadn't been observed.

He passed out of her sight, into the anteroom. She heard low voices outside. Brother Ismundus entered to take his place in Hugh's chair as the snoring presbyter startled awake, smiling as if from sweet dreams.

Antonia slipped out unnoticed. Hugh had already left the anteroom, but she had a good idea where he might be going.

She found him deep in prayer in St. Thecla's Chapel. This time, she made sure to examine closely the thresholds of the two adjacent doors that led up into the galleries. He had gone far beyond the crude bindings of cloth and dried herbs that common folk used to protect their henhouses from the depredations of foxes or to lure an unsuspecting sweetheart into falling in love. Like every threshold in the skopos' palace, meant to glorify God by the beauty of its ornamentation, these lintels had been carved by master artisans. As befit the chapel dedicated to St. Thecla, the vivid carvings represented cups and robes, her sigils. But when Antonia reached up to brush a finger over the shape of one of those cups, she felt the sting of magic on her skin. Hugh had glossed over the bright colors with a glaze. It stank of lavender and narcissus, harbingers of sleep and inattention. He had ground them into a paste and used a coating of them to disturb the disposition of any person who might climb to the gallery and thereby observe him.

But Antonia's mind remained clear. She took the narrow steps slowly, careful to miss the eleventh step, which creaked. The gallery was empty; everyone else was asleep, or at the feast.

But she was not entirely alone. Below, illuminated by a single lamp, knelt Hugh, golden head bowed in prayer.

Maybe she was getting a little obsessed with him. She would have to be careful. In part, she missed Heribert. She had always had someone to manage before, but of course she must never make the mistake of believing Hugh to be as manageable as Heribert. Not that Heribert had proved manageable in the end—damn Prince Sanglant.

Below, Hugh whispered words too softly for her to understand. The ribbon twisted and wound around and through his
fingers in a sensuous dance, one that, briefly, reminded her of
that one dalliance, three months of carnal pleasure as luxurious
as silk—

All at once, the ribbon went slack. The daimone had
escaped him. But he did not cry out. For a long, long time he
knelt in intense concentration and with his eyes shut.

Now and again she caught scraps of words, whispers spoken
as though to an unseen accomplice. "Change does not come
easily. . . . Let me not speak of torment, who sinned so grievously. . . . Fate guides her movements."

All at once, he threw back his head. By the light of that
simple lamp she saw such a look of bliss transform his face that
she might as well have caught him in the act of lovemaking.

Ai, God, if only she knew how to bind such emotion in,
gather it all to herself. People were so weak, and so transparent. Even as cunning a man as Hugh in the end wasted his
substance in the throes of ecstasy. Yet his yearning was as rich
as cream, and she could not help but drink it down as his lips
parted and he sighed as does a man who has at last achieved his
heart's desire and the fulfillment of his most pressing physical
need.

"Ai, Liath," he murmured, like a caress. Like rapture.

Antonia licked her lips.

He jerked back, eyes snapping open. He looked surprised,
almost bewildered, but the moment passed quickly and with
a grimace he gripped the ribbon tightly and shut his eyes
again, mastering himself. The ribbon twisted weakly in his
hands. A pale thread of aetherical light stabbed down, as
though from the heavens, winding down along his arm and
weaving itself back into the substance of the ribbon. The lamp
flared hotly, and he winced in pain.

"Damn!" he swore as the ribbon came alive, contorting and
thrashing like a snake trying to escape its captor, but he had
too tight a hold on it as he murmured words of binding. For

an instant she could actually see the bound daimone writhing within the confines of the silk ribbon before he tucked it away into his sleeve.

Standing, he was shaking, shaken by his unseen encounter, too distressed to take any notice of his surroundings as he tucked his book under his arm and hurried out of the chapel as though to escape an inferno.

He had learned to conceal from others the emotion that blazed in his heart. But Antonia knew how to watch and to listen, how to find out just those secrets that would serve her best when the time came, finally, for her to act. Anne's scope, for all her power, was too narrow. Anne thought only of the coming cataclysm, not of what could be built out of its ashes.

Antonia did not intend to make that mistake, but she knew she would have to have allies, whether willing or not.

Hugh did not return to the skopos' private chambers. He wandered by a roundabout and rather complicated way that led him, in the end, out along the parapet set on the cliff's edge, the high point of the Amurrine Hill on which stood the two palaces, symbols of the endless tension between spiritual and secular rule in Darre.

Here, in the waning days of the dying year, the night air had a fresh taste to it, the scent of change. In Aosta, the rains were drawing to a close. With the turn of the year, the rainy season would give way to the long drought that marked summer and early autumn. Meanwhile, in pots set at intervals along the wide parapet walkway, lilies and violets and roses had already begun to bloom. Some hopeful soul had hung myrtle wreaths from the tripods where lamps stood, their flames marking the path for anyone who walked abroad so close to dawn.

He made his way to one corner of the walkway, leaning far out over the waist-high wooden railing as though ready to test if he could fly. Wind whipped his robes around him, bringing them to life, or perhaps they, too, were being visited by a daimone coerced down from the spheres above.

The bell rang for Vigils, but here on the wall its call seemed unimportant compared to God's glorious creation laid out before them. The clouds had blown off to reveal the heavens in all their brightness.

She paused in a pool of darkness to look down toward the river running far below at the base of the hill. From this height, the shadowy ribbon of the river was glazed a silvery gray by the moon's last light. Almost full, the moon was setting now, Somorhas' bright beacon following behind. She studied the stars, pleased to find it easier to identify the constellations. Somorhas stood at the cusp of the Healer and the Penitent, in her bright aspect as the morning star. Red Jedu shone malevolently above, caught in the Sisters, who plot mischief, but steady Aturna shone within their house as well, with the promise of wisdom brought to their scheming.

He spoke unexpectedly, still staring out into the gulf of air. "Nay, do not step out into the light. I know you come from Sister Anne. The king is coming, and it is better if he does not see you."

At once, so easily, her mastery was overset. Her heart pounded erratically, and for an instant she felt as might a hen, come face-to-face with the fox himself. Was it possible he'd known all along that she was following and observing him? She touched the amulets hanging against her breast, hidden by her cleric's robes, and breathed herself back into calm. Nay, he did not call her by name. Perhaps he had heard her, but he hadn't seen her face. He wasn't sure exactly who she was. Her scheming was still safe as long as Anne didn't suspect her.

Silent, she stayed hidden from his sight.

"Tell Sister Anne, if you please, that I have considered what she had to say. But she must understand that I am loyal to my king."

The heavy tread of agitated footsteps echoed up to her. Someone was climbing the outside stairs. She shrank farther back into the shadows. The bell began to toll again, ringing out seven strokes, the call of death. Another bell, in a distant chapel, took up the stroke, and then a third, an echo ringing through the city below, leaden and somber.

Ironhead strode onto the parapet, breathing heavily.

"Mother Clementia is dead!" Stopping in front of Hugh he set fists on hips as if he expected Hugh to take the blame. "Now what are we to do? I need a skopos who will support me! You know how the nobles all hate me."

"My lord king, it might serve you better if you did not abuse thirteen-year-old girls in the sight of your noble companions and a hundred church folk."

Ironhead spat on the plank walkway. "I'll never win their love, so why should I temper what I do?"

"It's true that a bastard should not expect love," agreed Hugh smoothly, "but he may yet earn a measure of respect."

"Will respect earn me the new skopos' support, whoever she may prove to be?"

"Do not fret, my lord king. The right person will be chosen as skopos."

"Will she truly? So you have promised me before."

"Have I not accomplished everything that I promised you in Capardia, at the convent?"

Ironhead grunted, pacing in a tight circle bound by the railing and the stairs. "You promised me I'd win the crown and that Mother Clementia would herself place the circlet on my head. So it proved."

"Then what troubles you, my lord king?"

"I've gold enough to buy another thousand mercenaries, but King Henry has gold, too. Spring is upon us. Soon the passes will open. If he marches down into Aosta, he might bribe my army with Wendish gold and then where would I be? Without the skopos' support, I can't hold on to Darre, much less the rest of Aosta."

He flung himself against the railing so hard that Antonia flinched, afraid the wood would shatter and he go tumbling down, and down, to fall and break himself on the roofs of the houses built up against the base of the cliff.

But the railing held.

"Rumor has it that Henry has married Adelheid," Ironhead growled.

The glow of the lamp softened Hugh's pensive smile as he stared out at the city below. In the distance, torches marked the harbor. "I've heard rumors that seafolk, people with the tails of fish, have been sighted beyond the harbor, out in the deep waters. Do you believe everything you hear, my lord king?"

"I would be a fool to do so, and a worse fool not to think Adelheid won't offer herself to Henry in exchange for his help. She was last seen in Novomo and is known to have marched north over the mountains with what remained of her retinue and in the company of Princess Theophanu. What if the nobles choose to rally to Adelheid's cause? What if Henry claims the king's throne of Aosta by right of marriage to its queen?"

The bells ceased ringing. In the hollow silence, Antonia heard the whispering purl of the wind through the parapet railings and the myrtle wreaths. The lamp's flame flickered, faded, and died.

"With me at your side, my lord king," said Hugh mildly, "you have nothing to fear from King Henry."

XIII
A VISION OF
TIMES LONG PAST

1

SHE *has heard of the queens of the desert in stories told around the hearth fire by night. Many creatures stalk the wild lands, where humankind dare not tread. But she never thought to see them with her own eyes.*

Yet if she dreams, then is it true sight or only desire that causes her to look upon them, who prowl the wilderness? Perhaps it is a vision of times long past, and soon she will see the queen Arrow Bright, young and perilous, riding on the back of a lion queen out onto the sands to learn the mysteries of hunting from the ones who have long since proved themselves mistresses of the art of stalking and killing.

It must be a vision, because even as she watches she sees a small human figure step out from the shelter of a huge rock with his hands outstretched in the gesture of peace. Two black dogs, made small in contrast to the towering sphinxes, growl softly at his heels.

"Alain!" Adica jerked, and a hand pressed down on her shoulder.

"Quiet," whispered Laoina.

Adica lay in such shade as a boulder afforded. Rocks dug into her shoulder and hip, but she didn't have the strength to stand. Weakly, she groped to touch the bag her head rested on and found that it was her own fur cloak, bundled up. Just beyond it, within reach of her fingers, lay her pack with her precious regalia.

Laoina gasped, sudden and sharp. The ground shuddered. The boulder's shadow slid off Adica abruptly and the sun blasted her eyes. Laoina threw herself prostrate onto the ground. Rolling onto her back, Adica looked up into the inhuman face of a woman, looming above her. With a forepaw, the lion woman had rolled aside the boulder to expose the two hiding behind it. The boulder rested in the curve of her paw like a ball ready to be rolled along the ground.

Her silvery mane streamed out as though a wind raked it. The lion woman regarded them with amber-colored eyes. The slit pupils made her look far more inhuman than the Horse people; although the centaurs had horses' bodies, they had the torsos and faces—and eyes—common to humankind. The lion woman's face had a human cast, but Adica saw nothing of human intelligence behind it.

"I pray you," said Alain's voice, from behind the sphinx, "we come in peace. We mean no trouble to your kind."

The lion woman pushed the boulder away. It tumbled, crashing and rumbling, down to the base of the slope. Beyond it, nestled in the broad hollow at the base of the slope, lay the distant stone loom. Adica did not remember how she had gotten from there to here. Heat rippled in the air. Laoina had not stirred, but now the lion woman casually placed her paw, claws still sheathed, on the Akka woman's back, and rolled her over.

Adica struggled up to her knees. "I beg you, Lady Queen." Her voice had a hoarse squeak to it, parched dry. "We seek the tribe of humankind who are led by the holy woman, Brightness-Hears-Me."

The lion woman cocked her head to one side, listening to a sound Adica could not hear, and sat back on her haunches. She lifted the paw touching Laoina and licked it thoughtfully. She had wicked-looked teeth, sharp and plentiful. After an excruciatingly long while of grooming her paws, she rose and strolled away as if she had forgotten her captives. Perhaps she just wasn't hungry.

Laoina staggered up to her feet. She said something in her own language, an oath, perhaps, before speaking to Adica. "Never I think to see a *maoisinu* so big."

"What *is* that?" exclaimed Alain, crouching beside Adica. "Ai, God, we must get you out of the sun."

With a grimace and a groan, Adica struggled to her feet, still dizzy from the backwash of the spell that had woken the dragons. "Did you measure the stones?" she asked Laoina. "Where will we find the tribe of Brightness-Hears-Me?"

Laoina had only to point to the oasis below them, rising out of the desert. "We go, quick quick."

With Alain's support and the broad back of the dog called Rage to lean on, she managed to pick her way down the hill and across the sand and pebble-strewn flat, baked hard by the merciless sun. The journey seemed to take forever, as if the oasis kept receding before them. The lion woman had vanished. Maybe she had only been an hallucination.

The smell of water hit. They staggered forward into the shade of tall trees whose fronds waved in the breeze. It was much cooler within the shelter of plants. Resting, they sipped water as they gathered their strength. The sounds of an unseen human encampment drifted to them: singing, a hammer pounding on metal, the braying of a donkey and the indignant bleating of goats.

"Look!" said Alain.

A short figure swathed head to toe in voluminous robes approached them cautiously, both hands extended with palms out and open in the gesture of peace. Painted swirls and patterns of a deep blue color marked its palms. Adica quickly opened her own hands to show that they, too, came in peace. They followed their guide along a narrow path that led between gardens of dense bushes and trees laden with clumps of a tiny, green fruit. Purple-and-white flowers as broad as hands drooped toward the ground. Rushes lined the banks of a canal so narrow they could step across it, the rushes sliding and scraping along their thighs. Sweat streamed off Adica's back. Her legs prickled from the heat.

They crossed a second canal, wide enough that Adica was grateful to wade across, glad to get her feet wet. Finally, they came to the center of the garden where lay a pool of water about as far across as she could throw a stone, lined with rocks and cut by canals radiating out like six spokes of a wheel. Rage and Sorrow waded into the water to drink. Beyond this spring, small gardens bloomed with greenery, thickly scented herbs, young shoots of einkorn, and trees laden with fruit, reddish like apples but rather more swollen and round. Vines were staked out on hummocks of earth. Beyond the gardens lay tents, more than Adica could count at one glance. There stood among these tents one greater than the others: high and broad, the tent cloth so white that she had to shade her eyes from its brilliance. All around them, the people of the tribe of Essit went about their work. Most of them were covered from head to toe in flowing robes. Only their eyes and hands could be seen. A few, adorned with copper bracelets, worked out in the sun clothed in shifts and a loose head covering; these people had brands burned into their cheeks.

The children ran about naked, shrieking and giggling, pausing only to stare and whisper at the strangers, keeping their distance. Beyond the encampment, herds of sheep and goats and donkeys made a cacophonous racket.

Their robed guide led them to the holy tent. Soft pillows awaited the travelers beneath the pleasant shade afforded by a striped awning. While they reclined at their ease, two youths brought them wine in golden cups and a basketful of moist brown nutlike fruits. Only their hands were visible, soft and young, patterned with henna. A young person played a four-stringed harp. With brown eyes, thick lashes, and a delicately formed face, the youth could have been male or female; it was impossible to tell. A ring of brass pierced the youth's nose; bracelets adorned the wrists, and a brand marred her—or his—cheek.

Under cover of the rippling melody, Alain leaned forward. "A woman watches us from inside."

"Where? I see no one at the entrance." Adica bit into the nut-brown fruit. It was sweet, not nutlike at all. Delicious.

"She watches us," repeated Alain. Rage and Sorrow padded back from the pool, muzzles dripping as they flopped down in a shady patch and set their heads on their forelegs, content to rest. "Why did you need to measure the stone to find this tribe? Surely the loom where the sorcerer works her magic is always in the same place."

"The tribe of Brightness-Hears-Me does not live in houses, as we do. They have more than one loom in their land. When they move, the Hallowed One marks the loom nearest to her camp so that our magic weaves into that loom. The stones are arranged so that a line drawn between them points to the water hole where the tribe shelters."

When they were refreshed, a robed person motioned to Adica and Laoina, inviting them across the threshold of the tent. But when Alain rose to accompany them, Adica shook her head.

"No man may enter the tent of Brightness-Hears-Me. It is the law of their tribe."

"Will you be safe?" he asked in a low voice. "I don't like to leave you alone."

"Nay, beloved, there is no danger to me here."

After a moment's hesitation he sat back down, although he did not relax into the pillows.

It was not particularly dim inside the tent because plackets of material lay open along the sides, where wall and ceiling met, admitting light. Hard-packed sand made the floor. Six stakes had been driven into the sand, poles tied to them to make two triangles, one overlapping the other. Through these triangles, in the manner of threads of starlight woven through the stone looms, six women wove an intricate cloth out of blue, purple, and crimson threads. A shape was taking form on the cloth, but Adica couldn't see, yet, what it was meant to be. These women wore no face coverings, although shawls covered their hair and their pale robes covered the rest of them, flowing loosely over their bodies. They had dark complexions and startlingly brown-black eyes. All of them had hands hennaed in the way of the attendants outside, dots and zigzag lines painted onto their skin. The melody of their murmured conversation rose and fell as though it, too, were being woven into the cloth. The youngest among them glanced up to survey Adica with bold eyes, but looked down swiftly when her neighbor pinched her on the thigh.

The next curtain was drawn aside by an unseen hand, and they ducked low to enter a second, inner chamber. An old woman directed them to a basin gloriously shaped out of copper, where they washed their hands. This chamber was furnished with two chests carved with lion women, plush carpets, and a heap of pillows embroidered with flowers and vines. The curtains hanging on each side were woven of blue, purple, and crimson threads, and they, too, depicted the lion women in stately grandeur. The old woman rang a belt of bells hanging beside the innermost curtain.

The curtain concealing the farthest chamber lifted. Adica saw briefly into a dimly lit chamber: a table and chair wrought of gold sat on thick carpets and, beyond them, a filmy veil of fine linen concealed the back of the tent. A woman shuffled through, laden with the burdens of age. She wore the same flowing robes as did the others of her tribe, but her head and face were veiled by a linen shawl. Not even her eyes were visible, only a loosening of the weave so that she might see without being seen. According to the beliefs of her people, she had looked upon the presence of her god, and the divine radiance still dwelt in her face so brightly that it would kill any other mortal to look upon her.

"I greet you, Brightness-Hears-Me," said Adica respectfully,

waiting for Laoina to translate. "Grave matters bring me to
this land, which is strange and perilous."

Brightness-Hears-Me had a bit of a stutter. She spoke laboriously, yet there remained a profound sense of weight in her
voice, as if each word had been handled beforehand by her god.
"I greet you in return, Young-One-Who-Stands-Among-Us."
She paused then, waiting in a silence broken only by the murmuring chant of the women in the adjoining chamber. The
curtains and walls muffled the sounds of the outside world. At
last, she spoke. "From where comes this man who is not born
yet?"

"From the loom," said Adica, surprised. "The Holy One
brought him off the path leading to the lands of the dead, so
that he might be my companion until the last day."

"He cannot be dead," said the holy woman, "because he is
not born yet."

"Then how can he be here, in a man's body?"

"It is a mystery. His soul is not yet meant to walk on this
Earth."

Adica wondered if Laoina had translated the holy woman's
words correctly. Yet truly, none of the other sorcerers, including Adica, had ever looked upon the naked face of their gods.
Surely that changed a person. Surely that meant she might see
things other mortals could not comprehend.

"I fear I do not understand what you are saying."

Brightness-Hears-Me paused, as if listening, maybe to her
god. "Much of life remains a mystery. Even I, who have
glimpsed God's presence, am not given to know everything
that shall come to pass. Tell me what passes in the lands
beyond."

At Adica's direction, Laoina recited the events that had led
to their arrival here.

"What must we do if Horn is dead?" Adica asked, fearing to
hear the answer.

An uncanny silence settled over them. Adica could no
longer hear the murmuring made by the weavers, no sound at

all, not even the sigh of the tent's walls billowing in and out
with the wind. Had she gone deaf? That scritch was Laoina's
feet, shifting on the carpet. A chime rang faintly.

Brightness-Hears-Me spoke in a whisper, as slowly as if she
were repeating words dictated to her from an invisible source.
"If our companion Horn is dead, then we must raise our children to be warriors. There will be fighting in every generation,
unto uncounted generations, and the fighting will never cease,
for the Cursed Ones are our enemies from the day they first
walked among us, to this day, to all the days that will come.
Once my people were their slaves. The God of our people led
us forth from slavery and we came to this wilderness. Here the
servants of God who have the bodies of lions and the wings of
angels and the faces of humankind have protected us against
the wrath of the Cursed Ones. But even so the magic of the
Cursed Ones leans against us. Every year there are fewer of the
God's servants, for the Cursed Ones hunt them for sport and
for sacrifice."

She lifted a hand. The prophecy had ended. The attendant
came forward with a cup. It vanished under the veil; the holy
woman drank, returned the cup empty. Adica could hear
again: a child's laughter, the bleating of goats, the murmuring
of the weavers, a waterfall of notes made by the harpist.

In a more normal tone, staggered only by her usual halting
speech, Brightness-Hears-Me went on. "Go to the land of the
stone giants where the phoenix flies. The one with two fingers
will guide you. You must not walk into Horn's country by the
great loom that stands outside the city built by the tribe of
Horn. You would only walk into the knives of the Cursed
Ones. Go by the secret way. You are the young one. We rely on
your strength. The rest of us must wait. If Horn is dead, then
we must hope that the one she teaches as her apprentice is
ready to take her place."

"If her apprentice survived the attack," murmured Adica.

"We must prevail, or the Cursed Ones will make slaves of
all of us."

With that, they were dismissed.

Outside, Alain had managed to relax, seduced into a doze by the heat and the ease offered by the soft pillows. Adica stopped dead in the entrance, staring. He had never looked more beautiful to her than he did at that moment as he woke and looked up at her: his expression radiant, his eyes bright, even his hair somehow glossier, as though it had been washed in egg white.

He yawned, sipping at his wine. "I had such a strange dream," he said drowsily. He had such an expressive face, open and honest without being simple. "Petals of roses falling like snow. There was a wind at my back, huffing and blowing. I thought a huge creature stood behind me, beating its wings."

She shivered, as though a spider crawled up her back, recalling what Brightness-Hears-Me had said about him. But for once, he seemed not to notice her disquiet. He lifted a handful of the moist fruit toward her, like an offering, but as she bent to take them, one of the attendants gently pressed Alain's hand aside with a stick before their hands could touch.

"We are bidden to go," said Laoina.

Startled, they discovered that a new guide had appeared, this one also swathed in black robes and hood. Their supplies of water and food had been replenished. After hoisting their gear onto their backs, they followed the same trail past the spring into the riot of vegetation. It was unbelievably hot, even in the shade. The sun stood at zenith. They could not possibly walk back across the sands to the stone loom. When they halted in the shade of the last palm tree, their guide lifted a ram's horn to his lips. He blew, although Adica heard no sound issue from the horn.

A spit of dust appeared along a distant ridge. Three of the lion women loped down the ridge and across the flat with graceful strides, wings half open. Their eyes, so uncannily inhuman in a face so like to human form, examined Adica, Alain, and the Akka woman before they sank down to the ground, legs folded under them. The guide indicated their backs.

Laoina swore in her own tongue. Adica could not move, unsure which was hotter: the breath of the sun, or her fear. Alain stepped forward cautiously. His back bowed under the weight of the sun's heat as he crossed from shadow into sun. He hopped from one foot to the other, swearing at the heat of the sand, and finally dashed to the nearest sphinx. As he clambered awkwardly onto her back, his dogs trotted forward to sniff at the hindquarters of the huge creature. She lashed her tail, once, to drive them off to a respectful distance, then kneaded her claws in the sand as she made a rumbling sound in her chest, soft and threatening.

"Come." Alain looked delighted, like a child whose innocence frees it from fear.

Adica touched Laoina's elbow. "Come," she said, for she saw that the Akka woman was frozen in terror. "You have seen the dragons rising. Surely these creatures are not more perilous than dragons!"

"Only because we war against the Cursed Ones," muttered Laoina with a resigned sigh. "This I must do as my part." She made a complicated gesture, a sign against evil spirits, and without warning ran to the second lion woman. Adica stepped out onto the stingingly hot sand. The grass bound into her foot coverings sizzled as she ran. Jumping, she got her chest and belly over the forequarters of the third lion woman, then heaved a leg over so that she sat astride as she had once ridden on the back of the Holy One. Its rumbling purr shook through its body and her legs as it rose.

Rocked from her precarious balance atop it, she grasped at its shoulders, groped for a handhold, and finally hooked her legs tightly around its wings and simply threw herself flat against its neck where she held on as well as she could.

It proved, after all, easier than she had feared to stay on. Its stride was smooth and supple, although its rough fur chafed the skin of her thighs. Her pack of regalia bounced uncomfortably on her back, striking the same spot along her spine over and over, but she dared not let go with one hand even for an instant to adjust it.

The sun's light hammered her. They came up over the hill, and she saw the stone circle below them just as a wave of dizziness swept her. The air seemed to boil and the sands to heave and shake. Sparks spit from within the loom. Without warning, arrows hissed out from the stones. Laoina shouted out in pain. Adica's sphinx threw her head back, crying out, but no sound came from her open mouth. Her hind legs bunched under her as she readied to leap, all coiled power and fierce anticipation.

But the lion woman on whom Alain rode veered away at the last moment as a second arrow flight showered out of the stones.

"Cursed Ones!" cried Laoina.

Figures with the bodies of men and the faces of animals lurked behind the stones. The glare of the sun painted their feathered cloaks bright.

Her steed lurched, and Adica barely caught a leg around a wing as she slipped, dragging herself back up. If she fell now, she would be dead. The trilling war cry of the Cursed Ones rose from the stones. A dozen of them bolted out from the shelter of the stones. The sphinxes turned tail and raced away into the desert. Adica was too busy holding on even to call a spell of distraction.

The cries of the Cursed Ones receded in the distance. Faintly, Adica heard the blatting of a ram's horn, sharp and urgent. The sound faded as the sphinxes crested a hill and descended onto a plain so flat and devoid of vegetation that it looked as though fire had scoured it clean. Her head pounded mercilessly. A wind had come blasting off the sun, and sweat streamed down her back until her thighs became slick with it. Her skin rubbed raw against the sphinx's coarse fur coat as they ran on, and on, and on, endlessly on until she shut her eyes, hoping for respite, praying for water.

The Cursed Ones had learned the secret of the looms. All of humankind was doomed. There was nothing they could do to stop the Cursed Ones from winning the war if they could walk the looms.

Waves of dizziness spun her. She had a death grip on the sphinx's fur, finding the places where it was looser along the skin. Spots danced before her eyes. The earth radiated the sun's heat up like a mirror, battering her, and her vision faded to gray before she struggled back to consciousness. How far were they going? Where did the lion women mean to take them? Would she even manage to hold on long enough to get there?

As if in response to Adica's thought, the sphinx slowed to a walk together with her companions and unfurled her wings to provide a gleaming tent through which the sun's light filtered, muted and made pale. When Adica looked at the ground, her eyes stung with the jolt of heat and light, so she shut her eyes instead and rested her head against the creature's neck. Inside the shelter of its wings, the air flowed in cool currents around her as they went on, and on, but she could endure it now. She could hold on.

If only they could rid themselves of the Cursed Ones, she could do anything.

2

ALAIN'S heart was still pounding from the unexpected attack, arrows whistling darkly out of the stone circle, the bright flash of feathered helmets. Maybe Kel was right. Maybe the Cursed Ones were simply bloodthirsty savages bent on destruction and war. He licked his lips with a parched tongue. Reflexively, he groped for the water pouch tied to his belt, but an arrow had punctured it.

The sun slid westward. In time they came to a range of steep ridges carved into the earth as though a cat ten times the size of these had clawed scratches into the ground. The sphinxes brought them to shelter in the shadow of a cliff where the afternoon sun could not reach. A spring lay hidden among the rocks. Alain let Sorrow and Rage drink, then pulled them

back before quenching his own thirst. While Alain rubbed a
salve into the hounds' paws, Adica investigated the shallow
graze along Laoina's left thigh, festering from whatever poison
the Cursed Ones dipped their arrow points in. With spring
water and a mash of lavender, Adica cleaned the wound. When
she was done, Laoina leaned back against the rock face to rest.

Alain crouched beside Adica, stroking her hair. Even when
she acted strangely, as she sometimes did, she was a joy to
watch. Like Spits-last, she was full to overflowing with vitality, such a contrast to the remembered grief that often touched
her eyes that he always wanted to make her smile. She leaned
against him as he settled back against the rock. They shared a
hank of bread, but he dozed off with it still in his hand.

When he woke, it was gone. Sorrow and Rage sat with their
big heads on their forelegs, staring at him mournfully, hoping
for more.

Beyond the shadow of the rock face, the three sphinxes sat
enigmatically in the sun, tails lashing. One had her paws
crossed. Another licked a gash on her foreleg. Their gaze, on
their charges, did not waver.

"Surely mice feel like I do now, before being swallowed,"
murmured Adica.

He laughed softly, draping his arm comfortably over her
shoulders. "They will not eat you."

Content, she settled her head against his chest and dozed off
again. He sighed, well satisfied by her weight leaning against
him, the symbol of her trust. Wasn't this what mattered most
in life? They would live many long years together, raise children, rig a better plough, one with a coulter and moldboard.
Somehow it would all work out. . . .

A cough woke him. He started awake, shivering. Sunset
gilded the ridgeline in rose and purple. The sky had not a
breath of cloud in it. The line between earth and sky seemed
as stark as though it had been drawn by a human hand wielding charcoal and paints. He was alone except for Sorrow,

sitting on watch. What had coughed? He felt the prickle of an unseen gaze, not malevolent but merely curious.

He rose gingerly. His neck ached because he had slept at an awkward angle, and his hands, knees, and calves stung horribly, red from sunburn and beginning to blister. Thirst had dried out his throat. Fortunately the hidden spring, bubbling up among the rocks, flowed boundlessly. Moss grew along the bowl of rocks that bordered the spring, and he used this as a sponge to wash his face and arms.

"Where is Rage?" he asked Sorrow. "Find Adica."

The hound rose with a massive yawn and a grunt, yipped once, and padded silently away. Alain grabbed his staff and followed him. Spires of rock loomed above them, swathed in darkness. Only the eastern ridges still caught the last of the sun.

He met Laoina coming back around the rock face. "You come, quick." Laoina pointed to the sky. "Night come. Stars come."

They collected their gear before following the tracks. The cliff face gave way to a defile, descending in stair steps. Here, the air smelled of water. Hardy plants grew in the walls, finding any purchase that they could. Some had prickly skins, harsh to the touch, and others lay low along the ground, snaking through tiny crevices.

The defile ended in a steep wall. Here an unknown tribe had erected a stone loom of peculiar design, constructed out of pillars instead of megaliths. Adica walked among the pillars, measuring their distance and angle, glancing frequently at the sky as twilight fell. The pillars had the sheen of granite but the feel of snakeskin frozen into stone. The upper portion of each column was carved into the torso of a woman, arms pressed flat along a scaly gray side. Fanciful stonework decorated the capitals, stonework ropes and vines that half-concealed the sly faces of smiling girls. It took Alain a moment to see that these wreaths of vines and ropes were actually carven snakes.

A flash of gold caught his eye. He knelt at the base of one of the pillars. Sand poured over his hand as he fished out a gold necklace constructed of small squares of gold, each one impressed with the image of a winged goddess dressed in a layered skirt, attended by two lions and flanked on either side by rosettes like those that decorated the palaces of the Cursed Ones. How had it come to be lost here?

He held the necklace up against Adica's throat. "It looks most beautiful when worn by beauty." The gold squares looked uncannily cold against her skin, as chill as the touch of death despite their grave among the warm sands.

Shuddering, she pushed his hands away. "That is not mine to wear. Old magic haunts it."

Surprised at her vehemence, he buried it back in the sand. "I take not that thing which is not ours. Where are the lion women?"

She rose, glancing up at the heavens. "We must walk the loom. Come."

Rage growled softly, standing stiffly alert at the opening of a crevasse that thrust into the rock face blocking the lowest end of the defile. A threatening scent wafted out from the crevasse. Behind them, Laoina whistled a breathy melody as sinuous as a charm. Sorrow trotted over to Rage and took up the watch.

"Quick." Laoina pointed toward the dogs with her spear. "We go, quick quick. Some thing comes."

The first stars popped into sight overhead.

"I do not know how much time has passed," said Adica, backing away to find a vantage point to get her bearings. "Do you see the moon? Hei, let the days not have passed too rapidly, I pray you, Fat One. Let it not be too late."

"What must I look for?" asked Alain, coming to stand beside her. "Teach me how to help you weave the looms."

"Two Fingers' land lies west of here. So if we would travel west, I must weave west." She studied the sky, intent and purposeful as she held her mirror poised by her chest. "The stars do not move in relation to each other. But how high or low they stand in the sky can change. See there." She pointed to a bright curve of stars, glittering in the clear desert air. "At our village, the Serpent crawls along the hilltops. Here in the desert lands it gains invisible wings that allow it to soar. There is its red eye, that bright star. Yes, that one. Step back, now. I'll bind the first thread—"

Lifting her mirror, she angled the reflective face until the image of the star caught in it. She had already forgotten him as she fell into the rising and falling chant of her spell. So quickly, she pulled away from him, as though a chasm had ruptured between them. Yet how could he help but stare as she worked her magic? She looped her weaving around the stars known as the Holy Woman's Necklace, still high in the sky and setting toward the west, and wove a gate to western lands. He had never stood so close before. He could actually hear the thrum of the threads through the soles of his feet, deep in his bones. The gate arced into being just as the hounds yelped with fear and skittered backward. Alain raised his staff as they bounded into view. Night fell.

"Go!" cried Adica, caught in the maze of her weaving.

A sibilant hiss echoed along the stone cliffs around them. Laoina needed no more urging: she bolted through the threshold.

"Go!" cried Adica when Alain hesitated. "I will follow you."

"I won't leave you!" he cried. The hounds raced through the gateway, vanishing through the archway, abandoning them— or scared off.

What on Earth was dreadful enough to make his faithful hounds run off like that?

A grinding weight scraped along rock behind him. He whirled, holding his staff ready, keeping his body between the crevasse and Adica, but all he could see was shadow. A heavy footfall shuddered the ground as one of the lion women padded past him, eerily silent.

"Alain!"

A hiss answered Adica's call. A serpentine creature emerged from the crevasse, winding sideways in the manner of a snake. Except it wasn't a snake.

It had creamy-pale skin and a torso like that of a woman with the face of a girl newly come to womanhood, fey and curiously aloof. Her hair writhed around her head as though in a whirlpool of air, or as if her hair itself were alive, a coil of hissing serpents.

"Alain!" The gate glimmered, threads snapping. The sphinx leaped forward to attack, and Alain heard Adica's fading cry. He jumped back through threads sparking and hissing

into a blinding sandstorm.

Drowning in sand, he flailed wildly. He could not breathe.

Hands grabbed him. He stumbled as they dragged him along. Bowed down by the force of the sandstorm, he tugged up a corner of his cloak to shield his face. Sand dribbled down his chin. Dry particles coated his mouth, and every time he swallowed sand scraped the moist flesh of his throat until he thought his throat was on fire.

They stumbled over rough ground for an eternity as sand battered them, scouring his exposed skin. Certainly he could see absolutely nothing. All at once he felt a massive wall looming before him. A strong grip tugged him sideways, and he fell forward down a smooth slope and cracked his knees on stone. Far away up the tunnel, wind screamed. He spit and coughed and finally vomited a little, so choked with sand that he shook helplessly. His eyes stung with sand, and sand clogged his ears. His hair shed gritty particles with each shudder.

Where was Adica? Had she escaped the storm? He struggled to his feet just as a man spoke to him in a language he did not know. He spoke again in the tongue of the White Deer people, with an accent even stranger than that of Laoina but a rather better grasp of the niceties of the language.

"Rise, stranger. Walk forward, if it pleases you. A place we have for you to bathe yourself."

Alain squinted through sand-scoured eyes. A swarthy man
with a proud face and an aquiline nose examined him. Was
that compassion quirking up his mouth? With an elegant gesture, he indicated a tunnel lit by oil burning in a ceramic
bowl. Alain glanced back the way he had come. Three robed
figures hunkered down at the entrance, armed with spears.
They stared out into the storm, a void of wind and earth and
spirits howling in the air. What they feared beyond the storm
itself he did not want to consider, not after he'd seen the face
of that snake woman.

He had never expected to see so many strange things, like
visions drawn out of the distant past. The forest around Lavas
Castle boasted a herd of aurochs and the occasional chance-met
unicorn, swiftly seen and as swiftly gone, and there were
always wolves, but the great predators that plagued
humankind in the old legends, the swamp-born guivres, the
dragons of the north, the griffins that flew in the grasslands,
did not wander the northern forests and in truth were scarcely
ever seen and commonly believed to be nothing more than stories made up to scare children.

Maybe the three men were only guarding against their enemies, the Cursed Ones. It just seemed impossible that anyone
could navigate through such a storm.

"Where is the Hallowed One?"

"She came before you, before the storm hit. Come with me."

"I must see that she is safe."

The guide's glance was honed like a weapon, cutting and
sharp. "This to me she says you will ask. She already goes to
Two Fingers. I shall show this to you, from her, to mark she is
safe." He opened a hand to display one of Adica's copper
bracelets. "The dogs also came safely to our halls. Now, we
go." He turned and walked away down the tunnel.

Ceramic bowls had been placed just far enough apart along
the tunnel that the last glow of light from one faded into the
first share of light from the next as they walked. In this way,
they never quite walked in darkness and yet only at intervals

in anything resembling brightness. The rock fastness smelled faintly of anise. Alain shed sand at every step. Probably he would never be rid of it all.

The tunnel emptied onto a large chamber fitted with tents of animal skins stretched over taut ropes. The chamber lay empty. A goldworker had been interrupted in the midst of her task: her tools lay spread out on a flat rock next to a necklace of surpassing fineness, a pectoral formed out of faience and shaped into two falcons, facing each other. Two looms sat unattended; one of the weavings, almost finished, boasted alternating stripes of gold, blue, black, and red. A leather worker had left half-cut work draped over a stool. A child's wheeled cart lay discarded on the ground; a wheel had fallen off, and the toy cart listed to one side.

His guide waited patiently while Alain stared about the chamber, but at last the man indicated the mouth of a smaller tunnel. "If it pleases you."

This second tunnel, shorter and better lit, opened into a circular chamber divided by a curtain. The guide drew the curtain aside and gestured toward a pool. He wasn't one bit shy. He watched with interest as Alain stripped, tested the waters, and found them gloriously warm. With a sigh, Alain ducked his head completely under. Sand swirled up all around him before pouring away in a current that led out under the rock.

"You are the Hallowed One's husband," said the man as he handed a coarse sponge to Alain. "Are you not afraid of her fate eating you?"

"I am not afraid. I will protect her."

The man had a complexion as dark as Liath's, and bold, expressive eyebrows, raised now in an attitude of skepticism. "Fate is already woven. When the Shaman's Headdress crowns the heavens, then the seven will weave. No thing can stop what befalls them then—" He touched a finger to his own lips as if to seal himself to silence. "That we may not speak of. The Cursed Ones hear all things."

"Nothing will befall Adica," said Alain stubbornly.

The man grunted softly but, instead of answering, rinsed out Alain's clothing in the pool.

After Alain had gotten almost every last grain of sand out of the lobes of his ears and from between his toes, he examined his body. Winter had made him lean, and the work had strengthened him. He had welts at the girdle of his hips where the sand had worked down, and his heels were red and raw. Yet the sunburn he had gotten in the desert was utterly gone, not even any trace of peeling skin, as though days or even weeks had gone by in the instant it had taken him to step through the gate.

"You are a brave man," said the guide solemnly, handing Alain his wet, wrung, and somewhat less sandy clothing.

Alain laughed. It sounded so ridiculous, said that way. "Who is brave, my friend? I want only to keep the one I love safe." He began to dress, dripping as he talked. "What are you called, among your people?"

"It is permitted to call me Hani. What is it permitted to call you?"

"I am called Alain. Do your people always live in the caves?"

"No. Here we take refuge from the attacks of the Cursed Ones."

Here was a subject Alain could understand. When had the Cursed Ones first attacked? How often did the raids come these days, and from what directions? Hani answered as well as he could.

"Do you believe the Cursed Ones walk the looms?" Alain asked.

"It may be. Or it may be they beach their ships along the strand and hide them. That way they can make us think they know how to walk the looms."

"Then you would fear both their raids and their knowledge because you do not know how much they know."

Hani gave Alain an ironic smile, peculiar to see on that proud face. "This I am thinking, but the Hallowed Ones and elders of my people do not listen to me."

As they talked, each in his halting command of their common language, they walked back to the main cavern before ducking behind a hide curtain that concealed yet another tunnel. They made so many twists and turns, passed so many branching corridors, that Alain knew he would never find his way out again without a guide.

At intervals he heard down the maze of tunnels the sound of the storm screaming outside. Sand stirred up by its passage dried out his lips. But the sound faded as the passage dipped down to a circular aperture carved into the rock. Alain stepped high over a band of rock thrust across the corridor at the same time as he ducked to avoid the low ceiling; and passed into a world bathed in red, walls painted with ocher.

Hani bent, bowed, and murmured a prayer. A stickily sweet perfume hung in the air. They came into an antechamber carved out of the rock, stairs and doors, carved niches and stepped ceilings, all painted reddish orange. It was like step-ping into a womb, the ancient home of the oldest mothers of humankind.

People waited here, sitting or kneeling in silence, shawls draped over their hair. He saw no children. Laoina knelt here, head bowed, by a second doorway, this one carved out of the stone in imitation of a lintel and frame made of timber.

She shaded her eyes with a hand as though to shield them from a bright light. When Alain paused beside her, she glanced up with a grimace of relief. "We did not lose you! Wait with me."

He still did not see Adica. Ignoring Hani's startled protest, Alain stepped over the threshold.

Inside, torches illuminated three people, two of them veiled and the third Adica. The cloud of incense choked him. Sorrow and Rage sat on either side of the threshold, waiting for him.

In silence, with a bent head, Adica waited as the veiled man chanted over a swaddled bundle held in his arms. His free arm lifted and fell, lifted and fell, in sweeping motions in time to his chant. He was missing two fingers on that hand.

A wide-mouthed white-and-red pot sat at his feet, incised with spirals whose smooth line, like that of a wild rose, was broken by nublike thorns. He bent to settle the bundle inside the pot, and in that instant, the cloth covering the bundle parted enough for Alain to see an infant's face, gray and composed in death. Two Fingers covered the mouth of the pot with a lid.

The second adult stepped forward to place the pot beside a dozen similar pots, set neatly on shelves carved out of the rock within the niche. Then both retreated to the middle of the chamber, singing their prayers.

Adica saw Alain. Her expression was soft, and sorrowful, but a smile of relief twitched her cheeks as she touched a finger to her lips. Despite her occasional strangeness, he understood the language of her body well enough: she wanted him to stay where he was, so that he wouldn't interrupt the ceremony. Nodding, he stepped back to stand by the threshold between Sorrow and Rage.

The chanted prayers ceased. Silence struck the chamber, powerful and thick as the smoke from the incense. Yet it wasn't complete silence. The wail of wind whistled at the edge of his hearing, fading in and out. He thought, for an instant, that he heard a baby crying, but the sobs blended with that faint howl of wind to become an undifferentiated sound, low and long.

Two Fingers' assistant unhooked her veil to reveal a young face marked with severe features and a furious frown. She shook a string of stone, bone, and polished wood beads, shattering the silence. Alain heard the crowd in the antechamber rise and move away.

A curtain of shimmering cloth was hung over the threshold; strands of thread worn into a metallic glitter striped the fabric, gold wings woven into a blue-dyed wool hanging, further elaborated with beads and shells. Two Fingers let his veil fall. He had a solemn face, weathered by sun and sand, and a clean-shaven chin. It was difficult to tell how old he was except for the crow's-feet at his eyes. He spoke the conventional greeting, displaying his three-fingered hand with his palm out and open. The scar showed clearly, a cleanly-healed wound that ran raggedly, as though a beast had bitten off his fingers. "Why have you come, daughter? What news brings you?"

Adica told him the story of their hasty journey. Two Fingers listened intently while Hani and Laoina translated from behind the curtain. He interrupted at intervals for clarification, woven as this tale was through the barrier of imperfectly understood translations.

"Truly," Two Fingers said when Adica had finished, "we feared the worst. Now we must post guards at every loom, because the Cursed Ones raid as they wish."

"Have they learned the secret of the looms?" asked Alain. "Or are these raiding parties sent out to make you believe that they know more than they do?"

Two Fingers grinned. When he smiled, his face was transformed; he had a dimple. "Is this the husband of Adica who speaks, or my cousin's son Hani? It may be that they send out raiding parties who roam for many moons or even seasons. So have they done in the past, to plague humankind. It may only seem to us that they travel through the looms, when perhaps they cloak themselves in other magic that we do not understand. Yet what does it matter, if they have killed Horn and broken the weaving?"

"Do not say so," retorted Adica sternly. "We have walked a long path together. We cannot let them defeat us now."

"We must know for certain," Two Fingers agreed thoughtfully.

"How can I and my companions find Horn's people without walking into a trap?"

Once Hani's voice ceased, Two Fingers considered. Alain stared at the niche, with its offerings of pots. Did each one contain a dead infant? Was the thickly burning incense covering the smell of putrefaction? The red paint, like a coating of blood, lay heaviest along the inset stone walls of the niche.

Painted figures of women with heavy thighs and pregnant bellies reminiscent of the Fat One danced up and down the walls of the niche, celebrating the innocent dead or protecting them. It was hard to know which.

"The storm may last for days. There are some among my tribe who believe that the Cursed Ones afflict us with harsh storms to break our spirit."

"What do you believe, Two Fingers? The Cursed Ones know many secret things. Can it be they can weave the weather as well?"

He lifted his mutilated hand in a gesture of surrender. "I know little enough. Storms grow worse each year, so it seems. But I am not sure even the Cursed Ones can work such powerful magic that they can raise storms in a land so far from their own."

"They have ships."

"So they do. How does a storm benefit them when they are at sea, unless they can bend each breath of wind to their will?" Again, he made that dismissive gesture, glancing at his young assistant. The woman frowned back at him. Nothing seemed able to break her concentration, or that startling frown. "It matters not, for all will be decided soon enough. The month of Adiru comes to an end. Now the sun stands still—"

"Has so much time passed?" Adica demanded harshly. "When we left our tribe, we had just welcomed spring!"

Was it already summer? Adica had told him that time passed differently when one walked the looms, but how could that happen when only a pair of days had gone by?

"So much time has passed," replied Two Fingers with a solemn nod. "The time of weaving will not wait for us. It will come whether we are ready or not."

"We must be ready." Adica wore that stubborn expression which Alain had learned to respect.

Two Fingers nodded. "If we are to succeed, one among us must reach Horn's land to see if she yet lives. I will travel there with you."

"It is hard enough risking my own self," said Adica. "You must not risk yourself as well."

"Nay, for I have Hehoyanah to follow me." He gestured toward the young woman. "She will work my part of the pattern. You cannot be replaced, Young One, since you have no apprentice. Although it is true you have a powerful spirit walking with you." He gestured toward Alain, marking him with an astute glance. His dimple peeped again as his lips quirked up, but the smile was brief. "I must make sure you arrive safely in your own land."

Adica's shoulders stiffened. She yanked at the sleeve of her bodice the way she always did when she was irritated. "So easily do the old sacrifice the young. Does your apprentice embrace her fate gladly, that you have passed onto her so unexpectedly?"

Alain began to step forward, to soothe her, but thought better of it as Two Fingers' assistant lifted a corner of her veil up to cover her face, hiding her expression. Better not to interfere. This was out of his hands.

Two Fingers gazed on Adica blandly, as if the anger boiling in her heart slipped off of him like water. Yet his voice was not easy. "Do you think the old gladly bury the young?" He gestured toward the silent pots at rest in the painted alcoves. "Do not let your own eyes cloud what you see. I am sorry for the burden the young have been forced to share with the old. But we have no choice unless we choose to let the Cursed Ones win this war and subject all humankind to slavery."

Such words made Alain nervous. Why did everyone speak so stubbornly about fate and death? Adica was so young that although it was true that all people must expect to die in time, and perhaps untimely, she ought to have many long years to live. With Alain at her side.

The wind whined distantly, like the lost and fading wails of an infant torn from his mother's breast.

"Come." This time Two Fingers' curt smile did not bring out his dimple. "We cannot wait for the storm to falter of its own. We must walk the phoenix path into Horn's land."

From a ceramic dish resting in one of the niches, he scooped up a paste of red ocher and brushed Adica's forehead with the color, marking her. After a hesitation, he did the same to Alain. He veiled himself before the curtain was drawn aside so they could leave the chamber.

In the larger chamber, six people remained. Laoina looked relieved to see them, and she fell in beside Adica at once. Two Fingers spoke to each of his tribespeople in turn, a complicated and intimate phrasing that made Laoina shake her head in bewilderment.

Hani stepped up beside Alain. "In this way, the Hallowed One says good-bye to his family."

So it was. Two Fingers was taking his leave: a hand on a brow, a low string of instructions, the touching of two foreheads, like a kiss or a meeting of minds.

Last of all, Hehoyanah clasped hands with him. She had the kind of sharp pride that makes the expression seem naked, as though all veils between the inner fire and the outer mask had been torn away. Kneeling, she bowed her head to receive a blessing from him. Then she rose and crossed to Adica. She held up both hands, palms out, and Adica pressed her own palms against hers. The other woman's hands were shorter and stubbier, but they looked strong enough to wring the neck of any young man crass enough to insult her. She, too, had missing fingers and the same kind of raggedly-healed scar.

"So do we walk together," said the young woman. "I will know you when the time comes, Adica."

"May your gods and your people bless you for what is to come, Hehoyanah."

"There is but one God," retorted Hehoyanah, "who dwells in all places and is never seen."

"Tsst!" muttered Laoina at the same time as Hani grimaced, as one might when an otherwise tolerable kinsman starts in for the tenth time about the hunt where he single-handedly killed an aurochs. "How can one know of a god who can't be seen, and has no dwelling place?"

"I pray you," said Alain, stepping forward in astonishment. Only when they all stared at him, puzzled, did he realize that he'd slipped back into Wendish. With difficulty he groped for words in the language of the White Deer people. "Know you of the God who is two made one?"

"God is only one!" Hehoyanah objected. "God is not of flesh but of spirit."

Two Fingers chopped through this discussion with a brisk gesture. "So speaks the one whose face must be veiled, for she has looked upon God's spirit, and the radiance of the Holy One still shines in her face too brightly for mortal eyes. This is not the time, Daughter, for such talk as this."

"If I do not speak, then it is as if I am worshiping the idols myself!"

"By this means am I rewarded for sending you to dwell among a foreign people! Daughter, you will obey me in this. I do as the gods command me, and as necessity makes plain. My task is to rid humankind of the Cursed Ones. If all humankind falls under the lash of the Cursed Ones, then what can your god say to us and how may your god rescue us then?"

"God rescues those who believe," Hehoyanah retorted.

"Do what you have pledged, Daughter, for I have given you my teaching in return for your obedience. If I return, and you live, then you may do as you think right, because then I will not be here to argue with you. Come."

He walked out of the chamber, down the tunnel. Adica and Laoina followed him.

Alain hung back, beckoning to Hani. "I ask you, friend, if you will tell her that I know of the God she speaks of. She is not alone in believing."

Hani looked at him strangely. "Has this god walked so far as the White Deer tribe?"

"God do not walk."

"Then how comes the god to the north? How can the god live both in the desert *and* in the frozen wasteland?"

"How comes the sun to the north? If the sun can shine everywhere, then it is easy for God's presence to shine everywhere as well."

"Huh," Hani grunted, thinking it over but not looking convinced.

Rage whined, padding after Adica. Yet Alain could not bear to go without letting Hehoyanah know that she was not alone. "Please tell her I know this God. This God is mine, too." He drew the circle at his chest, the remembered motion coming easily to his fingers.

Hehoyanah gasped out loud. She spoke impassioned words, to which Hani replied, and her face transformed for a moment into a blinding smile. She bent to touch one of Alain's feet, and with that hand touched her own heart and her own forehead, bowing as though to give him obeisance.

As common folk had once bowed before him, when he was heir to the county of Lavas.

He recoiled, stumbling up against rock. "Nay, I pray you," he said in Wendish, "do not give honor to one who deserves no honor. None of that old life is left to me. It's a sin to grasp for that which was forbidden to me, which was never mine to take."

As if in shame, she pulled her veil across her face. Hani looked as though he didn't know whether to laugh or cry, an odd expression on features as finely sculpted with pride as his were. "Hehoyanah says that by this sign may one know the God's messenger. She begs that you forgive her for not recognizing the light of God's presence in your face." Dropping his voice lower, he sidled confidingly over to Alain, looking every bit the conceited prince about to commiserate with his noble companion over the inscrutability of women. "Do you know what she speaks of, friend? She's a little crazy ever since she came back from her fosterage."

All this time with Adica he had simply drifted, like a leaf on a river, content in the small harmonies of day-to-day life. The act of living by itself contained a great deal of joy. After all, he had glimpsed the other side of living, which is dying, and living looked a lot better.

"Do not mock her," he said softly. Taking her hand, he lifted her up. Tears glittered in her eyes, shining as the light caught on them. The rest of her face was hidden by her veil. "Go with God. May you find peace."

He and Hani crossed the threshold that divided the painted halls of red from those corridors that lay pale in the smoky light of burning pools of oil. After several turnings they caught up with Two Fingers, Adica, and Laoina at a crossroads where torches and gear lay stacked neatly on the ground: a pack of foodstuffs, four waterskins, a pair of sandals, a coat of striped cloth that Two Fingers put on, and a carven stick no longer than Adica's arm.

"Come, come," said Two Fingers impatiently. Hani knelt to receive the holy man's blessing before bowing respectfully to Adica as well. He exchanged a farewell with Laoina, a brief ritual peculiar to the Walking Ones, and last turned to Alain.

"I hope I can call you 'friend.'"

"That you may, friend."

They clasped hands. Hani turned and hurried away.

"Do not fear." Two Fingers unveiled his face as he started down a passageway.

They walked in silence into the darkness. The only light Alain could distinguish was that of the shiny surface of Two Fingers' coat, the lighter stripes almost luminous. Yet it was not the cloth that glowed; it was another light, insubstantial and yet unwavering, as though the sun's rays penetrated the stone to cast a diffuse net deep into the underworld. Patches of a luminescent growth stippled the walls of the tunnel, almost as if a creature formed out of pale fire had left a trail marking its passage.

He licked moisture off his lips. Was that heat radiating off the glowing patches that dappled the walls, or were they approaching something very very hot?

The tunnel took a hard rightward turn and dipped down, sharply up again, and now heat blasted them. Two Fingers drew out from a sleeve a gold feather that gleamed so brightly each least blemish on his hands—the white scar sealing off the stumps of his missing fingers, the topography of the skin wrinkled up over his knuckles, a callus on his forefinger, the faience ring on his right middle finger—was thrown into relief.

He set the quill lightly against his lips and blew. The melody that rose from that feather was not music, or even the hiss of a human's breath across the vane, but an unearthly sound that, like the whisper of the sun's rays across a hillside at dawn, could never be caught. An answering whisper came from the halls ahead. A deafening cry resounded around them. Sorrow and Rage whimpered and hid their heads against Alain's legs.

The cry was not repeated. A great beast rustled up ahead, slowing, settling, quieting, until all was silent.

Two Fingers led them forward.

They emerged into a narrow cavern. Pillars thrust up from the floor like racks of javelins and hung down from the roof as numerous as the spears of the great host. Silver and fool's gold glistened, seams of orange and green, and long patches of crystalline froth like the trail of petrified waterfalls. The cavern glittered by the light that shone from a phoenix, lost now to sleep, roosting on its nest.

Maybe it only seemed as big as a house because of the confined space. It had the head, beak, and body of a gigantic eagle. All its feathers gleamed gold except its emerald-green tail feathers, peeping out in a half-closed fan and marked with eyes: all of them closed in sleep. It roosted on a nest built of grasses and reeds, scraps of cloth, and whitened bones, some of which appeared human. A slithering bed of eyeless snakes writhed, hissing, under its body.

They had to walk past it to get through the chamber.

Alain tugged gently on the hounds' ears, pressing his face

right up against them. "Go with Adica," he voiced, too low to be heard over the hissing snakes.

He moved cautiously forward among the stone pillars. A jumble of items lay strewn across the cavern floor: stones, broken sticks, a fragment of a plank, a spear, a singed leather helmet, a deflated leather pouch, dry and withered, and fine necklaces and wristbands gleaming with the dull fervor of gold. When he stood close enough to fend off the phoenix's first snap, should it wake, he waved the others forward. The undertone of hissing from the snakes increased, and although the phoenix's eyes stayed shut, its tail feathers fanned out slightly. A half dozen of the eyes on its tail snapped open.

Those eyes actually *moved,* watching the intruders pass behind him. Although his back was to them, he could mark each of his companions crossing by the motion of those uncanny eyes, tracking first one, then the second, then the third. The phoenix muttered in its sleep. Its tail fanned out farther until green-gold feathers brushed the roof. Two Fingers blew gently on his feather a second time. As the breath of that sound echoed through the cavern, silence descended again except for the hissing snakes.

As Alain shifted back, making ready to follow the others, gold winked, a gleam half hidden by rubbish. He stooped, and rose with a gold feather.

A dozen feather eyes popped open at once. He actually started back, so surprised was he by that sudden wakening. A snake wriggled free of the fetid nest and fell, slithering, to the floor, tongue tasting the air. Seeking *him.*

He lifted the feather to his mouth and blew. The gold shaft breathed a low moan. Half the open feather eyes hooded, drooping, falling to sleep.

But there was still that damned snake. He had lost sight of it among the rubbish. A broken cup, disturbed, rolled sideways.

Edging backward, staff held so that he could strike down,

he stepped back through the pillared columns until he ran up
against Two Fingers' steadying hand.

"Now, go we quick." Two Fingers sounded like he was
about to start laughing.

Laugh they did, once they had gotten farther down the
tunnel and found a narrow cleft half blocked by rockfall where
they could stop and sit. Alain actually laughed enough, trying
to stifle it so that it didn't echo through the rock passageway,
that he had to wipe away tears.

"You are brave," said Laoina admiringly.

"Or foolish," agreed Two Fingers. He brought out flint and
a shred of dried mushroom for tinder.

Adica said nothing. She did not need to, with the hounds on
either side of her, the ones who knew how much he loved her.
All she needed to do was smile at him. A wan light emanating
from the gold feather illuminated her face. Oddly, the way the
light shaded her face made her old burn scar stand out starkly.
She reached to touch his cheek, smoothing a finger over that
place where, as she had shown him once in her mirror, he had
a red blemish shaped like a rose.

Maybe it wasn't the rush of overpowering love he felt for her
at that moment that caused the tinder to spark and burn.
Probably it was the flint. But the torch couldn't have burned
any brighter. He leaned over and swiftly kissed Adica on the
cheek before following Two Fingers.

The smoke from the torch made the narrow passages seem
even smaller, but as they walked on, the air became moist, the
walls dripped, and the sound of running water grew louder.
Eventually they entered a long cavern filled with water except
for a narrow walk along the cave wall. This underground
stream flowed from the far end of the grotto where a fall cas-
caded out of an opening, along the cavern, and into a natural
culvert nearby them. The hounds sidled up to the water, drank
their fill, and settled down on the ledge while the others
drank. The water had a rich almost salty taste but was so cool
and refreshing that mead could not have satisfied him more.

With a sigh, Alain leaned against cold stone and surveyed the cave. It glistened with moisture. Patches of blue-green moss gave a soft glow throughout the room. Two tunnels entered on the other side of the water. The water itself was clear, but shallow, perhaps only an arm's length deep. Slimy yellows, browns, and whites encrusted the bottom, and small pale white fish, salamanders, and eels thrashed wildly when the torch was held high to view them more carefully.

"Hrm huum," hummed Two Fingers thoughtfully, considering Alain. He had evidently exhausted his entire store of the language of the White Deer people, because he spoke in his own tongue and let Laoina translate. The noise of the cataract meant they had to yell in order to be heard. "How did you come by the gold feather?"

"I saw it on the ground. I picked it up."

Rage stood suddenly and let out a single "woof" that pierced through the tumble of water. Sorrow rose groggily from a nap, but his attention quickly sharpened as he focused on the tunnel across from them. Two Fingers quenched the torch in the water.

"Hsst!" They retreated into the tunnel from which they had emerged just as two figures appeared in the other entrance, illuminated by torchlight, spear points leading their cautious advance.

The Cursed Ones.

Rage barked threateningly. Alerted, the two scouts slipped back into their cave, and their shouts calling for aid blended with the roar of the cascade.

"Come." Two Fingers spoke urgently.

"Quick quick," Laoina echoed.

An arrow shattered against stone. Laoina clawed at her eye, stumbling, as Two Fingers pulled her down the tunnel. Alain called in the dogs as a group of Cursed Ones burst out into the cavern, spears and swords in hand. The leader leaped into the water, splashing quickly across the stream, and lunged forward to thrust at Sorrow. Alain deflected the spear's thrust with his staff, countering, but he was too far away to actually hit the warrior. As the Cursed One jerked back from the blow, he slipped in the water. Sorrow pressed forward, but Alain shouted sharply, catching him across the chest with his staff.

"Back!"

Cursed Ones screamed triumph as they charged into the water, brandishing their weapons.

"Alain!" cried Adica behind him.

"Go, Adica!"

Alain held them back, striking toward their heads, knocking a spear thrust off course, as Rage retreated in Adica's wake and Sorrow took one last bite at the foot of the struggling leader who, righting himself in the slippery stream, thought he could get a last kick in for free. In the confusion, Alain retreated with Sorrow. They cut into the tunnel as another arrow thudded against stone.

"We go back to the phoenix," called Laoina, ahead of them.

"Are you hurt?" Alain kept his balance in the blackness by keeping one hand in constant contact with the wall.

"Dust in my eye, nothing more."

But it was more than dust that pursued them. Shouts and ululating cries rebounded off the walls. A light flickered behind as the Cursed Ones brought torches forward to light their pursuit. Alain saw Adica running before him and farther, almost a stone's throw on, the faint figure of Laoina. The hounds had gotten ahead and were now trying to push past Two Fingers, who was leading them through the dark. They rounded a bend, and the light faded.

Alain paused long enough to turn and shout. "Haililili!" Then he rushed onward after the rest. Every score of steps he would yell back again, hoping to give their pursuers pause, believing he meant to charge out of the dark at them. But after the third time they began to yell taunts back at him. Even with Two Fingers' knowledge of the tunnels, the Cursed Ones with their torches were gaining ground.

A glow rose ahead. Golden phosphorescence striped the walls. Two Fingers halted in that jumble of fallen rocks where they had stopped to laugh so short a time before. Here the tunnel narrowed until only one person could squeeze through at a time. After the others crowded through behind him and Alain stationed himself to guard the cleft, Two Fingers lifted the gold feather to his lips and blew.

Adica's fingers brushed Alain's back, a reassuring caress on his neck. The hounds pressed up beside her, tails thumping lightly on rock. Two Fingers lowered the feather and retreated cautiously toward the phoenix's lair, Laoina at his heels.

"Go on," Alain murmured, afraid to speak more loudly for fear of alerting the Cursed Ones, but Adica didn't move.

Torchlight lit the rock face and made sharp angles stand out in relief. A spear point probed around the cleft. With his staff held vertically, Alain shoved the point aside and, using the rocks to protect himself, twisted within the cleft, striking the leading warrior so hard in the face that he staggered backward into the others.

"Run!" Pushing Adica forcibly before him, Alain fled with her and the hounds toward the phoenix's cave. They stumbled over bones and debris in time to see Two Fingers and Laoina escaping out the far passage down which they had first come. The tail-feather eyes had woken, all of them, searching the cavern. Snakes slid from the nest to fall in among rubbish and bones. The debris on the floor shifted, rocking, tipping, tumbling as black shapes writhed through the heaps of refuse. The Cursed Ones advanced from behind, voices ringing as they called out in triumph.

Recklessly, he shoved Adica forward into the cavern. Beyond, Two Fingers lingered at the far passageway. He lifted the feather to his lips as the phoenix stirred, cracking open one golden eye.

"Let it wake!" cried Alain. He shoved Adica hard onto the ground and fell on top of her just as a spear passed through the space where he had been. Sorrow and Rage raced toward Two

Fingers, fleeing in terror as a wave of heat filled the room, the restless phoenix opening its wings.

A snake slithered over his hand, cold and smooth. It had no eyes, but its tongue flickered ceaselessly, probing his skin with a stinging touch. A second, and third and fourth, followed; he felt a dozen or more writhing over his legs and the flicking darts of their forked tongues as they investigated him. Adica whimpered softly. He had never seen her truly scared before. Yet when a snake touched the skrolin armband, it hissed, spasming wildly, and at once the blind snakes scattered, leaving them alone.

Alain scrambled up, grabbed Adica by the arm, and they dashed after the hounds just as a volley of arrows and thrown spears clattered into the cavern, accompanied by cries and shouts.

Light rose as the phoenix woke fully, screaming its fury. Two Fingers yanked Adica into the safety of the far passage, tugging her into an alcove cut into the rock. The glare of the beast's uncanny feathers made the stone walls shudder, and where Alain crouched at the mouth of the narrow alcove, sheltering the others with his body, he could pick out every least sparkling granule in the ancient walls carved so long ago from the stone. The hiss of its breath steamed on his calves. It trumpeted frustration.

An instant later, shouts of alarm echoed weirdly along the rock as the pursuing Cursed Ones, emerging into the cavern, discovered the source of the light. The phoenix trumpeted again. Cries shattered everywhere.

"Where the phoenix nests, there can be no attack," said Two Fingers cryptically, hard to hear over the panic that had broken out among their pursuers.

It was terrible to hear and worse, in a way, when the screams and noises had faded, and the light fled, as the phoenix pursued the pursuers down the tunnel.

After a while, when all they could hear was a steady hissing undertone, Two Fingers relit the torch. Alain ventured uneasily into the cavern, only to find its surface boiling like water. All the snakes had tumbled out of the nest to make a seething sea. There was no way across except to wade through them.

"Ai, mercy!" muttered Laoina, wiping her injured eye. "I think I must die now."

"They are poison," said Two Fingers. "This is very bad."

"I have an idea." Alain slipped off his armband and fastened it to his staff. "Light all the torches, one for each of you, and walk closely behind me. I'll clear a path."

So they went, he in the lead and Adica immediately behind him, then the hounds with Two Fingers right behind and Laoina—brave Laoina!—bringing up the rear. The snakes writhed away from the touch of the armband, and he shoved it among them mercilessly as he broke a path through their ranks. Slender tongues flickered, tasting the air. The hissing of the agitated snakes rose in volume to become like a flood's roar. Behind, the others thrust and thrust again with the torches, cutting swathes of fire to keep the snakes away. Smoke hazed the cavern.

The boldest of their pursuers had been caught by the phoenix's first attack. Falling, gut ripped open, he had succumbed to the snakes, dusky skin purpling everywhere and swelling most horribly from their poison. He was a difficult obstacle to cross, because he was already beginning to stink.

Not quickly enough the far tunnel opened before them. Alain shoved Adica past him, then slapped the hounds along after. Two Fingers almost swiped him with his torch as the man leaped past, Laoina at his heels, coughing as she took in a lungful of pitchy smoke. Alain backed after them, poking at the slithering mass, which had already swarmed over the corpse, hiding it.

"Watch out!" cried Laoina, behind him.

His heel hit a soft obstacle. He stumbled, tripped, and fell hard into the grotesque embrace of a mutilated corpse that half blocked the tunnel's opening.

"Hei!" cried Laoina, stepping up next to him and thrusting her torch forward.

He groped for the haft of his staff, fallen over his knees. His other hand slipped on something cool and wet as he tried to push himself up.

A snake had found shelter in the opened chest cavity of the dead man. It curled free, out of the spume and blood, just as Alain set his hand in its way, trying to get purchase on the bloody ground.

Bit.

Unspeakable pain lanced up his stricken arm.

Laoina tossed the torch to land at Alain's feet. Snakes writhed away from the flames as she jabbed with her spear, catching the snake midway down its length. With a furious oath, she flung it off the point and back into the darkness of the cavern.

Alain scrambled to his feet, grabbing his staff. They retreated hastily, brought up short at the narrow cleft, where their companions waited beside two more gruesomely-torn corpses.

"The snake has bitten him," said Laoina curtly.

Two Fingers grabbed Alain's hand at the wrist. An ugly red swelling had already begun to deform the hand. "For this I have no cure," he said mournfully.

"Let me see." Adica raised the bitten hand to her mouth, but Two Fingers grabbed her arm and yanked her away.

"Do not! In the mouth, it will kill. In the hand, maybe he can live. Quickly we must go. If the phoenix returns, then are we all dead."

"Let's go," said Alain, biting hard at his lower lip. That small pain alone allowed him to stay standing. The pain had thrust all the way up to his head. Maybe he might split in half from the agony. But Two Fingers was right. Shaking so hard he could barely get his fingers to work, he untied the armband and shoved it up his injured arm. At once, strangely, the pain eased enough that he could think again. His little finger, below the bite, was beginning to puff up. "I will live."

"Quick quick," said Laoina, taking him at his word. Behind, they heard hissing, as though the eyeless snakes had come to investigate down the tunnel, guiding themselves along their trail with flicks of their forked tongues. One of the corpses was actually blocking the cleft. Laoina shoved it out of the way.

"Follow me," said Two Fingers.

They doused two torches and by a single light retraced their original path. They found another dead Cursed One afloat in the underground pool, his arms and leg leaking blood in rivulets that flowed toward the culvert. It wasn't easy to wade across that water, its clarity polluted by bits of flesh and innards drifting free of the cavity ripped into his stomach. All the pale fish and salamanders had vanished. Faint gold streaks made the walls glow, the sign of the phoenix's passage.

The cold water eased the pain in Alain's hand, although a second finger had begun to swell.

Two Fingers followed the phoenix's trail down a tunnel that ran as straight as an arrow's flight. One torch guttered out, and he lit the second, but even so they walked on and on until Alain's feet began to hurt from the unrelenting stone. He could not bend three of his fingers, but decided it was simply better not to look at them. Adica tried to talk to him, but he shushed her, afraid she would let her fear for him delay them.

The second torch spent itself, and Two Fingers lit the third. On they went. Eventually, the rock floor gave way to grainy sand.

Alain stopped to take in a deep breath. "Salt water." The sharp scent cleared his head. His headache eased. He could not close his hand. It felt like it had swollen to twice its normal size, but when he looked at it in the dim light, it didn't look much different.

Two Fingers extinguished the torch. There remained light enough to see Two Fingers place the partially burned torch onto a stack of other torches, some fresh, some half spent, set into a niche carved into the sloping wall. They emerged then out of a narrow cave's mouth onto a strand so long that, with dusk falling, Alain could see no end to it on either side. Heavy clouds engulfed the sky, an angry horizon marked by the receding storm. The wind stung his fingers, its touch like the bite of the snake all over again. Angry red stripes lanced up his forearm, to his elbow, but where they reached the skrolin armband they simply ceased, as though cut off.

"Let me see," said Adica, more insistently now. He held out his arm. Where her fingers probed gingerly, pain flared. He looked away, unwilling to see the angry swelling turn white where she pressed on it, as if it were already dead and rotting.

Sorrow and Rage took off running down the beach, stretching their legs at last. Many tunnels studded the cliff face that backed the strand. A ship lay beached on the sand, drawn up out of tide's reach: sleek curves and pale, gleaming wood.

Seeing him stare, Adica spoke as she continued to probe. In a way, her matter-of-fact voice took his mind off the pain and off the fear of what the snake's poison might be working in him. "Only the Cursed Ones build such beautiful ships, as fair as the stars and strong enough to sail out of sight of land. In such ships, the Cursed Ones crossed the world ocean. They came from the west many generations ago, in the time of the ancient queens. Here in human lands they crafted a new empire built out of human bone and human blood."

"Ai, God, look." He choked, wincing as Adica's touch reached the painful bite.

The phoenix had gotten here before them. The ship hadn't burned, but its sails had. The planks had scorched but remained intact. Dead littered the beach like flotsam.

Not even an enemy deserved a death like this one, rent to pieces, burned, and mangled.

"I'll make a poultice," said Adica, letting go of his hand.

"Where has the phoenix gone?" asked Laoina nervously, but she headed down along the shore to collect weapons off the dead.

Was that movement, out on the sand? He hurried forward to kneel beside a body, one among two dozen, a formidable raiding party with their bronze swords and spears, and wooden shields overlaid with a sheet of bronze embossed with cunning scenes of war.

Formidable, except that they were all dead now.

The man moaned, gurgling. His crested helmet had been half torn off his head, his wolf's mask ripped clean off, but the death wound had come when claws had punctured his lungs.

"Poor suffering soul," murmured Alain, kneeling beside him. His proud face reminded Alain bitterly of Prince Sanglant: the same bronze complexion, high, broad cheek-bones, and deep-set eyes, although this man's eyes, like a deer's, were a depthless brown. Despite his wounds, he hissed a curse through bloody lips when he saw Alain looming over him, and in an odd way, Alain felt he could understand him, a dutiful soldier defiant to the last: "Although you defeat me, you'll never defeat my people, beast's child."

"Hush, now," said Alain. "I hope you find peace, Brother—"

Laoina stepped up beside him and drove her spear through the man's throat. "Sa'anit! So dies another one!" She spat on the Cursed One's face.

Alain rose. "What need to treat him cruelly when he already dies?"

"How is a quick death a cruel one? That is better than the death his kind give to their human slaves!"

"So may they do, but that doesn't mean we must become as they are! If we let them make us savages, then we have lost more than one battle. If we lose mercy, then we may as well become like the beasts of the wild." With his good hand, he gestured toward the carnage left by the phoenix. Blood stained the sand and leaked in rivulets out into the sea, soon lost among the surging waves.

Laoina stabbed her spear into the sand to clean the blood off of it. When she looked up, she met his gaze, warily respectful.

"Maybe there is truth in what you say. But they still must die."
Then she flushed, looking at his wounded arm.

"I won't die," he promised her. But he thought, suddenly
and vividly, of Lavastine and of the way Bloodheart's curse
had, so slowly, turned the count into stone. Yet when Alain
touched his swollen, hot fingers they hurt terribly, and he
could still feel bone, flesh, and skin. Even to turn his wrist
caused enough pain to make him dizzy. But he wasn't turning
to stone.

The sea hissed as waves sighed up onto the beach and slid
away again, leaving foam behind.

"Hei!" By the cliff, Two Fingers pulled a bush away to
reveal a cave's mouth.

Alain stayed on watch while the others dragged out a slender boat, deep-hulled, with clinker-built sides, a steering oar,
four oar ports on each side, and a single mast, and shoved it
down over the sand and into the water before fastening down
all their gear and looted weapons as ballast. Alain whistled,
and the hounds came galloping back, eager and fresh, to pile
in with them.

Two Fingers unwound eight heavy ropes fastened to hooks
at the stem of the ship and flung them over the side. He stationed himself at the stem. While the boat rocked on
incoming waves, he drew a bone flute out of his pouch and
began to play.

They came, first, like ripples in the water. Two creatures
reared up from the waves, their bodies glistening as foam
spilled around them. They wore faces that had a vaguely
human shape, with the sharp teeth of a predator. The skin of
their faces and their shoulders and torsos had a sheeny, slick
texture, as pale as maggots. The first dove, swiftly, and slapped
the surface of the water with a muscular tail.

Alain stared. "He's summoned the merfolk! I never
thought——" He reeled as the boat rocked under his feet. How
long had it been since he had dreamed of Stronghand?

But he was dead, wasn't he? The dead did not dream, and he

had not dreamed of Stronghand since the centaur shaman had brought him to Adica's side. In a way, staring at the sea, it was like dreaming of Stronghand all over again.

If he was already dead, then he could not die again, even from a poisoned snake bite. He laughed, grasped Adica's shoulder, and turned her so that he could kiss her on the cheek.

"Maybe the poison makes you lose your wits," muttered Laoina.

Adica's frowning apprehension was as strong as the salt smell of the sea, yet she was too practical to weep and moan. She crouched in the boat and began to rummage through her pack while, as Two Fingers played the flute, the merfolk circled in reluctantly.

A second pair arrived, and a third, and suddenly the boat lurched under Alain, and he sat down hard onto the floorboards, clutching at the side with his good hand. His staff clattered against the sternpost. He caught it just before it tumbled into the water. The hounds settled down, whining softly. Laoina spoke soft words, as though she were praying, and stared in wonder and horror as the merfolk caught the ropes in their clawed hands and, to the tune of Two Fingers' flute, pulled the boat onto the sea.

A fourth pair arrived, then a fifth and a sixth, until there were always some circling and some towing, their bodies a slick curve against the dark waters. The strand and the cliff receded until even the gleam of the crippled ship left stranded on the beach vanished from sight.

Alain's arm throbbed steadily, all the way up to the armband. His ears rang slightly, and he felt feverish, or maybe he was only shivering because of the wind and the cold sea spray.

"Drink this." Adica set the rim of a leather cup to his lips, and he swallowed obediently. Afterward, she pressed a cool mash against the swollen bite and wrapped it tightly under a bit of wool cloth.

Night fell. Alain could not see the merfolk at all, yet the salt spray stung his lips and eyes and the boat heaved and danced under him as they pressed onward. His hair, his clothing, his skin: all were sticky with salt. Adica had fallen asleep under her fur cloak.

He dozed, and woke, cold, damp, and miserable with his head pillowed on Sorrow's massive back. Two Fingers stood tall and straight by the stempost, playing. Alain knew a spell when he heard one. Should Two Fingers falter, they might well be abandoned here in the middle of the sea, left to drift and, finally, die of thirst despite the wealth of water. Alain found a waterskin but drank sparingly, even though he had gotten very thirsty.

For a long while he sat in silence, in the darkness, his hand and arm hurting too much to let him sleep, as the boat split the waters and raced onward. The merfolk made clicking sounds so muted that at first he thought it was the hounds' nails ticking on wood. But the pitch and distance of these clicks changed and shifted: in this way the merfolk communicated each to the others, punctuated by sudden wild hoots and spits of water arcing skyward.

He swam in and out of waking as he shivered, dreaming that he could understand their talk: "Turn them out of their shell and into the world so we can eat them. Nay, the queen bids us. We cannot refuse her song."

Sometimes when they changed direction, swells hit them sideways and water spilled over the side. Every time cold seawater sluiced around his feet, he bailed while the hounds whimpered. Here, out on the sea, the two hounds scarcely resembled the fearsome creatures they were on land. To the merfolk, whose element this was, the dogs would no doubt be nothing more than a tidy morsel gulped down. Nor could the human passengers expect any mercy. He didn't like to think of what would happen to one who fell over the side.

The rhythm of the waves chopping at the underside of the boat lulled him into a doze even as his blood pulsed hotly in his hand. He slept fitfully, dreaming of a great chasm opening in the heavens as the earth split beneath his feet and plunged him into an abyss with no bottom into which he fell and fell and fell. . . . He had sworn to protect her, just as he had sworn to protect Lavastine, and now he had failed.

"Alain."

He started awake, almost crying out in relief to find that it was Adica, alive and well, shaking him gently. Her face was a shadow against the sky, like a ghost, nothing more than eyes, nose, and mouth.

"I feared for you, beloved." She touched his lips, brushed her fingers lightly over his forehead, and checked his pulse at his throat.

"I am well enough." He tested his hand but still could not flex it. It felt stiff as a board and twice as large as normal. But he could bend his elbow, very slowly.

Up by the stem, Laoina crouched behind Two Fingers, staring into the sea.

"You must see." Adica's voice had an odd hitch in it.

The waters sang around them, an eerie lilt, like the sea wind streaming through a hundred whistles. Light gleamed from the watery depths. He crawled over the nets splayed over the ballast and, clinging to the side, looked out over the waters.

There was a city under the sea.

A whorl of light, like a vast shell, spread across the seabed below them. It seemed to go on and on and on in a tangle of curving walls, accretions of alabaster or palest living shell coated with phosphorus that pulsed in time to the waves above, or some respiration of the sea unknown and unknowable to him and to all creatures who live in the world of air.

A crowd of merfolk rose to the brink of sea and sky to swarm around the ship. They, too, seemed trapped by Two Finger's flute. Their dance, as they swam in tight circles and spirals, winding in and out around the ship as it streamed through the waters, seemed born as much out of resentment as enchantment. Magic binds. They were powerless against the spell he wove.

At times, a pair of merfolk streaked in, taking over the ropes; the tired pair melted away, lost as they sank into the darkness. Their clicking and singing serenaded their voyage, yet it was no restful lullaby. 'What lies beyond the Quickening? How can magic out of the thin world bind us? We could eat them if it weren't for that shell. Do they breathe in the Slow, too?'

He was so tired that his drifting mind wove those noises into intelligible language. Were the merfolk simply beasts? Stronghand had not thought so. Stronghand had negotiated with them, trading blood for blood, the currency he knew best. They had shown signs of intelligence, and here lay greater evidence before Alain's eyes: a vast city.

How was it possible to know what was truth and what was falsely seen, the outer seeming that concealed the inner heart? How could one person ever pull aside all the veils that shrouded his sight and muffled his hearing?

At last the whorled city passed away and the swarming seafolk dropped behind, diving back to their home, all but the ones who towed their craft. At intervals a new pair surfaced abruptly to take the turn of ones exhausted. In this manner, as night passed, they went on, and at last Alain slept.

3

DAWN bled light over the waters and, as the sun rose, Adica saw birds, the harbinger of land. Driftwood bobbed thoughtfully along the swells. Whips of kelp slithered along the hull before being left behind. A trio of porpoises surfaced, blowing, and vanished.

Adica turned away from this appealing vista to examine Alain's hand and arm. Although the skin was still swollen to a bitter, nasty red, it looked no worse than it had yesterday. Surely, if it meant to kill him, he would be suffering more by now.

"There!" cried Laoina.

White flashed along the horizon. Was it land?

"It is a ship," said Alain.

"They will kill us if they catch us." Laoina hooked her elbow around the mast. She shinnied up the bar, trying to get a better look, and swore vigorously. "It is ship of the Cursed Ones."

Two Fingers did not falter, although he looked exhausted. The merfolk swam on, plunging through the waves with the ropes taut behind them. The ship creaked and moaned as it hit choppier waters.

Adica fumbled in her pouch, her hands cold and stiff and sticky with salt. She blew on her fingers to warm them before struggling to open the strings of the pouch, now swollen with brine. Inside, she found her tiny bundle of precious Queen's Broom and a braid of dried thistle. She twined the Queen's Broom into her bodice so that it wouldn't fall, and with some effort struck flame, with her flint, and set the braid of thistle alight.

As it burned, she sang a spell:

> "Flee now, thistle,
> The lesser from the greater,
> The greater from the lesser.
> Let there be no meeting
> And no bloodshed."

Fighting the rocking ship, she lurched toward the stern. The ship plunged down a high swell and she fell hard against the sternpost. Alain caught her with his good hand before she fell overboard. Hanging there, she watched the distant ship heave to and change direction. Had they spotted them?

Quickly, she fastened the Queen's Broom to the sternpost and, with the sting of the burning thistle still in her nostrils, sang the spell again.

As they watched, it became apparent that the other ship had

not seen them. It came no closer and in time vanished over the horizon.

Shoreline rose in the distance, more green than brown. They hit the first line of surf just as the ropes went slack and the merfolk rolled away, letting the swells carry them toward shore. The sea creatures lolled in the waves, watching. One bold merchild swam so close that Adica saw the tiny mouths snapping at the ends of its hair, like eels. Beady eyes studied the ship with greedy anticipation just before the merchild dove under the boat. Its back jostled the hull, rocking them enough that Two Fingers had to grab at the stempost to keep from being thrown over the side. Abruptly, the merfolk swarmed menacingly around the boat, only to retreat as the waves dissolved into breakers.

With the breaking waves throwing spray over them, Alain made to jump out of the ship and guide them in, but Two Fingers grabbed his good arm.

"Stay!" Laoina was quick to translate. "Beware the water. The merfolk have sharp teeth and do not wish us any kindness."

"True enough."

The merfolk stayed beyond the breakers, but one coursed in, in their wake, rolled, and spun away again, letting the outgoing waves drag it off the shore. When the ship finally scraped bottom, Alain leaped off, followed by the rest, and they dragged the boat up onto the shore, out of reach of the tide. The dogs yelped and bounded around, chasing their own tails, barking and racing.

Two Fingers waded out to his knees in the waves, facing the sea. The waters hissed and ebbed around his legs. He raised both hands. "Thank you, sisters and brothers. You, also, have done your share, if unwillingly. I return to you this bone that once belonged to your queen."

He flung the bone flute high and long. It disappeared into the waters. A swarm of bodies churned the sea where it had fallen. As suddenly, all trace of the merfolk vanished. The sea sighed in along the beach, and the morning sun drenched the sand with gold. The only sound was the water and the bubbling song of a curlew.

Far out, movement flickered. A single gray tail flicked into sight, slapped down. Then, nothing. The merfolk had gone.

"So." Laoina turned to take in the view. The beach itself, more pebbles than sand, stretched eastward out of sight, bounded on the west by a low headland evergreen with scrub and trees grown distorted under the constant pressure of wind. Hills rose up behind them, pockmarked with shallow caves. "Let's find shelter and something fresh to eat."

Two Fingers waded back to shore. They dragged the boat up the beach and sheltered it in a cave, blocking the entrance with driftwood, and stowing a cache of weapons, too many for them to carry. A trail led past shellfish beds, populated by a flock of annoyed oyster catchers, who protested, kleeping, as the four humans raided the rich tidal pools. Out of the wind, they found a hollow that showed signs of previous habitation: a fire pit, a lean-to woven out of branches, a pile of discarded flint shavings and broken tools. Shell mounds rose at intervals along the path. After collecting driftwood, Adica struck a fire.

They rested here, rinsing the salt out of their clothing and hair in a nearby stream.

Adica pulled Alain aside into the shelter of a copse of low trees. She was greedy for him. It was a curse to want someone so badly that you would make demands on him even when he was injured, but his sweetness was a healing nectar. He kissed her eagerly—he always did, like someone who has been denied water for too long. It was a little awkward, with him favoring his one arm, but wasn't it true that lovemaking was exactly the thing to take one's mind off pain and anxiety? So it had proved for her.

She dozed a little, after. Walking the looms made her so tired. Fighting the constant urge to worry and be afraid and angry at fate made her so tired. Live now, each moment, each kiss.

She woke to Laoina's call. The dogs swarmed over them, licking Alain's face, sniffing at his swollen hand. He laughed and shoved them away. For the first time, he could close his bitten hand halfway, and that made him kiss her so passionately that finally Laoina had to come and, with a laugh and a gentle prod of her spear, remind them that it was time to move on.

Their clothes had dried, stretched along a fallen log to catch the sunlight. It was a hot day, quickly felt as they walked.

They hiked a trail obviously used for part of the year, grown over but distinct, a pleasant path with heights and falls. The landscape of oak wood and pine opened frequently into bright clearings. Ivy twined up the oaks and the shrub layer grew in some places as tall as she was. The dogs often ran off to lose themselves in the leaves. She would hear them barking and rattling branches, never losing track of Alain but often out of his sight. Madder grew across the path, and butcher's broom spread in dense shrubs. It was very different than the forest she was most familiar with.

That night they sheltered in another campsite, made pleasant by the addition of several lean-tos, branches bowed and covered with thatch to provide shelter. The clouds had blown off, and the night was unusually warm and balmy, not one for hiding in a shelter.

"This is a winter camp," explained Two Fingers as he and Adica made note of the position of the stars. The Hare leaped higher here in the south.

"Look at the Sisters and the Bull," she said, as Laoina translated. "Can it be true that summer is here? We left my village at the spring equinox."

Yet what could she do? That was the curse of the looms, that they ate one's life like a hungry wolf eating you up in bites. All she could do was live in the day given her. It would have to be enough.

In the morning Laoina skinned and roasted three rabbits that had been trapped overnight in snares while Adica spread

a poultice of bramble leaves and comfrey on Alain's hand to
draw out the swelling. When they had done, they set the
campsite in order, buried their leavings, and set out. Laoina
hung the scraped rabbit skins over her back so that she seemed
to be wearing withered wings as she walked. She knew these
lands well enough to comment on familiar landmarks. She
had sojourned here for many seasons when she had come to
learn the language of Horn's people, and she knew the names
and uses of many of the plants, and recognized birdsong. Not
even Two Fingers had her knowledge of the land. He had, so
he said, lived with Horn's people when he was a boy, to study
with her—Horn had been a woman already when he was a
boy—but he had been so taken up with the arts of the ancient
ones and the caverns in which the secrets of her ancestors lay
concealed that he had often gone for days without seeing the
light of the sun.

"To the place of caves I will take you now, to see if there is
truth to the words of the Walking One from whom you heard
this grievous news."

The path grew steeper, clambering up goatlike along the
side of a ravine, and brought them to a plateau where oak
wood gave way to brush. Three goats fled into the forest at the
approach of the dogs. Two Fingers moved forward cautiously
into range of a watch post, somewhat the worse for weather-
ing: its plank roof had fallen in. A cistern lay beside it. He
sipped at its waters, declared them good, and they refilled
their waterskins while Alain clambered up to the topmost
part of the wall, finding that he could, with care, use his
injured hand to grip. When he found a safe vantage place and
beckoned, they climbed up beside him.

Stumps of trees littered the hillside, giving way downslope
to an extensive grove of olive trees and, farther down, irri-
gated fields woven together with an elaborate pattern of
canals. The town itself lay on a rise. Massively fortified with
earth walls and a wooden palisade, it looked impregnable to
Adica's eyes, yet the figures that walked its ramparts wore

the crested helmets and animal masks that marked the soldiers of the Cursed Ones. Some of the houses in the village lay in ruins, burned or torn down, and a few human figures labored at the tannery and in the fields, stooped with misery and despair. Fresh scars marked the earth just outside the rampart. Adica shuddered: she knew that the Cursed Ones had a habit of throwing the dead bodies of their slain enemies in pits, like offal, thus condemning their souls to haunt the living for eternity since the souls of the dead could not pass on to the Other Side without the proper ceremonies and preparation. She caught sight of a flock of hummocks, like sheep, to the north. There, almost out of sight, lay the tombs common to the tribe. They, at least, did not look disturbed. But in their midst she saw the uprights of a stone loom, and tiny figures standing guard. The Cursed Ones held the path in and out of Horn's country.

"Horn and her people will have taken refuge in the caves of her ancestors." Two Fingers made no other comment on the devastation.

They negotiated the broken walls of the watch post and fell back to the safety of the oak wood. Both Two Fingers and Laoina knew this trail well, although it was cunningly hidden and disguised by a series of dead ends, deadfalls, switchbacks, and false turnings. They came finally to a limestone outcropping where a cave mouth gaped, but Two Fingers led them past this inviting opening and down over the rocky slope, until with his spear he swept aside the heavily weighted branches of a flowering clematis. A small opening cleft the hillside, barely large enough for an adult. Two Fingers got down on hands and knees and clambered in without hesitation. Laoina waited, indicating that the others should go first. After commanding the dogs to wait, Alain followed the old man into the hill, more confident now that he had regained some feeling in his hand.

Adica crawled after them. The rock closed over her head, and, very quickly, darkness blinded her. It was slow going because of her hesitancy, but she heard the movements of the two men ahead of her and Laoina behind and in general the going was fairly smooth. The tunnel forked to the right, and suddenly she heard whistling and moaning: narrow shafts thrust skyward, a pipe for the wind. The tunnel dipped, hit an incline, and at the base opened out. By now it was pitch-black. She groped, found Alain's body, and held on to him as Laoina came up behind her. Night had never bothered her, nor her visits into the tomb of the ancient queens under the tumulus, but this place, narrow and clammy, had a presence that weighed uncomfortably, as though the earth itself had consciousness.

"Come," said Two Fingers, as Laoina translated. "Hold one onto the next, and follow me. There is a trap we must work around."

"You don't think they've laid in others since the attack?" asked Laoina.

"It may be. But I have certain charms upon me that will warn me."

So it proved. Three times he stopped them. Once, she heard a hissed conversation, words exchanged, and they were allowed to pass through a bottleneck so narrow that she had to squeeze sideways to get through. A hand brushed her head, checking for the telltale topknot worn by the Cursed Ones, and let her by without further molesting her. It was a good place for an ambush. She was blind as a mole; she could not even see her own hands in front of her face. How the others moved with any sense of confidence she couldn't imagine, and yet wasn't all their work as the Hallowed Ones, learning the secrets of the great weaving, itself like groping forward in darkness?

None among humankind knew the extent of the Cursed Ones' magic. They could call fire from stone and earth from water; they could cause wind to arise from flame and water to leach out of the air. They knew the power of transformation, and they could coax elementals from their hiding places among the ordinary places of the Earth. For this power they paid a price, and they paid it not just with their own blood but with the blood of their enemies.

So humankind had perforce learned other magic, those manipulable by the hands: smithing and pottery; plaiting and weaving; words and melody and dance. In such forms, human magic flourished, and in this way the ancient mothers and fathers had observed the turning wheel of the heavens and the way in which the shuttles, known as the wandering stars, moved an invisible weft through those stars which never changed position in reference to each other. Adica had listened at the knee of her teacher for years and been initiated into the greater mysteries, and into the secrets of the great working: That the stars in the heavens above were woven as though in a vast loom, and the power of those threads could be drawn down to Earth and woven into power made manifest here, on Earth.

All this had gone into the building of the stone looms that now waited in readiness across the land, set such great distances apart that she knew if she tried to travel between them on foot she could probably never reach them all in her own lifetime. But each loom, when woven with the living threads of the stars, made a gateway that linked it to all of the other looms, a gateway that might lead east and south on one night, depending on the configuration of the stars, and north and west another.

Yet the Holy One said there was a greater hand that worked the loom of the heavens, one that made changes unseeable by human eyes, since the span of any individual human life on earth was brief. This was the greatest mystery of all.

Out of the darkness bloomed light, stunningly bright, although it was only a small torch of bundled reeds, dried and coated with pitch. Two Fingers held it aloft as they negotiated a narrow plank bridge set across a chasm. By its light Adica saw ancient forms painted on the walls: the imprint of hands, outlined in red, heavyset horses speckled by black dots, four-legged beasts shaggy with long hair that drooped down their flanks, a horn marked with thirteen stripes.

She smelled other humans before she heard them. Two Fingers doused the torch, and in darkness she followed Two Fingers and Alain through another narrow passage, had to actually shimmy forward on her stomach for a short stretch, pushing her staff before her and with her pack hooked around her ankle to drag it after.

This hole opened out suddenly. She felt the presence of others—not all of them, perhaps, still among the living. She felt the touch of ancient ghosts and guardians and heard the whispering of people yet alive. A torch flared into life, but even before Adica could register the figures huddled on the floor of the cavern, she was hurled into a vision:

A herd of cattlelike beasts, horned and shaggy, thunders past. Birds explode up from their grassy hideaways, flooding the sky, and in the distance a huge beast with an impossibly long, sinuous nose and horns thrusting out on either side of its great mouth lumbers past, leading more of its kind toward an unknown destination. She sees people walking along the edge of a pine forest. They look very like the people she knows, but they are clad in skins and they carry tools of stone and bone. They have no metal and no pots she can see. Elaborately woven baskets and beads of ivory, shell, or stone adorn their clothing. Deer swarm by, a powerful herd coursing across the landscape

and she stood once again in the cavern, in the middle world, staring in amazement at the paintings that covered the ceiling of the cavern.

She stood alone: Alain had already followed Two Fingers to the center of the crowd where an outcropping of rock metamorphosed into two shaggy beasts, one carved higher up on the rock. She stepped carefully along the shadowed ground in their trail, examining the people who waited around her.

Was this all that was left of Horn's tribe? There were not more than twenty, half of them children. Many had wounds, and some were unable even to sit. At the center of this pathetic group rested a pallet woven out of sticks. On it lay a figure so heavily draped in copper ornament that Adica could barely make out that she had hair and features beneath a headdress of

beaten copper, a broad pectoral, armbands, bracelets and a
wide waistband worked into the shape of two axheads crossing.
Fine-boned hands rested on the pectoral, curved around a
small, gold cup. As Adica moved closer, she smelled the powerful scent of a potion sharp with aniseed. Red ocher smeared
closed eyelids, and a pattern of crescent moons marked the old
woman's face.

Horn had been named for the shape of her disfigured face.
To look at her from one side was to see a woman of advanced
years, wrinkled but keen. To look at her from the other side
was to see a face all slack and drooping, lifeless, and a
hideously vacant eye that, Adica supposed, saw such sights as
mortal vision could not comprehend.

She knelt beside the old woman as a girl moved aside to
make room for her. "Is she alive?" she asked, then saw the
feather laid across the old woman's lips stir, brushed by the respiration of the spirit still housed within that frail body.

"Badly hurt," said Laoina, translating Two Finger's words.
He turned away to speak to the girl who, despite her youth,
seemed to be Horn's apprentice. Dressed in a woven blouse
that fell as far as her knees, she, too, wore the copper ornaments common to those who had won a Hallowed One's
renown. Her hair was braided with pale shells and beads
carved out of bone, and she wore a pectoral so heavy that her
shoulders bowed under the weight of it—or maybe that was
only the weight of the burden that would come to rest on her
should Horn die and not be able to take her part in the great
weaving.

The girl would have to take Horn's place.

Alain had been wandering around at the edge of the torchlight, staring at the paintings. When Adica looked for him,
she saw him tentatively reach up to place his uninjured hand
over the broad palm—a grown man's palm—that had been
outlined in red countless generations ago.

A faint grunt sounded beside her. The feather wafted up,
blown by a puff of air, and Horn's eyes snapped open. For an

instant, Adica had the wild idea that the old woman was staring directly at Alain with her vacant eye. Abruptly, her left hand let go of the gold cup balanced on her chest and, trembling, grasped Adica's wrist. Her other hand, withered and limp, rolled away from the cup which, overset, spilled its aromatic brew down over her right side. If the hot liquid burned her, she seemed not to notice.

She spoke in her own language. Laoina was quick to translate as Two Fingers hurried over to crouch on Horn's other side. "Go by the silent road." Only half of her mouth truly moved when she spoke, giving her words a lisp, but Laoina had clearly spent many seasons listening by the side of the old woman and had no trouble interpreting the slurred sounds.

Two Fingers grasped her limp right hand and drew it back up to her chest. He set the fallen cup upright on the cavern floor, wiped its rim with a forefinger, and touched that moist finger tenderly to the old woman's lips.

"You are ill, cousin," he said as Laoina murmured a translation to Adica. "You are not strong enough to weave the loom."

Horn licked her lips as well as she could, tasting the liquid. "I am sorely hurt. I will not live long. But my apprentice died last year and this young one——" she indicated the girl with a movement of her good eye, "——knows too little."

"I will remain," said Two Fingers. "My niece can take my place in my own land."

"So be it," whispered Horn. She looked at Adica. "How will you weave at the loom while the Cursed Ones control our lands?"

"Adica must go on to Shu-Sha——" Two Fingers began, but Horn cut him off.

"Nay. We cannot risk her in that land." She coughed, as if so many words were a great trial to her, taxing what little strength she had. Liquid bubbled in her lungs, a deadly sound. After a pause during which all of them waited patiently, anxiously, Horn went on. "She will walk the silent road with this Walking One, daughter-of-my-heart Laoina. The Bent People will take her by their roads back to Queens' Grave. Laoina must go back to her home and bring to me her strongest warriors. We have too few adults left to attack the Cursed Ones ourselves. We must have a force strong enough to draw them off on the evening of the great working, so that Two Fingers can reach the loom and weave his portion. Only then will we be safe."

Horn coughed again, shaken with it, weakening perceptibly.

Alain ghosted in beside her and settled down like a hound come to rest beside its mistress. He set his good hand on Adica's shoulder and regarded the old woman with a compassionate gaze, neither too sorrowful nor too cool. "May you find peace, honored one," he said.

At the sound of his voice, Horn turned her head so that the slack side faced them full on. She seemed, oddly, to be staring at Alain again with her vacant eye, as though it was the only eye that could focus on him properly. Her labored breathing made an erratic accompaniment to the other sounds in the cavern: whispering children, a light and steady snoring from off in the darkness, the insubstantial footfalls of unseen dancers and pipers caught forever in their ancient ceremony, painted upon the rock ceiling. A faint horn call seemed to resound, but surely it was only a trick of the ears or the echo of a child's sigh.

Horn spoke in an altered tone, too resonant to come from that diseased throat. "You do not belong here, Wanderer," she said in the language of the Deer tribes. "Go back to your own place. Your father weeps for you."

Alain's expression altered, pain and bewilderment replacing sincere sympathy. "I have no home. I have no father. No mother. No kin. I came alone, with nothing, from the place I once lived. I will not go back." He stared fiercely at Horn's slack eye before turning to Adica. The light in his expression made her heart flood with joy. "Here, I have a home. I will not leave her." He clasped one of Adica's hands between his own. Even the grasp of his injured hand felt strong, now.

"Many are they who wait for you in that place," repeated Horn stubbornly. "I see your crown, brighter than stars. You have wandered off the path meant for you, and you must return. This is your fate, Wanderer."

Throughout this labored speech, Alain's hand tightened on Adica's until her fingers hurt, squeezed between his. Horn's words cut deeply, slicing open the scar that had sealed over her fear of dying. Was Alain to be taken away from her? Truly, she was no longer sure she could walk with the others, knowing where their path led, if she didn't have him beside her. She had come to depend on his companionship; it made her last days bearable.

Alain did not quail. "I will not leave her."

Adica recognized then, in his expression, the terrible pain he had suffered before. It was not only she who had found shelter in their bond. He had as well.

Horn snorted, made a whistling, throaty sound as a palsy shook her. Her apprentice rushed forward and bathed her face with what was left of the spilled potion, and this effusion calmed the old woman. When her body ceased its trembling, she lay slack, her good eye closed and the vacant eye staring unseeingly toward the ceiling as at a particular group of brightly-painted pipers dancing around an elk, coaxing it into their snares.

No one knew what to do at first. Cider was brought, along with rather fermented, withered, tasteless greens, and barley cakes that had been fried in lard and left to congeal in the recesses of the cave. Adica ate what was given her. She knew that, driven from their village and their stores, they had little enough to offer a guest.

Abruptly, Horn woke and, in her normal slurred whisper, began speaking where she had left off before Alain had knelt beside her. "Laoina and the Akka warriors she brings will shelter here, with my people, until the time comes for the great working. Afterward they will be free to return to their home. Those among my people who live will build a new village so that we need never again dwell in a place poisoned by the Cursed Ones. Those who die will catch up to me on the path that leads to the Other Side. Girl, take them to the Bent People. I still hold the power of fire over them, and they owe me one last boon." She fumbled with her good hand at an armband, her fingers slipping as she tried to tug it off. "Return this to the Bent People. They will do my will in this matter." Horn took in a breath, and as she let it out, spoke faint words. "Let that be the end of it."

A feather floated down out of the darkness and came to rest on Horn's lips. Adica waited for her to take in another breath, for the feather to stir, but nothing happened. Her chest did not rise. Her whole body slackened. The pale wisp that was her spirit rose out of her body, taking a form like that of the big-bellied woman carved into the cavern wall, so different than the frail, elderly body she now inhabited.

A wind rose sudden and strong. The torches blew out, plunging them into darkness. The pale substance of Horn's spirit twisted as the wind spun it around.

"Hear me! Hear me!" It spoke in a new voice, deep and booming. "She is taken! Come quickly, or all is lost. The Holy One has been captured by the Cursed Ones. We have not enough strength to rescue her. Come quickly, or all is lost!"

"Shu-Sha!" cried Two Fingers.

A thunderous knock resounded through the chamber. Adica leaped up just as the wispy spirit shattered into a thousand glittering lights, quickly extinguished. The young apprentice wailed out loud.

Quickly, the torches were relit, but Horn was dead, and her spirit had vanished into the darkness.

PART FOUR

A MIRROR ON THE PAST

XIV
JEDU'S ANGRY LAIR

1

THE flames scoured her clean. They emptied her of emotion, of her past, of all her links to any substance except fire, because she was fire. Long ago Da had constructed and then locked a door in the citadel of her palace of memory, hiding from her the truth of what she truly was. Even as the fire of the Sun consumed her, the pure fire of her innermost heart burned more brightly even than the blast of the Sun, waves of heat and golden towers of flame. The door remained in place, but now she could peer through that keyhole and understand exactly what it was she saw writhing and burning, the thing that Da had locked away from her: her secret soul, the blue-hot spark that had given her life and that permeated her substance.

I am only half formed out of humankind. She needed no words, no voice, because the fire itself was her voice. *The daimones who took me at Verna are my kin.*

I am fire.

Exultant, she reached easily into the blazing fire of the Sun and transformed it into wings. On these wings she rose on the updraft of an uncurling flare to the limit of the Sun.

Yet even so, to her surprise, she had not left everything

behind. Maybe she could never leave everything behind. She still had her bow and quiver of arrows; she still had the gold torque, cold at her neck, that bound her to Sanglant, and the bright beacon of lapis lazuli, the ring Alain had given her. But nothing else, only the fire that suffused the physical form she called a body.

Jedu's baleful glare bathed the horizon in a bloody red, the home of the Angel of War. The gates were guarded by a pair of sullen but dreadful daimones, carrying spears carved of crystal. Skulls dangled from their belts, and their faces shone with blood lust. She strung her bow and nocked an arrow, lit it so it burned.

They laughed, seeing how pitifully small she was. Although she was fire, they did not fear her. They were big as castles, with thighs as broad as a house and arms as stout as tree trunks.

"Pass through, pass through!" they cried mockingly, with voices that boomed and crashed. "We'll watch the sport while you're hunted down and killed, Bright One."

"I thank you," she said, seeing no reason to stay and quibble with creatures who looked ready to squash her like a bug.

She passed through the arch as their voices followed her, deep and resonant. "Go as you please, Child of Flame, yet you will lose something of yourself on the path!"

She tumbled into Jedu's angry lair.

2

AT dawn, Bulkezu ordered the vanguard driven forward with the lash to swarm the walls of Echstatt. Maybe the hapless men, women, and children would find mercy in the Chamber of Light, since they had certainly found none at Bulkezu's hands. He used his prisoners wisely, if one called ruthlessness wisdom. By pressing the unarmed mob up against the walls first, he ensured that Echstatt's defenders used up much of their precious store of arrows, javelins, and hot tar on folk who could do nothing to harm them in return.

Hanna refused to weep while Bulkezu watched her. He liked to watch her, just as he liked to make her watch each assault as his army struck deep into the heart of Wendar, having long since outflanked his pursuers. He was trying to batter her down, breach her walls, but she would not give in.

By midday the Quman breached the town's gates and the fires started. Smoke and flame curled up from houses, halls, and huts, melting the thin mantle of snow on the rooftops. Mounted on a shaggy Quman horse, surrounded by Bulkezu's command group as they surveyed their troops from a hillside overlooking the prosperous town, Hanna saw every bitter moment as the victory unfolded. Despair tasted like ash on her tongue as the winged riders started in on their usual slaughter, cutting the fingers off folk who didn't give up their rings quickly enough, dragging adult males out into the streets and killing any who resisted.

Smoke billowed into the sky as fires raged. A dozen riders hurried out of the church as it, too, began to burn, flames licking up through the roof. Four men held corners of the embroidered altar cloth; vestments, gold fittings, silver cups, and the deacon's bloodstained stole jostled in a heap at the center. After a moment, the glass window above the altar blew out.

In a prosperous town like Echstatt there was plenty to loot beyond fodder, provisions, and the church's treasure. Bulkezu's intentions remained a mystery to her, because he seemed remarkably uninterested in loot except in so far as it pleased his troops to enrich themselves with trinkets and slaves.

Now, of course, came the worst part as the Quman herded the surviving townsfolk out of the gates and onto their ruined fields. Bulkezu gestured, and the command group moved forward. Trapped between his warriors, she had to go along with them as they rode down to examine the captives.

An old woman limped, a trail of blood marking her stumbling path. A young man hugged a baby to his chest while at his side his pretty wife, her expression caught between terror and hopeless anger, slapped her screaming toddler into silence before clutching the now-stupefied child tightly against her as tears streamed down her cheeks. Children sobbed. A girl tried vainly to hold together her torn sleeve. A chubby man in steward's robes fell to the ground and lay there moaning helplessly, face buried in the dirt.

Smoke from the burning houses clouded Hanna's vision. Tears stung her eyes. The townsfolk saw her then, an Eagle riding among the hated Quman.

An elderly man dressed in a rich man's tunic stepped forward, raising his merchant's staff. "I pray you, Eagle," he cried, "intercede for us—"

A Quman struck him down. Blood pooled from the old man's temple into the depression left by the heel mark of the warrior's boot. A half-grown boy with a cut on his cheek screamed out loud, once, and an older girl who looked to be his sister clapped a hand over his mouth. There was a terrified silence. All of the townsfolk dropped their gazes and hunched their shoulders, as if by not seeing, by making themselves small, they would not be seen.

Bulkezu laughed. The sound echoed weirdly, muffled by his helm. He gestured, and the interpreter hurried forward, eager to serve. He had stolen a new tunic off a corpse about ten days ago and had recently gotten hold of a silver chain out of the ruins of a burned church. The finery made him vain. Hanna hadn't known his name before, but now that he had a half-dozen prisoners to use as slaves, he had begun to style himself "Lord Boso." Sometimes, if Bulkezu was in a magnanimous mood, Boso got to pick a fresh woman from among the newly-captured prisoners rather than accept the leavings after the Quman had done with them.

Bulkezu pulled off his helm. He spoke, and Boso translated.

"His Munificence feels a strong mercy weighing upon his heart. Be glad you do not face his wrath. Because of his good humor this day, he will allow the Eagle to choose ten from your number. The rest will become prisoners. It will become their good fortune to be allowed to serve their Quman masters."

Was this mercy? Hanna felt sick. The townsfolk stared at her, seeming not to understand his words. Already Quman warriors walked among the three hundred or so captives, testing the soundness of limbs, pinching the arms of the young women to see how pleasingly fat they were, prodding the few men who remained, those who hadn't been killed in the first assault or the final desperate fighting. Some men made good slaves; some did not, because they would always struggle. Bulkezu and his men knew how to tell the difference.

"What will happen to those left behind, the ones I choose?" she asked.

Bulkezu kept a stony face until Boso translated her words. His reply was swift and certain. "His Bounteousness gives his word that they will be allowed to stay behind, unmolested. Let the Eagle choose."

The reputation of the Kerayit shamans had protected her for this long. Bulkezu had not laid a hand on her, but perhaps he meant to win her regard using different methods, mercy and persuasion, if you called this mercy. She regarded him suspiciously, but he only smiled, looking ready as always to burst out laughing.

She made the mistake of looking again at the townsfolk. They were beaten, they were lost, but a few had managed to understand Boso's words. No matter how they struggled to keep their expressions blank, she saw hope flower in their eyes, she saw hatred burn for the choice she would be allowed to have over them.

The girl with the torn sleeve hissed. "Slave! Traitor!"

She wasn't talking to Boso.

The townsfolk all looked at Hanna; in their hearts they knew what she was, if she rode among the Quman. Fire hissed from the town, an echo of the girl's accusation. Boso whispered to Bulkezu, and the prince snapped a command. The girl was dragged forward, thrown down to her knees before him. She began to snivel and cry. She couldn't have been more than thirteen. He drew his sword.

"I choose her," said Hanna hastily. "I am a prisoner, too. I have no choice, I didn't ask to travel with them." These words she spoke to the watching townsfolk, but they didn't believe her. They hated her now anyway, whatever they believed of her, because she had the power of life and death over them, the power to choose who would remain free and who would become a slave. It was a cruel game to play with them, and with her. Hope is often cruel.

But if she didn't choose, then they would all suffer as Bulkezu's slaves.

He laughed as she choose them—the defiant girl, the young couple with the two small children, a man with the burly arms of a smith, a woman who reminded her of her mother and the teenage girl clinging to her side—because by the time there were only two choices left to make they were all begging and pleading to be chosen themselves, or thrusting their innocent children forward in the hope of saving them from the Quman yoke. So many.

Cold wind stung her cheeks, bringing tears. The Quman warriors shoved the desperate townsfolk back, away from Hanna.

Children wept. The boy with the cut cheek shuddered as his sister gripped him tightly, but no sound escaped him. The steward curled up and moaning into the dirt began to claw the ground as though he meant, like a mole, to dig himself in to safety. He was missing three fingers. His blood had spattered the front of his linen tunic.

"Two more," cried Lord Boso cheerfully. The townsfolk's fear excited him. His eyes ranged over the women who were left, measuring them, his own nasty gaze lit with greedy desire.

The Quman watched without expression, all except Bulkezu, who found the scene amusing. She hated him for his laughter. She hated him all the more because it would have been easier to hate him if he had been ugly, but even when he laughed, even when he reveled in her pain and in his captives's despair, when his laughter revealed a pitiless and ugly heart, none of that darkness marked his handsome face.

It wasn't true after all, what the church folk sometimes preached: as inside, so outside.

Let no one know she was weeping inside. She was the King's Eagle. It was her duty to witness, to save what she could. She picked out two more girls, both about the same age as the girl with the torn sleeve. Old enough to survive if they were left on their own. Old enough to be raped and taken as concubines if they were left with the Quman.

Boso cursed at her, having had his eye on one of them. Bulkezu finally stopped chuckling. With shuttered eyes, he watched Hanna, not the chosen ten being herded back to burning Echstatt. A captain called out the advance. A horn blew. Weeping and wailing, the rest of Echstatt's survivors were goaded and lashed toward the waiting army.

The captives stumbled along. One toddler, falling behind, was killed where it lay sobbing, a prod for the rest. Riding with the command group, Hanna soon outdistanced them, but their cries and grief stayed with her anyway, melding soon enough into the morass of sorrow that attended the Quman army: the mob of prisoners driven along with livestock and extra horses.

Late that afternoon the scene was repeated again when the vanguard reached a village. Soldiers drove a crowd of prisoners forward to take the brunt of the initial assault. When the first flurry of arrows trailed off, the Quman troops attacked, burned the palisade and houses, and rounded up prisoners. Bulkezu brought her forward again, to grant mercy to ten.

"I won't do it," she said. "You're only playing a game with me. You don't care about mercy."

Bulkezu laughed. As he spoke, Boso translated. "Then I will choose, and leave ten behind for the crows."

This time a woman spat on her, calling her worse names than "slave" and "traitor", and was murdered for her disrespect. But Hanna chose ten while the others huddled in hopeless silence or stared at her accusingly.

"Mercy is a waste of time," said Bulkezu as Boso translated. "People despise the ones who show them mercy."

"They feel I have betrayed them," said Hanna, "and maybe I have."

The vanguard set up camp an arrow's flight from the ruined village, upwind from the mass of the army and, more particularly, from the stinking mass of livestock and prisoners. But Bulkezu liked to survey his riches. He liked his luxuries, his silk robes, handsome gold trinkets, sweet-smelling women he did not treat badly as long as they did not resist him. Yet these were all things he could give up and leave behind without a moment's thought. What he enjoyed most of all, as far as Hanna could tell, was the misery he left in his wake.

With his night guard in attendance and Hanna perforce at his side, he rode back along the lines, weaving in and out through his troops, stopping at campfires, inspecting tents, until he reached the bloated crowd of prisoners mixed together with stolen livestock, cattle and goats and sheep bleating and lowing, chickens and ducks fluttering and squawking in cages, and every variety of donkey and horse, from scrawny asses to sturdy work ponies to an aged warhorse now ridden by four small children. Even cowed as the prisoners were by their fear of their masters, they still made noise enough to wake the dead. She could not count them all; in the last few days the numbers had swelled alarmingly as the Quman army swept into more densely inhabited areas. By now, she guessed there were twice as many prisoners as soldiers.

Winter had become spring, although here and there snow lingered on the rooftops or in the northern shadow of trees. Cold and wet made conditions wretched even for those who traveled in some comfort. For the prisoners, most barefoot and half without even a cloak to warm them, spring was deadly. Every night some lay down who would not get up again in the morning. Children too weak to cry whimpered. A man scratched the festering sores on his legs. A mother clutched an emaciated child to her breast, but she had no milk. Here and there knots of people huddled together, protecting precious stores of food gained from relatives who had by one means or another come under the protection of a man in the Quman army—a young woman to be his concubine, her mother to cook his meat and gruel or to mend his shirts, a boy to groom his horses or polish his armor.

While Hanna watched, a dozen soldiers rode up to look over the new captives. The guards rounded them up—easy to mark out the new ones because their look of terror hadn't yet been subsumed by numb despair—and prodded them forward. Bulkezu watched with that irritating half smile on his face. Other villages had been overrun today. Hanna saw prisoners who had not been among those she had seen taken, chief among them a pretty young woman who had just the kind of pleasingly plump figure that Quman men found attractive. Soldiers jostled each other to get close to her, to poke and pinch her, to check her teeth and test the strength of her hair; soon enough she was crying openly, so afraid that she wet herself. One man shoved another to get him out of his way. Curses flew fast and furious.

The smile vanished from Bulkezu's face as he urged his horse forward. At once, the jostling ceased and the men moved back obediently. His griffin wings hissed softly as a breeze rose. Bulkezu ruled his army with an iron hand. He did not tolerate fighting among his troops. Lord Wichman and his cronies would not have lasted a day among the Quman, no matter how great their prowess in battle.

He bent down from the saddle to touch the young woman's hair, letting it fall through his hands before lifting it up again, testing the weight and silkiness between his fingers. The young woman had wits enough to stop weeping, although maybe she was only shocked into a stupor.

Bulkezu had decided to take her for himself.

He called out orders. Then they all waited with that seemingly infinite patience the Quman had while two of the night guards rode away to the vanguard. Bulkezu whistled merrily while he waited; some of the soldiers contented themselves with other women, dragging them away from their families while cries of grief and fear broke out among the new prisoners. The young woman stood stiffly, bolt upright, only her gaze ranging as she looked for help, for succor, for escape— hard to say.

Hanna moved forward as the night guards returned with all five of Bulkezu's current concubines, to be handed over to the men who had been fighting over the new woman. One of them—the blonde who had been found hiding in a root cellar—threw herself down before his horse, crying and pleading, trying to grab his boot and hang on. Bulkezu, laughing, kicked her in the face and signaled to a soldier to drag her away.

Hanna used the cover of this mild disturbance to ride in close to the new captive. She bent forward as she passed, spoke quickly and in a low voice, hoping the girl had wits enough to pay attention. "No flattery. No whining. No fear. Don't cry."

Then she had crossed beyond her, not daring to turn to see how the woman had reacted. The blonde was still weeping as one of the soldiers who had started the fighting over the new captive hauled her away. The old captives merely watched, too ill, too weak, or too hopeless to react. A few enterprising children, grown wise from neglect, sidled over to the families of those taken away. They knew who had access to food: the ones who pleased their masters.

After all, the Quman treated their favored slaves no worse than the prisoners treated each other.

"Men are weak who fight over women," Bulkezu said suddenly in Wendish as he rode up beside Hanna. They now sat far enough away from the prisoners that none could overhear them.

"Why do you take so many prisoners, when all they do is suffer? They gain you nothing. What you want them all for?"

"I want them so Wendar suffers."

Truly, he killed them with neglect. "What do you gain by burning and destroying? How does it help you, how do you enrich yourself, by ruining Wendar? Do you hope to rule here? You would have done better to offer marriage to one of the king's daughters."

He spat. "What man of my people would wish to marry a barbarian's get? I'll take the king's daughter as my bed-slave if I want her."

"The king's daughters have their own armies. They aren't as easy to capture as these poor, defenseless townsfolk. What honor is there for a great warrior like you in defeating people such as these?" She gestured toward the prisoners.

His wings sighed as wind brushed through them. For a moment, she thought he had not heard her, or was not listening. His night guard, silent astride their horses, waited patiently. In a way, it was as if she and Bulkezu sat alone, separated from the army, from the hapless prisoners, from his personal guard, by the same unnatural mist that had protected him from the shadow elves.

She looked around, half expecting to see his shaman, but all she saw were soldiers, their campfires and bivouac tents, and the crowd of prisoners and livestock winding away along the track as they found a place to settle down for the night. Fields stretched away on either side, delicate shoots of winter wheat trampled into the mud. Farther away lay the line of trees and undergrowth, cut back by the villagers' need for firewood and building material. Smoldering fires lit the desolate village, now deserted. The ten lucky souls she had chosen for freedom had not stayed to see if Quman mercy would hold until morning.

"They hate me in my own country," Bulkezu said at last, softly. "The Pechanek elders have grown weak and cowardly. We were driven out of our pastures by the Shatai, and the southern Tarbagai is closed to us because of the Ungrians, those bastards, may their testicles rot. Now my sister's son is the favorite of the old begh, that son of a bitch, and he's handsomer than me, too."

Hanna looked him over, the smooth cheeks and vivid, almond-shaped eyes, the breadth of his shoulders under armor, the lift of his chin to draw attention to his handsome profile. He had tucked his helmet under his arm, a gesture eerily reminiscent of Prince Sanglant, the better, no doubt, to display his wealth of glossy black hair. "How can that be?" she said, having learned something of him in the last weeks. "Is there any man handsomer than you?"

"One," he admitted. "I saw him in a dream. But he had golden hair, spun from sunlight." He grinned, on the verge of laughing. "Women love a handsome man. Why, women already married have risked death to creep between my furs. Why are you so hard-hearted? I'll make you chief among my wives."

"I thought Quman men did not marry outside the tribes."

"Any man would be a fool not to marry a Kerayit shaman's luck if she offered herself to him."

"This one hasn't offered herself to you."

He laughed. "Yes, better that you stay out of my bed. I respect you now, but I wouldn't once I'd conquered your body."

"Which do you want?" she said, irritated by his games.

"I want victory."

"Against whom?"

"Against anyone who stands in my way."

A drum rapped smartly in the distance, answered by a second. He cocked his head to one side, listening to the message they brought. He whistled, turned aside his horse, and his night guard fell in around him. Hanna had no choice but to

follow; she couldn't escape their net. Twilight washed the prisoners to gray, but the darkening light could not hide the smell
of despair or the stink of diarrhea and sickness. An infant cried
on and on and on. Hanna was suddenly hungry, smelling meat
roasting up ahead, brought on the wind, but the appetizing
scent curdled in her stomach as they rode alongside the line of
prisoners, many of whom would not eat this night and had not
eaten last night or the night before.

While she feasted tonight, a child would die of starvation,
just as one had last night, and the night before. The Eagle's
burden had never weighed as heavily as it had these last
months, since her capture. She had to witness and remember,
so that, in time, she could report to the king. Sometimes that
was the only thing that kept her going: her determination to
report to the king.

Bulkezu moved out to greet the last raiding party, come in
to report. Truly, some things would be more difficult to report
to King Henry than others.

Prince Ekkehard and his companions had taken to wearing
princely Quman armor, cobbled together from armored coats
stripped off of dead men, felt coifs, looted Wendish cloaks
made rich by fur linings, supple leather gloves, painted
shields, everything but the wings, which they had not earned.
Everything but the shrunken heads, which not even Ekkehard
had the stomach for.

They had brought loot, and news. Lord Boso was called
back from the vanguard to translate as Lord Welf delivered the
report.

"Lord Hedo's fort was stripped of soldiers and easy to take.
The servants said his son marched west last autumn with fifty
men to fight in Saony."

"Who is fighting in Saony?" asked Hanna.

"Duchess Rotrudis' children." With his highborn arrogance,
meaty hands, and scarred lip, Welf looked remarkably like a
fool to her, especially when he could barely bring himself to
answer her just because she was common born. He only spoke

to her because Bulkezu had a habit of whipping, and once castrating, men who treated Hanna disrespectfully: not warming the water brought for her bath, not getting out of her way fast enough as she walked through camp, daring to look her in the eye, who bore the luck of a Kerayit shaman.

The loot gained at the fort was a fine haul: gold vessels; silver drinking cups; ivory spoons; and two tapestries.

"His Contemptuousness bids you keep what you have earned," said Boso, translating for Bulkezu. "For are you not brothers? Are you not honorable, in the way of all noble folk?"

How Bulkezu kept his expression blank Hanna did not understand, considering the insulting way Boso had of speaking. It was another one of his charades, the games he played incessantly with his prisoners, because even Ekkehard, for all that he now rode and fought with the army, was nothing more than a glorified hostage made much of and let range wide on a leash. Ekkehard had women, he had silks, he had meat and wine, and he had his own honor guard, which he evidently chose not to recognize for what it was: his jailers. Let him get dirty enough with raiding under Bulkezu's banner and it would be too late for him to go back to his father's hall and authority.

No doubt Bulkezu counted on it. He didn't care one whit for Ekkehard. He had just found a more amusing way to ruin him.

"I'm surprised, my lord prince," said Hanna, "that you would war on your father's people. Isn't that treason?"

Prince Ekkehard did not deign to reply, but Lord Benedict rose to the bait. "Lord Hedo did not come to King Henry's aid when the king's sister, Lady Sabella, rose in revolt against him. This is his just punishment. We are doing nothing more than seeing him rewarded for his disobedience."

"Aiding an enemy as he devastates your father's lands and cripples his people scarcely seems the act of a loyal subject."

"You'll regret those words," Lord Welf said hotly, "when you don't have a prince to protect you." He nodded toward Bulkezu.

"Nay, I don't have a prince to protect me." She lifted her right hand to display the emerald ring. "I'm the *King's* Eagle."

Ekkehard flushed, and his companions muttered among themselves, glancing toward Bulkezu, gauging his mood. Ekkehard's boys didn't like her. She didn't like them much, either, if it came to that; they were the real traitors. Yet were they any different than most of the nobly born, fighting their wars across the bodies of the common folk?

Bulkezu laughed as soon as Boso translated the exchange. He moved forward to ride beside Ekkehard, treating Ekkehard to flowery compliments delivered by a sarcastic Boso; how well he acquitted himself in battle, how many women he had won for his slaves, how terrible it was that his relatives had tried to consign him to the monastery when certainly any fool could see that he was born for the glory of war. Ekkehard lapped it up like cream. He even forgot about Hanna, trailing behind, she who carried the wasp sting of conscience because she never let him forget that he had turned coat and embraced Bulkezu's cause.

A scream shattered the sleepy twilight. Deep in the crowd of weary, worn-down, lethargic prisoners, an eddy of movement spiraled out of control like leaves picked up by a dust devil.

"Witchcraft! Demons! The Enemy has spawned among us!"

Panic broke like a storm. Prisoners pushed and shoved frantically, more afraid of an unseen menace in their ranks than of the dour Quman soldiers who guarded them. Terrified captives spilled across the invisible boundary into range of Quman spears. Like raindrops presaging a downpour, the first handful turned an instant later into a hysterical flood of ragged people desperate to escape the horror in their midst.

Even horses accustomed to war shied at the sudden agitation. Ekkehard's nervous gelding reared, backing sideways into Bulkezu's horse. The night guard, distracted by this threat to their leader, hastened forward.

Hanna saw her chance.

She kicked her horse hard and galloped for the trees. The forest gave scant cover. Pale trunks surrounded her, bare branches clattering in the breeze. She heard the singing of wings, high and light, and the pound of hooves as her captors pursued her. Ducking low, she pressed the horse through a stand of stinging pine, forded a shallow stream running in three channels along the forest floor, and skirted a massive bramble bush. Her cloak caught once in its thorns; she tore it free, nudged her mount around its tangled verge, and found herself facing Bulkezu.

Even under the cover of the forest, with dusk lowering, there was light enough to see his expression. He laughed. But he had his bow strung and an arrow nocked, and at moments like this, with that half crazy expression on his face and something more than laughter in his eyes, she could not bring herself to trust to Sorgatani's luck to keep her unharmed. Breathing hard, she reined up the horse and regarded him with disgust and resignation. And a sliver of fear.

He lifted the bow, aimed, and shot into the bramble, flushing out two escaped prisoners who had hoped to hide within the thorny refuge. Hanna recognized the adolescent girl and her half-grown brother, the one with the cut on his cheek, from Echstatt. The boy was gulping soundlessly, trying not to dissolve into hysteria, while his sister gripped his shoulders and managed a defiant glare.

Bulkezu chuckled. The movement of his shoulders made the shrunken head at his belt sway, knocking against one thigh. He pulled a second arrow out of his quiver and drew down on the boy. "Run," he said softly, in Wendish.

They ran, floundering out into the darkening forest. The child tripped. With a leisurely draw, Bulkezu marked the boy's back. Hanna kicked her horse hard, driving toward him, shouting out loud, anything to spoil his aim.

But the arrow was already loosed.

It whistled, the girl screamed and tugged at her brother; the point buried itself in the bark of a slender birch tree, less than a hand's breadth from the stumbling boy. With a strangled cry, the girl dragged him onward into the trees.

The night guard trotted up, but Bulkezu gave a curt command, and they made no move to follow the fleeing children.

Tears of elation wet Hanna's lips. "You missed!"

He laughed, that damned half-giggling guffaw. Sobering, he drew another arrow from his quiver and twisted it between his fingers. The wind whistled through his wings; she smelled a faint scent, like putrefaction, wafting toward them from camp.

"I never miss." His expression darkened. "Twice only, and they will suffer for it, when I have them in my hands again."

"Who could have defeated you, Prince Bulkezu?" She was too angry, at herself, at fate, at his arrogance, to watch her tongue, to curb her sarcasm, even if she knew it wasn't wise.

"Once, that Ashioi witch. Once, that smart-mouthed priest."

"You tolerate insults from Boso all the time. You can understand every word he says."

"Boso is a fool. A dog would make a more worthy lord. It amuses me to wait and let him spin a little longer. Now Zach'rias was a clever man. He made war on me with his tongue. I should have cut off his tongue instead of his penis. I didn't understand him well enough to know which would hurt him worse. My arrow missed its mark." He shifted in the saddle, lifting an arm to brush a finger along one of the griffin feathers bound into his wooden wings. The touch raised blood on his skin, but the wind wicked it away. A thin rain of snow spilled from a tree branch, a shower of white that melted where it touched the sodden, spring ground.

"But they only made me stronger, when they thought to humble me. Now I'm the only man born into the tribes who has killed two griffins, not just one." He did not smile. Nor did he laugh.

"You didn't wear those wings when you fought against Prince Bayan and Princess Sapientia."

A spark of mischief and cruelty lit his expression. "I wanted Bayan to know that even wingless I could defeat him and his noble allies." He laughed for such a long time that Hanna began to think something had gotten stuck in his throat. The shrunken head rolled along his thigh, staring accusingly at Hanna. "I'd never killed a lady lord in *battle* before," he continued at last, "so I thought it best to put my old guardian away and dedicate a new one." He laughed a little again, trailing off into giggles as he stroked the hair on his shrunken head and lifted it. "Do you know her?"

Bile stung in Hanna's throat. For a moment she thought she would vomit. Or ought to. No wonder the head, all twisted, blackened, warped, and nasty as it had become, looked familiar. She knew who had died in that battle.

"Judith," she whispered, "Margrave of Olsatia and Austra."

Another of the night guard rode up to deliver a report. Bulkezu listened intently, eyes crinkling as he concentrated. He had already forgotten the head. Slowly his expression changed. The only thing worse than his smiles and laughter were his frowns, and he frowned now as night fell and a warm breeze brought the fetid smell of camp to her nostrils, choking her. She could not bear to look at Bulkezu, not with Margrave Judith's head dangling there.

One of the guards lit a torch. Back at the army, more torches blazed into life like visible echoes of the one snapping brightly next to her.

Out of the night, screaming rose like a tide.

"What's going on?" she whispered, horrified. It sounded as if the Quman had turned on their helpless prisoners and begun killing them.

"What is the name for this thing that has crept into the ranks of the prisoners, this thing we must drive out lest it infect my troops?" He mused aloud, absently fingering the point of the arrow as he cocked his head to one side, listening to the distant slaughter. Snow dusted his black hair as a last shower rained from the pine tree under which he sheltered.

"First the demons slip invisibly into the body. Then the body turns gray and shakes. Then the noxious humors explode out of the mouth and the nose and the ears and the asshole, all the snot and blood and shit and spittle bursting forth. Zach'rias taught me the name for this thing."

She already knew. A cold worm of fear writhed in her heart, numbing her. She had thought the shadow elves the only thing more terrifying than the Quman. But she was wrong.

He nodded to himself, remembering the word.

"Plague."

Back in the camp, the killing went on.

3

THEY came down out of the Alfar Mountains into a summer so golden that it seemed to Rosvita that the sun itself had been poured over the landscape. In the north, the light was never this rich and expressive.

When they stopped to water the horses and oxen at midday, Fortunatus took off his boots and dabbled his toes where the cold mountain water frothed and spilled over exposed rocks.

"Ah!" he said delightedly as he wiggled his toes under the water. "I'd forgotten how pleasant it is to have feet that are hot and dry for a change. After that tedious winter and spring, I thought I would never be comfortable again."

With relief, Rosvita dismounted from her mule and found a flat-topped boulder to sit on. From this seat—no harder, really, than her saddle—she could survey the stream where the clerics of the king's schola had gone to wet their faces, drink, and stretch. Although the king preferred that she attend him at all times, she had obtained permission to travel with the schola, the better to keep an eye on her precious books and young clerics.

Servants brought soft cheese from the wagons. She nibbled at this delicacy as she watched animals being brought up in bunches to water downstream, where a fallen log dammed enough of the current that a watering hole had been hollowed out of the earth. A hawk drifted overhead, spiraling on the winds that brushed down off the high peaks, now hidden by forest and foothills. A woodpecker drummed nearby, and she saw its white flash among pine branches.

"The months weren't wasted entirely, Brother. At last I was able to make a great deal of progress on my *History of the Wendish People*."

He smiled sadly, not looking up from the play of the water around his feet. "So you did, Sister. I only wish Sister Amabilia were here to copy your words in a finer hand than that I possess."

"Truly," she echoed, "I wish she were not lost to us. I miss her."

Fortunatus sighed. He had never gained back the healthy stoutness that had made his features round and jolly; their adventures crossing the Alfar Mountains three times in the last two years had taken a lasting toll on him. "Will we ever know what became of her?" he asked wistfully.

"Only if we can trust dreams. I fear they lie as often as they tell the truth."

As she finished her meal of cheese and bread, she called to her servingwoman, Aurea, and bid her bring her pouch from her pack mule. Aurea brought both pouch and travel desk, which unfolded easily to make a stout surface on which to set the *History*. Rosvita wiped her hands on a cloth and only then turned the unbound pages to her final entry, made three weeks ago on their last day at the palace of Zur, originally a villa built in the times of the Dariyan empresses and now a way station where a royal party could break its journey for a day or a week.

Some said that fully two hundred thousand Rederii bar-barians were slain that day, either cut down by the sword or drowned in the marsh when they tried to make their retreat.

After this, the young margrave Villam moved his army against the city mentioned above, but the inhabitants now feared to stand against him and therefore they laid down their arms and asked for safe passage. In this way, the city and all its wealth and all the household furnishings fell into the possession of King Arnulf the Younger.

When the margrave and his companions returned to Saony, King Arnulf received them with gratitude and praised their victory. It so happened that the king's favored Eagle returned at this time from Arethousa with the news that the king had obtained what he most desired: an Arethousan princess who would stand in marriage to his son, Henry, a most radiant and worthy young man. When the glorious Sophia arrived with her splendid retinue, the royal wedding was celebrated with largess and rejoicing.

To Henry and Sophia were born these children: a daughter named Sapientia, a woman of merit, justly dear to all the people, who married Bayan, Prince of the Ungrians, and also a daughter named Theophanu, wise in all matters and of a cunning disposition, as well as a son named Ekkehard, who was invested as the abbot of St. Perpetua's in Gent.

Here she had stopped. The rigors of a mountain crossing, even in the fine weather that God's favor had at last granted them after several unsuccessful earlier attempts, had not allowed her to write more. Truly, the long winter and dreary spring had been inconvenient and uncomfortable, but she had had the leisure to work because they had stopped for as many as ten days at a time at various estates and palaces. What lay before them in Aosta she did not know, but she didn't suppose that war would bring many peaceful interludes during which she might have the freedom to work without interruption. It was very difficult to work while on the move.

At times like this, she remembered why so many of her spiritual sisters, women devoted to their books, preferred to stay in the convent rather than traipse about the countryside as part of the retinue of their noble relatives.

"Sister Rosvita!"

She looked up to see the king's favored Eagle at the side of the road.

"If you will, Sister Rosvita, Brother Eudes is taken ill again, and the king requests your presence."

Fortunatus padded over barefoot and took the unbound sheets carefully off the travel desk so that Aurea could fold it up. "I'll care for these, Sister," he said.

The mule was brought, and Rosvita mounted with a grimace. Her bones creaked and popped constantly these days. With Hathui as escort she rode forward along the lines, passing knots of soldiers and stands of dismounted horsemen like copses of trees. The road led down a steep valley, walled here by cliffs ribboned with slender waterfalls whose spray made little rainbows in the air, quickly seen and as quickly vanished.

Carefully, they picked their way down the path until they reached a broadening in the valley where the royal party had stopped to take advantage of a pleasant meadow as a haven for their noontime rest. The king and queen waited at their leisure while servants watered the horses and brought their sovereigns ale, cheese, and bread as well as greens plucked from the hillsides. Adelheid sat on a blanket, so big-bellied in her pregnancy that she found the ground a more comfortable seat than her throne.

Henry conducted business a short way away from her, consulting with his captains and stewards and noble companions and dispensing judgment over disputes that had arisen in the train. Occasionally he would refer two quarreling parties to Adelheid, and they would hasten over to kneel before her. A steward hurried forward to Rosvita and, taking her travel desk, set it up at Henry's side. She sat on a stool, trimmed her quill, and readied her ink as Henry listened to the complaints of a wagoner who had gotten into a fight with a Lion over a chicken looted from a farmer's shed. A knife fight had ensued, and both men had been wounded.

"Yet what of the injury you inflicted upon the householder

whose chicken you stole?" demanded the king. "Made you any recompense to her for the loss of the chicken?"

"Nay, but, Your Majesty, she was just an Aostan woman, not of our people at all." On this point both men agreed.

"Yet were she a Wendish woman, would you have treated her so disrespectfully? Will the Aostans rally to our cause if we treat them as we would our enemies? They are not meant to suffer as our enemies but to prosper as our subjects. Let both of you make her some restitution. I will send an Eagle back to the village with this fine. As for the two of you, you will dig privies side by side for a week, so that you may learn to work together."

He dismissed them, then beckoned to a steward. "Here is Sister Rosvita, Wito. Make your report."

Rosvita duly cataloged the steward's report. It had taken them three weeks to cross the mountains, moving at not more than five leagues a day. The weather had held fair, for the most part, and they had lost only twelve horses, eighteen wagons, and twenty-five soldiers, seventeen of them to an outbreak of dysentery that had luckily been confined to the rear guard.

When the steward finished, Henry's captains came forward to discuss the route, and Rosvita looked back over the hapless Brother Eudes' precise entries that in spare language told the story of the abortive attempt to cross the mountains last autumn, when the weather drove them back to the north and they spent a miserable winter moving from one palace to another pursued by sleet, snow, spoiled food, and a scarcity of ale and wine. It had been either too cold to travel or else not cold enough to freeze the ever-present mud slop that turned roads and stable yards into mires. The army had lost seventy-nine horses and forty-two cattle to foot rot alone, and ninety-four soldiers to lung fever and dysentery, mostly from that first awful outbreak. Indeed, Brother Eudes himself had barely survived that first outbreak of dysentery, and since then he had suffered several relapses, the worst after their second failed attempt to cross in the spring.

Henry sent his captains away, and for a moment peace reigned. Rosvita closed her eyes and listened to the murmur of Adelheid's noble companions and the laughter of Henry's personal retinue, most of whom had wandered down to the stream to cool their faces.

For an instant, Rosvita's hearing sharpened so intensely that she could hear Queen Adelheid speaking. "Yet a wealth of sun does not bode well. I do not like the sere golden color of the grass. There should have been more rain over the winter and spring. I see too little green."

"Sister Rosvita." Henry spoke in a voice that carried only to her ears. "What if it is true that his wife is the great granddaughter of the Emperor Taillefer? She could claim the empire."

Startled, Rosvita dropped her quill. Henry sat with his chin resting on a hand, elbow propped up on the arm of his throne. He stared into the distance, at the pine forest or perhaps at his fears and doubts. Marriage to Adelheid had lifted years from his face, but it also meant that he was even more rarely alone than during the years of his widowerhood. He rarely had opportunity these days to open his most private thoughts to her.

"The young woman has not proved herself fit to rule, Your Majesty, nor has she any retainers. A queen without a retinue can scarcely be called a queen."

"Yet according to my Eagles and other messengers, Sanglant rode east, gathering an army about him."

"The Quman lie east. Do you think he means to make allies of them?" She didn't mean the words to be sarcastic, but Henry glanced at her sharply, jolted out of his reverie.

"Nay, I do not believe any Wendish noble will make peace with the Quman. I think he means to fight them. But the Quman are not the only people in the east who have an army. It has been months since we had word of Sapientia and Prince Bayan, nor has Margrave Judith sent word nor any representative to my court."

"To what purpose would they revolt against you? How can Taillefer's lost grandchild be a threat to you? Queen Radegundis made no effort to put her son on any throne. She gave him to God's service, not to the trials of the world. Nor did his child ever make any claim to Taillefer's imperial throne, if she even survived infancy."

"But you believe a child was born to Taillefer and Radegundis' son."

"I do believe that, Your Majesty."

He frowned, regarding the trees again with an intent gaze. Rosvita realized all at once the main difference between Henry and Sanglant: Henry had the gift of stillness, and Sanglant could never be still.

"This bodes ill," he said softly. "I fear Sanglant has been bewitched."

"That is a serious charge, Your Majesty, and one that Prince Sanglant has already denied."

"He must deny it, if he lies under a sorcerous spell. Do you know for certain that he was not enchanted, either by Bloodheart or by that woman's influence?"

"Nay, Your Majesty, you must know that I cannot say for certain. We all saw that Prince Sanglant was much changed by his captivity in Gent. It is true that the woman Liathano held some kind of power over him, even if it was only the power of lust."

"Then you do not think him bewitched?"

Yet how could she answer? She, too, had seen the daimone suckling his child. She shuddered, remembering that abomination, and Henry smiled slightly, although the expression seemed more of a grimace.

Just as he seemed ready to comment further, a steward hurried up, followed by an outrider still dusty from the road. The man presented himself first to Queen Adelheid and then to the king. Adelheid got to her feet with the assistance of her servants and came to stand beside Henry.

"I am come from Lavinia, Lady of Novomo, to bring you

greetings." The man spoke only Aostan, but Henry could understand it well enough as long as the speaker chose his words carefully and spoke slowly. "She rides to meet you on the road, and show you honor."

Henry rose. At his signal the army began its ponderous gathering up, like a great beast getting its legs under it in order to rise and stagger forward.

The valley began to broaden noticeably, hitting a stretch as straight as though a giant had gouged it out with her hand. Cliffs became ridgelines peppered with rock ledges and out-crops, slick with overhanging ferns, brown from lack of rain, crisp moss, and oleander bushes whose white flowers hung like falling water down steep hillside clefts. Farmers had found room to plow fields and plant orchards, and the landscape began to be cut through with fields, clusters of huts, and neatly-kept orchards.

The captain of the vanguard shouted out the alarm, and an instant later a horn rang out. Below, a party ascended along the road to meet them. Banners flew in a stiff spring breeze flow-ing down off the foothills, gold and white, matched in splendor and number only by the bright pennants and banners of the king's army. Adelheid's personal banner bearing the crowned leopard at rest below the royal sun of Aosta flew at the center of a six-pointed constellation of pennants. These pennants bore the sigils of Henry's rule over the six duchies that made up his realm: Varingia's stallion, Wayland's hawk, Avaria's lion, Fesse's red eagle, Arconia's green guivre, and the red dragon of Saony, the duchy out of which his grandfather Arnulf the Elder had taken control of the kingdoms of Wendar and Varre. Behind these paraded the banners of his noble com-panions, those who had chosen, or been commanded, to accompany his expedition: Duchess Liutgard of Fesse, Helmut Villam, Duke Burchard of Avaria, and a host of other lords and ladies. His army wound back up the valley, lost finally around a bend. Strung out along the road in marching order, it was an impressive sight.

The king's vanguard formed a protective wall in front of him as Lady Lavinia advanced and, finally, dismounted in order to approach Henry and Adelheid on foot. She looked as if she had aged ten years in the year since Rosvita had last seen her. The line of her mouth was grim, and her hair had gone white. She knelt in the middle of the road in the dirt, opening her hands in the manner of a supplicant.

"Your Majesties, I pray you, I give myself and all the lands and people I control into your hands. My fighting men are yours to command. You must take what you need from my storehouses, although we are sorely pressed in these days by drought."

Henry seemed ready to speak, but Adelheid made a slight gesture that drew his attention, and he nodded, giving way to her. With assistance, the young queen dismounted. She walked forward to offer her hand to Lavinia.

"I pray you, Lady, rise. Do not kneel here in the dust. We have come as I promised you last year." Lavinia took her hand but did not rise. She seemed incapable of speech, caught in some strong emotion that made her lips work silently. The calm, decisive woman who had aided Adelheid last spring had vanished. "What ails you, Lady?" continued Adelheid gently. "You are much changed."

Lavinia's voice was coarse with fury. "You know that Ironhead took my daughter to Darre to serve as a hostage for my good behavior. Now he has taken her against her will as his concubine. She is only thirteen. I will have revenge for the insult given to my family."

"So you will." It was always odd to hear such a steely voice emanate from that sweet, pretty face, but Adelheid had been raised in a hard school and had survived a forced marriage, a siege, Ironhead's pursuit of her, and an escape managed only with the aid of forbidden magic.

"She is not the only daughter of a noble house used in such an ignoble fashion," continued Lavinia. "Others have come to Novomo, hearing of your approach. We beg you to let us support you. Ironhead has brought dishonor to our families. Yet we brought the shame upon ourselves by not rising against him when he pursued you, Your Majesty. You see that we are repaid by God for our sins, for there was not enough rain this past winter. I fear there will be famine if no rain falls soon."

She gestured toward the orchards and fields. In truth Rosvita could see that the winter wheat was stunted and yellowing, and the new leaves on pear and apple trees were already curling.

"I have brought King Henry of Wendar and Varre, as I promised," said Adelheid. "We have wed. I am pregnant with a child who joins the blood of both Wendar and Aosta."

Tears ran down Lavinia's face as she kissed Adelheid's hand. "Bless you, Your Majesty."

"Come then, Lady. Rise. We will not march to Darre on our knees."

"Nay, nay, we will not." Lavinia got up at once and came forward to kiss Henry's ring and offer him her allegiance, but it was clear that she looked first to Queen Adelheid.

"Who awaits us in Novomo?" asked Henry when Lavinia's horse had been brought and both the lady and the queen mounted. At his signal, the royal party started forward at a sedate pace. Lavinia's retinue split to either side of the road to let the royal party pass through their ranks, and for some while the cheering of Novomo's soldiers drowned out any attempt at conversation.

"Who awaits us in Novomo?" Henry repeated as Lavinia's retinue fell in behind, being given the place of honor behind Henry's noble companions and his cohort of Lions but before the king's clerics and schola and the rest of his army.

"Richildis, Marquess of Zuola. Gisla, Count of Placentia, and Gisla, Lady of Piata. Tedbald, Count of Maroca, and his cousin, Red Gisla. Duke Lambert of Uscar, who can bring all of the nobles of his lands if he calls them."

"That is half of the north country," said Adelheid. "Some of these refused to aid me when my first husband died. How can I trust them now?"

"It is true that some may be spies for Ironhead, but they have all come here to pledge their support to Your Majesties. They like Ironhead no better than I do. The drought has affected all of us, and we fear worse, because the Most Holy Mother Clementia, she who was raised to the seat of the skopos eight years ago, is dead."

Rosvita drew the Circle of Unity at her breast and murmured a prayer for God's mercy, just as others did, even and especially the king.

"May God grant her peace," said Adelheid. "She is my great-aunt."

"Truly, she comes out of a noble lineage," agreed Lavinia. Anger lit her expression again. "Rumor whispers that Ironhead means to appoint his cousin as the new skopos, although she is not even a cleric!"

Rosvita leaned forward over the neck of her mule. "Have you heard any rumor of a Wendish frater among Ironhead's counselors, Lady?"

"Nay, Sister Rosvita, although it is said that a Wendish-born presbyter held great influence with the ailing skopos. I have even heard it whispered that he used sorcery to keep her alive, for she suffered greatly from a palsy in her later years. No one knows whether this presbyter supports Ironhead, or defies him, although it's said that he tried as well as he could to keep young women out of Ironhead's rough hands. But I hear only rumor. No noble lady or lord who travels to Darre is safe from Ironhead. None of us dare go there ourselves, for fear he'll kill us outright. You know, of course, that he gained his lands and title by murdering his half brother, and that he murdered his wife when he had no more use for her."

"How many wait for us in Novomo?" The catalog of Ironhead's sins had made Henry impatient. "Who else will march behind our banners? What number of milites and horsemen may we expect?"

"The wars have taken a toll on us, Your Majesty. Perhaps seven hundred."

They rode on for a while in silence. The ring of harness serenaded them. The muted rumble of wagon wheels behind them sounded like distant thunder, but the sky remained cloudless, a hard blue shell.

"Shall we gather more support, Your Majesty?" asked Lavinia finally, as if she could bear the silence no longer.

"Nay," said Adelheid fiercely, "let us strike hard and immediately at Ironhead, before Lord John has time to respond and build up his army." But as she spoke, she looked toward her husband. It was his army, after all.

Henry stared ahead. They had come within sight of Novomo, its walls and towers rising where the land opened into a fine landscape of rolling hills and extensively farmed lands, fields cut by ranks upon ranks of orchards and vineyards. They had come down far enough that, looking north, Rosvita could again see the tips of the mountains touching the heavens, distant and cold.

Beyond Novomo the road ran south to the heart of Aosta. Some trick of perspective allowed her to see a distant, flat-topped hill studded with dark shapes that she first took for sheep. With a shudder of misgiving, she recognized the hilltop of standing stones. Through those stones she and Adelheid and Theophanu and the pitiful remnant of their armies had staggered over a year ago, in the spring, propelled to safety by Hugh's magic. A spike of dread crippled her heart. Certainly they had escaped John Ironhead's army, but they had not yet escaped the full consequences of letting a man accused of sorcery harness a most dangerous magic, one long ago condemned by the church, to help them. She could not erase from her mind's eye the sight of the daimone Hugh had bound. She still saw clearly its writhing fury, heard the resonant bass hammer of its voice, felt the damning chill that boiled off the threads of hard light that made up its body, if the creatures known as daimones even had true bodies.

She had seen what the others had not, and yet she had acquiesced. She knew in her heart that decision would come back to haunt them all.

"A well-fitted army with horses and stout soldiers can reach Darre in ten days," said Lavinia as they approached the gates of Novomo.

In Darre lay the key to the imperial throne that Henry had for so long dreamed of possessing.

"God march with us," said Henry. "Adelheid is correct. We must not wait. Let us feast this night in your hall. In the morning, we will march south."

It seemed the entire populace of Novomo turned out to greet them, running out to stand alongside the road or waiting in the narrow streets and leaning out of the windows in their crowded houses inside Novomo's walls. Their cries and cheers rang to the heavens. When they came to the steps of Lavinia's palace, fully two dozen noblemen and -women laid their swords at Adelheid's and Henry's feet.

The feast that night had the slightly frenzied spirit of a man coming down with a fever, punctuated at intervals by the distant rumble of thunder, so muted that Rosvita kept thinking she heard wagons passing by on the streets outside.

Some hours before dawn, rain broke over the town, and in the morning the army began its march south beneath a steady, light rain. God was smiling on Aosta again.

Five days' march south they met outriders ranging through low hills, looking for them. Light cavalry chased off these scouts, but by midday the road brought them to a fine vantage point and here, arrayed in battle order, they could see from the ridgetop down onto the central plain that stretched away south until it was lost in a heat haze.

Ironhead was waiting for them. His army lay encamped across the road, its flanks stretching well out to either side, with a makeshift palisade thrown up before his lines. Ironhead had wasted no time, and it was obvious that he had assembled a larger army than Henry's, fully two thousand mounted men or more to judge by the tents and banners, herds of horses, and horde of wagons.

"He must have had word we were coming," said Villam. "A rider could have left Novomo and changed off horses to get to him in three days, but it seems impossible to me that he could have acted so quickly and brought his army five days' march north from Darre in so short a time."

"Unless he has one among his retinue who has the Eagle's sight," said Henry softly, glancing at Hathui, who rode at his right hand.

Villam had not heard him, but Rosvita did. "If Ironhead commands the loyalty of a sorcerer, who knows what he may attempt. Certainly Ironhead does not have the reputation of an honorable man. I advise that you proceed cautiously, Your Majesty"

"So I will."

It was quite warm already and bid fair to become a fiercely hot day despite that they were eight days short of the summer solstice. Henry's brow had a sheen of sweat. Absently, he mopped his brow with a cloth and handed it to one of his stewards, come up beside him. Three captains waited at his back, one carrying the king's shield, one his helmet, and one the holy spear of St. Perpetua, sign of God's favor.

"Where is the queen?" he asked, looking back over his shoulder.

"She comes now, my lord king," said Hathui.

In the last five days Adelheid had grown increasingly clumsy with pregnancy. She looked ready to burst, and could only mount and dismount with difficulty, aided by a half-dozen servants. But ride she did.

"What is this?" she asked as the lines parted to let her through with her ladies and servingwomen riding in her train. Rosvita reined her mule aside to give place to the queen. "Ah! Ironhead has come to greet us."

"It seems the issue is to be decided sooner rather than later," said Henry.

Adelheid had a soldier's eye. She assessed the length and depth of Ironhead's force, and studied the banners. "He has more mercenaries than loyal troops. Might they be bribed to desert him?"

"It might be," said Villam, "but Ironhead will have thought of that himself, if he's as wily as they say."

Henry examined Adelheid. The heat had not withered him; he sat as straight as a young man, unbowed by the aches and pains of advancing age that Rosvita felt every day now that she, like the king, was forty-two—or was it forty-four?—years old. It was hard to keep track and not really important.

But infatuation can make a person young again, and Henry admired his pretty, young queen, just as he had so sweetly admired Sophia when they had married all those years ago; just as he had fallen hard for Alia, when he was only a youth of eighteen. Some men were taken that way, preferring attachment to lust, and in Henry, who had been given the regnant's luck, it extended to all of his friendships. His affections were strong, balanced only by those rare displays of his anger which, once kindled, could not easily be laid to rest.

"If battle is to be joined," he said now, with a handsome frown as he gazed at his pregnant wife, "it would be best for you to retire, my love, to the fortress of Lady Gisla, where we sheltered last night."

"I will take not one step backward in fear of Ironhead. I will ride myself into battle if need be rather than retreat!"

"Truly, you have earned the leopard banner your family bears, my heart. But as you know yourself, a battle can range widely, and what sorrow might there be in victory if you were jostled by some flanking movement—"

"I will not retreat."

Irritation flashed in Henry's expression, but the sight of her stubborn gaze fixed on Ironhead's distant army, the way she tilted up her chin when angry, softened him. "So be it. Will you lead the charge, my lady queen?"

She laughed, knowing herself outflanked. Although pregnancy had softened her features somewhat, blurring the sharp lines of her face, she had not lost the lightning-swift changes of expression that made her features so lively. She smoothed a hand down over the fabric of her gown where a placket of cloth had been added to accommodate her girth. A youth held the reins of her horse, solemn as he kept his hand up close to the bit so that it would make no sudden movement. "I would rather not ride all the way back to Lady Gisla's fortress, but I saw a stout little fort in good repair not more than a league back on the road. I would be willing to wait there, to be sure no harm comes to the child."

"My lord king." Hathui pointed toward the plain where a small group of riders broke away from Ironhead's line to ride toward them. They rode accompanied by three banners: that of the sun of Aosta, that of the presbyters' college, and a white banner bearing the olive branch that signified "parley."

"Do you suppose Ironhead wishes to negotiate?" asked Villam skeptically.

"We shall see."

Henry fell back from the front line. Servants hurried to set up the throne he used when traveling, with its back carved as an eagle's wings, legs fashioned as a lion's paws, and arms shaped in the likeness of fierce dragon visages, painted in bold colors. Adelheid sat beside him in a handsome chair that had been fitted with pillows and a special backrest for her comfort. Her ladies brought her the Aostan crown that was hers by right to wear; it and the royal seals were all that she had salvaged in her escape last year.

Henry knew well the proper use of ceremony. His stewards dressed him quickly in his robes of state, and Rosvita hastily anointed him with a dab of holy oil on his forehead before placing the crown of Wendar and Varre on his head. In such state, and with his court and all the noble ladies and lords of

Aosta assembled around him, he presided over a formidable gathering.

The sun beat down. Wind rippled through the assembled banners and bent the tall grass. The Wendish army, waiting beyond, made a thousand quiet noises, horses whinnying, men calling out, the creak of leather and the snap of cloth as they, too, held ready in case of a trick.

Henry did not rise when Ironhead's emissaries arrived and were allowed to approach the royal presence. But he looked surprised to see the man who strode at their head, brilliantly arrayed in handsome robes and the distinctive scarlet cloak worn only by presbyters. As beautiful as the sun. It always surprised Rosvita each time she saw him.

Hugh.

Henry had not ruled successfully for twenty years because surprises could overset him. One finger stirred, stroking the carven head of a dragon; otherwise he did not move nor give any further impression of amazement. The standard of the realm of Wendar and Varre stirred, belling out, then sagged back to conceal the bright animals embroidered there, the sigils of his regnancy.

He spoke in the king's most forbidding tone. "Hugh of Austra, son of Judith. Did I not send you to Aosta to stand trial before the holy skopos, on the grounds that you had soiled your hands with sorcery?"

Hugh bowed with the precisely correct degree of inclination, neither too proud nor too humble. "So you did, Your Majesty. I was judged and found wanting, but the skopos is merciful, may her soul be at rest. She saw fit to take me into her service so that I could serve God and the church in recompense for my sins."

"Yet who is it you serve," asked Henry in a dangerously soft voice, "when you walk forward now as an envoy from John Ironhead?"

"I serve God, of course, Your Majesty."

Henry's smile was as dangerous as his tone. "Wisely spoken.

Yet you still stand there, while my army and my loyal retinue stand behind me."

Hugh gestured to his servants, who carried forward a basket, which they set in front of him. "No man may serve two earthly masters, Your Majesty. This I know well enough, for I was raised by my mother, who has always supported you faithfully."

"So she has."

"I have always been your loyal subject. That is why I made a place for myself at Ironhead's court."

Truly it was said that God favored the virtuous, and Hugh appeared so devoutly virtuous—as though butter would not melt in his mouth—that Rosvita shuddered with foreboding and moved forward to stand beside the king, thinking that maybe she could deflect whatever sorcerous spell Hugh meant to cast upon them.

Adelheid put a hand over her mouth and nose, grimacing. "I smell something terrible."

Rosvita smelled it, too, a sour iron taste like the odor of magic. She touched the king's arm and bent to whisper in his ear. "Your Majesty, I beg you—"

Hugh was too fast for her.

He signaled. One of his servants whipped aside the cloth that covered the basket. Adelheid cried out, choked, and barely staggered out of her chair before vomiting on the ground while one of her ladies held her.

Henry leaped to his feet.

"I beg your pardon, Queen Adelheid." Hugh took the cloth from the servant and gently placed it over the grisly thing lying on straw in the basket. "I did not intend to upset anyone."

But the image of it had seared into Rosvita's mind. Even if she hadn't recognized that beak of a nose and those wretched features, frozen in a death grimace, she would have known anywhere the iron crown Lord John had worn to spite his enemies, now tumbled in blood-soaked straw.

Adelheid sipped wine and turned back, her face pale but her expression gloating. "It is what he deserved. Stick it on a lance. John's head is the banner that will clear our path to Darre."

The king walked to the basket and drew the cloth aside again. Henry had always been a cautious man, inclined to listen to others but to check for himself. He grabbed the head by its hair and hoisted it. Clotted fluids dripped from the severed neck onto the sodden straw. A spike had been driven through Lord John's temple.

"Very well," he said, calling over one of his captains. "Ironhead will precede us to Darre." He dropped the head back into the basket, which shuddered at the impact. He turned to Hugh. "His body?"

"In camp."

"His mercenaries?"

"Loyal by reason of the gold he paid them, not to his person. You will find, Your Majesty, my lady queen, that few will mourn Ironhead's passing."

"Yet such a large army of paid soldiers is doubly dangerous when left to its own devices. We'll have to negotiate carefully so as not to have a battle on our hands or a countryside laid to waste by marauders."

Standing under the sun's full glare, Hugh did not wilt; it seemed his natural element, as though the sun had been created expressly to illuminate his features. "You'll find their captains amenable to peace, Your Majesty. They'll not trouble your army."

"An ignoble fate for a warrior," mused Henry as the basket was carried away. "How did it happen?"

Hugh shrugged. "As you sow, so shall you reap. He had a violent nature, my lord king, and I believe that he was murdered while sleeping by one of the girls he had raped."

"So be it," said Adelheid. "God favors the virtuous."

"Is there aught else?" Henry glanced around his court, made quiet by the gruesome sight now mercifully concealed. He looked toward Hathui and, last, at Rosvita. Hugh also regarded her, one handsome eyebrow lifted as though in a question. Words stuck in her throat. The sunlight flared as the wind whipped banners into a frenzy, dazzling her. Mute, she could only shake her head. Servants hurried forward to divest Henry of his robes and crown.

"Come, Lord Hugh," said the king as his horse was brought forward. "Ride beside me."

4

IN his youth, Helmut Villam had built a strong fort at the confluence of the Oder and Floyer Rivers. In the forty years since its founding, Walburg had grown into a substantial town ringed by two walls and further protected by the Oder River on one side and a steep chalk bluff on the other. The Villams had enriched themselves on the spoils won in their wars against the heathen Rederii and Polenie tribes, and in addition to founding two convents and a monastery, Villam had commissioned a cathedral.

Despite the drizzle, Zacharias could see its square tower from their fortified camp set up around a ruined watchtower that overlooked the steep river valley.

He could also see a Quman army encamped on the river plain outside Walburg's palisade and double ditch.

If they captured him, he'd go for the quick death. Fear warred with hatred; neither could win. All that mattered right now was that he didn't see the mark of the Pechanek clan displayed from any of the tent poles. As long as Bulkezu was far away, he could survive the morning with a stalwart heart.

"My lord prince." Captain Fulk came in with the evening's report. "Everwin and Wracwulf killed another Quman scout and brought in his wings."

Under the shelter of an awning strung between the walls of

the ancient round tower, Prince Sanglant lounged at his ease on a pillow while he rolled dice with his daughter and her nursemaid. Soldiers sat around them sharpening swords, polishing helmets, and repairing harness. A handful of young lords sat uncomfortably in this rustic camp, used, perhaps, to more luxurious campaigns, but Sanglant rode without the extravagance of camp followers, concubines, and an extensive baggage train. Unlike most nobles, he shared the conditions of his soldiers. It was one of the reasons they loved him.

Several braziers had been set out, over which strips of meat roasted; smoke stung Zacharias' eyes as he ducked in from the back.

"This is the fifth group we've encountered and certainly the largest. Have we an estimate of their numbers yet?"

"Not more than two hundred, Your Highness."

Blessing jumped to her feet and dashed over to present Fulk, one of her favorites, with two of the dice. "You roll 'em," she said enthusiastically, as pure a command as Zacharias had ever heard. "You roll 'em, Cappen Fulk."

He grinned. Like the rest of the company, he would have walked through fire for his little empress, as they called her. "I'll roll them, Your Highness, but I've got to make this report to my lord prince first."

She glanced at her father, stamped her foot impatiently, but quailed at once when Sanglant frowned at her. With a fierce expression of disgust, she crossed her arms on her chest and glowered.

"I pray you, Your Highness, come sit beside me while you wait." The nursemaid's hoarse little voice was like a soft echo of the prince. "We haven't done carding that wool."

"Don't want to."

"But you shall," said Sanglant.

"Shall not!"

"Than I shall do it myself," said the nursemaid tartly, sitting back and beginning to card wool over the comb. "Because I like to do it and I don't want to share doing it with you."

This was too much for Blessing. She trotted over on her short legs and crouched down to get a good look, biting her lip fretfully. "Can I try? Can I?"

"Here, you hold the handle like this—"

Zacharias wiped raindrops from his forehead and sat down beside Heribert, who was playing chess with Wolfhere. "I can't take a turn around the camp without coming in to find she's grown another finger's span," he said, examining the little girl uneasily. She had lost her infant roundness. Her face had gotten leaner, making her blue-green eyes stand out even more than they had before. Wisps of black hair curled everywhere around her face where it escaped from her braid.

Heribert glanced at him. "It's not her doing."

"Nor did I say it was. But you must admit it's uncanny to see a child grow so quickly. It isn't natural. She must age a week for every day that passes."

"I thought it might stop once the daimone left us," murmured Heribert, looking round to see if the prince was listening, but Sanglant appeared to be deep in conversation with Captain Fulk. "But God know it hasn't. Lord bless us. She was born on the seventh day of Avril, on the feast day of St. Radegundis. One year and three months ago. Yet she looks like any well-grown three-year-old."

"It's your move," said Wolfhere patiently.

"Do you know, Eagle," said Zacharias irritably, "I think I particularly dislike that smirking little smile you wear on your face all the time. You know a lot more than you are telling us."

"So I do, but in the matter of the child I know as little as you do."

"Spoken contemptuously!"

"Hush, now," said Heribert. "No need to quarrel. If I've made peace of a kind with Wolfhere, so can you."

"I'm not meaning to quarrel," replied Zacharias, angry at himself for letting his envy of Wolfhere's knowledge get the better of him. "I just don't like secrets. You know well enough,

Wolfhere, that I'd be your pupil in whatever you cared to teach me, if you had a mind to. But you've made clear it that you won't teach me or anyone else. Except the absent Liath who, I swear to you, I'm beginning to quite dislike even though I've never met her."

"You jealous bastard," said Heribert with a laugh.

"It's still your move," said Wolfhere.

"I'll go." Zacharias ducked back outside, stepping over ropes staked down to hold the awning in place. Summer twilight painted the western forest, shrouded by low-lying clouds, in haze. Wind murmured through the trees, a counterpoint to the patter of rain. A mist had come up from the river, wreathing both cathedral tower and fortress tower in white. Beyond the palisade and ditch lay trampled fields, all that golden grain leveled by a malicious heart that reveled in destruction. A few abandoned hovels, homes of fisherfolk or tanners, stuck out as blackened hulks. Even the orchards had been hacked down, although intact gardens and orchards flourished within the safety of the walls.

The main force of the Quman army lay in wait by the front gates, but smaller encampments were scattered along the valley in a pattern Zacharias could not read. He wasn't a strategist. He'd never trained for war. Perhaps Bulkezu was only hiding in his personal tent, waiting to ambush him—

Nay, no use letting his thoughts tend in that direction. Fear crippled you. He had to beat it out of himself. That was the only way to defeat Bulkezu.

He had other angers he could nurse, to keep his mind off his fear of the Quman.

Why was Wolfhere so stubborn? What use were secrets? Knowledge only mattered if it was shared; people ought to be allowed to learn rather than be kept in ignorance. The thought of that old man sitting on everything he knew, the way a dragon might hoard gold, rankled.

"Out here," said the empress' voice, and Blessing appeared with her nursemaid and young Matto, her constant attendants.

She had a little wooden sword in her left hand and was waving it about enthusiastically. "Now we fight! Now we fight, Matto." When she saw Zacharias and the vista that lay beyond the low wall, she darted over to the wall, jumped several times trying to get a good look over it, and tested toeholds at the base of the wall before returning to Zacharias. "Lift me up!"

He hoisted her up in his arms and there she clung, hands on his shoulders, staring out with her eyes wide as she struggled to actually stand up on his arms to get an extra hand's breadth of height to see. "What's that?"

"That is Margrave Helmut Villam's city, called Walburg. Can you see that banner on the tower? That means his heir is in residence. All the people in the town have been besieged by the Quman army."

"Those Quman are bad," she announced.

"Yes, they'd like to break into the city and burn everything."

"But Dada won't let them. Dada will kill them all and make them go away."

Because Zacharias didn't reply at once, strangled by that plaguey fear, Matto strode forward indignantly. "Of course he will! There isn't anyone who can stand against the prince."

"Of course, lad," said Zacharias weakly as he gazed down on the distant army, their pale tents like dead maggots littering the ground.

Blessing wriggled out of his grasp and set out to climb the wall with Matto hovering behind her to make sure she didn't fall until at last, disgusted, she glared at him to make him move back a step.

"Let her take a few falls, Matto," said Anna as she watched the determined child struggling with a toehold in the wall. "She'll learn better that way."

Zacharias chuckled. "Where did you learn such wisdom, child?"

Anna shut her mouth tight. She hadn't trusted him since the day she learned that he refused to pray to God.

With a sigh, he turned away. The rain had stopped and a dense humidity settled in, almost thick enough to lick out of the air. Twilight closed in and restlessness seized him though he hadn't anywhere to go. He just had to be patient. He'd survived seven years as a slave of the Quman. Certainly he could survive one night of waiting and wondering. He could survive Wolfhere's damnable secretiveness.

He ducked back under the awning just as a cocky young soldier, windblown and rather dirty, entered from the other side to approach captain and prince.

Sanglant sat up with sudden alertness, setting down his cup. "Sibold. I'm glad to see you back safely. What's your report?"

Sibold had a rakish grin and a knife scar under his left ear, just the kind of reckless young man who would volunteer to ride out closer to the Quman lines to reconnoiter. He sauntered forward. "My lord prince. The ditches were well pleased to hide me, hating the Quman as they do. There are three banners flying in the Quman force. The siege is placed before the main gate, but there are two smaller camps, one southwest by the Floyer shore and the other north and east past the ferry. I saw four scouting parties, none above seven men."

Sanglant glanced at Wolfhere, who was still intent on his game with Heribert. "An Eagle's sight is as keen as rumor has it."

"Even if princes do not always trust it," murmured Wolfhere without looking up from the board.

The prince smiled but made no answer. He slipped a ring off his finger and handed it to the young soldier. "You risked your life to bring us that report. It will serve me well."

"Your Highness." With a sly grin, Sibold backed away before swaggering out into the misting rain, no doubt to boast to his companions and show off his prize.

Sanglant picked up the dice still scattered on the carpet. "We'll attack in the morning."

Now his noble companions roused.

"But my lord prince," objected Lord Hrodik, "all the Quman soldiers are mounted. Three hundred of them! We have only one hundred and thirty, even if they are all horsemen."

Sanglant grinned. "Therefore they will not be at too great a disadvantage." The prince took his dragon helmet from the sergeant who had been polishing it and turned it in his hands, examining the fearsome gleam of the dragon ornamentation from every angle before he balanced it on one leg. "Do you have a better plan, Hrodik?"

Thus challenged, the young lord fell all over himself apologizing and finally Zacharias could stand his whining and awkward flattery no longer. He slipped away to the corner given him to sleep where, rolling himself up in his cloak, he dozed off.

Only to wake, later, feeling Heribert's warmth at his back. The pad of a sentry's footsteps drifted to him on the breeze. Fear, like a breath of cold night air, had already gotten its claws into him. What if the Quman overran their camp? What if Prince Sanglant lost the battle sure to come in the morning? Would it be better to end his life by his own hand, or would that merely damn him forever? Had he the courage to throw himself in the path of a Quman arrow or spear? Or would they drag him away and make him a slave again?

He shuddered, thinking of the mark on his shoulder. What if they captured him and, seeing the rake of the snow leopard's claw on his shoulder, returned him to Bulkezu?

Death would be better. If he only had the courage to embrace it.

The night was hazy, the stars half hidden. The camp lay silent, shrouded in mist. A fire burned in front of the prince's awning, and two men sat there without speaking as the flames leaped and crackled: Wolfhere with his back to Zacharias, and a second person, fainter than the Eagle, sitting opposite Wolfhere. But that second person was no man; it was a woman, all bent with age, so thin she seemed without substance, like a shadow.

Zacharias shifted, raising himself up on an elbow. For an instant, he could see the other side of the fire without the flames sparking and twisting in his vision.

There was no one there.

He dropped, breath punched out of him. Mist streamed over the stars. Out in the forest, a wolf howled. Closer, a night creature rustled through the rocks.

Wolfhere did not move. From this angle, Zacharias saw through the flames again.

The woman's figure was still there, faded but clear. She was a shadow. He was seeing the shadow of a woman through the flames.

He began to push himself up just as a man crouched silently beside him and a strong hand gripped his shoulder.

"Let it be, Zacharias," murmured the prince. "Now is not the time."

"When will that time come?" he whispered harshly.

Sanglant did not relinquish that grip, forcing him down firmly until the ground pressed against his back. "When we're no longer fighting for our lives."

"That's me! That's me!" cried Blessing exultantly as her father rode out at dawn, resplendent in armor, tabard, scarlet cloak, and his magnificent dragon helm, with his army arrayed behind him. His banners carried no sigil; he rode with simple cloth-of-gold standards streaming behind him, in recognition of his royal birth, however left-handed it might be, and his daughter's imperial descent.

For Anna, waiting out the skirmishes was the hardest part of traveling in the prince's war band. Prince Sanglant was a grand fighter, but a reckless father.

"Come down from the wall, Your Highness," said Heribert nervously. "You might fall."

Blessing ignored him, bouncing up and down excitedly on

the ruined wall as she watched the soldiers ride away. "I'll
fight next time!" She brandished her wooden sword, which
was about the size of a kitchen knife, poking and thrusting
and hacking at the wind. Pebbles clacked and clattered off the
wall to thump onto the ground in time to the pounding of
hooves fading into the distance as the prince and his soldiers
vanished down the track.

Anna shifted anxiously as Heribert simply swept Blessing
off the wall and carried her—the little girl was too dignified to
struggle—to the half-ruined watchtower. They had to skirt
the traps; Matto and Everwin set the last two in place once
they had all ducked into the tower. The camp lay silent around
them, awning, tents, traveling gear stacked neatly, although in
fact everything of real value had been stowed in the watchtower. She scrambled up the stairs after Heribert and found a
place beside him at the top, where she could see out over the
valley. Blessing had tucked her face into Heribert's shoulder,
yawning mightily.

Fog concealed the valley except for the flames burning at
the top of the two gate towers, symbols of Villam resistance.
The defensive walls of Walburg looked stout and welcoming
right now, compared to the crumbling watchtower and the
little band of six men, not counting the clerics and the Eagle,
left behind to defend Blessing. At times like this she was sorry
she had left Gent and the safe routine of Mistress Suzanne's
workshop. Fool, fool, fool. She squeezed back tears, sure a sob
was about to burst out of her, but Matthias had trained her
well. If she cried, the Eika might hear her. She had never forgotten the lessons she had learned hiding from the Eika in
Gent. She knew how to swallow her fear and keep still, no
matter what.

The sun was rising in the east, but the wind had died. Fog
thinned into wisps along the two rivers. The sound of drums
beating loud and fast rose from within the castle walls. This was
surely not the doing of the prince, who preferred to approach a
fight in silence. Horns joined into the rancor, incoherent blasts

dragged out like the wailing of a stubborn two-year-old. Between the towers, the gate of stout timbers braced with thick iron bands swung open. Armored warriors advanced one by one to form a line before the open portal.

The Quman, whose defensive works were set more than a bowshot from the towers, scrambled for their horses, expecting the keep defenders to charge at any moment. For every mounted warrior who appeared at the gate, five Quman riders came forward to counter them. The wings made them seem ominous and even greater in number than they were. At last, after the banner appeared at the portal, drooping in the dying wind, the lord of the keep rode out to take up the foremost position. He turned to face his troop of four dozen mounted soldiers, his back to the Quman as if daring them to charge. Yet the Quman only formed up, waiting for orders or suspicious of a trap.

After a short span the lord of Walburg turned to face his foe, lowering his lance as if in salute.

Prince Sanglant's force, having reached the bottom of the wooded slope, broke out of the forest and onto the river plain. They advanced at a trot. As yet, a copse of scrub and open orchard obscured them from the main Quman army, assembled before the gate. The scouts stationed to guard against a flank attack fled back toward their camp, occasionally loosing an arrow toward the prince's force to keep them off guard.

It did not take long for the main Quman force to recognize the new threat. A Quman chieftain joined the gathering horde. He was easy to spot because his wings glinted as if each were a knife of polished steel. Half his force split with him, turning neatly and breaking into a charge as the prince's troops cleared the orchard. At a gallop, the two forces collided.

Zacharias, beside her, grunted softly, as though he himself had been hit. Heribert murmured a prayer. Blessing had two fingers in her mouth, sucking hard, as she squinted at the landscape below; it was impossible to tell if she understood what was going on.

Anna leaned forward. The sun was shining in her eyes and it was hard to see.

The prince, dragon helm gleaming, led the charge straight to the iron-winged Quman. Horse and rider disappeared under the prince's assault; the brilliant wings splintered and vanished as the fight swirled over them. Now, at last, Walburg's cavalry advanced as the gate closed behind them, blocking their retreat.

"How goes the fray?" Wolfhere's voice surprised her.

"Well enough, I think. Don't you ride with the prince?

He chuckled softly as Zacharias glared at him. "Nay, child. I'm too old for battle."

"Look," said Heribert softly. "They've routed them."

The field churned into chaos, Wendish soldiers pursuing the Quman, who scattered in all directions.

Sanglant split his group into three; his dragon helm could be seen chasing the largest surviving knot of Quman toward the river. Walburg's forces hunted down Quman as well. Anna lost sight of Walburg's lord where the slope and wood hid him from view, near where Sanglant had originally emerged.

"Quman!" From below, Matto called the alarm.

A group of fourteen Quman broke out of the trees and into the clearing, reining their horses aside when they saw the undefended tents, the ruined watchtower, and the square-walled little fort. Wolfhere drew his short sword and crept carefully to the parapet walk, avoiding rotted planks and gaps in the floorboards.

Zacharias yanked her down beside him. Through the gaps in the floorboards she saw Matto, Everwin, and the man everyone called Surly standing with spears to cover the breaches that riddled the first floor of the tower. From this angle she couldn't see Den, Johannes, and Lewenhardt, who were stationed elsewhere. She stuck her hand into an alcove in the stone wall, drawing out the long knife she had laid aside just in case. Zacharias and Heribert had staffs, but everyone knew that Heribert was pretty useless in a fight. How well Zacharias could fight was a mystery to everyone, but the look of desperation on his face made her almost feel sorry for him.

Heribert slid over to Anna. "Don't worry," he whispered. "They'll loot the camp and then ride away. They won't even know we're here."

"I kill them," interrupted Blessing. The cleric hissed softly and set two fingers over Blessing's lips. The little girl sighed disgustedly and shut her eyes.

By now the sound of horses crashing through the undefended camp and of men calling to each other in their harsh language carried easily. Fabric ripped. Pots clattered. A horse neighed. Anna took little comfort in Heribert's words. She hid the knife up her sleeve so that, should a Quman reach her, he might think her unarmed and easy prey.

What betrayed them she never knew. Maybe it was only curiosity on the part of one of the Quman soldiers.

She heard it because, crouched down, she could see nothing except her companions, the crumbling parapet wall, and the sky. A soldier must have investigated the stairs, where one of the traps had been laid.

A scream cut abruptly through the sounds of looting. A body fell, wetly, in awful silence. At once, the Quman shouted to each other and a rain of arrows spattered down along the parapet walk. One slammed into the wall above Anna and flopped over to clatter onto the plank beside Heribert. She peeped out over the wall.

Crazy Lewenhardt had found himself cover on a slab of wall broken off on either side and therefore hard to climb. The best archer in Sanglant's troop, he started shooting now, picking his targets carefully. A dismounted Quman who was advancing on the tower fell writhing, then scrambled backward with an arrow sticking out of his thigh. Another shower of arrows followed; Anna ducked. Through the floorboards she saw Everwin grab at a rope just as Matto yelled.

"Three of them, in the left breach!"

Rocks tumbled as a winged soldier pressed through, leading

with his spear. Either the rocks crushed him or he leaped out of the way; she couldn't tell as dust rose, screening her view. Surly was already hacking at the central breach, trading blows with an unseen foe. Shouts rose from Den and Johannes as Quman found the other usable stairs leading to the parapet. She heard the sharp "twang" of the last trap released. Wolfhere ran down the walk to aid them, but he hadn't gone more than ten steps when a Quman leaped onto the parapet between Wolfhere and the tower. The stone archway, all that remained of the old door, framed his frightful figure. His wings fluttered as the wind picked up; several feathers, scraped off from his climb, drifted out into the gulf of air beyond the wall.

Anna shouted a warning, leaping up as she drew her knife.

Lewenhardt's arrow took the man from behind. He staggered and fell forward just as Wolfhere, turning, struck him down. But he still wasn't dead. Anna ran forward as he groped toward the wall. She kicked away his spear, then leaped back as Wolfhere rolled him over and slit his throat.

"Wolfhere!" shouted Heribert desperately.

Anna turned to see Matto scooting up the narrow stair that led from the lower room to the upper. The youth jabbed his spear down, and down again with his right arm while his left arm was wrapped around Everwin, dragging him up as the other man kept kicking and kicking as though to shove away an enemy or to catch a step to propel himself upward.

"Damn," said Wolfhere casually. He tossed the dead man's spear to Anna. "Do your best, child." He turned back to help Den and Johannes, both of whom she could now see being pressed backward up along the other stairs.

Heribert set Blessing down and leaped forward to pull Everwin free. Amazingly, the child had fallen asleep. Zacharias was nowhere to be seen.

Anna ran over to stand beside Matto as he heaved himself up onto the planks. Once Everwin was clear, she thrust the spear into his hands, then pried loose rocks free from the wall with Heribert's help and started dropping them down the stairs as fast as they could get hold of new ones. Wings shattered. Men cursed. The angle and ferocity of their attack stymied the Quman for the moment.

"Anna, Anna, give me the baby!" Zacharias' voice called from below, from outside the guard tower.

Darting to the side of the tower overlooking the inner ward of the little fort, Anna peered over the side. Zacharias had actually climbed over the parapet wall and slid down the outside of the watchtower to the inner ward, where only the ruined square of walls protected him from their attackers.

A trio of Quman archers had Lewenhardt pinned down in his redoubt. Den was wounded, an arrow stuck cockeyedly out of one shoulder, and he had fallen back behind Johannes and Wolfhere, who retreated step by laborious step back up the stairs in the face of superior numbers. An arrow glanced off Johannes' helmet and he stumbled, only to be yanked out of reach of a Quman spear by Wolfhere.

"Rocks!" cried Everwin.

Two Quman riders leaped the fallen stones half blocking the entrance to the inner ward and pulled up inside. Zacharias shrieked in helpless fear and threw himself onto the ground in abject surrender. There was nothing she could do to help Zacharias, if he'd been so stupid as to leave the only refuge they had. But she could still, maybe, save Blessing.

As one of the Quman drew and aimed at the frater's prostrate body, Anna gritted her teeth and tugged another stone off the wall before staggering back to throw it down right on the helmet of the Quman soldier trying to push up onto the second floor. Matto cheered weakly as the Quman dropped out of sight. Blood ran from both his legs as he sat down hard, face pale, too weak to fight.

"They'll never take her," cried Heribert, grabbing the spear out of Matto's hands.

A horn rang clear and sweet. The Quman shouted to each other. The attackers below vanished between one breath and the next, and she heard them scrambling over rocks to get to their horses. The ring of swords over by Wolfhere ceased as abruptly. Anna ran over to the outer wall, standing on tiptoes and craning her neck just in time to see Wendish soldiers break out of the woods.

The lord of Walburg and twenty stout fighting men had arrived, thank God.

Good Wendish steel made short work of the last of the Quman. When they were all dead and sentries had ranged out to cover the ground, the lord pulled off his helm and coif to reveal that he was a woman.

"Well met, my lady Waltharia," cried Wolfhere from the parapet walk. To Anna's surprise, he was grinning, an odd expression on that normally secretive face. He shouted to the others. "Best go down and pay our respects."

Zacharias staggered out of the inner ward, having suffered no worse injuries than scraped knees and hands. Only Anna and Heribert had noticed his ignominious escape attempt, and if Heribert meant to say nothing, then Anna decided she would keep her mouth shut, too. Surly was dug up from the first-floor rubble; he'd taken a hard blow to the head and was only now waking, but otherwise looked unharmed. The rest straggled over, limping, cursing, but otherwise victorious.

"God save us," said Lady Waltharia as the motley defenders gathered before her. "I've never seen a more wretched crew than this one. Where's the brat?"

Heribert was carrying Blessing, who yawned sleepily and cracked one eye, twisted up her face in a delightful grimace, and decided against waking up. With another yawn, she snuggled her head against Heribert's shoulder and promptly went back to sleep.

Lady Waltharia dismounted to examine the child, although she was careful not to wake her. "Handsome little thing. Although I suppose she'd be so, with the prince for a father. Who are you?"

"I am Brother Heribert, my lady. Brother Zacharias and I constitute Prince Sanglant's schola."

She had a good laugh, friendly and open. "A schola, an Eagle, a brat, and this nut-brown creature."

"I am called Anna, my lady," said Anna stoutly.

"So you are, if you say so, but why on earth does a girl of your tender years ride with Sanglant's war band?"

"I am the nursemaid, my lady."

"Ah. A good thing, too, for the prince to provide his child with a nursemaid if he insists on dragging her about with his war band. Are you practical? Do you scare easily? Can you endure the pace of his army?"

"That's a lot of questions, my lady."

"Nor should you answer them, if you're wise. Here's a few likely looking youths as well," she added, marking Matto and the other five soldiers with a comprehensive glance. She was perhaps thirty years of age, a tall woman made imposing by her mail and swagger, with ruddy cheeks and light brown hair pulled tightly back in a braid. Sweat beaded on her forehead. One of her ears was missing the tip of its lobe, and her easy grin revealed a missing tooth. She beckoned to Wolfhere, who stepped forward respectfully. "So, Eagle, I hear a rumor that you've been banished again. Or that you deserted the king. It's so difficult to sort out rumor from truth, is it not? Ought I to send you on your way with the flat of my sword, or imprison you?"

Wolfhere smiled. To Anna's amazement, she could see that he genuinely liked this woman. He was always so reserved that it was remarkable to see a real spark of emotion in his face. "I am pledged to aid the prince, my lady. I throw myself on his mercy in this case."

She snorted, delighted by his reply. "On the mercy of the prince! Whom you tried to murder when he was but a mewling infant, if the old story is indeed true, and certainly my dear father believes it true, since he's the one who told it to me."

A sharp whistle, repeated three times, sounded from the trees.

"But I trust we can ask him ourselves," she finished, turning at the sound of riders approaching up the track.

Blessing woke up abruptly, lifting her head and squirming so determinedly that Heribert gave up in disgust and let her wriggle out of his grasp. "Dada!" she yelped ecstatically as streaming gold banners appeared among the trees. A moment later the prince himself rode into view, quite splendid in his gold tabard, scarlet cloak, gleaming armor, and the intimidating dragon helm, gold dragon plating sculpted onto the helmet in such a way that it looked as if the dragon was about to launch itself into attack.

He pulled up his horse and dismounted at once, had barely gotten his helm off before Blessing was on him, clamoring to be picked up. "Hush, Daughter," he said, laughing as he picked her up. He looked at Waltharia, who was admiring the fine figure he made. "It worked."

"It always does." She smiled as at an old memory, meeting his gaze straight on.

"Dada, look at me!" scolded Blessing, then shrieked with glee when he tweaked her nose.

"How is Hedwig?" asked Wolfhere.

Waltharia chuckled. "Hates you as much as ever, or so I assume from the stream of oaths she let fly when she realized last night that it was you who had arrived in the train of the prince."

"I shall endeavor to keep out of her way," murmured Wolfhere mildly.

"So you had better, if you value all your limbs." She turned back to Sanglant. "A timely visit, my lord prince. The Quman invested Walburg only six days ago. You saw what they did to the fields and orchards. There are a dozen farmers unaccounted for from the estates." She walked boldly up to him and fingered the hem of Blessing's tunic, smudged and ragged from play. The little girl eyed her suspiciously. "I am surprised, though, that you expose the child to so much danger, riding on campaign with you."

"Less danger with me than with any caretaker." Anna knew how fiercely he loved his daughter. She could see it in his expression now as he glared defiantly at Lady Waltharia, as if her good opinion mattered to him. "Better she die if I die than that she live without my protection."

"And her mother——? Ah. Best we leave that subject for another time, I see. I'll personally escort your schola and your nursery to the safety of my fortress."

"I thank you," he said stiffly, still looking irritated. He kissed Blessing. "You go with Anna, little one. Nay, no arguments now." Nor did he wait for arguments. He handed Blessing over to Anna's care and left again with his war band, thundering down toward the plain, no doubt to track down and kill as many fleeing Quman as he could.

Lady Waltharia did indeed escort them to Walburg, but she left them at the gates in the care of a steward and herself rode off to pursue their enemies.

Planks had been thrown hastily down over the outer ditch to accommodate the sally. Anna walked over, feeling safer that way as a servant led her mule. The planks shifted under her feet, and she had to throw out her arms to keep her balance before she reached solid ground. The next bridge led directly under the wall, guard towers looming on either side and murder holes spaced at intervals. She heard voices murmuring down the holes and glimpsed movement, soldiers watching from the safety of their fortifications. The gate creaked open; they passed through into Walburg itself.

For a city under siege it was remarkably clean and orderly. Avenues wrapped around the hill where the original fort had risen. Newer streets, all of them lined with plank walkways, radiated outward from the cathedral square. Tents had been thrown up in the square and in a handful of vacant lots in neat lines to accommodate refugees, but most of the unbuilt ground had been given over to orchards and gardens, provision against the siege. Smaller than Gent's cathedral, the basilica of St. Walaricus had a tidy look about it, everything squared off, the lintels painted with intertwined spirals and linked circles flowering into wreaths and the tower decorated with a carved tree on each face, painted silver.

"The Villam sigil is the silver tree," explained Zacharias as they passed through the cathedral square on their way up to the fortified palace.

"So it is," agreed Heribert, "but so also was St. Walaricus martyred by being hung from a tree by a heathen prince."

"Clever of Villam to dedicate the cathedral to Walaricus, was it not? Then he could have it both ways."

Heribert looked surprised. Anna liked him much better than she liked Zacharias, who had spit in God's face, but even so, he made her kind of uncomfortable just because he was always so tidy and clean even in the worst camp conditions. Sometimes she just didn't see the point of being so fussy.

"Do you think Villam chose to dedicate his cathedral to St. Walaricus just so he could display his own sigil upon the church tower without anyone calling him to account for such presumptuousness?"

Zacharias laughed. "Do you suppose Villam did not? He's a more clever man than I, friend."

"Than I devoutly pray we be spared his intrigues."

Zacharias merely smiled. Anna didn't trust him when he smiled, no more than she trusted the old Eagle Wolfhere who, like any wolf, looked as ready to bite you as to lick your hand.

The men-at-arms, even Matto, were led to the barracks, but Blessing and her personal retinue were given a tower room in the palace, good enough to see out along the river. There was a bed all downy soft, a smaller trundle bed heaped high with a feather quilt, and four sleeping pallets stacked against one wall. A half-dozen braziers heavy with coals warmed the chilly room. Anna sat cross-legged on the thick carpet since Zacharias, Wolfhere, and Heribert took the bench and chair. Blessing decided to sit on the table, right in the center, where she could command the servants as they brought in a hearty meal of chicken basted in mustard and parsley, a juicy broth, leeks cooked in butter, slices of veal with a mint sauce spooned over it, and honey dumplings.

The rich meal made Anna burp. She curled up at the foot of the bed, suddenly so sleepy that she wanted nothing better than a nap.

Woke to a shriek.

"Dada! Dada! See me up here!"

"Lord save us, Your Highness!" That was Heribert, frantic. "You'll fall to your death!"

Hiding from the Eika, Anna had learned to wake quickly and with all her wits intact. She leaped up in time to see Wolfhere grab Blessing bodily and sweep her down from the window ledge. The girl shrieked louder, if that was possible, twisted in Wolfhere's grasp, and bit his wrist, hard.

He yelped and dropped her.

"Now there's a child whose taste I admire." An elderly woman wearing the badge of an Eagle moved in through the door, leaning heavily on a cane. She measured each person in the chamber with a keen gaze more likely to chill than to warm. Even Blessing, drawing breath for a good, loud, out-raged scream, deflated abruptly, staring at the new arrival with puzzlement. "So, Wolfhere, I had prayed I might never have the pleasure of seeing you again."

"I beg your pardon, Hedwig," he said. "Out of respect, I'll offer no 'hail, fellow, and well met.'"

"I expected you'd be dead by now."

"I heard you were."

She snorted. "It will take more than five Quman arrows to kill me."

"I heard it was bandits."

She laughed dryly. "Quman weren't the only ones who have tried to kill me. The bandits you speak of soon learned their mistake. Lady Waltharia strung them up for their trouble in Cathedral Square. They hung there until the crows and ravens ate them down to the bone." She dug in one of her dangling sleeves and after a moment fished out a string of finger bones. "This is all that remains of them."

"A handsome trophy," observed Wolfhere.

"I keep it with me to remind me of what befalls those who make me angry."

He laughed, but Anna could see by the flush in his cheeks and the way he squinted his eyes all tight and shifty-like that he loved Mistress Hedwig no better than the elderly woman loved him. Anna scooted over to Blessing and made the child graciously accept the old Eagle's homage.

"So this is the child." They examined each other, the crippled old woman and the young princess. Blessing's hair had escaped its braid, and wisps curled around her sharp little face.

"I will sit," Blessing announced. She sat on the center of the carpet and gestured imperiously toward the bench, where Zacharias hastily moved aside to make room. "You will sit."

"I thank you, Your Highness, but if I sit it will be a day and half before I can get my old bones to lift me up again. I am bid by Lady Waltharia to bring you down to the feast. She means to serve you and your father most handsomely, as befits a margrave hosting a royal prince."

"I thought Helmut Villam was margrave here," muttered Zacharias.

The comment earned him a cutting look from old Hedwig.

Wolfhere hastened to explain. "Lady Waltharia is margrave in all but name."

"Her father isn't dead yet! He looked damned lively to me when I had the misfortune to be brought to his attention!"

Heribert shrugged. "The secrets of King Henry's inner court are hidden to me. I am only a lowly cleric from the schola at Mainni."

Wolfhere grunted, half amused by the elegant cleric's protestation. "Why do you think old Villam rides in attendance to the king? He and his daughter respect each other, but they don't get along. She's competent to rule the marchlands, and he can't live forever. He stays out of her way. It's a form of retirement, since he hasn't the temperament to abide the monastery. And better—" He glanced at Hedwig. When their gazes met, it was like blows being exchanged. "Better for all concerned than rebellion. It's been known before for a restless adult to rebel against a parent when no independence is forthcoming. Villam is a wise man, and he did better than most to raise an heir as wise as he."

"That you respect her as she deserves is the only good thing I have to say about you," observed Hedwig.

"So be it." Wolfhere raised a hand, as if in submission. "Let us not scrape old wounds raw, I beg you."

"Don't fight!" commanded Blessing, fists set on hips as she glared at them. She had such a fierce way of screwing up her face that it was—almost—impossible to laugh at her. In another year, it wouldn't be funny anymore.

"As you wish, Your Highness," said Hedwig without expression. "If you will allow me to escort you."

Anna admired Hedwig for the steady way she took the stairs, even though every step seemed to hurt her. The stairway twisted down, curving to match the tower. She'd never seen a tower so big built all of stone before except for the cathedral tower in Gent, and it had been square. This one was cold and dreary and dark, but once they reached the base they passed through an archway girded with a double set of doors, each one reinforced by an iron bar, and out into a sizable courtyard where soldiers swarmed. Anna smelled blood and excitement like perfume, the heady scent of a victory won. A great pile of wooden wings lay in a heap to one side. Feathers drifted in the air like a fine chaff of snow. Prince Sanglant stood by one of the troughs. He'd stripped down to almost nothing and now sluiced water over his bare chest and arms, washing away blood.

Blessing drew in air for a shriek of delight, glanced at Hedwig, and abruptly thought better of it. Instead, she yanked and yanked at Anna to get her to move faster as she trotted through the crowd. Soldiers gave way before her, calling out her name, as she made straight for her father.

As they came up behind him, he spoke without turning around. "Nay, little one, I'm in no mood for sport."

Sometimes, like now, the prince seemed consumed by a passion for washing that put Heribert's fussy ways to shame. Anna had never seen a person scrub as hard as he might do when he got in one of those moods. But she remembered the way he'd looked when he'd been chained in Gent's cathedral, two years ago. Maybe he could never scrape all that grime and filth away, or at least not in his heart.

Lady Waltharia's soldiers spoke together in low voices, watching the prince as he bathed.

"Nay, I'd not have believed it. I swear those Quman would have run from him even if he'd been alone."

"I've never seen a man fight so bravely."

"I heard he went mad when his banner bearer went down."

Lower still: "Is it true he can never be king?"

A sudden arc of noise ended in silence as Lady Waltharia entered the courtyard with a broad-shouldered lord in attendance. He was still armed, cheeks as flushed as though he'd been running. Drying blood streaked his blond hair, cut short to frame a square face. Waltharia had already shed her mail but the padded coat she wore showed stains of sweat around the collar and under the arms, and tiny discolored rings where her mail had pressed into the cloth.

At once, the soldiers broke into cheers.

She lifted a hand to call for silence. "Let Prince Sanglant be honored. If he had not struck, we would still lie under siege."

As the soldiers hurrahed and shouted, Matto ran up with Sanglant's feasting tunic. He pulled it on over his damp hair, a fine wool tunic dyed a mellow orange, embroidered with yellow and white dragons stretching like snakes along the hem and at the sleeves. He did not ask for quiet but got it anyway as he finished belting the tunic at his hips.

"Don't rejoice too much." Though he did not seem to shout,

his hoarse voice carried easily over the throng. "Drink your fill tonight, but remember that we have more battles to fight. This was only a small portion of the Quman army. Their leader isn't dead yet, nor are they running east like whipped dogs. *As they will.*"

The soldiers liked such words. They shouted his name, and then that of their lady and her husband, Lord Druthmar. The celebration carried them into the great hall. Prince Sanglant hoisted his daughter onto his shoulders where she shrieked and shouted with the best of them, her high voice lifting above the clamor. Anna thought she herself would be overwhelmed and trampled, but Matto and Captain Fulk closed in behind her, protecting her in a pocket of space behind the prince so she wouldn't be crushed. The months hadn't been as kind to her as they'd been to Matto, who had grown a hand in height and filled out through the chest. Although she never got bitterly hungry, she'd gotten lean. All the fat she'd earned in Mistress Suzanne's compound had melted away under the rigors of riding to campaign. Caught up in the rush of rough and ready soldiers, she felt like a stick thrown into a stream swollen with the spring flood.

It was hard to hear anything at the feast over the constant singing and toasts, the dull roar of a satisfied and triumphant assembly. Anna stood in attendance on Blessing, as always. At intervals, she nibbled at the delicacies heaped up on Blessing's platter as course after course rolled through: roasted goose with parsley and bread stuffing; a meat stew strewn with rose petals and sweetened with cherry preserves; oyster loaves; breads sprinkled with caraway and fennel; beef broth cooked with dill and leeks; a potage of ground hazelnuts, flour, and elderflowers; and honey dumplings again.

The victorious soldiers drank heavily. Lady Waltharia herself poured Prince Sanglant's wine through a gold sieve spoon that she had gotten, so she said, as part of her inheritance from her dead mother, who had been Villam's third and favorite wife.

Lord Druthmar seemed a steady sort of man, open, honest,

good-hearted, and not one bit chafed by his wife's authority. "We've heard reports that Bulkezu has captured Prince Ekkehard."

"Has Bulkezu asked for ransom?" Sanglant chased off a greyhound that was trying to lick grease off the linen cloth laid over the prince's knees. "Or do you think he'll kill him?"

Lady Waltharia sat down between the two men. Anna moved quickly to stop Blessing from feeding a choice morsel of meat to the rejected greyhound.

"It's only a rumor that the Quman captured Ekkehard," said Waltharia. "Prince Bayan and Princess Sapientia wintered in Handelburg. We heard that Prince Ekkehard was imprisoned there, but he escaped the biscop's custody and fled the town. The roads are cold and difficult in the wintertime, when he was last seen. I think he must be dead."

Sanglant sipped thoughtfully at his wine. "It's an implausible story. You know Bayan as well as I do. How could a youth like Ekkehard escape not just Bayan's but also Biscop Alberada's watch?" He shook his head. "For what offense is it said he was imprisoned?"

Blessing dropped her spoon. Anna crouched just in time to see the recalcitrant greyhound nosing the ivory spoon, licking off the remains of broth. She hissed, and the dog scrabbled away, kicking rushes up in her face. Half under the table, hands covered in rushes and a discarded bone digging into her knee, she heard Lady Waltharia's quiet reply.

"Heresy."

Did the hall quiet, or was it only the thick table and the heavy embroidered tablecloth hanging down to brush the floor that muffled the noise of the feasting multitude? Lord Druthmar began laughing at a joke told to him by the lord sitting at his right hand. Lady Waltharia had the prince's attention all to herself.

"It's been said that these heretics use evil magic to gain followers. It's also been said that God aided Ekkehard. Take your pick."

"I let the church folk quarrel about religion."

She chuckled and called for more wine. Anna felt it safe to emerge from under the table, wriggling back under the bench. Standing, she wiped off the spoon on her tunic so that it was clean enough to give back to Blessing.

Petitioners came forward to beg Lady Waltharia to allow them to return to their farms now that the Quman menace had fled. A poet begged leave to entertain them with the song that he had composed this very night in honor of their victory. Blessing's head drooped, her eyes fluttered, she yawned, and tried to climb into her father's lap to sleep.

"I'll take her to her bed." Sanglant rose, cradling Blessing in his arms. A great shout rose from the assembled soldiers, cheering him, and for the first time since returning from battle he smiled, acknowledging their tribute. He raised a hand for silence, and the crowd quieted, waiting for him to speak.

"Drink well this night," he called. "Tomorrow we hunt Quman."

With the soldiers' cheers still echoing, Anna followed him out by dark passages that led them not immediately to the tower but rather to the barracks, a long attic room built over the stables. Pallets of hemp and straw made lumpy beds, but they were a softer mattress than the plank floor. She could smell the horses below and even catch glimpses of them through warped floorboards. It was quiet in the barracks; most of the men still feasted in the great hall. Those who had been wounded in today's engagement had been carried up here to recover, or die.

With Blessing asleep on his shoulder, the prince visited each of the injured men, traded jokes, checked poultices, or quizzed them closely about what they had seen and done in the battle. A few were too injured even to speak, although one of these could at least grasp the prince's hand. One man had a gray face, as though the life drained quickly out of him. Anna knew all their names, Chustaffus, Fremen, Liutbald, and even reckless Sibold, who had taken a grim wound to his chest but joked in a lively enough manner when he saw his prince before him. Maybe he wouldn't die.

There were, of a miracle, only three corpses, hauled back from the battle and now covered with shrouds, but one was faithful Wracwulf, who had been given the honor this day of carrying the prince's golden banner. Sanglant knelt beside his body for a long time while Blessing snored quietly in his arms. After a while, Captain Fulk appeared to take his place with the dead. Only then did Sanglant take his sleeping daughter to the tower chamber where her bed waited. Anna carried a lamp to light their way. Once inside the room, she hung it from an iron hook set into the wall, then helped the prince wash Blessing's hands, sticky with grease and honey, strip her down to her under-tunic, and tuck her into the trundle bed. He stood over the child, watching her slide into a deeper sleep as intently as he had studied his wounded soldiers.

"You're a good girl, Anna," he said suddenly. With a poker, he stirred the coals in the brazier closest to Blessing. "What do you think? Should I leave her here at Walburg under Waltharia's protection while I ride east? Yet who can I truly trust? Can I trust anyone?"

"You can trust me, my lord prince."

He looked at her finally and grinned a crooked grin, a charming grin. She would have jumped out the window right then and there, if he'd asked her to; he had that kind of shining honor to him, so bright that sometimes she thought she could actually see it like a nimbus around him even though she knew it was only her heart that loved him, just as his soldiers loved him.

"So I can," he agreed, and her heart leaped with joy, knowing she'd won his trust in return.

He had remained still for a long time. Now he began to pace, working the length of the chamber, cutting it into patterns, squares and stars and circles, until she got dizzy watching him. She took off her shoes and lay down beside Blessing on the trundle bed. The feathers were so soft that she thought she might sink forever. She was tired, and she hadn't slept in such a comfortable bed since she'd left Mistress Suzanne's. But she cracked an eye open to see what he was doing. He had stopped by the door and stood there listening, hand poised a finger's breadth away from the latch. The latch creaked, shifted, and turned. He jumped back so that, as the door opened, it hid him.

Lady Waltharia entered the chamber alone. She halted a few steps in, surveying with an ironic smile the empty bed, the silent pallets, the table laid with a pitcher of cider and three silver cups, and the sleeping child. The door closed sharply behind her and she jumped, startled, and whirled around to see Sanglant laughing silently behind her.

She chuckled, sweeping her hair back over her shoulders. Somehow, between the hall and this chamber, her braid had come undone to reveal waist-length hair, still crinkled from its recent confinement in the braid.

"You haven't changed," she said as she crossed to sit on the edge of the bed, tying back the hangings so they didn't get in her way.

"Haven't I?" he asked, not moving from his place beside the door.

"You once told me you would never marry."

"Only because my father forbade it. I was captain of the King's Dragons. It was not my right to marry. Then."

"Maybe I'm wrong," she observed, rising to go to the unshuttered window. "You are not what you were." She leaned out on the ledge, hands braced on the wooden frame set into the stone opening. From the trundle bed Anna could not see what Waltharia was looking at, if indeed she was looking at anything except the sky and the stars. It was probably warmer outside than in. The stone walls had a way of holding damp and chill jealously inside them.

"What is she like? Your wife, I mean."

"Do you envy her?"

She turned. "I suppose I would have, once. But you would

have been too much trouble, even if I could have had you. My
father was right about that. I needed a more compliant husband." Because he remained silent, she grinned delightfully
and sat on the ledge. Wind stirred her hair. "He's a good man,
Druthmar. Good enough."

"He acquitted himself ably today."

"So he did. But he isn't you. You're the best stallion in the
king's stable. I can't help but admire so much handsome flesh.
Especially when I discover it standing half naked at my
trough."

He laughed. "I needed a wash."

"You can wash here. I can have water brought up."

"You're the one who hasn't changed."

"Perhaps not. In the old days before the church of the
Unities saved my ancestors from the Abyss, it was said that
certain priestesses of my people mated with stallions in order
to bring good luck to the tribe. I must be descended from one
of them."

He came forward finally and threw himself down on the
bed, lounging on his back with casual grace as he watched her.
From her place in the trundle bed, Anna saw him outlined in
lamp glow. The mellow light gave his tousled black hair a
silky sheen.

Waltharia remained seated at the window. "You married a
woman who claims to be the great granddaughter of Emperor
Taillefer and who has also been excommunicated and outlawed
for sorcery, one who hasn't been seen since she left Werlida in
your company. In truth, nothing remains of her but the child.
The same could be said, I suppose, about your mother."

His lips curled, although not in a smile. "What a great deal
you know."

"Do I? It seems to me that the person who believes she
knows a great deal most likely knows very little."

"A wise saying."

"My father taught me well." She walked to the table to
pour herself a cup of cider, letting the rim of the cup linger at

her mouth as she examined him over the lip. "What happened to your wife? Did you abandon her?"

His expression grew stiff. "More like she abandoned me. I have reason to believe she still lives. Whether she cares to return to me and the child I do not know. But you are right. The same could be said about my mother. How have you learned so much, out here in the marchlands?"

"I received a message from my father some weeks ago." She paused suggestively, lowering the cup. Anna almost sat up, eager to hear what would come next, but just in time she remembered that she was pretending to sleep. "He suggests that I support you as well as I am able."

"What does he mean by that?"

"What do you think he means? Why did you leave your father's court and turn your back on your father's authority?"

"Because he wouldn't listen to me. There is a cataclysm coming, and we must prepare for it."

"The folk who work my estates think the Quman raids are cataclysm enough."

"So they are, but they are nothing compared to what we will have to face."

She set down the cup and simply watched him for a while in silence. Anna examined her profile: a strong face, as proud as a margrave's heir must be but also clean like unstained linen. She had faint scars along her jaw below the mutilated ear, and a wine-colored birthmark in the hollow of her throat, easy to see from this angle, but nothing evil in her face, no hidden hatreds or petty jealousies. She knew what she possessed, and she wasn't afraid to rule what was hers.

"Of course, I am inclined to support you in any case, Sanglant."

"Are you?" He was either very drunk or very tired.

Her smile hadn't any answering softness in it. "We live in a time of troubles. Eika raid from the north while Quman strike at us from the east. Machteburg burned to the ground, did you hear that? For two years running there have been poor harvests in the marchlands. A hailstorm flattened a church south of here this spring. A two-headed lamb was born in Duchess Rotrudis' lands. A child here in Walburg was born with six fingers. Along the north coast a thousand birds washed up on the shore, all of them dead. Half of the fraters wandering in my lands speak heresy instead of truth, and the people listen to them. In a time of troubles, the land must have a strong leader."

"My father is a strong leader."

"So he is, but he thinks too much about Aosta and Taillefer's crown. We need a strong leader here in Wendar and the marchlands. Sapientia is weak, Theophanu is cold, and Ekkehard is young and by all reports foolish, if not already dead. But we march lords have not forgotten that Henry has one other child."

Sanglant had been resting his head on his hands, but now he pushed himself up. "What intrigue is Villam hatching?"

"My father loves Henry. No man loves the king better. But my father loves Wendar most of all." She fished into her sleeve and drew out a gold torque, holding it up. Its metal gleamed richly; light winked on the braided surface. "You no longer wear your gold torque, my lord prince. But you should."

He hissed sharply, taken aback by the precious ornament hanging so casually from her hand.

"I pray you," she went on, her voice sliding into a sweet languor as she dangled the torque from her fingers, "let me see how it becomes you."

Anna was old enough to understand what went on between men and women. That Sanglant was aroused was evident enough; he was flushed with more than the wine. Women were subtler but not always more difficult to interpret. Only a fool or a child would not have known what was on Waltharia's mind at this moment.

Blessing grunted in her sleep, rolled over, and nudged up against Anna, who squeezed her eyes shut and desperately tried to keep still even though Blessing's elbow was jabbed against her ribs.

"We wintered at Gent." That hoarse scrape in his voice gave his words a nostalgic tone—but in truth, his voice always sounded like that. "There was a woman there, a servant in the palace. Frederun. She wept when I left."

"Thinking already of the gifts she would no longer get from you."

"No. She was genuinely sorry to see me go."

"So will I be, Sanglant." She spoke the words teasingly, but he did not respond in kind.

"That's not what I meant. It didn't seem right somehow, to use her that way. It seemed as though I'd offered her something she desperately wanted and then snatched it out of her hands."

"I don't understand you," said Waltharia impatiently. "I am a woman, just as she is. You know well enough what appeal you have to us, or at least you once knew it well enough to encourage our sighs and offers, and I know you have never suffered a lack of interest on our part. She was lucky you paid her any attention at all."

"Was she?" he murmured, but Waltharia either did not hear or did not reply. Sanglant sighed sharply. Blessing gave a snorting sigh as if in answer and rolled away, flinging an arm out as she shifted. She had grown into a remarkably unquiet sleeper.

Lying still, Anna risked opening one eye.

Sanglant still sat on the bed, looking intent but rather rumpled, as though he'd already taken a few rolls in the hay. He fingered his hair, playing with the tips, needing something to do with his restless hands.

"Where is my schola?" he asked at last.

"They were given my leave to sleep by the hearth in the hall this night."

At last he rose, walking to the window, leaning out to stare into the night just as Waltharia had done before him. His embroidered tunic showed off the breadth of his shoulders and the tapering line of his torso and hips. Anna was old enough now to note that men were good-looking. Sometimes she peeked at Matto, watching the changes overcome his youthful body, but she had never precisely thought of the prince himself in those terms. He was too old, and too high above her. The night breeze breathed in his hair, stirring black strands along his neck.

"It would be treason to rise against my father," he said to the night sky.

"Walburg is a stout fortress, Your Highness. I do not doubt I can bide here safely, despite war and famine. But my people will not do as well, and if they suffer, then what kind of steward am I? Will there be anything left for my children, and my children's children, to rule? I cannot take that chance."

"I am not ready to take so bold a step."

"Do not wait too long, Prince Sanglant." Her voice roughened, and not only from passion. "Your child is precious, but children are easily lost in times like these." He turned back, startled, to regard her. Tears shone in her eyes. "Our daughter was but two years of age when she died."

"I was never told. She was to be placed in a convent. That's all I heard. My father made it clear that was to be the end of it, as far as I was concerned."

"And so it was the end of it," she said bitterly. "Is the church not the proper place for an illegitimate child? When a stallion is brought in to breed a mare, isn't he returned afterward to his master?"

"What happened?"

Anna feared to breathe, seeing how still the prince stood and knowing how well he could hear.

After a moment, Waltharia continued. "Bandits fell upon the party that was escorting her to the cloister at Warteshausen. I had them hunted down and hanged, and let their corpses rot to nothing on the walls. But that did not bring back the child." She smiled bravely, wiped her face, and downed another cup of cider. "There," she finished, setting down the cup. It rang lightly on wood. "I had done grieving, until you reminded me. It happened four years past, not yesterday. I lost my second son to fever two winters ago, and I pray to God every dawn and every night that I shall not lose the other three." Anger made her tears wither and dry, a heat that wicked them away. "I will not risk Villam lands and all that my father has left in my care so that Henry may run to Aosta seeking an illusory crown among foreigners."

"You risk Henry's wrath if you counsel rebellion. You could lose everything, even your life."

The fever had passed, leaving her calm again, the kind of woman who rarely lost control and then only when she really, really wanted to and was prepared for the consequences. She displayed the gold torque again, tracing the curve of the braid sensuously with her finger. Sanglant, shuddering, shut his eyes. His hands, lying open against the stone ledge, curled into fists.

She smiled as at a challenge offered and accepted. "We march lords must be prepared for anything."

He stirred at the window, opening his eyes. "Is that an invitation, or a proposal?"

"It's whatever you take it to be. Will you wear the gold torque, my lord prince?"

5

THE Eika fleet sailed out of Rikin Sound before a fair wind, two hundred and twenty-three longships and forty-six knarrs, the big-bellied cargo ships that plied the northern seas. Behind them came eight ships of various size and shape, captained by human allies. These were mostly young men from the merchant colonies that now paid tribute to Stronghand, restless youths eager to make a fortune looting Alba's rich towns and heathen temples.

At first the weather favored them, but they had no sooner

seen the shorebirds flying overhead, they had no sooner heard the first shout from the foremost ships, sighting the green hills of Alba, than a gale blew up from the southwest and scattered the fleet north and east.

Stronghand ordered his men to shorten their sails and they rode out the storm with ease, but it took six days for their mer-folk allies to track down the scattered ships and escort them back to a rendezvous at the Cackling Skerries off the rugged northeastern coast of Alba, far from the southern lands where lay the most prosperous towns, fields, and temples.

He met with his commanders on Cracknose Rock. Their skiffs were beached in a narrow strand strewn with coarse rocks as grainy as pumice. Cracknose Rock lay at the center of the Skerries, a fist of stone thrusting up defiantly out of the sea. Climbing to the top, scrambling on rock split and cracked and seeping water from every crevasse and depression, Stronghand could see the fleet riding at anchor in the choppy waters, most of the ships pulled well back from the scatter of rocky islets. Spray whipped off the sea. Breakers surged and sucked among the smaller rocks crowding like children about the foot of Cracknose. Dark clouds made iron of the sky. A pale promontory flashed in and out of view on the western horizon as a rainstorm occluded it at intervals.

The storm had made a few of his allies timid.

"What if it's true that the Alba tree sorcerers raised that storm?" said Isa's chief. "Our priests don't have the power to call wind and make the waves into mountains."

Stronghand set his standard pole at the center of the gathered chieftains. He pivoted around, gripping it, looking each of his commanders in the eye. None looked away. They had more pride than that. But he knew he could not trust them all.

"I have nothing to fear from the Alban tree sorcerers. They must fear me, although they may be too foolish to do so."

After a pause during which the chieftains fingered their spears in silence and a few regarded him as if they were thinking that it might be a good idea to run him through that instant, his littermate Tenth Son raised the expected objection, as they two had agreed beforehand. "It is foolish not to fear those with powerful magic."

"I am protected against their magic." He raised his standard. Feathers adorned it, bones strung together with wire and clacking softly against strings made of beads and scraps of leather that twisted in the breeze as they brushed against the desiccated skin of a snake. Chains forged from the spun and braided hair of SwiftDaughters, iron and gold, tin and silver, chimed softly. The bone whistles strung from the crosspiece clacked together, moaning as the wind raced through them.

"You may be protected, but what of us?" said Skuma's chief, a huge warrior with massive hands the size of a spade and skin as pale as powdered arsenic.

"All those I hold in my hand cannot be harmed by any magic thrown against me."

"What of spears and arrows?"

He grinned, displaying the jewels set into his teeth. "Not even I can protect your sorry hides from plain iron. Are there any among you who desire such a shield in battle? Do you fear to fight?"

They roared their answer as the wind ripped through their lifted standards, raising a hellish noise.

After a bit, the wind dropped enough, and their shouting ceased, so that he could speak again. "Those who faithfully follow me, I hold in my hand. Those whose hearts are not loyal receive no protection from me." He gestured toward the fleet before counting his commanders. "Who are we missing? Who has turned tail to run home?"

Eight longships and two knarrs were missing from those that had set out eight days before. One had been seen drifting lifeless on the open waters, and no captain had dared board it for fear that the tree sorcerers had poisoned its hull with their magic.

"It flew Ardaneka's banner," said Hakonin's chief. "Not one of Ardaneka's ships do I see now."

Some of his chieftains eyed the distant shore nervously. A blanket of fog had settled in over the headland, tendrils probing out onto the open sea before they were ripped to pieces by the wind. A warning whistle blew shrill and strong. At the fringe of the gathered assembly, right where the rock dropped precipitously away to the sea on its steepest side, his human allies huddled. They had pulled their cloaks up in a vain attempt to shield themselves from the battering of the wind, but now they exclaimed out loud and pointed to the northeast.

A longship was coming in, bucking in the swells. Its mast had been snapped off halfway, and shreds of sail draped the deck. Seaweed wreathed the stem of the ship. A half-dozen oars had survived the wreck, but not one body could be seen. Deep gouges marred the clinker-built hull, scars cutting through the red-and-yellow paint to reveal pale wood beneath. Rigging trailed behind like so many snakes wriggling through the sea, except for two lines drawn taut at the front.

The merfolk were hauling in the crippled ship.

Four merfolk surfaced near the strand, propelling a bloated corpse. Two swam in close enough to give it a final shove, and it scraped up along the beach, rolling against the pebbled shore until it wedged face up between two rocks, caught there. They watched in silence as the sea troubled its rest, trying to suck it out as waves receded, trying to force it in to shore as waves rolled in.

Even from the height of Cracknose Rock every soul there recognized the corpse. Like the rest of them, Ardaneka's chieftain bore distinctive markings on his torso. Seawater and feasting crabs had obliterated portions of the three-headed yellow serpent painted onto his chest yet, even with sea worms writhing in the rotting oval that had once been his face, enough could be seen to identify him.

Hakonin's chief hissed derisively. "Ardaneka's master only bared his throat to you after the battle at Kjalmarsfjord, when he saw no one else had the strength to resist you. It seems his faith in you was not strong enough to protect him from the tree sorcerers' storm."

"So it was not," remarked Stronghand.

They all agreed then, one by one, that Ardaneka's chief had been furtive and tricky, eager for gold and silver but reluctant to place his people in the front lines where they might take the brunt of an assault. His seamanship hadn't been anything to boast of, either, and he had only raided where the pickings were easily gained, not where he might meet real resistance.

"He was weak," said Stronghand at last, "and he was not loyal." He regarded his captains calmly, baring his teeth in a grin meant to provoke the irresolute among them. "That storm was only the first magic that the tree sorcerers will cast at us. But I do not fear them. Do you?"

None stirred. None dared show weakness, or hesitation, now that they had seen what the magic of the tree sorcerers had wrought.

Perhaps the tree sorcerers were in fact capable of raising a storm that great, although he doubted it. He did not doubt the danger the Alban wizards posed to those unprepared to meet them, but he had seen for himself that their magic did not reach far beyond their physical bodies: a shrouding fog, a temporary storm front blasting through a line of ships drawn up for battle, a mist to dazzle the minds of men swayed by their power and guile. The gale that had scattered his fleet had encompassed a vast swath of the northern sea, according to his own observations as his ship had ridden out the gale and to the reports he had received as his loyal captains had straggled in to the Crackling Skerries afterward.

Perhaps the tree sorcerers *had* called up that storm, seeing his fleet poised at their shore. But whether it was born out of the sea or out of their magic, he knew just how to make use of such opportunities, blown to him on the wind.

That was why he had told the merfolk, in the aftermath of the storm, to hunt down Ardaneka's ships and destroy them, each one. To bring him the chieftain's body, drowned and broken.

Let the capricious ones fear that they might be next to suffer under magic's cold claw.

Below, the red-and-yellow ship listed to one side. Seawater swamped the deck, and with a sucking sigh the ship sank under the waves, ropes slithering down until, at last, nothing could be seen except scraps of flotsam, bobbing on the swells. Waves battered the bloated corpse. One of the arms came loose, rotted away at the shoulder, and it rolled away like a lifeless slug. A ripple stirred its steady course; a ridged back sounded. Eels writhed, mouths snapping in eyeless faces, as one of the merfolk raised its gruesome head and, that fast, snatched the decaying arm. Limb and merman vanished beneath the gray-blue sea.

The headland emerged from a low-lying mist. Chalk cliffs gleamed invitingly where the sun lit them. Clouds scudded away northwards. Gulls screamed.

Stronghand raised his standard once more. The haft hummed against his palm as though a hive of bees lived within, but it was only the voice of the magic, always aware, always alert. Always awake.

The magic that protected him never slept, and never dreamed.

"Summer wanes," he said softly, making his commanders strain to hear him above the pound of the surging sea against the rocks and constant blowing rumble of the wind. "Alba waits. And they can do nothing to stop us."

6

IT all happened so fast: Henry's and Adelheid's triumphant entrance into Darre, Adelheid's labor pangs and her delivery of a healthy daughter in the presence of a dozen witnesses on the sixteenth day of Cintre, a mere twenty days after their arrival. The queen was too exhausted to be moved; the rigors of the mountain crossing in the fullest months of her pregnancy had worn her down. Henry could not wait, nor did Adelheid counsel him to tarry in the palace while she recovered.

So it was that a month later Rosvita found herself once again at the head of a triumphal procession riding into Darre. King Henry had made a brief progress through the northern counties and dukedoms of Aosta, restoring daughters and sons that Ironhead had held hostage and allowing the ladies and lords to feed and house his impressive army. Every gate opened to admit him, although it was by no means clear that every count, lord, and duke was overjoyed at the prospect of Queen Adelheid restored to her throne at the hand of the Wendish king. But the northern lords did not want to fight.

"As long as they don't want to fight this year, then we can hope for peace while Henry establishes his power in the south," said Villam as they halted an arrow's shot from the massive gates of Darre.

The magnificence of Darre still awed her. The city was built on five hills, with the two palaces—representing spiritual and temporal power—sitting at the height of Amurrine Hill. The city walls remained more-or-less intact from the time of the old empire, repaired and rebuilt over the course of the four hundred years since the last empress had died defending her throne from the invading Bwr horde. The Bwr army had left the walls intact and razed the temples instead, to show their hatred for the empire's bloodthirsty gods. Cut from huge stone blocks quarried to the east, the walls rose to the height of ten men, and it was said that a person might walk five leagues on those parapets and not come to the end of them.

Villam, too, admired the walls, but he hadn't done speaking. "A good harvest, a mild winter, the Jinna bandits beaten back out to sea—all these will pacify the Aostan nobles more than any battle can."

"So we must hope," replied Rosvita, "because if reports are

true, the southern counties will not yield easily. Is that the queen come to welcome us?"

Henry looked eager, seeing the crowd of folk gathered at the gate, but he was quickly disappointed.

"Clerics all," said Villam, surprised enough to show it.

Hathui rode forward to meet the welcoming party halfway. Presbyters in red cloaks and clerics garbed in robes of white sang a hymn of praise in strong voices. Incense rose in clouds from gold thuribles; even at this distance, the heady scent made Rosvita dizzy, or perhaps that was just the scorching heat of the summer sun. She had grown accustomed to wearing a broad-brimmed hat, like those Aostan clerics favored, but it was so hot that even such shade gave trifling respite from the heat. Fortunatus had remarked several times that it was so hot that not even flies troubled them.

The Eagle returned, escorting a single man resplendent in rich vestments surmounted by a scarlet cloak trimmed with gems at the collar. The blazing sun was not more golden than his hair. He knelt in the dirt before the king.

"Your Majesty, Her Most Blessed Majesty Queen Adelheid has sent me to receive you into the city and to escort you to her. She awaits you in the Ivory Pavilion."

"I had thought she would greet me herself, at the gates of *our* city," said Henry in a dangerously low voice. "I did not march the breadth of Aosta on her behalf only to be brought before her like a mere prince come to pay my respects."

Hugh wore no hat. Sweat gleamed on his brow, but he looked otherwise cool and collected as he lowered his voice to speak in a voice meant to carry no farther than the king and his closest companions. "The queen is well, my lord king, after the rigors of birth, but her physicians still confine her indoors in this heat. She had a pair of fainting spells some ten days after the birth, and they fear the sun might cause another."

Henry had the grace to change color, and his mouth, tightened into a line of annoyance, shifted subtly to mark concern. "Escort me to her at once."

They rode into the city to the accompaniment of cheers and garlands, thrown by the populace. Clearly, Adelheid had won their love in the month Henry had been gone. They blessed the Wendish king, foreigner though he was, for freeing them from Ironhead's tyranny.

But Villam leaned toward Rosvita, speaking in a low voice. "Do you see how they call for 'Father Hugh'? Look at their faces. The flowers are for the presbyter, not for the king."

Yet Hugh walked humbly enough beside the king, leading Henry's horse as though Hugh were the king's servant. He was, amazingly, barefoot, in the guise of a humble frater— except, of course, for the richness of his clothing.

"Do you think so?" whispered Rosvita. How could she tell, as garlands fell onto the avenue, a mass of lilies and roses, poppies and narcissus, to make a sweet carpet for the triumphant king? Villam cocked an eye, looking skeptical. When had he grown so suspicious?

The northern road struck straight through the city to the heart, where the twin palaces lay. Along the lower southern slope of Amurrine Hill, huge walls almost obscured the hill itself, but to the northwest a rocky escarpment fell away below the high parapets to the river beneath. The road ramped up, buttressed by a complicated series of arches, and they dismounted in the forecourt and gave their horses over to grooms.

In the month they had been gone, all trace of Ironhead, his whores, and his furnishings had been swept out of the palace. Arethousan carpets ornamented the corridors. Brass hooks set into the walls supported oil lamps fashioned into the shapes of animals: roosters and eagles, griffins and dragons, a pair of phoenix, and a flock of golden swallows. Every shutter had been taken down, every room and chamber thrown open to the light. A crowd of servants beat dust out of tapestries. A trio of girls polished the brass fittings on the doors.

The Ivory Pavilion was not the grandest hall in the palace, but the intimacy and richness of its furnishings gave it a grandeur that many a vast hall could not rival. Narrow window slits allowed a breeze to work through the chamber, but otherwise the thick stone walls as well as the shade of cypress trees in the gardens set to either side of the old building allowed the inhabitants some respite from the heat. They entered through a porch screened off by doors so cunningly carved in a pattern of intertwined roundels that those within could look out upon any courtiers who waited beyond, hoping for admittance.

The inner chamber was dim enough to need illumination: six handsome lamps in the shape of leopards with the flame licking out of their snarling mouths. The wainscoting was all of ivory, each plaque detailing a scene: battles, the martyrdom of saints, the journey of Helen and her founding of the ancient city of Dariya, stories depicting the queens and kings of Aosta and the trials of the Holy Mothers of the church side by side with heathen tales of gods and magic.

Queen Adelheid reclined at her ease on a couch, in the ancient Dariyan style, eating grapes and drinking wine while she conversed with a woman whose hair was as pale as moonlight. Rosvita would have thought her a simple churchwoman, except for the exceeding richness of her white cleric's robes, ornamented by eagles and glittering circles picked out in red-and-gold thread on silk. A nursemaid dandled a plump baby nearby.

The two women, one young and handsome and the other impossible to put an age to, looked up at the same instant as Henry and his companions entered the chamber. Rosvita saw it at once. Even Hathui caught in her breath with an audible gasp.

Adelheid, of course, wore no gold torque to mark her royal descent. It was a Wendish and Salian custom, one that had never migrated south of the Alfar Mountains. Nor could Aosta boast a true royal lineage. In truth, any of the noble families of Aosta might claim the throne for themselves, if they were strong enough.

But the mellow gold of a masterfully crafted torque gleamed at the throat of Adelheid's companion. The ends of the braided gold had each been formed into the face of an angel. The woman did not rise as Henry strode forward.

Adelheid did.

"Henry! I pray you, forgive me for not meeting you at the gates. My physicians—"

He kissed her warmly on either cheek before insisting she sit. "Rest, my heart," he said fervently, seeing that she was comfortably settled before he beckoned to the nursemaid. "Here is my sweet Mathilda. How fares she?"

The sleeping Mathilda looked healthy, red-cheeked like an apple at first blush, her limbs plump and her downy cap of hair as dark as her mother's.

"She fares well," said Adelheid proudly. "She eats well, and grows quickly."

"But not as quickly as your granddaughter," said the cleric seated on the couch next to Adelheid's.

Henry gave the baby back into the nursemaid's arms and examined this woman who had not shown him the least deference. King and cleric studied each other. A difficult winter and spring waiting in Wayland for the passes to clear, a grueling journey over the mountains, and a month spent in almost constant motion winning over or, at times, intimidating the Aostan nobles had not wearied Henry as much as his new bride, new child, and new throne had uplifted him. He had more silver in his hair but, like a crown, it ennobled him. A man half his age might well wish for as much vigor as the king possessed. Certainly Adelheid had never complained of his bed, and even now she gazed at him admiringly, seeing what a fine figure he cut in a rich tunic and with his hair still tousled from the day's ride.

But the cleric had vigor also. She wore arrogance with an ease that betrayed high birth and an expectation that others would bow to her authority. And she had stillness. She sat, hands clasped in her lap, and regarded the king with a thoughtful gaze unblemished by strong emotion. If she felt fear, or anger, or joy, no hint of it touched her eyes.

"Who are you, who sits while I stand?" he asked bluntly.

"I pray you, Henry," began Adelheid, reaching for his hand.

At the same moment, Hugh came forward. "Your Majesty, if I may be given leave—"

"Nay, Hugh," objected Adelheid, addressing him in a most casual manner. "It must be done, and done quickly." She turned to Henry. "We have had word from the south. Ironhead's cousin has raised an army to avenge him. Jinna raiders have put to shore in both Navlia and Tratanto. The Arethousan emperor claims the entire province of Aelia, and the Count of Sirriki begs for our aid in fighting off the pirates who have besieged his ports. Six of the northern lords refused my summons to come to court to make their submission. Untimely rain threatens the grape harvest in Idria, and the stores of rye here in Darre have all been taken by rot. Two deacons in Fiora were struck dead by lightning. There are rumors of a heresy taking hold in the northeast. Meanwhile, Mother Clementia is dead these three months or more, and the throne of the skopos remains empty."

"Surely the presbyters meet and hold council, as is their tradition," began Rosvita.

"The council of presbyters may argue for months," said Hugh quietly before bowing his head to await events.

Adelheid glanced at Hugh, as if expecting him to go on, but he kept his gaze lowered modestly, fixed on the parquet floor and its two tones of wood, blond and ebony, spreading out from his feet in a pattern of repeating squares. Like good and evil, the warring inclinations stamped into every human soul.

"The presbyters weave their own intrigues that have nothing to do with the security of Aosta," continued Adelheid fervently, taking Henry's hand again. "Many of them do not care to act in favor of restoring the empire. Yet those same clerics will not necessarily move against a strong hand setting the emperor in place."

"What are you saying?" asked Henry.

But Rosvita already knew, with that sudden, sure instinct that causes dogs to shy and birds to twitter in the hour before an earthquake hits. She had heard Sanglant's testimony. It did not take any great wisdom to add two to two and count up four. "You are Sister Anne, of St. Valeria's Convent."

"Liath's mother!" murmured Hathui, standing just behind the king. "I see no resemblance."

Henry was not slow to catch their meaning. "Are you the woman who claims to be the granddaughter of Emperor Taillefer?"

Anne did not rise. She lifted a single hand, like a queen calling for silence. "What need have I to claim such a thing when it is truth? Why else would I wear the gold torque of royal kinship?"

This argument stymied Henry, but Villam could not remain silent. "Any woman or man might put a gold torque around their throat and say what they will. In the marchlands, imposters sometimes ride into villages and claim to be clerics, or lords, or heathen sorcerers with the power to make birds talk and the rivers run with gold. What proof have you?"

Anne was neither amused nor angry. Her calm ran as deep as the ocean. "What proof do you desire? Is it not obvious?" She whistled, an unexpected sound coming from that ageless, composed face. A huge black hound trotted into view, emerging from behind a carved wood screen. Servants shied away, but it approached meekly enough and lay down submissively at Anne's feet.

"That looks like one of Lavastine's hounds," said Henry, examining the hound with the keen interest of a man who keeps a large kennel and knows the names of all his dogs. "I thought they were all dead."

"I do not know where the beast came from," said Anne, "only that it did come to me one day to offer its obeisance. I believe this hound is descended from the black hounds who were loyal to Taillefer. They are spoken of in poems, and I have seen them depicted in tapestries."

"There is one carved in stone in Taillefer's chapel at Autun, faithful in life as in death," said Rosvita, and while it was true that one might mark a resemblance, too much time had passed between the reign of Taillefer and this day to know whether this fearsome creature was itself the descendant, many dog generations on, of the emperor's famous hounds.

"Nay, Your Majesty." Villam crouched to get a better look, although he did not venture too close. "This is indeed one of Lavastine's hunting hounds. I recognize the look of it. The ears. The size. The breadth of its chest. It might as well have swallowed a barrel. I respected those hounds too well to forget them now."

"What do you want?" asked Henry.

"To serve God," said Anne. "That is all."

"If queen and king agree, then there can be no impediment to Sister Anne's crowning as skopos," said Adelheid.

Anne did not smile. "If I am skopos, then I cannot contend with you for the imperial throne that is rightly mine."

Henry smiled sharply. He eased his hand out of Adelheid's grip and gestured to his servants. Two stewards had already hurried in, and they hastily set up his traveling throne, with the dragon arms, the eagle-wing back, and the lion legs and paws to support it. Sitting, he set chin on fist and elbow on knee, regarding Anne more with curiosity than with animosity. "With what army do you mean to contend for the imperial throne?"

"God's favor and the right of birth ought to be army enough. So have you put forth your own claim, I believe."

He glanced at Hathui, who fingered her Eagle's brooch self-consciously, her expression fixed like stone. What was the Eagle thinking? What did Henry mean to do?

Like a good commander, he attempted a flank attack. "Is it true the woman named Liathano is your daughter? Do you know what became of her?"

"No more than I know what became of your bastard, Sanglant."

"Who does not trust you and spoke most damningly of your powers and your intent. You are a sorcerer, I believe, a mathematicus. There was talk of a cataclysm soon to engulf us. The return of the Lost Ones. A war, perhaps, or some other disaster."

"I pray you, King Henry, do not mock what you do not understand." As they had spoken, it had grown dark and the chamber dim. Wind rustled through the cypresses outside. Adelheid's banner, hung from the wall behind the couches, stirred, the cloth sighing up and settling down as though an invisible daimone's hand toyed with it. No one had lit lamps; even the servants watched in anticipatory silence as king faced cleric.

Even the servants understood that something monumental was at stake. Servants could smell the heady brew of a silent struggle for power sooner than anyone else.

"Very well," agreed Henry softly. "It's true I understand practical matters better than sorcerous ones. I know that a woman may not rule as queen regnant in Salia. But if you are indeed Taillefer's granddaughter, then you might well gain adherents enough to drag Aosta into a long struggle over the crowns, which none of us desire. Your aspiration seems reasonable enough, Sister Anne, but of what use can you be to me if I support your election as Holy Mother, skopos over all the church?"

Anne lifted cupped hands. A silvery sphere of light spun into being just above her palms. Villam muttered a prayer under his breath. Adelheid sighed sharply, like a woman in the throes of pleasure. Henry remained silent, watching.

Anne raised her arms and, as a woman tosses rose petals to the wind, flung up her hands. The silvery globe dissolved into sparks of shimmering white light, each one a butterfly swooping and fluttering throughout the chamber. The winged light threw the scenes carved onto ivory into relief: a lady with her falcon; the entombment of St. Asella; fair Helen on the walls of Ilios, calling the troops to battle; the tortures of St. John of Hamby, each one depicted in exquisite detail.

Anne stood. Each white butterfly spark bloomed with color—ruby, sapphire, emerald, carnelian, aquamarine, amethyst and rose quartz, banded chalcedony, iridescent opal—each one as lustrous as a gem. Their dance swirled around the chamber, making Rosvita's head ache at the same time as her heart exulted. Henry rose slowly, staring as butterflies swarmed around his head to form a crown of luminescent stars at his brow.

For an instant he gleamed there, crowned in splendor.

The sparks vanished, leaving them with a steady gleam of magelight and a cool, pale woman of vast power and middling height. Whispering, half frightened and half in awe, the servants hurried to light lamps as the magelight spun itself into delicate threads and, at last, into nothing, simply fading until it disappeared.

"Illusion," muttered Villam.

Hugh of Austra's gaze glittered just as brightly as had those dancing sparks. In his expression gleamed an unsettling *hunger*.

Queen Adelheid looked no different than he did, dazzled, thirsty for more.

Even Henry. God save them, even Henry.

"What do you want?" Henry asked again, his voice as hoarse as that of a famished man who has just seen a feast laid out on the table.

Villam's hand brushed Rosvita's fingers, a signal she could not read. Nor could she speak to ask him, not even whisper, not with the silence lying so deeply around them, a cloak thrown over the assembly.

Can we trust her?

Rosvita no longer doubted Anne's right to wear the gold torque. Granddaughter of Taillefer and Radegundis, daughter of Fidelis and the foundling girl Lavrentia; a mathematicus of considerable power. One could not ignore such a woman.

Anne bent to pick up a shard of glass, as blue as lapis lazuli, off the parquet floor. She displayed it in her palm, blew on it gently, and a brilliantly blue butterfly opened its wings and flew away, quickly lost in darkness. She did not smile as she addressed the king. A woman with so much power does not need to smile, or to frown.

"Do not turn away from me, Henry, Lord of Wendar and Varre," she said, untroubled by the agitated currents roiling around her. "For without my aid, you will have no empire to rule."

7

EVERY soul tainted by the touch of mortal earth is peppered with shadows and black recesses, caught where they are least expected: hates, loves, fears, passions, envies and angers, lies and truths. Every soul born on Earth can never be free of them. No matter how fiercely the cleansing fire rages, she will never be pure fire.

She will always be trapped in her body.

She hit the ground running, half crouched, bow ready. Here in the sphere of Jedu, a light snow fell. She loped over a plain marked by hundreds of small outcrops, tumbled boulders, heaps of stone, irregular folds, every lump and swell concealed under a blanket of snow. Cold flakes dissolved on her lips, swirling around her naked body. The only place she was warm was along her spine where her quiver gave her skin some protection from wind and falling snow. Her toes had already gone numb from the cold; each step was agony, like walking on needles. It was a bad place not to have any clothes.

It was a bad place to be trapped in a physical body. Looking back, she saw no gate, no entry point, only her footprints, steaming as the brief warmth of her passing was whirled away into the bitter air. She could only go forward. That was always the case, wasn't it? She could never go back.

She brushed snow from her hair, felt it tickle her eyelashes and dust the end of her nose. Flakes melted on her nipples and strung a mantle across her shoulders, rubbed clean at intervals by the leather strap of her quiver. Her ears stung. Despite the stiffness in her fingers, she kept her bow raised and an arrow taut. In Jedu's angry lair, anything might happen. She had to expect the worst.

It didn't take long for the worst to find her.

Thunder rolled and tumbled in the distance. Lightning flashed, sparks of brilliance on the horizon. She paused, seeing no storm clouds, only the steady gray bowl of a fathomless sky.

Not a storm at all. At first the figure looked impossibly small. In the time it took Liath to take in two sharp breaths, the creature doubled in size as the thunder of its footsteps rang in the air. As she caught in a gasp, it filled her sight, a monstrous giant.

The Angel of War.

In place of eyes she wore shining mirrors. Her mouth was huge and fierce, as red as poppies. Her black hair was as tangled as a bramble bush, and from it peeped two hideous horns, each one tipped with a stain of blood. For armor she wore masks, a hundred or a thousand or more covering her massive body. On each shoulder she wore a mask with mirror·eyes. On each elbow there hung another such face, a mask with mirror eyes, and on her knees there hung masks as well, faces glittering and shining with every least movement she made; even her abdomen and back bore faces, each one frozen in a leer or a grimace. With mirrors hanging upon every part of her body, it looked as if she could see in all directions.

She bore a spear and a sword, but not a shield. The masks—the mirroring eyes—were her shield.

Where the Angel of War walked, the ground came alive. Snow shuddered. What Liath had thought were rocks and boulders uncurled into living beings. She walked not on an empty plain but on a battlefield that stretched impossibly far in every direction, a plain of corpses, the detritus of war.

They didn't look very dead now. They were rising out of the snow, and they were all armed.

The easiest choice was to run.

But she had only taken two halting steps backward before she knew that running was no choice. The dead were everywhere, too many to count.

Thunder crashed. Jedu loomed, filling the sky. The angel's face bore that grimace of uncontrolled rage that turns a beautiful face hideous. Thousands of huge mirrored eyes stared at Liath, yet their gaze did not perceive her. In each glittering, faceted eye she saw, not herself but a death on the field of battle, the killing thrust, the mortal wound, the last breath and bubble of blood. There were more than enough suffering dead to fill the vast plain.

Out of the field of moldering bones and broken weapons, misty figures appeared, insubstantial at first but solidifying like wax sculpted into forms. To her left a phalanx of a hundred warriors moved into position, each man armed with a lancelike spear twice as long as any she had ever seen. She recognized these warriors from tapestries and frescoes, with their hammered breastplates and crested helmets: the soldiers who carried the banner of the old Dariyan Empire. Other groups of fighters cohered on the plain around her. Some of these cohorts she recognized, Aoi, Quman, or Eika. Others she knew only from stories or dreams, centaurs, men mounted on camels or huge elephants, a wild hunter leading his mastiffs, guivres and griffins rising in flight. Sounds issued forth, orders in a thousand languages, the cries of the beasts, the clamor of armies in motion.

In the sphere of Jedu, war was never finished.

Moving slowly at first, the armies began to advance. The phalanx at her left shuffled closer step by step, their hedge of sarissas leveled at her—nay, not at her but rather at a line of elephants formed up to her right. A clear trumpet belled the advance. The ground shook under that weight as the elephants advanced toward the phalanx, and toward Liath.

Arrows, darts, and slender javelins filled the sky as a thousand conflicts unfolded. A stone from a sling struck a glancing blow on her thigh. She fell to her knees, blood streaming down her leg. The elephants rumbled forward, and the men in the phalanx braced themselves against that charge.

One of the massive gray beasts lumbered forward directly toward Liath, trampling everything that came under its broad feet. Recoiling, she shot an arrow as it came into range. The shaft slipped between two armored plates protecting its throat and disappeared, buried deep. The creature bellowed in pain; its screams echoing along the line of elephants as they responded to its death cries. It collapsed to its knees after three more steps. Two men spilled from the carriage on top, one rolling clear while the other was caught under the rump of the beast as it pitched to one side and let out a weak, and final, trumpet.

Then the rest of the elephants passed her position and crashed into the spears. The phalanx dissolved as the massive forms shattered spear and bone. Elephants, skewered through limb and neck, went berserk, tossing and stomping on their riders, on their foes, on anything they could reach. Blood spilled on the snow. Behind the elephants, soldiers advanced, carrying great axes; their job was to finish off the shattered phalanx. She could not tell if they saw her at all, but she dared not wait to find out. Rising to her feet, she shot any creature that seemed to approach in her direction. They weren't real, after all. She wasn't really killing them because they were already dead. She was only protecting herself.

She fired ten times, and ten men fell dead or dying.

Jedu's expression warped, rage turning to sadistic joy. Liath reached to her quiver for another arrow. Only two remained.

Ai, Lady. These warriors were as much victims of Jedu's wrath as she was. She could remain here, trapped in the agony of war, or she could seek the gate that led to the sphere of Mok. With an effort, as the battle raged around her, she remembered her wings. She called fire and, with her wings burning at her back, lifted above the fray. Arrows that flashed toward her burst into flame, their ashes raining onto the carnage below.

Men screamed. Horses fell, kicking. The killing went on and on and on.

Let there be an end to it.

She nocked arrow to bow and drew Seeker of Hearts one more time, aiming true at Jedu's grimacing face.

Loosed the arrow. That blissful smile of joy melted from the angel's hideous and beautiful face to be drowned once again by an expression of rage. Her maw opened, exposing teeth like a thousand daggers; in that dark cavern, the arrow was lost at once.

Heart pounding, wings hissing at her back as she beat hard to stay aloft, Liath reached back for her final arrow. Her fingers touched silken coverts, the gold feather given to her by Eldest Uncle, which she had used to fletch her last arrow.

Before she could pull it free of the quiver, Jedu gave a cry, shrill and piercing, that caused every creature on the plain to shudder to a halt. Liath tumbled backward on the wind of that cry, fighting to control her flight, as the angel's words boomed out over the battlefield.

"Die a million deaths. Suffer for all eternity. No one, Daughter of Fire, enters Jedu unbidden. No flesh escapes my bite."

Then Jedu heaved out her chest, and sucked in.

With all her might Liath fought to fly higher, but she was drawn in despite her struggles. The mirror eyes grew huge and in their depths she saw the slain, and the slayer.

Ai, God. Some she knew. There a guivre, killed by Alain. There an Eika chief, falling under Lavastine's sword. There a Quman soldier, being drowned by Ivar. There Ironhead's pretty concubine, driving a spike through the sleeping king's head.

A lord outfitted in mail and helmet tumbled from his horse, dismounted by a spear thrust. The man who unhorsed him was no luckier; the impact of his own blow overbalanced him and he was thrown from his horse to land hard on the ground, losing his helmet, while a skirmish raged around him, made misty by the slant of light obscuring the mirrored eye into which she stared in horror.

It was Sanglant, except he was so young, scarcely more than a boy.

The stinking aroma of a charnel house dizzied her as the angel's mouth opened wider, to swallow her whole.

She twisted, reaching for Sanglant, spinning herself into the mirrored eye, into the grasp of her lover.

She landed on a soft cushion of long green grass. The blinding sunlight stung her eyes, but at least it was warm here. Yet she hadn't escaped Jedu's rage. Her horse, leaping over her, galloped off, and the din of battle still filled her ears.

She was not herself. She lay in a man's body, a lord of Hesbaye, nephew of the countess, risen in rebellion because his mother's portion had gone to his aunt at her death instead of to him. So inconsequential did King Henry think him and his rebellion that the king had sent his half-breed whelp against him, a child not more than fifteen or sixteen years of age, untried and unfit even with an older, wiser captain riding in attendance.

How was it, then, that the brat had unhorsed him?

A body slammed against him, pressing him into the grass. Ai, Lady, it was Sanglant, helmet lost and black hair streaming. He was so young, lithe, lean as a reed, not yet filled out with a man's height and breadth. Yet he still felt firm and reassuring, lying against her.

"Sanglant!" she whispered, having no breath to shout. "It's me. It's Liath!"

He slipped his arm across her chest, a broad knife clenched in his fist as he brought it to her throat. In a quick motion, the merest sting, the blade bit deep and her words choked and drowned in blood as she struggled to tell him. Her life gushed from her neck. She clawed toward her throat, anything to stop the blood, but he pinned her arms under his weight. Gasping, she looked into his green eyes, but all she saw was the rage of Jedu. Rays of sun melted holes in her vision; murky stains blotted out Sanglant's face. The world narrowed, sound faded, and all washed black.

The clash of arms and the jerk of her horse woke her as if from sleep. On her left side the begh, with his fearsome griffin feathers gleaming from the wings fastened to his armor and his iron visor making a mask of his face, urged their line forward. His standard billowed in a stiff wind, the rake of the snow leopard's claw that marked the proud warriors of the Pechanek clan. They charged and she, like her chief, lowered her lance. The banner of the Dragons amidst a mass of mounted Wendish and Ungrian soldiers surged forward to meet them.

The King's Dragon led the charge. Sanglant, older now, drove straight for her chieftain, his ax raised. With a deft shift of his point, the griffin rider slid his spear around Sanglant's shield and caught the prince just where his coif gapped to expose his throat.

The young prince fell back across the rump of his warhorse but still, somehow, managed to drag himself back up. He clung to the saddle, blood from the wound pouring down over his Dragon tabard, as the steed charged through the crowd and broke to the rear of the Quman charge. Behind, his Dragons raised a cry of alarm and fury.

Liath fought her horse back through the chaos to catch up to Sanglant. His helm had fallen askew and he was as pale as if all his blood had drained out through that horrible wound. He lay like a dead man over the withers of the horse. Tears streamed from her eyes as she called out to him and brought her mount up alongside his. He convulsed once, like a man spitting out his death, and heaved himself up to strike with the speed of a snake.

A crushing force came down on her head and for a moment she could actually see along either side of the ax blade protruding from her forehead, but all she really saw was the desperate look in her lover's eyes. Red seeped into her vision. She slid limply from the saddle.

Slipping in the blood and stink of one of her fellows, she scrabbled to gain purchase on the stone floor. The man creature had one hundred small wounds, one hundred rivulets seeping blood. The scent of his blood made her wild with hunger. She thrust aside the others, biting at their flanks so that they gave way, and trod on his chest, pinning him.

A glimmer of sentience sparked in her tiny mind. Was this man creature part of her pack? But hunger ate at her belly and he smelled so sweet. She lunged for the kill.

He was too fast for her. He caught her under the throat and like a dog bit down on her windpipe. Thrashing, fighting, she felt the wind crushed out of her, the air choked, the rich smell of blood and death fading, dulling, until the world was cold iron and for an instant she remembered the waters of her birth softly lapping around her and then even that sensation fled.

And she was fleeing Gent with the other RockChildren, running behind Isa's banner, but a figure that stank of captivity rode her down and with the strength brought about by madness clove her head from her shoulders.

And she had no body, not here where the perfume of flesh and blood made her thirst, an aching, ragged, raw pain. She had not wanted to come here. Torn from the halls of iron, she swayed in the hot blast of wind and sighed the name of the one she sought. "Sanglant." His blood would release her to return to her home. That alone she knew. But as she advanced with her sister galla, tasting his blood on the wind, he attacked, piercing her with the stinging tip of a griffin's feather. The sorcery that bound her to the halls of earth burned and snapped, and she was flung into agony.

And she shrank back in terror as the mounted man charged through her motley companions, cutting them down like reeds. She cried out, begging for mercy, as her last arrow spun uselessly to the ground.

Ai, Lord, why had she left her mother's house? She'd been a fool to argue with her brother, and a bigger fool to let anger drive her away, and the biggest fool yet to allow Drogo to convince her that there was wealth to be made and supper to be had by picking on hapless travelers. But she'd been desperate by then, and too proud to go home. She'd been so hungry, and Drogo had offered her bread if she'd join his miserable pack of bandits.

Sage and fern halted her backward stumble. "Mercy!" she cried. Then he was on her, death in his eyes.

Sanglant.

His sword came down, and pain obliterated everything else.

"Nay, Welf!" cried Ekkehard, stopping him with the point of his lance. "You'll not desert me now."

She wept in her young man's body. She had never known fear could hurt so much. "I'll never desert you, my lord prince. You know that. But it isn't right that we fight on the side of the Quman against our own countryfolk. It's treason."

Ekkehard flushed. "We've dirtied our hands too much to ever go back. Better to die in battle than hanging from the gallows."

They waited as the gold banners flown by their foes advanced. Frithuric and Manegold waited with stolid patience, but he could see, she could see, the despair in their eyes. How had they all been so stupid? How had they let Bulkezu seduce them? It was a good thing his mother wasn't here to see him now, the son who had dishonored the family name.

Drums and a horn call signaled the charge. Welf pressed forward as their horses broke from walk to trot to gallop, a roll like thunder filling his ears. He pushed his horse past the prince, so that he took the brunt of the impact. A lance struck him right over the heart. As he fell, he heard a cry of grief and anger, and a man's hoarse voice shouted Ekkehard's name in surprise.

Ai, Lord, it was Prince Sanglant!

The ground slammed into him, and the last thing he saw was the hooves of his horse, coming down on his head.

If she remained still, her feathers would blend into the silvery grass and only the keenest eye could observe her. Sanglant was intent on her mate, a silver-hued griffin asleep on the sunning stone. The prince's spear was poised as he prepared to strike. His eyes calculated his next move, as did hers. She would not let him kill her mate.

She pounced, he spun to meet her, but the advantage was hers. The shaft of his spear shattered under her attack, and her weight bore him to the ground. Her mate awoke at the noise, hearing her shriek of triumph. Calling shrilly, he shook himself free of sleep and leaped forward to assist with the kill.

Her claws pressed the prince's shoulders to the ground. But he hadn't given up. His knee jabbed hard into her belly, but she would not free him. She could not let him kill again.

Slewing her great head to one side to get a better look at him, she recognized at his throat a scar taken long ago, half hidden now by a braided gold torque. She had thought him dead, once before, and had died for her mistake. She screamed fury. The Angel of War danced at the edge of her vision. Razor sharp, her beak would cleave flesh easier than any sword could.

She would not die at his hands again. And again.

And again.

A growl rose in his throat as he tensed to fight her off. He yanked an arm free and grabbed desperately for her throat, ignoring the blood leaking from a dozen cuts scored along his fingers as he clawed for purchase at her iron feathers. She struck at his vulnerable eyes.

The last thing she heard was his scream as she fell free of the mirrors, spinning and tumbling in the blast furnace that was the wind of war.

Ai, God, she had killed Sanglant. She groped at her throat, thinking to find a bruise where he had tried in that last instant to choke her. Instead, her gold torque was missing. Gone.

With a scream of fury, she lifted heavenward on her wings of flame, beating for a sliver of light, like the moon's crescent, that drifted far above her. The world below had gone white as a blizzard of snow and wrath obliterated the plain, the dead and those who killed them, all vanished beneath a mantle of white. A broken spear rolled over the icy waste, caught by the wind's cold hand.

Mirrors winked like flashes of lightning half hidden by storm clouds. A wild laughter boomed like thunder, fading into the distance.

"Now you are bitten. Who has won, and who has lost?"

"I have escaped you," cried Liath triumphantly as she neared the silvery boundary and saw a gap splitting open in the gleaming shell that marked the sphere of Mok.

But Jedu's laughter had already lodged in her heart. And she could still feel blood, and life, spilling from her unmarked throat.

XV
EAGLE'S SIGHT

1

BULKEZU and his army cut a swath of misery and destruction through the southern portion of the dukedom of Avaria before turning north as summer waned, but Hanna never saw Prince Ekkehard weep for his father's ravaged kingdom until the day the vanguard of Bulkezu's marauding army came across the ruins of the palace of Augensburg. As the abandoned palace came into view, populated now only by weeds, insects, and a pair of red deer that sprang away into the forest, the young prince began to cry silently, tears streaming down his cheeks. Had he been there that day when Liath had sent the palace up in flames, desperate to escape Hugh?

Hanna could not now recall. She only remembered the terrible flames and the blasting heat that had scorched her skin when she had dragged Liath away from the inferno. Where were Folquin, Leo, Stephen, and her good friend Ingo now? Had they survived the winter in Handelburg? Would she in the end find herself facing them across the field of battle? Would any Wendish army ever confront Bulkezu, or would he simply march across the length and breadth of the land sowing desolation and terror for as long as he wished?

Bulkezu called a halt. His soldiers and slaves busied themselves setting up camp for the night and turning the horses and livestock out to graze on the lush grass. The site had been entirely abandoned. The forest had encroached upon the open space cleared around the palace grounds. It was a beautiful place, calm and peaceful if only because this one afternoon, at least, there would be no killing.

Hanna had seen enough killing to last her ten lifetimes. Each death was a scar cut into her heart, untold wounds that never really healed, only scabbed over with time.

"Sit here, my lord prince." Lord Welf steered Ekkehard to a camp chair, swiftly set up by one of their concubines, a blonde girl with the look of a cornered rabbit. As Ekkehard let the girl wipe the tears from his face with a scrap of linen, various slaves erected one of the round Quman tents behind him, deploying an awning to spare him from the afternoon sun. It was a hot day. Hanna sat in the shade of a tree, savoring the tickle of grass against her wrists as she leaned back. Her ever-present guards waited as patiently as stone to either side, not so close that they pressed in on her but not so far that they couldn't drag her down within ten steps if she made a run for it. One of them chewed on a stalk of grass as he surveyed the birds flitting among the trees. The other two stood there as stupidly as sheep, an easy illusion to cling to until one looked into their eyes.

Bulkezu came whistling cheerfully out of his tent, the first to be erected, leading the prettiest of his concubines, a plump young woman with waist-length black hair almost as luxuriously thick as Bulkezu's own. This was Agnetha, whom Bulkezu had picked out from the crowd of prisoners that awful twilight when plague had flowered in the mob. She was one of the few to survive that terrible night and she had, amazingly, saved a dozen of her kinsfolk from the slaughter. Bulkezu brought her to Ekkehard and indicated that she should kneel before the young prince. Hanna rose hastily and strode over.

Boso strutted up, as self-important as a rooster. "His Gloriousness cannot bear to see you snivel and whine like a sick child, Your Highness. Therefore, to raise your *spirits,* and your cock, he's giving you one of his well-used cunts."

Hanna had long since grown accustomed to Boso's coarse and arrogant way of speaking, but she often wondered what exactly Bulkezu did say to his interpreter and how much the Wendish man was twisting his master's words. As Hanna slid in behind Lord Frithuric, poor Agnetha caught sight of her but could do no more than look at her beseechingly. The young woman was too wise to protest, or even speak or cry, as she was handed from one man's tender mercies over to the other's.

However phrased, the offer dried up Ekkehard's tears. He was well supplied with women, of course, but Agnetha bore about her a certain cachet beyond the perfumes she wore because she was the best-looking woman currently with the army, and Bulkezu's besides. It was a grand gift to Ekkehard's mind, and he almost fell over himself thanking Bulkezu while the young woman knelt silently at his feet, trying hard to show no expression at all.

As Ekkehard nattered on, and Boso translated, Bulkezu began to look bored. A discreet hand signal, and quickly enough horses were brought for the Quman prince, his body-guard, and Hanna. Even Boso was left behind as the small party mounted and rode up to the hilltop to investigate the ruined palace.

Hanna saw no signs of rebuilding. The fire's destruction had been so complete that there wasn't anything left to salvage. Two years of rain and wind had washed the mantle of ashes off the hill, but blackened spars still stood in tribute to the sprawling palace that had once taken up half the height. The walls of the stone chapel were more or less intact, scored with the marks of fire. The shattered glass windows gaped vacantly and the roof had fallen in. Roof tiles littered the nave. Bulkezu poked through heaps of tiles with a spear but found

nothing of interest except a bronze belt buckle, warped from
the intense heat, that had once been fashioned in the shape of
a springing deer.

He laughed softly. "Would that I had such power." He
glanced up, caught by Hanna's silence, and peered at her with
an unnerving stare. "Do you know how this came about?" He
gestured broadly, encompassing the hilltop ruin.

She pressed her lips tightly together.

He smiled. "A broken lamp, oil spilled, or sorcery?"

At times like this, a fit of reckless fury would overtake her, a
wish to slam her fist into that handsome face and gallop onward
to freedom. But he had too many guards, more carefully placed
since her last attempt to escape, for her to try again.

He enjoyed her anger. He fed on it, and it made him laugh.
Although, of course, almost anything could make him laugh.

"Sorcery," he replied with satisfaction, as though she had
answered him.

Maybe she had.

He whistled sharply. After a bit his shaman, Cherbu, trotted
up on a piebald mare whose blotched coat bore a vague resemblance to the patchwork cloak and trousers worn by its rider.
The two men exchanged a few words, after which the shaman
dismounted, got down on his hands and knees, and proceeded
to sniff like a dog, following an unseen trail through the ruins.
Bulkezu followed him on horseback, singing—in that irritating nasal tone the Quman used for their favorite songs—to
entertain himself as he waited. Hanna recognized a song he
had once translated for her:

> "Has anyone suffered so much misfortune as I have?
> Who pities the orphan, or the little bird that falls from its
> abandoned nest?
> It would be better to be dead than motherless.
> But fate has already played this song.
> If my mother rose from her sickbed and kissed me now,
> it still wouldn't bring me any joy."

He paused. The shaman had vanished. Hanna looked around wildly, but she saw no trace of Cherbu or his patchwork cloak among the fallen beams and barren ground. The noises from camp, below them, seemed suddenly faint, shrouded. A cloud had covered the sun, granting respite from its glare, yet a thin line of light slithered through the wreckage like a snake.

An owl hooted. White flashed off to one side, and Hanna turned in time to see a huge owl settle onto the highest wall of the burned chapel.

"I'm here," she whispered, wondering if will alone, chiseled to a point and flung outward on a thought, would be enough to alert the owl to her presence among the Quman.

It raised its wings once, like a salute.

One of the guards drew, aiming an arrow at the huge bird, but Bulkezu spoke three soft words.

A billowing cloud of ash blew up from the ruins, making Hanna's eyes sting. She blinked rapidly, shielded her eyes with a hand, and when she dared look again, the owl was gone. The shaman, coated with a white layer of ash over his patchwork clothing, stood in the midst of the ruined barracks where five Lions had died.

"There," said Bulkezu. "That's where the fire started. He can taste it, you know."

"Taste what?"

"Magic."

"Why does he follow you, if he's so powerful? What do you give him to make him ride so far?"

Bulkezu laughed. God have mercy, how she had come to hate that laugh. "Cherbu is my brother. Our mother commanded him to serve me. Are you Wendish so uncivilized that you would disobey your own mother? It's true, isn't it, that you fight among yourselves more than you fight anyone else."

This struck him with such force that his laughter redoubled and he actually had to wipe tears from his eyes.

While she stewed, stoking her anger, she watched Cherbu pick through rotting planks and leaning wooden pillars singed by smoke and flame. Cold cinders crumbled under his hands as he marked a patch of ground with soot, then stamped around in a curious dance, singing in a reedy voice that occasionally slipped low.

Until a word she knew well slipped out of his throat, strangely accented but impossible to ignore.

"*Liathano.*"

She started, betraying herself. Bulkezu whistled. Cherbu shook himself, slapped the ground, and returned, humming under his breath. He had a habit of regarding his listeners out of one eye, tilting his head to the side like a bird. Bulkezu questioned him at length, but the shaman replied in short phrases and finally shrugged, ending the conversation.

"Where is she gone, this Liathano?" Bulkezu demanded with a frown, turning to Hanna. "My brother says she is a female, but that he can't smell her out. Where is she gone?"

At last Hanna smiled, letting anger bloom. "Why should I tell you?"

Her cool defiance provoked him; easy to see, when his nostrils flared like that and his horse shifted nervously under him, catching his mood. But his wrath only made her more stubborn. She stared him down as his dimple flashed, as he laughed but stroked the hair of his trophy head instead, almost caressing it. His brother spoke to him, glancing once at Hanna, and Bulkezu jerked as if he'd been struck. Without a word, he reined his horse around and rode down to camp. The set of his shoulders betrayed his rage. Half his guards followed him. The other half remained behind, watching with blank expressions.

But Hanna laughed, flushed with the satisfaction of having finally won a single, tiny victory.

Cherbu clucked his tongue, shaking his head from side to side so that his earrings swayed. When he spoke, although she couldn't understand the words, the tone could just as well have been her mother scolding Hanna and her two brothers if they whispered during Mass: "You know better than that . . ."

"I know, my friend," she said, and was surprised that she considered him no enemy, not really, despite the gruesome ornaments he wore. After all, she had not seen him lift a weapon or cast a harmful spell, not once. His cloak of magic protected Bulkezu from magic; that was all. He regarded her with a puzzled grin, since he couldn't understand a word she was saying. "I know I shouldn't make him angry. But right now it's the only weapon I have."

Such a frail weapon to fight back with, especially when fighting back made no sense. If she hadn't been Sorgatani's luck—well, then she'd be dead.

The light of the setting sun streamed golden across the open space, illuminating each suffering soul slumped in the grass, two or three hundred of them mixed in among the live-stock. It was hard to count with the sun's light shining in her eyes. By killing hundreds, Bulkezu had slaughtered the plague in their midst, but that didn't mean he'd stopped taking pris-oners.

Her anger was a small thing to lay as an obstacle in his path, but sometimes you had to make the most of what little you had.

By the time she got back to camp, Bulkezu seemed to have forgotten about the incident. A feast was laid, cheese and freshly baked bread salvaged from the small estate they'd over-run that morning, roasted venison, and mare's milk. Bulkezu never drank much wine or ale, preferring to watch Ekkehard and his companions drink themselves into a stupor. In general, Quman soldiers were a dour and unexciting bunch, not one bit up to the standards of carousing that she had grown accus-tomed to riding with Wendish or Ungrian nobles.

It was, thank God, possible to step away from the feast and relieve herself in what passed for privacy, given the three sol-diers who never strayed more than ten steps from her. The

Quman were not in the habit of digging ditches to use as
privies, but at least, like well-trained dogs, they tended to
choose one area at each place they camped for these necessities.
She remained at the outskirts of camp for as long as she could
and watched the stars twinkling in the sky above.

Where was Liath now?

She had no way to look for her. She did not dare attempt to
use her Eagle's sight for fear that Bulkezu would discover that
she possessed a skill, not quite magic but stinking enough of
sorcery, that he might try to force her to use it on his behalf.

A woman hurried out from the tent, making choking
noises. She dropped to her knees a few paces from Hanna and
threw up, mostly wine. The acid smell stung the air, then
faded.

Hanna dropped down beside her. "Are you well?"

It was Agnetha. She grasped Hanna's hands. "He's not
happy with me," she whispered frantically. "I did what you
said. No flattery. No whining. No crying. But he sulked.
Listen to him now."

Ekkehard had gotten hold of a lute and started singing,
obviously drunk. He had a clear tenor and a poet's talent for
shaping a phrase.

> *"Once in this bright feasting hall*
> *I laid eyes on the most beautiful of women.*
> *Yet now I return and find her gone*
> *the walls fallen,*
> *the hearth silent,*
> *no ring of cup or lilt of song*
> *to cheer my heart.*
> *Death has swept away all that I cherished.*

"What shall I do?" whispered Agnetha, retching again,
nothing but dry heaves now. She clutched her stomach. "Ai,
God, he said he would throw me to the wolves, to the common
soldiers. Tell me what shall I do, Eagle, I pray you."

"Lady shield you," murmured Hanna. A simple village girl like Agnetha hadn't the least idea how to be a concubine. And why should she have? Hanna had learned how to negotiate and observe at her mother's inn; those skills had served her well at court. "You can't treat each man the same. What Bulkezu liked isn't what the prince will want. Flattery for Prince Ekkehard. Tell him anything as long as it's praise. If he casts you off, beg to go to one of his companions. Manegold is vain and shallow. Welf is short-tempered but feels shame for what they're doing. Benedict is sharp. He'll see through bald flattery, and he likes to hit his girls. Frithuric likes men as well as women and mostly wants to be petted and kept comfortable. He's decent enough."

Agnetha's face was a pale shadow under the trees. "How do you know all this? Were you their whore before you went to Bulkezu?"

"I'm no man's whore, and never have been! I've spent time at court. An Eagle must learn to keep her eyes open and know those she serves."

Agnetha wiped her mouth with the back of a hand. She was dressed in a light shift, exposing rather too much creamy white breast only half covered by cloth and the silky fall of her long black hair. Even the normally impassive guards eyed her, such as they could see of her in the shadow of a tree with not more than a quarter moon to light the heavens. Maybe they had been among the dozen who had been fighting over her the evening she had come to Bulkezu's attention. "Lady save us," she murmured unsteadily. "When will it ever be over?"

"I don't know."

She was trying her best not to cry. "I try so hard. My mother and my four siblings, an uncle and three of his children and two cousins. I'm all that stands between them and death." She shuddered. "And I'm still more fortunate than most, all those poor dead souls. But sometimes I just don't know how I can stand another day of it." She sucked in air, coughed at the stench, and rose, squaring her shoulders. "I just have to. I just have to."

As she turned to go back into the tent, she rested a comforting hand on Hanna's arm. "At least I'm out of Bulkezu's tent. It's not that he hits you, but there's just something so cold and unnatural about him. And he's so ugly."

"Ugly?" Hanna almost laughed, but did not.

"With those slanty eyes and that complexion, like mud? That Lord Manegold is like the sun beside a nasty goblin, for that's all the beast is."

Since Hanna thought Lord Manegold even more vapid than the infamous Baldwin, and not nearly as pretty, she didn't reply.

"At least it's not so bad for me now as it has been for you all this time."

"For me?" Shame made her cringe away from the other woman. How had she suffered, compared to all those prisoners she heard screaming as the Quman cut them down?

"He watches you all the time. I know you've been his mistress longer than any other woman. I don't see how you can stand it and keep so calm and dignified. You're so strong! I guess that's why you don't think of yourself as his whore."

Maybe sometimes people could not hear the truth, and it was useless to explain.

"You're not even pretty, but I know he only rapes you because you're the King's Eagle. It's like raping the king that way, isn't it? I know he's trying to humiliate the king through you. I admire you for never letting him dishonor you."

Or maybe it was impossible for people to grasp the truth when the truth stood outside everything they knew.

Light shone as a lamp bobbed around back, away from the feast. She saw Bulkezu, escorted by one of his night guards. But he was only looking for her. She had been gone for too long.

"I thank you," she said to Agnetha. "I had forgotten the words to that song."

Agnetha saw Bulkezu. Her mask of stone would have done King Henry proud. She wasn't a stupid girl, only an innocent one, struggling to survive. "My lord," she said, dipping down to show him deference. When he did not reply, she walked with head held high back to the feast: no flattery, no fear, no whining.

"Sing me the song," whispered Bulkezu. He didn't laugh.

It had been a reckless day, and a certain foolhardy courage still gripped her. She stepped carefully as she came out from under the trees. She had always been quick on her feet, so her mother often said.

"My lord prince," she said softly, "I didn't expect to meet you here." Rude comments and nasty retorts bubbled up on her lips, but she choked them off. "Just an old song I used to sing as girls do. I'd forgotten the first line. It goes like this."

She had a decent voice, could carry a tune and entertain the inn customers without ever dreaming of running away to become a court poet. "'Golden is his hair and sweet is his voice; I don't want to love him, but I have no choice.'" She laughed, seeing the flash of dimple that could signal his laughter, or his rage. Hate burned hot in her. "I've seen him, the man who is handsomer than you. And he is."

His right hand twitched once, then stilled. "Why do you go to so much trouble to make me angry? I haven't touched you."

"You haven't touched my body. You've just brutalized my heart and my soul."

He regarded her for a while in silence. Behind, Ekkehard had begun, thank God, a more cheerful song, goaded on by Agnetha's giggling praise.

"Where is Liathano?" he said at last. "Lead me to her, and I'll let you go free."

"She already has a husband, Prince Bulkezu."

"I already have four wives. And a Kerayit shaman's luck."

"Or her curse."

That made him laugh, but the laughter did not reach his eyes. "Don't make me angry," he said at last, before indicating that she should follow him back to the feasting.

They continued north along the tributary. Three days and seven villages later, they came to its confluence with the Veser

River. The first sign of outriders came about midday when a scout was killed. Several larger scouting bands were sent out, and when they returned with their reports Bulkezu ordered a change in their marching order. As usual when they approached a fortified site, the prisoners were driven to the front as the army pressed forward through the trees.

"Ai, God," said Ekkehard when they halted at last on a ridgeline from which they could overlook the Veser River. "That's the fort of Barenberg. We're in my aunt Rotrudis' duchy now."

His companions regarded the distant fort in silence. The river wound north through ripening fields and orchards. This was rich country, indeed.

"I can't fight her," whispered Ekkehard, glancing toward Bulkezu, who had ridden up to the edge of the ridge. A steep slope cut away beneath the Quman begh. The wind sang sweetly in his griffin wings. Because he wore his helm, Hanna could not see his expression behind the visor, only that mask of iron.

"Whose banner flies from the tower?" asked Benedict.

Ekkehard made a choking noise as his face drained of color. Bulkezu reined his horse around and returned to them.

"Two banners," Hanna said as hope sparked. "The regent's silk, and Wayland's hawk. We seem to have met up with Princess Theophanu and Duke Conrad, Your Highness."

2

EVEN with an Eagle's sight to aid him, Sanglant and his troops spent three weeks following the meandering trail of Prince Bayan and Princess Sapientia as it wound through the marchlands of Olsatia, Austra, and Eastfall. He met up at last with their army at a slave auction in the ruins of the fortress of Machteburg. Easy enough to tell that Bulkezu's army had been here two months before: the mostly rotted bodies of unarmed prisoners lay in heaps along the outer wall where they'd fallen, killed by their own terrified countrymen deceived into believing that the mob of captives was the vanguard of the Quman assault.

Sanglant tracked Bayan down where he prowled the burned-out ruins, poking with a spear through the ashes of the central tower. The Ungrian prince looked no worse for wear, as bluff and fit as ever, with a becoming twinkle in his eye as he looked up to see Sanglant approaching him. He pressed through his retinue and hurried over.

"My friend!" Bayan clapped Sanglant heartily on the shoulder before enveloping him in a crushing hug. He kissed him on either cheek, as a kinsman, and finally let him go. "Alas that we meet in such troubled times."

"Troubled enough, it's true."

"What is this frowning face, my brother? I know this look of a man who is not sporting in the bed enough."

Sanglant laughed. "Is that the trouble you complain of? I thought you meant this war against the Quman."

But Bayan was not to be thrown off the scent. "How can this be? You look whole in all parts. Do the women not find you handsome any longer?"

The question made Sanglant unaccountably irritable. "Nay, I'm troubled more than enough by women. It was easier to travel in the duchies. I felt safe at night in monastic guesthouses, sung to sleep by the chaste music of God. Out here in the marchlands I'm tormented every night by yet another sweet lass asking prettily for my prince's seed to honor her family."

"Not two sweet lasses every night? From me you get no pity if you send them away without a taste. Five pretty Salavii slave girls I bought at the market in Handelburg this past winter. I must send them to work in the kitchens. Nor can I mention ever my beloved snow woman, whom I sent to her death for the sake of peace in my bed." He sighed, eyeing

Sanglant with a rueful expression. "Are you not traveling with this wife you married against your father's wishes?"

As with any wound, the pain did dull after a time, even if the ache of mingled grief, hope, and anger would never go away completely. The late summer heat cast a haze over the dead fortress. Luckily, they had arrived weeks after the worst of the stench had faded, although now and again a tickle of putrefaction teased Sanglant's nostrils, some bubble of gas released from deep within the mound of corpses.

"It might be best to bury the dead," he replied curtly.

Bayan had a way of quirking up his right eyebrow when he wished to ask an unwanted question, but refrained. "Now we hear report of plague in Avaria. We need none of that here to add to our distress. Already have I men at work digging graves enough to take all these poor innocent corpses. Maybe it is not right to call a corpse innocent, with maggots and flies crawling in its belly."

"Your Wendish is much improved."

"Your disposition is not. What happened to your wife?"

Sanglant took the spear out of Bayan's hand impatiently, stabbing at a gleam caught among the ashes, but all he came up with was yet another skull. He crouched to fish it out of the debris. It had come loose from its body. The lower jaw had been smashed in, probably by falling stone. A few shreds of flesh still adhered to the dome of the skull, trailing patches of reddish hair, but otherwise weather and insects had picked it clean.

"I haven't the stomach to tell the tale one more time. You'll find that my faithful soldiers and clever scholastics know the story by heart."

"Father! Daddy!" Blessing had escaped from Heribert and Zacharias again and with nut-brown Anna in tow came charging through the ruins, whacking at tumbled walls with her wooden sword as she passed. "I want a man, Daddy. I saw a man. I want him." She ran up, wiped soot from her cheek but only succeeded in making her face dirtier than it already was, and placed herself directly in front of Bayan. She set hands on hips and looked him in the eye. "This is a prince," she proclaimed, thought about what that meant, and leaned closer to Bayan and spoke confidingly. "Can you get me the man?"

"Who is this charming child?" exclaimed Bayan, delighted. "Why wears she a gold torque?"

"*I* am Blessing, heir to Emperor Taillefer." She was as arrogant as an empress, and he supposed he had only himself to blame. He adored her, utterly, helplessly, and that she had any self-control at all was entirely due no doubt to Anna's stern, no-nonsense attitude. Nothing scared Anna, not even Blessing's tantrums.

"What man does the young empress desire?" asked Bayan, managing not to dissolve into laughter.

"I saw a man in *chains*. I want him. I'm thirsty."

"We'll share ale, I trust, child. But first we see about the man in chains." He beckoned to his retinue, a dozen Ungrian noblemen and soldiers who watched Blessing with a mixture of amusement and interest that both irritated and pleased Sanglant. "Prince Sanglant? You accompany us? A party of Wendish and Polenie merchants camp here with a crowd of slaves among their goods. Some prisoners must be refugees from the fighting. They will have stories to tell about the Quman army."

Blessing had recently developed an aversion to being carried, so Sanglant slowed his steps as she trotted alongside. They crossed the fort's yard. Scorched roof tiles lay shattered on paving stones. A dead horse had been picked down to the bone by vultures. A pale blue tunic, ground into the muck, gave an incongruous splash of color to the grim destruction.

"What are Bulkezu's objectives?" Sanglant asked Bayan.

"Many times I ask myself this question. But how can I think like a filthy Quman?" Bayan spat. "To my shame, I hid all winter behind the walls of Handelburg, licking my wounds. Then I crawled out in the spring, but he rode west

long before and left me cowering in my hole. Feh." He spat
again, looking really angry now, a man with a grudge.
Gesturing broadly, he indicated Machteburg's ruins, the
once-proud border fortress reduced to rubble and debris.
"What else do the Quman want except slaves, gold, and
misery?"

From the height of the citadel, standing among the fallen
stones that had once formed the gate, Sanglant watched the
Oder River streaming northward below. Northward, toward
Walburg, where he had left Waltharia with a small garrison
and a gold torque. Her husband Druthmar stood nearby, chatting quietly with Captain Fulk. "He must want something
else. Or be driven by a whip we know nothing of." He
grinned, suddenly, and lifted Blessing up onto a block of stone
so she could see better. He turned to Bayan. "Where is my
sister?"

"Ah." Bayan's answering grin had a wicked edge. "Speaking
as we do of a whip. Come. She is down at the slave market
with my mother."

Sanglant's army had halted north of Machteburg on the
eastern shore of the river. To reach the slave market, a motley
collection of wagons, suspicious merchants, and nervous hired
guards who had set up for the night in an ancient ring fort, he
and Bayan rode south along the western shore, through the
ranks of the army marching under the command of Bayan and
Sapientia.

The Wendishmen had not forgotten Gent. They cheered
Bayan happily enough, but the sight of Sanglant made them
roar. Soon enough, the path was crowded on either side by
Lions and milites and young lords with their retinues, hastening forward to cheer him on. Even Bayan's Ungrians gave the
prince his due, shrill whistles that made him think his ears
might pop and that forced Blessing to clap hands over her ears
to muffle the sound.

Sapientia heard them coming. By the time they found her
emerging from the slave market, she had obviously prepared

for the meeting, stationing herself just where the old hill-fort gate, now fallen into ruin, pitched downward. Sanglant, dismounting, had to walk up the rise to greet her. From her position above him on the slope, she deigned to kiss him on either cheek in the greeting of a kinswoman.

"Sister," he said cheerfully enough, although he didn't see much answering warmth in her expression.

"Has Father sent help at last?" she demanded.

"Nay, he's ridden south to Aosta—"

"Always Aosta!"

Bayan made to speak, but Sanglant gave a quick lift of his chin to interrupt him. "He's ridden south to Aosta where lie other threats—"

"What can possibly threaten us more than Bulkezu and his army? Have you heard about the plague in Avaria? We've seen with our own eyes the trail of destruction the Quman army has left in its wake—villages burned and fields trampled. You can see yourself the dead he's left, there at the walls. All the folk hereabouts, those who survived, say the fortress is haunted by the unavenged dead. A child's ghost walks at midnight, crying for its mother."

"Many a child cries for its mother," said Sanglant, smoothly slipping into her rant, "but weeping for what we don't have won't defeat the Quman. Come, Sapientia, here is my daughter Blessing, your niece."

Aunt and niece eyed each other. Sapientia had weathered her first extended campaign well. She had filled out, gained color, and moved with more confidence. But as she examined Blessing, he saw the old dance of envy warring with interest in her gaze. "I thought she looked like you. But this can't be the Eagle's child. She's too old. Did you father her on some concubine before your imprisonment at Gent?"

He had learned to resign himself to the questions. Sometimes, the best answer was the simple truth. "Do not forget that sorcery runs in her blood. I can explain no better than you why she grows so fast. She was born in the spring, last year."

"She looks like a well-grown girl of three or four years of age," objected Sapientia, "not a toddling child of fifteen or sixteen months."

"So she does." He had learned to hide his fear. He did not understand what was happening to his daughter. At first he'd believed that the unearthly milk she imbibed from Jerna caused her to grow with unnatural speed, and maybe it had. But Jerna had left them, and Blessing still aged far more quickly than she ought. He had a bad idea that it would not end until Liath returned, as if a link bound Liath and Blessing so closely that what happened to one rebounded onto the other. If Liath only knew that, would she not return to spare her daughter?

She would, if she cared for them at all.

At moments like this, he wondered where his own mother had gone. Alia had deserted him, too—for the second time.

"You are a princess." Blessing had remained silent long enough.

Sapientia did not quite recoil. "I am King Henry's heir."

"Oh," said Blessing appreciatively, oblivious to these nuances, "I *like* him. He's my grandfather." Because she was a child who didn't mind sharing, she went on. "I am the heir of Emperor Taillefer."

"Does she say that to everyone?" asked Bayan as Sapientia's mouth pursed with disapproval and she looked ready to say something rash.

"Only to those who deserve it. Come, sweet heart, where is the man you saw?"

Blessing grabbed his hand and, after a moment's studious thought, grabbed Bayan's hand as well. "This way!"

Even Sapientia laughed. "She is indeed Henry's granddaughter."

"Since you are a princess," called Blessing as she dragged her escorts forward, "will you help me get the man?"

Anger sparked as quickly as amusement in Sapientia's face. "Not one to listen to others, no matter whose need is greater.

We could use these men in the army, and a few of these women, too, if they're willing and strong enough."

"An excellent idea," cried Bayan. "My lion queen has a keen eye for worth. It is you who must pick out the ones who can fight and serve."

"Think you so?" she asked, a flush making her cheeks bright as she turned to gaze at her husband. Sanglant had seen besotted women before; his sister looked no different, although she managed to keep her noble dignity intact as they walked together into the market.

Sanglant had never thought much one way or the other about merchants who trafficked in slaves. The heathen Jinna empire and the crafty Arethousans had an unending appetite for slaves, preferably boys cut to become eunuchs. Neither did Wendish merchants shy away from selling captured heathen tribespeople out of the east into servitude in the civilized west. These merchants had other wares available as well: linen and wool cloth; furs from the north; casks of salt; spoons of wood or ivory or tin; sickles, scythes, and hatchets of iron; whores, herbs, and spices, some more sweet smelling than others. But after a year confined by Bloodheart's chains, Sanglant could not help but notice the suffering of their human merchandise.

Blessing tugged him and Bayan over to a ragged group of captives bound hand and foot. They had the look of defeated soldiers, the kind of troublemakers who needed to be trussed up so they couldn't escape on the long march.

A Polenie merchant hurried up, bobbing up and down anxiously as he took in Sanglant's Wendish clothing and noble bearing and Bayan's Ungrian flair. He wore the typical Polenie hat, a pointed leather cap with a folded brim. "Your Most Excellencies," he cried in passable Wendish, "here have I strong men who I take south to the slave markets of Arethousa. Have you a care to purchase them now? I can give you good price."

Blessing marched up to the youngest of the captives, a lad of perhaps sixteen years with a blackened eye, bare feet, and the scarring of frostbite on his nose and ears. "I told you I would come back." She turned to the merchant, expression fierce. "Thiemo is mine."

"My lady—" began the merchant, glancing at Sanglant, not wanting to insult a prince's daughter.

The youth began to weep, although it was hard to tell whether his tears were those of joy or thwarted hope. "My lady, is it true? Have you come to ransom me and my comrades?" Then he, too, noticed Sanglant and Bayan.

"Your Highness!" cried the lad, flushing hotly. Five of the men with him dropped hard to their knees. Under their dirt, Sanglant recognized the tabards of Lions.

"God save us," murmured Bayan. "The heretics."

Sapientia came up beside Bayan. She frowned, and when she narrowed her eyes in that particular way one could almost actually see her thinking. "Can it be? Are these the heretics banished after the trial at Handelburg? How did they get here? Where are the rest of them?"

"Dead," said the eldest of the Lions. "Or better dead, considering what we ran into. Your Highness." He bowed his head respectfully toward Sanglant. "I know you are Prince Sanglant. It's said you're a fair man. I pray you—"

"Daddy, I want him."

"I don't know." Sapientia wrung her hands. "Biscop Alberada excommunicated them for heresy. How can we go against the church? We could be excommunicated, too. It's God's judgment upon them that they be sold into slavery as punishment for their sins." But she wasn't sure. Sanglant saw how she looked at Bayan, waiting to see what he would say. She was afraid to pass judgment herself.

Sanglant turned to the merchant. "These men are King Henry's Lions. I will ransom them from you for a fair price."

"One nomia apiece," said the merchant instantly.

"Remember," said Sanglant with a warning smile, "that I have an army and you have twenty guards. I could take them as easily as buy them, and since we stand on Wendish ground,

I would be well within my rights to restore their freedom because they are Henry's sworn soldiers."

"Forsworn," objected Sapientia, "because of heresy—"

"As long as the Quman army rides on Wendish soil, I do not care if they are heretics, foreigners, two-headed, or painted blue, as long as they will fight loyally for the king." He turned to the old Lion. "What is your name?"

"Gotfrid, my lord prince. We are none of us disloyal to the king. What God chose to reveal to us has nothing to do with how faithfully we'll fight."

Sanglant called to Heribert, who had been trailing behind with the rest of his retinue. "Give the merchant ten sceattas for his trouble."

"May God bless you, Your Highness," said Gotfrid. "We'll serve you well, I swear it. And so do these others swear."

The other four swore oaths hurriedly, with every appearance of gratitude and sincerity. Only the merchant didn't look happy, but he knew better than to protest.

Bayan stepped forward and spoke to the redeemed captives in a low voice. "The Eagle? Prince Ekkehard?"

Beneath the grime, Lord Thiemo's clothes had the cut, color, and richness of a lord's garb, and when he rose to his feet he had the slightly bow-legged stance of a young man who has grown up spending more time in the saddle than walking. "Dead," he said raggedly.

"Is this true?" asked Bayan.

"I fear it must be, my lord prince," said the old Lion. "It was winter. It was snowing like to drown us. And we were attacked by shadows." His voice dropped to a whisper and he glanced around as though expecting to see them materialize out of nowhere. "The Lost Ones."

Flushing, he struggled to contain the memory, and the fear. His companions murmured to each other, huddling together as if the mere mention of the creatures who had attacked them was enough to bring down a snowstorm.

Gotfrid went on harshly. "I never knew what happened to

the others, except for two of my men who were cut down by elfshot in the forest. We got scattered. We found Lord Thiemo, here," he nodded toward the youth, "in the woods, and escaped as best we could. In the end we got taken by bandits. They were merciful. They took our weapons, cloaks, and belts, but they sold us to the slavers instead of killing us." He wiped a tear from his eye. "That Eagle, she was a good woman. It pains my heart to have lost her."

Bayan murmured under his breath so softly that Sanglant knew the words were not meant even for Sanglant's ears. "As it does mine."

"Ekkehard is dead?" asked Sapientia. "Young fool." She wiped a tear from her eye as though she'd copied the movement from the old Lion.

"I heard otherwise," said Sanglant. "There's a rumor heard as far north as Walburg that Ekkehard has turned his coat and is riding with Bulkezu."

Lord Thiemo leaped up. "It's not true! Ekkehard would never act the traitor. He'd never betray the king. If his father had only given him what he deserved—"

"Quiet!" Blessing's voice cracked like a whip over the youth's protest. "Don't yell at my Daddy. I don't like that."

Just like that, the youth dropped to one knee before her and bowed his head obediently. "Yes, my lady."

No one snickered or even grinned as Blessing extended a hand to touch him lightly on the head. "Stand up, Lord Thiemo," she commanded. "But don't yell."

"I think such rumors are not true," said Bayan. "Maybe he fell, and his armor off his body was took, and now is being worn by a Quman thief."

"I think it's true," muttered Sapientia, "or at least that it could be true. If you dangled enough sweets and enough flattery in front of Ekkehard, I swear I believe he would do anything."

"Even that?" demanded Sanglant.

"You don't know him as well as I do."

It was hard, seeing the resentful purse of her mouth, the weakness that had troubled her heart for her entire life, to believe that she knew what she was talking about. She was always afraid that the person next to her at table was going to get a bigger cut of beef than she did.

"Come, Sapientia," said Bayan hastily, appearing to know his wife's moods very well, "you will judge which prisoners come free to serve in our army."

"Come! Come!" echoed Blessing, dancing from foot to foot. "I want to see." Not waiting for the others, she raced ahead, Anna and, belatedly, Lord Thiemo hurrying after her. "What's that?" the girl shrieked, pointing toward the far wall of the old hill fort where, seen through various carts and stalls, the palanquin belonging to Bayan's mother had come to rest. Her four slave bearers had hunkered down to wait. With the curtains pulled closed it was impossible to know from this distance what the Kerayit shaman was looking at, but Sanglant felt sure she was examining something worthy of interest. With Bayan and Sapientia beside him, he hastened after his child. His companions followed him.

Here in this quarter of the little market the slaves included Quman prisoners trussed up or shackled; even the children were considered dangerous enough to be bound. As they approached, poor Zacharias began nervously twisting one hand about the other wrist, as if remembering the chafing hold of a shackle. His right eye blinked alarmingly the closer they got to one sullen display of Quman prisoners.

"They stink so effusively," said Heribert, waving a scrap of linen cloth in front of his nose as they approached the wagons belonging to a Wendish merchant, a stout woman with the gaze of a stoat spying on an untouched nest of eggs. "Is there any way to clean them up?"

Zacharias' giggle was cut through by hysteria, barely suppressed. "Throw them in the river. They hate water." He wiped his brow and looked ready to jump in the river himself.

"Courage, Brother Zacharias," said Sanglant softly. Zacharias glanced at him in surprise and, with an effort, steadied his breathing and squared his shoulders like a man preparing for battle.

The merchant hurried forward to greet them. "My lord prince, I pray you are well come to this terrible place, and that you may find what you need here among my wares. I am called Mistress Otlinde, out of Osterburg, where your most noble aunt, Duchess Rotrudis, rules her subjects with a steady hand. My lord Druthmar! I have bided several times most rewardingly in the fine town of Walburg. Perhaps you may recall the fine silver silk damask my lady Waltharia selected from among my wares for your youngest son's naming day?"

"Alas," Druthmar replied, with a pleasant smile, "I do not."

Mistress Otlinde looked like the kind of merchant who recalled every least transaction she had ever made, not to mention the exact count of eggs she had sucked dry. "I pray you, let my son bring you ale. How may I help you?"

Sanglant's attention was caught by his daughter, who had bolted away from Bayan and gone to examine the palanquin and the four male slaves. Without warning, she grabbed the edge, hoisted herself up, and slithered in through the gaudy draperies protecting the woman concealed within.

Anna shrieked in protest. The Ungrians called out in shock and dismay, and Bayan grabbed for Blessing's small shod foot, just missing it as it vanished behind the curtains. The slaves leaped to their feet, as distressed as fowl caught napping by a fox. Bayan swore in Ungrian. He touched the curtain, jerked as if he'd been stung, and leaped back, face white.

"God have mercy!" cried Sapientia, not without satisfaction. She saw Sanglant and gestured broadly. "Look what trouble the child has caused already! How can we ever repair such an insult to a Kerayit shaman?"

Maybe she hoped to shame him into admitting he didn't understand the powers of a Kerayit shaman, but he'd ridden

with Bayan before, and where Bayan rode, his mother was
never far behind. He reached the palanquin at a run only to be
stopped by Bayan, who thrust out an arm to hold him back.

"Nay, my friend, I beg of you, go not to make it worse."

"My daughter—" began Sanglant.

"Please, Daddy, can you wait?" Blessing's voice sang out
from behind the curtains, as cheerful as a sunny summer day.
"I'm talking with the old lady."

Sweating, Bayan wiped his eyes and called for a cup of ale.
His interpreter, Brother Breschius, drew him aside and they
fell into a whispered conversation until a soldier hurried up
with a cup and a pitcher. The filled cup was passed around the
assembled lords, drained, and filled again.

As they drank, there was silence except for the click and
clack of beads swaying as the bearers shifted position again. In
this summer heat the four slaves wore little enough clothing
that Sanglant could not help but imagine Waltharia admiring
them. Strange to think that an old woman like Bayan's mother
might have something in common with Villam's heir, even if
it was only a lascivious eye for the male figure. Not many
women, or men for that matter, possessed Waltharia's easy
authority, blunt common sense, and playfully sharp disposition. How many times had he inadvertently found himself
comparing Waltharia to Liath over these past weeks? Liath had
none of Waltharia's winning qualities: she was secretive, serious, and not one bit accustomed to presiding in authority over
anyone except perhaps herself. But she was still the most glorious woman he had ever met, and even to think of her made
him heartsick with longing.

Yet did she think of him and the child at all, wherever she
had gone?

He heard Blessing's voice chattering away and the occasional murmured reply, but something about the heavy
curtains around the palanquin or the haze of magic known to
a Kerayit shaman kept him from understanding their words.
By his daughter's tone it was quite obvious that she was in fine

fettle, babbling happily. What on Earth could she and the old shaman have to talk about?

Unable to wait patiently, he examined Mistress Otlinde's wares, laid out over racks: tabby linens and diamond twills from the island kingdom of Alba, marten, beaver, and fox pelts from the Starviki chiefdoms, and a pair of small tapestries depicting the fall of the Dariyan Empire to the Bwr horde. Somewhere she had found two score of Quman, mostly women with tangled, greasy hair and stick-thin children scratching fleas and sores who sat huddled abjectly in the dirt, having long since given up any hope of escape or succor. But among them stood a dozen Quman men with deceptively bovine stares, as concealed, in their own way, as Bayan's mother was concealed behind her curtains. He knew that look; he'd seen it in other prisoners, the most dangerous kind. Any one of these men would happily claw out his eyes if he only got close enough to let them do it.

Zacharias glided up beside him, trembling a little, and spoke in a low voice. "They're out of the Shatai tribe. You can see the cloven hoof of the red deer cut into that man's shoulder."

"Are they allies of the Pechanek?"

"Nay, they never have been. There has been fighting in the Karkaihi pasturage the last few years. That's almost to the Bitter Sea."

He examined the prisoners. They eyed him, silent, betraying neither hate nor fear. He admired the grim aloofness with which they endured their fate. He'd never hated the Quman, not like Bayan. Years ago Bulkezu had ruined his voice and killed too many of his soldiers, but the Quman had never done him any greater harm than had most of his other enemies. They'd done no greater harm to him than he'd done to them in his turn.

"A Quman warrior takes hardship as well as any soldiers I've ever seen. How can I win their loyalty?"

Was that sweat breaking out on Zacharias' forehead. "What do you want of them, my lord prince?"

"If there are any willing to swear allegiance to my cause, why not take them into my army?"

"My lord prince!"

Captain Fulk had heard, as had Lord Druthmar, Lord Hrodik, and several of the other noblemen.

"Do you think it wise to allow Quman into our ranks, Prince Sanglant?" asked Druthmar. "What's to prevent them from murdering us in our tents at night once they have the run of camp?"

"Come, Brother Zacharias," said Sanglant, "how can I convince Quman soldiers to ride in my army, under my command, without having to watch my back ever after?"

"Will they take gold?" asked Lord Hrodik.

Zacharias laughed. "Yes, they'll take it and then murder you afterward to see if you're hiding any more on your person."

"Might they swear a binding oath?" asked Captain Fulk, "as a good Wendishman would?"

"They'd swear an oath as easily as they'd spit in your face just before they cut off your head."

"Are they such savages that they can't be trusted at all?" demanded Lord Druthmar. He was an able man and a decent enough companion on the march, but Sanglant had discovered that he lacked imagination and ambition.

Zacharias laughed, a choked sound that annoyed Sanglant. "I pray you, forgive me," he said at last, shuddering. "Griffin feathers, my lord prince."

"Griffin feathers! Like those my mother had at Verna, when she shot the creatures that attacked us."

"Just so. Bulkezu's feathers, those were." A nasty gleam lit Zacharias' gaze as he savored a memory. "I remember how she defeated him."

"Truly, a remarkable feat. If only she would have stayed to lend some of her skills to my cause. But she never told me it was Bulkezu she had bested."

Zacharias smiled wryly. After all, he, too, had been abandoned by Alia when she no longer needed him. He surely had no illusions about her loyalties. "Nay, my lord prince, do not think she tried to deceive you. I doubt she ever knew or cared about his name. But he'll not have forgotten her as easily as she forgot him."

"I suppose not."

"He's a madman, my lord prince. Nay. Do not shake your head as if I were a poet crowing for my supper. I mean it in truth. He is mad."

"So was I, for a time. But he wasn't so mad that he couldn't stalk and kill a griffin."

Heribert was listening. "It seems to me that a man must be mad to stalk a griffin. Are you really saying, Zacharias, that the Quman will follow a man wearing griffin wings even if he has nothing else to offer them? What of loyalty? Necessity? Family honor?"

"Have you ever seen a griffin, Heribert?" asked Zacharias.

"I have not."

"Then you'd not ask that question." He snorted, but not entirely with contempt. "Any man in the tribes can turn his back on his begh and take his tent and his herds and his family out into the steppe. Any man among them can live like a prince and his wife like a queen, if he chooses to leave the tribe behind. If he doesn't mind the solitude and is content with a small herd that he and his family can care for alone."

"Do you mean to say they're entirely faithless?" demanded Druthmar. "Not even honorable enough to swear vows and keep them?"

"They're the most loyal soldiers I've ever seen. Never once would a Quman rider complain of hardship. They'd die rather than utter one word against the begh they follow."

Lord Hrodik had taken a liking to Druthmar, who put up with him, and he exclaimed loudly in protest, looking as if he would like to spit at the helpless prisoners. "If you love them so much that you praise them like kings, then why did you flee from them, Frater?"

"I hate them," said Zacharias softly. "Never doubt that. They treated me like a dog, and worse than a dog." Sanglant had noticed now and again a certain expression on Zacharias' face, a way the disreputable frater had of wrinkling up his nose as at a bad smell, or as if he were trying not to snarl contemptuously—or yelp in fright. He had that look now. The frater looked the prisoners up and down and even swaggered forward two steps, well out of reach in case one should try to kick him. The Quman studied him with those unnaturally blank stares, then glanced away dismissively. But Zacharias wasn't done. A string of words emerged fluently from his lips, swift and sweet. The aloof demeanor of the Quman slaves snapped so fast that poor Lord Hrodik yelped, startled, and leaped backward. The slaves growled and swore, spitting. One yanked so hard against the cords that bound him that the post to which he and his comrades were tied, driven deep into the ground, rocked alarmingly. Druthmar drew his sword. Bayan's Ungrian guards came running. Sanglant laughed, feeling the old familiar surge as his heart pounded and excitement raced along his limbs.

Mistress Otlinde's hired guards bolted forward with their staffs and began beating the bound prisoners into submission.

It wasn't a pretty sight. The Quman who had howled curses at Zacharias hunched over, taking hard blows without a whimper. In its own horrible way, it was an impressive display of toughness.

But it was a waste.

"For the sake of God," said Sanglant harshly, moving in to drag off the most rabid of the hired guards, who was whacking away like a crazed man at the Quman now driven to his knees below him. "Hold!" The man whirled, thinking to strike the prince, but Sanglant caught his arm in mid-strike and held it, staring him down. After a moment, the hired guard shrank away, called off his fellows, and retreated to a safe distance, glowering. His victim spat out a few teeth and wiped blood off his chin. Staggering slightly, he stood, lifting his chin to look up at Sanglant, meeting his gaze. In the end, after a long battle, it was the Quman who looked away first.

"What was that?" Sanglant grabbed Zacharias' shoulder and spun him around. The frater was breathing hard, as though he'd been running, and sweat streamed down his face. "I would have been better amused if I knew what purpose it serves to beat them senseless."

"Forgive me, my lord prince." Zacharias could hardly speak because he was panting so hard, flushing and almost stammering. "I only wish it were Bulkezu trussed up in their place. My mother always told me I was better armed with my tongue than many a man who carries spear and shield."

"If they hadn't been tied up, they'd have torn you to bits," observed Heribert, who had retreated a few steps, letting Lord Druthmar's broad shoulders shield him.

Zacharias spoke again, hoarsely, still catching his breath. "Griffin wings, my lord prince. They'd never stab in the back a man wearing griffin wings." With a shuddering sigh, he strode off into the crowd.

"Nay, Heribert," said Sanglant quietly before the cleric could hasten after him, "he has his own demons to fight. Let him be for now. Yet I would gladly know what he said to them."

The Quman slaves had by now all picked themselves up, shrugging bruised shoulders, licking away blood that trickled down from their nostrils, all of it done awkwardly because their hands were tied up tightly behind their backs. Bayan and Sapientia hurried up, having heard the commotion.

"Do they trouble you?" demanded Bayan. "I can have my men kill every one, but first I must wait on my mother. She sometimes likes to take one of these—" He spat at the feet of the nearest one, shoulders taut and one hand on his sword hilt as if he meant to cut their throats himself. "—as a slave. But such maggots as this are unworthy even to be slaves."

"I think they're not really born of human blood," said Druthmar in a low voice. "You'd think it hadn't hurt them at all. There's no shame in saying what hurts when a wound is honorably won, or dishonorably given." He, too, glanced toward the hired guards, a motley-looking crew of mercenaries who had probably been bandits preying on innocent travelers two months ago.

"No shame," agreed Sanglant. He beckoned to Brother Breschius. "Do you know what my frater said to them? I know you have experience with the tribes."

"Nay, Prince Sanglant," said Breschius. "I was a slave among the Kerayit, not the Quman clans. I know a few words of Quman, it's true, and indeed I believe he made some comment about their mothers, but beyond that I could not understand what he said."

"What do you care what the frater said to them?" asked Sapientia scornfully. "They're only Quman. More beasts than people."

"They're soldiers. We have need of soldiers, I believe. If they aren't Pechanek Quman, then there's no reason we can't take them into our army as well and use them to fight Bulkezu."

Bayan stiffened as though he'd been spat on, turned abruptly, and walked away into the market.

Sapientia turned angrily on Sanglant. "You know how he hates the Quman. It was Quman who killed his son. How can you even suggest that we use Quman troops?"

"I'll use what I must to defeat Bulkezu. There is far more at stake here and now, Sapientia, even than this. As I will tell you when we have more privacy. Any man or woman who will fight for me, I will take into my army. If Bulkezu is not defeated soon, if the Seven Sleepers are allowed to act as they will without opposition because we quarrel about which men we deign to use to do our killing for us, then we will be no better off than that poor lad, led away in chains." He gestured toward Lord Thiemo, loitering like a faithful dog a discreet distance away from the palanquin as he waited for Blessing. "Nay. We'd be lucky to be slaves. More likely we'd be dead and our father's kingdom shattered and overrun."

The force of his words made her uncertain. He could see it

in her eyes: ought she to believe him? Object? Walk on? Call for help? Give a command?

He remembered the expression on Waltharia's face that night she had offered him a gold torque. "To rule, you must lead, Sister," he said softly, "or else stand aside."

Annoyance flared. "Where is your gold torque, Brother?"

"I left it with my wife."

"Who does not ride with you, I see."

"Who does not ride with me, as you see."

"Lady help us, did she abandon you and the child? Just as your mother abandoned you." She clucked reprovingly. "Alas, you and Father have left yourselves at the mercy of inconstant women."

But Sanglant knew how to play this game. "I pray you, Sister, do not speak so slightingly of your own blessed mother, Queen Sophia, for she was always kind to me even if all the other things they said of her were true."

Sapientia flushed bright red. She called to her ladies and strode off after Bayan.

Heribert stepped up beside him. "A fruitless victory, I fear."

"True enough. And ill gotten, may Queen Sophia forgive me, for it's true she was always kind to me. It was the Wendish clerics who would persist in never trusting her, just because she was Arethousan."

Blessing's childish giggle rang out, and she slid out from under the curtains, tumbled to her knees, and picked herself up before Anna could get to her. She allowed Anna to dust off the knees of her leggings and straighten her sleeves but hadn't a chance to speak before Sanglant lifted her up.

"That was rashly done, Daughter!"

Her sweet little face trembled, her mouth turned down, and the shock of his stern anger made tears well up in her eyes as she stared up at him in surprise. But she had to learn.

"You might as well stick your hand into a nest of wasps as crawl in where you're forbidden to go!"

"But—"

"Nay, I'll hear no more from you now, Blessing. You went where you were not permitted and did so without asking permission. Because of that, you may not walk around camp anymore today. Anna, take Blessing back to my tent and see that she stays there the rest of the day. Matto can help. Lord Thiemo, you'll stand guard over her. Do please kindly recall that you take orders from me, not from my daughter, who is after all barely more than an infant."

"Y—yes, my lord prince," stammered Thiemo, who had the grace to blush.

Blessing began to shriek in protest, then broke down into hiccuping snivels as Sanglant handed her brusquely into Anna's arms. "But, Daddy—"

He grasped one of her little hands in his and caught her chin with the other, so that she had to look at him. "Is this how Emperor Taillefer's heir returns through camp, crying like a helpless child taken prisoner in war? You'll take the punishment you earned, and you'll take it proudly."

She gulped several times, fighting down tears. Anger swelled, easy to see as she screwed up her mouth in a pout. She bit back several protests, then, finally, squirmed out of Anna's grasp and marched away with her back stiff and her hands clenched in fury. Anna and Thiemo hurried after her.

"Let me go," said Heribert softly at his side.

"Nay, my friend, she'll only twist you into softening the blow. I can't trust you with her when she's in this mood. As soon as she starts sniffling, you'll run out and fetch her honey cakes, anything to sweeten the punishment. I'll keep you with me, in case I need sweetening."

"Well," said Sapientia, sauntering up with an ill-disguised smirk on her face. She had seen the altercation and now returned with Bayan in time to savor the girl's scolding. "I trust we have seen more here than we had cared to see." She turned to her husband. "There are perhaps a score of slaves in the whole market worth freeing. I'll have my stewards take care of the matter. I trust we may leave the rest to rot in their chains." She indicated the Quman. "Don't you agree, Sanglant?"

Bayan kept quite still, neither speaking nor showing any emotion except that both his hands were clenched, and Sanglant thought it prudent to retire from the field on this matter, at least. "We've a long road, hunting Bulkezu," he agreed mildly.

She lifted her chin to examine Sanglant with what she evidently considered regal command. "Now that you have come to aid us with your troops, you may join our war council tomorrow night. We'll be leaving Machteburg the day after." She beckoned to her attendants and she and Bayan moved away together through the throng that had gathered, mostly soldiers come to survey the merchants' encampment and get a closer look at their commanders.

A youth pressed through the crowd in the opposite direction. When he saw Sanglant, he changed course.

"What is it, Matto?" asked Sanglant as the lad hurried up.

"The old man wishes to speak urgently to you, my lord prince. He says he's seen news."

The phrasing sent Sanglant's heart racing. He had a tremendous sense of impending action, that moment before a storm surge breaks over the wharf. They left the market. A ferry raft took them over the river to the neatly-laid-out encampment where his army, fully three hundred mounted cavalry as well as a number of other fighters, had set up their tents. The ditch being dug around the perimeter was almost complete, the easiest defense against a surprise cavalry attack should there be Quman lurking in the woods. Wolfhere waited for him in the shadow of his tent's awning, out of the sun. Blessing had gone inside the tent to sulk. He could hear her companions talking in low voices; Lord Thiemo seemed to be telling the child some kind of story about a phoenix. Harmless enough, and it might serve to keep her out of trouble for the evening.

"What news?" he asked Wolfhere. They walked away from the tent, giving them some privacy to converse. Only Heribert and Druthmar attended them. The rest of the pack waited restlessly under the awning, sipping mead.

"I found Hanna," said Wolfhere in a troubled voice. "I'd looked for her through fire and water both these past months. Since I couldn't spy her, I thought she must be dead—"

"Who is Hanna?" asked Heribert.

"The young Eagle I rode with when we took you over the mountains," snapped Wolfhere. "Or do you even remember her?"

Heribert wisely did not answer, although it was clear by his puzzled expression that he did not really recall her.

But for Sanglant the name sent off a cascade of memories: how he'd first seen Liath during a sally outside the walls of Gent; the way her braid swayed along her spine, sensuous and inviting although she wasn't the kind of woman who meant to be inviting, not after the life she'd lived and the abuse she'd suffered at Hugh of Austra's hands. Hanna had called Liath a fool for marrying him. "She seemed a wise and honest young woman," he said at last, surprised to find himself smiling. It had been a long time since thoughts of Liath had made him smile.

Wolfhere's smile in answer was as soft as a tender kiss. "Truly, Hanna is more than she seems, so I've discovered. She wasn't dead at all but held captive and concealed by Quman sorcery."

Sanglant swung round. "*Quman* sorcery!"

"Bulkezu's taken her prisoner."

"Ai, Lord. A grim fate, indeed. Was Ekkehard with Bulkezu as well?"

"I did not see him, my lord prince. I saw her only briefly because—" It was so unlike Wolfhere to hesitate, to show any uncertainty, that Sanglant set a hand on the old Eagle's arm to coax him. Druthmar had the patience of an ox, if rather more virility, and he had evidently heard so many awful things about Wolfhere from Hedwig that he found the old man fascinating, in the same way one stands watching from the safety of a bench as a scorpion skitters around the room.

At last, Wolfhere sighed. "Because of the owl."

"Owl?"

"Many eyes watch," observed Wolfhere cryptically. "But what I saw where the owl dispelled the mists I recognized easily enough. It was the royal palace at Augensburg, burned now, all in ruins. That's where I saw Hanna. As briefly seen and as briefly gone again, but without question it was her, surrounded by Quman soldiers. That means that Bulkezu and his army ride north along the eastern bank of one of the tributaries of the Veser River."

"God save us," said Druthmar. "Bulkezu has struck into Wendar. I thought he still wandered in the marchlands."

"Duke Burchard took a force south to Aosta, to support Henry," said Sanglant. "There's no one to stop Bulkezu from riding all the way north along the Veser to Osterburg."

"How can he hope to take Duchess Rotrudis' city?" asked Druthmar. "He'd have to besiege it for months."

"Truly, perhaps we're going at this wrong. Why lay in a siege at all, if he can just ride around them? Why go north to Osterburg when he could as easily strike west into Fesse and western Saony? Duchess Liutgard also rode south with my father. Who is left to protect Wendar?"

Yet the next night at the war council their debate hung up time and again not on the threat Bulkezu and his army posed but on the veracity of Wolfhere's testimony.

"You've no proof Bulkezu is in Avaria riding north along the Veser," said Sapientia for the third time as certain of her attendants nodded agreement. "I can't believe you let that Eagle Wolfhere ride with you, after the king outlawed him. That's as good as rebelling outright against Father's authority—"

"Which I have not done, Sister." Like an ill-trained hunting dog, Sapientia kept veering back to the already gnawed bone instead of forging forward on the trail of fresh meat. "Yet he has served me well. I might never have found you and Bayan if not for his Eagle's sight."

"Dearly bought," she retorted, "if it means losing Father's trust."

"How much trust can any of us place in the words of an outlaw?" demanded Lady Brigida, Sapientia's favorite, a florid woman with, Heribert had murmured, more hair than sense.

The lords standing at Sapientia's back murmured in agreement with Brigida's complaint. Even Thiadbold, the scarred, redheaded captain of the two cohorts of Lions who marched with the princess, nodded his head uneasily.

"Yet I wonder what news Father gains of us in Aosta?" mused Sapientia. "Surely he has reached Darre safely by now. Can't your Eagle tell you that?"

"His army has come to Darre, so it seems. No Eagle's sight is perfect, and there are certain glamours and amulets that can veil that sight."

Murmurs rose from the assembly, hearing of such witchcraft.

"Nor have we heard from Princess Theophanu," interposed Lady Bertha, who despite being Hugh of Austra's half sister seemed to Sanglant the most sensible of the nobles traveling in Sapientia's train. "None of her messengers have gotten through to us, if indeed she has been able to send any."

"All the more reason to return to this matter of Bulkezu's army." Sanglant hoisted his cup and found, to his annoyance, that he had drained it. Bayan's Ungrian servants, two of them eunuchs, were as well trained as Bayan's Ungrian soldiers. A smooth-cheeked man hurried up with a pitcher of wine, a strong vintage that had already begun to make Sanglant's head swim. The Ungrians didn't cut their wine with water.

"If Bulkezu does intend to march on Osterburg," said Sapientia, "he'll be trapped for months in a siege."

Sanglant sighed, and for the first time he looked directly, and beseechingly, at Bayan, who had spoken not one word since the council began.

"If it is true," said Bayan finally. He paused. Every soul fell silent. It was easy to see who really commanded the army, although by every right and privilege the Wendish folk, at least, belonged to Sapientia. "If·it is true we can trust this Eagle's sight, who says to us that for months there lies a cloud of sorcery over the land that hides Bulkezu. But I know the power of magic. None better than I! Maybe now the cloud parts and the Eagle gets a look. So. If it is true Bulkezu rides north along the Veser, then what prevents him from swinging wide, around this city, and going on his merry way, as Prince Sanglant says? Bulkezu can leave a force of small size camped outside the walls, and with this force he can·trick Duchess Rotrudis so she will believe he sets a siege at her gates. Then, if she so believes, she will not harry him until for her and for Saony it is too late."

"And he can do as much damage as he likes," agreed Sanglant. "Or he could strike west before he even reaches Osterburg and go for Kassel or the Rhowne heartlands near Autun. The best we could hope for in that case would be that he drives all the way to the western sea and spends his fury laying waste to Salia."

"What do you think we should do, Prince Sanglant?" asked Captain Thiadbold from where he stood behind the seated ladies and lords.

"I say we march hard and try to reach Osterburg before he does."

"Impossible," protested Lady Brigida. She giggled, as she was wont to do when she became nervous.

Lamps lit the interior of the spacious tent. By their fitful light, Sanglant saw the faces of the others, most of them regarding him with interest and mounting excitement. On the table around which they sat the leavings of their evening's feast congealed on platters of brass and pewter: chicken and goose bones; an eviscerated bread pudding with only the crusty sides and burned bottom left; fried griddle breads; small, sweet honey cakes; and berries flavored with a mint sauce—the kind of things easily prepared on the march. "Then even if Bulkezu strikes west, we'll still be in position to pursue him no matter where he rides before autumn rain and winter snows make the roads impassable."

Soldiers nodded. Lords and ladies murmured noises of assent.

Bayan coughed, clearing his throat. "I have to piss," he said cheerfully, standing, "but how I hate to piss alone! Prince Sanglant, will you join me?"

Sanglant laughed. "Ah, my friend, what man could turn down such a proposal?" He rose, drained his cup, and only staggered slightly as he made his way through the assembled crowd in Bayan's wake.

Bayan's boisterous humor vanished as soon as they got outside. His faithful Ungrian guards, the kind of hard, hearty men who would rousingly toast you with a beaker of strong ale one moment and beat you to a pulp the next if you offended their master, kept watch as Bayan strode over to the horse lines. He did his business quickly and waited, whistling softly under his breath, until Sanglant was done as well.

"Now, my friend," he said quietly, "we must have the talk."

"Ah, the talk. Which talk is that?"

"You are not a fool, my good friend. So I will not insult you with lies, but I will speak the truth."

"You're scaring me, Bayan. Are you going to tell me I have to sleep with Lady Brigida lest she take her retinue and ride home in a rage? I'd sooner sleep with Bulkezu than with her. Or maybe with her warhorse."

Bayan snorted, amused, but he shook his head and paced down toward the end of the horse lines, Sanglant following alongside, careful not to step in any fresh manure. The night was cloudy, although comfortably warm, lit only by sentry fires, the dozen lamps hung around the periphery of the royal tent, and the distant reddish flare of a bonfire burning away the remains of the dead at Machteburg. South, Sanglant could see the scattered fires of the merchants' camp up on the rise where the ancient ring fort lay.

"So." Bayan hadn't Sanglant's height but he was as broad

through the shoulders, not at all gone to fat as some noblemen his age often did. He turned to face Sanglant squarely. In this dim light Sanglant could not make out his expression. "Do we agree that Bulkezu threatens Wendar?"

"Of course."

"This other cataclysm you have mentioned. But I cannot see it. The fire of Bulkezu's army burns too brightly before me. What does it matter if your sorcerers intrigue if we all are heads dangling from Quman belts?"

"True enough. What did you bring me out here to tell me?"

"Let us speak bluntly. She has not your charisma. She has not your prowess on the field, and not your intelligence. But you are a bastard, and I am Sapientia's husband. Henry named her as his heir, not you. What if you raise your sword and demand to lead the army? Maybe even you have no intention to cause her soldiers to stand behind your banner, but if you do so, then you shame her. If you shame her, she will have no choice except to withdraw. And so, my friend, will I."

"I'm not accustomed to being commanded by anyone except the king."

Bayan shrugged. "So. If there is to be no agreement between us, then we must split our armies."

"We have a better chance of defeating Bulkezu if we hit him with our forces combined. You know that as well as I do."

"So I do."

"And you know our wisest course, if what the Eagle says is true, is to ride west to Osterburg and use it as our base to hunt down Bulkezu's army."

"So I do. But I am the one who married the heir to Wendar and Varre. I did not marry her so that it falls to me to stand back and allow a bastard to command me. I mean no offense to your mother or yourself, you understand. I give you the truth because I respect you. I am knowing you well, Sanglant. You will do what is best for your father's realm."

The heady courage given him by too much strong wine made him reckless. "Do you know, Bayan, that my father wished me to marry Adelheid of Aosta and take the king's crown in Darre?"

"Your father is a wise man. You would have done well to heed him instead of running off after a witch. Then you would have been fighting in Aosta and Henry would stand here to drive out the Quman."

"Nay, my friend, it's not as simple as that. It's but a small step from reigning as king in Aosta to reigning as heir to the Holy Dariyan Emperor."

"This is only a story, I think. You are not married to Adelheid. Your father is. You are not in Aosta, taking the king's crown. Your father is. That still leaves you and me out here, on this fine summer's night, taking a piss by the horses." He neatly sidestepped a pile of stinking manure, as graceful as ever. Bayan was not a man, Sanglant reflected, to challenge to a drinking contest. "Tell me what you intend, Sanglant. Will you contest your sister's authority? Or will you yield to her?"

"Ai, God! You ask too much!"

They had walked far enough that a nearby sentry fire illuminated Bayan's face as he smiled wryly, with the barest edge of anger, carefully honed. "Wendish pride."

A rent in the clouds revealed the quarter moon rising along the treetops. The charnel smell from the funeral pyre tainted the air as the wind shifted, then died. Sanglant shook his head, but as much as he fought to remember what it had been like to be the King's Dragon, whose life was forfeit for Wendar's safety, he just could not go back, not anymore. "There's sense in what you say, but you ask too much. Am I to bow my head when I've never bowed before any person but my father? Not even for you, Bayan, and there's few people in this world I respect as well as I respect you."

That edged smile did not waver. Bayan's lips ticked up, briefly, as if in a spasm of anger, but he did not lose control. "I will not ask you to bow your noble head, even to me, although by right you ought to. But if our armies will join, then there can be only one commander. That one must be Sapientia."

"God have mercy, Bayan, let's not mince words, if you insist. That one may be Sapientia in name, but it will be you in fact. As it is now."

"So, how does this trouble you? You will have as much chance to influence her as I do, will you not?

Sanglant laughed harshly. "I'm not sleeping in her bed, God forgive me for suggesting such a thing."

"Bowing the head is not easy to learn, so I admit. Then let us here agree to defeat Bulkezu together. We go our separate ways after. Sapientia also is Margrave of Eastfall, I think you remember. When she becomes queen, I can persuade her to grant the margraviate of Eastfall into your care. I want Bulkezu dead. I want to drive the Quman back east where they belong. And so do you, Sanglant. If you did not, you would not be here now." They had reached the end of the horse lines and crossed now, by unspoken consent, toward the first line of sentries. "But I do not forget your Wendish pride."

"Nor your own damned Ungrian conceit."

"Henry accepted Ungria's offer, not Salia's. Thus did he choose a consort for to marry his eldest legitimate child."

The night air had finally cleared the cobwebs from his mind. He halted, tipping back his head to watch as clouds swirled over the face of the moon, hiding it again. "I never had a child before," he said softly.

"Now do you understand me?" Bayan stood beside him, also watching the moon as it slipped free of the cloud cover, a trembling light drifting hazily behind misty streamers of night haze. "A child of my blood will ascend to the throne of Wendar and Varre. Beware what words you teach your small daughter, Prince Sanglant. The great Emperor Taillefer has been dead for a long time. His power fled with him to the grave. But few, I think, forget the noble feast he presided over. Be cautious, I pray you, in parading a child who has learned to say those sweet-smelling words, 'I am the heir of Emperor Taillefer.' The wolves are always hungry."

3

POOR Lord Manegold, vain and shallow, had to carry Bulkezu's standard when they rode down from their position on the ridgetop to the parley. He looked like he'd rather be dead, no matter how many encouraging words Ekkehard muttered privately to him before the prince was escorted away to wait nervously with an honor guard close around him, just to make sure he didn't attempt to escape.

The negotiations for the parley had taken an excruciating day conducted first through scouts, then through emissaries sent from camp to fort and back again with various demands, offers, and compromises.

Bulkezu went in full battle array, wings gleaming in the steady summer sunlight. He descended from the ridge with one hundred picked riders at his back, Lord Manegold at the front holding up his standard, and Hanna beside him, her hands bound to make it clear she was his prisoner. Boso had dressed himself in the richest clothing he could scavenge, and he looked as ridiculous as a dog fitted out in a lord's cloak and jewels, trotting along at his master's heels.

Midway between the ridgeline and the outer palisade of the fort stood a large pavilion, sides raised up like wings to let the breeze through, the neutral ground on which both parties would meet. A force of one hundred mounted men waited beyond the pavilion.

Princess Theophanu had already arrived. Her face was as expressive as the blank mask-visor on Bulkezu's helmet. Only the crease of her mouth held a gleam of emotion, difficult to interpret, as they approached over the grass and crossed into the shade afforded by the raised wings of the tent.

The princess had Henry's cunning. Seated in a chair almost as elaborately carved as her father's traveling throne, she allowed Bulkezu to come before her as though he were a supplicant. Duke Conrad the Black fidgeted at her back with the same kind of restless energy Prince Sanglant had, a man who would rather be fighting than standing. There were, besides them, two noble companions in attendance, a richly-dressed girl of ten or twelve years of age who stood behind an empty chair placed next to Theophanu's, and three stewards ready to serve goblets of wine.

Bulkezu's riders halted the precise distance back from the pavilion as Theophanu's cavalry waited in the other direction. He rode forward with Hanna and Boso to his left, three of his captains to his right, and Cherbu at his back. The wind moaned through the wings of his riders. Light rippled along iron coverts as the breeze coursed through his griffin wings, lifting a seductive melody into the air. He surveyed the positions of his troops, and of hers, the placement of her chair and of the one set ten paces away, facing her, that remained empty for him. With his helmet on, it was impossible to see his face. He looked back toward Cherbu, and the shaman made a sign with his hand, briefly noted. Satisfied, Bulkezu pulled off his helmet and tossed it to one of his captains, who caught it neatly and tucked it under his arm.

Theophanu remained silent. Conrad watched, shifting restlessly as Bulkezu dismounted and indicated that Hanna and Boso should dismount as well. The second captain took their horses' reins and led them to one side, out of the way.

Hanna met Conrad's gaze briefly; the power of his physical body was mirrored in the keen strength of his gaze. He had very dark eyes, almost black, the legacy of his Jinna mother's ancestry. The girl rested a hand on the back of the chair while she examined Bulkezu with a scornful expression similar to that of the duke. By coloring and features, it was obvious that she was his daughter.

Boso stepped forward. "His Magnificence Prince Bulkezu hears your pleas with interest and a kind heart, and by reason of his generosity and liberality has chosen to hear you out rather than attack and destroy your army outright."

"He wants gold," muttered Conrad darkly.

Theophanu's expression did not change. "I pray you, Prince Bulkezu, please be seated and let my stewards serve you wine."

Boso translated while Bulkezu kept his gaze fixed on a point midway between Conrad and Theophanu, that remarkably believable look of blank incomprehension on his face. Once Boso had finished, Bulkezu gestured, and Boso hurried to fetch a folding stool. Saved from the abbot's chamber out of a burning monastery, the wooden stool had caught Bulkezu's fancy because of the griffin heads carved into either end of the side rails, each one plated with gold. On this seat, Bulkezu deigned to sit. His wings rustled as he settled into place, refusing with a raised hand the silver goblet of wine brought forward by a stone-faced servant. Boso took it instead, draining it too quickly.

Conrad, at last, dropped down into the chair placed next to Theophanu. The three regarded each other in silence. Bulkezu had a slight smirk on his face.

At last, Theophanu spoke. "Tell your master that I prefer to negotiate bluntly. We will offer him two thousand pounds of silver to leave Wendar and Varre."

By now, Hanna recognized a few of the words as Boso translated, but only a few; Bulkezu made no effort to teach his prisoners his language, thereby allowing Boso more authority over the slaves because he was the only go-between. Once Boso had finished, Bulkezu lifted a hand. His third captain hurried forward to offer him a gold cup filled to the brim with fermented mare's milk, which he sipped at thoughtfully before he replied.

Boso translated. "His Fearsomeness, Prince Bulkezu, wishes you to understand that your noble brother, Prince Ekkehard, is even at this moment a prisoner with his army. Here is his ring and his banner."

The ring was displayed, the banner unfurled, and then put away.

Duke Conrad muttered something under his breath, and his

daughter patted her father on the shoulder and bent to whisper in his ear, an intimate gesture so endearing that Hanna was stricken by a sudden longing for her own father.

Theophanu's expression did not alter. "A ring and a banner can be taken off a dead body."

Boso was allowed a short whip, which he used on his whores and on recalcitrant slaves. It was his only weapon. He prodded Hanna with the butt of the whip now. This was why she had been brought.

She took a step forward. "I am known to you, I believe, my lord princess. I was taken captive west of Handelburg together with Prince Ekkehard and four of his companions. One of his retinue rides there." She had to gesture toward Manegold with her chin because her hands were tied. "I swear to you on my honor as a King's Eagle that Prince Ekkehard is alive and in Prince Bulkezu's hands."

Theophanu spoke softly to her stewards and they hurried forward to offer more wine, but Bulkezu again refused, and Boso again drained his cup. "Three thousand pounds of silver and one hundred gold nomias in exchange for your departure, and the return of Ekkehard and his companions." For the first time Theophanu acknowledged her presence, a glance, no more, that touched and fled, light as a feather. "And the Eagle."

Boso spoke. Bulkezu replied. "His Gloriousness will not ransom the Eagle. Five thousand pounds of silver and an equal measure of gold for the prince. And Duke Conrad's daughter, for his bed."

Conrad's head snapped around as his daughter stiffened, looking indignant and frightened. Abruptly, the interpreter gave a grunting moan, grasped his belly, and without a word or excuse to anyone bolted onto the grass. He hadn't gotten more than one hundred paces before he doubled over and began to retch. Bulkezu sipped at his mare's milk. By the way his dimple flashed in and out on his cheek, Hanna could tell he was working very hard not to laugh.

"Good Lord," said Conrad, observing the stricken interpreter. "I'd heard rumors. Do you think they've brought the plague with them?"

"You must consider it, Conrad," said Theophanu. "All the more reason to make short work of this. The girl in exchange for their departure."

He rose threateningly, dark cheeks changing color. "Marry him yourself, Theophanu. You've wanted a husband for a long time now."

"When my father returns—"

"*If* your father returns."

She went on as if he had not spoken. "When my father returns, I'll do my duty at his command. It's long past time for you to do yours and give your daughter up where she's needed. Times are desperate."

"And will get more desperate still without *my* support." The angrier he got the louder he spoke; they had given up murmuring as they argued. "Why should I aid you, Theophanu? Why should I aid Wendar at all, now that your father seems determined to desert us in favor of chasing down imperial feasts into Aosta? He's stripped Wendar of its army, and cleaned out my warehouses and levies in Wayland, so what will you use to fight the invaders—"

"For God's sake, my lord and lady," Hanna cried, "he can understand every word you say!"

She had never known anyone to move that fast.

He hit her so hard across the face that she actually blacked out. Of the gap between the pain of the blow and the ground smashing into her shoulder, she remembered nothing. Acid burned in her throat. Lights danced in her vision. She couldn't feel her legs. Distantly, she heard Boso's wretched coughs as he heaved up again, and again.

"I would not try that, Duke Conrad," said Bulkezu pleasantly. "I'm protected from harm by a cloak of my brother's weaving. But I won't hesitate to signal if there's any trouble. I can have Prince Ekkehard's head delivered to you," he snapped his fingers, "like that, if you wish it. Perhaps you've noticed my companion on the march, who grants me her strength. Don't you recognize Judith of Austra?"

Hanna still couldn't make any of her limbs work, but her hearing had sharpened.

"Oh, my God," said Conrad. "For God's sake, Milo," he said in a low voice, "take my daughter back to the fort. At once." After a stifled protest, footsteps moved hastily away.

"I would grieve at my brother's death," said Theophanu smoothly, as if nothing untoward had happened, as if she and Conrad hadn't betrayed their secrets, as if Bulkezu hadn't walked them through the oldest trick in the ancient tales. As if Wendish quarreling weren't the greatest weakness of all, just as Bulkezu had said. "As I mourn for Margrave Judith. But alas, Prince Bulkezu, just so we understand each other, he is only King Henry's third child."

"His fourth, surely, or did one of the elder two die?"

Sensation returned to her fingers. She got her bound hands under her and pushed herself up. Her head spun, and she almost threw up as she got to her knees. Conrad and Theophanu became four, and then eight, and slowly receded back into two.

"I believe we have told you more than enough," said Theophanu, "without receiving anything in return. Give me the Eagle. She's of no possible use to you."

"How can you know what is of use to me?" He called an order in his own language. Her right eye was already swelling shut, and the whole right side of her face throbbed agonizingly. Dust kicked into her face as she coughed out spittle colored by blood. Hands grabbed her and jerked her roughly to her feet. The fast movement was too much. She threw up, but the man holding her had no mercy. He simply dragged her away as she vomited. The world darkened as she fought unconsciousness.

Was that Theophanu, asking in that passionless voice to have the Eagle returned? All she could distinguish as the light hazed over and she gasped for air was Bulkezu's hated voice answering.

"Five thousand pounds of silver and one thousand of gold, and I'll ride past Barenberg with my army and leave it and the lands around it untouched."

She passed out.

She woke at the touch of hands pressing a poultice against her throbbing cheek. The cool mash reeked of mustard, and it stung. She opened one eye. Struggled a moment, panicking, until she realized the other eye was swollen shut, not gouged out.

Cherbu sat next to her, humming under his breath. He held a cup to her lips. Warm liquid steamed up her nose. The smell soothed her headache. Sipping, she got a bit of the broth down without feeling queasy, was even able to lever herself up and swallow the rest. The light in the small tent had splintered into dozens of colors. It took her a moment to realize that she was lying inside the shaman's patchwork tent, on a sheepskin. The ground lurched violently under her, and the patchwork ceiling swayed as they began to move.

Cherbu slipped out through the tent flap and leaped down. She caught sight of mounted men, a tree lurching past, and the sun shining through leaves before the tent flap slapped back into place. The wagon jolted on; despite the jerky motion, she fell into a fitful doze, starting awake whenever she was flung to one side or the other because of a hole or bump. At intervals Cherbu returned to change her poultice or give her a fresh infusion of broth. Strangely, despite the uncomfortable journey, she felt increasingly better as the day wore on and could even eventually crack open her right eye.

She felt, in truth, mildly optimistic when the wagon lumbered to a halt and she heard the familiar noises of folk moving about setting up camp. She peeled the poultice off her face before gingerly climbing out of the back of the wagon. She needed to pee, and wanted to get a look around.

Her legs and arms worked. Her face still hurt, but she could actually open and shut her eye and squinch up her cheek without much pain. She found enough privacy around at the front of the wagon to do her business, then surveyed the situation, the placement of the army, herds, and captives in a broad clearing surrounded by forest.

Maybe there was a chance they had forgotten about her.

Maybe not.

There came Cherbu with a cup of steaming broth. She drank it gratefully. Hunger stirred; her belly growled softly. Cherbu beckoned, and she followed him to the round tent surmounted by the Pechanek banner. Bulkezu strolled out to meet her with a smirk on his face, a cold light in his gaze, and, amazingly, Boso at his side.

The interpreter looked much improved, remarkably so, since she had last seen him throwing up during the parley, but perhaps it was only glee over her impending punishment. "Be afraid, woman. His Dreadfulness has had enough of your disobedience and disrespectful words."

Was it actually possible that Boso hadn't realized what had happened at the parlay? Didn't he know that Bulkezu could understand him? Or was she the fool, thinking all along that Boso hadn't known? She staggered, head swimming, and fought to keep her balance, to keep her dignity.

"His patience is at an end because you've made him very angry."

A cold fear crept into her gut as the silence dragged out. A few slaves stopped to stare, but Bulkezu's guards chased them away. He wasn't one for the big public gesture, not like the Wendish nobles, who raised up and threw down their favorites in the middle of court so that everyone could see. He was a man who kept his grudges personal.

Boso actually sniggered; so aroused was he by the expectation of her imminent downfall that he forgot to be sarcastic. "You can keep your clothes and your Eagle's cloak, so no one forgets who you are. But all other protections Prince Bulkezu withdraws."

She found her voice, hoarse as it was. "You mean he's going to hand me over to Princess Theophanu?"

Boso guffawed, giggling helplessly. Bulkezu's expression didn't change. Four guards came forward. If she fought, they'd see how desperately frightened she was. Hadn't Sorgatani's luck protected her? Wouldn't the Kerayit shaman watch over her? She looked toward Cherbu, but he had already wandered away into the trees.

Had she really believed in any savior but Bulkezu's whim, which had now turned cold?

"You thought yourself better than the rest," said Boso.

"No more than did you," she murmured, but she could barely get the words out. It hurt to talk. The impassive guards moved in around her, lances raised. She took a step back, flushed and perspiring as the sun slid out from behind the clouds and beat down upon her.

They advanced, and she retreated, step by step, until she realized that they were driving her, as they would drive a cow or a ewe, back to the miserable crowd of prisoners scattered like so many wilting flowers through the clearing. No longer was she Bulkezu's honored hostage, his model prisoner. She was just one more hapless captive left to stagger along in the wake of the army, one short step in front of the lances of the rear guard.

Most of the captives had collapsed in the grass, trying to cover their heads against the glare of the sun. Few had survived the night of the slaughter, and perhaps because of that, the plague had not surfaced again in the train of Bulkezu's army. He had raced ahead, leaving the plague behind, but he still took prisoners and he still dragged them along for his amusement, for his assaults, for whatever sick reason he had, if he had reasons at all beyond laying waste.

A few, those not yet so weakened by their ordeal that they noticed nothing beyond the next sip of gruel, raised themselves up to watch as Hanna was pressed back into their midst. More than anything, she noticed the stink of so many unwashed bodies, open sores, pools of diarrhea and urine and vomit spreading from those too sick to crawl away from their own sickness, all of it a sink of despair. Flies buzzed everywhere, feasting on infected eyes and filth-encrusted hands. Surely plague was hiding here, waiting to burst out again as it had that awful night.

Ai, God, if truth be told, she was more afraid of the plague than she was of Bulkezu.

A man sporting a black-and-blue eye and drooping folds of flesh at his chin heaved himself up from the ground and spat at her. "Whore! I see you got what you deserved at long last. I hope you got pleasure of what that demon gave you, while he was giving, because you'll get no such pleasure here."

His comrade, a tall man dressed in rags, lurched forward to grab for her. "I'd like a taste of his leavings!" He got a hand on her shoulder.

She ducked, by some miracle found a stout stick in the grass, and whacked him across the face. He was a lot bigger than she was, but she'd been eating and he hadn't. Staggering, he stumbled back and sat down hard. Pain stabbed through her cheek, but she dared show no weakness.

Yet no one laughed, or protested, or reacted at all. Most of them were too ill and exhausted even to care, even to hate. The Quman guards moved off, leaving her standing in the midst of the pack with a pounding headache and a swollen face.

"I am also a prisoner, a commoner from Wendar, just as you are. A King's Eagle, taken captive in the east—"

Even a starving man can feed on hate, if he's nothing left to him.

"Whore and traitor," said one of the women listlessly. She had a bundle of dirty rags clutched to her chest, but it was only when she shifted that Hanna saw she held a sickly child, eyes crusted shut with dried pus. Flies crawled over the child's pallid face, but neither it nor its mother had enough strength to brush them away.

In the distance a river ran noisily. She smelled water,

although the trees hid it from view. Most of the prisoners were looking at her now. Good Wendish folk, just like her.

The tall man coughed and braced himself on his hands as he caught his breath. When he grinned, she saw that all of his front teeth were missing. "You'll have to sleep sometime."

She spoke to the others. "Don't you see? The more we quarrel among ourselves, the easier his victories come."

No one answered. After a bit, the tall man and his companion dragged themselves off to the edge of the group. As for the rest, they were too weary, too hungry, and too apathetic to do anything but lie back down on the ground and close their eyes.

The Quman guards did not stop her as she gathered grass and, after several abortive attempts, wove a shallow basket and lined it with leaves. They shadowed her as she made her way through a narrow patch of woodland to the river's shore and knelt in the shallows. Upstream she saw only forest, but far downstream she saw a line of smoke rising into the sky.

Had Bulkezu taken Theophanu's bribe and ridden on, bypassing Barenberg? There had been no battle today, and this river looked broad enough to be the mighty Veser, flowing north toward the Amber Sea.

The basket held water well enough that she could carry it around to those folk too exhausted, or too afraid of the Quman, to walk to the river themselves. Best to start with the weak ones. They hadn't the strength to spit at her and were usually grateful for the water.

When she brought it to the mother with the sick child, she met suspicion first.

"What do you want with me, whore?" asked the woman, shrinking away. "Haven't I been punished enough by the beast?"

"I'm a prisoner like you," Hanna repeated. "It's true I've been treated better, and fed, and allowed to ride. But that's not because I'm the prince's whore—"

"The Wendish prince?" The woman's spirit flared as anger gave her strength. "Some say it's the king's son himself who rides with the beast. Is it true?"

This was hardly the way to convince these poor souls that she wasn't a traitor, too, but Hanna saw no reason to lie to them about his identity. "Yes, it's Ekkehard, son of Henry."

The woman spat. Perhaps she'd been passed over by the Quman soldiers because of the wart on her nose and lice-ridden hair, or perhaps she'd simply been raped and discarded during the attack on whatever doomed village she had once lived in.

"A royal son like that would be better dead than a traitor." But she accepted a sip of water. The child, too, drank, but he couldn't open his eyes. His whimpers tore at Hanna's heart.

"Here. I'll soak a corner of my cloak in water and maybe we can clean his face."

"If you wish," said the woman in a dull voice, "but he'll die anyway. My poor baby. Nothing can save us now. If the beast and his men don't kill us, then hunger will. Or the plague. I heard there's plague everywhere south of us now. So maybe it is God's mercy on us for living a Godly life."

"How can you say so?" demanded Hanna, aghast.

"Better to die of hunger or have your throat slit than to die of the plague. Have you seen what they look like after? I heard it from my cousin. She'd seen it, one man, two years back. He died outside her village and they let the dogs eat him. None of them touched him, not even the deacon. She said you shake and turn gray, and dying people scream that they're being eaten alive from inside, there's so much pain. Then the demon inside you spits you all out, through your mouth and nose and eyes, through your skin and your asshole, all blood and snot and shit and every stinking thing that it's eaten out of you and chewed with its poison—"

"That's enough!" said Hanna sharply. People had crept close to listen and some had begun to moan in fear. "No use catching your death standing out waiting for the snow when there's nothing you can do to stop it whether it comes or not. That's what my mother always says."

"Is your mother still alive?" asked one of the prisoners.

"I pray she is. She's in North Mark—"

"Ah," said a thin old man with a spark of curiosity left in his expression. "That would explain your accent and that light hair. How'd you come to be a King's Eagle?"

"The same way any do, I suppose. They were looking, and I was available."

This earned her a few chuckles as she continued to wipe the child's face, trying to moisten the crust around his eyes enough so that she could wipe it off without hurting him.

"What got you captured, then?" demanded the mother.

About fifty people had clustered close to watch and listen. The two men who had assaulted her sidled in as well, staring with a bitter, unsparing hatred, as if she were responsible for everything they had suffered and lost.

"I was riding from the east last winter. I left Handelburg at the order of Princess Sapientia, she who is heir to King Henry, to bring word to him of the Quman invasion. I was caught out in a snowstorm, in a forest, and was myself captured by the Quman."

"You've been with the beast all this time?"

She didn't see who had asked that question. "So I have," she admitted, wetting the corner of her cloak in water again, trying to squeeze the caked gunk off it.

The tall man pressed forward. He'd found a stick, too, although he used it to support his weight. "And you didn't whore with the beast all that time? How then are you so clean and fat, Eagle? Where did you get that ring?"

Quicker than she'd thought possible, he struck. His first blow glanced off the side of her head. She fell hard as the mother screamed, and the jolt when she caught herself on her arms sent pain stabbing into her injured eye. Head stinging like fire, she groped for and found her stick and brought it up just in time to catch his next blow on wood. Her stick shattered, and she scrambled backward, crablike, as his stick thwacked down in the grass first to her right and then to her left.

He raised it again. Fury knotted in her stomach. She threw herself forward and slammed into him, knocking him down. They wrestled. A thistle prickled on her back, and she flipped him over and jammed him face down into it. He shrieked, shuddered, and fell still.

Thank God for all that fighting with her elder brother Thancmar. Thank God her adversary had been so weakened by hunger. Breathing hard, she grabbed his unbroken stick and rose, staring down his trembling companion. Beyond, the Quman guards watched impassively, arms crossed.

Her face throbbed.

What had happened to Bulkezu's promise to the owl's master to see that she came to no harm? Blood leaked from her temple where the stick had caught her, and her ear throbbed painfully.

"I'm a King's Eagle, damn you," she said harshly, "and I received this ring from King Henry's own hand in recognition of my service to him. What you do to me is as if you were doing it to the king himself."

"Where's the king, then?" Tall Man's comrade confronted her. Now that he stood, she could see by the way his tunic hung on him how much flesh he'd lost. "Why hasn't the king come to aid us?"

His words were echoed by other prisoners, many more of whom slunk closer to see what the commotion was all about. "Where is the king while we're suffering here?"

"I don't know," she admitted. But she had a good idea where he might be, and she didn't want to tell these people that particular story. The crown of Emperor Taillefer would seem a sorry treasure to them who had lost everything, had watched their homes burned, their fields trampled, their daughters and sisters being raped, and their townsfolk slaughtered. "I don't know. But I know this, my friends. We'll all die if the strongest among us don't help the weakest."

"Easy for you to say, eating like a queen and sleeping between the beast's silks. Maybe he threw you out now, but that doesn't change what you were before."

She pointed the stick at him and let the end press against his sternum, pushing hard enough that he skipped back a half step. No one laughed, or even spoke. They had fallen silent. "It's true I ate the food he gave me, and ate better than any of you have. But I never slept between his silks. He never raped me." She let the stick fall to her side, keeping it ready for a fast strike, and turned so they could all see her Eagle's badge. "He didn't dare touch me." She hesitated. A complicated kind of hope and cynicism warred in their expressions. What did these folk know of Kerayit women and shamans who had the body of a woman joined with that of a mare? "He didn't dare touch me because he didn't dare insult King Henry. For what he does to me it's as if he does it to the king himself. He knows in the end that the king will have revenge. For me. For all of us."

As would she, by God.

At that instant, she knew what she had to do. Bulkezu had forgotten one thing when he'd thrown her out of his tent.

"But the king needs our help. And I need yours."

The guards did not stop her as she gathered firewood at the fringe of the forest, although maybe they thought she was crazy for thinking of building a fire on such a hot day, especially when she had nothing to eat. Twilight closed over them as she laid sticks for a fire. Wool thread teased off the sleeve of her tunic made a bowstring and a supple branch the tiny bow, wood scraps and dry leaves the tinder, and a notched wedge of wood a cup for her hand. With the bowstring looped around a stick, she drilled the end of that stick into the tinder until friction woke heat, heat smoke, and smoke fire.

Flames licked up through the kindling. Prisoners gathered around, as many as could stand doing so in order to block the view of the Quman guards, and the old man began telling a story.

"Here we begin by telling the tale of Sigisfrid, who won the gold of the Hevelli. He was born out of a she-wolf and a warrior—"

Hanna sat cross-legged by the fire, letting the tale drift past her, riding the flow of the words. Under Bulkezu's constant watch, she dared not use her Eagle's sight. But here, among the prisoners, she was free.

"See nothing, not even the flames," Wolfhere had told her. *"It is the stillness that lies at the heart of all things that links us."*

"Liath," she whispered. The fire wavered, and for a moment she saw faint shadows of men clothed in armor, she heard the clash of arms, but the vision faded into the snap of flame. Liath remained hidden from her. Was she dead?

Was everyone she cared for dead?

"Ai, God," she whispered, "can I not find you, Ivar? Where have you gone?"

A new log made the fire flare with blue streaks of heat, hot and bright. Were there women moving in the flames? Queens walked under a grave mound, one young, one old, and one as golden as the sun, but they held out empty hands and by the hard flint gleam in their eyes she knew them for the old gods, the Huntress, the Fat One, and the Toothless Hag who cuts the thread of life.

Ivar was lost to her.

For a while she sat mired in grief while some other hand fed the flame and the fire burned merrily on, twisting and popping.

She is the owl, gliding over the treetops, searching for the one she has lost. The streaming wind carries her far to the east, to the land where the grass grows as high as a man. Two griffins stalk at the edge of sand, closing in on their prey.

Tents shimmer in the distance, but it is the woman wandering on the shore of the desert who catches her eye. Here, among the Bwr-folk, Sorgatani has no need of veils or concealment. As she walks, she speaks passionately to her companion.

Hanna has never before seen the Bwr shaman so clearly: her glossy gray mare's coat and the creamy color of her woman's skin. Her face and upper body are striped with green-and-gold paint. Pointed ears, tufted with coarse black hair, peek out through her unbound hair which falls like silver water all the way to the place where her torso slips easily from a woman's hips into a mare's shoulders. She holds a bow in her hands, the horn curve carved with the semblance of pale dragons.

"Why can we not attack?" Sorgatani is saying fiercely, hands gesturing wildly. "He spits on us by holding her prisoner."

"She had a chance to come to you," replies her companion. "Now she suffers the fate she chose."

"Is there no way to rescue her? Is our magic of so little use?"

"Do not forget that magic protects him as well." She shakes her head as might a cleric surveying the ruins of her once magnificent church. "We are not what we were. Our numbers are much diminished because of the plague. Now is our time of greatest weakness, so we must use caution. We dare not reveal ourselves too soon. But do not fear—" She glances up, her gaze sharp as an arrow. "Who watches?"

In that moment it took her to inhale a gasp and let it out again, Hanna sees Wolfhere, brow furrowed, staring at her through the flames.

He is gone as though a hand wiped him clean off a slate. Lamps burn, brighter points of light within the leaping fire.

A familiar voice is speaking. She had heard it so often that it takes her several breaths to get over her surprise that, after all these months, she is listening to Prince Bayan. "If it is true Bulkezu rides north along the Veser, then what prevents him from swinging wide, around this city, and going on his merry way, as Prince Sanglant says? Bulkezu can leave a force of small size camped outside the walls, and with this force he can trick Duchess Rotrudis so she will believe he sets a siege at her gates. Then, if she so believes, she will not harry him until for her and for Saony it is too late."

Hazy figures too indistinct to see clearly shift within the fire. She can make out none of their faces, but the man who speaks next she recognizes immediately as Sanglant. "And he can do as much damage as he likes. Or he could strike west before he even reaches Osterburg and go for Kassel or the Rhowne heartlands near Autun. The best we could *hope for in that case would be that he drives all the way to the western sea and spends his fury laying waste to Salia."*

"What do you think we should do, Prince Sanglant?" How have they all come together? How many have gathered? For surely that voice belongs to Captain Thiadbold, of the Lions. Seated figures obscure him, a host of grim warriors holding a council of war. Lamplight shoots blinding lances across her vision, so that all she can do is hear.

"I say we march hard and try to reach Osterburg before he does."

His words fade as a hand catches her shoulder and draws her backward. Briefly, so briefly, she sees a black-haired child asleep on a bed of furs, and it seems as though a flame burns at the child's heart, blue-white and almost a living thing, twisting and hissing.

"Liath," she whispered, starting out of her trance as the hissing rose in pitch. She fell back and caught herself on her hands.

Cherbu sat on the other side of the fire, whistling death onto the fire. Flames curled and died, subsiding into red coals. Ash settled. A cool wind stirred the forest. Far away, a wolf howled despairingly.

"So." Bulkezu crouched behind her, his hand gripping her shoulder. This time, he wasn't going to let go until he got what he wanted. "Where is she?"

The prisoners had all slunk away or pretended to sleep. She could scarcely blame them for abandoning her to those whom they had no power to resist. No doubt they were happy to have escaped punishment. The night guards stood farther back, half hidden by darkness. That she could see them at all was because of the waxing quarter moon, riding high over the treetops.

A scarecrow danced under the nearest tree, dangling from a rope. Nay, not a scarecrow but a man. She recognized him by his clothing: Boso, hanged by the neck.

An owl hooted, but although she glanced past the swaying corpse, she saw no sign of the bird. Maybe that sound was only a lingering hallucination from the vision seen through fire.

Maybe hope woven together with fear made you see those half truths that made living bearable, when otherwise you would only lie down and die.

Bulkezu spoke again, and this time his hand tightened on her shoulder. His breath, sweetened by mint, tickled the side of her face that he had bruised. "Where is Liathano, the sorcerer who can raise such a fire that it consumes an entire palace?"

Trapped. Beaten. Maybe it had all been a trick to force her to reveal what slight power she had, the knowledge called Eagle's sight.

She fell forward to hide her face in her hands. She knew her shoulders were shaking, shuddering. Pray that he believed it was utter defeat convulsing her.

She thought hard about Ivar, the way he had laughed at his own stupid jokes, the time they had hidden in the branches of the lovers' oak and rained a basketful of pine needles down on her brother Thancmar and his sweetheart, the expedition to old Johan's house to recapture the russet chicken, endless races in the meadow, the first and only time he kissed her, before Liath came, before Liath had unwittingly ensnared him.

When there were enough tears, she lowered her hands.

"Osterburg," she whispered. "She's at Osterburg."

XVI
INTO THE DARKNESS

1

HORN was dead, and her spirit had vanished into the darkness. As keening and crying broke out, Adica struggled to stay calm. Was that Horn's soul she had seen, twisting upward? Had she really heard Shu-Sha's booming voice? Had they any chance of defeating the Cursed Ones if the Holy One had been taken prisoner?

Alain knelt beside Horn's body, but before he could touch the slack corpse, her young apprentice yanked his hand away.

"Shu-Sha calls for our aid," said Two Fingers. "Yet how can it be that she has called to us over such a great distance, using Horn's body?"

There was no time to ponder such questions. "We must go quickly if we are to have any chance to save the Holy One," said Adica. "Horn said there was a path we could take."

Two of Horn's people came forward and spoke in low voices tô Laoina. "Come," said the Akka woman. She led them into a tunnel, torches bobbing alongside.

Two Fingers examined Alain's injured hand by torchlight. He shook his head, raising a puzzled eyebrow. "It heals," he said, before turning to grasp Adica's hands in his own. "Weave well, little sister." Then he was gone, so fast, and the light vanished with him.

Probably she would never see him again.

She caught in a gasp of pain. The darkness was like claws, tearing at her, exposing the fear she had so ruthlessly shoved away all this time. She struggled to fight it back down, to seal it up so that it would not betray her.

In the darkness, Laoina spoke in the tongue of Horn's people and was answered by a man. She translated. "This person has come to guide us. We must climb down into the heart of the Earth. There lie paths unknown to humankind, where the Bent People live. They are the ones who can guide us on unseen roads to the fort of Shu-Sha's tribe." Another hurried dialogue ensued, and Laoina went on. "This man says, where we go, dogs cannot follow. Dogs we must leave."

Alain did not raise his voice. "I will not leave them."

Laoina sighed sharply as the unseen man replied. "He says you must stay here, then."

Would Alain leave her to stay with the dogs? Adica thrust the ugly thought aside. "I won't go on if he does not. Let a way be made to bring the dogs with us."

An argument ensued. Other voices joined in, whispers cutting in from the darkness.

"They are not liking this stubbornness," explained Laoina. "They say they understand the mountain roads and you do not. They ask, do you mean to jeopardize all the coming generations of humankind for the sake of two dogs and this man?"

"Who can say they are not more important than you and I can know?" Her own teacher had spoken with this imperious tone, and many of the people in the Deer tribes had resented her for it even while fearing her. Adica had chosen a different way, but now she fell back on what she knew would work. "Are we to leave behind a man who can be seen by an eye that is blind to the mortal world? If he must walk only with spirit guides, then so be it. Find a way it can be done, and do it quickly."

There was silence, followed by Laoina's soft translation. Footsteps padded away, unseen. "They beg your pardon, Holy One. We must wait while they fetch what we will need."

Alain put his arms around her. She rested her head on his chest, closed her eyes, wanting peace even for a brief while. He said nothing; he did not need to. He would stay with her until the end. That was what the Holy One had promised her. Sorrow and Rage pushed against her, moist noses slipping between the braided cords of her skirt to wet her skin. Laoina shifted, tapping at the floor with the butt of her spear as she waited. The erratic rhythm lulled Adica. Alain's body was so solid against hers. He hummed softly, as patient as the wind.

Let her fall forever into this moment and none other, let all that came before and all that would come after not exist, only this. She dozed, or slipped into a vision; in the darkness it was hard to tell.

She walks into a blazing hall of light. Brightly dressed people throng the hall. They are so many that she cannot count them, far more even than all the folk who live in her village. How can a single building be so large that it can hold such a crowd? Their speech, their songs, the platters on which they eat, the tide of food flowing in and out of the hall, all this overwhelms her. Surely she has fallen into the Fat One's hall, overflowing with plenty. She never thought it would look so bewildering, a path with no landmarks she can recognize.

Yet there is one other wandering like a lost soul through the hall, unseen by any of the feasting multitude. At first she believes it is another woman, naked except for the bow she holds in her hand and a single arrow fletched with a phoenix's feather. Naked except for her hair, hanging like a veil across her torso. A ring blazes with blue-white fire on her hand.

Then she recognizes her mistake. It is not a woman but a creature of flame in whose heart burns a blue-hot fire as bright as the blazing ring.

Then she recognizes her mistake. The stranger is woman and fire both; one cannot be untangled from the other.

Sorrow's warning bark woke her. Her left foot, wedged

against the wall, had fallen asleep. She stamped it until it stopped tingling, turning the dream over in her mind. She could find no hidden meaning in it. Best to let it rest for now.

"Come," said Laoina.

They made their way without lights along a tunnel that sloped steadily downward. The barest luminescence gleamed along the walls, fungus growing on knobs of rock. The growth gave off just enough light so that she could see her feet and hands and the dim figures of the others, walking before and behind her. Their guide was a man, lightly dressed, as thin as a reed. The tunnel ended abruptly at the lip of an abyss where a flimsy woven ladder vanished into the chasm.

"How do we get the dogs down?" asked Laoina.

The guide lit two torches before bringing out rope. A series of ladders linked ledge to ledge down a cliff face so vast that the meager glow from the torches only made the cavern and rock wall bulk ominously beyond the frail arc of light. It was a laborious task to lower the dogs from one ledge down to the next, especially having to light their way with torches, swaying at the ends of rope, that spat pitch and burning flakes of ash at erratic intervals. Alain did most of the work, never complaining despite the pain it must cause his healing hand. Adica took her turn as well, bracing, paying out line, catching the big bodies and letting them down onto narrow ledges, some of which were small enough that two people couldn't stand one beside the other. Her arms ached and her back was a belt of pain by the time they reached the bottom. A spark of hot ash stung her eyelid. The only mercy was that the dogs, perhaps aware of their predicament, were as gentle as lambs. If only they had weighed as little.

But Alain would never have left the dogs behind. Nor would he ever abandon her.

As soon as they were all safely to the bottom, the guide extinguished the torches anxiously, as though their light was a forbidden luxury. Laoina whispered prayers, and Alain spoke softly to the dogs in his own language. Deep within the earth, the sweat cooled on her body and she shivered as a breeze brushed her face. As warm as dragon's breath and just as sulfurous, that breeze made her light-headed. To think even for a moment of the mountain of earth above her was to panic. How could air alone hold up heavy rocks and the weight of spans of earth? Surely it must all come tumbling down on top of her head. Fumes danced around her head. Spots of light flashed into existence and winked out, disorienting her.

In the instant when one of those lightning flashes illuminated the night, she saw the guide kneeling before the cliff face as though he prayed. He made a strange movement with one arm. Chimes rang out high and sweet.

Light flooded the chasm.

She shielded her eyes, blinking furiously, blind. As abruptly, the light vanished. The dogs barked. A body bumped into her.

"Holy One." The honorific sounded much the same in any language, even squeezed by fear as it was now. He slipped an armband over her hand and up past her elbow.

"He says, you must give this to what creature comes to the summons, and tell them of Horn's wishes." Laoina's voice shook as she translated. Adica had never heard her sound so frightened. "Then they must do as Horn wishes. That is the bargain."

"What creature—?"

He scurried away without answering. She heard him scrambling up the ladder.

"He abandoned us," whispered Laoina hoarsely.

"What does he fear?" asked Alain out of the darkness.

The air eddied around them as unseen things set in motion whirled into life. The sulfurous breath of the underground wind blew hot in her face, and she coughed until her eyes watered. Light bloomed. That glow came in part from the armband she wore, twin to the armband now gleaming softly on Alain's arm.

"Skrolin," she whispered.

"Look!" Laoina stood clearly visible in the soft light. The

beads woven in her braids gleamed eerily. She pointed toward a low tunnel so smoothly faced and perfectly ovoid that fear kicked Adica in the gut. This was no natural tunnel. Someone had shaped it.

Sorrow and Rage growled, standing stiffly, ears alert. A bubble of light expanded out of the tunnel. No human creature held that lamp, and no flame known to human folk or their Hallowed Ones burned within the globe the creature carried, dangling from a chain. Laoina dropped to her knees. The dogs lunged, but Alain caught them by their collars and dragged them back with all his strength, straining and cursing.

Adica had seen so many marvels that one more could not jolt her. She had known since she was a child that many strange and unknowable creatures walked the Earth, and that humankind was young to the land. She had glimpsed the skrolin in the tunnels when the Cursed Ones had kidnapped her, but she had never seen one as close and as clearly as she did now.

The grotesque figure came to a halt before them. Bent and gnarled, it did not have skin as humans had skin, nor was it scaled like the lizards and snakes that crawl along the ground. Its skin glittered the way granite did when caught in sunlight; leprous growths more like crystalline rocks or salt cones than a scabrous disease encrusted that skin. The pale bulges that seemed to be its eyes clouded and cleared as if mist boiled within. Bent and gnarled, it wore an assortment of chimes and charms which rang softly as the spherical lamp swayed back and forth at the end of its chain.

She found her voice. "We have come from my sister, known to me as Horn." She extended her arm to display the armband. Without any acknowledgment, the creature turned and walked with a rolling gait back into the tunnel.

"So much unknown to me lives here in this country," murmured Alain. As the light receded, they followed down this smoothly surfaced tunnel road. Adica had never seen a path so straight and so easy. The creature leading them did not look back. They walked for a long time until without warning the tunnel ended on a ledge bordered by a railing that brought them up short.

Nothing in her life or experience, not even that one sight she had had years before of the great city built by the Cursed Ones, had prepared her for the vista that opened before her now. The skrolin lived not in dank and dark caves in the ground but in a city so vast and complicated that it made the great temples and palaces and gardens built by the Cursed Ones look like crude models fashioned by children. Just as mice might gnaw a maze of tunnels through a round of hard cheese, opening up the very heart of the cheese as they nibbled outward, so the skrolin had fashioned their city into and out of the rock itself, that made up the heart of the Earth.

Their guide fingered a series of bumps and grooves carved into the railing; a gate swung open to reveal a stairway carved into the cliff. Down these steps they descended into a labyrinth of pillars and archways clothed in jewels. Caverns spun one off the next as though an ancient hand had woven thread into stone. No surface was unpolished, and so many patterns and markings had been incised into every sloping wall that she thought it must be a language read by fingers. Indeed, their guide kept a hand in contact with these surfaces, its fingers rubbing and tapping in a complicated code.

They did not walk far before their guide steered them to a vessel that looked like a giant shell scoured clean and fitted out with pearlescent benches. It took all three of them to hoist up the dogs, and they clambered in uneasily after. Their guide hopped over the high side with unexpected grace to take its place at the stem of the vessel.

The vessel lifted right up off the ground. Laoina yelped in surprise. Alain gasped out loud as he steadied himself on the backs of the dogs. Adica bit her lip rather than make a sound; she didn't want their guide to think that she, a holy woman, was awed by their magic.

But she was: stunned and even terrified as they floated through the cavernous city. It seemed to stretch on forever, winding corridors, lengths of dark tunnel that opened at intervals into caverns born out of a thousand prickling lights or streaked with veins of gold and copper. This was mystery and power displayed on a scale so vast she could not comprehend it.

How had she ever thought the Cursed Ones powerful? They were as children, compared to this.

The guide's eyes—if they were eyes— remained turned away from them. Even their awe did not interest it. Yet Adica did not feel unwatched. The many adornments, bits of metal, rods of silver, square plates of gold that flashed and winked when any light diffused over them, seemed alert. Adica sensed magic hoarded within them, a mute life, aware but unspeaking. A few of the skrolin they passed halted to regard them as one might a curiosity, but most hurried on their way uncaring. She saw none performing any manner of work she recognized: no one scraped hides, gutted fish, wove baskets, built pots, or chipped obsidian into tools. She saw nothing resembling the magic of the smiths, who worked with fire blazing as they wrought sorcery into copper and tin. She saw no fields, nor flocks, but when they came at last to a vast river whose banks were chiseled out of the rock itself, she saw a thing she could finally recognize, built on such a vast scale that it took her breath away.

"Truly," Laoina muttered, clenching her hand until her knuckles whitened, "there is more to this world than I ever dreamed."

Adica knew a market fair when she saw one. The wood henge was the market for all the Deer tribes, where they gathered at the great festivals, three times a year. Peddlers and merchants might linger for days or even weeks at the Festival of the Sun as people gained time free from their fields and flocks to trade. One time, when Adica had been a child, the Horse people had come to the midsummer fair. Their tents and wagons had made of the henge a vast fair unlike any other she had seen, exotic and colorful, and folk had lingered there long past the usual seven days of meeting, but soon afterward the first of the raids made by the Cursed Ones had come, and the Horse people had never traveled so far west again. Adica had also seen the lively market of Shu-Sha's city before it was burned by the Cursed Ones, and she had seen, from a distance, the great slave market where the Cursed Ones sold and bought human slaves.

Was it possible that all those other markets were but shadows of this one? Here, along this river, lay a market built out of stone, a long avenue fronted on one side by a cunningly paved road and, on the other, by the river. For the river was also a road for those who traveled its ways as easily as a human walked a path.

The skrolin were trading with the merfolk. Could it be that skrolin and merfolk alike lived lives completely oblivious to what took place beyond sea and cave?

What merchandise passed from hand to hand she could not see; the vessel did not slacken its pace except to accommodate the flow of crowds who at intervals crossed the thoroughfare where other vessels such as this one skimmed past. A long wharf, decorated with shells and mosaics on the riverside and soaring into archways and pillars carved like elongated dragons on the land side, marked the border where the two folk came together. In troughs cut into the wharf, merfolk lounged at their ease, eellike hair writhing languidly around their heads. The skrolin, who looked quite dry and encrusted next to the sleek, moist forms of the merfolk, crouched comfortably on their squat legs next to low tables and basins in which, it appeared, merchandise was displayed. The only light illuminating this scene emanated from the stone itself, so diffuse and cool that it felt murky, like looking through water.

In a way, the cloudy light made the vista seem more dream than real, like that city seen beneath the sea, too strange to comprehend.

Adica could not have run the length of the marketplace without becoming winded, but it did come to an end at last. Alain had not uttered one word, only stared, while Laoina muttered imprecations and prayers under her breath. The only noise their skrolin guide made came from the tinkling of the adornments hanging from its body.

At last, they turned away from the river to quieter venues, stopped deep in shadow. Their guide disembarked before a simple stone structure, longer than it was wide. A second skrolin emerged from the building. The two communicated by tapping each other so rapidly that in the dim light Adica could not make out the individual movements of their fingers. Then their guide shooed them out of the vessel, rather like pesky rats being swept out of a clean house, before it climbed back into the shell and vanished into the darkness.

"You are the animals who live in the Blinding." The skrolin's voice grated like rocks. Words came awkwardly to it, and although it spoke in the language of Horn's people, Laoina had a hard time understanding its pronunciation. But no Walking One succeeded without a good ear. Whatever fear and awe Laoina felt, she did what was expected of her.

"We are not animals but human, people like yourself." Adica displayed the armband before touching the other jewelry she wore to show that her people, too, had the skill of making.

"So is our bargain, that we must help you because of the child who was lost." With a delicate claw it brushed the armband she wore. "What wish you of us? In haste, we give you what you need so you may leave."

"Passage to the land of the tribe of Shu-Sha, which borders the lands of the Cursed Ones."

Without warning, the skrolin turned and shuffled into the stone house. The door shut in Adica's face as she tried to follow; it bore no latch she could see, nothing to pry open. Smooth as wood, its surface had the grain of rock but she suspected it was neither substance.

"With such allies, surely we could defeat the Cursed Ones," she said.

"I knew nothing of this," repeated Laoina, as in a daze. "I thought I knew so much! How powerful their gods must be, to watch over such a place!"

"There is only one God, Female and Male in Unity," said Alain. "They who created all creatures and all places. Even these."

Laoina snorted. It was an old argument, one the two had had before. "I have not seen this god. Where do you keep it? In your pocket? Or your sleeve?"

"God are everywhere. As God are part of each one of us and of the world, so we in the world are part of God."

Before Laoina could reply, the door whisked open and the skrolin beckoned. "Come."

With its shuffling gait, it led them into the house and down a flight of stairs. It soon became so dark that they had to feel their way along the steps; Alain, helping the dogs, fell behind. The skrolin did not seem inclined to slow its pace to accommodate their clumsiness, but just when Adica could no longer hear its chuffing and wheezing, it halted so they could catch up.

She had lost count of the steps and knew only that her thighs and knees were aching when the stairs bottomed out. They stood in a vast chamber, echoing with loud booms. A hot blast of air struck her in the face. She was completely blind. A clawed hand scraped her arms, then shoved her forward unexpectedly. She collided with a slick wall, banged her knees on a bench, and sat down hard. Laoina crashed into her, swore; then the dogs were barking.

"Alain!" Booms and clanks drowned out his reply. The walls hummed. A jolt slammed her against the wall. One of the dogs was trying to climb up on her, paw digging into her thigh. With an effort, she got the dog off of her, groped, caught Laoina in the armpit, tried to rise, suddenly panicked, and then Alain found her and sank down on the bench beside her, holding her tightly.

"The armband is gone," she whispered. "They took it."

"I have mine still, but it casts no light here."

After a long while, waiting in silence, they realized that nothing had changed. The floor rocked slightly and steadily, as a boat would, but no waves slapped their hull. It was too dark to see anything.

"Are we at sea?" Laoina asked finally in a whisper.

"I think not." Adica searched out their surroundings by touch. They might as well have been sealed inside a huge acorn; she found no trace of door or shutter, beam ceiling or dirt floor, only unknown patterns and textures covering the walls. "We are trapped."

"Nay, do not say so," objected Alain. "Let us wait, sleep, and restore our strength. Maybe what seems dark now will seem more clear after."

"Good advice," agreed Laoina. "Even from a man whose god fits in his sleeve."

Alain laughed. His laughter made the darkness lighten, although there was in fact no actual change. They shared out water and a portion of the remaining provisions between the five of them. Afterward, Adica listened as Laoina settled down, making herself a nest, such as she could, for sleep. The Akka woman's breathing slowed and deepened. The dogs panted, and then began to snore.

Secrets lie buried in the dark, where they fester and rot. Wasn't it better to be truthful, no matter how harsh truth was?

"I'm going to die," she murmured, finding Alain's body and pulling him close.

"No, you're not! The Holy One sent me to protect you. I'll see you safely through this. I'll see you safely to the great weaving you've spoken of. Don't you believe I can do that?"

She rested her cheek where his shoulder curved into the soft vulnerability of his throat. Tears slid from her eyes to course down his skin. "Of course, my love. Of course you will."

She could not go on. Grief choked her.

He found by touch the knots that closed her bodice. The darkness, and the silence, lent an intensity to their touching, just as rage and sorrow did: rage at fate for tearing from her the life she could never have, with him; sorrow at the loss that would come. Death did not mean as much to her, at that moment, as losing him. She had learned to live in solitude, even when she was married to Beor, but she had never understood how lonely her life had been until Alain had come to her.

His fingers found and caressed a nipple as she slid his skin tunic up his thighs and straddled him. They rocked there, falling into the pulsing rhythm of the floor shuddering under them. Cloth bunched up and spilled free as they moved. She caught her hands in his hair and pulled his head back to kiss him.

Let it last forever.

In her dreams she sees the fire-woman again, pushing, pushing, pushing as she struggles forward, trying to press her way through the glittering, golden crowd that swarms around her like bees buzzing and stinging.

"Let me pass!" the fire-woman cries frantically. "You must not give her the skopos' scepter. You must not trust her!" But she cannot get through. No one even notices that she is there, astounding as that seems, given the way she blazes.

The hall in which they stand looms impossibly high and long. The figures robed in gold cloth who stand somewhat above the others, placed on a platform built at the far end of the hall, look half the height of normal humans. Maybe that is just a trick of the lamplight.

Maybe it is all a trick. Dreams and visions can be false as well as true. But Adica knows in her gut that this is a true vision. The only thing she doesn't understand is why it matters, or where in the middle world she stands, if she stands in the middle world at all.

She lifts her staff, surprised to find it in her hand. "Come, Sister, do not despair," she cries, because the look of anguish on the fire-woman's face touches her deeply. She has known anguish and isolation, too. "There is usually an answer if you only know where and how to look."

Eyes as blue as pure lapis lazuli widen in alarm. This time, the fire woman turns, and sees her.

2

IN the sixth sphere there was always enough food, and everything shone with the golden light of plenty, courtesy of the empress of bounty, known in ancient times as the goddess Mok. But Liath despaired from the moment she entered the regnant's feasting hall in the palace at Darre, just in time to hear King Henry rise to toast the woman who would, in a week's time, be invested and robed as the new skopos, Holy Mother to all the Daisanite faithful.

"Let us pray fittingly to God, who have shown us Their mercy by bringing us a new skopos renowned for her wisdom, piety, and noble lineage."

How could they crown Anne as skopos? How could they trust her, who was the greatest danger of all? How could she stop them when not one soul in the hall was aware of her presence?

She pressed through the celebrating throng to the side of Sister Rosvita, who had interceded for her before. But although the good cleric looked thoughtful rather than pleased, concerned rather than joyful, nothing Liath could do caught her attention. The sardonic cleric seated beside Rosvita, who kept making sarcastic asides, brushed at his shoulder when Liath tugged at his robes, as though brushing at a fly. He didn't even look up.

She dared not ascend to the high table, where Hugh sat in the place of honor between Queen Adelheid and the new skopos. Hugh would not heed her; he had ensnared Adelheid and Henry both. Obviously he had become Anne's favored ally, even though Anne had seen him at his worst, abusing her own daughter. Hadn't Anne let him take Da's *Book of Secrets*? Had she guessed all along what he could become and meant to twist him to her own purposes, or was it Hugh who had twisted Anne?

Did it even matter? Hugh's goals, at least, Liath could comprehend: he wanted knowledge and power. All that mattered to Anne was destroying the Ashioi.

Without allies, Liath wasn't sure how she could stop her.

"Come, Sister, do not despair. There is usually an answer if only you know where and how to look."

She turned.

The woman facing her was obviously human, not tall but not particularly short either, with black hair neatly braided, a broad face and a generous mouth, and a livid burn scar marking one cheek. But she was dressed so primitively in a tightly fitted cowskin bodice with sleeves cut to the elbows and an embroidered neckline, and a string skirt whose corded lengths revealed her thighs as she took a step forward. At each wrist she wore a copper armband incised with the head of a deer. The metal winked, catching lamplight, and Liath blinked hard, recognizing her.

"I saw you kneeling before a cauldron. Where is Alain? Is he living, or dead?"

The woman shuddered as at the passing of a cold breeze, making a complicated sign at her chest, a hex to drive away evil spirits. "He lives. He is my husband."

"Living!" murmured Liath as hope flowered in her heart. "At least he is free, and alive."

"The Holy One brought him to me from the land of the dead. Is this that land?" The woman gestured toward the merry folk feasting in the hall as they celebrated the coming investiture.

"Nay," she said bitterly, "this is the land below the moon, but I cannot reach them. I cannot stop them from doing the very thing they must not do."

"I do not understand," admitted her comrade, coming forward to stand beside her. "I thought this might be the Fat One's realm."

"That land I do not know."

"Of course you know it. The Fat One is the giver of all things, pain and death as well as plenty and pleasure. Can you not see her hand here as well, in this place wreathed half in light and half in shadow?"

"Who are you? Where are you from? Where is Alain now?"

"I am called Adica, Hallowed One of the Deer people. I come from the land of the living but it is true that I walk now in the land of dreams and visions, as you do. Alain sleeps beside me, in the heart of skrolin country, deep within the earth."

"Now I am the one who does not understand," said Liath with a smile.

A horn blew. Like curtains rippling in wind, the hall shuddered as a rich, golden light spilled over the scene, folding like days running together. Had the world come undone? Was the belt twisting?

Liath staggered, dizzy, and found herself grasping her new companion's hand in a sober hall lined with dark wood and filled with a crush of people, as silent as ghosts.

The empty throne of the Holy Mother stood upon a smaller dais wrought entirely of ivory and gems which was itself placed upon a larger dais carpeted in gold and red. A procession worked its way forward through the throng, presbyters cloaked in silken cloaks, clerics swinging thuribles as the smoke of frankincense rose in stinging clouds, giving Liath a headache. Bouquets of roses and lilies wreathed the base of lamp stands and ornamented the closed shutters. Anne walked at the forefront, escorted by Hugh and three other presbyters, all of whom were far older than he was. He outshone them as easily as the sun outshines the moon.

"Ai, God," said Liath desperately, "I cannot let them make

such a mistake. But I'm trapped here, because I'm walking the spheres, not standing in Aosta. I can't stop it now."

Adica had a serious face but such a pleasant expression that the words she said next shocked Liath, so agreeably were they spoken. "Yet if she threatens you and your people, then you must do whatever it takes to stop her. Can't you kill her?"

"Even if I had the power, I just can't," she whispered, "It would be unnatural."

As Anne reached the steps leading to the lower dais, her four companions stepped aside. Only the skopos could set foot on the ivory steps leading to the Holy Mother's seat. When she set her foot on the highest step, she turned to look back over the crowd. Liath saw clearly the resemblance in her stern features to that of her grandfather's death mask, rendered in stone in the chapel at Autun. None could mistake her who had seen Taillefer's recumbent statue. Here, in flesh, stood his missing heir, child of the son born and raised in secrecy to spare the infant boy a potentially fatal contest for the imperial throne.

With Anne as skopos, sovereign over the holy church, who would truly be more powerful? Henry, or Anne?

"Is killing unnatural when we hunt deer to feed ourselves? Is killing unnatural when we seek to protect our children from that which would harm them? Is killing unnatural when we fight off our enemies who wish to burn our villages and enslave us?"

"That's not what I meant." The hall had fallen into such a profound silence, waiting for Anne to take her seat, that Liath had a crazy notion that she had gone deaf. But her voice still worked. "She is my mother."

"Your mother? But you have a heart of fire."

Adica touched Liath over her heart and closed her eyes. Lips pursed, expression intent, she swayed her head from side to side as though seeking, listening. Her eyes popped open, but her irises had rolled back in her head, leaving only the whites visible. A thin line of drool dribbled down her chin.

She spoke in a hoarse whisper not at all like the easy tone she had used before, as though her inner sight had made a voice for itself out of smoke and ash. "Child of Flame, look inside yourself. *She is not your mother.*"

The ring on Liath's hand flared with a blinding blue light. Cold stung her finger, shooting up her arm until it stabbed into her heart.

She screamed.

She heard their booming voices, far away, calling her "*child.*"

She knew it for truth, because truth hurts far more than a lie.

"Did Alain send you, to protect me?" she cried when she could speak again. "To guide me?" She understood the trap of Mok now, the obstacle laid before her: the trap of false obligation. She had believed blindly, without trusting in her own judgment and wisdom and instinct. "If I am not the heir of Taillefer, then I am free of his shadow and of his burden. I am free to act as I must."

She pulled off the ring and thrust it into Adica's hands. "I pray you, Sister, keep this for him in return for the help he gave me. Let it protect him, when he is in danger, as he has protected me. If he ever needs me, I will come to him."

"Where are you going?"

Liath let her wings of flame flower into life, but she was sorry to see the other woman step back in awe. "To the sphere of Aturna, the Red Mage, who rules with wisdom's scepter. To find my mother."

Without the ring to bind her to Mok's realm, Liath rose easily on a draft of wind cloudy with incense as, below her, Anne took her seat in the throne of the Holy Mother and grasped the jeweled scepter wielded by the skopos of the church of the Unities.

3

SILENCE and stillness startled Alain awake. He was lying in the dirt with Adica's weight pinning his left arm to the ground and Sorrow licking his ear. Jagged pebbles stung his rump. He groaned, shifting to pull out from under Adica, and sat up, rubbing his hand. It hurt to touch it, still, but once he chafed the prickling needles out of it, he could close it into a firm fist. The snake's poison had neither killed nor crippled him, but he still had that faint ringing in his ears.

Dust motes floated in a shaft of daylight that cut through a cave's mouth. His staff, their empty provision sacks, and Adica's pack with her holy regalia all sat on the earth nearby. Rage whined in the dim recesses of the cave, scratching at the rock face that closed off the back. Laoina, with her spear, was poking at the rock wall as though to flush out snakes. Adica slept, hands clenched. Sorrow sniffed Adica's ear, then flopped down beside the Hallowed One and rested his huge black head on his forelegs. Doleful eyes regarded him. He rubbed Sorrow's head with his knuckles, and he grunted contentedly. Rage yipped, padding over to get a pat as well.

"Where are we?" Alain asked, picking up·his staff. He tested the height of the cave's opening and measured the tumbled boulders. They could climb out, but it would be difficult to hoist the hounds out.

Laoina turned. "I am thinking it is a good thing that these Bent People do not want humans as their slaves, because to me it looks like they have powerful magic. They have ships that can sail through rock, maybe. How else could we have come here? By some sorcery the vessel carried us under the land to the country of Shu-Sha's tribe. When I was an apprentice to the Walking Ones, I met a man who walked all the way from Shu-Sha's tribe to Horn's tribe. That was when the Cursed Ones destroyed the stone loom and the fine city built by Shu-Sha's people. That man left at the waxing quarter moon, and he saw three full moons before he came to Horn's tribe. That's a long path to walk in one journey. I don't know what magic the Bent People used to make us sleep so soundly, but I'm not thinking we slept as long as three courses of the moon."

"That's a long way," he agreed, thinking that maybe Laoina had lost her mind or gotten confused. Something had changed about the way she spoke, too; the hitches and pauses had vanished, as though the language of the Deer people flowed more easily from her tongue. And anyway, he could not explain any better than she could the things they had seen in the city of the skrolin. "How do you know where we are now?"

She indicated the opening behind him. He scrambled up, scraping his knees. Dirt rained on his head from rootlets stirred as he pulled himself out where he could see. At first it was too bright to recognize anything, but gradually the patterns of light and shade resolved into a rugged defile plunging deep into shadow. The far slope was covered in spiny bushes clinging desperately to the precipitous slope. At the top of the ridge opposite, he saw a massive wall rising up out of the hill like a waking dragon.

Laoina tugged on his foot. "Come back down, quick. That fort belongs to the Cursed Ones."

He dropped back down. Adica still slept. Rage snuffled along the cave's wall. "I thought you said we were in the land of Shu-Sha's tribe."

"So we are. But the Cursed Ones have killed or enslaved most of her people and have driven the rest into hiding."

"Why do the Cursed Ones hate humankind so much?"

She regarded him with a quizzical look. "They need blood, or else their gods will turn against them. Maybe, too, they are like old man Joa, who buried ten skins and six stone axheads in the ground so nobody else could have them. Then he died, and when a girl accidentally found them two summers later, the skins were no good anymore. So maybe he did keep them for himself by spoiling them for anyone else. There are some people who are always wanting more, an extra piece of deer meat even though they already have enough, a handful of extra spear points even if another person must go short."

"You think the Cursed Ones are selfish in that way."

"Don't they have enough already?"

"I don't know," he admitted. He sighed sharply. "If this isn't the land of the dead, then where are we?"

"In the land of Shu-Sha's tribe—" But she broke off, seeing that wasn't what he had meant.

"I have seen dragons, and a phoenix, and lion women. I have seen a great city beneath the sea, where the merfolk live. I have seen the land underground where the ones called skrolin bide. I've seen the Cursed Ones, and I think they look very like the man I knew as Prince Sanglant." He fingered the head of his staff, rubbing his thumb along the snarling dog's mouth, touching each carven tooth. "The valley where your people live I saw in my dreams. But other people lived there once, who called themselves the RockChildren and whose mothers were like living stone."

Laoina looked troubled. "These I have not seen, my friend. I know of no people calling themselves children of the rocks. As for the rest—well, I am a Walking One, so I have seen many things, more than most. I admit that the city of the Bent People and the sea city of the merfolk confuse me, for how can it be that they have such strong magic and we have so little knowledge of them?"

"They live in rock and in water. How could we know of them, who live where we cannot?"

"Then why do they not show themselves to us? Nay, there is an answer already. What if they do not care for those of us who live where they do not? What if they do not need us as the Cursed Ones do? Maybe we have nothing they want."

"I have seen merfolk in my dreams," he murmured, thinking of Stronghand. "But they were like beasts. Such creatures could not have built a great city." He knelt beside Adica, stroking her hair, wanting to wake her up gently. "All that matters, here and now, is that I protect Adica. But sometimes I just don't understand where I am."

"Maybe it is better that way," she said softly, but when he looked up, surprised at the compassion in her tone, she had turned away as if to hide her expression.

Adica still did not stir, although she breathed evenly enough. He kneaded her clenched hands but could not get them to open, tapped her knees, stroked her under her chin, but she gave no response. At last he sat back on his heels. "She's in a trance." He'd seen it before; it was one of the things that made her a Hallowed One, fits taking her, convulsions, long sleeps. "How do we escape this cave?"

Laoina made a sign against evil spirits, then spat. After that she crouched beside Alain and regarded Adica dispassionately. After all, she must have been used to the twitching and drooling, the blank stares or the sudden unbreakable sleeps, since her younger brother was the Hallowed One of the Akka tribe. "First we must wait for night."

Maybe there was a more harrowing way to descend into a defile overlooked by a ruthless enemy's fort than on a moonless night with an unconscious woman tied to your back and the knowledge that your two faithful companions, left in a shallow cave, would die of thirst if for any reason you didn't return to them within two days. At the moment, Alain couldn't think of one.

Laoina climbed right below him, murmuring directions: a ledge off to the right broad enough to brace his left foot; a fall of shale to be avoided; a sturdy root grown out of the hillside, suitable for grasping.

Better to imagine himself blind as he negotiated. His arms ached horribly, and his healing hand had begun to hurt like fire. His fingers were scraped raw, and he kept inhaling dust stirred up by his passage. Adica wasn't particularly heavy, but she was a dead weight, and the ropes that bound her to his back cut into his chest and hips. Her breath tickled his neck, but she did not respond at all. Maybe she would never wake up.

Nay, better not to think like that. He had sworn to protect her, and he would.

Laoina had many skills. She, too, was heavily laden. The only things they had left behind with the hounds were the last of their provisions and all of the water, poured out into a shallow depression in the rock. She was a patient climber and a good guide as they crept down the steep slope. It was a different world than the one he knew, even than the one he'd grown used to at Queens' Grave. The tough shrubs smelled different, resinous or sharply aromatic, and bore narrow-bladed leaves. Many of the plants had thorns that stung his skin or caught in Adica's corded skirt. Once they came across a narrow cave mouth where a large bird had built its nest, now empty. Here he rested on his side in a hollow of twigs lined with grass and hair and skin and the bones of the small creatures it had carried here to feed its young.

"When we make war," he said to Laoina, who was crouched beside him, "it's like feeding the bones of our children to our enemy and even to ourselves, isn't it?"

"They'll eat our children whether we fight them or not." Wind sighed along the slopes, rustling the shrubs around them. "I'd rather fight."

"That isn't what I meant—" Out of the gulf of air, he heard a man's laughter, high and sharp.

They kept still, knowing how exposed they were, yet surely with only the stars to light them they couldn't be seen from above.

"Come," whispered Laoina. "There's better cover along the stream."

They half slid down the last incline before it bottomed out where a stream cut through the rock. Alain was so scratched up that his skin wept trickles of blood. The pain in his injured hand had settled into a dull throbbing. Laoina held branches aside as they pushed through the dense curtain of trees to get

to the stream itself, a gurgling channel of water flowing over
exposed rocks, but he still stung everywhere from branches
scraping him. With Laoina's help he untied Adica's limp body
and finally settled on slinging her over his shoulder like a
sack of turnips, except maybe a sack of turnips was less
unwieldy.

It was hard work wading downstream in the darkness, even
with Laoina testing every step before him and with his staff to
steady himself. He slipped once on a rock that tipped as he
brought his weight down on it. The butt of his staff glanced
off a stone and flew up as he fell down to bang his knees so
painfully that tears flowed, warm salt tears sliding away into
the cold spring-fed waters.

"Let me carry her," whispered Laoina.

"Nay. I can manage. She isn't a burden to me."

The sound of wind and water serenaded them; otherwise, it
was silent. Where had the laughing man gone?

Stars blazed above. The Queen's Sword rode at zenith,
almost directly above them. Adica called the Sword by a different name. She called it the Heron and had shown him how
the stars outlined its broad wings, head tucked back against its
shoulders, and trailing legs.

He braced himself on the staff and, with a grunt, pushed up
to his feet. Adica moaned softly, whispering inaudible words.
Crickets chirped. A whirring insect brushed against his face.
He flailed, taken by surprise, just as Laoina hissed sharply and
grabbed his arm. He heard the man's laughter again, closer
this time and answered by a second voice. A rustling disturbed the trees. He heard a grunt from the same direction
he'd heard that laughter, a "gaw" of pain, a cry, broken off and
rolling into a horrible gurgle.

Throats slit. Men dying silently.

A child swung out of the branches just in front of them and
landed nimbly in the stream. She—or he—held a bow in one
hand and with the other gestured impatiently. A length of
white cloth was tied around its hips; otherwise, the child was

naked except for sandals and dark stripes painted across its thin chest.

"Come," whispered Laoina urgently.

They cut away into the underbrush, Alain stumbling over the rough ground as he followed Laoina and the child. They hadn't gone more than a hundred steps when a dozen figures blocked their path, each one armed with a round shield and a short sword. Because they were all painted with dark stripes across their bare chests and faces, they were hard to distinguish in the darkness since the blend of shadow and light against their skin made them fade into the night and the vegetation. Their leader, a stocky young man, spoke quickly to Laoina.

"You heard our call."

"We did. Where is the Holy One?"

"No one knows. But it is certain that the Cursed Ones have taken her prisoner. The Horse people are on the move."

"What must we do, then?"

"Go quickly. The queen needs the strength of the deer girl." He nodded toward Adica, looked again, and hastily came over to examine her. "She is caught in a vision," he said to Laoina, ignoring Alain. "We must get her to Queen Shuashaana at once." Without asking permission, he began to untie the ropes holding Adica over Alain's shoulders.

"Let them carry her," said Laoina as Alain began to protest. "You are tired."

"The hounds." It was the one point he was fixed on, like an arrow shot true.

"Ah." She turned back to the leader, and the two fell into an intense exchange that he was too tired to follow. "So it will be," she said at last to Alain as three men separated themselves from the others, trading packs with their comrades. "Once the Cursed Ones find the bodies of their patrol, this defile will swarm with them like hornets. You must get your dogs now, before the sun rises, or you will never get them. We will take the Hallowed One to Shu-Sha's camp. These men will help

you with the hounds. That one—" She pointed to a middle-
aged man wearing a necklace of jet beads. "—is trained as a
Walking One and can speak for you. I will go to be the words
for the Hallowed One. Then you will follow after."

"I can't leave Adica!"

Laoina cut him off. "Then must you leave your dogs. One,
or the other. We will go swiftly to Shu-Sha's camp. The
Hallowed One will be safe with these warriors, even until you
come."

Looking them over, he thought she was probably right. The
dozen warriors, three of them women, looked strong, determined, and ruthless. He hated to leave Adica, knowing that
the Cursed Ones might still ambush the party carrying her,
but clearly these people knew the ground better than he did
and he already knew they would kill. To follow her now, he
would have to abandon Sorrow and Rage.

"Very well. So must it be. I will take the waterskins." He
kissed Adica's warm cheek before a man hoisted her over his
back. She gave no response. Her hands remained clenched,
and it was hard to make out her features in the darkness. She
was only a shadow, really, blurred and indistinct. As the other
party faded into the darkness, he lost sight of her hanging
helplessly off another man's back.

Fear for her made tears burn hot in his eyes. It gnawed at his
gut, but he forced it to keep still, to crawl into his aching arms
and legs and feed them with its dark energy. He would catch
up to her in Shu-Sha's camp. By believing it, he would make
it happen.

He turned toward his new companions, who eyed him with
interest. Two of them looked so alike that for an instant he
thought he was seeing double. They wore, like him, neatly
trimmed beards, but they had coarse, wiry black hair.

"We should take water. The hounds will be thirsty. I am
called Alain."

The man wearing the jet beads looked him up and down.
He had silver in his beard and a swarthy complexion. "I am

called Agalleos. These two are my brother's sons, born together, Maklos and Shevros. Be quick."

The twins parted the bushes, stationing themselves up and downstream from Alain as he filled all four waterskins. "How did you come to stumble upon us?" he asked.

"The queen saw you in a vision. She sent us. The Cursed Ones have a fort here. She feared they would capture you. Then that would be the end. You would have been sent to walk the spheres. *Skau!*" He hissed the word, making a sharp gesture at his throat like a knife cutting into the skin.

"What does this mean, to walk the spheres?" The phrase niggled at the back of his mind, but he couldn't place where he had heard it.

"Hurry," said Agalleos. "We must get these spirit guides and be gone before dawn."

They waded back up the creek. Alain smelled death before he saw it. Luckily, the tumble of corpses was mostly hidden in the darkness, five soldiers lying dead under a sycamore tree where Agalleos' party had caught them. They had been only a few hundred paces behind Alain and Laoina when they had been struck down.

Maklos whistled softly, like a bird, and pointed to the scar cut through the undergrowth where Alain and Laoina had thrashed down from the hillside. The waning quarter moon was rising. Agalleos scooped up mud from the streambed and streaked Alain's arms, legs, and face with it. They started up with Shevros in the lead.

The twins clearly had experience climbing rugged hillsides; they swarmed up so fast that Alain, less sure of where to place his hands and feet, had finally to ask them to slow down. The moon rose higher. They rested at the abandoned nest and continued on, glancing over their shoulders toward the fort looming darkly on the ridge behind them. They weren't anxious, precisely, but they were as taut as strings pulled tight. How keen sighted were the Cursed Ones' sentries?

Shevros reached the cave mouth first. Low growls trembled

in the air. Alain scrambled up beside the young man, heaved himself over the lip, and slid down inside. Sorrow and Rage practically bowled him over with their greeting. When he'd gotten them down, he let them drink. Agalleos dropped down beside him, struck fire, and got a torch burning before moving into the cave, wary of the hounds.

"Are your spirit guides too heavy to grow wings?"

"They have no wings. But we have rope."

Keeping well back from the hounds, Agalleos prowled the cave, thrusting the torch into every crevice and hole in the limestone wall. "It was the Bent People who brought you here? On what manner of ship or beast did you travel?"

"I don't know." Alain did his best to describe their journey, but gave up after Maklos, who had climbed down after, snorted loudly, and skeptically, when Alain told of the great marketplace where skrolin and merfolk traded their wares.

"Peace," said Agalleos sternly. Maklos had a cocky lift to his chin, the kind of young man who believes, with some justification, that the young women of his acquaintance persist in admiring him. "He and his brother are learning to be Walking Ones. That's made my brother's son believe he knows more than he does." His tone changed as he addressed the young man. "Do not forget the lesson of your cousin, who thought he was smarter than the rest of us and became food for the crows!"

Sorrow padded over to Maklos, sniffing him up and down while the young man held very still, one hand twitching at the hilt of his sheathed sword.

"Nay, it matters not," said Alain, whistling Sorrow back. "I have seen many things hard to believe. Have you seen the Bent People with your own eyes?"

"Not I." Agalleos shook his head. "Nor any I know. It sounds like a good tale told at the fireside to me. But our great queen Shuashaana knows many things beyond the understanding of simple men like you and I. She is a woman, isn't she? She is a word worker, a crafter, I think you call it in the language of the Deer people. She is the heir of Aradousa, who was mother of our people, the daughter of bright-eyed Akhini." He finished his examination of the cave's depths, easily plumbed, and returned to Alain. "There are caves all through these hills. My grandfather called them 'the mouths of the old ones' and he said people would get lost in them and never come out."

Maklos grunted. "An old man's smoke dreams!"

Agalleos eyed him sharply. "Say what you will about the old stories. My grandfather was a wise man. I do not ignore his wisdom." Then he grinned at Alain. "Lucky for us that you're a Walking One, too. That makes it easy to talk."

"I'm not a Walking One."

"How comes it that you speak our language, then?"

"I only know the language of the Deer People, and that of my own country."

Agalleos measured the hounds, and then Alain. "This is a mystery," he admitted, "since I started speaking to you in my own language once it seemed to me you understood me well enough."

"How can that be?" demanded Alain, alarmed and confused by Agalleos' statement.

The sound of a horn calling soldiers to battle rang faintly in through the cave's mouth. Shevros scrambled in through the opening and jumped down to stand beside his brother. The resemblance between the two was uncanny; Alain could tell them apart only because Shevros had a scar on his belly and because Maklos had belted his linen kilt—the only clothing except sandals that the men wore—lower along his hips than the other two, exposing a great deal of taut belly.

"The Cursed Ones come," said Shevros. "The horn has been raised at the fort. They have found the dead ones."

Agalleos frowned. "This is bad. They will swarm like locusts into the defile. Now we cannot go down again by the low ground."

"Are we trapped here?" Alain asked.

"There is a longer road back. We must move quickly, before light comes."

It wasn't easy to wrestle the hounds out of the cave's opening, nor to maneuver them into position. Alain carried Sorrow as a heavy weight draped over his shoulders, and brave Maklos took Rage. Shevros led the way, climbing up toward the ridgeline above, while Agalleos hung back at the rear. Clouds drifted across the crescent moon, but Alain still felt the prickle of unseen eyes watching his back as they ascended. The horn blasted thrice more. Calls and shouts drifted to them across the gulf of air. Just as they reached the ridgetop and let the hounds down, throwing themselves on the rocky ground to rest, a line of torches sprang into life along the fort's walls, spilling out the unseen gate and scattering like falling sparks down the slopes of the defile.

Agalleos regarded Sorrow and Rage solemnly. "From here we know only two paths which can lead us safely back to the camp of our queen. But the shorter of these the hounds cannot walk."

"Even with ropes, and our assistance?" asked Alain.

"Even so. It is a worm's path, underground and underwater. We cannot risk it. We will have to go north and circle around the river."

Maklos hissed sharply.

"Go soon," said Shevros. "Look."

Torches had reached the bottom of the defile and a dozen now began to search for a way to climb while the rest followed the course of the stream. Cursed Ones spread everywhere, as numerous as a nest of baby spiders spilling into life. Pink painted the eastern horizon, the brush of dawn.

"Will Adica reach Shu-Sha's camp safely?" Alain whispered, horrified that he had let her be carried away. He should have gone with her to see her to safety. Yet Sorrow, lying beside him, whined softly, and Rage licked his hand.

"Nothing is certain," agreed Agalleos, "but theirs was the safest, swiftest path. Oshidos is a strong fighter, and they'll go anyway through the labyrinth. The Cursed Ones have never caught any of our people in there."

With an effort, Alain buried his fear. What use would he be to Adica if he got himself killed by the Cursed Ones because he was worrying about her? "Very well. North of the river, if that is the only path. I have come a long way with these comrades, and I won't abandon them now."

"Crazy outlander," muttered Maklos.

"I can see they are powerful spirit guides. The gods have woven a mystery about you, comrade." Agalleos pushed himself up to a crouch, poised and ready. "To get out of Thorn Valley we'll have to go by way of the Screaming Rocks. Shevros, you lead the way. Maklos, you'll take the rear. You must set the trap and follow by the ladder."

Maklos seemed pleased to have been given the dangerous assignment. Alain could imagine him boasting of it afterward to his admiring sweethearts.

If they got back safely.

So began the scramble, first along the ridgeline, using boulders and scrub for cover, and after that dropping down into the next canyon over where an escarpment of eroded limestone pillars thrust up out of a tangle of vegetation to form a landmark. Thorn Valley was aptly named, a steeply-sloped vale covered entirely with bushy undergrowth sporting thorns as long as the hounds' claws. There was no way they could get through that.

Shevros vanished into one of the cavelets worn out of the pillars. "Go," said Agalleos, glancing behind them. On the ridgeline behind them, a torch appeared, then a second. Inside the cave, cunningly concealed where a fallen boulder seemed to be crumbling into the sloping walls, lay a tunnel. Shevros had shinnied partway down; Alain could see his shield, glinting where he'd strung it on his back. Alain moved to follow him, but Agalleos held him back.

"He must release the trap before we can pass through."

The cave smelled of carrion, enough to disturb the hounds,

who wanted to find the source of the scent. Abruptly, Shevros'
shield vanished. Alain crawled after him through the dusty
tunnel, which dipped down and rose up, emerging into the
midst of thorns in a cavelike hollow carved out of the tangle of
growth. He could barely see the sky through the skein of
branches above, but a person standing on the ridge certainly
would not be able to see the people scuttling along underneath. Broken thorns crunched beneath his feet as he followed
Shevros down a dim tunnel hacked out of the vegetation. They
waited until the others joined them.

"The trap is sealed again," said Agalleos.

They went on, careful of hands and shoulders as the slope
steepened. In this way, they headed down into the ravine.
Alain had his hands full making sure the hounds did not
tumble into the tearing wall of thorns. After Maklos had eased
his passage through a tight opening a hand's measure of times,
Rage decided to befriend the cocky young man and even went
so far as to lick his face, which made Maklos spit and sputter.
Agalleos trailed at the rear, often lost beyond twists and turns.
How much labor had it taken Shu-Sha's tribe to cut this
labyrinth under the thorns?

Shevros halted at a crossroads to wait and, as if divining
Alain's amazement from his expression, spoke. "The queen's
magic is strong." Then he scrambled on, bent over like a
hunched old man as he scurried down the right-hand fork.

Alain's hand was beginning to hurt again, but he gritted his
teeth against the pain and went on.

They emerged out of the last thorn tunnel by shinnying
along a depression dug alongside a huge boulder that brought
them into a confusing jumble of boulders and scree wider
across than an arrow's shot, the tail end of a massive avalanche
that had ripped down the western slope and torn through the
thorny cover. Alain expected to hear the wind moaning
through the rocks, to hear anything except silence, but all he
heard was the scritch of Agalleos' feet as the man walked forward to survey the devastation. It was still morning, early

enough that the eastern slope of the valley remained in shadow. The calls and answers of the Cursed Ones' scouts rang in the air as they continued their search down the eastern ridge. Sun crept steadily down the broad western side of the valley; it would reach them soon enough. With heat already rising from the rocks, it promised to be a blistering hot day.

"Come." Agalleos gestured.

The fall of rocks, tumbled, fallen, shattered, loose shale and streams of fist-sized rocks snaking paths through larger brethren, made difficult going. It was hard to be quiet as they crunched over pebbles, negotiated a field of boulders as big as sheep, and squeezed through clefts made by two boulders fallen one up against the next. Shevros knew the twisty, dusty lanes well; he led them unerringly, never hesitating. Had he spent his entire life, from childhood on, engaged in this game of life or death, one step ahead of the Cursed Ones? Alain could not think of the child who had swung down before them, at the stream, without shuddering. So young to be sent out already on the hunt, to be trained for nothing but war.

No plants grew within the rockfall except for an occasional dusting of lichen. No birds flitted to catch his attention. But there was one sign of human encroachment: here and there, tucked away under ledges, caught around a jagged line of sight, scattered out in the open, lay human bones, picked clean by scavengers, scattered by wind and erosion or caught in spring streams that had, by now, dried up. The sun rose higher, light cutting down. The rocks grew hot to the touch as they picked their way forward, bearing on a diagonal line ups-lope.

"Why are they called the Screaming Rocks?" Alain asked at last when they paused to catch their breath in the shadow of a leaning slab of rock, some giant's finger torn loose from the escarpment above. He let the hounds lap water out of his cupped hands, their dry tongues eager on his palms. "I thought there would be pipes in the rock, some natural sound."

Agalleos smiled softly. Shevros had gone ahead to keep watch. Alain saw a corner of his kilt flapping out as the breeze caught it; otherwise, the young man was hidden from view. Maklos had dropped behind to guard the rear.

"It is not the wind that screamed here. In my father's youth the Cursed Ones set fire to the great city of my people, the one built in the time of Queen Aradousa. A battle raged among these rocks for days. It was the men who screamed, the ones who had been cut down, injured, left for the scorpions or the crows, left to die of thirst in the sun, because no one could reach them."

"Who won?"

Agalleos picked up a finger bone and rolled it along his palm. "Death won. My father died somewhere in these rocks. His body was never found. As you have seen, he had many companions on the road to the other side. The Cursed Ones do not like this place. Queen Shuashaana says that is because they can still hear the screaming of the ghosts who were never laid to rest."

Alain heard nothing but their own small noises: Rage's snuffling, the press of Agalleos' feet as he shifted. A golden eagle glided overhead. Wind picked up, casting grit into his face.

"Come," said Agalleos. "We are almost there."

They reached the far side of the slide although by this time they had climbed well up the western slope. Above them the valley's slope cut into a long escarpment, dark and brooding, that ran all the way down the rest of the broad ravine. Beyond the slide, thorns grew in profusion. It was hard to see where they could go from here. Maklos caught up with them, grinning like a boy ready to play a trick on his rival.

The sun had reached zenith, so bright and glaring that its light seemed like an actual weight. Alain was slick with sweat, and the hounds were laboring. His hand was swelling again. He hunkered down in such shade as he could find—there wasn't much, with shadows so short—and shaded his eyes to stare back across the valley. Was that movement on the eastern ridge? Hard to tell.

Agalleos pointed. "Twenty or more of them." After a moment, Alain thought he saw a darting movement at the fringe of the distant thorn growth, there on the eastern slope, but when it fluttered up into the sky, he realized it was only a bird.

A horn call rang out. Had the Cursed Ones found their trail, or were they giving up?

"It's clear," said Shevros, stepping out from a shadowed cleft, a natural chimney forged by unknown forces long ago.

"We must tie rope to the dogs, in case we need to haul them up," said Agalleos.

Alain looped a harness of rope around their chests, backs, and bellies so they wouldn't choke. He led them into the cleft; although it was still oppressively warm, the shade gave some relief from the heat. The builders had taken advantage of a natural incline already present in the escarpment when they chiseled out the steps. Climbing was hard work because the stair steps were not even. Whoever had hewn them out of the rock had merely worked with what was already there, so at times he had to take tiny steps, followed by a big lift. He was soon breathing hard. Shevros, in front, seemed scarcely winded, as though he climbed such staggering heights every morning before he broke his fast.

After about one hundred steps they came to the trap, a swaying bridge woven out of branches and rope and, poised above it, a lattice gate that held back a jumble of stones overbalanced into a horizontal cleft. Soldiers triggering the trap would be crushed once they were strung out on the bridge, and once the bridge was broken, it would be impossible to continue up the trail.

Maklos waited as the others negotiated the bridge. The hounds whined, nervous of the shifting ground, so Alain had to lead them across one at a time.

"How will Maklos follow us?"

"There's a ladder hewn into the rock. There, you can see the beginning of it."

"He's going to climb straight up the rock face?"

"There are hand- and footholds. You can't see them from here."

Below, Maklos whistled, still grinning.

"Has he a sweetheart? I'll be sure to describe his daring in great detail to her."

Agalleos chuckled. "Then you'll have an audience of ten or twelve."

They climbed on, resting frequently. Once or twice they had to hoist the hounds up steep sections, but in the end they reached the top. Alain's legs ached and his injured hand throbbed painfully. Scrub grew thinly here; the jumbled ridge-line was mostly rocks. They backtracked to the edge of the escarpment, a dizzying drop that looked down into Thorn Valley and beyond. A vista of rugged country unfolded before them. To the south and east, a line of sharp ridges and defiles gave out suddenly into a gulf of air and beyond that lay a hazy lowland, yellow with summer and bright with heat and color.

Shevros spat. "That is the country of the Cursed Ones. May they all rot."

It was the longest speech he had yet made. "Why do you hate them so?" asked Alain.

Shevros gave him a disgusted look and turned away, slipping gracefully back into the cover of the rocks.

"We are driven from our homes by the Cursed Ones," said Agalleos. "They destroyed our cities. Many of our people have died. Many more who escaped the ruins of our towns walked east to the country of our cousins, the tribes of Ilios, to beg for refuge, to make a new home if they can. Of course we hate them."

"I was driven from my home."

"Do you not hate the one who forced you to go?"

He shook his head, thinking of Geoffrey. "He did not

understand what he was doing. He thought he was right, that he was only taking back what belonged to him."

"Well," said Agalleos, "you are young. Come."

A cistern lay hidden within the rocks, enough water to drink their fill and even wash the dust off their faces and hands. To Alain's surprise, he found Maklos there, chatting with his twin and looking pleased with himself.

"They've lost our trail," he said to Agalleos. "They came no farther than the rotting pillars."

"Good." Agalleos sluiced water over his head, letting it dribble down his face in streams. "We'll not lose this route today, then. Tomorrow it may save another one of us." He measured the sun's height, now halfway down to the western horizon. "We'll go on at dusk. I want to cross the Chalk Path at night."

Alain welcomed a chance to sleep. He woke, smelling smoke and cooking meat. Agalleos had built a fire deep in among rocks, letting dry tinder and many smoke holes disguise its presence. Sorrow and Rage were already eating, cracking bones in their haste to wolf down their meal. Shevros had snared a dozen small rock partridges, quickly devoured by the hungry companions. As the sun's rim touched the western horizon, they shouldered their gear and walked north and west where the ridge spread into a large massif. There remained light to move quickly along the spine of the ridge. By the time it was too dark to move easily, they'd reached the high plateau which all the ravines and defiles and ridges spilled out of.

"Will the others have reached safety by now?" Alain asked when they stopped to water the hounds at another hidden cistern.

"Long since," replied Agalleos. "Now we rest until moonrise. After that, we must walk quietly. No speaking."

Alain was given leave to sleep while the others stood watch. No doubt, they understood better than he did what to watch for; they knew this land, while he did not. The injury to his hand made him woozy as exhaustion hit. He slept, grateful for his companions' generosity.

They woke him at moonrise. With the heavens so clear the waning moon still gave enough light to negotiate the rocky ground as they hiked onward into pine woods. The night was alive with birds and insects. The ground litter, parched by summer, crackled under his feet. Now and again craggy outcrops, like uneven rock blisters, thrust up out of the earth, devoid of any vegetation except a few tenacious grasses. It was easy to see the stars through the thin foliage. The River of Souls streamed brightly across the sky. Had he already begun to forget the names of the constellations that Deacon Miria had taught him? The Heron struggled upward as it sank into the west; the Eagle, likewise, was beginning to slip west out of the zenith. Yet which was the name Adica had taught him, and which from his old life? Did it even matter anymore? This was his life now. He had given everything else away in exchange for his life; all that mattered was what he had here. Knowing that, at the end of this detour, Adica would be waiting gave him strength. A shadow of fear fluttered up, like a bat out of night. Had she woken from her trance? What if her vision trapped her? What if she never woke? He pushed fear aside. He had sat patiently beside her while she suffered through worse trances than this, last winter; it was the burden of being Hallowed One. As long as he watched over her, she would be safe. The sooner he returned to her, the safer she would be.

The Chalk Path shone before them, cutting straight through the forest like a line of power outlined in gleaming white. They approached cautiously, listening for other travelers, but the night remained silent. Gray teased the eastern sky. Dawn was coming. Chalk marked a road wide enough for two horsemen to ride abreast. It struck east and west as far as he could see, an unbroken line demarcating the chalky surface of the even road from the uneven forest loam and litter on either side.

They paused just beyond its border. Agalleos drew a pouch out of his gear and poured a mess of seeds, chaff, and scraps of herbs and torn petals into a hand.

"Stay close together. Walk swiftly. We must cross as soon as I throw these up, or else the Cursed Ones will know we have passed this way."

"How can that be?" Alain grasped Sorrow's collar tightly but let Maklos take hold of Rage.

"The Chalk Path marks the border of those lands that the Cursed Ones consider their own. It tracks any who walk on it. Once their scouts find our crossing point, they would be able to track us for days just from the dust on our feet. Queen Shuashaana's magic will conceal us. Now. Go."

He flung seeds and chaff into the air. They bolted across the path as the mixture drifted down, shimmering like sparks around them, and tumbled panting into the scant cover of the trees beyond. Agalleos and his companions ran onward, eager to get out of sight of the road, but Alain turned to look back.

No footprints marked the path where they had crossed.

He saw no sign of their passage at all. Even the seeds and chaff had vanished. A last drifting flower petal, as light as down, spit brightness as it burst into flame and, a finger's breadth from the betraying chalk trail, winked out of existence.

They traveled all that day overland, resting that night in a ruined town, long abandoned although soot still streaked the tumbled walls. Here they ate a meal of smoked venison and crumbling waybread, flavored with aniseed and very sour.

"This road is longer than I thought," said Alain as he reclined on a bed of leaves. Clouds hid the stars, although no rain fell. "How far have we come? How far have we left to go?"

Agalleos knelt beside him, constructing a hidden fire pit with stone and tiles. Shevros and Maklos had gone out to set snares. Birds were easy to catch in the wilderness that the war had made of these lands. "Queen Shuashaana's magic is too powerful even for the Cursed Ones to defeat. That's why she's stayed here when most of our people, those who survived,

have walked away to find new homes. The hills of this part of
the country have many caves and tunnels worn into them,
because of the soft rock. The queen sealed the labyrinth with
her magic. There is a gate there, that she wove, where you can
step from the land of the Cursed Ones into the loom outside
her camp. But to walk is a path that takes many days. We
must go north, and then cut back south and west."

"Except for the worm's path you spoke of."

Agalleos grinned. "Truly. The worm's path cuts back
through the underside of the hills into the labyrinth. That
saves three days' walking. But the worm's path is for young
men." He sat back from his work and patted his midsection.
He hadn't much fat on him, but certainly he was stockier than
his young companions, having an older man's girth. "I fear I'm
too round to crawl on the worm's path any longer, although I
knew it well when I was a boy." He picked up a few tiles.
"Nay, friend. Rest your hand. I can do this myself." A quail's
whistle sounded out of the dark, and he answered it, low and
sweet. Shevros appeared carrying a string of partridges and two
pheasants. "Be patient," said Agalleos as he built a fire.
"Caution will serve us well. Three more days."

By dawn, Alain could eat his fill of the juicy meat, and
there was plenty to carry for the day's journey. Soon after they
started out they bypassed a watchtower, set on a low-lying hill.
From the shelter of the trees, Alain saw helmeted sentries atop
the wall.

"That tower belonged to Narvos' clan," murmured Maklos,
with a look that suggested he still took the loss personally.
"The Cursed Ones took it when I was a boy."

"All this was our country once," said Agalleos.

"And will be again," retorted Maklos.

They looked each at the other; something about the lightning shift of expressions, their grim frowns, made Alain shiver
as at a touch of cold wind or the frozen lips of an evil spirit
kissing his heart. They moved on into the forest, heading
north into broken country.

By midday they reached the river. It was nothing at all like the great northern rivers, the Rhowne and the Veser, with their wide banks and streaming current. No Eika ship could have navigated this river; it was too rocky, too shallow, more rapids than river, really. The ford was guarded by an outpost of Cursed Ones, an earthen palisade, a stone tower, and two concentric ditches to protect against attacks. A road struck north, paved with stones, a magnificent piece of engineering.

"Their armies are moving north and west now," whispered Agalleos, "to fight the Horse people."

Alain told them about the group that had attacked at Queens' Grave and kidnapped Adica. "Do you think they can walk the looms? Is that how they came there?"

Agalleos fingered his beard, as if the topic made him uncomfortable. "I've heard it said. I've never seen it, nor why should I have? I am not a Hallowed One, to be allowed to glimpse the magic of the heavens. The Cursed Ones have strong legs and growing armies. They have roads, and their own cursed magic. Why should they need to steal what little we have?"

"To make us their slaves," said Maklos. "They would leave us with nothing but our deaths. Even our deaths they take from us, to give to their gods. This isn't even their land. I wish they'd go back into their ships and let the sea swallow them up."

"But don't the Hallowed Ones have some great weaving planned?" asked Alain. "Isn't their magic enough to defeat—?"

Agalleos slapped a hand against Alain's mouth. "Speak not of what is forbidden. We are not Hallowed Ones. It is not allowed for us to hear such secrets or even speak of their existence."

Shevros was staring at Alain as though he'd sprouted horns in place of his ears. Rage growled, and Agalleos, glancing at the hounds nervously, took a step back.

Maklos, standing closest to the edge of the wood, hissed softly. "Uncle. Come see."

Alain's face still stung from the unexpected blow. His heart raged, and yet he was ashamed of himself as well. What right had he to delve into the secrets known to Adica and her companions, that they had suffered and died for, that they had trained long years to master? Yet the more he knew, the more likely he could help Adica. Resentment flared. What right had the Holy One to thrust him into a world he did not understand, to command him to play his part, and yet never tell him the truth?

He had so many questions. How was it he could understand his companions? Was it because this was the afterlife? Yet he hadn't been able to understand Two Fingers, or the folk in the desert, or the Akka people. Instead of the afterlife, perhaps this was simply a different life. Truly, people did not seem so dissimilar here, even if their customs and secrets were unfamiliar to him.

Sorrow licked his hand.

In any case, wasn't it the Holy One they had come to Shu-Sha's land to rescue? Once they had rescued her, she could answer his questions.

"Hsst!" Agalleos beckoned to Shevros. "Do you see that standard? What mark?"

Alain eased forward so that he, too, could see. Visitors had come to the outpost, a procession of at least two hundred people, most of them soldiers dressed in bronze armor and helmets and carrying the long spears that he now recognized as typical of the Cursed Ones.

"The blood-knife." Shevros' eyes were sharpest. Alain could not quite make out the insignia marked on the white standard, a narrow length of cloth bound vertically along a pole. "Look there. The high priest's feathers."

Shevros' words struck the others to silence. They watched from concealment as the retinue entered through the gate and disappeared behind the palisade bank, but they had all glimpsed the figure wearing a magnificent headdress composed of iridescent blue-green feathers.

With a heavy voice, Agalleos spoke. "There can only be one reason the high priest of Serpent Skirt would leave his temple in the City of Skulls. He must be going out to oversee the return of an important prisoner. Or to kill her."

They looked at each other, then, the uncle and his two young nephews. They were speaking not with words but with their expressions. Questions were asked, a decision made, and Alain did not yet even understand what was going on.

But they did.

"I'll go back," said Shevros. "I know the worm's road best." He grinned, just a little, as he looked at his twin. "I know you, Maklos. You'll not be content if you don't go forward. I wish you glory of it. Just don't get yourself killed." He grabbed his twin by the shoulders and kissed him soundly on either cheek.

"What's going on?" demanded Alain. They looked at him as if they had forgotten he was there. Agalleos' words penetrated far enough to waken in his mind the conversation he'd had with Laoina in those last moments before they'd parted. Rage whined. At the northern gate, the priest and his escort appeared again, supported by a dozen men from the outpost as they marched to the ford and began the crossing. "You think that party is going to fetch the Holy One, from wherever she is being held prisoner."

"We must follow them," said Agalleos. "We cannot risk losing their trail. Shevros will return by the worm's road to the camp and alert the queen. Then she can send a raiding party this far, at least. That way, maybe, we can rescue the Holy One. Otherwise—" He shrugged, making the gesture, at his throat, of a knife slitting the skin.

"I have to go back to the camp, to Adica."

"If you must, then go." Agalleos said the words without anger or accusation. "But if you go with Shevros, you must go now, and you must leave your spirit guides with us. We'll take care of them as best as we are able. We'll bring them safely back to you, if we can."

Shevros was already shedding most of his gear, taking only

a knife, two waterskins, and a pouch of food. His shield, his spear, even his sword he left behind.

"Ai, God," murmured Alain, sick to the depths of his heart. The hounds gazed at him patiently. Tears welled in his eyes but did not fall.

Shevros, ready, turned to look at him expectantly, waiting for his decision.

"Why is the Holy One so important?" Alain asked finally, hearing the words tumble out, feeling as might a man scrabbling for a branch to grab onto as he slides over the edge of a cliff.

"Without the shaman of the Horse people," said Agalleos, "so I have heard, the Hallowed Ones cannot work their magic. That is all I know." He glanced impatiently toward the ford, where half of the priest's party had already crossed. A raft had been brought for the man wearing the feather headdress. "That is all I *need* to know. I am theirs to command in the war against the Cursed Ones."

"The Holy One brought me here," murmured Alain. "She saved my life."

There wasn't really any choice. He had a debt to pay. Honor obliged him. And anyway, he could never abandon the hounds.

"I'll stay with you."

4

SHE dreamed.

Seven jewels on the seven points of the crown worn by Emperor Taillefer, all gleaming, yet they recede before her, or she falls away and upward, and their light spreads out until a band of darkness lies between each discrete point, like a thousand leagues of land between them, a vast crown of stars straddling the land itself. But where the brilliant light winks, it turns over in the manner of a restless beast as she walks into a cavern heaped with treasure. Young Berthold, Villam's missing son, sleeps peacefully, gold and silver his bed. Six attendants lie in slumber around him. Their respiration breathes a soft mist into the air, churning and twisting, and through that mist she sees into another landscape where a woman with wings of flame wanders through a cold and barren land. The winged woman's face is turned away, but surely she knows her; surely she has only to speak to touch her

"Sister, I pray you. Wake up."

She woke suddenly, into the darkness. A lamp hovered overhead, held by the nervous hand of her servant Aurea.

"Sister."

"What is it, Brother Fortunatus?"

He sat on the edge of the bed, holding her hand. She could feel how cold her hand was in contrast to the warmth of his fingers. "Are you well enough to rise today?" he asked, glancing anxiously toward the door, still hidden in the early morning shadows.

Aurea set down the lamp and frowned at the cleric, although her heart wasn't in it. Rosvita had long suspected that Aurea had taken a liking to Fortunatus, but he had vowed his life to the church and, unlike certain of his brethren, kept steadfastly to his pledge of chastity and devotion to God. "I told you not to be bothering my lady," she said, "even if it's true she's much better."

"You were ill, too, Fortunatus," said Rosvita.

"The summer fever afflicted many of us, Sister," he agreed, "but I am well enough now."

"You're too thin. I can see that you're still tired."

"This would not wait, Sister."

She sat up. She was light-headed but otherwise felt hearty enough, even hungry. "If you will, Brother."

He retreated hastily to stand in the hall outside. Three young clerics hurried in to fuss over her as Aurea helped her with her morning business and dressing.

"Sister Rosvita! You look so well today!" That was young

Sister Heriburg, short, stout, with a bland, amiable face and the hands of an angel when it came to writing.

"Sister Infirmarian says not one soul died last night." Sister Ruoda marched over to the window and threw open the shutters while timid Sister Gerwita shrieked in protest. "Nay, for if the contagion is dying, then the air isn't contaminated anymore, and I must say, begging your pardon, Sister Rosvita, but it smells in here."

Rosvita laughed while Aurea, eyes wide, tucked her mouth down into tight-lipped disapproval. But the young women were themselves a breath of fresh air, as the ancients would say. She watched them bustle around, setting the place to rights: straightening the blankets, closing the two books Rosvita had been reading, wiping sand off the table, cleaning the pen that Rosvita had forgotten last night when she had worked at her *History* until fatigue drove her to her bed. They were so young, so clever. So energetic. She remembered being that enthusiastic once, overwhelmed by the glory of the regnant's schola.

"Now that you are better," said Sister Heriburg, who wasn't as bland as she looked, "I'll have the servants bring our pallets back here. You ought not to have to sleep alone."

"Even in the kitchens they're saying no one died last night," Aurea commented as she helped Rosvita with her robes. "The local folk say that when a dawn comes with no dead, then the fever is spent and autumn will follow soon."

"That would truly be a blessing." Rosvita sat patiently while Aurea brushed out her tangled hair, braided it, and pinned it up at her neck, a cloth cap sewn with a net of jewels tucked up and over her hair. Fortunatus, obviously agitated, crept back in and seated himself on the bed again, since Rosvita had taken the only chair. "What troubles you, Brother?"

"Messages. I saw an Eagle ride in. She'd come from the north, from Princess Theophanu, but instead of being taken to Queen Adelheid, she was led away to see Presbyter Hugh."

"Perhaps the queen was asleep. She's been up many nights

with the infant." She hesitated, seeing his distressed expression. "Surely there's no rumor of any unseemly intimacy between queen and presbyter."

"Nay." His grin flashed, and a familiar spark of mischief lit his expression. "None but what you've just whispered yourself."

Ruoda could not have been above eighteen years, but she had never learned to school her tongue. "They're a handsome couple, when they hold court together as they do now, with King Henry out on campaign in the south."

"Queen Adelheid is devoted to the king!" protested Heriburg indignantly.

"Truly, and so would I be if he'd given me back my throne, and fathered my child."

"Hush, infant," said Fortunatus as mildly as he ever could. Like Rosvita, he liked the bustle and hubbub now that their numbers had increased again. He turned back to Rosvita. "Not one soul in Darre has a bad word to say about Presbyter Hugh. Why should they? There's no man with gentler manners or a more noble bearing." Did sarcasm twitch his lips as he spoke? For once, she couldn't tell.

"He is handsome," said Aurea unexpectedly. She did not usually offer an opinion, nor was Rosvita accustomed to asking one of her. "But I haven't forgotten that time at Werlida, with him and that wicked Eagle and good Prince Sanglant caught between them. Like my mother said, wolfsbane is a lovely flower to look at, but it'll kill you the same as rotten meat."

"A fine expression," murmured Fortunatus with a chuckle, looking at the servant woman as if he'd never noticed her before.

She flushed. Aurea was old enough to be steady yet still young enough to think of marrying, if she found a husband who could offer her the security to make it worth her while to leave the king's progress. So far she had not. And Brother Fortunatus certainly was not going to be the one to offer. Rosvita wondered if she would have to let the young woman down gently. Here in Darre, with such a high concentration of presbyters, she had seen mistresses aplenty, set up to live in small houses close by the Amurrine Hill. It was easier, in truth, for women to resist the whisper of temptation, since they had been granted hearts less susceptible to rash impulse. Even so, too many clerics turned their ears to the seductive voice of the Enemy.

Humankind was weak, despite what the blessed Daisan had preached. It was always a struggle.

"I pray you, Aurea, I would have bread, if there is any."

"Of course, my lady." Still red, and with a hand on her cheek to cover her blush, Aurea left the chamber.

"Sister Gerwita, now that I am better, I would like Brother Eudes and Brother Ingeld to attend me today as usual." The young cleric nodded obediently and hurried out. Rosvita regarded Heriburg and Ruoda in silence, and they returned her gaze steadily. They were so young, but they had come from Korvei, chosen expressly by Mother Otta to be at Rosvita's service. She sighed, understanding the need for allies, and returned her gaze to Fortunatus. "Go on, Brother. I trust we are alone now and cannot be overheard."

He glanced again around the room, as if expecting to see a spy hidden in one of the corners, but, like Rosvita, he trusted the two girls. Enough light crept in that the painted walls swam into view: geometric borders framed by flowers and, within these, a series of murals depicting the deaths of the martyrs: St. Asella walled up alive in an anchorite's cell; St. Kristine of the Knives; St. Gregory torn apart by dogs; the hundred arrows that pierced St. Sebastian.

"Do you remember the convent of St. Ekatarina?" he asked.

"How could I forget any of the things that happened there? Queen Adelheid trusts Hugh now because of the aid he gave us."

"Sorcerous aid."

Heriburg started, but said nothing. Ruoda leaned forward eagerly, her scarf slipping to reveal honey-colored hair.

"True enough," agreed Rosvita. "Now we are all stained by it. Knowing what powers he has, we cannot speak against him, since we stood aside and let him use those powers to help us escape Ironhead."

"I beg you, do not be so hard on yourself, Sister." He paused, like a fox about to snatch an egg, and then slipped a hand up his sleeve. She heard rustling. "Do you recall the young lay sister, Paloma?"

"The young dove? Poor child, she will soon be withered by that hard work, and in such a lonely place."

"She is here."

"Here! In Darre?"

"Hush, Sister." Was that sweat on his brow? Was he really so anxious? A breeze stirred the stuffy room, enough to waft away the worst of the closed-in smell. She had been cooped up here for many days, recovering from the fever. "I did not recognize her, but she knew who I was. She contrived to meet me after chapel, after Vigils, out among the hedges where I usually go walking until Lauds. She said she'd come from the convent at the order of Mother Obligatia, with a message for you, but that she could not get near enough—because of your illness."

"She could have come to one of us!" exclaimed Ruoda.

"You were not at St. Ekatarina's," he retorted. "She did not know you." He turned back to Rosvita. "She brought this to me instead."

He drew a tightly rolled length of parchment from his sleeve and handed it to Rosvita as though it were a sleeping snake that might bite. She unrolled it on the small table beside the east-facing window. As the sun nudged up over the horizon, its light splayed across the table, illuminating the lines drawn into the parchment before her.

"A map."

Fortunatus rose to stand beside her, leaning on the table. Ruoda and Heriburg crowded behind him. They had all seen maps, mostly drawn in the time of the Dariyan Empire, in

monastic libraries and at the schola at Autun. Emperor
Taillefer had commissioned mapmakers to mark the bound-
aries of his holy empire but those that remained from that
time looked rough and unpolished compared with the efforts
of the ancient scholars. The great library in the skopos' palace
also kept a number of crumbling maps from the old days, frail
papyrus that flaked away at a touch. This map was crudely
drawn and freshly, even hastily done; inkblots had not been
scraped off; the coastline of Aosta—well mapped by the sailors
and merchants of the old empire—was barely recognizable; off
the western coast only a simple oval, marked "Alba," signified
that large island even though Rosvita had seen in Autun a map
delineating the southern coast, made in the time of Taillefer's
grandfather, who had married his younger son to the Alban
queen.

"What are these marks?" Fortunatus pointed to scratches,
like chicken's tracks, set here and there across the land, erratically spaced, each one numbered. "Some of the numbers are
repeated. What can they signify?"

Even without her dream, she would have known them. She
had never forgotten reading in the chronicle kept by the holy
sisters of the convent of St. Ekatarina. She had never forgotten
the conversation she had had that fateful day.

"Mother Obligatia said that the abbesses who came before
her believed that the stone crowns were gateways."

"So they proved to be," said Fortunatus, "but that does not
explain—"

"Nay, Brother, look what she has written here."

He frowned. "I fear my Arethousan has never been good,
Sister. You know my failings. What does it say?"

"Heriburg, would you read it?" Rosvita read Arethousan
easily enough, but it was always good to let the young ones
shine.

The young cleric colored, looking pleased, and read the
Arethousan letters carefully. "'We have done what we can. Is
there a pattern?'"

"What does it mean?" asked Ruoda, never able to keep silent for long.

"These are the stone crowns. That number marks the number of stones reported to stand in each circle. There is Alba, with two crowns recorded, one which has seven stones and one which has nine. Here, the coast of Salia. South of Salia lie the lands where the Jinna heathens have made inroads. East of Salia, Varre, and Wendar. This is North Mark, where I came from, thrusting out into the Amber Sea."

"What is this land, here?" Fortunatus pointed to a faint line drawn in to the north of the Amber Sea.

"That must be the Eika shore. East of Wendar lie the marchlands and farther east—I see there is nothing marked here. All wilderness."

"The lands of darkness," he murmured.

"Just so. The Alfar Mountains lie to the south of our home-land, and here is Aosta. There, along the coast of the Middle Sea, lies Arethousa."

"'Beware Arethousans bearing gifts.' I see no stone crowns in the heretics' lands."

"Neither do I. Yet it is hard to say whether that is because there are none, or only because the good sisters of St. Ekatarina had not heard of any. They could mark only those they knew of, and surely they do not believe they know everything."

"So few of us do."

She smiled, hearing his old, wickedly sweet humor. "Is there a pattern here, that you can see?"

His sharp smile quirked. "No circle that has only one stone."

"Or even two. That would be a fine philosophical question for the skopos' schola, would it not?"

"No doubt St. Peter the Geometer would have something to say on the question of how many points make up a circle," said Ruoda.

"I will let you lead the discussion, Sister," said Rosvita with another smile. Ruoda had the grace to blush, yet Rosvita did not like to scold the young clerics under her supervision for loving their learning a little too much. Age humbled one soon enough, as she knew from her aching back and the headache still afflicting her, a last vestige of the summer fever. Both Heriburg and Ruoda had gotten sick, but they had recovered so very quickly; let them believe that youth and rude good health would protect them a little longer. The world would teach them otherwise soon enough.

Fortunatus crossed abruptly to the window, leaning out as if to make sure no birds had come to perch on the sill to listen. At last, he turned back. "The little dove had a spoken message for you as well, Sister. I am to meet her tomorrow after Vigils to bring her your answer."

"Can she not come to me?"

"She said she feared she had already drawn attention to herself by asking after you. I know not what she is afraid of, but I swore to honor her request. She seemed to find me trustworthy."

Rosvita smiled. "Do not look so downcast, Brother Fortunatus. Good behavior has quite ruined your reputation as a reprobate, but I am sure you will recover in time." Ruoda giggled. When Fortunatus had chuckled, even if weakly, she went on. "Pray tell me what message Mother Obligatia has sent."

"A puzzling one, to be sure. A woman seeking refuge has come to the convent, where she remains for now in the guesthouse. She wishes to be admitted into the convent as a nun. She calls herself Sister Venia and says she took part of her education at the schola in Mainni and part of it at St. Hillary's in Karrone. By her accent and bearing, the good mother believes she is a woman of noble background, either from southern Varre or from the kingdom of Karrone. She seems well educated and familiar with the skopos' palace. The good mother wishes to know if you know aught of her. She is an old woman, kindly, unaccustomed to physical labor but very learned."

"I know of no such woman." She glanced at the two girls,

who merely shrugged. They had come south with Rosvita and the king and knew even less than she did. "Was there anything more?"

"That is all the girl told me. Truly, Sister Rosvita, I wonder that Mother Obligatia would not welcome more dedicated nuns. Her convent was dwindling. It must not be easy to lure novices to such an inhospitable place."

"Alas, that we must all be suspicious in troubled times. I tell you truly, I am hesitant even to ask here in the palace, among the clerics, for fear that I should, like Paloma, draw attention to myself."

"We could ask," said Ruoda. "All the elegant Aostan clerics think we are hopeless Wendish barbarians anyway. If we're careful, no one will think anything of our questions."

"Especially if a question about the existence of Sister Venia is only one among many," murmured Heriburg. For such a tidy, quiet soul, she manifested a startlingly roguish gleam in her eyes now and again.

Rosvita's father, Count Harl, had trained his most spirited hounds that way: by giving them a little more freedom with each lesson rather than beating them into submission. "Very well, but do not—"

The door opened without warning. Rosvita slapped her hands down over the parchment, although truly it was vain to attempt to hide it. Aurea entered carrying a tray of bread and wine. Her face was flushed, as though she had been running.

"My lady! There's a presbyter here from Lord Hugh. You're to go at once to attend the queen." She began to set the tray down on the table but pulled up short, seeing the parchment.

Rosvita rolled it up. "No word of this to anyone, Aurea. Do you understand me?"

"Yes, my lady." She asked no questions where they were not wanted. That was one reason Rosvita had kept her in her service for so many months.

"Fortunatus, I must ask you to keep this with you for a little longer." She handed him the rolled-up parchment. After

a pause, he tucked it up his sleeve. "Go and see what is keeping Ingeld and Eudes." As he left, she seated herself again
while Aurea poured wine into her silver cup and sliced off a
hank of bread. Her stomach growled for the first time in days.
"Let him in, Ruoda."

Lord Hugh's messenger was a stout, diffident presbyter,
older than Rosvita, with a placid manner and neat hands.
"Sister Rosvita, the queen requests your presence." He waited
a moment, then went on in his slow way, which made it easy
to understand him. "It gladdens my heart to see you eating,
Sister. Everyone knew how ill the summer fever took you. It's
always northerners who take it hardest, it seems."

"I thank you, Brother—Petrus, is it not?"

"You are kind to remember me, my lady."

Was Hugh kind to use a senior presbyter as his errand boy,
as if Petrus were no better than a common steward? Or was he
only showing Rosvita the respect he felt she deserved because
of her status as one of Henry's cherished counselors?

"Let me but finish, Brother Petrus."

The meal was quickly taken, shared with the young clerics
and with Aurea, who finished up anything left over.
Normally Rosvita might not break her fast until after the service of Sext, but with illness she knew she needed to eat more
frequently in order to gain back her strength. Girls, of course,
would eat whenever they could. Petrus had the habit of stillness. With folded hands, he bowed his head and shuttered his
eyes. His lips moved in a silent prayer. Unaccountably she
felt needled by his calm piety. Why should she not trust
Hugh? He had shown nothing but complete loyalty both to
his king and to God in the weeks since they had arrived in
Aosta. In truth, some said—although never within Hugh's
hearing—that Henry and Adelheid would have faced far
more resistance had Hugh not quelled Ironhead's mercenary
troops.

Fortunatus arrived with the rest of her retinue in tow: timid
Gerwita, serious Eudes, the Varingian brothers Jehan and

Jerome, and Ingeld, who was very young but recommended particularly by Biscop Constance herself. Bolstered by their presence, like a noble lady with picked warriors at her back, she let Petrus escort her through the Hall of the Animals and outside along an arcade surmounted by a procession of saints, each one lovingly carved into the marble.

Hugh received them outside the queen's apartments. "I pray you, Sister Rosvita, be of good cheer. We have news from Wendar that comes ill today, with Princess Mathilda still feverish."

The men had to wait outside. Not even Hugh entered the queen's private apartments. Rosvita found Adelheid still seated in bed while one of her servingwomen finished plaiting her wealth of dark hair, tying off the end of the braid with a gold ribbon. A net of gold wire interlaced with tiny sapphires dressed her hair.

Two noblewomen had been allowed to sit on stools beside the bed. Rosvita recognized the two Gislas, neighbors in the region of Ivria. They had obviously been arguing.

"This cannot go on," Adelheid was saying firmly. "Jinna pirates have attacked the coast thrice now, this summer, and because you two are feuding over a plot of land, no one can join together for long enough to end the raids."

"But, Your Majesty—!" began the one called Gisla the Red, for her bright red hair.

"Nay, I have made my judgment. You both have children of marriageable age besides your heirs. Your second son—isn't his name Flambert?"

"So it is, Your Majesty," replied Gisla the Red, "but—"

Adelheid turned to the other Gisla. "Flambert shall marry your third daughter, Roza, who I believe is now thirteen years of age."

"But, Your Majesty—!" objected the other Gisla.

"They shall take the disputed lands as their own, and on their children I shall settle the title Counts of Ivria. Then you shall both have a share in lands none of which were wholly yours to begin with, but which came empty of a lordship by reason of the Jinna attacks."

Gisla the Red bowed her head. "A fair judgment, Your Majesty." Was it what she had been after all along? Rosvita did not know her well enough to judge.

The other Gisla had more objections, but she knew better than to make them now. "I will bow to your wishes in this matter, Your Majesty, but I will expect your assistance with provisions and troops in order to drive out the pirates."

"You will have it." Adelheid gestured to her servingwomen, and as they came forward to assist her to rise, the two noble-women moved back into the crowd of courtiers, each one immediately surrounded by a faction eager to hear her side of the dispute. Adelheid's women robed her in the southern style in an overdress heavily embroidered at the neck and elbow-length sleeves and belted three times round with a supple cloth-of-gold belt ornamented with cabochons.

She settled herself into the queen's chair and gestured. "Sister Rosvita."

"Your Majesty." She knelt, and her three clerics hurriedly followed her lead. For all her timidity, Gerwita had a particu-larly graceful way of moving that would serve her well at court. "I trust Princess Mathilda is recovering?"

"So she is. The physicians say she will be healthy in another week. She is still a little feverish, but she is nursing well again."

"God be praised, Your Majesty. What news from Wendar?"

Adelheid's frown made her forehead crease slightly, presag-ing lines to come. She was still too thin. The birth, followed two months after by the fever, had weakened her more than anyone publicly admitted, but her color was good. "That is why I have called you to attend me, Sister. I need your coun-sel." She beckoned. A travel-worn Eagle came forward from the cluster of women attending the queen. "I pray you, Eagle, repeat your message for the good sister."

The Eagle was about the same age as Aurea, older than

Adelheid, and unusually tall. She had big, callused hands and surprisingly delicate features, weathered by hardship. "As you please, Your Majesty," she said obediently before closing her eyes, marshaling the words she had memorized. Her voice was high, at odds with her height and broad shoulders.

"Her Highness, Princess Theophanu, sends greetings to her most honored father, King Henry of Wendar and Varre, and to her beloved cousin, Queen Adelheid of Aosta. Ill tidings stalk the land. There have been reports of plague in the south. Varingia suffered a bad harvest last autumn, and there is drought in the land this spring. A Quman army has struck west through the marchlands and has been reported as far west as Echstatt in Avaria. They burn and pillage, leaving nothing behind but ruin. No news has come from Sapientia's army since last autumn except rumors of a battle. I fear for the marchlands and indeed even for the heartlands of Wendar if this tide goes unstemmed. To this end, I have left Biscop Constance as regent in Autun while I ride with what forces I can muster to the east. Yet I lack troops, with so many taken south to Aosta. Duchess Rotrudis has taken ill, and her children are quarreling over their portions, all but her son Wichman, who rode east and vanished with Sapientia's army. Prince Ekkehard left Gent in Wichman's train and has also been swallowed up by the fighting in the east. Duchess Yolande claims that the Salian war for succession has bled away her fighting force, since many of her nobles have been forced to defend their borders from renegade bands pushed east by the fighting in Salia. Duke Conrad has pledged his aid, but there is further news that makes me hesitant to trust him. He has married Princess Tallia. That is why he was not in Bederbor last winter. The deed was done while Constance was riding progress through Arconia, and when she returned Lady Sabella had already given Tallia into Conrad's hands. It is rumored that the girl is now pregnant. I pray you, Your Majesty. Let matters be settled quickly in Aosta. We need the army here in the north."

Despite the questions burning to be asked, Rosvita remained silent a few breaths longer, in case the Eagle had not done. She knew better than to interrupt; an ill-timed interruption might jumble an entire message.

"What do you think?" asked Adelheid at last. A servant brought a cup of wine for the Eagle, who retired gratefully to a bench.

So much ill-starred news made Rosvita's head spin. "I am thinking that King Henry will not be glad to hear of this alliance between Conrad and Tallia. Conrad should have asked Henry's permission to wed the girl, since Henry is Tallia's guardian, in default of her mother, Sabella."

"The one who is imprisoned at Autun," mused Adelheid, who had until six months ago been ignorant of Wendish intrigues, "for leading a rebellion against her brother."

"Even so."

"Is this alliance an advantage to us?"

Rosvita had to shake her head. "I fear not. Tallia has a claim to the throne of Wendar, just as Conrad does. Some would argue—as did the Varren nobles who followed Sabella's revolt—that Tallia's claim to the throne of Varre is stronger than Henry's."

"You believe Duke Conrad to be ambitious."

"I do, Your Majesty. He is also strong-minded, a man of bold temperament."

"And poor judgment?"

"That is harder to say. I would not speak ill of a man as powerful as Conrad without good cause. He has offered none yet."

"Will he come to Theophanu's aid?" A servant came forward with a tray to offer her wine. The cup was, like Adelheid, a thing of beauty: carved sardonyx decorated with a filigree of gold wire studded with cabochons, an echo of those in her belt. Like Adelheid, it looked delicate, easily broken should it be dropped and smash into the floor. But Adelheid's youthful prettiness made her easy to underestimate.

"It would be foolish of any noble in the kingdom to let the Quman range freely," said Rosvita.

"Won't the Quman just return to their homelands come wintertime? Can't they be bought off?" Adelheid sipped at her wine before setting down the cup restively. "If only it were true that such raiding could be easily squelched. Yet how can we spare any troops from Aosta? The situation remains troubled here. Even in Darre there are still disturbances on the streets, people calling for this cleric or that biscop to be named skopos in place of Mother Anne. Bandits rule in Tarveni, and the noble houses of Calabardia refuse to send representatives to pledge loyalty to our reign. Henry fights in the south, but even so, half the southern provinces still lie in the hands of Arethousan thieves. I have pledged troops to rid my subjects of the Jinna pirates who plague our coasts. If Henry returns to Wendar now, all this will fall apart." Her passionate gaze would have broken a man's heart. "I know what it is to be a noble child at the mercy of her relatives' ambitions. When I became pregnant, I swore my child would not suffer what I suffered when I was young, thrown to the wolves. I swore that she would inherit what is rightfully hers, in a land at peace. What shall I do, Sister Rosvita? What do you advise?"

"Send the Eagle on to King Henry, Your Majesty."

"I could go myself!"

"Nay, you are right, Your Majesty, in remaining in Darre while the king rides out to consolidate your allies." And knock a few reluctant heads together, or frighten them into swearing allegiance. "You must consolidate your power here so that the king can return to a place of firm ground. If you leave, Darre's support may crumble. No one questions your right to reign as queen."

"No," agreed Adelheid, more calmly, "they do not."

"Has there been news of the king, Your Majesty? As you know, I am but recently risen from my sickbed." She did not feel it necessary to tell Adelheid that her clerics brought her gossip every day. No doubt the queen guessed as much.

"They have laid in a siege at Navlia. Lord Gezo had made certain pacts with Ironhead and now refuses to hand over the greater part of the treasure which he took from Ironhead in return for supplying mercenaries. Duchess Liutgard was lightly wounded in the fighting. I confess, there has been some talk of her marrying again."

Something in Adelheid's expression alerted Rosvita. She said, carefully, "Has there been? Shall there be an open competition or does the duchess have anyone in mind?"

Adelheid had the courtesy to blush. "I have suggested to Henry that Prince Sanglant might be an appropriate husband for a woman of Liutgard's rank and lineage."

"Ah." To get hold of her thoughts, now whirling violently, Rosvita folded her hands and bent her head, the better to contemplate the neatly laid out zigzag flooring, white stone alternating with black, beyond the pillow on which she knelt. Rosvita was certain that neither Liutgard nor Sanglant would welcome such a match, but she did not care to say so out loud. Liutgard had come early to her duchy and would not suffer any man for a husband who might try to rule with or for her. "Any gesture that opens the path of reconciliation is a welcome gesture, Your Majesty. Princess Theophanu's message said nothing about Prince Sanglant."

Adelheid smiled thinly. "So it did not, Sister. There are some who say that the king was too lenient with his bastard son." Her eyes were bright in the soft light of morning shining in through the eastern windows to illuminate the handsome murals along the western wall, all of them depictions of scenes from ancient tales like the Lay of Helen and the conquests of Alexandros, the Son of Thunder. "Indeed, there are some who say that Henry's marriage to the Arethousan woman Sophia ought never to have been recognized as valid. There are some who say that her children, too, should have no rightful claim to the throne."

5

FOR three days they traveled fast through sparse woodland, well away from the road so that they would not be
spotted. They rarely lost sight of the blood-knife banner.
When they had a clear view down onto the road, it was easy
to mark the progress of the high priest because of the startling headdress he wore, his feathers so lustrous that they
seemed shot through with rainbows. Now and again they
had to detour wide around a village and its vineyards and
fields, careful not to be seen. The first time, Alain asked why
they did not stop.

"Surely the folk here would aid us, if they all hate the
Cursed Ones so much."

Maklos pointed at the people working in the fields. It took
a moment for Alain to realize that humans and Cursed Ones
worked side by side, recognizably different only because of
their complexions and because the Cursed Ones were, in general, shorter than their comrades. Some of the humans even
wore their hair up in that distinctive topknot.

"They are slaves," said Agalleos.

"They are dogs, licking the feet of our enemies," retorted
Maklos. He spat to show his disgust.

"They seem harmonious enough to me. Look. Do you see
them laughing, there? See how that woman—she's as human
as you or I—stops to touch that man, as she might her own
brother—"

"He is no man." Maklos spat again. "He is a Cursed One.
May he rot—"

"Hush," said Agalleos. "My friend," he said to Alain, "you
are a foreigner and do not understand what you see. Slaves may
smile and bow, hoping to be spared the whip. Magic may
twist a person's mind until she sees colors that are not there.
Now, come. We cannot bide here or we'll lose track of our
party."

Maybe so. There was so much he did not understand. Here
in these lands even the houses were different, built of pale
bricks and roofed with wooden shingles. But as they journeyed on he saw other villages where humans and Cursed Ones
worked and lived together. The only places where the Cursed
Ones lived separately was at the small forts, spaced a day's
march apart, where the high priest and his escort sheltered
each night.

That third night as they bedded down in the pine woods
within sight of earthworks, Agalleos could see that the matter
still troubled him. "You have not walked in those villages,
friend Alain. You have not walked in the ruins the Cursed
Ones made of the town where I lived as a boy. We follow the
high priest and his escort, yet can you say you have looked into
his eyes, have you seen his expression? We are too far away to
know any of those people except by the color of their cloaks.
That does not tell us what lies inside their hearts."

They lit no fire that night because the terrain had forced
them close in to the road, well within sight of the low
embankment and the wooden watchtower. Maklos took the
first watch. Much later, Agalleos woke Alain for the final
watch and lay down next to Maklos. Rage and Sorrow both
slept; better to let them lie. They had come a long way
without complaint, good comrades that they were. None
better.

Alain leaned against the trunk of a pine, taking in the night
sounds: an owl hooted, insects chirped, Maklos snorted softly
in his sleep and turned over. After a while he moved cautiously to the edge.

The woodland had been cut back about an arrow's shot on
all sides of the little fort, an astounding amount of work.
Sentry fires burned on either side of the gate, illuminating the
glitter of rectangular shields set up along the embankment
like a palisade. There was no moon, but the stars burned piercingly, so bright that for a moment he had an odd desire to
weep with joy at their beauty.

A single figure passed the limit of the sentry fires and, lighting its way with a lamp, moved slowly into the clearing toward Alain's hiding place. The man swung the lamp from side to side, searching low along the ground. Twice, he crouched and, knife glinting in the lamplight, gathered plants best reaped on a moonless night. Alain dared not stir. Something about the figure seemed familiar to him, a haunting ache, a teasing memory, but he could not say what. Darkness shadowed the man's face, but as he came closer, Alain could see that he wore odd garb, not much more than a loincloth tied in a knot and draped loosely at the hips and, over his bare chest, a hip-length white cloak. Beaded sheaths covered his forearms and calves. Was that a feather stuck in his hair, bobbing in and out of sight as the lamplight caught its color?

The man crouched to investigate a spray of leaves among the ragged grass, lifting the lamp up at such an angle that all at once Alain saw his features boldly outlined.

It was the shadow prince, but not dressed as a prince in martial array and certainly not a shadow.

This man he had seen and exchanged words with in the ruins above Lavas Holding while an unseen shadow fort burned down around them. This man had led a column of refugees past Thiadbold's cohort of Lions after Alain had negotiated a hasty truce, if there could in truth be any true intercourse between shades and people.

Maybe he gasped.

Maybe knowledge, like a knife-edged flower, opened in his heart. If the shadow prince was alive, Alain certainly could not be in the afterlife, because shades could not dwell on the Other Side; otherwise they would not be trapped as shades on Earth.

"Who is there?" said the man, lifting his head. He doused the lamp, but he had a habit, not unlike that of Prince Sanglant, of tipping back his head as though he were sniffing the breeze, trying to catch a scent.

A sentry moved out from the fires, crossing the grassy clearing quickly. "Is there anything wrong, Seeker?"

The prince waited a few breaths, still listening. Alain was achingly aware of the creak of the trees, the sigh of the wind through lush summer leaves, the soft snort of Sorrow, a stone's throw behind him, as she dreamed.

"Just an animal."

"You shouldn't be wandering out here, Seeker," continued the soldier sternly, hands gripped tightly on his spear. "There are bandits still, you know what beasts the Pale Ones are. They'd rip you to pieces and then eat you raw. That's what happened to my cousin. I hope we kill them all."

"Even the folk in those villages we passed? Even the Rabbit Clan lady who sells incense in Western Market? Even the sailors on *White Flower*, whose captain is a half blood?"

The soldier gestured toward the sentry fires and the earthen walls, eager to return to their safety. "Wild dogs can be taught a few tricks, but they're never tamed. And they'll bite you when you try to feed them."

"Hu-ah," said the prince softly, "so swift a judgment and so harsh a cut." He touched thumb and forefinger to the wick on the lamp, and fire flared, so startling that Alain jerked back, thumping his head on the tree behind him.

"What was that?" The soldier raised his spear threateningly and took a step toward the forest's edge.

"A deer. Come, let's go back." The prince lifted a square of cloth overflowing with leaves and stems; tying diagonal corners gave him a means to carry his bounty. "I've got what I wanted."

Waking his companions at the first blush of dawn, Alain heard a horn call, low and trembling.

Maklos grabbed his weapons hastily. "They're off early today."

"No need to hurry," said Agalleos mildly as he stretched out the kinks that sleeping on the uneven ground had left in his body. "Aih! To be young again!" He grimaced. "I'll never be free of these knots in my neck! There's only one road, so we can't lose them. We'll reach the Spider's Fort by afternoon. I wager they'll stop there for the night."

"Why so?" demanded Maklos. "Aren't they in a hurry?"

"There's a crossroads there, lad. West and north runs the path into enemy lands, as far out as they've forced the border. To the southeast they can march by the Carrion Road and cross the Chalk Path by the Bright River. It's but a day's march from Bright River to the City of Islands. They can sacrifice a prisoner there as easily as they can in the City of Skulls."

"What is a Seeker?" asked Alain. When Agalleos looked at him strangely, he explained the encounter he'd had.

"Have you learned the language of the Cursed Ones as well?" asked Agalleos, surprised. Maklos had already started out and now, half hidden in the trees, turned to wave them forward impatiently.

Alain gathered up his gear, staff, pack, and the shield left by Shevros, while he gathered his wits as well. "I told you before: I only know the language of the Deer people, and that of my own country."

They looked at each other, each seeing distress and bewilderment in the other man's face. Rage whined and nudged Alain, urging him to move on.

"Come," said Agalleos. "No doubt your spirit guides have given you some gift you weren't aware of."

No doubt. But his thoughts were so jumbled that three times that morning he tripped over roots and once slammed right into the trunk of a tree.

"Hsst!" Maklos sprinted back and shook him. "Keep alert! You could get us all killed."

It was like chasing down flustered geese. For some reason, his hand—the one that had been bitten—began to throb again, although it hadn't pained him since the day they'd crossed the Chalk Path. There went one goose which he had chased before: How could he understand Agalleos and Maklos? How could he understand the speech of the Cursed Ones?

And there, crossing its path, drawing his attention, another: The prince was no shadow. He was alive. He had been a shade in the world Alain had once known, a vision from times long past.

What did that make him now?

Spider's Fort had been built over the ruins of another town, thick stone walls raised on a low hill to make it a fortress. So many old ruined walls wandered out onto the grassy land around that the brooding watchtowers and massive walls did give it the look of a many-eyed spider nesting at the center of its web. There were many more soldiers here, and even a camp set up outside the walls on flat ground extending out to the southeast: circular pavilions of white cloth dyed a pale gold under the light of the setting sun. Soldiers were driving stakes into the ground at an angle along the east-facing slope, like a defense against cavalry.

"Do you think they have the Holy One here already?" Maklos grinned. "I can sneak in along the old stone walls and get a look inside."

"No, I must go," said Agalleos. "When I wasn't more than Maklos' age, I spent a season here as a soldier." He spat, as though ridding himself of a bad taste. "Even then, we were losing the war. The Cursed Ones spread their net wider every year. So far have they come."

"Nay, I must be the one to go." As the other two began to protest, Alain lifted a hand. "I can understand their language. Can you?"

"Truly," admitted Agalleos, "I can't understand their speech." Maklos crossed his arms and grimaced, hating to miss his chance for a daring raid.

"Even if I can't get close enough to see into the fort, I can at least hear the gossip of the sentries. What do you know of these old walls? Is there one route better than the others?"

"Along the northern slope you'll find the ground dug through with old trenches and fallen walls. You can move in close, this way." Agalleos drew in the dirt with a stick. "The fort's walls thrust out like a ship's prow at the narrow end of the hill." He scraped a deep line diagonal to the walls he had outlined. "Move up along this cleft. To your left you'll see an old terrace that used to be an herb garden. There was an old stair there that was hidden by the queen's magic before the soldiers had to abandon the fort. In the corner of the garden, where three walls come together, find the carving of a lion woman. This is the sign that will open the weaving and let you through." He showed Alain how to place his hands and press them over the mouth and eye of the carving. "Go up the stairs. There's a hidden place where you can see into the fort."

"So be it," said Alain.

He ate, and drank, and fussed over the hounds, waiting for nightfall. He took only his staff, a knife, and a water pouch, refusing the shield, spear, and sword offered to him by Maklos. "The staff is the only weapon I use," he said, "and a shield will only get in my way."

Agalleos slipped a small stoppered bottle out of his pouch, opening it. "We have little enough, but this is a good time. Open your left hand." He poured oil onto Alain's palm. "Now rub this into your face from right to left, saying these words: 'Let the swift god Erekes place his hand upon my brow and make me invisible to all my enemies.'"

Alain hesitated. The oil smelled faintly of lilies but also of something tart and displeasing.

"This is men's magic," said Agalleos. "Go on."

Starting at his ear, he rubbed the oil into his face while murmuring the words. Oil tingled on his lips, but he felt no different.

Night brought the waxing crescent moon, already low in the west but bright enough together with the light of the stars that Alain could creep away from their hiding place out onto the open ground. The ground was mostly flat, but here and there pocked with depressions and rubble, easy enough to move through without too great a risk of being seen whether or not the magic worked. Fires burned on the walls above. He heard the noises of camp, men singing about ships and the sea, in odd contrast to the dust sliding under his feet, the hanks of dry grass his hands closed over at intervals, and thick patches of fennel rising up before him.

Once he had to lie low as a patrol strolled past. Maybe the spell hid him, or perhaps only the shadows did. He rose as soon as they were safely away and continued on in a crouch, hurrying from the refuge of a ditch to the lee of a fallen wall, scraping his knees on ragged stone, smelling the parched odor of the earth. The ground rose steeply beneath his feet. Above, torches burned, the edges of their flaring light obliterating the nearby stars. Figures moved along the walls, but their gazes were turned farther out, across the open ground to the concealing woodland beyond.

He scrambled up through the rubble of tumbled walls that had once ringed this lower slope of the hill. In an odd way it was as though those old sharpened senses, borrowed through dreams from Stronghand, remained with him. Grass sighed under the touch of the wind. Insects burrowed. An owl passed overhead, calling a warning that no man but he could hear: "Beware! Beware!"

He hoisted himself up a chest-high embankment and rolled onto an open ledge. A wave of scent smothered him, lavender and rosemary gone wild, rue and sage a heady aroma like a cloud around his head. The moon sank low along the horizon. He crawled on hands and knees through the overgrown garden and found the place where three walls met, two of them old ring walls and the third yet lower again, an ancient foundation almost consumed by the hillside. Because it was dark, he used touch to find the sphinx with her arching wing, powerful forelegs, and hindquarters carved statant into the stone. He placed a thumb in the sphinx's mouth, a forefinger in its eye, and a little finger in a cleft carved under the wing.

A musty exhalation of cold air kissed his face. The moon touched the western horizon, sinking fast. He stumbled forward and banged his knees on stairs carved into the hill, too dark to see. He crept his way up using staff and hand, an arduous climb because of the darkness. After ninety-seven steps—he counted every one—he saw a reddish light flickering and bobbing to his right; a wall cut off his forward progress, and he had to turn right and follow a narrow passage barely wide enough to squeeze through because it was half filled with rubble. Fifteen more measured steps brought him to an embrasure cut into the rock, a hidden alcove from which he looked down onto a broad forecourt that fronted the main gate with its twin, square towers.

Soldiers gathered, ready to march. Their torches made the courtyard flare ominously, all smoke and fire and the glitter of bronze helmets and shields. The standard of the blood-knife fluttered in their midst. A slender figure cut through the ranks of soldiers to speak to the standard-bearer. Alain recognized him at once: the prince, whom the guard had called "Seeker." The two spoke as the soldiers waited in patient silence. Then the prince hurried away, ducking inside a low doorway, lost to Alain's view.

The high priest came from farther down the forecourt, where a wall broke Alain's line of sight. His feathered headdress gleamed in the light of torches held up to either side of him. Ranks of spears bobbed alongside, a fence around their prisoner, trapped between two small wagons.

Because of her horse's body, she stood a head taller than her captives, but her proud and beautiful head was bowed and her eyes were blindfolded. Her thick hair lay tangled and dirty over her shoulders. Bruises and unhealed cuts mottled her naked torso, and she limped, unable to put her full weight on her right foreleg. Her arms were tied behind her back, resting on her withers. Ropes bound her belly and back, held taut out to two wagons, one before and one behind, so she could neither bolt nor kick. She was jerked to a halt as the wagon drivers pulled back on their reins. The gates were unbarred and men hurried to open them.

They weren't going to wait until daylight to take her away.

Her fine black coat, once glossy, was streaked with dirt and blood and coated with a dusting of ash. She shifted, favoring her injured leg. One of the drivers snapped his whip, a curling "snap" against her croup that made her lurch onto the injured foreleg and cry out in pain. Soldiers laughed to see her suffer. The heavy gates thudded against the towers. The way lay open for the high priest's party to march out.

Alain stumbled backward, almost tripping when he reached the stairs. The smoky light of torches had blinded him. He counted each step so as not to fall, but feeling with his feet and his hands into the darkness it went so slowly. Was that the jangle and clank of their movements, as the troop moved out? Could he actually hear wheels grinding against dust as the wagons rolled down the ramped gateway?

Or was that only the wind moaning through cracks in the stone?

Or the whisper of men speaking in low voices?

Ninety-seven steps brought him to the concealed entrance. His hands traced the carven wings of the sphinx, sleeping forever in stone. He paused at the juncture of the three walls, seeing a pale light gleaming on the small ledge that harbored the overgrown herb garden, and stayed hidden in the shadows.

Someone stood there, back to him, a soldier with a crested helm wearing a hip-length white cloak. Bronze greaves protected his calves. The wind caught the cloak and whipped the ends up to reveal a finely molded cuirass decorated with boiled leather tasses that reached halfway to his knees.

"You're wrong," he said as he turned to face some other person, who was hidden by the curve of the wall. "They will fall before us because our armies are stronger than theirs. They are no better than packs of wild dogs." The pale light limned his profile as it came into view: it was the prince, but he was now dressed in the garb of a soldier, the same clothing Alain had seen him in before when he had appeared as a shade in the ruins above Lavas.

How strange, that he had changed clothing so quickly.

"Then you underestimate them," said his unseen companion. Their whispers made their voices sound much alike. "That is why we still fight."

The prince laughed harshly. "This war will only be over when the pale dogs and the shana-ret'zeri cease to hunt us, and that they will never do. Because they are still beasts, they cannot live peacefully, nor will they ever let us live peacefully."

"Spoken like a soldier."

"Do not mock me, brother. You know they are our enemies."

"I know there will never be peace as long as our leaders persist in thinking they are beasts."

"Tell me you did not cry with joy when news came to the blood-knife lord that the witch who calls herself Li'at'dano was captured!"

The name made Alain slip in surprise. Pebbles fell in a spray, skittering onto the ground at his feet.

But the unseen man was already talking; neither seemed to have heard. "She is not even the most dangerous of those who oppose us. But at least once she is sacrificed, her power is lost to our enemies."

"We don't need magic to defeat them."

"If you think so, then you are a fool."

"You have been listening to the mumbling of the sky-counters again. We have spears and swords enough."

"Why will you never listen, elder brother? Spears and swords will never be enough."

"What great magic are the pale dogs hiding? How will they rise up and defeat the Feathered Cloak and her sorcerers? What are they waiting for? The witch mare will be taken to the temple of He-Who-Burns, and there she will walk the spheres. So we will be rid of her. The rest will die or surrender or flee."

How could it be that this man, who was alive and not a shade, knew of Liath? Wasn't she already walking the spheres?

Or was it Liath he was in fact speaking of? She was no "witch mare."

"That is what I am afraid of," said the other man as he stepped at last into Alain's line of sight. He carried the pale light, a simple oil lamp flaring and flickering as the night wind teased it, held away from his body to illuminate the face of the prince. "That as we march our armies out to the frontier and leave our cities unprotected, the pale dogs are hiding and hoarding their magic. That is how they will strike us. That is why the sky-counters have sent out raiding parties to the four winds."

"To be eaten by guivres, clawed by sphinxes, and smothered in sandstorms!"

The man carrying the lamp shifted, and all at once the light shone on his face.

Which was a twin to that of the soldier prince. Here was the Seeker again, dressed in simple garb and adorned by feathers.

Maybe Alain made an involuntary squeak of shock. Maybe his foot slipped. The next thing he knew, the soldier had spun around and lowered his lance, balanced to slide right into Alain's belly.

"Who's there?" he demanded, squinting into the darkness.

"Do not act rashly." The Seeker laid a restraining hand on his brother's arm. "I have smelled this one before." He lifted the lamp to shoulder height. He had a young face, handsome and proud, but not cruel. Feathers bobbed in his hair as he lifted his chin. "Come forward. You are trapped."

With his staff held in his right hand, Alain stepped forward cautiously into the light.

"I am only one man," he said quietly, "and I do not understand this long war. Wouldn't you live more easily if you could make peace?"

The soldier hissed through his teeth. He held his lance steady, but did not lunge.

"Do you not mean to stab the pale dog through at once and have done with its barking?" asked the Seeker with some amusement. Seeing them together, side by side, Alain could now detect certain differences of stance and expression——the soldier tense and slightly thinner, as grim as death, and the Seeker with a gleam like mischief in his expression and a sardonic lift to his mouth. Otherwise they looked exactly alike except for their clothing.

"What are you doing here?" demanded the soldier as the point of his lance hovered an arm's length from Alain's abdomen. "How did you come to our walls without being seen by the sentries and patrols?"

Alain touched his own face, but the taste and feel of the oil Agalleos had given him to rub into his skin was long since wicked away by wind and night. Before he could answer, he heard the distant sound of barking, all at once, as though the hounds had been surprised out of sleep.

Hard on that sound, the darkness came alive as the blat of conch horns rose out of the east. A rumble like distant thunder shook the earth. Torches flared at the edge of the woods. Alarms rose from the fort's walls, and men shouted out warnings as, along the entire northern sweep of forest, lights bloomed and, in the hands of shadowy figures, swept in toward the fort.

"Now what say you, brother?" cried the soldier. "Do they walk forward offering the gold feather of peace? Do they send emissaries with tribute? No, they strike like wolves in the night." He struck. Alain dodged aside as the prince caught himself and jerked back for another try.

"Hold your point!" cried the Seeker. "These are the Horse folk come for their witch. This one, he does not belong here."

"Then we shall be rid of him." The soldier struck again. Alain knocked the point aside with his staff and leaped back toward the wall as the prince pressed his attack.

"Brother! Behind you!"

Two massive creatures scrambled up the lower slope. One, lithe and swift, closed faster than the other. The lamp held in the Seeker's hand flared as the leading centaur burst into the

herb garden, trampling waist-high lavender. The soldier spun
to meet her.

Ai, God. Like the Holy One, she was beautiful. Long black
hair blown back revealed full breasts, each glimmering in the
pale light like a perfect moon. As with her hind legs she
jumped, she raised high in her hands a club bristling with
spikes. She bore down on the prince. He held his ground and
thrust, catching her between those breasts. Her momentum
pushed the spear point out her back as he scrambled backward
to the low wall ringing the ledge. The club came down too
late across the haft of the spear, splintering it as her body collided with her killer. They both tumbled over the retaining
wall, vanishing from sight.

The second centaur let loose a piercing scream as she arrived
too late to do anything but avenge her companion. She
charged the Seeker, who danced this way and that, at some
advantage because he could dodge more swiftly than she could
turn her bulky body, until at last his enemy cornered him
near Alain. She hadn't the lithe beauty of her dead companion;
broad shouldered and barrel-chested, breasts almost lost in
her muscular arms and chest, she reared up, fore-hooves striking and club lifted for the killing blow.

Alain thrust his staff up, catching the club at the apex of its
arc. She twisted, her fore-hooves knocking Alain hard to the
ground, and reared again, ready to strike him, but he pushed
his staff between her rear legs and with the weight of his body
twisted it around. The wood did not break. She tumbled back
onto her flank. He leaped to force his weight down onto her
heaving shoulder, pressing his staff against her neck.

"We must save the Holy One!" he cried.

"I am Sos'ka." She twisted her head around to catch sight of
the Seeker, standing stock-still against the wall. "Bar'ha and I
were sent up here to find the one called Alain. Why do you
fight me, if you are that one?"

The Seeker had pulled his knife, but he did not advance.
Amazingly, he hadn't lost his grip on the oil lamp. Alain eased

up on his staff and rose. Sos'ka regained her club and righted herself, getting her four legs under her and with some difficulty staggering upright. When she saw the Seeker, hatred swept clean her expression. She lifted the club and danced toward him.

Alain stepped between them. "No. No more killing."

She shook her head, making a noise more like a whinny than a word. Where her black hair had been bound back, her ears, pointed and tufted, showed through. She examined Alain briefly with eyes slit vertically, their color impossible to make out in the night. "Come," she said at last, with only a final, swift glance at the Seeker, who had not moved.

Maybe this young prince, so uncannily like the other, would not die today. Maybe his brother had or was soon to become a shade, caught forever in the shadows of the world.

"Quickly." Sos'ka grabbed Alain with a burly arm and helped him mount awkwardly onto her back. He righted himself, clamping his staff under his arm as she turned, cleared the wall easily, then half slipped, half cantered down the slope. He had to grasp her mane, which ran all the way down her spine to her withers, to stay on her back. Although she was as surefooted as a goat, the ride was rough.

He glanced back to see the Seeker bending to pick an object from the ground. It gleamed, sweetly gold, almost as bright in the night as the oil lamp. As Alain slapped his hand over his tunic, feeling for the phoenix feather, he saw the soldier prince push himself away from the body of the dead centaur just below the ledge. At once, the Seeker jumped forward to help his brother to safety.

"Beware!" Sos'ka cried, and he held on for dear life as she jumped a ditch and landed hard on the other side.

He felt at his chest again, but the phoenix feather was gone, lost in the struggle. It was too late to go back now. The battle rose out of the darkness before them.

Alain held tight to Sos'ka as she cleared the worst of the rugged ground and galloped wide around the fighting that

had erupted in the encampment. Pavilions burned, fire illuminating the scene with a sickly glow. Cursed Ones fell, and
centaurs stumbled, cut down. Screams cut the air. The horrible scent of charred flesh stung at his nose and made him
choke. Torches ringed the fort. Flaming arrows made arcs of
light across the night sky.

"To the southeast road," he yelled, almost coughing out the
words. She cried out, a whinnying call, and about four dozen
centaurs split away from the attack to follow her, half of them
carrying torches. They pounded onto the road, hooves striking
sparks on stone, and broke into a gallop. The stonework, the
fruit of the Cursed Ones' fabled engineering, made the road so
even and smooth that they could move swiftly and without
much fear of stumbling. Even so, he could tell from their fury
that no obstacle, even night, would come between them and
the one they sought, not now that they were so close.

The high priest's party had made good time and, truly,
looked to be making better time still, since the men had all
broken into a steady soldier's trot. Their rear guard shouted
the warning, and half the troop—perhaps three dozen—
stopped to meet the threat. They fanned out into a line, spears
lowered, as the rest of the troop hastened on. The blood-knife
banner bobbed away into the night shadows, a pair of torches
casting light onto the sigil. The two wagons, with the Holy
One tied between them, lumbered on.

The centaur charge hit the line of spearmen like a storm
surge, flattening them. Four centaurs fell, but the rest poured
past even as those soldiers who weren't writhing on the ground
cast their spears after them. One centaur lurched forward,
wounded in the thigh, and collapsed. Alain had to look away
as a group of soldiers leaped on her, stabbing.

Seeing that their pursuit hadn't slowed, the rest of the troop
pulled up to face the centaurs. Sos'ka's coat was slick with
sweat. Froth bubbled at her mouth as she shrieked in battle
frenzy and charged for this new line. Alain tightened his knees
along her withers, desperate to stay on, and couched his staff

like a lance. The Cursed Ones formed their final line, spears ready, swords poised.

As they broke over the line Alain slapped a spear's thrust away and struck the soldier across the face, knocking him hard to the ground. Sos'ka's club swiped close by Alain's head as she swung it down onto the helmet of a Cursed One. The force of the blow shuddered through her body as her club crushed the man's skull. The dying soldier's sword drew a shallow cut across her shoulder and down Alain's thigh as the man fell beneath her hooves.

They broke past the line and, with some effort, she slowed, danced sideways, and turned to meet a new press of soldiers. Her club struck wildly in grand arcs from side to side. Half the time Alain had to duck her swings, but he thrust his staff toward one face, then another, hitting them hard to keep them off-balance. She reared as a soldier cut at her legs, and Alain slid from her back. Amazingly he landed on his feet and had enough balance to jump forward, catching the soldier's sword against his staff. With the sword still embedded in the wood, he shoved the flat of the blade into the face of its owner, stunning the soldier. Wrenching his staff free, he struck a blow that sent the man to the ground.

The wagons had lurched to a stop as the drivers fought to control their panicking horses. The high priest, with his rainbow headdress thrown carelessly to one side, leaped out of the back of the lead wagon and, ugly obsidian knife in hand, ran forward to Li'at'dano. The centaur shaman was still trussed, trapped and helpless as she threw back her head and neighed. The Cursed Ones fought furiously to keep her rescuers away. All they had to do was hold long enough for the priest to murder her. No matter how hard Alain pushed, for every one he knocked aside, another leaped forward to take that one's place.

The priest cried out. "May He-Who-Burns take this offering!" He struck.

The centaurs cried out in fear and helpless fury.

Light ripped down from the heavens. The burning flash was followed by an explosive clap that threw every person to the ground.

Then it was silent, for the space of two breaths, or two hundred breaths, impossible to tell because his skin tingled so sharply that the sensation obliterated all his other senses. Blood trickled from one ear as his sight returned, and he pushed up to his knees. His hair had come alive, twisting like the living hair of the merfolk.

Only the Holy One still stood upright, unable to collapse because of the ropes binding her. Her flesh was burned and her black hair, mane, and coat singed. The priest had been thrown twenty paces away, his burned and contorted corpse smoking. Fire danced along the hem of his cloak and died. The obsidian knife lay at the centaur shaman's feet, melted into a puddle of steaming glass.

Alain staggered to his feet just as the drivers fell from the wagons, clothes burned off their bodies, and stumbled away toward the safety of the woods. One of the horses, caught in the traces, tried to rise, but could not. Alain kicked down a nearby soldier who tried to stand. He made it, barely, to Li'at'dano. As he cut the ropes, she collapsed gracefully to the ground. Centaurs struggled up, their manes and hair standing straight up like that of frightened cats. Sos'ka was not among the standing.

The Cursed Ones were slower to rise. Some crawled away. Other were killed by those centaurs who recovered first, but Alain could do nothing to help them, any of them. All he could do was help the shaman to rise. This close, he saw the horrible bruises across her torso, the marks of a whip, and the mangled stump of one ear, its tip cut clean off.

At last, Sos'ka appeared at his side, singed but living. "In the wagon," she said. It was not easy to get Li'at'dano in, and a tight fit besides to place a centaur's body in a bed meant for carrying two-legged creatures and their cargo. When they had done, other centaurs had already unfastened the stunned horses and harnessed themselves in their place.

"What did she do?" Alain asked, leaning on the wagon to catch his breath. His hair was finally beginning to settle. A huge scar marked the center of the road.

"Li'at'dano wields the weather magic," said Sos'ka. "She called lightning."

A new herd of centaurs galloped up, wielding torches like clubs as they scattered or killed the rest of the Cursed Ones. Only now could Alain hear the distant clash of battle by the fort, fading as wind rose up out the dark, a rushing in the nearby trees. He heard barking, coming closer.

Sos'ka whistled, and a centaur with burnt-butter-colored skin and a glossy gray coat trotted up. She carried a bow, with a quiver of arrows slung over her back. "He'll need to ride if he's to come with us," said Sos'ka.

"He is not," said Gray Coat. "His companions come now, on the backs of Ni'at's foals. They must return to their own herd with this news."

"Let him come before me." The Holy One's voice was soft, labored, yet it still sang sweetly. He turned to look. The shaman lifted her head, seeking; she seemed blind, although her eyes were open.

"Here I am," he said, reaching out to touch her questing hand.

"Yes." She caught hold of his fingers, her grip uncomfortably strong. "You are here. What is it that you wish to ask me?"

How did she know? "Are you the one called Liathano?" He stumbled over the pronunciation, trying it again. "Li'at'dano."

"I am called Li'at'dano." A thin smile teased her swollen lips. "But there is one who will be given my name in the time yet to come."

"Ai, God." Her words shuddered through him like the tolling of a bell. He glanced around at the centaurs looming and pacing, impatient to go, to get their rescued shaman to a place of safety where she could heal. But he still had so many questions. "Where am I, truly?"

"You are here."

"Where was I before? Where was I when I was alive?"

"You are alive now."

"Alive where?" The words caught on his tongue, all tangled and heavy. He could barely speak. "Alive *when?*"

A dozen centaurs pounded up, Agalleos and Maklos clinging to the backs of two roan mare women. Agalleos looked grim. Maklos seemed, as he dismounted, to be flirting with the pretty creature he had just ridden in on. Torches shifted and bobbed in the darkness as more gathered, retreating from the battle at the fort.

And he remembered: the soldier prince hadn't died. He wasn't a shade. He remained as alive, at this moment, as Alain was. "Ai, God. I'm not in the afterlife, am I?"

"No," she said sadly, "you are not. I found you only because the one you call Liathano dragged you off the path that leads to the Other Side."

"You mean I was truly dying." Bitterness took hold of him as he blurted out his next words. "I served the Lady of Battles as she bid me. I died on that battlefield."

"You did not die only because the fire's child dragged you off the path. I saw you in the crossroads between worlds and lives, in the place where all that was and that is and that will be touches. There I got hold of you, and I brought you here. To this time. To Adica." Pain creased her features, but she managed to speak. "Who needs you."

Ai, God. Adica!

Rage and Sorrow swarmed him then, bounding up fearlessly through the herd of gathering centaurs, leaping over the corpses of the dead, and jumping up to lick his face.

"Down! Down!" he said, almost laughing. Almost crying.

Gray Coat lifted a conch shell to her lips and blew. She bent forward to touch, respectfully, one of the hooves of the shaman. "We must go. Our rear guard cannot hold off the Cursed Ones forever. You must be well away before they march out in force."

"Yes," agreed Li'at'dano. "I fell for their traps once. Not again." She laid her head down and, with a ragged breath, closed her eyes.

Alain lifted his hands from the wagon's side just as it lurched forward, pulled by two strong centaur women. Torches lined the roads, and an eerie whistling rose from the assembled centaurs as the wagon passed through their ranks.

"Come," said Agalleos, taking Alain by the arm. "We must go with them."

"But we have to go back to get Adica!"

"The road back is closed to us now. The Cursed Ones will roam everywhere because of this. It isn't safe."

"But—"

Sos'ka trotted up. "Here is my cousin," she said, indicating a husky centaur who bore a remarkable resemblance to Sos'ka: shoulders the width of Beor's and muscular arms. Like all the others, she went naked, not a scrap of clothing. "She will carry you for the first part of the road."

"Come," said Agalleos.

Rage and Sorrow nosed against him, licking his hands. In the distance, a shout raised from Spider's Fort. Already the mass of centaurs had fallen in to follow the wagon, torches fading into the distance as they picked up speed.

Alone, he could not make his way back to Shu-Sha's camp through unknown country now surely buzzing with agitated soldiers on the lookout for creeping enemies. In a way, it seemed like losing the phoenix feather was a terrible omen. Anger and fear warred within him, until he remembered the Holy One's whispered words about Adica: "Who needs you."

No matter what came next, he would find a way back to her.

XVII
POISON

1

AFTER twenty days marching west, the armies moving in parallel columns under separate commanders, they began to get sporadic and possibly exaggerated reports of a large Quman force moving north along the Veser River, closing in on Osterburg. Just as they were. The thought of facing Bulkezu again made Zacharias so sick that he could scarcely bring himself to eat.

Rumors flew violently among the troops, often accompanied by fistfights. Who would command, when the battle came that everyone was hoping for? Henry had *said* that he meant Princess Sapientia to be his heir, her soldiers argued; but he never anointed her, Sanglant's loyal followers retorted. They had heard the king offer Aosta and its crown to Sanglant. Didn't that count for anything? Not if he'd refused it, the answer went. He was still a bastard, after all, even if he was a great fighter and leader.

No one could answer that objection satisfactorily: he was still a bastard, after all.

It was rumored that Princess Sapientia was pregnant. When at last the call came down through the ranks that there would be a trial by combat to determine who had the right to command, everyone knew that she would therefore choose her husband as her champion. The church sometimes used such trials to determine which person God ordained as victor when an irreconcilable dispute was brought before a biscop. Only one could win, and that one would win the right to command the combined armies, now almost three thousand mounted warriors, a huge force with more lordly and monastic retinues joining up every day as they marched west, gathering strength and resolve.

The road in this region of Saony was more a wagon track, but at least the local residents at the villages and estates had heard rumors of the atrocities committed by the Quman army to the south and were, for that reason, only somewhat reluctant to give over stores of their newly harvested grain to the army.

They set camp early that night where three grassy meadows cut a swath of open ground through woodland. Sheep and cattle grazed, watched over by shepherds. The commanders ordered half the beasts taken from the herds to feed the army and sent the rest on their way to discourage hungry soldiers from stealing what they wished under cover of night.

The two armies gathered just before twilight in the central meadow, where a slope ran down to a stream. Grass grew abundantly. The soldiers took their places on the slope while servants set up a pavilion by the stream's edge for those nobles privileged enough to attend Princess Sapientia: Bayan's Ungrian retainers, Lord Wichman, the Polenie duke Boleslas, Hrodik and Druthmar, Brigida with her levies from Avaria, a lady from Fesse, and several nobles from the marchlands who had joined to avenge the damage done to their lands by the Quman.

Prince Bayan's mother had been brought forward in her palanquin, but of course, with all the veils drawn and curtains closed, no one could see her nor ever would. She had a new slave, one of the ones she'd bought at Machteburg: a well-built

Quman youth standing beside one of the carrying poles. Like the other three, he watched without expression as the proceedings unfolded, as though he was both deaf and mute. Had the old woman ensorcelled all those who served her? Had she cast a love spell over Sapientia to make the princess besotted with her husband?

"It does seem odd to me, said Zacharias to Heribert, glancing around to make sure no one was paying attention to them, "that Prince Bayan commands her army in all but name." They stood behind the chair, placed to the left of Sapientia's, set aside for Blessing.

"Does it? That's not what puzzles me. King Henry must have guessed that whatever man married Sapientia would be likely to rule as her equal, not her consort. Bayan's a good man, but he isn't Wendish and he's scarcely a Daisanite. How can Henry think the Wendish nobles, much less a duke as proud as Conrad, would accept a foreign king reigning over them?"

Behind them, Blessing shrieked. She was crouching on the edge of the stream, half lost in the rushes that crowded the shore, tossing stones into the water while Anna, Matto, and Lord Thiemo hovered next to her to make sure she didn't fall in.

Zacharias smiled derisively. "Do not ask me, Brother. I am only a common-born frater."

"So you are," agreed Heribert amiably. "But much cleaner than you were when we first met you. As outside, so inside. I still value your insight."

"I have nothing insightful to say on this subject. Of the king's progress and its intrigues I remain ignorant, as befits my station."

A shout rose from the assembled armies. Blessing leaped up, tottered unbalanced on the edge of the stream, and was caught by Thiemo, who escorted her back to the pavilion. She climbed up to stand on the seat of her chair.

"Here, now, Your Highness," Heribert said reprovingly as

she clung to his shoulders, trying to get a good look out along
the meadow. "Remember your dignity."

"Look!" Lord Thiemo's words were echoed by those nobles
clustered under the shade of the pavilion. "Here they come."
He pointed toward the two riders approaching the pavilion
through the grass, one from the north and one from the south.
Both horses were being led, giving their approach a dignified
pace suitable to the gravity of the occasion.

"Why Wolfhere?" Zacharias demanded, feeling the familiar
gnaw of envy at his gut as he watched the old Eagle leading
Prince Sanglant's horse.

Heribert's answering smile was bittersweet. "This isn't easy
for him, you know. Best to remind everyone from the outset
how far outside the king's approval he stands."

It took Zacharias a moment to realize that Heribert was *not*
speaking of Wolfhere.

Bayan and Sanglant were both outfitted in their armor,
although they weren't wearing their helmets. Sanglant wore
his sword slung over his back, in the manner of a traveler,
while Bayan's sword was belted at his hip. Bayan wore a tabard
of snow-white linen with a two-headed eagle embroidered in
red, the sigil of Ungria, and dagged ends in alternating red
and white that flowed past his knees. Sanglant wore a plain
gold tabard, without any identifying sigil, his only ornament
the magnificent dragon helm, which he carried under one
arm. Sapientia moved forward with a trio of ladies, one holding a tray set with two silver cups and a second carrying a
pitcher. The third, a cleric, stood slightly to one side.

"She doesn't *look* pregnant," muttered Lord Thiemo.

"Hush, my lord," said Anna sharply, the way one would to
a wayward brother. "A woman may be waxing without being
full. It's said she hasn't burned holy rags for three months. If a
woman isn't bleeding, then she must be pregnant. That's what
they always said in Gent."

"I've seen cases where women weren't bleeding but nevertheless were not—" began Zacharias, but Thiemo cut him off.

"Nay, Anna is right. I was wrong to speak so." He looked at her, and she at him; an odd alliance, when you thought of it: the young lordling and the nut-brown common girl, almost a woman. Zacharias could not shake the feeling that there was something more to it than their devotion to Blessing. Even Matto, standing behind them, had been drawn in although he had at first been jealous of Thiemo. They formed a tight circle that ringed the little girl.

The two combatants came to a halt about ten paces apart. Sanglant took the reins from Wolfhere and handed the Eagle his helm. Bayan exchanged helm for reins with his Ungrian groom. Then the riders moved around so they sat side by side as though poised for a race. They did not look at each other.

The cleric raised her arms. "Let the trial begin."

Sapientia poured ale into the two cups. Three noble witnesses from each army examined them and proclaimed themselves satisfied that they held an equal amount. Carefully, the cups were handed up, one to Bayan and one to Sanglant.

All this time, Blessing clung to Heribert's shoulders and did not speak one word, only stared, wide-eyed.

Those on foot stepped back, to leave the field clear for the duelists. Captain Thiadbold of the Lions stepped forward and raised a horn to his lips.

He blew.

The two armies erupted in cheers and whistles as the two riders urged their horses forward, each man holding the reins in one hand and the full cup in the other. Neck and neck, they raced across the meadow, reached the woodland fringe, turned their horses neatly and rode back at a canter. They passed the cleric side by side, neck and neck, and pulled up. The crowd fell silent as they handed their cups to the cleric and she compared the level of ale remaining.

She raised a cup. "Prince Bayan, the winner!"

Shouting and laughter drowned out everything else as Bayan, laughing, demanded a full cup of ale. Sanglant, too, took a freshly poured cup; he downed it in one gulp and asked for a second. Although he had a smile on his face, his expression was grim.

Blessing began to cry. "He lost," she said, and then, in a lower and more furious voice, "he lost on purpose."

"Nay, sweetling," said Heribert sternly, "he didn't lose. He did what he had to do for the kingdom, and don't ever think otherwise. Defeating the Quman matters more than anything right now."

She was not to be consoled, but she kept her sorrow quiet, as her father had ordered her earlier that day, and buried her head in Heribert's shoulder. Such a big girl, she was getting to be. So quick to understand the twists and turns of intrigue that plagued the nobly born.

Zacharias glanced back at Thiemo and Anna, fallen to whispering as the celebration continued on the field beyond and the armies began to disperse back to their tents. He knew they weren't lovers. Anna was not really old enough, in truth; she couldn't be more than thirteen or fourteen. Anyway, Prince Sanglant would never have allowed it—a little piece of hypocrisy that rather cheered Zacharias. It was good to know that even the most admirable of men might succumb to weakness now and again. It made Zacharias feel better, since his own weaknesses seemed so bold and starkly drawn in contrast. He had so very many of them.

Blessing wiped her face on Heribert's sleeve and wriggled out of his grasp, jumping down to the ground. Heribert was frowning, fingering a leather cord he had recently begun to wear around his neck.

"You don't like it," said Zacharias softly, seeing the other man's gaze on the mob out in the field, surrounding the two contestants. Sanglant had downed his fourth cup of ale.

"It's what the captain of the Dragons would have done," replied Heribert, "but he isn't captain of the King's Dragons any longer."

"Nay, Brother, you know yourself that the greatest threat isn't even the Quman. Or so you've told me."

"True enough." Heribert saw Wolfhere cutting his way through the crowd toward them. "Sister Anne is the greatest threat. So be it." He moved forward to meet Wolfhere.

Heribert and Wolfhere had gotten thick as thieves lately, plotting and scheming with Sanglant while, as always, Zacharias was left out in the cold, as ignorant as a beggar's starving brat. Envy made him dizzy as he watched the two men—elegant cleric and elderly commoner—meet and exchange words. Did they not trust him? Did Wolfhere speak against him? Was Zacharias somehow deemed less loyal than the turncoat Eagle? Little use in continuing his feud with Wolfhere, but he could not help himself; that was yet another of his weaknesses, that he held grudges as tightly as a drowning man clutches a spar and would not let them go even when they no longer did him any good. He wasn't even as good a man as any one of that ragtag group which had remained behind in the ruined fortress that day months ago outside Walburg. Not one of them had betrayed Zacharias' shameful behavior to the prince. Not one had mentioned it, even though they had all seen him bolt and run, ready to abandon the child they were fighting for.

No wonder no one trusted him.

In his nightmares, and they were plentiful, he still saw those two Quman soldiers pulling around and making ready to shoot him. Sometimes he wished that they had.

Behind, Blessing grabbed hold of Anna's hand and led her back to the stream's edge while she chattered on in her piercing voice. "Tell me again about the phoenix!"

Wolfhere and Heribert bent heads together, speaking intently as Heribert's frown deepened. Zacharias crept closer, but their voices were so low that he couldn't make out more than phrases and words, nothing to make sense of. After a bit, the prince himself strode up, none the worse for his heavy drinking until you saw the way his eyes tightened with anger despite the pleasant expression masking his face. He took hold of Wolfhere by the shoulder.

"Tell me truly, Wolfhere, is this Eagle's sight illusion or real?"

"Alas, my lord prince, it has never lied to me in all my days."

"Then your sight is more truthful than your tongue, Eagle. Anne made skopos with my father's blessing!" He glanced toward Bayan. The Ungrian prince, as jovial as ever, was accepting the congratulations of various nobles from among Sapientia's train. No one begrudged him his victory; he had proved himself worthy, even if he was a foreigner. "Pray to God, Heribert," he looked around and saw Zacharias, "and you, too, Zacharias, no matter what you believe now. Pray to God to grant me patience to endure what I must for the sake of the kingdom, and the wits to learn intrigue." He laughed harshly, drawing his little retinue away from the crowd, seeking his daughter where she splashed merrily in the stream, pretending to be a bird rising from the water. "Bloodheart taught me well, although he never meant to do me any favors. If his dogs couldn't tear out my throat in Gent, then these dogs surely will not do so now. Ai, God, to think that my father offered me the kingdom and I turned it down!"

"Your Highness!" said Wolfhere, surprised. "What do you mean?"

"No matter." Sanglant lengthened his stride, moving out through the grass away from the rest of them as he called to his daughter. He wore a leather cord around his neck and now, restless, he pulled it out to cup his hand over a round leaf of silver engraved with various signs. "My father would not have named Anne as skopos and fallen victim to her lies if I had been at his side, advising him. She would never have gained such influence if it had been me who had ridden to Aosta with Adelheid as my queen."

He stopped dead as his daughter crowed in triumph, having escaped Thiemo's efforts to catch her, and turned on Wolfhere. "Or you could be telling Anne everything that you've learned while riding with me. You could be hiding from me what she tells you."

"So I could, Your Highness. And I could kill your daughter while she sleeps. Lord Thiemo is a good boy, but not my match."

"The old wolf is wise and subtle. Tell me, Wolfhere, how does one learn intrigue?"

"What sort of intrigue do you wish to learn?"

"The intrigue of the king's court. It's said that you were my grandfather Arnulf's favorite. You, a common-born man. Folk must have hated you because he listened to you above all others."

"So they did. And your father most of all."

"Nay, truly? I thought he hated you because you tried to drown me."

"Well, that didn't help. But Henry hated me long before that. He envied me my place at King Arnulf's side. Young men are prone to jealousies, my lord prince, and strange fancies. Yet Arnulf always knew Henry's worth. There was never any doubt in his mind which of his children had been born with the luck of the king."

"What of Henry's children?" Sanglant glanced back toward the crowd of nobles gathered to celebrate Bayan's victory. Sapientia stood beside her husband, bright and happy, handsome and shining, yet beside the Ungrian prince she looked as light as a feather, ready to float away at the least puff of wind. She hadn't any weight.

"Ah." Wolfhere smiled, baring his teeth as a wolf might when it snarls. "What *of* Henry's children? Don't forget that he has another child now, the infant Mathilda, born to Adelheid. A strong, healthy girl, though she is still a suckling babe."

"What are you suggesting?"

"That Henry's children by Sophia aren't the only ones who can inherit his throne, Your Highness. He has two others. The newborn Mathilda. And you."

Sanglant glared at Wolfhere until the old Eagle fidgeted, looking curiously nervous in the face of the prince's obvious anger and grief. "Find my wife, Eagle. Why has your Eagle's sight failed you? Has she hidden herself from you? Where has she gone?"

Wolfhere had no answer for him.

"I pray you, my lord prince," said Heribert quietly, "it is like poison to the skin to handle it too much. Nor should you display it openly."

Sanglant started, glanced at the silver medallion in his hand, and slipped it back under his tunic.

Only then, with the three men standing close together, did Zacharias realized that all three—prince, cleric, and Eagle—wore similar amulets concealed under their clothing, a protection against sorcery.

2

HOW long ago it seemed that she had had the leisure to sit in the scriptorium and work uninterrupted on her *History of the Wendish People!* It had been so long that the blessed Queen Matilda, of glorious memory, to whom the work was dedicated, had died without ever seeing a finished work. These days, Rosvita wondered if there ever would be a finished work.

As she moved through the sunny scriptorium, she noted the scribes busy at their work, clerics from the king's schola copying out capitularies, deeds, and charters as well as letters pertaining to the king's business here and in the north. So many rounded shoulders, so many busy hands. Now and again clerics looked up from their work to nod at her or ask for advice. More by accident than design, she was now in charge of Henry's schola. Queen Adelheid had her own schola, made up of clerics from Aosta and overseen by Hugh, who had been assigned as the Holy Mother's official emissary to the Queen.

"Sister Rosvita, ought we to be writing this cartulary to establish the county of Ivria? Shouldn't that properly be done in the Queen's schola?"

"Nay, Brother Eudes, we mean to establish King Henry's right and obligation to rule in these lands so that none will protest if the skopos agrees to crown him as Emperor. Therefore, any grant must come from Henry and Adelheid together." She walked on, pausing where light streamed in to paint gold over the parquet floor.

"Sister, we have heard another report of heresy, this time from Biscop Odila at Mainni. How are we to answer?"

"Patience, Sister Elsebet. The skopos has already indicated that she will hold a council on this matter next year. Write to Biscop Odila that she must confine those who will not recant so that they cannot corrupt the innocent, but by no means to act rashly. Avoid at all costs any public trial, until after the council, because it is in the nature of people to make martyrs where they can. We must beware making martyrs of these heretics. Can you render that in your own words, Sister?"

Elsebet had been with a schola for ten years, just the kind of cleric who did better if given a little independence to work. She smiled sharply. "Of course, Sister Rosvita. I am glad that the charge of the king's schola has fallen to you. In truth, the skopos' clerics and presbyters rule with too heavy a hand for my liking. I daresay the custom is different here in Aosta than it is in the north."

Farther on, Ruoda and Heriburg sat side by side, one white-scarfed head and one pale blue one, intent on their copying.

"How comes the work?" Rosvita asked quietly as she paused beside them.

They had, open on the lectern above them, the *Vita* of St. Radegundis. Heriburg was continuing the copy started by Sister Amabilia, and Ruoda had begun a second copy, which Rosvita hoped to send to Korvei for safekeeping.

"Well enough." Ruoda had blotted a word and now scraped the offending ink away with her writing knife.

Heriburg was ruling a blank sheet of parchment. She did not look away from her work as she answered, her voice so low that Rosvita had to bend nearer in order to hear. "We dared

not speak to you this morning, Sister, because of the many visitors you had in your chambers. We have more gossip than you
could possibly want—"

"Never underestimate how much gossip can be useful to the
king, Heriburg. Go on."

Ruoda's smile flashed but she looked up only to read the
next line from the *Vita*, above her, and to dip her quill in the
inkpot.

"A Sister Venia came to the palace in the train of the Holy
Mother, Anne, when she first appeared here last summer. An
elderly woman with white hair and a pleasant, round face,
well spoken, well mannered, well educated, and nobly born.
She was heard to say only that she came out of the noble lineage of Karrone. Soon after she arrived a presbyter was heard to
claim that she was his cousin, a granddaughter of the
Karronish princely family who had been made a biscop and
then detained for black sorcery, but he died soon after of
apoplexy and could not therefore substantiate his claim. No
one liked him anyway, so we hear. But in any case, Sister Venia
made no enemies while she was here."

"*Was* here?"

Heriburg studied the newly-ruled parchment, frowning as
she measured the space and the amount she could fit into it
and where she would break the words. She had left space for an
illustration, but that work would go to Brother Jehan.

"Now she is missing, Sister. She was last seen in those desperate days after the death of the Holy Mother Clementia,
may her memory be blessed, and before the arrival of Queen
Adelheid and King Henry."

"A strange thing, too," murmured Ruoda, pausing to trim
her quill, "because until we reminded people of the woman, it
was as if everyone had forgotten her."

"I hope you did not draw attention to yourselves."

Heriburg glanced up, her face as bland as pudding but her
gaze as sharp as pins. "Have you ever noticed the similarity in
Dariyan of the words 'forgiveness' and 'poison'? 'Venia' and

'veneni.' Many in the palace still wonder about Ironhead's death, and about the death of the Holy Mother Clementia, may God have mercy on her. It is only a small slip of the tongue to introduce another name, and clerics are in truth the worst of gossips, given encouragement."

"Have you told Brother Fortunatus this news? He's still waiting to meet with the lay sister from St. Ekatarina's."

"We informed him last night, Sister. He hoped to meet with the lay sister just before Lauds."

"I thank you, Sisters. You did well." Ruoda grinned, as if expecting the praise, but Heriburg dropped her gaze humbly. A gem, and a jewel, as Mother Otta often said of her best novices, worthy to serve in the regnant's crown. "Now back to your work. It will not do for everyone to see you gossiping here with me."

Farther on stood the stool and sloping writing desk set aside for her personal use. With a sigh of relief and hope, she settled down, trimmed four quills, and studied the words she had written out that morning, copying from her wax tablet: the final days of Arnulf the Younger.

> At that time, having taken both Wendar and Varre fully under his control, he was called by his army Lord, King, and Protector of all. His fame spread to all lands, and many nobles from other realms came to visit him, hoping to find favor in his sight, for truly it could be said of him that he denied nothing to his friends and granted no mercy to his enemies. Having at last subjugated the eastern tribes and having thrown the Eika raiders back into the sea, he announced his intention to make a pilgrimage to the holy city of Darre for the sake of prayer.
>
> Yet within a week of this announcement, his infirmities so disabled him that he was forced to retire to his bed.
>
> He called together the leading nobles of the realm and in their presence designated his son Henry as regnant. To his other children he granted honors and lands of great worth as well as a share of the regnant's treasure, but Henry was made ruler over

his sisters and brothers and named king of Wendar and Varre and the marchlands.

After his will had been made legal and all in attendance had acclaimed Henry as king, so passed away that great lord, who had by his efforts united Wendar and Varre and, being first among equals and matchless in all those virtues governing mind and body, stood as the greatest of all regnants reigning in all the lands. He reigned for eighteen years and lived to see the age of four and fifty. He was buried in Quedlinhame before the Lady's Hearth. That day, many wept and all mourned.

She wiped away a tear. The memory of that bitter day, which she had witnessed as a young woman, still had the power to move her. She rubbed the parchment with pumice before taking up knife and quill to begin writing.

Here ends the First Book of the Deeds of the Great Princes.

She had to scrape away the last letter and write it again, but at last, with a quiet chuckle, she sat back and surveyed the final sentence. Hard to believe that this portion was, at long last, concluded. Yet truly, there would be no rest for the wicked: she still had to write the second part, her chronicle of Henry's reign so far. Sometimes it seemed the work would never end. There was always more to tell than space to tell it.

She dabbed her quill in the ink pot.

Here begins the Second Book—

"Sister Rosvita." Fortunatus came up behind her. He bent as if to examine the parchment, keeping his voice low. "Paloma did not meet me this morning. She has been patient, but I swear to you that yesterday when I met her, she was frightened. I convinced her to remain one more day. . . . but now I fear—" He broke off as a man wearing the red cloak of a presbyter walked into the scriptorium, marked Rosvita, and headed along the aisles toward her.

"We'll speak later, Brother."

The vault of ceiling made the scriptorium an airy place, filled with light. Watching Brother Petrus approach, Rosvita had leisure to examine the painted frieze at the far end of the room: martyrs and saints receiving their crowns of glory from the angels.

"Sister Rosvita." He inclined his head. She hid a smile, regarding him somberly. She had the king's confidence, the respect of the schola, and the ear of the queen. A presbyter like Petrus, however nobly born, did not wield as much influence as she did, and he knew it. "I have been sent by Lord Hugh to request your presence in the skopos' chambers."

Rosvita sighed, setting down her knife and handing the still wet quill to Fortunatus. He could only nod, frustrated and helpless, as she left him in charge of her history.

They crossed out of the regnant's palace and into the gilded corridors of the skopos' palace, dense with silence as a mere handful of presbyters, clerics, and servants hurried along the halls on their errands. No wall here was untouched; murals, friezes, paintings, or tapestries covered every wall. Columns were inlaid with tiny tiles or painted bright colors. Sculptures filled the courtyards and lined the colonnaded arcades down which they walked, in blessed shadow, while the sun beat down on empty graveled pathways beyond. This time of year, even as afternoon drifted toward twilight, no one walked under the sun because of the heat.

It was as quiet as if a spell lay over the palace. Pausing once at a break in the wall where she could see out over the city, she marked how the river dazzled as it wound through the streets, crossed in four places by bridges. A stuporous haze hung over Darre. Had even the buildings fallen asleep?

Pray God autumn would come soon, with cooler weather. She was sweating freely, had to dab at her forehead with her sleeve. They crossed into the heart of the palace and came to a door set with the skopos' seal, a private audience chamber. Brother Petrus stood aside. Rosvita entered alone.

Mercifully, the Tile Chamber was dark and cool, surrounded by thick earthen walls and decorated with pale tiles, set out in geometric patterns said to represent the path of the soul as it ascends through the seven spheres toward the Chamber of Light. The skopos sat in a simple chair notable for its high back carved in a pattern of linked circles. Her ferocious black hound lay at her feet, growling softly as Rosvita approached but not raising its head. The chair, elevated on a low dais, presided over a set of benches, five deep, set in a semicircle facing the dais. A table stood between the foremost benches and the dais step.

Only five people inhabited the chamber: the skopos, Hugh, a servingwoman dressed simply in a pale shift belted with rope, and two elderly people wearing the garb of clerics. One lay on a couch in the shadows, half hidden, silent. Hugh and the other man stood at the table, holding open a scroll. A lit lamp stood at either end of the map, but it seemed to Rosvita that their light did more to illuminate Hugh's handsome face than the faded markings on the scroll.

"Pray approach, Sister Rosvita," said the skopos in her cool voice, extending her right hand.

Rosvita came forward cautiously, well aware of that huge hound so close that it could rip off her hand with one bite, but it did not react beyond another soft growl as she knelt on the steps to kiss Anne's ring, the seal of her office. "Holy Mother, you honor me with your summons."

Not a flicker of a smile touched the skopos' face. She might have been carved in stone. It was hard to imagine anyone more regal sitting in that chair, though. Henry had been wise to grant her the skopos' throne. That way, she could never challenge him for the earthly throne. "If you will, Sister, examine the scroll."

Hugh moved aside to make room for her at the table, nodding with what appeared a genuine smile as she took her place beside him. The other man, older, with a severe face lined with old resentments and a more recent illness, examined her disapprovingly.

"It's papyrus," she said, "and so likely ancient. These symbols marked at the border of the map are not of Daisanite origin. I would say they are heathen and probably meant to represent heathen gods or perhaps the seven heavenly bodies. It is a map." She touched it hesitantly, because something about its markings made a bell chime in her mind. "Here are mountains, a river, a forest, and the sea." She pointed at each as she spoke the word. "It seems the map represents the placement of seven sites, towns perhaps, or temples. Hard to say. Here are six scattered through the land equidistant from the seventh, which lies in the center, ringed by mountains. Each site is represented by seven marks, like arrow points, which echo the larger design: six in a ring around a central seventh."

"What is it a map of, Sister Rosvita?" asked Anne.

The elder man grunted. Hugh took a step away from the table.

Rosvita had learned in a hard school not to betray surprise, and she did not do so now, as an inkling of what she was looking at lit in her mind. "Perhaps the continent of Novaria, Holy Mother. This sea could be the north sea, and here might be the middle sea, and these the Alfar Mountains. It is a crude representation, if so, but I have seen sailors' maps that show a similar outline of the coast. I have myself crossed the Alfar Mountains three times and know that they stand in about this place."

"What do you know about the coming cataclysm, Sister?" asked the Holy Mother. "About the attack of the Lost Ones, who wish to regain their empire and enslave all of humankind?"

"Nothing more than what I have heard, Holy Mother. Prince Sanglant spoke of a cataclysm, as did his mother, when they sojourned briefly at the king's progress last spring. But they both left when it appeared to them that the king was not willing to heed their words."

"Did you heed them?"

"I would need more evidence, Holy Mother. I confess it is a difficult story to believe. I have read many chronicles in my time. Many times good souls have cried out to warn the regnant of a coming disaster only to discover that they were mistaken in their reading of the stars, or the omens, or the Holy Verses themselves. God's will is a difficult book for mortals to read."

"Are you learned in astronomy, Sister?"

"I confess ignorance in such matters. I learned no more than any apt pupil would in a convent. I can recognize the constellations and I can identify the wandering stars in the sky." She smiled slightly. "I remember that Aturna takes twenty-eight years to circle the zodiac, while Mok takes twelve, but I confess I cannot recall the periods of the others. Somorhas and Erekes lie between Earth and the sphere of the Sun, so they are often lost in the glare of the Sun. Somorhas appears as both Morning and Evening Star, never at the same time, and sometimes disappears altogether. I pray pardon, Holy Mother. Early in my studies I became enamored of history, and I neglected the other arts in its favor."

"So it appears," said the skopos, yet by no means did she speak reprovingly, only to note what she had heard. A bell rang softly. The servingwoman hurried to the door, spoke there with an unseen servant, and returned to the Holy Mother.

"The emissary from Salia, Your Excellence."

"Let him in."

A portly man, flushed from the heat, knelt on the steps to kiss the skopos' ring. "Holy Mother." He dabbed at his face with a handkerchief, but it might have been fear of the hound and not the heat that made him sweat so freely. "I am at your service."

"Here is Brother Severus," said Anne to the emissary, indicating the elderly cleric. "You will take him personally to

Salia on your return, and see that his every wish is fulfilled. He is my personal representative."

"I am at your command, Holy Mother." He spoke Dariyan with the distinctive Salian accent, the soft "v" hardening, the hard "gn" going soft. "I do not know if we can cross the pass this late in the year. I've gotten word that there've already been heavy snows in the northern passes, quite untimely."

"But you have heard no reports from the western passes, Brother. I feel sure that if you leave at once, you will have a successful journey."

He eyed her with a mixture of awe and apprehension. Perhaps he had heard the rumors that she was a powerful sorcerer, exactly the sort of person whose activities had been condemned as recently as one hundred years ago at the Council of Narvone. It was not something ever spoken of out loud and certainly never to her face.

Or maybe he was only afraid that the black hound was going to lunge to its feet and rip his face off.

"As you command, Holy Mother. We can leave in the morning, if that is your wish."

"It is." Anne dismissed him, and the servingwoman escorted him to the door. After a silence, she rose and, with the hound at her heels, came down to the table, smoothing her hand over the ancient papyrus. It had gone yellow with age, flaking at the edges. "What evidence do you need, Sister Rosvita, to be convinced of the danger that awaits us all if we do not act?"

"Perhaps it is impossible to convince me, Holy Mother, without hard evidence, but that does not mean I cannot see the purpose to preparing for such an eventuality, in case it comes about. Yet why would Sanglant's mother come to Henry and offer an alliance if her people wish only to enslave and dominate us? Can a dialogue not be started?"

"With whom? Where is the Aoi woman now, Sister? Where is Prince Sanglant?"

"I cannot answer either question."

"The Aoi woman has returned to her people to raise an
army, now that she sees that humankind have no will to fight.
Prince Sanglant also left to gather an army."

"For what purpose? How do you know this?"

"Surely you know of that skill commonly called 'Eagle's
sight'? Eagles are not alone in making use of it."

The wick of one of the lamps hissed as it came to the end of
the oil. The servingwoman hastened to refill the belly of the
lamp while Rosvita caught hold of her thoughts, for once so
horrified that she could not even voice mindless pleasantries to
pass the awkward moment. If Anne could use Eagle's sight,
then she could spy on anyone.

Anyone.

Yet even Anne could not spy on people constantly, and then
only one at a time, using such methods. Every skopos was
known to have spies, clerics moving through the palace in
Darre and the courts of far-flung regnants, reporting back
what they observed to the Holy Mother. How was this different?

"Where is Prince Sanglant now, Holy Mother?"

Odd, and troubling, to see annoyance brush its sharp claws
across that normally serene face. "Well hidden," said Anne,
reaching to scratch the hound's ears, and by this means concealing her expression as she went on, "no doubt with the aid
of his mother's magic. Why conceal himself if he has nothing
to hide?"

"Why indeed?" Rosvita glanced away to see Severus examining the map while Hugh listened with obvious interest.
"Yet I have not forgotten the Eagle sent by Princess
Theophanu, who spoke of troubles at work in the land, including Quman raiders."

When Anne straightened, her features displayed as impassive a mask as ever. "Be assured that I have looked, Sister
Rosvita. I have seen no Quman army."

"You do not think Prince Sanglant might be raising an
army to fight the barbarians?"

"I do not know the mind of Prince Sanglant. Wendar is plagued by much unrest in these days, which comes in many guises. A wise mind recognizes these troubles as a sign of the cataclysm to come, for the earth itself shifts and trembles, knowing the dreadful fate that awaits it when the Lost Ones work their terrible magic to force their return."

"It is difficult to argue against you, Holy Mother, considering the extent and depth of your knowledge."

"So it is," agreed Anne. She lifted a hand. At once several servants, previously unseen, hurried out of the shadows. The cleric reclining on the couch was lying, it now transpired, on a litter, which made it easy for the four servants to carry her out of the chamber. Even so, Rosvita could not *quite* get a glimpse of that person, only that she was small and dark. How strange that she should observe the whole and yet never speak or be spoken to. Yet it was too late to discover who she was now.

Brother Severus retreated, as did Hugh, with a smile and a bow, and at last the servingwoman went out and shut the door behind her. The black hound yawned, displaying fearsome teeth.

"Now you will tell me, Sister," said Anne, facing Rosvita, "why you persist in not trusting me. I have served as Holy Mother for only one month. Have I given offense? Have you heard aught of me that leads you to believe that I am plotting evil?"

For an instant Rosvita felt the thrill of panic, but she knew how to think fast. "Only this, Holy Mother. Hugh of Austra was sent south to face charges that he had soiled his hands with black sorcery. Now he stands as an intimate in the queen's counsel and you have allowed him exceptional authority within the college of presbyters."

"Most of which he had already earned by his own efforts during the last days of my predecessor, Clementia, may her memory be blessed. Is it my trust in Hugh that you do not trust?"

It was hard to judge Anne's age. She might have been about forty years of age, as Rosvita was, or ten years older. Time had not marked her smooth face but neither did she look young; the weight of time, wisdom, and rank cloaked her. She had power, bone-deep and solid, and if she chose to support Henry, then truly there was nothing he could not accomplish. For that, Rosvita was willing to forgive much, if it were true that Anne meant to support Henry rather than merely use him for her own purpose, to thwart the return of the Lost Ones.

Rosvita knew better than to voice such doubts aloud. There were, after all, so many other questions that could be answered, now that she had the opportunity to ask them. "I am a historian, Holy Mother. The good abbess at Korvei, where I received my education, said I would be both saved and damned by my curiosity. I confess freely that I have read the chronicles, and I do not entirely understand your genealogy. I beg pardon if what I say appears rude. Pray trust that it is only the sin of curiosity that leads me to ask."

"You doubt that I am the descendant of Emperor Taillefer?" Was that a flicker of anger, or of amusement? Impossible to tell. The hound growled rather louder than before. Its whipcord tail thumped once against a table leg, almost rocking it.

"I have in my possession the *Vita* of St. Radegundis, as you know, Holy Mother." It wasn't easy to keep her voice even, not with that huge hound glowering at her.

"I have seen it." How coolly she spoke those words, considering that the *Vita* had been written by her own father, a man she had never met. "When you have finished the copies your clerics are making, I will gladly take such a blessed work into the library here, Sister."

Rosvita knew how to swallow regret, although it hurt. "That would be most fitting, Holy Mother. But although I was blessed by God as the vessel through whose hands the *Vita* would pass on its way to you, I am puzzled by the circumstances surrounding Fidelis' marriage. That he was hidden in the cloister and raised as a monk, I can understand. That he succumbed in his autumn years to temptation, I can understand and in truth I pity him, for despite his great age and wisdom it seemed to me that he still thought of the woman with affection and regretted to the end of his life any harm that might have come to her because of his weakness." It was a long speech, and a convoluted argument. She had to choose her words carefully. "But I have never fully understood the identity of your mother, or what happened to her after. How were you then raised, and in what secrecy, with what education, to find you awake to your ancestry, so learned and so wise, and yet unknown to those of us who have studied the chronicles for all of our lives?"

"I was raised by Sister Clothilde, handmaiden of St. Radegundis and later servant to Biscop Tallia, my aunt. My mother was called Lavrentia. She was the unwanted child of a noble family in Varre. It is common for families to place inconvenient children in the church."

Rosvita smiled bitterly, remembering how her brother Ivar had been thrust into the church with no calling and no love for his new position. Count Harl was not a forgiving man, and no doubt rash, impulsive young Ivar had given him trouble one too many times. "So it is, Holy Mother. We can only pray that they all come to serve God with an honest and open heart."

The skopos murmured a blessing in response, fluid and almost mindless, a habit to one raised in clerical surroundings. The hound sat. "She died, and in any case she was very young, not more than fifteen years of age. Sister Clothilde knew well what trouble might erupt in Salia should it be known that a legitimate descendant of Taillefer still lived. She knew that the Salians only let women rule as co-regnants, never alone, and she knew that were it known that I lived, some powerful Salian lord would take me hostage, raise me, and marry me to his son so that his son could claim the kingship of Salia through his use of my body."

"Truly," murmured Rosvita, "a barbaric custom."

"Not so different than King Henry's marriage to Queen Adelheid."

That stung. "Adelheid fled to Henry and begged for his help, Holy Mother. It is true that theirs is a marriage dictated by politics and expediency, but there is true affection and respect as well."

The hound growled, yipping once, threateningly. The skopos mounted the steps and sat, placing her hands on the arms of the chair, which were without any decoration except the polished luster of gold leaf enveloping the wood. She gave a soft command, and the hound at once lay beside her. "Sometimes I wonder, Sister Rosvita. Does God come first in your heart, or does the king?"

"I serve the regnants of Wendar and Varre, as I was raised to do, Holy Mother."

"And I serve humankind, as I was raised to do. Biscop Tallia and Sister Clothilde learned of the threat posed by the Lost Ones, so I was raised to follow in their path, to save humankind by casting the Lost Ones back into the Abyss. Will you aid me, or will you be an obstacle, Sister? The king heeds you. You are well respected, and it is obvious that the king's schola and much of his court will follow your lead, should you chose to speak in my favor. Or against me."

Pray God that her face and voice betrayed nothing. Pray God that no hint of suspicion should fall on her. "Then that is why you were raised in the arts of the mathematici, Holy Mother. That is why your daughter was raised to know those arts as well. Yet such arts still remain condemned by the church you now preside over."

"Condemned because of envy, directed at my aunt, Biscop Tallia, the wisest and most selfless of women. Yet I understand your meaning, Sister Rosvita. I must move cautiously so as not to arouse anger and fear. What we fight, we have fought for long years in secrecy, seeming to sleep and yet remaining awake. It has been our fate and our duty to prepare while humankind slept, oblivious to the approaching danger."

Curious, but never a liar. Rosvita had prided herself for all these years on her honesty, yet was it not said in the Holy Verses that pride was first to fall? "It is a solemn charge, Holy Mother. Pray do not suspect me of ever placing any obstacles in the path of righteousness."

Anne raised a single eyebrow, although it was difficult to tell whether she was surprised, pleased, or skeptical. "As long as we work together as allies, we are therefore in harmony. You may go. Pray be at your leisure to attend me when I next call for you. There is also this matter of reports of heresy in the north to consider. A council must be called, and I am minded to command you to preside over the proceedings."

"I am yours to command, Holy Mother." She was offered the holy ring. With some trepidation, she mounted the dais and kissed it. This time the hound did not even growl, but she could feel the weight of his presence so close beside her. Thanking the Lady for small mercies, and glad to see that she still had all her fingers, she made her own way to the door.

Hugh waited outside in the anteroom, leaning on a windowsill and examining the courtyard beyond, a small garden yellowed with summer's heat. A fountain in the shape of a phoenix trickled at the center, with a fruit-bearing tree growing at each corner. Pears, figs, and apples drooped from weighted branches, awaiting harvest. Smiling amiably, he turned to greet her.

"Sister Rosvita. I was about to walk back to the royal palace. May I escort you?"

"The honor would be mine."

They strolled along shaded arcades. Brother Petrus followed ten steps behind, carrying an unlit lamp.

"I am sorry you could not attend Her Majesty yesterday. We went outside the city to oversee the grape harvest at one of the royal vineyards."

"It is well for Queen Adelheid to get out more," agreed Rosvita. "I am happy to see that she is recovering her health at last."

They spoke for a bit of inconsequential things: Princess
Mathilda, Aostan architecture, the rituals of the grape harvest. What game was Hugh playing? Yet at times like this,
she wondered if he had truly changed. By all reports, and by
her own personal observation, he was pious, discreet, benev-
olent, eloquent but gentle, grave in his authority and yet as
humble as a beggar, affable to every person yet with such an
elegance of manners that he never seemed common. Surely if
he were irretrievably stained by the evil inclination, then that
mark must somehow show in his outward form. But it did
not. It had become something of a joke in the schola that
when queen and presbyter rode out into the streets of Darre,
folk gathered to acclaim her authority and to marvel at his
beauty.

They stepped out from a colonnade to cross a courtyard on
a graveled path, white stones crunching under their feet.
Afternoon shadows drew long across the neatly raked garden
and crisscrossing paths. Above, parapets rose, visible beyond
the roofs of the palace.

"The Holy Mother means to appoint you to oversee a council on this heresy that troubles the north."

"So she has given me to understand. I fear I am not qualified
to lead such an investigation."

"Nay, Sister, do not say so. You are respected by all. It is
well known that your judgments are made without any regard
to your own personal inclinations. I cannot think of any person
in the church who is as widely trusted as you are." They
stepped onto the portico that framed the entrance, three monumental arches, that led from the skopos' palace into the
forecourt of the royal compound. Rosvita had never gotten
used to the speed with which the sun set here in the south; no
long, lingering twilights common to summer days in the
north. Darkness was already falling, drowning them in shadow
beneath the heavy arches. She could barely make out the elongated figures of saints carved into the facade, pale forms
looming above them, stern but merciful.

"I am troubled, Sister," said Hugh softly. Brother Petrus waited obediently behind them, just out of earshot. In the forecourt beyond, torches were being lit, placed in sconces around the court, light flaring and smoke streaming toward the heavens. A dozen grooms hurried out from the open gate that led in to the stable yard. Distantly, from the direction of the road that led down into the city, she heard shouting and cheers.

She said nothing, only waited, and after a moment Hugh went on. "What would you do if you discovered an ancient text in whose words you read an account of the very heresy that even now pollutes the kingdom?"

"What do you mean? It's well known that the Arethousan church remains in error on certain matters of doctrine. At least one of these—these arguments over the nature of the human and divine substance of the blessed Daisan—are part of the heresy as well. Everything I have heard indicates that the heresy comes out of the east."

He stood in profile, visible in the twilight only as a shade, like a man caught between the living world and the dead. "I do not know where to go. I believe I have found an account written by St. Thecla herself in which she describes the flaying and redemption of the blessed Daisan, just as it is said to have happened in this poisonous heresy."

"A forgery." But she could barely force the words out. That such a statement should come from Hugh, of all people, set her completely off-balance. She was either a fool, or he was a consummate actor, but he seemed to her eyes, and to her instincts, to be truly distraught.

"I have labored to prove exactly that, but I fear—"

"Make way for King Henry!"

Soldiers raced to stand at attention in the spacious fore-court. Cries of acclaim rose from the city below as the king and his retinue neared the gate.

"This is unexpected." She had to yell to be heard over the clamor.

"Come." He drew her forward by the arm.

Queen Adelheid appeared, framed by the huge bronze doors that opened onto the entryway of the great hall, just as the first horsemen rode into the forecourt. They bore the banners of Henry and Adelheid. Behind them came the king himself and his closest companions: Duke Burchard of Avaria, Duchess Liutgard of Fesse, Margrave Villam, several Aostan nobles, and of course his stalwart Eagle, Hathui. No man there, nor woman either, outshone Henry. He was hale and healthy, not one bit the worse for the wear after a summer campaigning in Aosta's brutal heat. He dismounted, handed his reins to a groom, and hurried to greet Adelheid. But even as he led his entourage into the hall, he spotted Rosvita.

"My good counselor!" Thus summoned, she cut a path through the crowd to his side, Hugh trailing modestly behind her. "Come, Sister, you will sit at my left hand while we eat."

Supper was laid at the feasting tables, nothing magnificent, but sufficient for soldiers ridden in from the field. Adelheid sat at Henry's right hand in splendid robes she had somehow contrived to be wearing—as though she had known he was coming. Maybe she had. The king could have sent a courier, but if he had, then why, Rosvita wondered as she took her place at the king's side, had she and the schola not heard the tidings?

Had Hugh stopped her on the portico so she could witness the king's arrival and understand that she had less power than he had, in his graceful speech, claimed for her?

Nay, she chided herself, you are grown too suspicious.

A steward brought a basin of water and a cloth so that Henry could wipe the dust of the road off his hands and face. Servants hurried in with a clear broth, followed by roasted game hens basted in mint sauce. When the first bite of hunger had been calmed, Adelheid rose with cup in hand. "Let there be an accounting of the summer's victories!" she cried, to general acclaim.

Hathui recited a clear if undramatic account of the army's successes: three packs of Jinna bandits put to the sword; seven sieges brought to a peaceful conclusion, although Lord Gezo was still holding out in Navlia; emissaries from Arethousan potentates who were not eager to fight the Wendish king's army despite the fact that they were usurping lands in the south that belonged to the Aostan royal family; feasts and triumphal parades through a host of towns in central Aosta.

Henry remained somber throughout this recitation, and he left the feast early, taking a small coterie with him as he walked to his private apartments. They stopped to view the sleeping princess. As Henry leaned over Mathilda's bed, admiring how much she'd grown, Rosvita bent close to speak softly in his ear.

"I sense that all is not as you wish, Your Majesty. Be sure that I am ready to listen, should you desire a counselor's ear."

He stroked Mathilda's downy soft brown hair. The baby stirred, slipped her thumb in her mouth, and with a snort fell back to sleep. "Aosta is a thornbush, and the news from Wendar has not cheered my heart. Was I mistaken to leave Theophanu as regent?"

"You could not have known the Quman would invade, Your Majesty."

"Am I chasing a dream, Sister?" His hands, callused from so many years of war, traced the curve of the baby's ear; he had a delicate touch.

"Nay, Your Majesty. If the Holy Mother is right, then we must have a strong leader in the years to come. Taillefer's crown would unite many who might otherwise refuse to march behind the Wendish banner."

"If report is true, civil war rages in Salia. If I could only secure Aosta, then I might turn my eyes west to Salia next."

The words startled her, and worried her. "You would never be regarded as anything but a usurper in Salia, Your Majesty, if you will forgive me for saying so. I must advise you to strengthen your position in Aosta first—and not to neglect the troubles in the north."

His sharp gaze, his thoughtful expression, reminded her of the silent calculation, often unseen by others, at work in his mind. "Ought I to return to Wendar, do you think?"

"In truth, Your Majesty, I fear you are caught between the lance and the spear. If you leave Aosta now, all that you have accomplished so far may crumble. Yet if you do not return to Wendar, worse may follow."

"I had thought to leave a peaceful realm at my back," he said, not without bitterness, "but I see it is not to be. Yet I thank you, Sister, for your honest words." He straightened up, smiling as he caught Adelheid's hand and drew her to him. "Now, my friends, to bed."

There was a great deal of merrymaking as they escorted the king and queen to their bed and at length retired to leave them in peace. Courtiers dispersed quickly to their own private revels, but before Rosvita could return to her chambers, she was waylaid by Helmut Villam.

"I pray you, Sister, a word."

She smiled, genuinely happy to see him. "You're looking well, Margrave. You have weathered the summer's heat better than I have."

"We weren't cooped up within city walls. And I admit, Sister, that I found the women of Aosta most accommodating." His smile turned abruptly to a frown as he drew her into an alcove backed by a hideously clever marble fountain carved in the shape of a medusa's head, every hair a snake and each snake's mouth trickling water like clear poison. "I am distressed by the reports I hear out of Wendar and the marchlands."

"An Eagle came through Darre some weeks ago, sent by Princess Theophanu. Have you heard other news?"

"A messenger from Geoffrey of Lavas reached us, and it broke my heart to hear the lad speak. 'By the love you bear me, and by the honor you gave to my daughter by designating her as the rightful Count of Lavas.' He begged Henry to come home. Troubles. Drought and famine, and bandits come north from Salia to haunt the roads. Even talk of the shades of the Lost Ones, ranging out of the deep forests to plague folk with elfshot."

"Ill news, indeed."

Villam hadn't finished. "I had hoped to get a message from my daughter, in Walburg, but I have heard nothing. Tell me, Sister, do you think that Henry ought to remain in Aosta or return to Wendar? It is by no means clear to me that he and Queen Adelheid control enough of Aosta even now that they can expect the imperial crowns to be handed to them without a fight."

"Surely they can simply take the crowns. No one else is vying for them."

"That is the risk, is it not? If Henry allows himself to be crowned while Aosta remains in turmoil, with Jinna pirates and Arethousan thieves still in control of half the country. . . ." He trailed off, extending a hand to catch water from one snake's mouth and wiping his forehead. It was so dark in the alcove that Rosvita could only see the movement, not his expression.

"Yet if Henry retreats to Wendar, then this foray into Aosta might be seen as a defeat," she pointed out.

"True enough. Those who make trouble might begin to whisper that he has lost the regnant's luck."

Some tone in his voice alerted her. "Are such words being uttered, Villam? Surely not."

"I do not like Aosta, and even less do I like the intrigues of Aostan nobles. There is something untrustworthy about the entire lot of them. Nay, Sister, I think we neglect the north at our peril. That is what I will counsel the king: that we should return as soon as possible."

"That will depend in part on the passes over the mountains. Some may be closed by snowfall."

"If that's so, we must bide here until next spring."

Rosvita turned to survey Ruoda and Heriburg, who were regarding her with wide eyes and startled expressions. Lamplight played over their youthful features. "'I have been told I had cousins at Bodfeld!' How could I have forgotten? *Bodfeld*."

"Have you cousins at Bodfeld, Sister?" asked Ruoda. "I thought you came from the North Mark. I didn't know the Counts of the North Mark had kin in eastern Saony."

"Nay, they don't, child."

"Shhh!" hissed Heriburg to Ruoda. "She's still thinking."

"After the death of her husband, the child was taken from her and given to a monastery to raise. And the girl called Lavrentia was sent south—found by Wolfhere and sent south!—and so came by accident, or by God's design, to St. Ekatarina's. Maybe the only place she could have remained safe."

"Safe from what?" asked Ruoda. Heriburg kicked her in the shin.

"That is the one terrible secret that would destroy her position. That would force the council of presbyters to revoke the ring."

"Oh, my God," said Heriburg, as though the words had been forced out of her. "You're talking about the Holy Mother."

She realized, then, that they were staring at her, aghast. "Daughters, you must speak of this to no one. Truly, you can see how ugly and destructive rumor can be. I have no proof. I have only suspicions. I may be wrong."

"Wrong about what?" demanded Ruoda. "What is the terrible secret?"

"Ai Lady," Rosvita murmured. "Sin laid upon sin. Tomorrow, my children, I must ask you to do a horrible thing, to soil your hands with binding and working—"

"Sorcery?" asked Ruoda eagerly.

"We must all have amulets of protection, of concealment."

A sharp rap on the door caused them all to start, as though

God in Their guise as Eternal Judge had come calling on account of their sinful thoughts. Heriburg actually shrieked, so startled that she let go of the map, which rolled up with a snap. But it was only Fortunatus, wiping sweat from his brow, winded and distraught. He hurried in, stopped dead, and looked at each of them in turn. "What's happened?" he asked. "What's wrong?"

Having come so far, even knowing that it might be possible for Anne or any other adept to be watching her right now, she had to speak.

"Sister Clothilde is dead, and so is Fidelis, and the hapless nephew from Bodfeld. All the other principals. Only Anne and Lavrentia—and Wolfhere—remain. That is why they are looking for her. To make sure no one discovers that Liath's father was Anne's half brother."

"Incest!" whispered Ruoda in the tones of a gardener gratified to find all his roses in glorious bloom.

"May God have mercy," murmured Fortunatus.

"Terrible enough," continued Rosvita, "horrible, indeed. But there's still a piece missing. Why did Sister Clothilde remove an unimportant girl from a convent near the seat of the Counts of Lavas? Why does that nag at me? It might only be coincidence."

Fortunatus grabbed the map off the table and slid it up his sleeve, as if he expected guards to tromp in the next instant and arrest them all for treason. "The hounds. That hound the skopos keeps by her. Doesn't it look like Count Lavastine's hounds? Aren't the Lavas hounds very like the ones described in the poems about Emperor Taillefer?"

"You see them in all the tapestries," said Ruoda. "I never thought about it before, but that hound the skopos keeps by her is very like the emperor's famous black hounds."

"'He and his daughters led their black hounds with leashes around their necks, and in their excitement the hounds snap at any person who comes near them except for their master and his children, for even the dogs in their dumb loyalty bow before bright nobility."' Heriburg blushed when the other three looked at her. "I beg your pardon. I knew the entire poem by heart before I entered the convent."

"No." Rosvita stepped away from the window. "We're asking the wrong question. We should be asking not how the black hound comes to attend the Holy Mother Anne, granddaughter of Emperor Taillefer. We should be asking how, and when, such hounds came to attend the Counts of Lavas."

A scratch came on the door and Aurea peered in. "My lady!"

"Ai, God," swore Fortunatus. "I forgot Sister Gerwita. She was quite out of breath." He was sweating, if possible, even more than before.

"You have news, Brother," said Rosvita, not needing an answer. His expression was answer enough.

Aurea opened the door all the way to admit poor timid Gerwita, who was indeed panting so hard that Rosvita herself hurried over to help her to the bed. "Dear God, child, I hope you are not falling ill."

"Nay, Sister, it was just the stairs and the heat. In truth, my heart aches for the suffering I've seen. There is so little we can do to help them." She wiped a tear, or sweat, from her cheek. The lamplight washed her thin, pale face to ivory. "Alas, Sister, that we come bearing such tidings. Brother Fortunatus told you . . . didn't he?"

"Nay, he's had no chance."

"We found her, Sister." Gerwita sighed heavily, shoulders drooping.

"Gerwita found her," said Fortunatus sternly, never one to take credit where he had not earned it. "She was the only one not afraid to tour the plague houses and the poor houses and the infirmaries. She only took me there to identify the body."

"God have mercy," breathed Rosvita, seeing all too clearly where this would lead. "Go on."

"Found who?" asked Ruoda.

Gerwita waved a languid hand, unable to speak. Fortunatus went on. "Paloma, the lay sister from St. Ekatarina's Convent.

Dead of the summer fever, so the sisters at St. Asella's infirmary reported. But she had none of the bruising on the cheeks. Her eyes weren't sunken in. You know how they look. I think she was murdered, Sister, for when I met her yesterday before Lauds, she was as healthy as I am."

3

IT was obvious even from the outside that Osterburg's walls were in poor repair. But a mob of prisoners, whipped forward with the lash, could not breach them, not with so many determined defenders pouring hot oil and a rain of arrows down on their hapless foe. Most of the captives died in agony at the base of the walls while Bulkezu and his army watched in a silence tempered only by the whisper of their wings in a steady autumn breeze. There was nothing Hanna could do to stop the killing, nothing she could do to save them.

Nothing.

By the time rudimentary siege engines were brought forward on the third day of the siege, the defenders had plugged the gaps with piles of rubble and quickly erected palisades. To Hanna's eyes, it looked as though they had ripped down entire houses for the beams and planks thrown up to fill in the weak spots, but of course from this distance it was hard to tell.

All she could do was pray that Osterburg would not fall too soon. All she could do was pray that what she had seen with her Eagle's sight two weeks ago had been a true vision, not a false one.

"Eagle." Prince Ekkehard's concubine, Agnetha, had been weeping. She wiped at her eyes as she joined Hanna on the slope between the begh's tent and the prince's. The guards glanced at her and away, pretending disinterest. "Tell me what I must do, Eagle. They took my uncle away yesterday. I was barely able to save his sons from being sent out as well." Two dark-haired, ragged boys knelt on the dirt outside Ekkehard's tent, heads bowed in prayer or in grief. "But they took Uncle away for the attack. I know he must be dead now." She began to cry again. "I should have gone in his place. Look at how many are dead, and I'm safe and dry and not hungry."

"There's nothing you could have done." But her words sounded hollow. In truth, she felt hollow. "Nothing."

Even had she demanded that Bulkezu cast her back into the crowd of prisoners, that he let his soldiers lash her forward with the rest, he would not have done so. That one night she had spent in the mob had only been a ruse to catch her out, to see what magic she might be hiding. After that, he had reeled in her leash once again and kept her close by his side, always close. She had never known that hate, like a fever, could burn you out until you were only a husk.

She had seen so much death and cruelty that she wondered if it had crushed her heart. She hated herself for ever thinking of Bulkezu as a handsome man. Outward beauty meant nothing if the heart within was misshapen and monstrous.

Bulkezu's pavilion and the main encampment stood on a low rise overlooking the river valley from the west. The Veser River flowed northward, mighty and broad, meeting a tributary that flowed in from the east through rugged countryside right where the fortress city had been built to take advantage of such a good defensive position. The Quman army had trampled the fields outside of the city, on the west bank of the Veser, although most looked as though they had already been harvested.

"They must have good grain stores," said Agnetha suddenly, betraying her background as a practical farm girl. Not even the rich gowns that Ekkehard dressed her in could disguise the strength of her callused hands. No doubt she had hoed many a field and wrung many a chicken's neck in her time, before she'd been forced to accept the privilege of gracing a captive prince's bed. "And with rivers on two sides, good access to water. They'll be hard to take, as long as the walls hold."

Hanna glanced at her, surprised. "You've learned a thing or two about war."

"So I've had to," replied Agnetha bitterly. "Prince Ekkehard and his companions talk of little else." Although she was already speaking in a low voice, she leaned closer and whispered so softly in Hanna's ear that Hanna strained to hear. "He's terrified. That's his aunt's city, and you can see by the banner that she is in residence together with his cousins. All he's done the last three days is pray to God to not force him to commit treason against his own kin."

"It seems late to worry about that."

"That may be, but what else was he to do, taken prisoner and all?"

"He could have refused to fight on Bulkezu's behalf."

"And been killed instead? His own kin haven't treated him with respect, have they? Why shouldn't he resent them?"

"Is that what he tells you?" asked Hanna.

"Why shouldn't he tell me? Who else will listen to him?"

Hanna examined the pretty young woman. Not even red and swollen eyes could ruin the promise of her full lips and fuller bosom, nor tarnish the glory of her thick, dark hair. For all Ekkehard's faults, he was still a prince of the royal house, with fine manners, an elegant figure, and his own share of Henry's charisma. Thrown together with him in desperate circumstances, learning the best ways to smooth his feathers when he became agitated, comprehending that his protection could perhaps save her remaining family: nay, she could not find it in her heart to blame Agnetha for becoming his champion, in her own way. People did what they had to, to survive.

All the ferries and fords upstream along the Veser River were in Quman hands, and no doubt Bulkezu was in the process of sending out soldiers to take over those ferries a day's ride downstream of the city as well. The army fanned out along the eastern bank of the Veser, striking east into the forested country that lay between the two rivers, probing, burning, killing any poor soul unlucky enough not to have heard the warnings and retreated to the safety of Osterburg's decrepit walls. The main part of the force waited outside the city, ready for another assault once the siege engines had done their work.

"There are so many of them," whispered Agnetha hopelessly. "No one can ever defeat them."

Despite everything, Hanna still hoped a fierce hope. "They just look like so many because of the way they swarm over the ground. Look there." She pointed to the three fires burning about a stone's throw from Bulkezu's pavilion. "Haven't you seen how they signal to each other, using smoke?"

One of the boys kneeling by Ekkehard's tent leaped up and raced over. "You better come." He pulled at Agnetha's sleeve. "His lordship wants you."

With a glance, a murmured word that Hanna could not understand, Agnetha hurried away. As she went, the distant "thump" of the two catapults being released shuddered through the air. Hanna held her breath, trying to keep her gaze on the missiles rising, and then falling. A cloud of dust rose from within the walls, followed by a stream of smoke as the fire rags caught in thatch.

So it went as the morning passed and the afternoon bled away. Smoke rose at intervals but always got put out again. Hanna paced, four guards in ever-present attendance on her. Prince Ekkehard and his companions stayed in their tent, praying. Now and again she caught sight of Bulkezu's griffin wings below as he rode down to the ferry, over to the catapults, and then vanished north of the city. Cherbu rode beside his brother, easily identifiable because he wore no wings. A few pathetic prisoners, bloody and limping, fled west into the woodlands beyond the open fields, but Quman scouts rode after them and herded them in, driving them back toward the main encampment. At last, Hanna walked with a sick heart to the prisoners' compound, a makeshift corral guarded by the youngest and most inexperienced Quman soldiers, the ones who would more likely overreact to any least sign of activity among the prisoners and who were therefore the most dangerous sentries.

She did what she could, bringing water to the prisoners, tending wounds. Her guards watched without interest and made no move to stop her. They knew that any of these little things she did were useless. But she had to do them in order to live with herself, in order to sleep at night.

She had to listen to their stories, in order to report them to the king. Surely the king would be as horrified as she was, hearing of his loyal subjects driven forward at spear point to take the brunt of the assault, caught between a sure death, if they did not advance, and likely death if they did. One man had spent the night buried among the dying, hearing their screams and moans; even as he spoke, he kept slapping his ears as though he still heard their cries. Another had crawled to safety through a field of blood; his skin was covered in it, cracking and flaking off when he clenched and unclenched his hands. A woman had seen her own son fall with an arrow in his eye, and during the night she had crawled among the dead, searching hopelessly and desperately, until her sobbing brother had dragged her away before she could get cut down by the defenders on the wall or the Quman in the field.

There was no sign of Agnetha's uncle among the ones who had escaped the carnage.

Hanna noticed first that the attention of her guards slipped away from her as they pointed toward the trees and the encampment's flags, barely visible above the foliage. The smoke had changed. Three fat balls of smoke puffed up and dissipated. One of the guards whistled sharply, beckoning to her as he touched the handle of his whip. She wasn't the one who would be struck if she didn't obey immediately.

They got to Bulkezu's pavilion just as he rode up, attended by a dozen of his favored captains. His gaze marked Hanna, but that was all, before he called his brother over. The two spoke rapidly, words blending together so that she could pick

not even one common word out of the conversation except a
name.

Bayan.

Cherbu hemmed and hawed. He frowned and spat. He
scratched his crotch and pried a tiny stone out of the sole of his
shoe. Bulkezu wanted him to do something that he clearly did
not want to do. But in the end he acquiesced, muttering and
mumbling as he walked away with his odd, rolling gait. He
had stripped down to almost nothing because of the heat, and
the tattoos that covered his body seemed to shudder and move
where sweat glistened, trailing down his dark skin.

Bulkezu returned his attention to the scouts who rode up at
intervals and gave their reports. Hanna was too nervous to
understand even a single word. Around her, men began breaking down tents and pavilions. Cherbu made a circuit of the
camp, hopping from one leg to the other while he sprinkled
dust onto the ground at intervals. His singsong chant inter-
wove with Bulkezu's laughter every time a new scout rode in.

What was going on? Were they abandoning the siege? Had
Prince Bayan tracked them down at last?

Ai, Lord. Maybe Ivar was with him. Maybe Ivar wasn't
really dead.

Prince Ekkehard emerged from his tent with his four
faithful companions behind him, but they stopped short,
caught cold, when two Quman soldiers rode up and dumped
at Bulkezu's feet the body of a Wendishman dressed in the
light armor of a scout and wearing the badge of Princess
Sapientia. Ekkehard grabbed his battle banner out of Welf's
hand and tossed it back inside the tent. Standing with his
friends, he could no longer be identified as a royal prince of
Wendar.

Bulkezu held up a hand for silence. He had taken off his
helm. The wind streamed through his beautiful hair, making
it writhe like snakes around his shoulders. Below, the Quman
army was pulling back from the walls; on the far shore of the
river, groups of ten and twenty riders moved toward the

eastern bank, gathering into larger cohorts as they returned from their far-flung foraging.

"Arm for battle, Prince Ekkehard," said Bulkezu. "The time for fighting is soon upon us." At last, he met Hanna's gaze. "When I have destroyed their army, and burned their city, then you will lead me to the witch called Liathano."

4

THAT day, the ninth of Setentre, the feast day of St. Mary the Wise, six of the ten scouts sent far forward of the army did not return. That evening, Prince Bayan called a war council so that all the nobles and commanders could hear the reports of the four who had survived.

But before Prince Sanglant led his personal retinue to the council, Zacharias had the pleasure of watching the prince make his Eagle squirm. "It worked well enough with Hedwig."

"That is what I am trying to explain, Your Highness." Wolfhere was actually sweating, although in truth it was an unseasonably warm evening, muggy with the promise of a thunderstorm looming on the horizon. "Princess Theophanu had three Eagles in her entourage, and the only one who has the gift of the Eagle's sight is no longer with her. I can use my sight to see where the princess is—"

"At Quedlinhame. Not here, where she ought to be."

"—but without another Eagle with sight to communicate with, I can't know why she is there, or what she intends, nor even how large an army she has with her."

"What of the missing Eagle?"

"As I told you. She rode south to Aosta. Soon after, I lost track of her."

"*Lost* track of her?"

"Just so, Your Highness. We are not the only ones seeking to conceal ourselves."

One of Sapientia's stewards rushed up, and Heribert stepped aside to speak to the man.

"Which would explain, I trust, why you did not see the Quman army lying in wait for us at Osterburg? Or, as I've heard, Liath and I when we lived at Verna. Indeed, now I see the limitations of your Eagle's sight, if it is so easily clouded by sorcery."

Wolfhere lifted both hands in a gesture of surrender. "In truth, no more than one of every five Eagles has ever had even an inkling of the Eagle's sight. It's a secret we guard—"

"Or hoard."

"—and one that not all Eagles can, or should, master."

"Well," said the prince. He beckoned, and Heribert came over to him and whispered in his ear. Sanglant smiled sourly. "We must go, if they are waiting only on us." He glanced around the sprawl of his encampment, fires flowering into life as twilight spread its wings over the army: a few cloth tents but mostly men hunkering down to rest on their cloaks. Every man there kept his armor on and his weapons and helmet beside him, now that they knew the Quman were close by. They had marched through open woodland this day, an easy march, seeing nothing.

Too easy. The Quman scouts ranged wide and saw everything; everyone knew that. Bulkezu was sure to already know exactly where they were and how many soldiers they had. He was only playing with them, letting four enemy scouts escape the net of his own scouting line to lure his enemies into complacency. Zacharias had begun to entertain thoughts of running away, into the woods, but then he would only be caught by a Quman scout and dragged back to Bulkezu. But probably they were all going to die, anyway, in whatever battle was sure to come. He just hoped it would be quick.

"You're pale, Brother Zacharias," said the prince. "You'd best come with us. We'll need to know what you know about the Pechanek clan. None here knows them as well as you do."

He couldn't even answer, only shake his head, fear choking him, as Sanglant picked out his most trusted commanders to attend him: Lord Druthmar, Captain Fulk, Sergeant Cobbo, even the lapdog, Hrodik, who at least had the knack of obeying orders.

Bayan and Sapientia held court at their huge tent, all the sides strung up from trees, making it an open air pavilion where every important noble could gather. The crowd parted to let Sanglant through. He took the place of honor at Bayan's right hand, with Heribert and Zacharias given leave to stand behind him and the rest of his captains fading back to find places in the crowd. Blessing, as usual, sat on her father's lap. She had a stick, carved into the shape of a sword, but she had learned patience in the last few days and now held it over her thighs, her little face drawn into an intent frown as she listened to Bayan quiet the crowd and call forward the surviving scouts.

Of the four scouts who had managed to return, three were Ungrians and the fourth a wily marchlander out of Olsatia, one of Lady Bertha's trusted men-at-arms. Not one of Princess Sapientia's Wendish scouts had come back. The marchlander had seen a man in Wendish armor strung up in a tree, missing his head, but she hadn't stayed to investigate.

"The main army lies on the west bank of the Veser River," said Bayan after the reports were finished. "We'll cross the Veserling tomorrow and continue to march west through the rough country between the two rivers."

"Wouldn't it be better to move northwest along the Veserling, where the marching is easier," asked Duke Boleslas of Polenie, aided by his translator, "and move directly to relieve the siege on Osterburg?"

Bayan shook his head. "The Quman rely on archery. If we approach through rugged country, they'll have less chance to break up our line of march with arrow shot. We would be easier targets marching along the river valley."

Prince Sanglant said little as Bayan outlined the order of

march. There was little to say, reflected Zacharias. Bayan was an experienced soldier. He knew what he was doing.

A misty rain fell part of the night, enough to break the heat but not so much to make anyone miserable. In the morning the army set out, a process that took a goodly length of time as each legion or cohort or war band waited its turn and then moved forward. Because of the dampened ground, they raised little dust, a mercy for those marching in the rear. It also meant that they wouldn't betray themselves to the Quman too soon, although surely by now the Quman knew exactly where they were.

It was the tenth day of Setentre, the feast day of St. Penelope the Wanderer, as Heribert was quick to remind him, warm and muggy with that coiled snap in the air that heralded a thunderstorm. But as they marched and the sun rose to zenith, as the trees sweated last night's raindrops onto their heads, no thunderstorm blew through to break the heat. Zacharias rode two ranks behind Prince Sanglant, praying that he wouldn't vomit out of plain fear. His stomach roiled, as disturbed as the air and the wind, waiting for the coming storm.

Once, shouts rose, and a messenger galloped down the line, pausing to speak to Prince Sanglant before continuing on, back to where Prince Bayan rode with his Ungrians. Rumor filtered back to the group around Zacharias. Outriders had clashed with Quman scouts. Skirmishes had broken out across their line of march. The Quman were retreating, falling back toward the Veser, still several leagues away. It was hard to know what was true and what falsely hoped.

They crossed the Veserling in the afternoon at a ford controlled by a contingent of Lions under Princess Sapientia's command. She had crossed first, in the van, with three legions, and left soldiers behind in case Quman horsemen crossed the river and swept around in an attempt to divide their forces. The Lions left behind to guard the ford were already digging in, calling to each other as they worked.

"Ho, there, Folquin, you idiot! Don't drop that log on my head, if you please."

"Lady's Tits, Ingo, if you keep getting in my way I'll scar that handsome face of yours, and then your sweethearts won't want you anymore, and the Quman will probably refuse to cut off your head for a trophy!"

It was amazing how quickly a crude palisade could go up when the workers were lashed by the goad of fear. Strange how these kept joking as they labored. Zacharias felt he could hardly speak, as though he'd lost his tongue.

How would Bulkezu cut it out? Where would the knife's edge first touch flesh?

The jolt of water on his legs brought him back, hazy, clinging to the saddle as his horse plunged into the river. The current streamed past, trying to drag him off, but he had clung to life for this long that he hung on with bitter strength as the horse made for the opposite bank. This time of year the river was wide but shallow, a silty greenish-brown color. A branch swirled past him, then, strangely, a mangled glove. At last the horse struggled up the shore and he was at once directed to the right, leaving a trail of water drops as he followed the others along a narrow trail cut through the forest, mostly oak and hornbeam here along the river, fairly open, with a dense layer of crocus, hellebore, and wild strawberry carpeting the ground. They regrouped north of the ford where someone had years ago cut a clearing into the wood. An old shack lay tumbled down, good for nothing more than breaking into firewood. In all, as they gathered into their command groups, Zacharias estimated they had about five hundred mounted soldiers: Sanglant's legion, made up of his own personal retinue, Gent's irregulars, and Waltharia's levies.

"We'll make camp here, with the river at our back," said the prince. Lord Druthmar and Lord Hrodik hurried off to give their captains the order to dig in for the night.

Bayan and his Ungrians had just crossed when a scout rode

up to Sanglant's position. "Come quickly, my lord prince. There's news! The siege has been lifted!"

A cheer rose raggedly from the men standing around, echoed by others, farther away, as the news was relayed out to them. Sanglant only frowned. "I'll come," he said, hauling his daughter up on the saddle in front of him. "Heribert! Lord Thiemo. Zacharias. Wolfhere. Fulk. Lord Druthmar. You'll attend me. The rest, be mindful that we must be ready. An attack might come at any moment."

At the ford, Duke Boleslas and his Polenie were crossing; behind them waited the baggage train, lost to Zacharias' sight where it snaked back into the woodland on the other side of the Veserling. Sanglant's party rode on upstream, where Bayan's Ungrians had made camp next to Sapientia's Wendish legions.

The princess and Bayan held court where three logs had fallen together in such a way that planks could be thrown over them and chairs set up on this raised platform. As they rode up, and Sanglant handed his horse over to Captain Fulk to hold, an argument broke out between two lords standing right in front of the makeshift platform. One of them Zacharias had never seen before; the other was the infamous Lord Wichman, second son of Duchess Rotrudis of Saony, known throughout the army for impressive deeds of valor as well as an absolutely vile temperament. Some said he couldn't be killed, for many had tried, and not all of them were Wendar's enemies.

"—swore you wouldn't molest, but then I found that you'd forced her not even just once but three times before you left for Gent!" said the other lord, a brawny fellow with a bald spot and a fleshy face.

"Who's to say I forced her," sneered Wichman, "or that she didn't ask for it, wishing for a bull instead of an ox?"

The other lord swore violently, leaped forward, and grabbed Wichman's throat in his beefy hands. Prince Bayan turned bright red with anger as he jumped up, but before he could act, Sanglant had cut through the crowd and hauled the first man off Wichman.

"I beg you, Cousin, pray leave off strangling your brother." His hoarse voice rang out over the rising clamor. "He may well deserve it, but we need him to fight the Quman."

Laughter coursed through the ranks of the assembled nobles. A good family quarrel broke the tension. Bayan leaned down to whisper in Sapientia's ear.

Gagging and rubbing his throat, Wichman spat on the ground, careful to aim away from the prince. "Ai, Lord! She was just his concubine, common born. Easy enough to get another one, if she didn't please him."

The brother was struggling in Sanglant's grip, but even a man as stout and broad as he was couldn't quite get free. "She pleased me well enough, before you spoiled her!"

"Lord's balls, Zwentibold, that was—what?—two years ago? She's forgotten you by now—"

"She's *dead*. She hanged herself after you raped her."

The crowd had drawn back away from the brothers, but Zacharias couldn't tell if the nobles were appalled at the tale or only worried that one of the two men would draw a sword and accidentally injure a bystander.

Unexpectedly, Sapientia rose, signaling to Bayan to sit down again. "I pray you, Sanglant, let go of our cousin Zwentibold." She took a spear out of the hands of one of the men-at-arms standing below the platform and, from the height, drove the point into the ground between the two men. "Place your right hand on the haft," she commanded imperiously. Not even Duchess Rotrudis' sons, who both wore the gold torque that signified their royal birth, dared disobey a public order made by the king's heir, especially not when so many of her husband's picked soldiers crowded around, smiling grimly with their spears in hand.

"Now swear by Our Lord and Lady," she said when both men gripped the haft, glaring at each other with a hatred as palpable as that of the looming thunderstorm. "Swear that until the Quman are vanquished, you will do no harm to the other, for the sake of peace in our ranks and for the sake of the realm itself."

Put to the test in front of the entire assembly, they had no choice but to swear.

Sapientia's triumph was easy to see in her expression. At that moment, she looked truly as the heir ought to look: bold, stalwart, and ready to lead. But it was Bayan who stepped up beside her and raised his voice.

"Lord Zwentibold has brought us valuable news: The Quman army withdrew this morning from their siege of Osterburg." A cheer rose, but it died away when Bayan lifted a hand for silence. "Lord Zwentibold was therefore able to ride out of the city with three full cohorts of mounted men and make his way to us. But if Bulkezu withdrew his soldiers, it was only to prepare to meet us. We have no good count of their numbers, and they are in any case difficult to count because of their habit of ranging wide and moving quickly. Do not believe that they can defeat us, because God are with us."

This ringing statement produced another cheer, during which Bayan whispered into Sapientia's ear. When the cheering died down, she grasped hold of the spear's haft again and called out. "Let every leader swear peace and mutual help to one another. Tomorrow is the Feast of the Angels, when the heavenly host sing of the glories of God. We will fight in the name of Our Lord and Lady, and they will ride with us. Do not doubt that we will defeat the Quman once and for all time."

5

THAT morning, Antonia rose early, prayed, and paced, knowing it important to keep up her strength. At the appropriate time, she waited by the curtained entrance to the guest quarters, head bent and hands folded in the very picture of perfect repose. But in her heart she fumed over the petty insults and grave wrongs the mother abbess and nuns at the convent of St. Ekatarina had done to her.

For three months she had bided here, as quiet as a mouse, as humble as a sparrow, a most unexceptional guest. And yet Mother Obligatia persisted in treating her as an enemy.

A woman's voice, raised in prayer, lifted with heartbreaking beauty: "The longing of the spirit can never be stilled."

As quickly it was lost: a shift of air in the dusty corridors, perhaps, or the singer inadvertently turning her head so that her voice didn't reach so far. A bell tinkled softly. Antonia suspected there were secret hidey-holes from which they observed her. Of course, growing up as a noble child in a royal house, she was used to constant observation. Years of education in the church and the years she had spent presiding as biscop of Mainni, when she was never alone except for moments spent in the privies, had served to hone her skills, to teach her how to present to the world at all times the smooth mask of humility on her face.

Still Mother Obligatia suspected her.

A scrape of sandal on rock caught her attention.

"Sister Venia?" The raspy voice of the lay sister, Teuda, sounded from beyond the curtain.

"I am ready."

For three months they had followed this ridiculous routine. Teuda led her along empty corridors hewn out of stone past the chapel to the tiny library where, in the hours between Terce and Nones, she was allowed to read. At midday, Sister Carita, with her unsightly hunchback, escorted her to the service of Sext and then back to the library. After the brief service of Nones, Teuda led her back to the guest quarters, where she languished until Vespers, the only other service she was allowed to attend with the sisters. Even her meals were delivered to her in the guest quarters, where she ate alone.

To treat a sister nun in such a fashion was a mockery of charity! They did not trust her.

Sister Petra was already at work, making a copy of the chronicle of St. Ekatarina's Convent. She nodded to acknowledge that Antonia entered but did not greet her. In truth, except for Mother Obligatia and the lackwit, Sister Lucida, the other nuns acted around Antonia as though they were under a vow of silence. Only Teuda, as a lay sister, was allowed to speak to her, and she said as little as possible.

From Terce to Sext, Antonia studied several interesting and obscure works on theology and philosophy: the apocryphal *Wisdom Book* of Queen Salome; a complete copy—very difficult to come by—of the Arethousan Biscop Ariana's heretical and quite scandalous *Banquet*, regarding the generation of the blessed Daisan out of the divine substance of God; the *Catechetical Orations* by Macrina of Nyssa. But once she had returned from the midday service, she took down the final and of course thereby unfinished volume of the convent's chronicle. She would finish it today, and then there would be no more reason to delay her mission.

The light lancing down through the shafts carved into the rock shifted over the four writing desks as the hours wore on. The silence was broken only by the scrape of Sister Petra's quill and the occasional crackling of vellum as Antonia turned a page. Otherwise, they might have been entombed, suffering the ecstacy of oblivion.

She caught a whiff of cooking turnips, fleeting, gone.

Strange, she mused, as she read the final entries. *In the year 729: The queen took refuge in the arms of St. Ekatarina from those who hunted her, together with certain noble visitors from Wendar. A party of clerics from Wendar stayed one week in the guest hall. A blight struck the wheat crop in the vicinity of Floregia. Jinna bandits killed every member of the house of Harenna, leaving their palace and fortress in ruins and their lands without a regnant. The palace of Thersa, eight stones, and ruins.*

Two years ago, Queen Adelheid had found safety here, fleeing Ironhead. Two years ago, Father Hugh had sheltered here as well and by an act of sorcery had aided Adelheid's escape.

In the year 730: Lord John, called Ironhead, was crowned king at Darre.

Now Ironhead was dead and Adelheid was queen. Antonia had to admire a mind that worked as subtly as Father Hugh's, laying out a torturous path often obscured by false doors and then following it to the end.

The rest of the entry for last year did not interest her, a record of certain disasters, called omens, that had befallen various peasant communities and local districts. No doubt the people had sinned in some grievous manner and were being punished by God, as they deserved. That was the usual reason for famine, drought, plague, and the blight of leprosy.

No hand had yet recorded the most important events of the current year, 731: the death of the skopos and her replacement by Anne; Adelheid's triumphant return and her restoration to Aosta's throne.

Probably, now, they never would.

Teuda, the lay sister, appeared at the door. Her time was up. As Antonia tucked the volume back onto its proper shelf, straightening the corners, wiping a smidgeon of dust from the corner of the book placed next to it, she wondered if she would be able to salvage this chronicle from the chaos sure to follow. There was a great deal of valuable information here, and it was obvious to her that the abbesses of St. Ekatarina's had known far more than they chose to let on. Why else record, in plain sight, the stone crowns scattered around the continent? In their own way, they were making a map. They knew the crowns were a key.

But she couldn't tell if they understood what those keys unlocked.

With a smile for Sister Petra, who had just set down a newly trimmed quill and now wiped ink from her fingers in preparation for services, Antonia left the library and dutifully returned to the guest hall. She tided herself up, revived herself with some wine set aside for this purpose, and went to pray at the small chamber where an altar stood. There was a cunning screen set into the altar itself, a concealed alcove so that an observer on the other side could look into the tiny chapel without being seen. She had noticed it within days of her arrival and could now tell if someone was lurking behind it, spying on her. There was no one there now; they would all be at prayer.

She spent a while making sure everything was ready. Then she knelt before the altar to pray, and to wait.

God would grant her triumph. Who else would see that God's work was done properly on Earth, if not her? She asked, of course, for forgiveness. Sometimes the blood of innocents had to be spilled in order to bring about the greater good for humankind.

In due course, as she always did, Sister Lucida arrived to escort Antonia to dinner. A halting footfall followed by a scraping sound as she dragged her cane along the ground preceded her appearance in the archway that separated the tiny chapel from the main guest hall. As the lackwit sucked in a breath, she snorted and gurgled, breathing hard, eyes blinking away tears. The light in the guest hall always made Sister Lucida cry, as though she had caught sight of angels in the streaming rays. She looked around aimlessly for a bit, head bobbing; it was difficult for her to focus.

At last, she fixed on Antonia and hobbled over. She grinned, displaying about ten teeth, all she had left. Her voice was a cross between a goose's honk and a pig's snort. "S—supper! Praise God!"

"Pray kneel beside me a moment while I finish my prayers," said Antonia with a gentle smile. She even helped Sister Lucida with the difficult task of kneeling, grasping her firmly around the back to hold her tight.

Then she slipped a slender knife out from the girdle wrapping her waist and thrust it, decisively, swiftly, up between Lucida's ribs, into the heart. As she held it steady, it pulsed to the frantic beat of the nun's heart. Lucida's mismatched eyes widened in shock and fear. She opened her mouth, but no sound came out, only a strangled croak.

"Pray, keep still, Sister Lucida, or you will surely die at this moment. As long as my hand holds the knife firm, then you will stay alive."

A whimper escaped the nun's lips, nothing more. A single tear slid from her right eye, trickling down her poxmarked face.

Antonia closed her eyes, the better to concentrate. The familiar syllables poured as smoothly as cream from her lips. She did not understand them, of course, because they came from the ancient rituals known to the Babaharshan priests, but their efficacy was undoubted. "*Ahala shin ah rish amurru galla ashir ah luhish.* Let this blood draw forth the creature out of the other world. Come out, creature, for I bind you with unbreakable fetters. This blood which you must taste that I have spilled makes you mine to command. I adjure you, in the name of the holy angels whose hearts dwell in righteousness, come out, and do as I bid you."

The iron-forge scent stung her nostrils. The breath of its being, shuddering into her view, stirred her hair. A galla swayed at the edge of her vision, a dark, towering shape, like a tall reed, reaching from floor to ceiling of the stone chamber.

Lucida, seeing it, jerked convulsively in terror. The knife in her chest wrenched sideways. Her heart's blood poured out of her, a river of scarlet gushing onto her robes, flowing away onto the stone floor. With a grimace of distaste for the mess, Antonia released her and let her drop. She stood and took a step back as the shadow that was the galla brushed past her, smelling the rich tang of innocent blood. Where its substance flicked over her, she heard faintly its agonized screaming, like the whine of a raging storm heard through thick walls. The middle world was torment to the galla; that was why they were so easy to control once they were brought over. Though it wavered, tiny tendrils lapping out to touch the flowering lake of blood, it could not resist the very thing that would bind it to her will.

It drank.

She had to cover her nose with a perfumed sleeve to muffle the stink of blood and the stinging forge-tang of the creature.

Soon enough, it had finished. Lucida was, amazingly, still alive, still conscious, her eyes wide and staring and one hand twitching. Life ebbed quickly. A last whimper escaped her as her soul fled. Antonia was relieved that the lackwit nun had died quietly. Not everyone did.

Still, it was an effort to raise her hands to pronounce the final command. "I adjure you, creature. This is your task, and you will do as I command. Kill the woman whose true name is Lavrentia, the mother of Anne."

Obedient to her will, its dark substance trembled, and it moved away immediately, its bell-like voice tolling the name of its victim. Passing through the rock itself, it vanished from her sight, but if she concentrated, she could see with its senses as it forged forward on the track of its prey.

Mother Obligatia—once known as the novice Lavrentia—assembled all unsuspecting with her nuns in the refectory, laying their simple meal out on the table.

Now, at last, Antonia allowed herself to totter to the stone bench carved into the wall, back by the entryway. She sank down, shaking horribly, all the strength drained from her limbs. It might take her hours to recover, and the link that bound her to the creature she had summoned still sucked at her heart. When she had been a young woman, sorcery hadn't taken so much out of her. Age had weakened her. In truth, unless she could divine the secrets of immortality, she hadn't many more years before she might become too weak to impose her will on the church.

Resting, eyes shut, she prayed for strength and health and long life in order that she could continue to do God's work on Earth. On the floor nearby, Lucida's body cooled and stiffened.

XVIII
THE FIELD OF BLOOD

1

ANNA found it hard to sleep, especially after listening to the intimate council held late that night under an awning strung up between three trees to give shelter while Prince Sanglant and Prince Bayan conferred, each man attended only by two trusted captains. Sapientia sat beside Bayan, but in truth she hardly spoke, mostly listened. She seemed as nervous as a rat caught in a box.

"You know these children born out of Duchess Rotrudis," Bayan had said. "Are Wichman and Zwentibold the best of them? Or are they the worst?"

"Zwentibold merely lacks imagination," Sanglant replied. "The sisters are as bad as Wichman, in their own way. There's a younger boy, too."

"God save us," murmured Bayan, apparently without irony.

Blessing had already fallen asleep. She stirred, snorting as she turned over, and Anna shut her eyes firmly, hoping that neither of the princes would notice that she was still awake. When Bayan went on, she peeked again, watching the figures silhouetted in lamplight as the awning swayed above them, stirred by the night's wind.

"Then can trust be put in the news Zwentibold to us brings?" asked Bayan. "His mother dying. Conrad rides to Wayland on a flimsy excuse, or as we call it, a lame horse."

"It is in Conrad's interest to protect his western provinces from the civil war in Salia."

"That horse still limps," retorted Bayan, glancing at Sapientia. "With sweet words he can sing to all three sides, and when they have done fighting each of the other and lie weak, so he marches in to take what territory he wishes."

"Do you know Conrad well?" asked Sanglant.

"By his reputation I know him."

"Ah."

"You do not agree?" Bayan laughed. "The crow of gossips says Conrad wishes the kingship of Wendar for himself. Also I hear he married Henry's niece, this Tallia, who wears a gold torque. Her mother is the elder sister of Henry, is she not? What does Conrad intend?"

"It's true that Conrad likes to be his own master, beholden to none. He may wait until we spend ourselves and our men driving out the Quman, and then send out scouts to see what remains. I don't know. What troubles me more is that Theophanu has retreated to Quedlinhame."

"She fears the Quman," said Sapientia.

Sanglant shifted impatiently on his camp stool, lifting his empty cup for more wine. "Only a fool doesn't fear the Quman," he said, hand drifting to touch his throat. "Theophanu does not lack courage, Sister. But she may lack an army, in which case she would have been foolish indeed to meet Bulkezu on the field. According to Zwentibold's report, she turned west before anyone in this region knew we were coming. I expect she retreated to Quedlinhame in order to protect it—"

"You always take her side," said Sapientia suddenly, falling silent again only after Bayan laid a hand on her arm.

"—or to have a base from which to harry the Quman, in case Bulkezu took Osterburg and afterward chose to strike west into the heart of Saony. A wise enough decision, from a strategic point of view. But why has she such a meager army at her disposal?"

"Our father took Liutgard *and* Burchard and most of their host into Aosta, as well as many more, his own and others."

"Theophanu should have been able to draw from Varingia and Arconia," said Sanglant.

"True enough," reflected Bayan. "No news to us has come of the western duchies. Maybe they have troubles with Salia, too."

"Maybe they do," echoed Sanglant.

Anna could tell that he didn't believe it. Anna could tell that something deeper was troubling him, and if the bold prince was troubled, then how could she possibly sleep? She tossed fitfully, dozing, waking, hearing a rumble of thunder that faded and did not sound again. The heat lingered, although a sprinkle cooled down the worst of the mugginess, thank God. After that, the erratic drip-drop of moisture trickling off leaves kept her awake. The river ran behind them, and once she heard voices raised in song, like the angels beginning their choir, but the rustle of wind through the autumn leaves muted the sound.

Like God's glory, snatched away just as the fallen soul came within sight of it. Had she been wrong to let Lord Thiemo tell Blessing the story of the phoenix? What would the prince do when he found out that Blessing was already beginning to ask questions about the martyrdom of the blessed Daisan, and the glory of his Holy Mother, who is God of all Creation?

Surely it wasn't wrong to tell the truth? Surely those young monks she had seen, with their paintings and their piety, hadn't been lying? Surely it wasn't a heresy, but the truth, concealed for so long. With the land itself torn by war and plague and famine, wasn't it fittingly brought back into the light?

But she was only a common girl, struck dumb by God's hand, recovered through a miracle, nursemaid to a princess by God's will. How could she tell what was true and what was false? How could she know what was God's will and what the Enemy's lies? The only thing she really knew was that Prince Sanglant would be very, very angry when he found out about the stories Lord Thiemo was telling his daughter.

At long last dawn gave color to the air. Where the sun's rays touched the ground, mist steamed up, making streamers of gauze among the trees. The river was cloudy with mist. She could barely see the other bank, although she heard the Lions at work, chopping, hammering, and swearing, as they prepared a blockade for the ford.

The army, stirring like an ill-tempered beast, made ready to march. Prince Sanglant kissed his daughter and sent her with her retinue to stand on the royal platform—the planks on which Sapientia and Bayan had held court the evening before—to preside as the army moved west in marching order. Anna stood behind Blessing's chair while Heribert answered the young princess' endless questions.

"Why isn't my Daddy riding first? They don't like him."

"Nay, it is no insult to your father, sweetling. It is Princess Sapientia's right and duty to lead the vanguard. She is King Henry's heir and must prove herself as a leader."

"Why?"

"If she hasn't the luck and the leadership to command troops in battle, then she cannot reign."

"But she's married to Prince Bayan."

"He's a foreigner, who can only rule as consort, not as regnant, over the Wendish."

"Why—?"

"Hush, Blessing, no more on this subject if you please. Sapientia commands two legions."

"What is a legion?"

The army made a great deal of noise, horses neighing, men shouting, the tramp of feet, and the crack of branches as they pressed forward along the road, which wasn't much more than a track through the forest barely wide enough to accommodate two wagons abreast.

"A legion is an old Dariyan term, from the old empire. It designates a unit of soldiers who fight under one high commander."

"How many soldiers?" Blessing asked.

Anna tried to count as Sapientia's Wendish cavalry rode past, in lines of four, but she lost track after forty.

"That depends on what authority you read," said Heribert, slipping into that way of speaking he had when all his fine education grabbed him by the throat. At times like these, Anna found him difficult to understand. "Some say several thousand infantry—that's foot soldiers—and a few hundred cavalry. Some say a thousand men, organized in ten centuries, or what we call cohorts, each group consisting of one hundred men."

Sitting on the platform, the army seemed to take forever to go by. "Is that a thousand men?" asked Anna. She thought about this for a moment, remembering the sums Raimar and Suzanne had taught her when it came time to count up thread and wool and cloth so that you wouldn't get cheated. "If it was two legions, then it would be two thousand men, wouldn't it?" The number dizzied her. She had to shut her eyes and just listen to the fall of hooves on the track and the persistent drip of moisture from the damp leaves.

"I'd guess not more than eight hundred under Sapientia's command," replied Heribert. "We aren't truly an army the way the old Dariyans had armies. We just use the Dariyan words."

"Why?" asked Blessing. These days she was full of "why."

The last of Sapientia's horsemen rode away down the track. After a gap, a new banner came forward, following the path of the first. "Here is Lady Bertha and her legion of Austran and Olsatian marchlanders," said Heribert.

"Why?" repeated Blessing.

"Why do we use the old words? To remind us of the strength of the old empire."

"I will be emperor," said Blessing, "so I'll call my armies legions, too."

Lady Bertha's legion was perhaps half the number of those who had ridden out with Sapientia. After she had passed, Sanglant rode forward, saluting his daughter, and headed down the track with Captain Fulk and his men, Lord Hrodik's Gentish irregulars, and Lord Druthmar and the contingent from Villam lands. Prince Bayan and his Ungrians, the biggest and most experienced group of fighters in the army, came next, followed in their turn by Lord Zwentibold, Lord Wichman, and their legion of skirmishers and cavalry from Saony. Last came the baggage train under the command of Duke Boleslas, the Polenie duke with his bright silver tabard and feathered helm, the peacock of the army, as Sanglant had called him one night after the prince had been drinking too much.

The wagon in which Blessing was to ride trundled to a stop before the platform, and Blessing allowed Lord Thiemo to help her into the back as Heribert folded up her chair. Although she could ride a pony, she wasn't old enough to do so under the circumstances, so they had tied her pony behind the wagon. As she settled down among sacks of grain, Captain Thiadbold of the Lions knelt before her.

"Your Highness, your father Prince Sanglant has charged me and my cohort of Lions to see that you remain safe until we come within the walls of Osterburg. I pray you, Your Highness, if there is any trouble, do as I command, and we'll see that no harm comes to you."

"I don't like riding at the rear," said Blessing.

He grinned, then hid the smile quickly, not sure of her temper. "Nay, but there are many fine and valuable things necessary to victory here in the baggage train. It is no insult to be left to guard them, Your Highness. Nor is it any insult to you to ride with the baggage train. Do you see?" He pointed toward the painted wagon belonging to Prince Bayan's mother. "You are not the only warrior who rides with the baggage train."

The sight of the wagon convinced Blessing not to argue.

Duke Boleslas rode up with a dozen frilled and colorful attendants to either side of his brightly caparisoned horse. He bowed before Blessing. "Your Highness," he said, before riding away again, circling toward the tail end of the train as the wagon lurched forward and they began moving.

Because the ground was still damp from the night's brief rain, there wasn't too much dust, but Anna could still tell that eight legions of fighting men had passed this way before them. Dirt soon coated her lips and tickled her nostrils. Any overhanging branches were snapped back or torn off by the press of bodies.

A feeling of dread grew in Anna's heart as they rolled onward and the sun rose higher. Would they be able to hear the clash of arms, ahead of them, when the vanguard met the Quman? Was it true that every Quman soldier carried a shrunken head at his belt, as a trophy? She touched her own neck, wondering if they chopped the heads off children, too, or if in Quman eyes she was old enough to be married or taken as a slave.

But at least, here in the rear guard, they were a long, long way from the front, where the battle would be fought.

By midday they came up along a ridge and caught a glimpse of the Veser River in the distance. Weapons and armor glinted in the trees below where the rest of the army wound away before them, closing in on the river plain.

Blessing stood up on the cart and grasped the shoulders of the good-natured wagoner who was driving. "Look!" she cried in her piercing voice. "I see the Quman army."

Anna stared, thinking for an instant that she saw a dark stain, like a plague of locusts, swarming over the river plain; then the road dropped into a cleft that steadily widened into flatter ground as it opened into broken woodland, oak and hornbeam and the occasional pine or beech. The tree cover gave them occasional protection from the glaring sun, but she was sweating, even though she didn't have to walk. The Lions, striding steadily alongside, had their helms thrown back and wiped their faces frequently.

Was that a growl of thunder in the distance? She couldn't decide whether a storm would make things better, or worse.

The wagon jostled along the trail in an even rhythm, jarred by an occasional bump. None of this bothered Blessing, who finally got bored, curled up among the lumpy sacks, and fell asleep after making Anna promise to "wake her up for the battle." Anna envied the child her ability to sleep so easily. The load of grain made a sturdy pillow, and Anna was able to fashion a little awning out of tent cloth so that Blessing's head remained in shadow as the wagon rolled along through changes of light and shade.

A group of at least one hundred Lions marched ahead of them and, in front of them, perhaps one hundred Polenie horsemen with their colorful striped tabards. Lord Wichman and his brother, with the Saony legion, rode too far ahead to see from here.

There was just room on the track for two wagons to move forward side by side. For a while, Anna watched the painted wagon belonging to Bayan's mother, but the beaded covering over the window never parted to reveal a watching face. Six male slaves marched behind the wagon. Two walked at the front, leading the oxen which pulled it. In this heat, they had all stripped down to loincloths. They were probably the most comfortable people there: no armor, no weapons. If they were nervous, they didn't look it. She tried to imagine what feelings they had, but even though once in a while one would glance at her, feeling her gaze on him, not one ever cracked a smile or turned his lips down in a frown. They just walked, obedient to their mistress' will.

The rest of the train followed in their dust, supply wagons, a few carts holding injured soldiers, carts holding the pavilions and camp furniture of nobles who could not go to war without their comforts and other visible signs of their rank and importance, the closed wagons bearing the princess' treasure, and several carts belonging to the church folk, which contained their precious vessels and golden altar cloths for the nightly service.

Lions marched alongside all the way down the train, together with other infantrymen. Now and again she caught sight of horsemen farther out in the forest. At the rear, she knew, rode Duke Boleslas and the remainder of his troops. Heribert sat on the open tailgate, lost in thought.

Lord Thiemo, Matto, and the other six of Sanglant's soldiers designated to escort Princess Blessing rode off to the right, working their way through the trees.

"Why are all the infantry back here, Brother Heribert?" she asked finally.

Heribert started, as if he'd forgotten Anna was there. "I'm no expert in strategy," he said with a smile, "but even I know that the Quman are all horsemen. Best to engage them on the field with cavalry."

"Why did Zacharias have to ride with Prince Bayan?"

"I thought you didn't like him?"

"I don't. I think it's better he's taken away. He's worse than a heathen. He used to be a good God-fearing man, and now what is he?"

"A very troubled one, I fear, and as good as he can be, in his heart. Nor should you hate him, child. He's done you no harm." She frowned at him, not liking to be lectured. "I'll say no more," he went on. "Since Zacharias was a slave to Bulkezu for seven years, Prince Bayan wants him nearby in case he sees or hears anything of importance, so he can warn Bayan."

"But not Prince Sanglant."

"Prince Bayan is the commander of this army. That is, I mean—" Amazingly, he blushed. "Princess Sapientia is the commander of this army, and I beg you, Anna, do not ever mention that I said otherwise."

Surprised to hear a cultured noble cleric *beg* her for anything, she began to answer when shouts and the blast of a horn sounded from the rear. Heribert hopped off the wagon, stumbled, and righted himself just as a rider galloped past, heading forward along the line.

Lord Thiemo cut in close, followed by the others. "It must

be a Quman patrol," he said to Anna, glancing at Blessing. "Nothing to worry about."

Lewenhardt had an arrow held loosely in his bow, and he was scanning the woods nervously, but through all that open woodland Anna saw no sign of winged riders. From the rear, the clash of arms rose singing on the wind. A few arrows fell among the wagons, and as she stared, shocked, at a white-fletched arrow skittering over the ground, a hard *thunk* shuddered the wagon. An arrow quivered in the side, the entire point buried in the wood. Chustaffus, who had refused to be left behind at Walburg even though his injured shoulder had crippled his sword arm, shouted in alarm as an arrow skated a hand's breath past his nose, and he rocked back, barely able to stay mounted.

"My Lord," swore Lord Thiemo, staring into the woodland as a misty fog coursed through the trees.

Only it was not mist but a hundred, or more, pairs of wings.

The Lions cried out warnings. They broke into a trot, and the cursing driver of their wagon whipped the mules forward.

Behind, men shouted and screamed, and for one horrible moment as they jolted into a broad clearing, she heard a cry ringing out above the clamor.

"Duke Boleslas is down!"

Panic broke through the line of wagons. Riders scattered, and in the chaos the only thing Anna could think was that the Lions were holding formation as they shouted at the wagon drivers to head for a little knoll, topped by a copse of trees, that sat at the far end of the clearing. The rain of arrows thickened.

"Ai, Lord, Thiemo," cried Heribert, "if this is a Quman patrol, then each of them must be shooting four bows at once."

More of the wagons broke free into the clearing, but it was already too late. The foremost group of Polenie horsemen had charged left into the trees to head off the Quman attack. As the lines collided a noise like rumbling thunder filled the air as weapons clashed.

Blessing woke. "Where's Daddy?" she cried.

Lewenhardt leaped onto the wagon, standing literally over the child, bracing himself with a foot on either side of her body. Thiemo, Matto, Surly, Everwin, Den, Johannes, and Chustaffus made a ring around the cart. Heribert hastily mounted Lewenhardt's horse, falling behind as more wagons raced forward, desperate to escape the Quman.

Anna got to her knees, staring. Back in the woods, the Polenie standard bobbed awkwardly. The battle was all confusion, half lost under the shade of trees now that the sunlight burned her eyes. It seemed like everywhere she saw Quman wings, crowding into the ranks of Polenie horsemen. A horn blew another long blast before stuttering to silence as the first Quman horsemen broke through the Polenie line, as the handsome Polenie riders scattered from the battle, fleeing or dying.

Blessing tried to push to her feet, but Anna shoved her back down as another rain of arrows spattered around them. Everwin swore, yanking off an arrow that lodged in his chain mail. Matto was bleeding where an arrow had cut into the leather cheek strap of his helmet.

The worst thing about the Quman attack was its silence: no horns, no trilling cries, only the whistle of their wings where the wind sang in them. At last, inevitably, the Polenie standard sank into the fray and the last of Duke Boleslas' cavalry—had there really been three or four hundreds of them?—were lost to sight, leaving only infantry, half of them running, or falling, or battling as well as they could against superior numbers.

"We're going to die," said Thiemo.

"Shut up," snapped Surly. "I hate whiners."

The wagon surged forward, neck and neck with the painted wagon in which Bayan's mother rode. Her slaves trotted alongside, easily keeping up. Their calm expressions, almost of indifference, hadn't changed.

"Ho! Princess!" An old Lion gestured wildly. "Move along!" The first line of the Lions had reached the knoll and already

were frantically digging in, chopping down trees, anything to
make a barrier against the horsemen.

Back in the forest, it had begun to rain. Thunder grumbled
ominously, and wind whipped the treetops. The Quman were
everywhere. Was this their entire army, that had cut around to
attack them from behind? A large contingent galloped past,
far off to the right side, heading toward the rear of the unsuspecting Saony legion. Others surged up to catch the last of the
wagons. A carter was killed, cut down from behind as he
whipped his horses. Another man threw himself from his cart
and tried to take refuge under the bed, but he got trampled
before he got to safety. Without dismounting, Quman warriors
began to pull the contents from the carts. Chests were spilled
open and bags dumped in the mud to see if they held anything
of value.

Half of the Lions fell back to form a line between the forward half of the baggage train and the part that was already
being overrun. A number of other infantrymen joined up with
them, although in truth hundreds must have already died or
fled into the forest, hoping to escape back the way they'd
come.

"Get down, girl!" cried Lewenhardt as he dropped to his
knees. A shower of arrows fell around them. Someone was hit;
Everwin, maybe, or Den. Anna threw herself forward over
Blessing. The child wriggled and protested, trying to get free
so she could see.

"Lie still!" Terror made Anna's voice no better than a croak.

Lewenhardt jerked to one side as an arrow passed his ear. It
buried its point in the neck of the driver, whose head kicked
forward. He twitched a few times, slumped as the reins slipped
from his hand, and toppled from the wagon. At once,
Chustaffus slid gracefully from his mount to the driver's seat
and got hold of the reins with his good arm. Behind the
twelfth rank of wagons, all they could now hope to save, the
rear guard of the Lions stepped back in good order, a single
step at a time. The Quman, those who weren't looting the rear

wagons, hesitated, unwilling to assault the well-ordered company now that they didn't have surprise on their side.

The knoll lay but a spear's throw away. A rough palisade was already rising as Captain Thiadbold ordered the defense. As their wagon rolled in, it was commandeered at once to fill in a gap in the wall. Anna leaped off the wagon just as Thiemo pulled Blessing free. A moment later, Lions got their shoulders under the wagon's bed and tipped it up on its side. Its contents spilled everywhere. A bag of grain ripped, and wheat poured onto the ground while men hurried over it, unheeding. As the other wagons trundled up, they were corralled to fill in gaps in this makeshift redoubt; even oxen and horses were tied up across such gaps. Only the painted wagon of Bayan's mother was left untouched.

But it was already too late.

A Quman captain with magnificent eagle feather wings had whipped his unruly men into formation. The line split. The main force of the Quman and their leader attacked obliquely on the right flank of the retreating line of infantry, while a smaller force circled around the left, still launching arrows as they rode. Anna hauled Blessing up the knoll to crouch in the shelter of a beech tree, her arms wrapped tightly around the little girl.

So close. Arrows fluttered through the branches. Men shrieked in pain. The line of retreating Lions curled back, trying to protect their back, and to protect the last of the wagons now racing for the knoll. It was impossible that they wouldn't all be killed before they reached the knoll. They were less than a bow's shot away.

Lewenhardt took aim and loosed his arrow. The Quman leader's horse tumbled, throwing him to the earth. A shout of triumph rose from the retreating line of Lions. The old Lion at their center shouted orders. In groups of three and four, men broke from the center, running to extend the flanks so that the line kept extending—at the cost of the center, so far unchallenged. Most of the wagons had now reached the knoll, been

tipped over, and set up to fill in gaps, but they didn't have
enough to make it all the way around the knoll.

A few arrows launched from the knoll landed among the
Quman attacking the left. A band of ten Lions charged off the
knoll to prevent that line of their comrades from being outflanked. On the right the Quman horse rode up to the line but
balked at the hedge of spears and shields retreating evenly
before them.

"Gotfrid!" cried Thiadbold from the knoll. "Close up!"

As Lewenhardt and other archers shot rapidly, and accurately,
the line still out in the clearing moved backward at double step.
Leaving a dozen of their men dead on the field, the Lions closed
up the gap. A ragged cheer rose from the Lions waiting for
them on the knoll. It was a small, bitter victory, probably short-
lived. The rear guard was gone, obliterated, except for them.

Far away, Anna heard the ring of battle breaking out as the
Quman hit the Saony legion from behind.

"They're going to wrap up the line of march one legion at a
time, from the rear." Heribert was white in the face, breathing
hard, as he grabbed Blessing's arm and tugged her up to the
top of the knoll.

"Won't go!" cried Blessing, waving her wooden sword,
which she had managed to salvage from the overturned wagon.
"I have to fight, too!"

Anna slapped her on the rump. That got her going.

All across the clearing, Quman continued to upset and loot
the captured baggage. The leader, now on a new mount, began
organizing the attack against the knoll. Riders spread out in a
circle around the knoll and moved in. Near the top Heribert
found an old oak with a bit of a hollow burned out, where
some traveler had once hidden out from a storm. Anna shoved
Blessing in against her protests and stood with her own body
blocking the opening.

The eight slaves had brought Bayan's mother, discreetly
concealed in her litter, to the top of the knoll. Now they
crouched around her.

Anna smelled rain, approaching fast.

Quman riders closed. Because their arrows came from all directions, it was impossible to find a tree that could protect on all sides. Some lord's concubine, a woman with beautiful blonde hair now fallen free over her shoulders, began to curse and throw stones at them—until she was shot dead through the chest.

Lewenhardt and the other archers made them pay dearly. Every arrow Lewenhardt loosed struck human, or horse flesh. The Quman were no fools. Every person on the knoll who picked up a bow was quickly dropped by a hail of arrows. Many of them aimed specifically for the young archer, but he had a way of shifting, almost like a twitch, that moved whatever part of his body was endangered out of the path of the incoming arrow. Still, he bled from a dozen scratches on his thighs and arms. A young boy, a carter's son, wounded in the leg, scrabbled about gathering spent arrows and placing them at Lewenhardt's feet.

But even with the wagon redoubt, gaps loomed. Even with a strong cohort of Lions and various stragglers, the Quman outnumbered them, and as far as Anna could tell, their enemies had no shortage of arrows.

Five Quman riders made a sortie for one of the gaps, where Thiadbold himself with a brace of Lions held the opening with shields raised. The enemy fired at the men's feet, all they could see except the tips of their helms.

"At them!" shouted Captain Thiadbold, leaping forward with an arrow quivering in the sole of his boot. He hurled his spear, taking one of the Quman in the throat as his men surged forward with him. Well-placed ax blows caught arms or legs, and Lions dragged three of the riders down to the ground, where they died in a flurry of blows. The last one fought his horse round, thinking to flee, but old Gotfrid had readied his throwing ax, and he threw it with all his might. The rider slumped forward with the handle of the ax sticking out from between the wings and the blade embedded through split plates of lamellar armor.

To the right, another group of Lions tried a similar sally, but as they lurched forward, their leader was caught in the eye by an arrow. Dismayed, his companions scrambled back for cover.

The arrows kept coming. It seemed like between one breath and the next, fully a third of the Lions lay dead or dying and most of the others were wounded several times over. But they would never surrender. They endured the storms of arrows, waiting for that moment when their spears and axes could bite. But there were so many gaps now, too many to hold.

"Look," said Heribert, but Anna had already seen it.

Rain swept toward them over the treetops.

"Let me see!" shrieked Blessing, her voice muffled within the oak hollow. Her small fists pummeled the back of Anna's legs as she fought to get out.

The Quman riders pressed in. Some grabbed the carts and dragged them back while others attacked. Old Gotfrid dropped his shield so that he could concentrate solely on his spear work. His spear point snapped Quman faceplates and caught men in their vulnerable throats. He did not hesitate to strike horse or rider. He was a veteran who did not waste his energy. He did not throw half the blows of the younger Lions, but each one counted. Gotfrid's companions defended him with their shields, well aware of the damage he would do if they could keep him alive.

The eagle rider bore down on Thiadbold's group, which held a gap between a wagon and a cart. The ox which had once filled much of that space lay dying from numerous arrow wounds. The horse had been cut free and had bolted away. As the Quman leaped the ox carcass, the eagle rider struck at Thiadbold. Thiadbold caught the blow on his shield and pressed in, driving his sword deep into the horse's belly. The rider kicked him in the head as the horse collapsed. Another Quman thrust, striking Thiadbold in the side. Thiemo struck the spear haft down with his sword, splintering it, as Matto, Surly, and Everwin waded in with their swords. They traded a fierce exchange of blows, but Everwin staggered back, his face covered in blood. Den, who still had an arrow protruding from his side, joined the fight, as did Johannes, and Chustaffus with his one good arm.

Then it was hard to see, or maybe that was only tears in her eyes. Was it starting to rain?

The remaining Lions gave ground step by hard fought step. Captain Thiadbold was back up, accounting himself well; his mail had saved him. Anna whispered a prayer, brushing her hand in the remembered gesture, a circle drawn around her Circle of Unity.

Remembering that day long ago in the cathedral in Gent, when the Eika prince had let them go. Remembering the way her voice had choked in her throat when, in Steleshame, she had heard Count Lavastine's heir tell her that he had once given a wooden Circle, such as hers, such as the one the Eika prince had worn at his throat, to an Eika prince. But she had not spoken; she had not asked, to see if it were the same prince. She had not closed the Circle.

That was why God had punished her.

In ten more steps, the remaining Lions would close in on her position, and then they would have no farther to retreat. Heribert raised his staff, making ready to fight, with the most desolate look on his face that Anna could imagine. He looked brave enough, but it was obvious from his stance that he would be no threat to his attackers. He glanced at her. "Try if you can to be taken prisoner, with the princess," he said in a low voice. "If you ever see him again, tell the prince I died fighting."

Raindrops spit on her face. Out in the clearing it had begun to rain harder, but Quman riders continued their looting undisturbed.

So far away, as in a dream, she heard the ring of Wendish horns calling a retreat.

The Quman were going to kill them all.

Not even the Kerayit princess' weather magic could save them now.

The tip of the wooden sword poked out between Anna's calves. Blessing wriggled and shoved forward as Anna staggered; the little girl thrust out her head, blinking as she surveyed the gruesome scene, as the wave of sound, grunts, cries, sobs, calm commands, and the screams of wounded horses, swept over her, as raindrops slipped down her little cheeks.

"Don't worry, Anna," she said in her self-assured voice. "My Daddy is coming to save us."

2

THE gatekeeper who guarded the narrow entrance to the sphere of Aturna looked remarkably like Wolfhere.

"Liath!" The gatekeeper held his spear across the open portal to bar her way. Black storm clouds swirled beyond; she could distinguish no landmarks on the other side. "Where are you? I have been looking for you!"

"What do you want from me, Wolfhere? Who is my mother? Tell me the truth!" As she stepped forward, the tip of the arrow she held in her right hand brushed through him, and he dissolved as does an image reflected in water when it is disturbed. Had it really been Wolfhere, seeking her with Eagle's sight, or only a phantom sent to tease her, or test her? Frowning, she passed through the gate.

Storm winds bit into her naked skin. Blades of ice stung her as she pressed forward, leaning into the howling gale. It was so bitterly cold. Gusts of icy wind boomed and roared. Her hair streamed out behind her, and she had to shelter her eyes with an arm, raised up before her face. In her left hand she held Seeker of Hearts and in her right her last arrow, fletched with the gold feather Eldest Uncle had given her. These alone remained of all the things she had started with. These alone, but for her own self.

The cold winds numbed her. Her lips cracked, became so stiff that she could not even speak to call out, to see if any creature lived in these harsh realms that might rescue her. Shivering, aching, battered by the freezing gale, she could only battle forward as her fingers went dead, as the pain of cold seeped all the way down to her bones.

It was so cold, a vale of ice.

She was going to die out here. Not this night, but another one, tomorrow perhaps. There weren't even the pigs to keep her warm. She was going to die, or she was going to turn around and walk back into the chamber where Hugh was waiting for her, just as she had done that winter night in Heart's Rest when she was only sixteen. Just as she had done that awful night, when she had given in to him because it was the only way to save her own life.

But it hadn't been the only way. Da had hidden her power from her in order to conceal her from Anne, who was hunting her. Da had never taught her how to fight, only how to hide and how to run. Hugh had understood that better than she ever had.

She wasn't a powerless girl any longer, frightened and helpless.

She called fire, and the cold blast of icy air split around her. The clouds melted away like fog under the sun.

Aturna's realm dazzled her. She walked along the floor of a vast ravine, its distant walls so far away that their height was lost in a haze. Waterfalls spilled down on either side, flashing, blinding, as light sparkled off the falling waters. Daimones danced within the brilliant waters, too bright to see except for one with salamander eyes. Ahead, a pair of huge gold wheels thrummed around and around, the source of the wind.

In the vale of Aturna, home to the sage of wisdom, nothing was hidden from her, who could now look long and deeply within herself into the cold darkness that weighed her down.

She had relied on the strength of others for too long: Da and Hanna, Wolfhere and Sanglant, even Anne, who had made promises and never kept them. Even Jerna, whom she had ripped out of the world and back into the sphere of Erekes when she had needed her help to cross the poisonous sea. In the end, she could never reach out fully to others: not to Hanna and Ivar, who had befriended her with honest hearts; not to Sister Rosvita, who had sensed a kindred soul; not to Thiadbold and the Lions who had offered her comradeship; not to Alain, who had given her unconditional trust. Not even to her beloved Sanglant and her precious Blessing. She could not trust them until she trusted herself.

Almost as if that last thought brought it into existence, a staircase came into view, hewn of marble and rising up between the golden wheels. Tendrils of mist played around its base, and its height was lost in a bright blaze of fire, like a ring of flaming swords: the entrance, she knew at once, to the realm of the fixed stars.

Home.

The unexpected thought made her stumble to a halt. Her heart hammered alarmingly. She thought she would keel over and die right there, because she could not catch her breath. Flushed and sweating with exhilaration and astonishment, hope, and dismay all at once, she crouched to steady herself, resting her fist on the ground.

A white-haired figure sat with head bowed on the first step. He was dressed in a plain cleric's tunic. As she caught her breath, rose, and stepped forward, he raised his head.

It was Wolfhere.

Nay, not Wolfhere. That was only the guise she saw, the man with secrets who knew more than he let on.

"You are the guardian of this sphere," she said. "I would ascend the steps."

"You have come a long way," he agreed, "but I warn you, you have only one arrow left. Use it more wisely than you did your others. There is one close to you whom you can save, if you can learn to see with your wits rather than act on your fears."

He moved aside.

She hesitated. Was it a trick? A test? But she had to ascend to reach her goal. No other way was open to her now.

She set her foot on the first step. "I thank you," she said to the guardian, but he was already gone.

The steps felt smooth and easy beneath her bare feet. As she climbed, sparks and flashes like lightning shot off the thrumming wheels that spun high in the air on either side of the stairs. The brilliant light of the wheels grew more intense as she climbed. Through clouds of gold drifting above she saw into a chamber of infinite size. Nests of blue-white stars glowed hotly, the birthplace of angels. Thick clots of dust made strange and tangled shapes where they billowed across an expanse of blackness. A faint wheel of stars, like an echo of the golden wheels on either side of her, spun with aching slowness. Beyond all this lay silence, deep, endless, unfathomable.

A flash of blue fire caught her gaze: the crossroads between spheres and worlds. Its flames shuddered and flared, bright one instant and then fading as if that fire pulsed in time to the heart of the universe. In flashes she saw through the distant crossroads into other worlds, other times, other places, glimpses half seen and quickly gone:

a girl standing with her arms full of flowers; a woman seated at a desk, writing with a strange sort of quill on sheets of paper, not vellum, her black hair pulled back in a ponytail and her dark coat cut in a style Liath has never seen; Count Lavastine's effigy in stone, with two stone hounds in faithful attendance; an egg cracking as a barbed claw pokes through from inside the shell; the slow trail of molten rivers of fire as they shift course; a centaur woman galloping across the steppe, expression alive to the beauty of speed and power; a woman dressed only in a corded skirt, suckling twin infants; Emperor Taillefer himself, proud and strong, at the height of his power, as he watches his favorite daughter invested as biscop.

Inside a pavilion, Ironhead's concubine, the pretty one with black hair, smooths Lord John's hair back from the crown of his head in a gentle gesture as he sleeps. Then she takes a stake and, with a hammer blow, drives it through his temple so hard that the point of the stake cleaves his skull to pierce the carpet below. Blood pools, changing color as it snakes out in a stream along the ground, drawing her gaze along its twisting length until Liath sees the man watching from a shadowed corner in the tent.

Hugh.

He lifts his head, as if he has sensed her. She bolts down another branch of the crossroads, forward in time.

Longships ghost out of the fog wreathing the Temes River. With heartless efficiency, silent and almost invisible, they beach along the strand below the walled city of Hefenfelthe. The great hall built by the Alban queens rises like the prow of a vast ship beyond the wall, long considered impregnable. Because of the power of the queens and their tree sorcerers, Hefenfelthe has never been taken by fighting. Eika warriors swarm from the ships as mist binds the river, concealing them. A torch flares by the river gate. The chain rumbles, and as the vanguard races up to the walls, the gate swings open. What cannot be gained by force can be gained by treachery. Stronghand pauses as three men dressed in the rich garb of merchants scurry out of the gate, signaling frantically as they hurry forward to welcome the army they betrayed their own queen for. His lead warriors cut down the traitors. No man can serve two masters. If they would betray their own people for mere coin, then they can never be trusted. His army pours past the bodies, although dogs pause to feed on the corpses and have to be driven forward. He waits on the shore as the sun rises, still obscured by mist. The first alarms sound from inside the city, but it is already too late. Threads of smoke begin to twist upward into the heavens, blending and melding. . . .

She paused, aware again that she stood far up the stairs, the sphere of Aturna glittering below, beyond the golden wheels, and the universe opening beyond her.

A silver belt twisted through the gulf, marking the path of the country of the Aoi, now drawn inexorably back toward Earth. It was impossible to tell one side of the ribboned surface from the other or if it even had two sides at all but only one infinite gleaming surface. With her gaze she followed it down past the spheres descending below, each gateway a gem cut into a sphere's bright curve, all the way down to where Earth lay exposed below her, too broad to encompass with her outstretched arms here at the height of the spheres. Its curve, too, was evident where the line of advancing dawn receded to the west and night rose in the east. Taillefer's crown gleamed, spread out across the land, seven crowns each with seven points, the great wheel set across many realms and uncounted leagues: the vast loom of magic.

She saw:

Far below a battle rages. On a knoll a child brandishes a useless wooden sword while all around her Lions fight and die under the assault of winged riders, the Quman. Is that Thiadbold, calling out commands? The Lions fight bravely, but their numbers thin as the winged riders attack again, and again. It is only a matter of time.

As though struck by lightning, she recognized that dark-haired girl. She plunged down into the world below the moon, bow in hand.

How has Blessing come to be so old, four years of age at least? Ai, Lady! Has so much time passed? Has the child grown, knowing nothing of her mother? Will she die likewise, motherless and abandoned?

Liath sets her arrow to the bow, makes ready to draw.

But whom shall she shoot? There are fifty, or a hundred, or two hundred Quman riders swarming around the knoll and, farther away, another equally large group attacks and routs the rear of a legion of Wendish soldiers. She recognizes the banner of Saony, but this is only a minor distraction.

She must save her child.

Yet against so many, one arrow will not be enough to save her.

To shoot now is to waste the only weapon she has left.

Ai, Lord. Where is Sanglant?

They had at last gained a good view of the plain and the Quman army set in battle order not far beyond when one of Bayan's Ungrians came galloping up.

"My lord prince!" The captain had served in several embassies and spoke Wendish well. "Prince Sanglant! Prince Bayan commands you to turn your line about—"

"Turn my line about!" Sanglant's anger cut the message short. What was Bayan plotting now, demanding that he turn his line away from the enemy and thus lose the honor of engaging the Quman in battle?

"Look, my lord prince!" cried Sibold, who had been given the honor this day of carrying the banner.

Only a short stretch of woodland separated them from the open fields where the Quman gathered. The vanguard of the Wendish army could be seen, banners flying, as they emerged from the wood and split apart into regular lines to face the Quman across the broad gap. For a moment Sanglant admired the brisk efficiency of Sapientia's troops, drilled and trained by Bayan over the winter. Was it jealousy that made him hesitate? Did he fear that Sapientia would acquit herself well, as Bayan clearly meant her to do? Wasn't it necessary to give her a chance to prove herself fit to command, and therefore to rule?

He turned back to the messenger. "Go on."

"My lord prince." The man loosened the strap on his helm and tipped it back for relief from the heat. "Prince Bayan orders you to turn your legion and ride to the aid of the rear guard. The Quman swung wide and sent an entire wing of their army to destroy the rear. Duke Boleslas and the Polenie are hard hit, and the rout has already reached the Saony legion, which is scattering—"

"My daughter?" asked Sanglant, as the cold battle fury descended.

The messenger flushed. "There is no news either of your daughter's whereabouts or those of Prince Bayan's mother. The entire rear has collapsed."

He waited for no more. "Captain Fulk! Send Sergeant Cobbo to alert Lord Druthmar that we are turning. He will ride at the rear of our unit. I'll take the van myself. Sibold!"

Horns rang out. The banners signaled the turnabout. These were not battle-hardened troops, as his Dragons had been, but he had seen their willingness to follow over the last few months. This would be their true test.

Goaded by his fury and his fear, they rode recklessly, at full bore. He trusted them to keep up. Let the unworthy fall behind. He would kill every Quman himself if he had to.

They swung wide through the open woodland as they pounded past Prince Bayan's Ungrians, who whooped and cheered to give them courage but who nevertheless kept moving toward the plain. Why hadn't Bayan himself turned around to meet the threat from behind?

No time to think of that now.

A gap had opened between the Ungrian rear guard and the van of the Saony legion, under the joint command of the two quarreling brothers. Stragglers appeared, running through the trees: soldiers on horseback, a few hapless camp followers on foot, screaming warnings when they saw the prince and his legion. He lifted a hand; Fulk blew the horn twice, and the entire mass of men—not less than six hundred riders including Druthmar and his marchlanders—came to a stop as Sanglant brought several soldiers to a halt.

Their stories varied wildly. The entire Quman army had hit the baggage train. Lord Zwentibold was dead. Duke Boleslas was dead. Duke Boleslas was in league with the Quman. All the wagons were burning.

One man had seen the Lions forming up around a knoll; from his brief, panicked description, Sanglant recalled the little hill. He had noted it, as he always noted strategic landmarks, when he had ridden past earlier.

Signaling to Fulk, he started forward. Soon enough they heard the clash of battle ahead. Breaking into a gallop, Sanglant led the charge.

The Saony legion, taken unawares from behind by the Quman, had dissolved into scattered bands of stalwart men fighting for their lives while the rest fled or were cut down from behind. Sanglant saw Wichman's banner, still bobbing aloft, before he lowered his lance and let the weight of their charge carry them into the Quman line. In their heavy armor, his Wendish auxiliaries bore down and trampled the more lightly armed Quman riders, just overran them. Sanglant knocked one man from his horse, then thrust his lance deep into another Quman's unprotected belly before letting go of the haft and drawing his sword. With a cry, he lay about on either side, driving his way through the Quman. Feathers drifted on the air. Bones cracked. Horses stumbled, wounded, and fell, plunging their riders to the ground. A shout of triumph rose from the Saony men who had so far survived, and they redoubled their efforts.

"Call the advance!" cried Sanglant over the noise, pulling away from the fighting so that Fulk could gather his men again. Wichman had rallied half the remaining Saony troops. There was no sign of Zwentibold. Sanglant signaled, and Lord Druthmar joined him. "Use your men as the other claw of the pincer. Now that we've shaken up the Quman line, you can crush them between your group and Saony."

"As you command, my lord prince." Druthmar called out orders as Sanglant withdrew from the battle with half of his soldiers.

Fulk blew the advance. Sibold raised the banner high, thrice, and with Sanglant still in the lead, they rode in haste for the baggage train. Behind, the battle raged on as Druthmar drove his soldiers back upon the flank of the Quman, catching them front and rear.

But as shadowy figures fled through the forest on all sides, refugees from the fighting, Sanglant could think only of the baggage train. Pray God his daughter still lived. He should have left her at Walburg, with Waltharia; he knew it, and guilt burned him, but he had to push it aside. If he let guilt cloud his mind now, then he was risking the lives of the men he commanded. There would be plenty of time for guilt later, when this was done.

A crowd of prisoners came into view, being herded by a half-dozen Quman soldiers. At the sight of this new force, the Quman abandoned their captives and rode away, unwilling to stand and fight. The prisoners cheered hoarsely at the sight of the prince and his golden banner. But Sanglant strained to see through the open forest. Was that the knoll, ahead? He heard cries, and the ring of fighting. He heard rain, and the growl of thunder.

"There!" cried Fulk.

A broad clearing opened before them. Wagons and carts had been abandoned all across the grassy expanse, now wet under a light rain whose front stopped, uncannily, just before the knoll. Careless Quman, lured by the riches carried in a prince's train, had given up the fight to loot. Not all of them were so undisciplined, however. Wagons had been thrown up to make a palisade around the knoll, but this line had now been abandoned as the remaining Lions were forced to retreat up the knoll. Despite the tiring run, Resuelto stretched out into a gallop, feeling his rider's anticipation.

"Fulk! Take Cobbo's company and kill those looters."

A third of the men peeled away, bearing down on the enemy now scrambling for their horses, trying to ready their weapons before they got trampled or swept away. A few Quman threw down their weapons and dropped to the damp ground, trying to surrender—

He didn't see what became of them. The Quman's leader had pulled back from the attack on the knoll to meet Sanglant. Both men wielded swords. Sanglant parried, and cut, cleaving the other man through shoulder and wing. With a shove, he toppled him from his horse.

A Quman rider collided with Resuelto, but the steppe pony was dwarfed by the Wendish war steed. The jolt made the gelding stagger, but the Quman was knocked to the ground. Resuelto reared and plunged down. The Quman died quickly, but the pony still struggled, trying to rise.

At last Sanglant reached the overturned wagons. Above, a score of Lions fought desperately against the onslaught of winged warriors. A cheer rose from the Lions as they caught sight of their rescuers. They attacked with renewed strength, using their shields to shove the winged riders off-balance as Sanglant, now closely followed by Lord Hrodik and his Gentish followers, fell upon their flank.

Sibold and the rest of Sanglant's company had circled the base of the knoll to pinch off the attack from the other side. While many men who bore a banner simply followed and defended, not so Sibold: the reckless fellow seemed to enjoy dropping the banner in the face of his foe and then closing for the kill while the enemy was still confused. Pressed from all sides, the Quman broke and scattered, running like deer.

The Quman who had pursued the attack up onto the hill were now cut off, and the hundred or so Wendish warriors at Sanglant's back whittled them down until there were not more than two dozen Quman left, many dismounted and wounded, now surrounded.

Sanglant knew one word in the Quman tongue. "Surrender!" he cried now.

A few of the Quman cursed. The rest remained silent, unyielding.

Between one breath and the next, the rain stopped falling.

Red-haired Captain Thiadbold stood at the height of the knoll, commanding what remained of the stalwart Lions. He stepped forward. "No mercy!" he shouted into the unexpected silence. "Kill them all!"

With cries of glee and fury, the Wendish soldiers fell upon the cornered Quman. The fight was short and desperate. Lord Hrodik fell, pierced in the side, but soon the last of the Quman was beheaded by a Lion's ax after having been knocked prone by old Gotfrid, the Lion Sanglant had rescued from a slaver's chains.

Blessing burst into sight as though she had exploded out of a tree. She leaped for her father's arms. Sanglant scooped her out of the air and held her tight, face pressed against her hair. She smelled of rotting logs. But she was alive.

"I was waiting for you," she cried, scolding him, "but it took you so long to come and kill the bad men."

"I know, sweetheart," he said, trying not to weep for joy at holding her, unharmed. "They won't hurt you now. I must go to fight at the front. The battle against Bulkezu is yet to be joined."

"Didn't you kill Bulkezu? Wasn't that dead man him?"

"Nay, Daughter." Tears stung his eyes. They always did, when he had to view the carnage, so many good men down. "This was only a feint, an attempt to roll us up from behind and catch us between two claws." He kissed her and handed her into Heribert's waiting arms as the cleric staggered down the slope, face pale and robes streaked with blood. Quman blood smeared Blessing's cheek and stained her tunic where she had pressed against her father's tabard.

"Thank God," said Heribert. That was all.

Anna crept forward to sink down next to the cleric. A moment later young Matto and Lord Thiemo, limping but mobile, pushed their way out of the crowd as well. Were they all that remained of the men he'd left behind to guard Blessing?

Fulk and his company had slaughtered any remaining Quman and now hunted through the scattered remnants of the baggage train. None of the ill-gotten loot from the train would ever arrive in the eastern plains, nor would any of these rich fabrics and glittering jewelry ever adorn Quman women.

"My lord prince." Captain Thiadbold knelt before him, bloodied but not bowed. The groans of wounded men, Wendish and Quman alike, made a horrible din around them. "What is your command?"

"Set up a field hospital." Sanglant glanced around and caught sight of Wolfhere, who had done his part in the fighting but now moved through the battlefield, searching for wounded who could be pulled free. "Eagle! You'll stay with the Lions. There must be men here who might still live if they're cared for. These wagons can be set to rights, and loaded. Be ready to march as soon as you can."

"What of the Quman who are injured?" asked Thiadbold. "My men will kill them willingly enough."

Sanglant hesitated. "Nay. Save those who can live. The Lord enjoins mercy, and I'll have it now. Our enemy may yet prove of use to us."

Wolfhere glanced at him, a strange expression on his face, but he said nothing. Instead, he hurried down the knoll to organize the freed prisoners and surviving soldiers into a work detail. Thiadbold merely shrugged and rose, calling to his men.

Captain Fulk rode up. "My lord prince. The Quman are routed."

"Sound the horn and rally the men. We must return to Prince Bayan."

Sibold raised the gold banner high so that all could spot the prince's colors as Fulk blew three staccato blasts on the horn. Almost all his men reassembled; Lord Hrodik had fallen and was possibly dead, but the prince guessed that he hadn't lost more than ten men in the attack. If only the Lions, and Duke Boleslas and his Polenie, had been so lucky. He could see the line of battle, and the dead, stretching east into the forest, a clear trail of bodies and blood showing the way the earlier battle had fallen out with the Quman chasing down the fleeing baggage train and the Polenie trying desperately to stop them.

No use dwelling over what was past. No time for regrets in the midst of battle. Knowing the real battle could be joined at any moment back on the Veser plain, Sanglant raised a hand to signal the advance. Paused. The skin between his shoulder blades crawled, as though an arrow had been aimed to pierce his back. He glanced back over his shoulder.

Captain Fulk moved up beside him. "Do you see anything, my lord prince? I believe we killed them all. They'll not be back to trouble your daughter this day."

"Nay, it's not that, although we have to win the battle at hand before we can be sure we're free of trouble." Sanglant had a momentary illusion that hornets were swarming all around his head, but it sloughed off quickly. Yet he still could not shake the sense that someone was watching him. "Ai, Lord, Fulk, it's hard enough knowing the danger my sweet child faces every day, that I've brought on her. Lord knows I've done things I'm not proud of these last months, but God forgive me, I still think of Liath constantly. Will I ever see her again?"

"I pray that you will, my lord prince."

At times like these, battle was almost a relief. Better to fight than to dwell on his grief and his fears. He lifted his hand again, calling for a new lance to be brought for him.

A crack of thunder splintered the air around them. Horses neighed, rearing. Men raised their voices in alarm, but as suddenly quieted. As though silence itself commanded attention, men began to look around. Sanglant, too, looked back over his shoulder to see a tiny figure descending from the knoll. A veil concealed her face, but her ancient hands, gnarled with arthritis, betrayed her age. Scarcely taller than a child, Bayan's mother wore rich gold robes elaborately embroidered with scenes of griffins and dragons locked in battle. When she commandeered a horse from a soldier—who promptly dropped to his knees as though felled—and mounted with assistance from one of her slaves, Sanglant saw that the robes were split for riding. Hastily, he rode over to her as soldiers reined away, made superstitious by the stories they had heard and by the uncanny behavior of the rain.

"My lady," he began in Wendish, "I pray you, forgive me for not knowing the proper address for a woman of your birth and rank." Though she was mounted now on a huge warhorse whose size dwarfed her, she did not look ridiculous. Sanglant towered over her. "I beg you, you will be safer here in the rear now that we have—"

One of her slaves stepped forward. "Stand not in the way of the holy woman." He was a huge man with a dark complexion

and thick shoulders and arms, not the kind worth tangling
with in a fight unless necessary.

"She is safer—"

She rode away. Her feet didn't even reach the stirrups.

"The holy woman has seen that her luck is in danger," said
the slave. "She must go."

Her luck?

That quickly, Sanglant remembered the old Kerayit custom,
that a shaman woman's luck resided in the body of another
person.

Her luck was her son.

This time when he raised a hand, twin horns blared. In the
distance, he heard the answering bell of Druthmar's horn.
Afflicted all at once with a horrible sense of foreboding,
Sanglant signaled the advance. With his forces marshaled and
Druthmar waiting farther down to join them, Sanglant led
them back along the road at a trot.

*Long ago, at besieged Gent, when she saw him for the first time, he
had been wearing that same dragon helm, splendid and handsome.
Just as he was then. Just as he is now. Desire is a flame, a torch burning in the night. No traveler can help but be drawn toward it.*

Ai, God, she misses him. She misses the feel of him.

*But she has to go on. She has to choose wisely, never forgetting that
she isn't truly on Earth but rather ascending the last sphere.*

*No creature male or female can harm him. Remembering this, she
stayed her hand through the worst of the fighting. In battle, truly,
Sanglant can take care of himself. She hasn't forgotten the lesson she
learned in the sphere of Jedu, the angel of war.*

*She hasn't forgotten the horror of being killed, over and over again,
by the one she loves.*

*But those hornets bother her. She saw them as aetheric darts sting-
ing at his face and hands. He shook them off, but it is obvious to her
that another hand works magic, hoping to harm the prince. She touches*

the golden robes of the old woman, the veiled one, but although the crone starts around surprised, feeling her touch, the woman cannot see her, only sense her gaze. The old woman has a face so wrinkled that it is hard to see the soul beneath, like an insect protected by its carapace. Despite her great age, her hair is still as black as a girl's. Her complexion is dusky, and her dark eyes are pulled tight at the corners in the shape of an almond. These features mark her as a steppe dweller, a woman from the eastern tribes, the people who live on the endless plains of grass with their herds and their tents.

She has powerful magic, the air hums around her as though infested with bees, but it isn't her magic that threatens Sanglant. Regretfully, Liath leaves Sanglant, Blessing, and the old woman behind and speeds onward, an arrow on the aetheric winds binding the Earth. She has become the bow.

Skirmishes are being fought far into the woods and as far away as the twin rivers, flowing northward to join at the base of Osterburg's walls. Such melees do not warrant more than a glance. She seeks, and she finds two armies massed for battle just beyond the woodland, gathered on open ground. The Wendish fly the banner of Princess Sapientia, the sigil of the heir of Wendar and Varre, six animals set on a shield: lion, dragon, and eagle, horse, hawk, and guivre. A large force of Ungrians bearing the sigil of the double-headed eagle comes up behind the Wendish line, ready to strike at the center of the Quman line.

Already the Quman archers fire at will, to soften up their enemy, but the Ungrians give as good as they get, and the Wendish legions swing wide and begin a steady advance toward the flanks. The Quman force seems larger than it is. From this height, like a hawk circling, she sees that the wings they wear make them seem as if they have more soldiers than they really do.

Brute force will win this engagement today, unless that magic she tastes in the air and feels like a prickling along her skin turns the tide.

A rumble like thunder rises as the armies shift forward and charge. Dust billows into the air. The Wendish and Ungrian forces shriek and cry out, voices ringing above the pound of hooves, but the Quman *advance in uncanny silence, goaded on by their prince, whose griffin wings shine and glitter in the sunlight.*

Just as the two armies meet in a resounding clash, she finds a thread spanning the wind. Aetheric hornets gleam along its length, buzzing and chattering as it extends toward the armies. She speeds backward along the thread. Beyond the Veser in a makeshift camp, desperate prisoners huddle, awaiting the outcome of the battle, but the thread leads her an arrow's shot away from the groaning, helpless captives, back across the river to a low rise on the east bank over-looking the plain. The glimmering thread curls into a line of horsemen: a dozen guards, one light-haired person dressed in ragged Wendish garb, and a strange man stripped down to trousers patched together from a hundred different pieces of fabric. Blue-black tattoos cover his torso; they seem to writhe and shiver as he chants. Unlike the other Quman warriors, he wears no blackened and shrunken head dangling from his belt, but his ornaments are gruesome enough: earrings made from shriveled human noses, a needle piercing the septum of his nose and each end of it adorned with a withered human ear.

He is a shaman. The thread of hornets spins out from his voice, twisted into life through the words of his spell.

The woman beside him raises her head. In that first instant, Liath does not recognize her because of the hatred that mars her expression as she gazes over the field of battle. Hate distorts the heart, leaving scars, as it has scarred her own heart. Remembering this, she knows her.

"Hanna!"

Hanna shakes her head as though to chase away annoying flies. Her hands are tied in front of her; she is a captive, forced to watch as the battle unfolds. The smooth wood of Seeker of Hearts feels cool against Liath's palms. One arrow will not rescue Hanna, not with a dozen guards, and because she does not exist on Earth in bodily form, she cannot manifest fire. It is only her consciousness that has fallen to Earth; her body remains above.

But the Quman shaman is up to some mischief. Ought she to kill him? Might his magic alter the outcome of the battle?

She rises aloft on wings to survey the field of blood where the invisible spirit of Jedu now roams, where men kill and struggle. Sanglant and his men have not yet come into view. The gleaming thread unwinds across the carnage. In close quarters, Wendish spears and swords and chain mail hold up well against the more lightly armed Quman. Seen from Aturna's heights, as from a ridgetop looking into the future, Liath feels sure that Princess Sapientia and her allies will win.

They don't need her help.

At that moment she hears the faint cry of a voice she has never heard before that yet reverberates in her heart. She rises, seeking a broader view; the battle recedes below her. In her last glimpse she sees the hornets swarming forward to buzz around the banner of the Ungrian prince, the commander. Far away, too far away to aid him, the ancient Kerayit woman screams in horror and rage. Clouds bear in from the east. Lightning blinds Liath. Thunder cracks, and back where Blessing stands among overturned wagons, turning her head to stare gleefully at the heavens, it begins to rain.

"Lady, blessed saint, defend us!"

A shrill scream, cut off with an awful gurgle.

Liath smells the sharp iron scent of galla. With one step she covers weeks of travel, she leaps the towering Alfar Mountains and tumbles down into a weird landscape of rock chimneys and narrow plateaus rising like pillars out of barren ground. Someone has carved a convent into one of these vast rock pillars, a refuge in times of war. A scream echoes again, and she slides between rock, seeking the one whose prayers have touched her heart and reached her ears.

In a warren of rock she finds six nuns cowering in a chamber carved into the stone. Seven windows admit a gleam of afternoon light, obscured by the terrible creature advancing down the length of the refectory. The table, laden with platters, cups, and a stern meal of porridge and bread, has been overturned. Cooling pease porridge lies in spatters on the floor. One of the women is screaming convulsively, utterly panicked. Back by the door lies a jumble of disarticulated bones, steaming slightly, as though the soul of the person who just inhabited that body is trying to form itself into a ghostly specter. The old mother abbess, golden Circle of Unity held high, limps forward, past her nuns, making the sign of exorcism to drive the creature away.

But a Circle of Unity and honest faith will not turn back a galla bound by blood. Liath fits arrow to string, draws—

And hesitates. Who bound the galla? Who has sent it on this deadly errand?

She has only one breath to decide. The galla is here, and before she draws her next breath it will consume the old abbess just as it consumed the poor woman who had been standing in the doorway.

She looses the arrow. The gold fletching gleams, and sparks, as the arrow explodes in the slender tower of darkness that is the galla's insubstantial body. With a shriek of agony, and of joy, it vanishes, released from the bonds of magic that dragged it here to this world. Its unfulfilled purpose kicks back along the pale link that ties it to the sorcerer who called it. Briefly, Liath sees an elderly, apple-cheeked woman seated in a chamber with a bloody body nearby. The woman jerks as the rebound hits her, then faints.

"Go now!" *cries Liath, trying to catch the attention of the six women.* "Bind the sorcerer who has done this."

Perhaps they hear her, even above the hysterical sobs of one of their number, who cannot be consoled.

The old abbess gestures. "Hilaria! Diocletia! Go at once to the guest hall to see if Sister Venia is safe. But take rope, and a sleeping potion." *Leaning heavily on a cane, she takes four steps forward and bends, picking up a gold feather. There is no sign of the arrow.*

She glances up. All at once, staring, she seems to see Liath hovering in the air before her. Her eyes widen. "Who is there, in the shadows?" *Despite her infirmities and great age, her voice remains strong.*

"Fear not," *says Liath, but she thinks the old woman cannot see her, for she is no more substantial on Earth right now than the galla was.*

Some eyes are keener than others. The old woman squints, looking surprised, puzzled, hopeful. "Bernard?" *she asks, voice gone hoarse all at once, as though she might weep.* "Is this my sweet son Bernard, who was torn from me? Your face— Nay, you're a woman. Who are you?"

Who am I? And who are you, who sees in me the image of a lost son named Bernard?

Liath takes a step forward

and found herself back on the marble stairs of Aturna, almost at the top. Bow and arrow were gone. She was naked, alone; she had nothing, except herself.

The realm of the fixed stars blazed before her, white hot, as terrible as a firestorm.

But they were waiting for her, clustered at the lower limit of the border: spirits with wings of flame and eyes as brilliant as knives. Their gaze fell like the strike of lightning. Their bodies were not bodies like those known on Earth but rather the conjoining of fire and wind, the breath of incandescent stars coalesced into mind and will. The sound of their wings unfurling in pitiless splendor boomed and echoed off the curving gleam of Aturna's sphere. Far below, the golden wheels spun madly, powered by that fiery wind that is the soul's breath of the stars.

She recognized their voice.

"*Child*," they said as she climbed the last step and without hesitation walked into their joyous embrace. "*You have come home.*"

3

THE Quman resisted the heavy charge at first, holding firm under the leadership of their prince, who rode with them. But the sheer weight of the Wendish cavalry at either flank and the Ungrian mass in the center broke them at last.

Zacharias watched, exulting, as first the left flank and then portions of the center sagged and gave way, as the infamous Quman soldiers, hardened and grim, began to turn their horses and flee. If Zacharias had believed in God, he would have offered up a prayer at that moment. He mopped his brow instead. Thunder pealed behind them. He smelled rain, although it was impossible to hear much of anything over the cacophony of battle that raged on the river plain before him. He waited at the rear with Bayan's command group and the prince's adviser, Brother Breschius. Prince Bayan had ridden forward with the charge, but he disengaged from the line and rode back to them, calling for a messenger.

"Ride to the Wendish banners. My wife must now pull back from the fighting. The day is won, and it makes no matter for her to keep fighting. In the rout, this is when folk may come unexpectedly to grief." The messenger rode off at a gallop. Bayan called for water. Loosening the straps of his helmet, he tipped it back so that he could drink. "Brother Zacharias, what will Bulkezu do next? Surely you know him best of all of us."

Zacharias chuckled nervously, not liking the way everyone was looking at him. "Bulkezu is as clever as he is mad. I cannot know his mind."

"I pray you, Your Highness, put your helmet back on," said Brother Breschius. "A stray arrow might come from anywhere."

Bayan grunted, finished his drink, and pulled his helmet back down. For a quiet moment, such as could be had watching over the battle as the Quman line retreated even farther and began to break up all along its length, he watched, measuring the movement of the various units, their strengths and weaknesses, commenting now and again to his captains and sending messengers or receiving them. Princess Sapientia had not yet disengaged from the fray.

"Damn," swore Bayan, swatting at his helm. With a curse, he undid the straps of his helmet again. "Damn hornet." He pulled it up, exposing his face as he tried to bat away something Zacharias could not see. "It stung me!"

The arrow, coming out of nowhere, took him in the throat.

Without a sound, he slid neatly from his horse. His blood drenched the ground.

And the world stopped breathing.

No man spoke. The air snapped, stung—and screamed, like a woman's voice. No person ought ever to have to hear a woman scream like that, naked grief, raw pain. Thunder boomed directly over them. Wind howled out of the east, flattening Zacharias. The horses spooked, bucking in fright, and he actually fell right back over the rump of his mount and hit the ground hard while around him Ungrian captains and lords fought to control their horses. He cowered under the fury of the storm while Bayan's life's blood trickled across the ground to paint Zacharias' fingers red.

As abruptly as the storm had hit, it ceased. Leaves fluttered through the air, stilled, and fell. A deadly quiet shrouded the land. Below, the conjoined armies seemed to pause.

As though Bulkezu had been waiting for this moment, the griffin-winged rider called for the advance, and the fleeing Quman gathered themselves together and struck hard at the faltering Wendish and Ungrian line. Princess Sapientia's banner was driven back as if before the lash.

"Oh, Lord, I beseech you, spare his life," said Brother Breschius, dismounting to kneel beside the prince. He took hold of the prince's limp hand, touched a finger to gray lips, then wept. "My good lord Bayan is dead."

Just like that, the command group disintegrated. The cries and ululations of the Ungrian lords resounded off the hilltop. They had lost their prince, their luck, their commander; for them, the battle was over. The double-headed eagle banner was furled, and along the center of the army, as Ungrian soldiers caught sight of the furled banner, the center bowed backward as they retreated.

"Ai!" cried Zacharias, scrambling up. Blood dripped from his hand. He caught sight of his mount galloping away toward the woods. He was trapped on the rise, easy prey for Bulkezu. With a groan of despair, he threw himself back down on the ground. "We are lost!"

Horns belled in the distance. A great shout of triumph rose from the rear lines as the gold banner of Prince Sanglant burst

out of the trees at the head of his troop of horsemen, many
hundreds strong.

Sanglant recognized a line about to break, and he knew what
to do about it. With one comprehensive glance, he took in the
situation on the field: Bayan's furled banner, the retreating
Ungrian troops, Sapientia's wavering troops on the flanks.
Only Lady Bertha's Austrans, on the left flank, were holding
their own. That would change if the rest of the army lost
heart.

Was Bayan wounded, or even dead?

No time to consider. He lifted his hand. Fulk raised the
horn to his lips and blew the charge. Drums rolled in time to
hoofbeats.

The noise deafened him, but even so he shouted, letting his
voice ring out. "For Wendar!"

Urging Resuelto forward, Sanglant led the charge. The dis-
couraged Ungrians parted before them. At the sight of his
banner, they rallied, falling in to form up behind his soldiers.
With Sibold at his right hand and Fulk, Malbert, and
Anshelm around him, he slammed into the forefront of the
Quman line. It broke, riders falling, the press of the Quman
disintegrating. Yet another line of enemy riders closed from
the second rank. He set his lance and directed his charge for a
small group of wingless riders, Wendishmen perhaps, traitors
seduced by the promise of gold and slaves. Something about
their shields—

One of the soldiers pushed his horse past the leader to take
the brunt of the impact. Sanglant's lance struck him right
over the heart, and the man fell to the ground. As he drew his
sword, he slammed a Quman rider hard with his shield to
unseat him, got his sword free, and cut at the wingless leader.
Only then did he recognize the scarred and battered shield of
the boy cowering before him.

"Ekkehard!" With an effort, he twisted his wrist so that the flat of the blade caught his young half brother in the helm, knocking him to the side, although the lad at least had enough horsemanship to keep his seat and ride past. His three other companions threw down their arms and yielded. Only the one lay dead, trampled by his own horse.

"Get them out of here!" he shouted before he pressed forward with Fulk and Sibold on either side and the rest of his men moving up around him as Anshelm dropped back to take care of Ekkehard. Druthmar's banner flew proudly over to the right. Along the left flank, Lady Bertha had pushed her advantage and now swung wide to roll up the struggling Quman flank arrayed against her. Away to the right, past Druthmar, Sapientia was acquitting herself well enough, emboldened by his success.

But he knew that the Quman would not fall until their leader did. Griffin wings flashed in sunlight as the clouds scudded away on a stiff wind. With a cry of triumph, he carved his way to Bulkezu. This fight would be very different than the one six years before when the Quman begh had ruined his voice and almost taken his life.

Bulkezu turned to face him. Even through the clash of battle, Sanglant heard him laughing as they closed. Sanglant had the advantage of height—the Wendish horses were simply larger than the stolid Quman ponies. He rained blows down on Bulkezu, but the griffin warrior parried every one with shield or sword. Sparks flew as his griffin feathers notched Wendish steel. But in the end brute strength won, and a massive blow sent Bulkezu's sword spinning from his grasp.

Bulkezu threw himself into Sanglant, punching with his shield. Grabbing hold of Sanglant's belt, he dragged the prince from his mount. They both tumbled to the ground as the horses broke free and bolted, leaving them on foot as the battle raged around them.

Bulkezu pulled his dagger as he tried to break Sanglant's grip, but Sanglant wrapped his shield around Bulkezu's back and struck him in the face with his pommel. With each blow a large dent appeared in the face mask and the iron began to crack. A trickle of blood oozed from the eye slots as Sanglant struck a fourth time.

Bulkezu jerked back, twisting his shoulders to one side so that the griffin feathers cut into Sanglant's left arm. His shield fell to the ground, its leather straps severed. Bulkezu caught his lower arm and shoved it hard, twisting all the while, to drive the sword into the ground. He thrust with his dagger at Sanglant's head. The blow scraped gold flakes from the dragon helm. Sanglant caught the frame of a wing with his boot and shoved. The wing snapped off. They rolled on the ground. Bulkezu's other wing snapped, shedding griffin feathers along the earth as they wrestled, each trying to get the upper hand.

Sanglant caught sight of a Quman rider bearing down and barely got hold of his sword, whipping it up to parry the blow that would have crushed his head. Bulkezu kicked him away and scrambled up, lost at once in the turbulent sea of fighting. Sanglant killed another Quman rider before Fulk cleared a space for him to remount Resuelto.

"Bulkezu?" he shouted as Resuelto pranced away from the griffin feathers, which could even cut into hooves.

Bulkezu had vanished, impossible to trace without his griffin wings. The Pechanek standard swayed and, abruptly, collapsed under a Wendish charge. A roar of triumph rose from the Wendish troops as the Quman line disintegrated. The Ungrians, rallying round, cried out Sanglant's name.

Between one breath and the next, battle turned to rout. The bravest Quman warriors soon found themselves isolated and surrounded and in this way they perished in the midst of their enemies.

"Send messengers!" the prince called to Fulk. "Let all the fords and ferries west and east be on their guard."

He and his captains withdrew from the field, letting the soldiers do the rough work of slaughter, those who could catch the fleeing Quman now scattering in all directions. Back on a rise they found Brother Breschius and a dozen Ungrian noblemen preparing Bayan's body for transport, stripping him of his armor. Sapientia was already there, keening like a lost child, scratching at her cheeks in the old way as she mourned her dead husband. Her attendants had to restrain her twice from throwing herself onto his bloody body.

Sanglant surveyed the scene with a dull heart. All of Bayan's liveliness was gone, fled; what remained was only a husk. He wept openly, honoring Bayan with his grief, while Anshelm washed and bound the cuts on his left arm where the griffin feathers had laid open his skin. They stung like crazy, but they didn't hurt half as much as the pain of seeing Bayan dead.

Captain Fulk rode up with the latest reports: Lady Bertha had followed a large contingent west, toward the Veser; Lord Wichman, recovered from the near rout of his forces earlier, was engaged in a lively slaughter of any Quman soldier he and his men could get their hands on; Thiadbold's Lions had captured a lordling, son of a begh, but it wasn't Bulkezu. Prince Bayan's mother had been found, with her slaves keening around her: she, too, was dead.

"Where is my brother Ekkehard?" asked Sanglant quietly, not wanting Sapientia to overhear. He could not predict how she would react to the news of Ekkehard's treachery.

Fulk nodded wisely. "We've taken him to the baggage train and put him in the custody of the Lions, my lord prince. They're levelheaded enough to treat him calmly. What of Bulkezu? Do we pursue?"

"Nay. I doubt we've more than an hour of daylight left to us. Send Druthmar to the baggage train. I want my daughter escorted forward at once under heavy guard. I'd best go pay my respects to my aunt and remind her whom she has to thank for saving her city and her duchy. Sapientia and I will ride to Osterburg together, with Bayan's corpse."

"But Prince Bulkezu got free—"objected Sibold. He stood in his stirrups, alive with excitement as he held the gold banner aloft in victory, as his gaze scanned the field beyond.

Broken wings littered the field, obscuring bodies. Feathers drifted on the wind. A roan kept struggling to get up but could not stand. Carrion crows circled. In their haste to retreat the Quman had scattered into packs of two or ten or twenty, hard to catch but easy to kill once they were ridden down. Many escaped into the forest, fleeing east like frightened rats toward their distant home.

Sanglant shook his head, eyes narrowing as a soldier dismounted beside the distant roan and knelt to examine its wounds. Sapientia sobbed on, and on, and on, brokenhearted. He wiped away tears from his own cheeks, thinking of the toasts he could no longer share with Bayan. "Tomorrow is soon enough to hunt Bulkezu. He may already lie dead on the field."

"And if he does not?" asked Fulk.

"I've never heard that any Quman can swim. He'll have to cross at a ford or ferry. My soldiers will be ready for him."

4

FROM a rise on the east bank of the Veser River, Hanna watched in silent exultation as the two armies engaged. Even from a distance she could see that the Wendish were better armed, and that the weight of their larger horses and bigger shields gave them an advantage despite the crippling heat. Sweat streaked her forehead, and her tunic stuck to her back. With her bound hands, she swatted at a cloud of gnats swarming around her face. The ropes made her awkward, so she couldn't hope to escape, or to interfere.

Not until too late did she realize why her hands had been tied, so that she could not possibly disturb the other battle going on, the secret one. Not until Cherbu stopped muttering and chanting did she hold her breath, abruptly aware that something was about to happen. A shout of despair and confusion arose from the Ungrian ranks. Prince Bayan's banner, no bigger than her hand seen from this distance but still easily recognizable, was furled, as they would do if he were dead.

Dead.

She knew then, seeing Cherbu's solemn face, that the Quman shaman had killed him with magic. He sighed, dismounted, and laid himself flat on the ground, all four limbs pointing out like those of a sea star, as though he were awaiting his fate. Was that a single tear, trickling down one cheek?

The storm hit.

The first blast of wind actually tossed her from her horse. She hit the ground, taking the brunt of the fall on one hip, and lay there, stunned, while thunder cracked around them and lightning flashed so close that horses screamed and she smelled burning. A cloudburst swept through, flattening the grass.

Then all stilled. She took in two shuddering breaths. Her skin tingled alarmingly, as though she had been stung by a thousand hornets. Her face, where Bulkezu had hit her, throbbed painfully, and her hip ached as she rolled over to push herself up. A spear drifted lazily in front of her eyes. The guards, at least, had not forgotten their duty.

Stiffly, cautiously, she got to her feet, gritting her teeth as pain shot through her hip and up into her shoulder. The stink of charred flesh made her gag.

Cherbu was dead, his body blackened and contorted. He had been struck by lightning. Her stomach clenched. She stumbled away, dropped to her knees, and vomited.

A ragged cheer rose from the ranks of her guard. Surprised to hear their cry, she raised her head in time to see Bulkezu, his griffin wings a glittering beacon on the distant field, leading a charge to smash the Wendish army. The Ungrian legion began to retreat. Tears stung her eyes, but she choked them back, swallowing bile as she stared helplessly. Yet wasn't this her duty? To witness and remember, so that she could report to the king? She straightened up proudly, though it hurt to stand. No matter what happened, she had to be strong enough to defy Bulkezu. If he defeated her, then it would be as if he had defeated King Henry. Maybe that was the game Bulkezu had been playing with her all along.

So when the horns rang and a gold banner emerged from the wooded lands farther east, she could not help but cry out in hope and triumph. Who bore the gold banner? What prince or noble lady had come to Sapientia's aid?

Dust obscured the scene. The guards muttered nervously around her as the clamor of battle drifted up to them on a stiff breeze blowing in from the east. It was impossible to see who was winning, and who was losing. Impossible to know anything except interpret the shouts and cheers and commands ringing faintly from the field.

At first, she didn't recognize the rider making a dash for their line, galloping out of the haze of battle with about a dozen Quman soldiers at his heels. The shattered wood frame of his wings trailed over him, shedding bright feathers. Griffin feathers.

As Bulkezu rode up, she laughed to see him humbled, but when he yanked his battered helm and featureless face mask from his head, her laughter choked in her throat. Blood ran down his face from a gash at the corner of one eye where the mask had been driven into his skin. A flap of skin hung loosely; she even saw the white of bone. His terrible expression made her shudder as, with the tip of his spear, he poked his brother's corpse. Without comment, he turned and, signaling, headed south at a brisk pace. By now he had about thirty soldiers following. She saw no sign of Prince Ekkehard and his companions.

They swung south a ways before cutting east, pushing their horses to the limit. Twice they came across knots of Wendish soldiers and, after a skirmish, broke free. But they always left a few men behind, wounded or dead. After the first time she tried to escape under cover of such fighting, Bulkezu tied a rope around her neck and, using it like a lead line, forced her to ride directly behind him. When she let her mount lag too far behind, the noose choked her. When she crowded him, hoping to injure his horse or make it stumble, he turned and whipped her across the face with the only weapon he had left: a stick.

Her nose was bleeding and her hip had gone into spasms by the time it got too dark to ride any farther. In any case, the horses were winded, blown. It was at least a week past the full moon, and the waning crescent hadn't yet risen. They had to stop, taking the time now to eat and drink what little remained to them.

There were about two dozen left, creeping through the forest, signaling to each other with hisses and whistles. From ahead, they heard shouts and the noise of horses and fighting. Bulkezu yanked her rope and dragged her forward. By this time she could hardly walk; the pain in her hip stabbed all the way up to her head, and her teeth ached. They took refuge in dense cover on the edge of a clearing. Leaves tickled her face.

He pressed a hand over her mouth so that she couldn't cry out. Where he held his head against hers, blood from his wound seeped onto her cheek, warm and sticky, and where the blood snaked in between her lips, she swallowed reflexively, tried to jerk away, but could not. No one had ever called Hanna, born and raised to hard work, a weakling, but Bulkezu had a grip like iron chains, almost as though he wasn't really a man at all but some kind of unnatural daimone.

A party of Wendish horsemen, at least fifty strong, had cornered a much smaller party of Quman soldiers in a little hamlet. The fleeing Quman had taken refuge in two cottages and now used this cover to take shots at the enemy.

A lord rode into view, followed by a dozen lordlings, all swearing and laughing as they taunted the trapped Quman. It made no difference to them that they trampled the gardens and kicked over the fences and now-empty chicken coops of the farmers who lived here. Probably the families had taken refuge in Osterburg. Hanna recognized Lord Wichman as he called forward six archers. Fire bloomed along six arrows and made a beautiful arc as the arrows lofted into the air and landed on thatch roofs.

A few of the Quman tried to break free of the burning death traps but were shot full of arrows. The rest chose to die, burned alive, in silence.

Bulkezu grunted, retreated back into the wood, and they moved on. The damp ground made the going rough. Soon enough her boots were caked as she shed mud and picked it up with every step. After a while the soldiers had to take turns carrying her. After an interminable gray journey, bounced and jounced while the throbbing in her hip slowly receded into a merely agonizing torment, she smelled horse manure, heard the rush of a river, and was dumped unceremoniously into the rotting remains of an old hovel. She could see nothing, only hear, as Bulkezu and his surviving men whispered to each other, settling in around her.

Under the collapsing roof the ground was dry. She grimaced as she straightened out her leg, rolled onto her back, and used her palms to massage the knot in her hip. The pain eased.

That was when she heard the Lions.

At first she didn't understand the melange of voices, blending as they did with the rush of the river behind her.

"There! Coming out of the water!"

"Behind you, you idiot!"

"Got him!"

"God be praised!"

Fading again. She thought maybe she had dozed and heard the words in a dream. Strange that one of those voices should sound so like that of her old friend Ingo. Hope plagued her, making it impossible to sleep as the night dragged on.

Bulkezu squatted down beside her.

"You lost." She no longer cared what happened to her. She no longer cared if he killed her. Or at least, at this moment, her hatred drove her. "Now what can you do except run like a whipped dog?"

"I am still the only man in the tribes to have killed two

griffins," he said, but he did not laugh. He grunted, softly. She hoped the pain of his wound scalded him. She hoped he was suffering. "The beghs cannot turn their backs on me. One defeat does not mean the end of the war."

"What do you want? What have you ever wanted?"

He was silent for so long that she sat up, brushing moldy straw from her lips with the backs of her hands. Thirst chafed her throat.

Still, he said nothing. A shroud of silence fell, broken only by the sound of the river. This river didn't have the deep strength of the Veser. It flowed more lightly, singing over rocks and shallows, the bass melody of its main current almost lost beneath these higher notes and the constant roaring rush of wind through the trees. It reminded her of the rushing river after the battle at the tumulus, when Bayan's mother had called down a flood that had swept away the vanguard of the Quman pursuit, that had blocked the river, delaying Bulkezu's army long enough that Bayan and Sapientia had been able to lead their battered troops on an orderly retreat.

Was Bayan truly dead? What had happened to his mother? Was it her magic that had struck down Cherbu?

She could stand it no longer. "If the luck of a Kerayit shaman dies, what happens to that shaman?"

"She dies."

"Why did you risk killing Prince Bayan's mother, yet won't risk killing me? Don't you all fear the Kerayit weather witches?"

"Any wise man does. But it was our only chance. The other prince was protected from Cherbu's magic, so I had to strike Bayan." Small at first, then growing, he giggled, that nasty, gleeful, mad laughter. "I've been wanting to get rid of him for a long time, anyway. But I do regret losing Cherbu." Nothing in his tone gave credence to this statement.

"Surely Cherbu understood that if he struck against Bayan, then Bayan's mother would avenge her son."

"Cherbu didn't like me anyway. He was jealous that I was the elder born and that he had to obey me."

"Did you care about him at all?"

He made no answer, as if she'd spoken to him in a language he did not understand.

"Then why not have me killed, if the wrath of my Kerayit shaman will not strike you but only the person whose hand strikes the killing blow?"

"Nay, it's not your young shaman I fear. It's the owl who watches over you, who is the messenger of the Fearsome One."

Hanna thought that she actually heard fear in his voice, quickly surfacing, as quickly gone. He rose and went outside so fast that he kicked dirt up into her face. She spat, wiped her mouth. Two guards crouched in the doorway, watching her. One held the rope that bound her at the neck. With a sigh, she lay back down

No Lions' voices serenaded her as she dozed, waking at intervals with questions chasing themselves through her thoughts. Ai, God, what other prince was Bulkezu referring to? Who flew the gold banner she had seen emerging from the woods? Was it Sanglant who had saved the day? Was it possible that Liath was with him, hidden by magic?

The darkness lightened at last. When they came for her, she was able to walk without too much discomfort while one of the guards led her horse. They moved downriver a short way before attempting a crossing, but the first man to dare the water got caught in the swift current, not deep but strong. He slid off his saddle and his wings dragged him down. The horse fought the water before being lost to sight in the predawn twilight.

The soldiers made certain signs, as though to avert the evil eye. Even Bulkezu seemed unwilling to test the waters, although Hanna would gladly have swum, given the chance. She had never feared the water, but she was fiercely glad to see that they did. If they stayed here, trapped by the river, eventually their enemies would catch them.

A twig snapped behind them. A warning whistle shrilled,

cut off abruptly. The Quman soldiers spun around, raising their weapons—those who had them.

She saw her chance. She yanked hard on the rope, jerked it right out of Bulkezu's hand in that instant when his attention jumped away from her, and leaped into the river. Flinging herself forward, she hit the water with a mighty splash, head going under. When she surfaced, she floundered toward deeper water, thrust forward as Bulkezu cursed behind her and shouts rang out. A host of men broke out of the trees to surround the band of Quman and their horses.

The current caught her. With bound hands, it was hard to keep her head above the water. The trailing rope caught in a snag and dragged tight.

"Hanna!"

Just as the noose pulled taut, choking her, just as her vision hazed and the water closed over her face, a hand gripped her. The rope came free, cut through, and she went limp, letting herself be hauled to the bank through the streaming water and thrown up on shore like a fish gasping for air.

"Hanna! We thought you were dead!"

Coughing and spluttering, she rolled onto her stomach and heaved a few times onto rocky shoreline. At last, she looked up to see the concerned and horrified faces of four very familiar men: Ingo, Leo, Folquin, and Stephen, her good friends from the Lions.

"Bulkezu!" she cried, heaving again as she struggled to her feet, but Ingo caught her easily as she staggered.

"Nay, we've captured a group of them, the ones that had you prisoner. Are you saying that lord with the broken wings is Prince Bulkezu himself?" He laughed aloud and punched Folquin merrily on the shoulder. "Won't we have a great prize to deliver to Prince Sanglant!"

"Ai, God," whispered Hanna. "I'm free."

Her legs gave out completely and, while Ingo held her, she broke down and sobbed uncontrollably, a storm of tears she could no longer restrain.

5

ROSVITA rose at dawn and, after prayers, studied the first
of the books Heriburg and Ruoda had found in the palace
library the day before. This copy of the prose *Life* of Taillefer,
by his faithful cleric and counselor Albinus, said in his time to
be the most learned man in the world, confirmed what she
already knew. Taillefer had had four daughters who lived to
adulthood. Three had entered the church, including the
famous Biscop Tallia. The fourth girl, Gundara, had after certain unnamed embarrassments been married to the Duc de
Rossalia, the most powerful noble in the kingdom outside of
Taillefer's own family. Albinus said nothing more about
Gundara's life, only mentioned that a set of rich bed curtains,
three Belguise tapestries, a square table engraved with a depic-
tion of the universe set out as seven spheres, and four chests of
treasure including vessels of gold and silver were allotted to
her in Taillefer's will.

"Here is the *Chronicle* of Vitalia." Ruoda opened the next
book to the appropriate chapter. The cleric and deacon Vitalia,
at the Salian convent of St. Ceneri on the Eides, had written an
extensive history of her cloister, and it was owing to her superior understanding as a woman that they could therefore
discover more of the details they desired to know. In the civil
wars following Taillefer's death, the great emperor's nephew's
cousin Lothair had emerged triumphant in the end and been
crowned king of Salia in 629. Yet he had never been strong
enough to claim the imperial title.

Eika raids that same year had devastated Rossalia, and the
duc had died defending his lands, leaving Gundara a rich
widow overseeing the upbringing of three children. Lothair
had himself claimed Gundara, sending his first wife to the
convent in order to marry Taillefer's daughter. In the opinion
of Vitalia, he had been cursed by God for this sin of arrogance and greed by having his old age disrupted by various

rebellions hatched against him by his sons, all of whom quarreled incessantly.

"It still says nothing of the fate of Gundara's other children by the duc de Rossalia," observed Ruoda. "The eldest boy, Charles, inherited the dukedom when he came of age, married Margaret of Derisa, and had a son to inherit after him. What are you looking for, Sister Rosvita?"

The crisp writing on the yellowed page gave no hints. It spoke only of words copied by a scribe, events recorded by a hand long dead. "At times I feel as though a mouse is nibbling at the edges of some secret knowledge hidden in my heart. If I only give the mouse a while longer to feast, then it will uncover what I wish to know. If I can only be patient."

She glanced, frowning, at Heriburg's bandaged hand. The girl had burned herself yesterday trying to scratch magical sigils into a tin medallion. The incident had frightened and disturbed them all, and for now Rosvita contented herself with hanging sprigs of fennel and alder branches over the doors and windows to ward off evil spying.

"My lady." Aurea appeared in the door. "Brother Petrus has come."

It was time to attend the king, although Rosvita thought it strange that a presbyter came to fetch her rather than one of Henry's own stewards. She took Fortunatus with her and sent the young women to the schola. They joined Henry and the court for midday prayers in the king's chapel while, as was customary in Aosta, Queen Adelheid and her entourage prayed in the queen's chapel. A colonnade connected the two buildings, and here Henry brought his retinue after the service of Sext concluded, to the royal garden.

"Walk with me, Sister Rosvita," the king said as he strolled out into the garden.

Statues of every beast known to the huntsman stood alongside gravel paths bordered by dwarf shrubs or hidden beyond the taller ranks of cypress hedges. Stags and wolves, boars and lions and aurochs, guivres and griffins and bears glowered and threatened. Yet their threats weren't nearly as great, Rosvita thought, as the busy courtiers of Aosta with their bland smiles and charming manners.

Beyond a square fence lay a captivating floral labyrinth whose twisting paths were delimited by beds of hyssop and chamomile, bee-flowers, a purple cloud of lavender, and the last pale flowers of thyme. Summer had leached away the strong fragrance, but there was still enough lingering that, when Henry opened the gate and beckoned to her to follow him onto the narrow paths, it was like walking into a perfumed sachet.

She knew the path better than he did and had to guide him past two wrong turns until they reached the bench placed at the center, surrounded by a circle of neatly trimmed rose-bushes. From here, they looked back out over the low box shrubs as Adelheid emerged from the queen's chapel, attended by Hugh and her ladies. Seeing Henry, Adelheid disengaged herself from her courtiers and struck out across the garden toward them.

"Let me speak quickly, Sister." The summer's campaign had tired Henry out. New lines nested at the corners of his eyes and he favored one leg. "It has become known to me that there is serious trouble in Wendar, more serious than any-thing here in Aosta. Duke Conrad has married against my will. There are rumors he seeks to raise himself up as a prince equal to me, in the west. A Quman army has invaded in the east. Merchants bring stories of an Eika attack on Alba, more like an invasion than a raid, that might disrupt trading for many years. Plague, famine, and drought all trouble my loyal nobles. How can I reign in Aosta if Wendar falls into ruin? In truth, Aosta has suffered for years these manifold trials. Another year of campaigning and I surely can be crowned as emperor without any powerful noble family raising arms against me. But in my heart I know it is the wiser course to return to Wendar now. Yet I would hear your words, Sister, before I make any public pronouncement."

"This is a grave charge you set on me, Your Majesty."

He nodded. "So it is. Villam has already made his opinion clear. He counsels that we ride north as soon as we can, given the rumors we've heard of early snow in the mountains. If we do not make haste, we'll not be able to cross the passes until next year. I cannot tell what might happen in Wendar over the winter and spring if I am not there to set things right. What do you advise, Sister Rosvita?" His gaze was keen, almost merciless. He wore an ivy-green tunic today, trimmed with pale silk, and the hose and leggings that any nobleman might wear, but no person, seeing him, would mistake him for anyone but the king.

"I pray you, give me a few moments to think."

Adelheid reached the gate, had it opened for her by one of her servingwomen and, with a sweet smile on her pretty face, threaded inward along the intricate paths. She knew this labyrinth well.

"There are those who advise against returning to Wendar." He watched his young queen with an odd expression in his eyes, like a man who is pleased and exasperated in equal measure. His gaze flicked outward to where Hugh stood in conversation with Helmut Villam, Duchess Liutgard, and other notables. "I have heard rumors."

"So have I, Your Majesty, and I see no reason to believe what gossips will whisper. Speaking evil of others is a sin that hurts not one but three people, the one who is spoken of, the one who speaks the falsehood, and the one who listens to such slander. Queen Adelheid is an honorable woman, and a clever one. I do not believe you have any reason to fear that she has dishonored your marriage."

In truth, how could any woman even think to look at another man if she was married to Henry? It beggared the imagination.

He plucked a beautiful blood-red rose from the nearest bush. "Yet even the freshest bloom has thorns." He twisted a petal off the stalk and touched it to his lips. "What do you advise, Sister?"

"If you return to Wendar, you must not let it be said that Aosta defeated you. Yet if you remain here, and your kingdom is weakened because you are not there to steady it, then your position here is lost. Wendar and Varre is the kingdom your father gave into your hands, Your Majesty. Do not forget that you are, first of all, a Wendishman, born out of a long and illustrious lineage to a bold and warlike people."

"My queen," he said, with a genuine smile, as Adelheid came up to them. Henry's return had lightened the young woman; she laughed delightedly when he offered her the rose, although she was careful to check for thorns before she took it from his hand.

"Greetings to you this fine day, Sister Rosvita," she said most cheerfully as she inhaled the fine fragrance of the rose. "I fear that you and the king are plotting, and that all my intrigue is for naught. You have seen the troupe practicing in the arena, have you not? I meant it to be a surprise."

In this way, chatting amiably, Adelheid drew them back into the embrace of the court. Feasting followed that day and the next, food and drink like the flow of a river, never ending. Petitioners came and went. A troupe of acrobats entertained with rope tricks and hoops and balls, and poets sang the praises of king and queen.

Rosvita enjoyed a feast as much as anyone, but nevertheless she was relieved to escape late in the evening on the second day. She had no opportunity to speak privately with the king, or even with Villam, who seemed quite overtaken by admiring women, all of them young and most of them attractive. Even the king's Eagle, Hathui, remained busy pouring wine, delivering messages, and serving at the king's side. Tomorrow the feast would continue, but the royal court would cross the courtyard that separated the earthly from the spiritual palace and join the skopos in her great hall for a meal worthy, so it was whispered, of an emperor.

Fortunatus made small talk as they walked back to her chambers. "Do you suppose the acrobats will perform for the

Holy Mother as well? Those girls might as well have been monkeys. I've never seen such tricks on a rope. And that juggling! Did you know that when I was a child, I saw a trained monkey perform? The harvest failed that year—you can imagine I recall that!—and we heard later that the traveling players had been forced to sell everything they owned to get out of Mainni, to escape the famine. The monkey was made into mincemeat, and every person who ate of the sausage made of its flesh sickened and died."

"An edifying story, Brother. I do not know whether to feel more sorry for the hungry souls who suffered, or for the poor creature abandoned by its master and then slaughtered."

"It bit me," he added, lips quirking up mischievously. "I only tried to pet it. I couldn't have been more than six or eight years of age. So I think maybe the players sold it because it was a nuisance. Or perhaps it was just a story my sisters told me to make me cry, thinking I would be next to die because of the mark it left on my thumb." He held up a hand and, indeed, a fine white scar cut raggedly across his thumb.

She laughed. "So it's true you've always been the one getting into trouble, Brother. I thought as much."

He had the sweetest grin; it was one of the things she loved him for. "Nay, Sister, I am innocent. It is only that I strive to follow your example in curiosity."

Aurea saw them coming and opened the door but did not follow them inside, where Ruoda, Heriburg, and Gerwita waited, standing at the table with a large book open before them. They started guiltily as Rosvita entered, but Heriburg, at least, had the presence of mind to turn one vellum page slowly, as though she were only browsing. Once the door was shut, Heriburg turned the page back.

"We found it!" cried Ruoda triumphantly. "Or at least," she added, with a blush, "Gerwita did."

"What have you found?"

Gerwita, too shy to talk, indicated that Heriburg should explain. "These are the *Annals of Autun* from the years when

Biscop Tallia held the biscop's crosier. They end with the Council of Narvone, when Biscop Tallia lost the biscop's crosier and the see of Autun by command of the Holy Mother Leah, third of that name. It seems the Holy Mother and her advisers were determined to break the power Taillefer's daughters held over the Salian church."

"A matter of great historical interest," agreed Rosvita, "but what has that to do with the question we were speaking about two days ago?"

Ruoda sprang forward and pressed a forefinger onto the page. "We found Lady Gundara's other children. See, here! A girl, called Thiota, was given to the church but died before she could take her vows. A younger son, called Hugo, betrothed at the age of four to the infant daughter and only child of the Count of Lavas, called Lavastina. So," she finished triumphantly, "thus the hounds."

"Nay," said Gerwita faintly, "for the Lavas hounds didn't come into the possession of the Counts of Lavas until Count Lavastina's son Charles Lavastine inherited after the death of his mother. Most said it was a curse set on him by the Enemy, that Charles Lavastine killed his own father and mother because he feared they would have a daughter to supplant him." When everyone looked at her, she clasped her hands tightly before her and seemed eager to shrink into the bedcovers. "The story is well known in northern Varre, Sister. My family comes from that region, near Firsebarg Abbey."

"Was it never spoken of that the Counts of Varre were therefore related to the Emperor Taillefer?" asked Rosvita.

Gerwita shrugged, looking horrified to be the center of attention of fully four persons. She wrung her hands nervously. "No."

"That seems unlikely, given that Taillefer had no other known legitimate descendants," said Fortunatus.

"In Salia, daughters cannot inherit a title, only sons," said Ruoda, "and in Varre, sons inherit only if there are no daughters."

"Gundara would have been wise to settle her younger son in a place where he could be easily lost, and easily retrieved should his older brother die without an heir." Rosvita drew the lamp closer to the old pages of the *Annals*. Her eyes weren't as keen as those of her young assistants. She admired the refined minuscule common to annals written during the reign of Taillefer, but the words themselves told her nothing that her clerics had not already mentioned: the boy, Hugo, betrothed at the age of four. No indication of his upbringing or later career graced these pages, intended as they were to vindicate the actions of Skopos Leah as she brought down the power of Taillefer's most powerful daughter, Biscop Tallia. Perhaps the child was sent to Varre to be raised with his intended bride, hidden in plain sight, the Emperor's grandson who by reason of his birth to one of the emperor's daughters could never contend for the Salian throne. But his children, should he survive, might still marry back into the royal lineage.

"Was Charles Lavastine the only child of Lavastina and Hugo?" Rosvita asked of Gerwita.

"Nay, Sister. Count Lavastina died in childbed almost twenty years after the birth of Charles Lavastine, giving birth to her second child, another boy, called Geoffrey."

"Ah, yes." Rosvita remembered the story now. "He would be the grandfather of the Geoffrey whose daughter became count after Lavastine's untimely death. There was a trial—"

Ruoda, it transpired, had a cousin who had witnessed the trial for the inheritance of Lavas county. She would have spent all night telling the particulars of the strange behavior of Lord Alain and the Lavas hounds and the victory of Geoffrey and his kinsfolk, but it was late, and there was much to do in the morning when, Rosvita supposed, Henry would at long last announce his intention to return to Wendar before snow closed off the mountain passes.

They made ready for bed, Fortunatus retiring to the adjoining chamber while Aurea laid down pallets for the girls and a straw mattress for herself by the door.

It seemed to Rosvita that she had scarcely fallen asleep when she was rudely awakened.

"Sister Rosvita! Wake up!" A single lamp lit the dark chamber, hovering and cutting the air as the person holding it shook her.

"I pray you!" Rosvita swung her legs out from under the linen sheet, all she needed on a warm night like tonight. Her shift tangled in her legs as she squinted into the darkness. Amazingly, none of the girls had woken. Perhaps that thumping wasn't a fist pounding on her door but only the hammer of her heart. "What is it?"

"Come quickly, Sister. A most terrible act—"

Abruptly, Rosvita recognized the voice, shaken now, warped by horror and tears. "Is that you, Hathui? What trouble has brought you to my chambers this late in the night?"

"Come quickly, Sister." It seemed the pragmatic Eagle was so overset that she could only repeat these words.

Frightened now, Rosvita groped in the chest at the foot of her bed for a long tunic and threw it on over her head. She had only just gotten it on, and it was still twisted awkwardly sideways, when Hathui boldly grabbed her wrist and tugged her urgently. Rosvita got hold of a belt and stumbled after her, banging a thigh against the table, stubbing her toe on the open door, and at last hearing the door *snick* closed behind her. Hathui lifted the lamp as Rosvita hastily straightened her tunic and looped the belt twice around her waist.

"Do you trust me, Sister?" the Eagle whispered hoarsely. In Hathui's gaze, Rosvita saw terror and a passionate rage, reined tight. "You must trust me, or you will not credit what I have seen this night. I pray you, Sister, it may already be too late."

"The king is not—" She could not say that grim word because once spoken it could not be taken back.

"Nay, not dead." Her voice broke. "Not dead."

"Sister Rosvita." Fortunatus appeared at the door. "I heard noises—"

"Stay here, Brother. Do not sleep until I have returned, but by no means follow me nor let the young ones do anything rash." He nodded obediently, pale, round face staring after them anxiously as the two women hurried away down the corridor.

With an effort, Hathui spoke again. It seemed that only the movement of her legs kept the Eagle from dissolving into hysterical tears. "Not dead," she repeated, like a woman checking her larder yet again in a time of famine to be sure that she still has the jars of grain and oil she had set aside for hard times.

They came to a cross corridor, turned left, and descended stairs and by a route unknown to Rosvita made their way along servants' paths to the great courtyard that lay between the regnant's palace and the palace of the skopos.

"Where are we going?" murmured Rosvita, risking speech.

"Not dead," repeated Hathui a final time as she paused behind a pillar that might shield her lamp from prying eyes. Her face, made gray by shadow, loomed unnaturally large in the lamplight as she leaned closer to Rosvita. "Spelled. Bewitched. *I saw it happen.*"

She shifted, drawing a leather thong over her head. "I almost forgot this. You must wear it to protect you against the sight." She pressed an amulet into Rosvita's hands. The silver medallion stung Rosvita's palm.

Did the king protect himself against the sight of his own Eagles, or was he already suspicious of Anne? As Hathui moved out into the courtyard, Rosvita caught her arm and drew her back.

"Nay, Eagle. You must tell me what you saw before I take one step farther. Here." She retreated backward into the shelter of an alcove, where travelers could refresh themselves and wash their faces before they entered the regnant's hall. A fountain trickled softly, but when Hathui held out her lamp, a leering medusa face glared out at them, water dribbling from the mouths of its snake-hair into the basin below. The Eagle gasped out loud and turned her back on the hideous sculpture.

"What I saw . . . nay, first put on the amulet, Sister."
Rosvita obeyed, and Hathui went on. "I sleep in an alcove of
the king's chamber. I woke, for I swear to you that an angel
woke me, Sister. I woke to see the bed curtains drawn back and
Hugh of Austra holding a ribbon above the king's sleeping
form. The ribbon twisted and writhed like a living thing, and
in truth, for I can scarcely believe it myself, I saw a creature as
pale as glass and as light as mist pour out of that ribbon and
into the king's body. King Henry jerked, once, and opened his
eyes, and the voice he spoke with then was not his own."

Rosvita caught herself on the lip of the basin. Water
splashed her hand and cheek, spitting from the mouths of
snakes. "Hugh," she whispered, remembering the passage he
had read from *The Book of Secrets* that day when she and
Theophanu and young Paloma had overheard him in the guest
chapel at the convent of St. Ekatarina's. Remembering the
daimone he had bound into a silk ribbon that night when he
had helped Adelheid, Theophanu, and the remnants of their
entourages escape from Ironhead's siege of the convent. "A
daimone can be chained to the will of a sorcerer, and if he be
strong enough, he can cause it to dwell in the body of another
person, there to work its will. 'Until one mouth utters what
another mind whispers.'"

"Can it be true, Sister?"

"If you saw what you describe, it cannot be otherwise. But
I tremble to think it might be true." Her heart was cold, not
hot. Her hands seemed frozen, and her mind clouded and useless. The amulet burned at her breast. "Yet where was the
queen?"

"Ai, worst of all! She stood to one side and watched him do
it! Cool as you please she told her servingwoman to tell the
skopos that the deed was done and that from now on matters
would proceed as they knew was best." Calm, practical, levelheaded Hathui, a common woman with so much good sense
and simple courage that she had been granted the king's signal
regard, broke down and wept, tears flowing down her cheeks

in echo of the monstrous fountain behind them. But she was able to do it silently, so that her sobs would not alert the night guards.

Rosvita took the lamp from her hand. "Do you know where Villam is?"

"I went to him first, but when we got back to the king's chambers, the king was gone and his steward said he had gone to hold an audience with the skopos. Villam sent me to rouse you. He said we must meet him in the skopos' palace. He thought if we got hold of King Henry before the spell bit too deep—"

Shock gave way to a curious, almost luminous clarity. Even in the darkness, with a waning quarter moon and the lamp's faint glow their only light, she could see the medusa's face, carved out of a marble so white that it seemed to gleam, leprous and pallid, an evil spirit sent to overhear the complaints of travelers come to burden the regnant with their petty cares and quarrels.

"Villam is in danger." The words tolled in her heart like the knell of death, singing the departed up through the spheres toward the Chamber of Light. "We cannot act hastily, for they have power against which our good faith avails us nothing. We must catch Villam before he does something rash. Come."

Hathui knew the servants' corridors in the skopos' palace well, since she often carried messages from regnant to skopos. A pair of guards at the entrance to the kitchens chatted amiably with her for a few moments about the current favorites for the horse races to be held in three days, then let her through without questions. Quickly, Hathui led them into the main portion of the palace. Even in the middle of the night a few servants walked the back corridors, carrying out trash or chamber pots, hauling water for the many presbyters and noble servitors of the skopos who would need to wash in the morning. None seemed suspicious when Hathui asked if they had seen the king; the Eagle had a natural gift with words and an

easy confidence, although it clearly cost her to put a careless
face on things. But in the end, servants saw everything: the
king, escorted by Presbyter Hugh, had gone up to the parapet
walk. They had not seen Queen Adelheid.

A spiral staircase of stone led from the guards' barracks all
the way up to the parapet walk. By the time they reached the
top, Rosvita was puffing hard. The night air, pooling along the
walk, had at last a hint of autumn in it. A breeze cooled the
sweat on her forehead and neck. Hathui started forward along
the walkway, which angled sharply along the cliff's edge overlooking the river below, now hidden in darkness.

"Wait." Rosvita took the lamp from the Eagle and, wetting
thumb and forefinger, snuffed the wick. "Better that we
approach without being seen."

They waited for their eyes to adjust, but fanciful lamps
molded in the shapes of roosters, geese, and frogs rode the
walls at intervals, splashes of light to guide their path along
the narrow walkway. Wisps of cloud obscured the stars in
trails of darkness. Was that Jedu, Angel of War, gleaming
malevolently in the constellation known as the loyal Hound?
Hathui, walking ahead, put out a hand to stop her in a pool of
shadow between two broadly spaced lamps.

A faint stench of decay rose off the river, the dregs of
summer. According to the locals, only the winter rains would
drive it away. The wind shifted, and Rosvita pulled her sleeve
across her nose to muffle the smell.

She heard voices, two men, one angry and one as sweetly
calm as a saint.

With Hathui beside her, she moved forward cautiously,
hugging the interior wall, until they came to a sharply angled
corner of a main tower and could see onto a wider section of
the walkway, set between the square tower at their back and its
twin, opposite. Three men stood there, one silent beside a
landing that led to a second set of stairs, one leaning gracefully
on the waist-high railing that overlooked the abyss, and the
third halfway between the two, as though to make a shield of

his body. Even without the light of two lamps set on tripods, Rosvita would have known two of them anywhere.

The bell rang for Vigils.

"But Margrave Villam," said Hugh most reasonably as he rested against the railing while the wind played in his hair and lifted the corners of his presbyter's cloak, "you do not understand fully the gravity of the dangers facing all of us, which remain hidden from mortal eyes. Like my mother, I act only to serve the king."

Villam seemed ready to spit with fury. She could see it in the way he held himself as he took a single threatening step toward Hugh, the way his hand brushed his sword's hilt. Hugh was unarmed. "You! Sorcerer! I never knew what you did at Zeitsenburg, but the whole court knows what your blessed mother thought a fitting punishment for you, her golden child! To humble you by making you walk into the north like a common frater. What would she say to this night's treachery?"

"What treachery is that? King Henry walks beside me to meet with the Holy Mother. Who has been speaking to you, friend Villam?"

Villam glanced at the man standing rigidly beside the stairs. In that moment, Rosvita realized that she *had not recognized him*; his posture and stance were utterly wrong, not her beloved king's at all. "Your Majesty," Villam entreated, "do we not ride out in two days' time to return to Wendar, where the people cry out in hope that you will soon come to aid them?"

"We will not return to Wendar," replied Henry in a voice that rang hollow, like a bell.

"But the news from Theophanu! The Quman raids that devastate the marchlands! Geoffrey in Lavas, besieged by drought and famine and bandits. What about Conrad, who may already be plotting? Two Eagles have come, pleading for your return! Your Majesty!"

"We will stay here and unite Aosta, and receive our crown, Adelheid and I, crowned as emperor and empress. We will send emissaries to every kingdom, to each place where a stone crown is crowned by seven stones, and there they will await their duty to save all of humankind from the wicked sorcery of the Lost Ones."

"But, Your Majesty, it is not practicable. The emperor's crown will fall quickly from your head if you lose Wendar to the Quman, or to Conrad, who has married your niece! What of Sapientia, fighting in the marchlands? What of Theophanu, who sends an Eagle to beg for your swift return? Aosta must wait until you have settled affairs in Wendar!"

"And Mathilda anointed as our heir."

"Your Majesty!" The soft chanting of clerics and presbyters, intoning the service of Vigils, floated up to them even as Villam sounded ready to weep. "Your Majesty. Your children by Queen Sophia—!"

"Mathilda anointed as my heir," repeated Henry. With his arms clamped tightly against his sides, he moved only his lips, like a statue, like a slave caught in fear for his life.

Villam drew his sword and turned on Hugh. The presbyter had not moved but only watched, one hand stretched out along the railing, his slender fingers stroking the stout wood railing as a woman might pet her cat. "You've bewitched him! That is not the king's voice! That is not the king! You've used foul sorcery to pollute his body and imprison his mind!"

Impossible to say what happened next. Villam lunged. Hugh moved sideways, pantherlike, as graceful as one of the acrobats she'd admired yesterday evening. He even had a startled look on his face, as though surprised. But Villam hit the wooden railing with a crash, sword still raised.

The railing splintered and gave way. Villam staggered outward, cried out as the sword slipped from his fingers, but he had only one arm to grasp with as Hugh reached out to him and it was not enough to save him. He fell. Hathui gasped out loud. Her hand closed on Rosvita's and held on there, as tight as a vise, but neither woman moved as Villam's shriek of outrage and fear faded to silence. Nor did King Henry make any least acknowledgment that his eldest, dearest, and most trusted companion had fallen to his death right in front of his eyes.

After a moment in which Rosvita thought she had actually gone deaf, the distant voices from various chapels in the palaces and down in the city reached heavenward again; she knew the service so well that scraps of melody and words were enough to reveal to her the entire psalm.

> "I cry aloud to God when distress afflicts me,
> but God have stayed Their hand.
> In the darkness of night, have They forgotten me?
> Can the Lord no longer pity?
> Has the Lady withdrawn Her mercy?"

"Come out," said Hugh. "I know you're there."

How soft his voice, and how delicate. Not threatening at all. An eddy in the breeze roiled around her as suddenly as an unseen current turns a boat in the water of a swift-flowing river.

"Come forward, I pray you," he said.

She slipped her hand out of Hathui's strong grasp, trying to shove the Eagle away, trying to give her the message to run, to flee while one of them could.

Who would come to their aid? Whom could they trust?

Stepping forward into the light, she said the only thing she could think of to give the Eagle a hint of her thoughts. "A bastard will show his true mettle when temptation is thrown in his path and the worst tales he can imagine are brought to his attention."

"Sister Rosvita!" Hugh looked honestly surprised, as though he had expected to see someone else. "I regret that you are here." He whistled. Four guards clattered up the stairs, pausing only to bow before the king before they knelt in front of Hugh. "Take her into custody. Beware what wild accusations she may speak, for I fear her heart has been touched by the

Enemy." Henry stood rigid, watching as though he were a stranger, his expression cold and hard. Certainly his features had not changed, but he looked nothing at all like the king she knew. "Come, Your Majesty, we must attend the Holy Mother."

But as Hugh crossed to the stairs, he paused beside Rosvita, frowning. "I had not hoped for this, Sister Rosvita, nor for what must come now. You know how much I admire you."

"Traitor," she said coolly. The shock of Villam's death burned in her heart, but she would never let Hugh see how much it hurt. No doubt he could crush her in an instant. All she had left her were her wits. She had to spin more time for Hathui to escape.

"Is it possible that all I have ever been taught is wrong? That the outer seeming does not reflect the inner heart? Can it be that you have stolen from some more worthy soul that handsome and modest aspect which you wear as though it was given to you by God? Do so many trust you because of your beauty and your clever words while darkness eats away at your heart? Do you not fear the judgment of God and the terrors of the Abyss? Can it be that you have corrupted the queen and the Holy Mother both, with your bindings and workings? What would your mother say were she to stand before us now, seeing what I saw?"

"Enough!" His anger, sparking suddenly, died swiftly as he got control of himself. "'The purified and serene mind has forgotten the passions,'" he said, as if to himself, as if reminding himself of a lesson he had not yet learned and wished devoutly to comprehend.

"'Virtues alone make one blessed,'" retorted Rosvita.

He sighed and moved on.

"What must we do with her, my lord?" asked one of the guards.

"Take her to the dungeon. I'll deal with her later." He and Henry descended the broad steps and soon the lamp he carried was lost to view.

The chief guard made no effort to speak to her, merely gestured with his spear. She saw no reason to fight them. They led her back the way she had come, along the walkway, to the guards' staircase that spiraled down into the palace and farther yet, into the bowels of the hill where lay the dungeons in which those wicked souls were confined who had come afoul of the church. The dank air caught in her lungs, but even when she was marched down a dark corridor, thrown into a cell scarcely wider than her outstretched arms, and left in blackness to sit on moldy straw, she did not, entirely, despair.

Ai, God, Villam was dead, murdered by some trick of Hugh's.

King Henry had become a puppet dancing to another man's strings, possessed by the very daimone Hugh had freed from the stone circle at St. Ekatarina's Convent.

But in those last moments, caught by Hugh, and on her trip down to this dungeon, there had been no sign of Hathui.

6

DUCHESS Rotrudis was dying. The cloying smell of her sickness made her bedchamber almost unbearable. Sanglant stood as close as possible to the window although, even so, no freshening breeze stirred the air inside the room. Even with torches burning to give light and with incense set in three burners around the chamber, it stank.

Her dutiful daughters argued by her bedside, ignoring the half-conscious woman moaning faintly on the bed.

"Nay, I was born first. Deacon Rowena will confirm it!"

"Only because you've offered her the biscopry once Mother is dead! Everyone knows that because I have the birthmark on my chest, it means I'm firstborn."

The two young women looked ready to come to blows, and their respective attendants resembled half-starved dogs preparing to fight over a juicy bone.

Lord Wichman sprawled on the duchess' chair, legs stretched out in front of him and arms crossed on his chest, wearing a smirk on his face as he watched his older sisters shriek and quarrel while their mother suffered unregarded beside them. He hadn't even kissed his mother's hand when he'd come in the room; he hadn't looked at her at all except for a single grimace as he took in the shrunken body of the once robust woman.

"I pray you, Cousins," said Sapientia, attempting to step between them, "this dispute avails you nothing. Surely your mother knows which of you was born first. Surely a midwife attended the birth."

"The midwife is dead, poisoned by Imma!"

"Liar and whore! We weren't more than five years of age when the old woman died. I had nothing to do with it. But you've never answered how the deacon's record came to be burned up six years ago."

"Oh! As if it wasn't you who had the idea to do it, Sophie!"

Wichman had paid more attention when his brother Zwentibold was brought in on a litter to be placed by the hearth, where he, too, was now dying, from wounds taken on the field. Zwentibold remained silent except, now and again, when a tormented groan escaped him and the pretty young woman who was evidently his current concubine hastened forward to dab his lips with wine. It was easy to let the gaze linger on the curve of her body under her light gown, hiding little, promising much, and easier still to notice that Wichman never took his gaze off her.

"How can it be you don't know which of you was born first?" demanded Sapientia, looking from one sister to the other. The two looked alike mostly in their broad faces and ruddy complexions, big women with years of good eating behind them. Imma had her mother's nose, while Sophie bore the red-brown hair that had, evidently, distinguished their dead father. The innocent question unleashed a torrent of abuse and accusations, hurled from one to the other.

"She always favored you!"

"Nay! She only pretended to favor me because she wanted to keep me on a leash like a dog. You're the one who got all the freedom. You're the one who gained because everyone thought you must be angling for the title!"

"I pray you, Cousins, this is no way to show respect. Duchess Rotrudis can hear every word—"

"As if she hasn't enjoyed every word of it, the old bitch!"

"Hah! You licked sweetly enough the honeycomb when it still had honey on it!"

Looking half their size and having none of their shrill stridency, Sapientia was helpless to stop them while, all around, nobles and attendants crowded in, eager or aghast to see such a show. Sanglant watched as Sapientia tried to calm them down, to no avail. She saw what needed doing, but she hadn't the authority to do it. They saw no reason to listen to her.

Wichman rose and stretched before padding over to Zwentibold's litter. The pretty attendant shrank away, but there was no way, here at Osterburg, that she could escape the son of the reigning duchess. Zwentibold had taken her, after all, with or without her consent, and Wichman clearly had decided to follow where his brother had first plunged in.

Just as Wichman, smiling with that ugly spark of unrestrained lust that marred his features, slipped a hand up the girl's rump and tested its roundness, Sanglant strolled forward. He got hold of Wichman's other arm and jerked him forward to stand beside his sisters. Wichman resisted, pulling away.

"I would not if I were you," said Sanglant softly. "I claim her, and I'll cut off your balls if you touch her. You know what my promise is worth, Cousin."

Fuming, Wichman raked his hair back from his head and shot a leer back at Zwentibold's concubine. But he stayed where he was, next to Sophie.

Sanglant placed himself between Imma and Sophie. Even Sapientia moved instinctively back to make room for him.

This close, the smell from the bed filled his nostrils, and he had to fight not to gag. Duchess Rotrudis' skin hung on her in folds. Her once ruddy cheeks were sallow, her eyes sunken and dark. Sanglant wasn't even sure she was aware of what was going on around her.

He remembered her well enough from the days when she had been healthy. He'd never liked her, but no person could ever have said that Rotrudis did not rule the duchy of Saony effectively and with an iron hand.

"I pray you, Cousins," he said, "answer me truly. Do you hate each other more than you hate your blessed mother? Or the other way around?"

Silence crashed down, broken only by a single gasp of amazement from one of the stewards and a low murmuring whimper from the duchess. Had she heard, or was she merely drowning in the pain of her illness?

"For it seems to me that she must have disliked you mightily if she went to so much trouble to be sure that you would fight to the end of your days, never knowing which was truly the firstborn. She must have known, unless the midwife dropped one of you and picked up the other. If you do not know now who is eldest, then it's your mother who chose not to tell you, for her own reasons."

Wichman laughed. "She played you for fools!" he crowed. "All these years, never letting you know which God meant to be heir. She must have known all along, and just wanted to watch you dance, you stupid cows."

Sophie slapped him. He grunted, grabbed for her, only to be slugged by Imma, coming to her sister's defense. The concubine began to cry, huddled by Zwentibold's unconscious figure. Rotrudis stirred, clawing at the bedclothes, and a choked word escaped her, lost beneath the noise of her shouting children and their agitated attendants.

"Silence!" shouted Sanglant.

"Silence!" repeated Sapientia, when the noise had died down enough that she could be heard.

Everyone turned to look at Sanglant. "There's another child, isn't there?" he asked.

When it became obvious that his sisters did not intend to speak, Wichman replied. "Reginar, the little prig. He's abbot of Firsebarg Abbey now, and good riddance."

"Then he'll not be in a position to contest the inheritance?"

That got their attention.

"He's youngest, and a boy," protested Imma. "He's in no position to expect to inherit the duchy."

"Isn't it the case," continued Sanglant, "that King Arnulf the Younger settled the duchy on Rotrudis when he named Henry as his heir? Surely it must have occurred to you that if your stewardship displeases the king, he can find another worthy child out of Arnulf's many grandchildren who is fit to inherit the duchy."

"How dare you suggest such a thing!" shrieked Sophie.

"With what authority do you dare speak to us in this arrogant manner?" demanded Imma.

"With the authority of the army that sits outside your walls and which saved you from being sacked and murdered by the Quman."

Was that a faint cackle of amusement, coming from the emaciated figure on the sickbed? Impossible to tell, since the sound was drowned out by the protests hurled at him by her outraged children. Sanglant merely smiled, took Sapientia by the arm, and drew her out of the chamber and down the stairs to the lower level.

"You've angered them," she said.

"They're no better than a pack of jackals. But that will keep them sober for a few days."

She glanced at him sidelong. Her eyes were still red from crying, but at least she did not attack him for usurping her authority. Marriage to Bayan had restrained her worst impulses; perhaps it had also accustomed her to following a stronger personality's lead. "Would Father disinherit them? Is that what you hope to inherit? The duchy of Saony?"

"Nay, it's not what I want. But it's of no benefit to the kingdom to leave a pack of fools and quarrelers in charge. Don't forget that our great grandfather, the first Henry, was duke of Saony. This is the base of our family power. The regnant would do better to name Theophanu as duke in Rotrudis' place." He paused, waiting for an outburst, knowing how Sapientia envied Theophanu, but his sister said nothing, only listened. They crossed the length of the great hall in silence, their footfalls sounding lightly on wood as Sapientia's attendants followed at a discreet distance, whispering among themselves. Torchlight made fitful shadows dance on the walls. Many noble folk, those who hadn't the rank or the connections to be admitted to the duchess' private chambers, had crowded in to wait, and they, too, watched and whispered as prince and princess walked past. "Theophanu has as much right to the duchy as any of them do, and she's more fit to rule."

"She's at Quedlinhame. She could be called here."

"It might make them think twice if she brought her retinue here. But neither you nor I have the authority to name Theo as Rotrudis' heir."

"*I* have the authority. Father named me as his heir!"

He stopped her from speaking by taking hold of her wrist and drawing her out through the double doors to the porch. Lamps hung from eaves, rocking in the breeze. A haze covered the night sky, obscuring the stars.

"Do you, Sapientia?" he asked quietly. "Do you have the authority?"

She burst into tears.

The courtyard of the ducal palace remained busy even this late at night: carts bringing in dead, wounded, or loot from the battlefield; servants attending to business despite the lateness of the hour; soldiers at rest, having nowhere else to bed down. The population of Osterburg had swelled, due to the siege, and even here within the confines of the ducal palace one could smell the press of bodies. The constant buzz of lowered voices ran like an undercurrent at the edge of his hearing, phrases caught and lost, curses, muffled laughter and heartfelt weeping, whispered gossip. In such close quarters, he had learned to shut it out.

"They won't follow me," she said hoarsely through her sobs. "They don't trust me. It was Bayan they followed and trusted all along. I could have reigned with Bayan at my side, because he made me strong. Now what shall I do?"

He guided her across the courtyard to the chapel. Lamps ringed the stone building, and an honor guard of Ungrian soldiers stood with heads bowed on either side of the doors. As one, they went down on one knee when Sapientia approached, but when she took the arm of Lady Brigida to go inside to pray, the captain of the guard beckoned to Sanglant.

"My lord prince, what do you intend for the morning?"

"We must leave at first light to hunt down as many of the Quman as possible. If we break their back now, then they won't be able to raid again, not for a good long time. Perhaps not ever, if God so wills it."

"Without our good lord, Bayan, we cannot remain long in this country," said the captain, with an expressionless glance at the woman interpreting for him.

"Then bide with me as long as it takes to destroy the Quman. That is all I ask."

"For your sake, my lord prince, and for the honor of our good lord, Bayan, we will follow you a while longer."

The Ungrian captain's translator was also his concubine, a wiry spitfire of a marchlander who had become infamous on the march for whipping to death a captured bandit whom she claimed had once raped her sister. A persistent rumor dogged her that the man had been neither bandit nor rapist but rather her innocent husband, come to fetch her back to their farm, and that she'd killed him in order to stay with her Ungrian lover. Sanglant had certainly noticed her around camp, and he certainly noticed her now. She looked like the kind of woman who would draw blood in the midst of dalliance, and you'd never notice until afterward.

"I pray you, Prince Sanglant," she added after she had translated the captain's words, "you know the Ungrians as well as any man, so they say. Are they men of honor? He's offered to take me back to his home, but he already has a wife and I'm only a common woman, not the sort a man like him would marry. He says he'll care for me and any children I have by him, as if they were legitimate. Do you think that's true?"

"Ungria is a long walk from the marchlands. Once you've gone there, you'll likely never see your old home again."

She spat on the ground, anger strong in her eyes. Her captain grinned, quickly hiding his amusement at her fierce demeanor. Or perhaps he was only nervous that Sanglant had somehow insulted her, leaving him caught between avenging the insult and angering a prince, or losing his honor by doing nothing. She was canny enough to observe his discomfort and spoke a few quick words to him before returning her attention to Sanglant. "I've nothing to return to, back in my old home. But I won't doom myself and any children I might have to poverty or slavery."

"No man or woman knows what lies in the future. Anyone who tells you otherwise is lying. But even Prince Bayan had more than one wife before he married my sister, and all of his children are considered legitimate, with a right to share in his wealth. Even if it's true your captain can only have one wife who is recognized by the church, I suppose he still prefers the old ways. If he doesn't beat you now, then he's scarcely likely to beat you once he returns to Ungria. I see no reason why you would suffer for living there, except that it's a foreign land and like any foreign land a hard place to raise Wendish children."

"You're a bastard, too, aren't you?" She toyed with one end of her girdle, wrapped tightly around her waist. Handsomely embroidered and finished with gold thread, it was a rich garment for a woman of her station. "What do I care if my children are half-breeds and more Ungrian than Wendish as long as they have a better station in life? Why shouldn't my sons hope to ride in a lord's war band, and my daughters to guard the keys to a chest of treasure that they can administer and dispense? In the village I grew up in, not one family owned a horse. Now I ride instead of walking!"

Her words struck him powerfully. He had hoped for so little all his life, raised to be captain of the King's Dragons, raised to serve Wendar and the regnant, nothing more. But he didn't want to walk that path any longer. He no longer had the stomach for it. He had a child to consider.

"Go to Ungria," he said softly, "and I pray that God go with you."

Inside the chapel, Bayan's body lay in state before the Lady's Hearth. His mother lay outside the city's walls, hidden in her wagon, guarded by her slaves and by a contingent of Ungrian troops. Rumor had it that her attendants had asked for a barrel of honey in which to preserve her body.

Brother Breschius lay prone before the shrouded corpse, still weeping, heartbroken at the loss of his lord. Sapientia fell to her knees beside him. She had to be held up by two of her attendants, and a third woman threw a light shawl over her head to hide her face from the clerics and mourners assembled in the church.

But Sanglant had cried all his tears at dusk, when he had ridden in through Osterburg's gate beside Bayan's limp body, thrown over a horse. He caught Heribert's eye, and the cleric squeezed through the crowd and hurried over to him.

"What have you heard?" asked Sanglant in a low voice.

"Little enough. They're still too grief-stricken to think beyond Bayan's death. He was a good man."

"True-spoken words." He considered his weeping sister and her dead husband, illuminated by the gleam of lamps. A mural, obscured by the shadow of night and the shifting oil flames, washed the wall behind the Hearth: the martyrdom of St. Justinian, who had chosen death over marriage to a heathen queen. "Sapientia could become duchess of Saony."

"An odd choice of words, my lord prince. I'm not certain I understood correctly what you just said."

"Nay, you heard well enough, Heribert, but never mind. Stay a while longer, if you please. I've set the fox among the hens up in my aunt's chamber. I'm sure they'll be speaking of it here soon enough, and I'd like to know what they're saying."

Heribert's smile was mocking. "A rough attempt at intrigue, my lord prince, but it will serve as a beginning."

"Darre wasn't built in a day." He laughed, choked it back as the people nearest him turned around to stare, wondering who would be so crass as to disturb mourners in such a manner. Luckily, Sapientia had not heard him. "Where did I hear that line? I'll be turning into a cleric soon."

"Nay, my friend, no one is going to mistake you for a cleric."

A shout of grief from outside broke the even murmur of prayers. Soon other cries and lamentations could be heard. A man burst into the chapel. "Lord Zwentibold is dead!"

Sanglant moved to the Lady's Hearth and knelt there, offering a prayer for Bayan before he got up and went outside. These crowded spaces chafed him. He needed room to move. In the dark courtyard he caught sight of a familiar figure sauntering toward the gates with an unwilling woman in tow.

"Wichman! Cousin!"

Wichman had wasted little time in getting hold of Zwentibold's concubine. No doubt he intended to drag her down to a safe house in the city where Sanglant would never find her among so many refugees.

With a grunt of disgust, Wichman stopped, turning to face him. The concubine twisted her wrist free of his grasp. She looked ready to bolt, but she hesitated as she saw Sanglant walking up to them. She straightened, smoothing her gown down over her stomach. The weave of the cloth was silky enough that it clung to her, revealing the shape of her breasts, suggesting the length of one thigh and the hidden treasure that a man might gain access to, should he win her favor—or simply take possession of her. Pretty enough, ripe and willing: no wonder Zwentibold had taken her.

"I thank you," said Sanglant to Wichman, staring him down, "for bringing her to me. I have been at the chapel, praying for the dead."

Sanglant knew men well enough to see Wichman consider fighting him, but the notion, briefly held, ebbed quickly. Wichman didn't dare challenge him. They both knew that. At last, Wichman spun and stalked away.

"My lord." She dipped in an awkward obeisance, half bow, half bend that displayed an arousing expanse of breast. He could actually see the tips of her nipples where her neckline cut low. Her voice shook, as though she suppressed tears. "You have my thanks, my lord prince. I am ever so feared of Lord Wichman, after what he did do to my sister."

Nay, truly, no one was ever going to mistake him for a cleric. "What is your name?"

She had a strong accent. "I am called Marcovefa."

"Are you from Salia? How came you here to Osterburg?"

Her gaze was more shy than her body, which she shifted ever more closely toward him, close enough that he kept expecting to feel the cloth of her gown slipping over his hands, inviting him to touch what lay beneath it. "My sister and I came as attendants to a noble lady out of Salia. Her parents married her to Lord Zwentibold to get her out of the way of the war."

"Which war is that?"

"Well, truly, my lord prince, the king's brothers and cousins and his eldest son are all fighting over the crown of Salia. Men do fight over what they most desire." Her shy gaze, the way she looked up through her eyelashes at him, provoked him to take a step away. It was a desperately warm night even for early autumn. When had it gotten so hot? "My sister Merofled came to Lord Zwentibold's attention after our lady was taken ill. But Lord Wichman raped her one day, and she couldn't stand the shame of it. I fear me, she hanged herself." With the back of a pretty hand unweathered by work, she wiped a tear away. "I have no family left to me. My parents are dead. I suppose I may have a brother left alive in Salia, but I don't know how I'd ever go back there. My sister was my family. Now she's dead, and I'll never meet her again, not even in the Chamber of Light, for she took her own life. I hate that Lord Wichman. I beg you, Your Highness, do not let him take me, for why should I not join my sister in a criminal's death if I'm forced to endure his cruelty?"

Now she did lean against him, clutching for support at his shoulders while pressing all that soft and voluptuous flesh against his body. With an effort, he pushed her gently away.

"Where is Lord Zwentibold's wife now?"

"In St. Ursula's Convent, my lord prince. She's ever so ill, and she prays to God to heal her."

"What will she do now that Lord Zwentibold is dead?"

She wept, with evident sincerity. "I know not, Your Highness. He was a decent man, the best of that sorry lot!" Flushing, she ducked her head. "Begging your pardon, my lord."

"Would your lady take you back, if you went to St. Ursula's?"

"Live a nun's life? That wouldn't suit me, praying all day!" She sidled closer, pushing her hips up against his, letting her hands wander. "But you would. I could please you, my lord."

And why not? Liath had abandoned him and might never return, just as Alia had abandoned Henry. Alia had never cared about Henry at all.

But Henry hadn't let his anger twist him to do what he knew wasn't right. Perhaps Zwentibold's concubine was a decent woman doing the only thing she knew to make a place of safety for herself. Perhaps she was simply an opportunist, wanting beautiful clothes and rich food where she could get it. Another man, or woman, might take what he could get when he could get it and carelessly cast it away afterward, without thinking of the consequences. But Sanglant knew now how it felt to be abandoned. He had heard Waltharia mourn the death of the young child they had made together, the child he had never known, had not been permitted to know.

What if Frederun, back in Gent, had gotten with child by him? What would she do with a bastard child and no family to help her? Had he even sent a message to discover what had become of her? He had left her behind with less thought than Liath had left him.

"Nay," he murmured, knowing these thoughts unfair to Liath. Hadn't he heard his wife's voice in Gent? Hadn't she cried out to him: *Wait for me, I beg you. Help me if you can, for I'm lost here.*

His anger at his mother had deafened him. He had wanted, and had chosen, to believe the worst. Maybe, if he ever found Liath again, he should wait to hear what she had to say.

"But if you will not have me, what am I to do?" pleaded Marcovefa, still pressed against him.

"My lord prince."

"Thank God." He turned away from Marcovefa as his good friend hurried up to him, lamp in hand. "Heribert, you are come at just the right time. See that this woman is given sceattas, enough that she might set herself up in some business if she has any craft, or that she might return to Salia, or dower herself into a convent."

Heribert raised one eyebrow, but his expression remained grave. "As you wish, my lord prince." Marcovefa had flinched back at Sanglant's words, but now she slid closer to Heribert, perhaps thinking to work her wiles on him. Sanglant smiled slightly, then frowned as Heribert went on. "You'd best attend to your brother. There's trouble."

It was a relief to climb the steps in the stone tower, the oldest part of the ducal palace, where noble prisoners were kept in a drafty chamber behind a stout door ribbed with iron bands. He had set his own men to guard Ekkehard's door, knowing they would allow no mischief from folk who might otherwise be eager to harm the four men who had branded themselves as traitors.

"Trouble," said Sergeant Cobbo, acknowledging him. Everwin, beside him, smiled nervously. "Captain's inside with the noble ladies."

"Which noble ladies would that be? Not my sister?" He had visions of Sapientia trying to pulp Ekkehard with her broadsword, but despite his youth Ekkehard was still taller and bigger than his elder sister, having inherited Henry's height if not yet his breadth.

"Indeed, your sister. And Margrave Judith's daughter, Your Highness. They're both angry."

He laughed curtly, thinking of Marcovefa's tempting flesh. "And I'm damned thirsty, not having had a drink for far too long. We'll see who's most ill-tempered."

Cobbo opened the door for him. He walked in to find Lady Bertha with four surly looking soldiers at her back and Ekkehard cornered between the hearth and a table by a raging Sapientia.

"It's your fault!" Sapientia was screaming. "Bayan wouldn't be dead if not for your treason!" She flung herself on Ekkehard, who raised his arms to protect himself from her fury.

Ekkehard's three companions were being held back by main force by Sanglant's soldiers as they tried to come to his aid. One wore linen bound around a head wound. Another's arm was in a sling. Their dead comrade lay shrouded under a blanket on the chamber's only bed. Not even Sanglant had dared suggest that the poor boy be given a place in the chapel beside Bayan and the other noble dead.

"My lord prince." It was clear by the expression on Captain Fulk's face that he was relieved to see Sanglant.

"Sapientia." Sanglant crossed the plank floor in a half-dozen strides, grabbed his sister's shoulders, and pulled her off Ekkehard. "Don't let your grief for Bayan drive you to anything rash. God, and our father, will see that he is punished for his crimes."

"I'll see him hanged!" she cried, but she collapsed, weeping, into Sanglant's arms, and he beckoned to her attendants, who hastened to her side, pried her off him, and led her away.

Bertha's soldiers moved aside quickly to let them through, but as soon as Sapientia left the chamber, Bertha herself stepped forward. "What do you suppose King Henry intends to do with a son convicted of treason?"

"I stand as surety for my brother Ekkehard. What he did was wrong, but he's young and may be forgiven once for being misled."

"Brother!" Ekkehard threw himself against Sanglant. He still had a youth's slenderness, no doubt because he was scarcely more than sixteen, but when he wrapped his arms around Sanglant, he held tight enough that Sanglant wheezed before pulling him off.

Bertha smiled. She had the look of her mother, cunning, sharp, and strong, and none of Hugh's fabled beauty.

"You and your legion fought well in the battle," added Sanglant.

"And lost a fair number of my good marchlanders," she replied tartly. "I promised my elder sister Gerberga I'd bring her a reward for the sacrifice we Austrans and our cousins from Olsatia have made to rid Wendar of the Quman scourge. She lost her husband to a Quman raid last winter. And surely you know that Bulkezu himself is rumored to have killed our mother."

Even a man as unused to intrigue as Sanglant could see where this was leading. "She wants a royal prince as recompense."

"He's young," observed Bertha, looking Ekkehard over with the same cold regard she might reserve for choosing a new horse. "Not to my taste, but I'm sure that Gerberga will feel her loyalty to King Henry has been amply rewarded if she is given his youngest child as her new husband."

"A rich prize, indeed. Unfortunately, Ekkehard is abbot at St. Perpetua's in Gent."

Bertha laughed. "And my bastard brother Hugh is, so they say, a presbyter in Darre, confidant of the Holy Mother. Vows to God may be conveniently put aside if earthly cares demand it. Your sister Sapientia wants to hang the boy for a traitor because she wants to avenge herself on him for Prince Bayan's death." A hard woman, she softened for one instant, touching her cheek as though a fly had tickled her. "He was a good man. If you're a wise one, Prince Sanglant, you'll convince your sister otherwise. Wendar will suffer if kin kill kin, as this boy should have known. I think my suggestion would serve us all best."

"We shall speak of this later. Ekkehard will be sent to Quedlinhame meanwhile, to the care of our aunt, Mother Scholastica. I'll be leading the army out at dawn, to pursue what remains of the Quman."

Bertha didn't waste words or energy. She understood the uses of fast action on campaign. "We'll speak of this later," she agreed. With a final glance at Ekkehard, she left with her men.

"I—I don't want to be hanged," whispered Ekkehard, still clinging to Sanglant's arm.

"You should have thought of that before you went over to the Quman."

"But surely you'd not allow them to kill me in such a dishonorable way. I didn't have any choice once Bulkezu had captured me—"

"Spare me your excuses, Ekkehard. You've been a fool, and now you'll suffer the consequences." He glanced over toward the bed where that shrouded figure lay. "Ai, God, what was his name, the one I killed?"

"Welf." Ekkehard had obviously been crying, and he began weeping again. "He threw himself in front of me. He saved my life."

"I think he wanted to get himself killed," muttered one of his companions.

"He managed it well enough," observed Sanglant. "Isn't that the way of war? I've a piece of news for you, Ekkehard. One of your comrades, Thiemo, still lives—"

"Thiemo is alive! Where is he?"

"He serves another prince now. I'll let him know you're alive, but he's no longer yours to command. These other three—" They stammered out their names: Benedict, Frithuric, and Manegold. "You may return to the monastery or choose to suffer whatever fate Prince Ekkehard suffers. Which will it be?"

For all their youth, for all their foolishness, for all their crimes against Henry and Wendar, they knelt most graciously and proclaimed their undying loyalty to Ekkehard. They would walk with him wherever it led, even unto death.

"So be it." Sanglant was glad to see that they had that much honor. He left them to stew, and to worry, and returned to the chamber allotted to him.

The bells rang for Vigils.

Blessing, Anna, and Zacharias slept, while Matto and Chustaffus stood guard and Thiemo played dice with Sibold, waiting up for their prince. The chamber was spacious enough to boast two tables and three beds. Wolfhere had pulled his camp chair over to the cold hearth. There he sat, staring into the ashes as though the dead fire still spoke to him.

He glanced up as Sanglant crossed to stand beside him. A few charred sticks lay in a heap to one side where they'd tumbled as they'd burned.

"You seem troubled," said Sanglant quietly.

When Wolfhere made no answer, he sank down beside him. Grief at Bayan's loss cut hard as Sanglant watched the old Eagle reach out with the poker to disturb the charred sticks, mixing them into the heap of ashes. Dust rose from the hearth, and settled again. Bayan had managed to juggle four wives and not get himself killed; he'd even put one aside when the marriage to Sapientia had been offered to him, and he'd not been poisoned or bespelled with impotence by his cast-off wife. Surely he had the cunning to deal with Wolfhere. Impossible to think of Bayan's corpse decaying and his soul fled.

Thoughts of death choked him. "What is wrong? Have you been using your Eagle's sight? Surely my father isn't—?"

"Worse." Wolfhere's voice actually trembled. "Anne remains skopos. Henry returned to the palace safely after his campaign in the southern provinces. But then, unless my sight betrays me, what came next—" He could not go on for a moment, and when he did finally speak, his voice was a hoarse whisper. "This much have I deduced from what I can see, although truly Anne's sorceries have clouded the truth."

"For God's sake, go on!"

"I never thought Anne would stoop so low."

"Did you not? I never had any doubt."

Wolfhere's sharp glance only made Sanglant smile bitterly. "So be it. You're wiser than I, my lord prince, but I have known her far longer than you have. My whole life in her service—" He could not go on.

"And my father, whom you swore to serve? I pray you, Eagle, tell me about my father!"

Wolfhere shuddered. "Possessed by a daimone. Puppet of Anne and Hugh. What role Queen Adelheid plays in all this I cannot tell. Ai, God! That such a thing should come to pass! He has even declared that he means to anoint the infant, Mathilda, as his heir."

Anne and Hugh. Whatever else Wolfhere said faded as a rush of anger roared like wind, blinding him. "He should never have trusted them. Yet who is worse, the man who trusts the untrustworthy, or the one who turned his back when he knew what dangers lay in wait for the unwary?"

Wolfhere rested head in hands, looking ten years older at that moment, utterly weary. "What can we do? It is hopeless if they have already gained so much."

"Nay, do not say so," said Sanglant as he stared at the hearth. A single spark glinted among white coals. "We are not done yet."

They rode out at dawn. Considering the disrepair of the walls, Sanglant found it amazing that the Quman hadn't broken through in any of a half-dozen gaps. Perhaps they hadn't managed it only because they hadn't had time. According to Lady Sophie, Bulkezu and his army had arrived a mere three days before Sanglant.

He surveyed the army riding at his back: noble lords and ladies and their eager retinues, the Ungrians bearing the body of Prince Bayan in a barrel of wine, leading them in death as well as life, and Sapientia, subdued and silent. His daughter was laughing at something Lord Thiemo had said. Although the poor boy had wept when told that Prince Ekkehard lived, he had seemed relieved to be told that he could not return to him. Fulk rode at the head of Sanglant's personal escort, the captain's keen gaze missing nothing as they headed down the road leading east.

A rash course, that he meant to take now, but the only one left to him. All along, ever since he had turned his back on his father at Angenheim, he had known this was what he would have to do. He had just never suspected that the stakes would be quite so high.

Drastic measures for drastic times.

He kept Lord Wichman beside him, not trusting him anywhere else. "Your mother?" he asked politely.

Wichman laughed coarsely. "The old bitch. She's stubborn enough to live on for months. I pray she does, if only to torture my sisters. Do you mean to disinherit them?"

"I am not regnant, nor have I been named regent, to pass such a judgment. I believe a messenger has been sent to my sister Theophanu at Quedlinhame. Sapientia must also be consulted."

"So you say, Cousin, but she's nothing without Bayan." Wichman's thoughtful look gave a unfamiliar cast to his usually arrogant and lustful features, as though another man peered out, seeking to be heard. "He was a right prick, but Lord knows we all respected him." He hiked up his chain mail to scratch his crotch. "Did the woman please you? I had to content myself with a couple of warty whores down in the town. Maybe I ought to think of getting married. I could use a good setup like Druthmar, there, with Villam's daughter. Lady Brigida is still looking for a husband, so they say."

"I understand that Lady Bertha, Judith's daughter, remains unmarried."

This sent Wichman into howls of laughter, picked up by his cronies once they had heard the joke, and the conversation quickly grew so crude that even Sanglant could not stand to hear more of it. He rode ahead with Fulk and Wolfhere beside him, falling in with the solemn nobles who attended Princess Sapientia at the van.

South of the city they came to the battlefield, swarming now with looters, ravens, crows, scavengers, and the ever-present vultures circling overhead, waiting their chance. Most of the Wendish nobles had been hauled off the field last night, and now the common soldiers were being carted off to mass graves. The Ungrian priests had their own rites, which he purposefully ignored. The Quman, of course, would be burned. Feathers torn off broken wings rose like chaff on the dawn breeze. A woman wept over the body of a loved one. A cart rumbled past, piled high with corpses.

Farther away, ragged folk wandered the edge of the battle-field like ghosts, stunned and bewildered. Was that young woman with long black hair as lovely as she seemed from this distance? She walked at the head of a pack of about a dozen thin, frightened people, some of them children. They huddled for a while staring over the battlefield while Sanglant watched them. At their backs stood a line of trees set along the length of a fallow field, still green from the recent rains. At last, they turned and trudged toward Osterburg, the towers of the palace stark against the pale rose sky as the sun lifted free of the eastern forest.

The army picked up the pace but hadn't gotten halfway through the open woodland toward the Veserling ford when they met a triumphant band of Lions marching in their direction with the last of the baggage train—that which hadn't been able to get in last night—rolling along in two neat lines behind them. Their ragged banner flew proudly, and Captain Thiadbold called the halt and gestured to a Lion next to him to step forward and greet the prince.

"Prince Sanglant! Your Highness, I am called Ingo, sergeant of the first cohort. See what a fine prize we have brought you!"

Sanglant saw the Eagle first. She looked exhausted, and when she saw him she wept.

"My lord prince," she cried, pressing forward on the horse they had given her to ride, "is Liath with you?"

She needed no answer, nor had he any to give her, knowing that his expression spoke as loudly as words might. She covered her eyes with a hand, hiding fresh tears.

She wasn't the only prize the Lions had brought in. Beyond all expectation they had captured the greatest prize of all, trussed and tied and forced to walk like a common slave. His face looked horrible, the flap of skin torn away from his cheek still weeping blood although someone had attempted to treat it with a poultice. Impossible to know how much pain he was in. His gaze had a kind of insane glee in it as he laughed, hearing Hanna's question.

"I should have known a Kerayit shaman's luck would not crack so easily. You lied to me, frost woman!"

"Yes!" she cried, turning to him in fury. "I lied to you! I lied to you! She was never at Osterburg!"

"Silence, I pray you!" When he had silence, Sanglant spoke again, a single word: "Bulkezu."

The Quman prince's wings were completely shattered, but a few bright griffin feathers remained to him, dangling by threads from what remained of his harness.

"Hang him," said Hanna hoarsely.

"Nay, let me kill him!" cried Wichman, riding up, and the cry rose throughout the ranks as soldiers clamored for the honor.

Sapientia drew her sword and rode forward, calling to the Lions to haul Bulkezu out in front of the line. "I'll have his head in recompense for the death of my husband!"

Men crowded up from the back to see the spectacle, all of them yelling and taunting the twenty or so Quman prisoners, who stood their ground with expressions of blank indifference. Bulkezu laughed, as though to spur Sapientia's anger further. She shrieked with fury and lifted her sword.

"Quiet!" Sanglant's voice rang out above the outcry. He rode up beside Sapientia and caught her arm before she could strike. "Nay, Sister, we'll have no killing of prisoners. Not when they can serve us in another way."

"Hang him then, as the Eagle says! Then everyone will know with what dishonor we treat heathens!"

"He'll serve us better alive than dead."

The words brought disbelieving silence as men murmured and Sanglant's pronouncement was passed by means of whispers to the rear ranks. Only one person had the courage to speak up.

"He's a monster," cried Hanna. "You must see that justice is done for all the ruin he's caused. I witnessed it, in the name of King Henry!"

"Worse ruin will come if we do not fight the enemy that threatens us most. Lady Bertha. I pray you, come forward."

Bertha rode up with her standard-bearer at her side and, with only a cursory acknowledgment of Sapientia, placed herself before Sanglant. Without question, Judith's daughter had summed up the situation quickly. She had a cut on her face that hadn't been there last night, and one hand bound up in linen—she was not a person he would care to face on the battlefield, strong, cunning, and ruthless.

"I'll give you what you want," he said, "if you'll pledge me your loyalty."

Sapientia gasped. "I was named as Henry's heir! This is my army—"

"Nay, Sister. This is *my* army now." He beckoned Heribert forward. "I'll have it now," he said in a low voice. "It's time."

With a brilliant grin, Heribert fished in the pouch hanging from his belt and brought out the gold torque that Waltharia had offered Sanglant months before. The prince took it, twisted the ends, and slid it around his neck. The heavy gold braid rested easily there. He had forgotten now natural its weight felt against his skin, the tangible symbol of his rank, his birthright, and his authority. His soldiers raised their voices in a deafening cheer. Sapientia's face washed pale, and she swayed as if dizzied by the noise.

Sanglant rode forward to take the rope bound to Bulkezu's neck out of Ingo's hand. "My army," he repeated, "and Bulkezu is *my* prisoner." The Quman chieftain said nothing, only watched, but his lips quirked up as if he were about to break out laughing. Sanglant turned to address Judith's daughter. "Lady Bertha, have we an agreement?"

"Ekkehard to marry my sister in return for my troops riding under your command? I'll accept that exchange." She grinned. "I was hoping there might be more fighting."

He stood in his stirrups, half turning to survey the soldiers winding back into the woods, awaiting his command. He pitched his voice to carry toward the rear ranks. "The war is not over yet, although we've won a great victory here. The threat to Wendar from the Quman is ended. But our enemies have not been defeated. Now I'm riding east. Who will ride with me?"

Not one among that host refused him.

XIX
THE UNVEILING

1

ADICA returned home just after sunset, stepping from southern heat to autumn chill as she crossed through the gate woven of starlight and set foot on familiar ground. She stood shivering and coughing as her lungs made the adjustment, as she struggled to place herself in the wheel of the year. The heavens were unbelievably clear. A full moon rose in the east, washing a silvery light over the sky that obscured all but the brightest stars.

Those bright stars told her what she needed to know. By the position of the Dipping Cup, swinging low in the north, and the trail of the Serpent along the southwestern horizon, she knew that the autumn equinox would have fallen just before the last new moon. That being so, the sun was only a short way from reaching the nadir of the heavens along its cyclical journey, and therefore she had less than a moon's cycle left to her before that night came in which all the alignments of the stars and the heavens were in place for the great working.

She would never see another full moon.

She would never again lie with Alain and caress his body with only the moon to watch over them.

Unable to help herself, she wept. Far to the south, Shu-Sha's weaving would tens of days ago have faded into sparks lost in the night, just as Alain and the men left behind to guard him had been lost. She twisted the lapis lazuli ring on her finger and with an effort wiped away her tears. Shu-Sha had scolded her more than once during the five days she had dwelt in her hall down in the southern lands.

"Do not mourn over the happiness you were fortunate enough to possess, lest you turn that joy into grief. Be glad that you had what others may never in their lives experience. The gods have dealt kindly with you, Daughter."

It was impossible to argue with Shu-Sha, the great queen, who with her vast girth and magnificent beauty was often called the living embodiment of the Fat One, most powerful of the gods because she held both life and death in her hands. The people ruled over by Queen Shuashaana did not call their goddess the Fat One in their own language, of course, but in her heart Adica knew it was the same power who lived in both places no matter what name was used.

As a child, she had learned to stifle her tears and get on with it. She slung her pack over her shoulder and set off for the village. Her people had been busy. The lower embankment circling the tumulus had a stout palisade of logs set around it as far as she could see under moonlight. Piles of fresh earth alternated with crude shelters built for the workmen on lower ground between the ramparts. A whistling man came walking around the curve of one rampart, saw her, and stopped short. He put a horn to his lips and blew, three times, to alert the village.

"Who is there?" she called, not recognizing him, but he ran away. He had recognized her, and feared her, just as they all had in the days before Alain had come.

The lower ramparts overlapped to make a cleft between them, an easily defended opening. The workers had dug a steep ditch here and lined the bottom with stakes; planks thrown down over the ditch made a bridge. Two adults stood on sentry duty, but they shielded their eyes and murmured polite greetings without looking at her.

When she emerged from the cleft she looked down the slope at the village and, by aid of the moon's light, surveyed the change two seasons had wrought. In the time she had been gone, the villagers had finished building the log palisade around the village, with watch posts set up at intervals and a double tower on either side of the gate. Torches burned at each watch post. Sentries stood by the torches, looking out into the night. How strange to see her peaceful village transformed into a camp made ready for war. How strange to see the serpentlike earthworks bristling with wood posts, like the ridged back of a sinuous dragon at rest.

It ruined the peace of the landscape. Yet they could only live in peace and without constant fear once the Cursed Ones were defeated. Her own sorrow, her own life, meant little compared to the life of the tribe. She hardened her heart as she descended the path.

The plank bridge had been drawn back, exposing a fresh ditch lined with pointed stakes. Lifting her staff, she shook the bells, calling out to the guard at the gate.

"Hallowed One!" By chance, her cousin Urtan stood on gate duty this night. Soon enough, the gate was opened, the plank bridge thrust across, and she welcomed inside.

"Where is Alain?" Urtan asked. Other villagers, alerted by the horn call, hurried up as torches ringed her.

"We despaired of you, Hallowed One!"

"The Fat One is merciful, Hallowed One. She brought you back to us!"

Beor shouldered through the crowd, pushing forward to see her. "Where is Alain?" he demanded.

Thinking of Alain made her so tired that she thought she might fall down where she stood, only no one here could touch her to lift her up again. Only Alain could do that.

"Let me sleep," she said hoarsely, unable to say more. She had to choke her heart as in a fist; she dared not start crying now.

Mother Weiwara came forward, looking prosperous and healthy. "Let the Hallowed One go to her bed," she said sternly to the folk crowded around. She escorted Adica to her cottage and crouched outside, just beyond the threshold, as Adica ducked under the door and dropped her pack on the floor, then sank onto her knees on the musty pallet.

"You have been gone a long time," said Weiwara through the door. "More than two seasons, now. The dark of the sun is only half the moon's cycle away—"

"I know."

"Oh, Adica." Once, Weiwara had been her dearest friend, two girls growing up together. With the darkness hiding them each from the other, she had the courage to touch that lost friendship again, despite the evil spirits that could smell the threads binding one person to another and use those links to sink their claws into the unsuspecting. "Where have you been?"

"On a long journey. I'm so tired. I lost Alain." His name caught in her throat. She had to pinch the skin of her neck with a hand to strangle a sob. "But do not fear, Mother Weiwara." Her voice was little more than a whisper. "The working will go forward. Soon you will be freed from fear."

If the weather held. If the Holy One still lived. If Laoina reached her people in time to lead a strong band of warriors to the aid of Two Fingers, in the land of Horn. If they could drive the Cursed Ones away from that stone loom, and so link up with the others. If Hehoyanah did as her uncle asked, and joined the weaving. If no Cursed Ones attacked the tents of Brightness-Hears-Me. If Falling-down did not die. If she herself did not break of sorrow.

"Tell me what you saw," breathed Weiwara in a low voice.

She began to object but caught the dismissal before it passed her lips. Alain had taught her how to listen to others in a way that allowed her to see past the words to glimpse the heart. Was that curiosity, even wistfulness, in Weiwara's tone? Did her old friend conceal a hankering to see distant lands and strange sights?

Sometimes telling is the only way to make the pain end, or at least lessen.

She told Weiwara the story of their long journey, of the strange creatures they had seen, of the unknown cities they had glimpsed, of the ambushes they had avoided. She even told her of the vision she had seen of the banquet of plenty, burnished by gold, and the woman with fire in her heart who had given her a ring to return to Alain. As she told the story, she pressed the ring into her cheek.

"But I didn't see Alain again. When I woke from my trance, I was in Shu-Sha's palace, where Laoina and the others had carried me. Alain had gone with three of the men of Shu-Sha's tribe, back to get the dogs. He never came. I waited there for five days, but he never came."

Wind breathed through the chimes hanging around the outside eaves. A cow lowed from a nearby byre. If she stopped now, she would fall into pieces and never be able to go on.

"Tell me about Shu-Sha," said Weiwara, as though she had seen into Adica's heart. "What is her palace like? Do the people of her land look the same as we do? What do they eat?"

"Queen Shuashaana is powerfully fat. You've never seen a woman with so much power in her body, thighs as big as my hips and arms as big as my thighs. Her belly is as large as a cauldron and her breasts are like melons."

"She must be very powerful," whispered Weiwara in awe. "I wasn't even nearly that fat when I was pregnant with the twins."

So drowned had Adica been in her own fears and sorrows that she hadn't thought once to ask of doings in the village. So much might have happened since she was gone, and yet she had to be careful how she asked, never to mention any person by name who might thereby become vulnerable to the darts of the evil spirits listening around her.

"I hope the Fat One's favor still smiles on the village."

"Spring and summer passed swiftly, Hallowed One. There were two raids by the Cursed Ones north of here, at Seven Springs and Four Houses, and some people were killed but the Cursed Ones were driven off. Dorren came from Falling-down to tell us that we must fortify Queens' Grave. We had work parties from the other villages all summer to build the palisade on the lower embankment, to protect the stone loom. One time just at the autumn equinox a scouting party shot arrows at us, but both palisades were finished by then, so they left when they saw they could do no damage with such small numbers. Still, we've sent for war parties from the other White Deer villages, in case they come back. The Fat One has blessed us with three births and no deaths in the moons since you departed. Her favor has been strong over us."

"May it continue so," prayed Adica softly. "Forgive me, Weiwara, to speak of fate when the spirits swarm so near to me, but one thing troubles me. Since you are Mother to our people, it falls to me to ask you."

"I remember our friendship. I will not turn my back on you now."

Adica sighed, shuddering. "Promise me that you will lay me beside the ancient queens, if you can."

Adica smelled Weiwara's tears. "You will be honored among us as if you were one of the queens of the ancient days. I promise you that. No one in this tribe will ever forget you, as long as we have children."

"Thank you."

"Is there anything else you would ask of me?"

To think of lying down alone on her old pallet made her think of the queens, asleep under the hill, but she knew she had to sleep, to keep up her strength just as she had to eat. So Shu-Sha had told her. Nothing mattered more now than that the great weaving be completed successfully.

"I will sleep. You must look to the village now, and I will prepare for what is coming."

Amazingly, once Weiwara had left and she lay down undressed on her pallet, covering herself in furs, she dozed off easily. Weariness ruled her. She slept, and she did not dream.

But the morning dawned cold and ruthless, nor had sleep softened her heart. She rose at dawn and did what she could to air out her bedding. She examined the dried herbs hanging from the rafters, weeding out lavender that had gotten eaten away by a fungus, burning a tuft of thistle too withered to be of use.

Already, at dawn, villagers gathered before her house.

"Hallowed One, the birthing house hasn't been purified properly."

"Hallowed One, my daughter got sick after drinking cider, but Agda says it was the berries she had, not the cider. There are still five jars left. Maybe evil spirits got in them, or maybe they're still good."

"Hallowed One, is it true that Alain didn't come back with you? My dog got a thorn in his paw and one of the geese has a torn foot—"

It was a relief to be busy. She dressed, broke her fast with porridge and goat's milk, and went first to the birthing house. After three new births, it desperately needed purifying; she smelled spirits lingering in the eaves, making it dangerous for the next woman who would enter to give birth here. As she examined the outside of the house, testing how the thatch had weathered the summer, looking for birds' nests, spiderwebs, and other woven places where spirits might roost, she glanced occasionally back at the village.

Manure from the byres was being carted out to the most distant fields in preparation for the winter. Beor and his cousins were slaughtering a dozen swine to feed the war parties, camped up beyond the embankment, and his sister had just brought up a big pot of hot boiled barley to catch blood for a black pudding. Young Deyilo tended a flock of geese out on the stubble of a harvested field.

Getsi appeared with a covered basket. She had grown a

hand in height since Adica had last seen her, and the shape of her face had begun to change. In another year she would approach womanhood. But Adica would not be the woman guiding her across that threshold.

"What do you have there?" she asked the girl, more sharply than she intended.

"My mother has been collecting herbs and flowers for you. Where shall I set them?"

"Here, Daughter," she replied, a little shamefaced, pointing to the ground just in front of the door. "Your mother will have my thanks. This thatch needs beating. You've had a frost that loosened it."

"It's been cold early this year," agreed Getsi. "I'll get my sister to come do it. My mother says I'm not strong enough to do it right yet."

"You'll soon be."

Getsi smiled, careful not to look her in the eyes, and loped off back to the village, lithe and eager.

Best to keep busy, and not to think on what she had lost. She completed her circuit of the birthing house before kneeling down before the basket, uncovering it. A rush of scent billowed up, dust dancing as wind caught and worried at dried summer milfoil, placed at the top. Beneath them she found small woven pouches containing flower petals or juniper berries, and beneath these butterwort, betony, and mint leaves, the bundled stalks of tansy and five-leafed silverweed, as well as lavender so fragile that it crumbled at a touch. She laid the contents of one of the pouches on her knees to sort it, sheltering the light petals from the breeze: eglantine and wild rose, made pale by age.

A horn call blared: the alarm from the village, a triple blast to call every person in to the safety of the walls. Shocked, she simply froze, lifting her head to stare as children shrieked and men and women dropped what they were doing and went running.

The horn sounded again, a single blast followed by silence,

followed by another short blast. She heard shouts and cries turn from alarm to amazement as people streamed out of the gates, running to meet what a moment ago they had been running from.

Still she did not move.

A dozen horsemen appeared around the southern flank of the great tumulus, the Queens' Grave. In the next instant she saw they were not horsemen but the Horse people. One of them carried a rider, a human like herself. Running among the centaurs came two huge black hounds.

Petals slid unheeded down her thighs, catching in the cords of her skirt. Never could she mistake him for anyone but himself, nor would she ever mistake another man for him. She leaped up, rose petals falling in clouds around her, trailing after her, as she ran to meet him.

He pushed through the crowd gathered to stare at the centaur women. They gave way, seeing his purpose. Breaking free, he hurried forward and caught her in his arms, holding her as tightly as if he never meant to let her go, his face pressed against her hair.

He said nothing. She wept helpless tears of joy and relief, and after a while he pulled back to kiss them away, although even he could not catch every one.

"Hush, Adica. I am come safely home. The Holy One is rescued. We couldn't return south to get you because of the war, but when we learned that Queen Shuashaana had already sent you home, my friends agreed to bring me here. All is well, my love. All is as it should be."

"I love you," she said through her tears as the hounds bounded up, great bodies wriggling like those of pups in their eagerness to get a greeting from her. "I was so afraid I had lost you."

"Never," he promised her as he embraced her again. "Never."

Held within that warm embrace, she knew she would not falter now, not even when it came time to walk forward to the death that awaited her. She would not go gladly, never that, but she could go with unhesitating steps because she had been granted strength and joy by the gift of love.

2

PALACES floated on a river of fire, each linked to the last by means of bridges as bright as polished gold. At intervals brilliant sparks flew up from the river of fire in the same way sparks scatter and die when a blacksmith strikes molten iron with a hammer. These sparks lit on her body as she met the embrace of a host of creatures, daimones whose substance was made entirely of fire.

Where they touched her, crowding around, she burned. Her hands burned, her skin burned, and fire from within broke the bonds of the binding Da had wrapped around her so many years before. He had tried to seal her away from herself. He had crippled her for so many years, but in this place his magic held no power. Sparks pierced the locked door behind which Da had hidden her soul, melting the lock until the door swung wide and vanished in a cloud of steam, and she burned until her flesh was consumed and fire within met fire without.

She was like them. She had a soul of fire no different than their own.

Joy struck at her heart like lightning. The universe changed into purity around her, and in her heart and in her soul she knew she had entered a place existing beyond the mortal limits of humankind. Even her bow, Seeker of Hearts, had vanished. She had nothing of Earth left to her, nothing binding her to Earth any longer.

In the embrace of fire she burned for an eternity, or perhaps only for one instant.

Then she found her voice. "Who am I?"

Here in the realm of fire their voices thrummed as though they were themselves taut strings on which the music of the spheres played out its measure. **"Step into the river of fire, child. Here nothing can be hidden that you call past, which binds you, and future, which blinds mortal eyes."**

She let herself fall, and the river swept her into the past.

She knows this handsome villa, its proud architecture and well-built structures, an entire little cosmos sufficient unto itself. She recognizes the vista of craggy hills and of forest so dense and green that the midday summer sunlight seems to drown in leaves. Fields surround the villa, a neatly tended estate. Not one weed grows out of place. Even the bees never sting. This is the place where she was born and spent her early childhood.

She knows this pleasant garden, once languid with butterflies and now made gold by a profusion of luminous marigolds. But the prize bed of saffron is quite simply missing, scorched and trammeled. A man stands with his back to the rest, surveying the ruined saffron. The other five weary, somber figures gather around the seventh of their number, which is in fact a corpse. It is one of these who kneels, face hidden, to gingerly examine the prone body.

One of the Seven Sleepers has died in the struggle, and Anne for the first time loses her majestic calm. She shrieks anger, an expression that on her face looks so startlingly wrong that it takes a moment for Liath to realize how much younger Anne is, here in the past. She has her grandfather Taillefer's look about her, well built and excellently proportioned, with fine eyes and a dignified manner. She cannot be much more than thirty years of age, strong and extraordinarily beautiful in her prime.

"We were to bind a male daimone!" she cries, outraged at their failure. "It was to be the father! I was to be the one who would sacrifice my blood and my purity to bear a child."

"This is the second death we've suffered," says Severus, "although in truth I haven't missed Theoderada's incessant praying these last six years." Taking years away from his face has not improved his sour aspect. "Can we risk a third death?"

"We must," insists Anne as she glowers at the dead woman, crumpled on the ground, robes burned to nothing and her skin ash-white, still hot to the touch. "We must have a child born to fire who can defeat this half-breed bastard being raised by King Henry. Do you doubt that all is lost if we do not counter the influence of the Aoi? Do you wish to set their yoke over your neck?"

"No," says Severus irritably, having been asked this question one too many times.

Meriam sighs as she regards the dead woman. "Where will we find another to join our number? Poor Hiltrudis was too young to think of dying."

"Aren't we all?" snapped Severus. His arms are burned, his cheeks flaming as though with fever. Blisters are already forming along his lower lip, and his eyes weep tears.

The youngest among them, a slight woman with wispy pale hair, stands back with a hand over her mouth to stifle the horrible stench. They are all marked by burns. "I'm afraid," she whispers. She glances toward the seventh of their number, the man standing a stone's toss away from the rest with his back to them. Light shines in a nimbus around his body, which by its position conceals something standing in the middle of the charred saffron. She begins to weep silently in fear. "I'm afraid to try again. You didn't tell me it would be like this." She gestures toward the corpse. "Hiltrudis didn't know either. How could you not have warned us?"

"Hush, Rothaide," murmurs Meriam, taking the young woman's arm. "Surely you understood all along that sorcery is dangerous."

The man kneeling beside the corpse looks up. At first, Liath does not recognize him. He looks so much younger than when she knew him, with only a trace of silver in his hair. He is even a little homely, the kind of man whose looks improve as he ages. "If we try again," says Wolfhere, "it will surely be worse. Can we not make do with what we have? We succeeded beyond our expectations."

Anne makes a noise of disgust, turning away. "Then I am forced to act alone, if I must. This day's work is no success."

But the man standing in the ashes with his back to the others sighs softly. "She's so beautiful."

"Go!" says Anne suddenly, caught by that voice. "Leave the body. I must think."

They are not unwilling to retreat to salve their wounds. Meriam leads away the weeping Rothaide, Severus limps after her and, after a moment, but hesitantly, Wolfhere goes as well, not without two or three backward glances at Anne. The butterflies have begun to return, fluttering around her like winged jewels.

Then Anne is alone with the corpse and the man standing with his back to her, who has not, apparently, heard her command to the others.

"Bernard," she says softly.

Surprised to hear his name, he turns.

Ai, God, it is Da, but so much younger, about thirty years of age and, by all appearances, a few years younger than Anne. Liath never knew he was handsome. She never really understood how much she looks like him, even with her golden-brown skin and her salamander eyes. The years of running took their toll. The magic he expended to hide her scarred and diminished him. This is the fearless man, face shaven and hair trimmed in the manner of a frater, who walked ardently into the heathen lands of the east without once looking over his shoulder. But that was all before her birth, before their flight, before that day when, by crippling her, he crippled himself.

Liath never understood until this instant, seeing Anne's expression, how much Anne hated him because he is beautiful to her eyes. She never understood until this instant how much power Da had, and how he shone, as luminous as the sun and with a glint of sarcasm in his eyes. She only remembered him, only had memories of him, from after the fear had sucked him dry.

"Bernard," Anne repeats, "you have been the thorn in my side for long enough. I know you have never cared about our work to save humankind from the threat of the Lost Ones. I know you joined us only to satisfy your intellect and your curiosity. We've suffered you all these years because of the strength of your gift, not for your loyalty to our goals. But the time has come for you to be of use to me. Can it be possible that you have at last seen a creature you desire more than you desire knowledge?"

Anger chases laughter chases longing across his expressive features. He steps aside, and Liath sees what they have caught in a cage made not of iron bars but of threads like spider's silk, billowing as the breeze moves through them.

She is fire, incandescent, a living creature bound by magic beneath the moon, where she does not belong. She wears a womanly shape, scintillant and as bright as a blue-white sun, and her wings beat against the unbreakable white threads, but she is hopelessly trapped. Heat boils off her, but the cage neutralizes these streamers of flame, and when she opens her mouth to scream, no sound comes out.

"You can have her, Bernard, because I can see that you desire her. But only if what transpires now remains a secret between you and me."

He is torn. He suspects that to agree will compromise him in some unintended way, but even as he struggles, Liath knows he will lose because he has fallen in love with the fire daimone, a creature so beyond mortal ken that even to call it down to Earth brings death.

"How can this be?" he asks hoarsely. "If it caused poor Hiltrudis' death just to cast the binding spell, how can any flesh dare touch pure fire?" He raises an arm, then blushes, hot and red.

"First we must send the others away, to give Hiltrudis' body a proper burial and to seek a seventh to make whole our number. There are certain spells known to me that can soften fire into light so that her substance will not burn you. But it will be up to you to win her acquiescence." She eyes him as the daimone writhes, trying to get free. "None of this comes without a price."

"What must I do?" He is already caught. He will agree to everything, because desire has trapped him in a cage of surpassing beauty, in the guise of a woman with wings of flame, daughter of the highest sphere, the soul of a star. He will agree to anything, if only he can have her.

Anne brushes a cinder, all that is left of a thread of saffron, off her sleeve. "First, this sorcery will weaken me. I will be an invalid, and you must care for me until I recover. Second, the others must believe that the child was made of my seed, not yours, that between us we freed this creature and captured another, a male, who could thereby impregnate me. The child must be thought to come of Taillefer's lineage. Yet not

*just from Taillefer's lineage, but legitimately born. To that end, you
must marry me in a ceremony sanctioned by the church."*

"Yes," he says absently, obviously too distracted as he stares at the
daimone even to point out the gaping holes of illogic in this proposal.
The woman-creature has calmed enough, now, to furl her wings and
with apprehension and anger survey her prison.

"Last, the child will be mine to raise."

"Whatever you say," he whispers, because the daimone has caught
sight of him. She has no true distinguishable features, no human
mask of a face, yet those are eyes that see him, that mark his presence,
and she does not recoil as he returns her gaze boldly. She watches him,
blazing and effulgent, the most magnificent thing he has seen in a life
that brought him face-to-face with many wondrous creatures. He does
not fear her. He is too much in thrall to desire, the man who until now
had remained faithful to his vow of chastity despite the many tempt-
ations thrown in his path.

Whatever you say.

The words haunt Liath.

The corpse is carried away and buried fittingly. The next day,
Anne and Bernard are joined in holy matrimony in the chapel, with
the others looking on as witnesses. Wolfhere paces restlessly throughout
the ceremony, looking ready to spit. Rothaide, Meriam, and Severus
leave for distant parts, although Wolfhere lingers for a handful of
days like a man in the throes of suspicion, believing that his wife is
contemplating adultery. Only when his Eagle's sight shows him the old
king, Arnulf, bed-ridden with a terrible fever, does he leave, hastening away to the side of the king he has pretended for all these years to
serve faithfully.

When Wolfhere is finally gone, Anne can at last work her spell,
but hers is a devious mind and she has the means to punish the only
man for whom she ever actually felt unbearable physical desire. The
fire of the daimone's soul is tamed, her aethereal body is given a semblance of mortal substance, but in this process her features are molded
so that they resemble Anne herself.

Trapped and diminished, the daimone turns to the one who shows
her kindness and affection. Fire seeks heat when it is dying. Bernard

*is not unaware of the way Anne has turned his wish back onto him,
so that when at last the daimone surrenders to his patient courtship of
her, it's as if he is making love to Anne herself, her face, her body, but
lit by aetherical fire from within, like Anne in the guise of an angel.
With that wicked, sardonic humor that made him able to withstand
much suffering in his eastern travels, he even calls her "Anne"
although Anne lies as helpless as a newborn in the villa, tended by
Bernard hand and foot because he remains as good as his word. His
entire universe has shrunk to this villa, to the care he gives faithfully
to the invalid who has made his wish become truth, to the sphere of the
fiery woman-creature he worships and makes love to.*

*Maybe what he feels for the daimone is love and maybe it is only
lust, a craving brought on by a glimpse of the high reaches of the universe, too remote for the human mind to comprehend. But if what he
feels is not love, then it is hard to say what counts for love in a cold
world.*

*Because the world is cold, and the universe disinterested in one
insignificant man's feelings, however strong they might be. Certain
laws govern the cosmos, and not even love can alter them, or perhaps
love is the unmoving mover that impels them forward.*

*Seed touches seed, by means unknown to humankind and perhaps
influenced by the tides of magic. A seed ripens and grows, and the
child that waxes within the creature born not of Earth must build a
mortal body in which to live.*

It happens so slowly that in the end it seems to happen all at once.

*The child consumes the substance of the mother to make itself. All
her glorious fire is subsumed into the child she births, and the birth
itself becomes her death. All that she was she has given; even her soul
is now part of the child. She herself, the brilliant creature bound and
trapped months ago, is utterly gone.*

*That she existed at all can only be seen in the newborn's remarkable
blue eyes, as bright as sparks.*

*He weeps for a long time, broken, pathetic, until Anne appears sud-
denly at his side, hale and hearty now that the spell which drained
her strength has been dissipated by the death of the daimone.*

"So," she says, examining the baby as if for flaws, "this is how lust

ends, in death and despair." She seems pleased to have found a way to escape this fate, since lust's cruel hand brushed her as well. She surveys Bernard's bent form with disdain. "Give me the baby now, as you promised."

"No," he says, clinging to the naked little thing, still slick from the birth. Where he made for his love a childbed for her labor lies only a soft blanket, nothing else, no trace of her.

"She killed her mother, the one you loved."

"I know." He weeps, because Anne has trapped him, as she meant to all along. She knew, or guessed, what would happen. He fell as did the angels long ago, tempted by carnal desire, and now all he sees at his feet is the yawning Abyss. His heart's strength is broken at that moment. In the years to come, his body's strength will be broken as well, bit by bit.

But he loves his daughter anyway.

After all, the child is innocent. If anyone is guilty, it is Anne for the ruthlessness of her ambition. If anyone is guilty, it is the other five sorcerers, for aiding her with willing hands. If anyone is guilty, it is he.

He will never stop punishing himself. And because he is weak and imperfect, like all human souls, in the end he will punish his daughter as well, even if he never intended to harm her.

Anne wins. She has the child she wanted, the husband she lusted after, but she has kept her body pure, a matter of great importance to her, who thinks of all other human beings as tainted and unworthy. Bernard stays, because he is completely compromised now, because he is guilty, because he has learned the meaning of fear.

He stays. He names the infant after an ancient sorceress he read of in a book years ago while sojourning in Arethousa: Li'at'dano, the centaur shaman, mentioned in the old chronicles many times over many generations. Some called her undying. All called her powerful beyond human ken. In the western tongue the consonants soften to make the baby Liathano.

He calls her Liath.

He stays with the Seven Sleepers, toiling under Anne's unwavering and unforgiving gaze, caring for his beloved child, until the day *eight years later when the fire daimones come looking for their missing sister. Time passes differently in the upper spheres; an eyeblink may encompass months and the unfurling of a wing years.*

That is when he flees with his daughter. That is when he expends the untapped potential of his own magical powers to lock away her soul and her power, which shine like a beacon, so that no one can follow them. Especially not Anne. Especially not the fire daimones, kin to the woman-creature he loved and murdered.

Did he run to save himself? To save Liath? Or to save the only thing he has left of the woman-creature he loved? Did he lock away Liath's true self to hide her from Anne's machinations, or to conceal her from her mother's kin, so that they could never find her and take her away from him?

Anger was a river of fire, molten and destructive but also cleansing and powerful. She never understood until now how much she despised Da for being weak. At moments she even hated him because she loved him, because she wanted him to be strong when maybe he never could be, because maybe all along without knowing it consciously she guessed that he loved someone else more than he loved her. Because she hated herself for being weak, hated that part of herself, broken and crippled, that had chained her for so long.

The river of the past, that which binds us because it has already woven its chains around us, flowed easily and without any obvious transition into the future, the unreachable destination where we are blinded by possibility, by hope, by unexamined anger, and by fear.

She walked into the future with the river of fire streaming around her and she saw

King Henry strangled by a daimone as a pretty child resembling Queen Adelheid mounts the imperial throne, her mother standing protectively beside her.

Sister Rosvita, aged and leprous, lies dying in a dungeon. A discarded shoe, its leather eaten away by rats or maybe by her, rests just beyond her outstretched hand.

The Lion, Thiadbold, who more than once showed her kindness, drinks himself into a stupor in a filthy tavern by sipping ale out of a bowl. He has lost both his hands but somehow survived. Isn't it a worse fate to live as a cripple, helpless except for what leavings others throw to you as to the dogs?

Ivar on trial for heresy before the skopos. The Holy Mother Anne condemns him and his companions to death, but he smiles, wearily, as if death is the outcome he has been seeking all along.

Hanna dead, by her own hand. The wounds that killed her cannot be seen on her skin.

Sanglant, still fighting and always fighting because he will never give up until his last breath, as the she-griffin strikes for his exposed chest.

Blessing stands by a window. Liath scarcely recognizes this magnificent creature, newly come to womanhood, tall like her father and with a creamy brown complexion, eyes green, or blue, depending on how the light strikes them or on the color of gown she is wearing. She is as beautiful as all the promises ever made to a beloved child. Then the door opens, and the girl turns. She shrinks back. Pride and youthful confidence turn to terror as the man who has come to claim her for his bride steps through the door.

"Hugh!"

Liath screamed her outrage as anger bloomed into wings at her back. Her kinsfolk, wings hissing in the aether and voices booming and muttering like thunder, stepped back to give her room as she leaped up and out of the river of fire.

Despite everything, Da had not abandoned her. Nor would she abandon her own child. Never would she abandon her own child.

Yet was it already too late?

Because Da did nothing but run the last years of his life, he had taught Liath to run, to turn away, to hide herself. She couldn't even truly love the ones she wanted to love, because she could not reach out to them, not with her heart entire. She had taken the key and thrown it away long ago, escaping from Hugh, but she hadn't understood then that she had also walled herself away, that the city of memory Da had taught her to build in her mind's eye was another barrier against those who sought to embrace her with friendship and love.

Ivar had never threatened her. But she had seen his infatuation as a threat. She had disdained him because she did not know how to be his friend.

Hanna had given her friendship without asking anything in return, but Liath had walked away from her to go with Sanglant.

Yet she had not even been able to love Sanglant with a whole heart. She had loved him for his body and his charisma but she had never truly known *him*. He remained a mystery; despite his protestation that he was no onion with layers of complexity and meaning to be uncovered, he was not as simple as all that. No one ever is. She had never looked to see what lay beneath the surface, because the surface was easy enough to polish and keep bright.

Ai, God, even Blessing. She had watched Sanglant love the baby unreservedly. But she had always held a part of herself back, the crippled part, the part that had never learned to trust.

The part that was afraid of being vulnerable, killed by love, and by hope, and by trust again, and again. And again.

"No," she said, from this height looking down over the glorious palaces and the river of fire, looking down at her kinsfolk gathered in a flock beneath, hovering halfway between the heavy silver sheet of the sky and the river's flashing, molten surface. "I'm not ready to leave them behind because I don't even know them yet."

She opened herself to the measure of their wings and let them see into her heart, into the burning bright soul that was the gift her mother had given her. "Maybe this will be my home one day," she added, "but it can't be now."

"Child," they said, in love and as a farewell.

What need had they to mourn her leaving? The span of one mortal's years on Earth might pass in the same span it took to cross one of those shimmering bridges that linked the golden palaces: a thousand steps, or a song. Her soul was immortal, after all, and half her substance was fire.

She could return.

"So be it," she said. Eldest Uncle had taught her that in the secret heart of the universe the elements can be illuminated, touched, and molded. She reached, found fire, and drew out of the invisible architecture of the aether the burning stone that marks the crossroads between the worlds.

Blue fire flared all along its length. She stepped through to find herself landing with a surprisingly hard thump in the midst of flowers, heavenly blues, blood-soaked reds, and so many strong golds and piercing whites that her eyes hurt. Her buttocks and hips ached from the impact, and even her shoulders were jarred. She was stark naked, hair falling loose past her breasts and down her back. In a heap beside her lay her cloak and boots, her clothes, her sword, belt, and knife, and her quiver, although it was empty. All her arrows were missing. Her bow and Sanglant's gold torque lay tumbled on top, as though all this had fallen here in company with her descent.

She was back in the meadow of flowers, in Aoi country.

Still shaking, she reached out to touch the cold, braided surface of the gold torque, frowning as she picked it up, no longer hers to claim. No longer hers to fear and retreat from.

Anne is not my mother.

She laughed out loud, awash in an exhilarating sense of freedom.

"So," said a man's harsh voice not ten paces away, "more than one day and one night have passed, Bright One. Feather Cloak's protection no longer shields you. Now I will have your blood to make my people strong."

Startled, she looked up to see fully fifty Ashioi surrounding her, fearsome animal masks pulled down to conceal their faces. Every one held a weapon, and the one in front had lowered his spear to point at her heart.

Cat Mask and his warriors had come to kill her.

3

HOME.

He had come home, and Adica was here, whole and alive, waiting for him, just as he had hoped and prayed and dreamed. For the longest time he simply held on to her, wanting never to let her go, breathing in the lavender scent of her hair, but at last he became aware of the hounds butting into them and the villagers, around them, waiting to greet him.

That, too, took a while. Even Beor laughed to see him, and he was surprised how happy he was himself to see all these familiar, cheerful faces. His people, now. His home.

He had to make Sos'ka and her comrades known to Adica and Mother Weiwara. In fact, he had to interpret for them all since the Horse people did not speak a tongue known to the tribes of the White Deer folk. The centaurs made a pretty obeisance to Adica, honoring her as a Hallowed One, and it was agreed that they would stay until after the dark of the sun to help protect her and only then return to their own tribe. All the children wanted a ride, and the haughty centaurs relented enough to let the youngsters be helped up onto their backs. Meanwhile, Urtan, Beor, and the other men insisted on showing Alain the hard work the villagers and other work parties had done over the spring, summer, and early autumn.

"See what a fine palisade we've built!" boasted Beor, as though he had achieved a personal victory against the Cursed Ones by hoisting logs into place. "Although I notice that you came back only after all the hard work was done."

"Queens' Grave is ringed by a wall!" exclaimed Alain, amazed by how the wood posts changed the aspect of the great tumulus, making it look rather like a slumbering porcupine. "How could you have done that in only two seasons?"

"We had work parties from all the other villages, Two Streams, Pine Top, Muddy Walk, Old Fort, Four Houses. Even

Spring Water. It took us all summer to build it, and I think we must have felled the forest all the way from here to Four Houses!" All the men laughed, but no one disagreed.

"Who cares about the work we did?" cried Kel. "You must tell us all the things you saw!"

"I hope you will," agreed Urtan, chuckling, "if only to keep this fly from buzzing all day. We haven't had a moment's peace from him since you left."

"You should have taken me with you!" protested Kel when all the men laughed. "I wouldn't have faltered! When will you tell us the tale of your journey?"

"Patience," replied Alain, laughing with the others, although in truth he was looking around to see where Adica had gone. She had retreated from the village quietly, with all the attention shifting to the centaurs and to him, and he finally spotted her in the distance by the birthing house, finishing some hallowing task.

Urtan chased the other men away, even Kel. "Go on," he said.

Alain hurried along the river to the birthing house, the hounds loping alongside, but he was careful not to cross the fence onto ground where only women were granted leave to walk. On the other side, Adica picked flower petals off the ground, expression pensive as she searched among the low grass for each precious one, those that hadn't blown away. Had she changed so much since the first time he had seen her, or had he?

She had certainly seemed attractive, that day almost a year ago, especially wearing that provocative corded skirt whose every shift along her thighs revealed skin and glimpses of greater mysteries, but he would not have called her pretty, not with a slightly crooked nose, the livid burn scar on her cheek, an overly-generous mouth, and a narrow chin.

Now he knew that she was beautiful.

"Adica."

She looked up. Her smile made her beautiful, the light in

her face, the ragged lilt of her voice, the graceful confidence of her movements as she came to embrace him by the fence, the shadow of sadness in her expression that he struggled every moment to wipe away, so that she would know nothing but joy.

"What's this?" asked Alain when he could finally bear to let go of her. He lifted her right hand and studied the lapis lazuli ring adorning her middle finger. "This looks very like a ring I once gave to a woman who needed my help."

"So you did. I met her in a vision trance, and she gave it to me. She thought you needed it."

He shuddered, but maybe that was only the cold breeze on his neck. "What magic can make a ring travel through visions? Where did you see her? You were in a trance when I saw you last. Ai, God, I have so many questions. I know now you came safely to Queen Shuashaana's palace, and that she returned you here. Did Laoina return to her tribe? I feared I had lost you, beloved."

"Nay," she said, almost in tears as she buried her face against his chest and just held him. Sorrow and Rage settled down nearby, willing to wait her out. After a while, she was able to go on: she had woken out of her vision trance in the care of Shu-Sha and, after a few days waiting for Alain and recovering, Shu-Sha had sent her home alone through the stone looms. "I only got back yesterday. I thought I'd lost you."

"But you did not. I told you I would never leave you. How many times do I have to tell you?" He smiled and kissed her. "Tell me about the ring."

She described the trance, but her words did not really make sense to him. Was it truly Liath she had seen? Was Liath dead? Or was Adica simply unable to describe the place he had once known, the halls where nobles walked and feasted and where the church reigned in splendor? Had Adica's vision shown her the future, or the past?

"I thought I heard the prince speak of Liathano," he said, remembering his conversation with the two brothers, "but he was talking of the Holy One, who is called in her own tongue Li'at'dano."

Adica clapped hands over her ears. "I must not hear the holy name, lest it burn me!"

"Nay, beloved, do not be frightened. It was given to me freely. Why can't I share it with you?" He sighed, shaking his head. "Maybe I am afraid to say it myself. She told me there was one who would be given her name in the time yet to come. But if that's so——" He shook his head. The only explanation that occurred to him seemed so outrageous, so disorienting, so *impossible*, that he fled to the refuge of the answer the centaur shaman had given him in the end. "I am alive *now*. Nothing else matters. I will not question the good fortune that brought me to your side, Adica."

She tugged on the ring, to pull it off.

"Nay, you must wear it. The stone will protect you from evil."

"Alain," she began, hesitant, almost choked, "there's something I must tell you." She stopped, looking past him with a sudden expression of relief. "Mother Weiwara!"

"I thought you might like help, Hallowed One. I can gather up the herbs and petals you spilled. I know you would like to finish the purification, so you can be alone with your husband sooner." With a smile for Alain, Weiwara crossed the fence and the two women walked away, Adica leaning toward her friend, whispering urgently.

Surely it was not his fault that the wind lifted their murmuring voices and brought them to his ears.

"What must I do? He doesn't know."

"Haven't you told him?"

"I can't bear to. What if it frightens him away from me?"

"Nay, Hallowed One, do not say so. You know that isn't true. The Holy One sent him. He won't desert you."

Adica's answer was lost as the two women ducked inside the birthing house. A moment later Weiwara emerged and, with a dismissive wave at Alain, started picking up the pouches and petals scattered on the ground.

Alain knew a command when he saw one. He retreated to the less complicated companionship of the men, who were engaged at this time of year in various projects preparing the village for winter. Urtan set him to work with Kel and Tosti binding thatch for the roof of the men's house, which had developed several leaks during the heavy spring rains. From the roof he could look out over the village and up to the tumulus. Most of the older children had been set to making torches, stuffing and binding wood chips with tow flax or hemp and soaking these flambeaux in beeswax or resin. Women sat in the doors of their houses, weaving baskets. Crab apples had been piled up in heaps to sweat. Now and again he saw men walking along the embankment or hauling water or firewood up through the cleft where two ramparts met and overlapped.

But the best part of being up on the roof, besides listening to his companions as they discussed the girls they wanted to marry or just to kiss, was that he could keep an eye on the distant birthing house and then, later, on Adica as her tasks took her around the village. Everyone could tell his mind wasn't on his work. His friends had a good time joking with Alain about just what exactly it was he might do in the evening: guard duty in the tower, wash the geese, scrape skins, sleep.

Their good-natured conversation and cheerful company made the time pass swiftly, because in truth he was waiting for the afternoon's feast. Because in truth, even the feast, feting the centaurs, welcoming him and Adica home, passed with agonizing slowness. Night came quickly at this time of year, and Mother Weiwara made sure to chase them off to bed at dusk even if she could not restrain his friends from singing lewd songs as he tried to slip away, leading Adica by the hand.

Laughing, they ran through the dark village to their house. They needed no lamp to light their way. They needed nothing more than each other as they fumbled with clothing and fell backward onto the bed, the feather mattress giving way beneath them as they pressed together under furs.

What things he said then to her he could not remember nor was even really aware of. Just to touch her was like a delirium, a drowning. Maybe they had drowned twice or even three times before they exhausted themselves enough simply to lie side by side in the darkness, her shoulder fitted under the curve of his arm and her head resting on his shoulder. She had thrown a leg over his hips, and they rested this way for a time as she nuzzled his neck, planting butterfly kisses along his throat and occasionally on his lips. Outside, he heard one of the dogs get up and pad restlessly all the way around the house before settling back in at the threshold. He found the ring on her finger and twisted it around, teasing it off over her knuckle and sliding it back on.

"What didn't you tell me?" he asked. "There's something you're keeping from me."

Her kisses ceased, and she sucked in a breath as if she had been slugged in the gut.

"I overheard you and Weiwara speaking today. I know other people have said. . . . things. Whispers. Comments. What is it that you fear to tell me?" His voice cracked a little. Now that he had found a home, he hoped for all those things any person wishes for: a mate, shelter and food, a community to live in, and children to follow after him. But perhaps it wasn't to be. "I know maybe you tried to tell me before, but I didn't want to hear it. If it's about a child, Adica. You know that no matter what, I will never leave you."

She let all her breath out in a rush. "It's true," she said in a low voice, face pressed against his hair as he shifted to try to hear her. "I'll never have a child. It's—it's part of the fate laid on me as Hallowed One."

No need to pretend it didn't hurt to have it spoken plainly. He had begged God to soften Tallia's heart so that they might make a child together. He had prayed for hours, hoping against hope to give Lavastine the grandchild the dying count longed for. But in the end, God were wiser than the human heart.

He knew now that Adica's soul was as bright as treasure, and that he'd been deceived in Tallia all along, small and crabbed as her soul had been, frightened and selfish and hollow. He pitied Tallia now, seeing how trapped she had become in her own lies. Yet it seemed cruel for God to deny Adica what she deserved.

He could not argue with fate. Nor would he deepen Adica's sorrow by trying to protest what he had no control over.

"It's true we'll be sad that we can't make a child between us. But surely, beloved, we need not turn away from raising children. God know that there are orphans enough needing shelter. Wasn't I one of them? Didn't a kind man take me in?"

He wept then, a little. It had been so long since he had thought of Aunt Bel and his foster father, Henri. Had they ever shown him anything but the same kindness they'd given to their own kin? Whatever the truth of his birth, they had raised him with their own. They had opened their hearts. Maybe it was up to him to do the same for another child, now that he had found his true home.

"Did he?" She held him as if she meant to crush his ribs. She was so tense. "Did kind folk take you in?"

"So they did. I told you the story. We'll find a child, Adica. Or two children. Or five. Whatever you want. That's how we can serve God, by giving a home to a child who needs one. That's good enough. But just in case—"

"Just in case?"

He rolled over on top of her, pinning her beneath him. "God help those who help themselves. Urtan says something like, but I can't recall how he says it."

"'Prayers can't make a field grow unless seeds are thrown in with them.' *Oof!* You're crushing me. What does that have to do with—" She gasped as his fingers tweaked a nipple.

"Just so," he agreed. "Maybe a child won't come from your womb, but there's a certain ritual a man and woman must go through to get a child for themselves, and I don't think we ought to neglect it."

"Again?" She laughed.

Again.

Morning came. The day passed uneventfully. Adica had so many duties that she barely got to see her. At dawn she rose to welcome the sun; after this she meditated up at the stone loom, in practice for the great weaving that she and the other Hallowed Ones would weave in only seventeen days. At midday they ate, and all afternoon she tended to the villagers or to the visiting warriors camped up on the hill, ministering to the sick, chasing away the evil spirits that thronged around the village, checking the newly slaughtered swine for disease, reading entrails for signs of good and bad fortune, watching the flights of birds for clues about the course and severity of the upcoming winter.

So the next day passed as well, and the one after. There were acorns to be gathered, swine and geese to be fattened up before the winter slaughter forced them to choose which would be killed and which kept through the cold season. More adults, mostly young men, walked in to Queens' Grave every day from the other villages, sent to guard the Hallowed One. Alain helped build shelters for them behind the safety of the embankments. He took his turn at watch, and in the afternoons tried with Urtan's and Agda's help to build a catapult while nearby Beor trained his growing war band how to fight with staves, halberds, and clubs. Bark or skins sewn together over a lattice of tightly interwoven sticks made crude shields.

The trickle became a flood as more warriors and, increasingly, whole families with their flocks walked from the nearby villages to crowd in to Queens' Grave, setting up an entire village of crude shelters within the safety of the ramparts. Everyone expected the Cursed Ones to attack as the days grew shorter and the nights colder. Alain discussed with Sos'ka and her companions the various ways the Cursed Ones often attacked: at dawn, on the wings of fog, just before sunset, now and again at night. Beor and the other respected war leaders listened, interjecting comments occasionally that Alain translated. The big man's hands were always busy, binding spear points to hafts, fletching arrows, grinding the tips of antlers into sharp points. Pur the stone knapper now had two other stone knappers working with him as well as five apprentices. The first catapult had a hitch in it, so they started building a second. Torches burned all night along the palisade wall and up on the ramparts, and they had to make numerous expeditions into the forest to haul in cartloads of wood or armfuls of cow parsley and hemlock whose hollow stems, stuffed with fuel, made efficient little torches easy to hold in a hand. They hauled and stored so much water that he thought they might drain the river dry.

On the eighth day after he had returned, the centaurs proved their worth as sentries by driving off a small party of Cursed Ones who had come to lurk at the edge of the woods. After that, the entire community stayed on alert. Folk rarely left the safety of the palisade and then only in groups of ten or more, even if they only walked the short path leading from the village gates to the outer ring of ramparts.

"We'd better rebuild your old shelter up by the loom," he told Adica that night, when they were in bed. She listened silently. She seemed so intent these past days, like an arrow already in flight.

"I didn't like it up there," she said at last. "I was in exile, a stranger to my own people."

"But now I'm with you. You'll be safer there. We'll ask the centaurs to bed down up on the ramparts as well, since their hearing is so keen. The old shelter is still there, most of it. It hasn't fallen in so badly that I can't fix it. We'll bring our furs. Maybe the ground will seem a little hard at first—"

"Hush." She sighed sharply, then kissed him until he had no choice but to be silent as she worked on him the magic he most desired.

But she made no objection when he took Kel and Tosti up to rebuild her shelter. She even let him carry her holy regalia and her chest of belongings there, together with the furs and bedding, although he left her herbs and various small magical items in her house so she could fetch them during the day as she went about her duties.

She seemed to care little where she slept, as long as he lay beside her. Yet only at night did her warmth get turned on him like fire. In the day, even sometimes at night when they lay together, she grew more distracted, more distant, with each passing day, as though the arrow receded farther and farther away, leaving him and all of them behind.

The moon waned. Frost laid a coat of ice on the ground. The stars pulsed in the clear sky. For days there had been no clouds at all, although occasionally he heard thunder rumbling in the distance. At the new moon Adica woke before dawn and with only the adult women made the ceremony for the new month, hidden to men's eyes. Anxiety gnawed at Alain. Envy ate at him. He hated every moment she spent away from him, although he could not have said why. Had happiness made him jealous? Yet what had he to be jealous of, who had her all to himself in the nighttime? Urtan had released him from the duty of nighttime watch, and not one adult sent up to do extra duty in Alain's place complained. Strange, too, how after so many months of easiness, all the villagers and especially their White Deer cousins had stopped looking at Adica. He recalled now how nervous they had seemed around her when he'd first come to Queens' Grave, but their uneasiness had waned and he'd forgotten about it as the months had passed and they'd made a place for themselves in the village. Now they feared her again, unspoken, apologetic as they talked to her less and ignored her more but continued to ask for her help when a fungus got into their stores of emmer or a sore afflicted their baby. Even Weiwara turned her children's faces away when Adica walked by.

"She's gathering power for the great working," she said, looking shamefaced, when Alain confronted her one day. "It's dangerous for any of us to look upon a Hallowed One in the fullness of her power."

"What about me? I don't fear her. I've taken no ill effects."

"Oh." Her smile was taut, not really a smile. "You're her mate. You're different, Alain. You have the spirit guides to guard you against evil."

"It's true that the Hallowed One's power can bring evil spirits into the village," Urtan said, when Alain asked him. But he fidgeted, clearly uncomfortable. "She doesn't mean to. She'd do nothing to harm us. Not she, who is giving everything—but that's her duty, isn't it?"

"I can't talk about it," said Kel, flushing bright red. "I'm not married yet. I have to go help my uncle split logs."

Alain went to Beor finally, hoping the man who had once been his enemy might prove more frank. But Beor only said, "She's a brave woman," and would not meet his gaze.

So it went, until the day came that she walked to each house in the village and made a complicated blessing over it, to insure good health and fortune over the coming winter. As if she wouldn't be there to watch over them. He followed along with her with Rage and Sorrow at his side, staying out of her way. It took half the day, but he finally understood the depth of her fears. He understood the solemn feast laid out that night: haunches of pork basted in fat and served with a sauce of cream and crushed juniper berries, roast goose garnished with watercress, fish soup, hazelnut porridge, a stew of morels, and mead flavored with cranberries and bog myrtle.

He was woozy with mead by the time they walked the path up into the ramparts and ducked into their shelter. The cold night air stung. They snuggled into their furs, kissing and cuddling. Adica was silent and even more than usually passionate.

"Is the great weaving tomorrow evening?" he asked softly.

"Yes." Even holding her so close, he could barely hear her whisper.

"You'll be free after the weaving? No more demands made on you, beloved? You'll be free to live your life in the village?" He heard his own voice rise, insistent, angry at the way

Shu-Sha and the others had used her. She was so young, younger even than he was, and he thought by now he'd probably passed his twentieth year. It wasn't right the other Hallowed Ones had made her duty such a burden.

A few tears trickled from her eyes to wet his cheeks. "Yes, beloved. Then I will be free." She drew in a shuddering breath, traced the line of his beard, touched the hollow of his throat, drew a line with her finger down to his navel and across the taut muscles of his belly. "I don't regret the price I must pay, I only regret leaving you. I've been so happy. So happy." She kissed him, hard, and rolled on top of him. She was as sweet as the meadow flowers and twice as beautiful.

"I don't want to sleep," she whispered afterward. "I don't want ever to leave you."

The notion dawned hazily in his mead-fuddled mind. "You're afraid of the weaving."

"Yes." She broke off, then continued haltingly. "I fear it."

"You're afraid you're going to die. I don't like the sound of that."

"Every person fears death. You're the only one I know who isn't afraid of dying."

"I'll come with you tomorrow." Obviously he should have thought of this before. The Cursed Ones might still attack. She and the other Hallowed Ones had to thread a weaving through the stones, a great working of magic. That much everyone knew, but the workings of sorcerers of course remained hidden from all but the Hallowed Ones themselves, just as only clerics could read the secret names of God. Knowledge was dangerous, and magic more dangerous still. But he would risk anything for her. "I'll stand beside you at the working. You know I'll never let any harm come to you. I swore it. I swear it."

"As long as we both live, I know you will never let any harm come to me."

"I'll never let you leave me." After a long while, after he made plain to her the depth of his feeling, she slept.

But he could not sleep. He dared not move for fear of waking her, who was so tired. He dared not move, but as he lay there his heart traveled to troubled lands. He kept seeing over and over again the dying child held in the arms of its starving mother, to whom he'd given his cloak that day he'd ridden out hunting with Lavastine. He kept seeing the coarse old whore who had taken in Hathumod on the march east, to whom he'd given a kind word. He kept seeing the hungry and the miserable, the ones crippled by disease and the ones crippled by anger or despair. He kept seeing Lackling, the way he threw back his crooked head and honked out a laugh. He kept seeing the guivre, maggots crawling out of its ruined eye.

So much suffering.

Why did God let the Enemy sow affliction and grief throughout the world? Ai, God, didn't the natural world bring trouble enough in its wake, floods and droughts, windstorms and lightning? Why must humankind stir the pot to roil the waters further?

Could magic ease war and bring peace? He had to hope so. He had to believe that Adica and the other Hallowed Ones knew a way to coax peace out of conflict and hostility. That was the purpose of the great weaving, wasn't it? To end the war between the Cursed Ones and humankind?

In the morning, Adica carried her cedar chest out of the shelter, threw Alain's few belongings out over the threshold and, before he realized what she was about, set the shelter on fire.

"Adica!" He grabbed her, pulling her back as flames leaped to catch in the crude thatched roof

She was shaking, but her voice was steady, almost flat. "It must be cleansed."

Sorrow and Rage whined, keeping their distance from the blaze. Up here on the highest point of the hill, with the stone circle a spear's throw away, they stood alone as the flames licked up to catch in bundled reeds. The refugees from the other villages had built their shelters down among the ramparts, well away from the tumulus' height and the power of the stones. A few children scouted out the billow of rising smoke, but older children snatched them away and vanished down the slope of the hill. No one disturbed them. The shelter burned fiercely. A huge owl glided through the smoke, but when he blinked, it vanished.

Rage raised her head and loped away toward the lower ramparts. Many folk were climbing onto the walkway set inside the palisade, squinting toward the village below, pointing and murmuring.

Smoke rose from the village like an echo of the smoke beside them. It took him a moment to identify the house in the village that had caught on fire.

"That's our house!" He tugged her forward to see.

She said nothing. She did not seem surprised.

"The only time people burn houses is when—" The knowledge caught as tinder did, burning as hot as the fire. "You *do* think you're going to die!"

"Nay, I don't think it, love. I know it." She didn't weep as she held his hands. She had gone long beyond weeping. She held his gaze, willing him not to speak. "I could not bear to tell you before, my love. That I have been happy is only because of you. Everything that is good you've brought to me. I would never have it otherwise. But my duty was laid out long before. I will not survive the great weaving."

Panic and disbelief flooded him. Heat from the flames beat his face. It could not be true. He would not let it be true.

"I'll never leave you, beloved." His voice broke over the familiar words, spoken so often. Had they been meaningless all along? He hated the fixed, almost remote expression that now molded her features into the mask of a queen far removed from her subjects. "I'll walk with you into death if I have to. I won't let it happen. I won't. I won't lose you!"

"Hush," she said, comforting him, embracing him. "No need to talk about what is already ordained."

But he would not give it up. He had stood by while Lavastine had died. He hated the grip of helplessness, a claw digging ever deeper into his throat. "No," he said. "No." But he remembered the words of Li'at'dano, that dawn when he had fallen, bloody, dying, and lost, at the foot of the cauldron. That morning when the shaman had healed his injuries and given him a new life in a place he did not know. He remembered what Adica had said, the first words he ever heard her speak.

"Will he stay with me until my death, Holy One?"

Li'at'dano had answered: *"Yes, Adica, he will stay with you until your death."*

"Hush," she whispered. "I love you, Alain. How could I wish for anything more than the time we were given together?"

"I won't let it happen!" he cried, anger bursting like a storm.

Was that thunder in the distance, rolling and booming? There wasn't a cloud in the sky. The shelter roared as flames ate it away. Smoke from the village, from their house, billowed up into the clear sky. The shrill cry of a horn cut the phantom calm lying over the scene. The adults stationed up on the palisade walkway, along the rampart, all began crying out, pointing and hollering. Rage, down at the cleft, began barking, and first Sorrow and then all the other dogs joined in until cacophony reigned.

"The Cursed Ones!" cried the people, clamoring and frightened. "They have come to kill our Hallowed One!"

Alain ran down through the upper ramparts and clambered up onto the walkway to see for himself. The Cursed Ones had come on horseback, more than he could count. He recognized their feather headdresses, short cloaks, and beaded arm and shinguards flashing where the sun's rays glinted off them. Many wore hammered bronze breastplates. Each warrior wore a war mask, so that animal faces hid their true features. He saw only lizards and guivres, snarling panthers and proud hawks.

With shouts and signals, they spread out to make a loose ring first around the village and also around the tumulus; he quickly lost sight of two dozen outriders who swung around to the east. The largest group, perhaps ten score, formed up on the stretch of land lying between the village and the hill. The sun's light crept down the western slope of the tumulus as the sun rose over the stones.

Adica, puffing slightly, clambered up beside him. Her expression had altered completely from only a few moments before. She no longer had any comfort left to give him. She no longer had any thought except for the task she had to complete when evening came. "They'll have to attack. Their only hope is to stop me from weaving my part of the working. They'll be trying to strike at all seven of us, each in our own place." She glanced up at the sky. "With the gods' blessing you and the others released the Holy One from the Cursed Ones' bondage so she could work her weather magic. The skies are clear. We have only to survive the day, and then we will be free of their curse forever."

He stared, trying to measure the force gathering in the village, where Beor, Urtan, Kel, and the others sheltered. Here, along the ramparts, even children armed themselves with clubs and staves. Hooves sounded below him as Sos'ka and her companions came up underneath the walkway. They had no way to get up the ladder to see over the palisade.

"What is the Hallowed One's wish?" Sos'ka cried. "We are here to protect her."

They had prepared for many things but not for an army of hundreds. He faltered. How easy it was to be reckless with other people's lives! But centaurs and human fighters watched him intently. They would not falter, no matter the cost. They had walked a harder road than he had, and for many more years. Determination would carry them forward.

Yet he had seen the Cursed Ones close up as well, and surely the Cursed Ones held determination close to their hearts, too.

No wonder war was a curse.

One of the Cursed Ones rode within a bow's shot of the village and loosed a burning arrow. It sailed over the palisade to land, sputtering, in the dirt. Another arrow flew, and a third and a fourth, then a shower. Children ran toward the safety of the houses, only to be driven back when the thatched roof of the men's house caught and began to burn, twin to the fire that consumed Adica's house, another funeral pyre.

Sorrow and Rage panted below, gazing loyally up at him. It was easy to think now that his heart had died of sorrow yet again. It was easy to act because he knew he, too, would die. It was simply not possible to go on living without her.

"Adica, you must go up to the stone loom. Their arrows can't reach you there. I want ten adults to attend her. Make sure she's covered and safe. You'll have to lie low all day, beloved. Can you do that?"

She nodded.

"What shall we do?" asked the woman called Ulfrega, war leader of the Four Houses warriors.

"We'll need fighters all along the palisade. That's our weakness."

"Not the cleft and the ditch?"

"The planks are pulled back, so the Cursed Ones can't charge through. Set a force with spears there, behind shields, and the best archers up along the palisade. That's the first place they'll try to break through. If somehow riders break through, you must brace the hafts of your spears in the dirt and hold them steady. Then they'll drive their horses into the points."

She nodded. An arrow sailed lazily overhead and skittered along the opposite embankment, rolling downslope to end up at one of the centaur's hooves. "What of the villagers?" she asked.

"Beor can lead them well enough. He'll let their archers use up their arrows as long as he can. It will help us that the Cursed Ones are caught between two pincers. They have to protect themselves from both sides. And we have a few tricks planned, things they can't expect. Just pass the word along the palisade that none of you are to shoot arrows unless you come under direct attack. Have children pick up any arrow that falls in to us. We can shoot it back at them."

In the village, a third house had caught on fire.

"Sos'ka, you and your comrades must keep a perimeter watch all around the hill. If any place on the embankment is weakened, send one to alert me, and we'll send reinforcements. If they break in behind us, we are lost. Ulfrega, you must remain here to command if I'm called away. Adica!"

She still watched the movements of the Cursed Ones and, farther, the smoke pouring up from the burning houses. A fourth house in the village caught fire, but people hurried to soak the thatch of the adjoining council house roof with water.

A line of Cursed Ones rode closer to examine the tumulus. One rash soldier with a fox mask rode in and, whooping, twirled a sling around his head. Stones peppered the palisade. A dozen archers rode close enough to shoot.

Alain took hold of her arm roughly and tugged her down, while folk around them gasped to see him handle her so. "You must get back to safety."

"Where will you be?" A single tear snaked down her cheek.

"I will always be with you. I'll follow when I can."

She climbed down the ladder. A dozen adults formed around her and hurried away up through the higher embankments, toward the stone circle.

"Shall we shoot at them?" cried one of the archers near Alain.

"Nay, they're no threat to us yet. Let them waste their arrows."

Beor's archers had begun to return arrow fire, and the archers of the Cursed Ones retreated to their main force, content evidently with the mischief their arrows caused in the village: five houses burned merrily now. Smoke boiled up into the sky, and ash fell everywhere. Yet the Cursed Ones waited as an unseen drum counted the passing with a steady rhythm that seemed to reverberate up from the earth. Leaning against the palisade logs, Alain felt that throbbing rhythm, oddly soothing, drawing his mind away, causing memories to flower as his attention drifted.

Up among the ruins near Lavas Holding, he sees the shadows of what had been, not the shadows of the ruins lying there now. The lantern's pale light and the gleam of stone illuminate the shadows of the buildings as if they stand whole and unfallen. This filigree of arches and columns and proud walls stretching out as impossible shadows along the ground is the shade of the old fort, come alive as memories twist forward. . . .

Liath stands in front of a heap of wood. Everything is damp. Even the air sweats moisture; in a moment it will start to rain. All at once, fire shoots up out of branches, licking and crackling. Falling to one knee, Liath stares at the fire as a gout of flame boils up toward the sky. Are those shadows dancing within the flame? She stares, intent, as distant then as Adica has become now, and draws from her tunic a brilliant gold feather.

Ai, God! He knows that feather, or knew one like it: a phoenix feather like the one he plucked from the cavern floor. In her hands, it glints fire. The veil concealing the shadows in the fire draws aside, burned away by its pure light, and he can see:

An old man, twisting flax into rope against his thigh.

Why does he look so familiar?

Rage barked, startling him. He rubbed his eyes as the folk around him murmured uneasily. Below, grass and stubbled fields bled a gauzy mist into the air. The enemy faded beneath the sun as if they had only been illusion all along, first darkening to shadow and then lost in a shrouding fog that seemed to drift up out of the earth itself. Mist boiled forward over the ground, spreading out in a broad front that would engulf both village and tumulus. Not a single rider could be seen beneath that veil of fog. The Cursed Ones had hidden themselves with magic.

The wind shifted sharply, blowing in from the east, and as it gained strength, the magical shroud shuddered and gave ground, catching out a handful of riders, the vanguard, who scrambled to return to the cover of the fog. A thud rang out from the village.

"The catapult!" cried Alain

A large pot came sailing over the wall and vanished into the mist. Beor had unleashed the first surprise. Shrieks and panicked whinnying floated out of the drowning fog as bees, now free and agitated, took their vengeance upon the Cursed Ones. The mist rolled back to unveil one force advanced almost to the village gate and the other closing in on the tumulus. The enemy soldiers, their magic exposed and disrupted by the bees, fell back to regroup as the White Deer people showered the foremost riders with arrows. A third force of Cursed Ones could be seen circling around toward the east side of the crown.

"Sos'ka!" he called. She had sent eight of her comrades away along the tumulus already. "Follow that group to see where they're going!" She cantered away.

The vanguard nearest him, retreating, reversed itself suddenly and charged for the ramparts. Arrows rained down and, after them, a hail of stones from slings. Children screamed. The man standing next to Alain jerked backward, spun, and fell to hit the ground below with a smack. Blood pooled under his body. The Cursed Ones leaped off their horses and hit the embankment running, scrambling up toward the parapet.

"Don't waste your spears!" Alain cried, but even so some threw away their spears by trying to strike at the enemy below them, in vain.

Yet what point did it serve the Cursed Ones to come up against the palisade, which they could not climb without ladders? The soldiers held their shields high, protecting one among their number, a woman dressed more lightly than the others, as she raced forward to throw herself against the wood. Where she touched the posts, wood flowered to life as fire.

"Water! Water!" The cry came down the line. Buckets of water were handed up to those on the walkway, who spilled them over even as the Cursed Ones continued to shoot arrows at the defenders. The villagers dropped rocks on top of the shields, battering them down, and a ragged cheer rose out of the ranks when the sorcerer was struck directly on the head with a big rock and went tumbling back down the slope.

"They're bringing ladders and planks!" Ulfrega's powerful voice rang out from the cleft, where she had taken charge of the defense. "Spears, stand your ground. Archers, hold until they're closer!"

The sorcerous mist rose as a cloud near the village. A second *thump* sounded; the second pot of bees arched up from the catapult and fell precipitously, but this time the Cursed Ones were ready for them as they charged out of the mist to escape the bees behind them. Fire bloomed in two more of the village houses. Cries and shouting and screams echoed everywhere. Tendrils of smoke obscured the fields. Thunder cracked, and clouds pushed in from the west, ominously dark.

"Alain!"

Sos'ka galloped up, sweat running all along her flanks, her expression grim. "There was another force waiting in ambush apart from the one you saw. They've almost broken through on the eastern slope, by the sacred threshold to the queens' grave. Come quickly!"

He scrambled down the ladder, leaping off the fourth rung to the ground, almost landing on the corpse. He grabbed a pair of girls, not much younger than Adica, who were cowering under the walkway. "You! Go to Ulfrega. Tell her she must hold the entrance now. You! Run up to the Hallowed One. She must find a way to counter their magic, if she can."

He jumped up, got his belly over Sos'ka's flank, and swung a leg over.

"Stay down," said the centaur.

He clutched her mane, head ducked low as she trotted along at a jarring rate, negotiating barrels of water and cider, stores of grain, shelters, and four wounded men who had crawled away from the palisade. At last she broke free of chaos and opened up to a gallop. The sounds of battle roared around them, shouts echoing behind and before. She knew her way well through the maze of the ramparts, blind alleys, and earthen mounds that made up the hill's defenses. Fighters manned the palisade walkway, thrusting with spears or heaving rocks over the side. Now and again they passed a zone of unexpected calm, where nervous guards waited, craning their necks to get a look down the palisade to knots of fighting.

He had heard these sounds before. Memory dizzied him.

The Lions hold the hill as Bayan's army retreats across the river. The first cohort stands the rear guard, and Alain keeps step with his comrades as they retreat up the hill with their fellows. The ramparts lie in a maze around them, ancient embankments curling around the hill's slopes.

He remembered these embankments, but when he had seen them last they had been so old that they had fallen in ruin and were half washed away under the brunt of time and wind and rain. He had fought in this place before. Yet the earthworks around him now were newly raised; any fool could see that.

He had fought here before in the time yet to come. This is where the Lady of Battles had killed him.

The curve of the ramparts brought them into sight of a ferocious fight. Cursed Ones had gotten over the palisade, and now Sos'ka's centaurs and a score of White Deer warriors grappled hand to hand, pounding with clubs, thrusting with knives. A roan centaur parried a spear thrust with her staff, flipped her opponent to the ground, and stove in his head with a well placed kick. Fire licked up the palisade. A shout rose from the enemy, unseen on the other side as they pushed forward.

A woman with her animal mask torn free slid over the posts, dropping to the walkway. She braced herself, met the charge of a man with the cut of her bronze sword, then dropped to one knee as she lifted her other arm high and spun a sling briskly around her head. Let fly.

"Down!" cried Sos'ka.

He ducked. A kiss of air brushed an ear as the stone shot past his hair. The second bounced off his skrolin armband with a *snap*. But the third slammed into his temple without warning.

Pain stabbed through his head as he tumbled off Sos'ka's back. The ground hit harder even than the stone.

"But I swore to serve you," he whispers, astonished, because he really never thought that this of all things would happen to him. He never thought that he would be the one to die on the battlefield.

"So you have served me." The voice of the Lady of Battles, as low and deep as a church bell, rings in his head. "Many serve me by dealing death. The rest serve me by suffering death. This is the heart of war."

"Adica!" He bolted up, struggling to sit, gaze blurring as the sun glared in his face. Familiar hands pressed him back.

"Hush, my love. Lie down." Her tears fell on his face. "I feared for you." She kissed him. For a moment, he saw two of her, his dear Adica sitting next to the Hallowed One in her antlered garb, haughty and aloof as she knelt before him.

Why wasn't the sun rising beyond the stones? He saw it, swollen and hazy, riding low over the indistinct palisade in a blaze of vivid red-gold. Smoke drifted in streamers among the distant trees.

Nauseated, he lay back, and after a moment, beyond the agonized throbbing in his head, he heard the clash of battle. "What happened?"

"You were hit in the head by a stone."

It was a struggle to recall what had happened. "They've broken through on the east slope, by the sacred threshold!" He got up to his feet before she could stop him and staggered, catching himself on one of the hounds before he could fall. It was hard to tell which one; he couldn't quite focus.

"Adica?" He turned, and saw her.

She had bound on her gold antlers and bronze waistband, the regalia of a Holy One, a woman of power. He could still hear the battle, but the sun now set in the west.

"How long?" he demanded hoarsely. Where once had lain the birch shelter where they had slept, and made love, now lay smoldering coals and white ashes lifting on the dusk breeze.

"All day," she said. "We've held them off all day."

At what cost?

He saw, then, that what he had first thought was the setting sun was in truth the village in flames, all of it burning or fallen in. The palisade had been breached in a dozen spots; in some places fire had eaten it away. Bodies filled the ditches, pinned on stakes or simply broken. He could not see what had happened to the villagers, but what remained of the Cursed Ones still fought desperately along the tumulus, trying to break through. Yet as desperately as they fought, the White Deer people fought more desperately still. He caught a glimpse of Sos'ka down by the cleft. Streaked with blood, she vanished in a hail of spears. The other hound ghosted in just as he sagged forward, and he caught himself on that strong shoulder.

"Are they all dead? Did I lie here all day, while they died?"

Behind him, she spoke. "Beor and the other fighters broke out of the village in the afternoon to try to reach this place. When the attack came, Weiwara led the children and old people into the forest. I made a prayer for them. I burned pine leaves, to grant them invisibility. I hope some made it. It will be safer for them there."

"Kel? Tosti? Urtan? Beor?"

"I don't know what became of them." Her tone sounded so distant, too calm, as though Adica had gone and the Hallowed One, a detached, unapproachable woman he didn't really know, had kidnapped her form and now walked the Earth in his beloved Adica's body.

The sun's lower rim touched the horizon.

"Alain." *Her* voice, so sweet to his ears.

He turned. She had come forward. They stood alone on the height, with the stones behind her and the fighting raging all around. Every last soul had gone down to try to stem the Cursed Ones, just for this one final hour. That was all she needed now.

Weeping, he caught her by the arm. "Must you do this, Adica? Ai, God. How can I bear it?"

"Think how many will die if we do not succeed. Think how many have already died, protecting me!" Anger flared at last. "My heart grieves to leave you, Alain. You know how much I do love you. But don't stand in my way. Don't break the love we share by bowing to selfishness. My life does not belong to me but to my people. And it does not belong to you either."

"You lied to me! You knew all along!"

Blinking back tears, she kissed him. "I couldn't bear to see you unhappy."

She kissed him again. Hugged him for a long time, arms wrapped tightly around him. And left him, walking proud and tall, her antlers towering above her as though they would touch the heavens. She walked to the calling ground. She set her feet in that chalk circle, with her head raised proudly as the light waned and twilight crept up the eastern sky, although the last purple-rose of sun's glow lingered in the west. The bowl of night began to fill up with darkness. The last glint of the setting sun caught and tangled in her shining antlers, making her seem no longer human.

She had lied to him all along. But had her lie been any different than the one he had spoken to the dying Lavastine? She had only wanted to spare him pain and fear.

He broke forward to came up behind her. "So be it. Then I'll die with you." Behind him, Sorrow and Rage whined.

Her back stiffened, tensing as she heard his words. She did not answer, but neither did she tell him to leave. The first star winked alive in the dusk sky, brilliant Somorhas setting in the west, almost drowned in the last glimmer of the sun. With a shuddering breath, she raised her mirror to catch its light. Stars bloomed quickly now, as if in haste, and with her staff she wove them, one by one, into the loom. Through the soles of his feet he heard the keening of the ancient queens and the cries of anguish from the battlefield. Threads of starlight caught in the stones and tangled into a complex pattern made strong by the bright light of Mok shining on the cusp between Healer and Penitent.

She had other names for the stars.

"Heed me, that which opens in the east.

Heed me, that which closes in the west."

Did he hear other voices, an echo of her own, singing along the gleaming spell, tangled in the threads of light woven through the stone loom?

"Let the shaman's beacon rise as our weaving rises.

Answer our call, Fat One."

As she wove, she wept. He saw it, then, the cluster of seven stars he knew as the Crown of Stars but which she called the Shaman's Headdress. As it rose in the east, she caught its light in her mirror. That light tangled around him, and he grew so dizzy that he would have fallen over if the hounds had not shouldered under him to hold him up. Above, stars wheeled slowly, ascending out of the east, climbing, climbing, until he realized that the spell had woven around him as well, that they were caught inside it as time passed, as the night wheeled forward from dusk to midnight. The Shaman's Headdress crept up the sky. The battle raged on, torches blazing along the walls, the cries of the wounded muffled by the throbbing ache in his temple where a bruise swelled. A child screamed, sobbing frantically.

"Let what we have woven come loose.

Let each on our place hold the pattern."

She sang their names, her voice unbearably beautiful as it echoed along the glittering threads of the spell. "Spits-last. Falling-down. Adica. Hehoyanah. Brightness-Hears-Me. Two Fingers. Shuashaana!"

It was midnight. The Dragon rose in the east, and in its wings rose Jedu, the Angel of War, near to the pale rose star of the ancient one, the Red Sage, known as Aturna. The Lady of Plenty, brilliant Mok, set in the west as the Penitent laid down his heavy burden, touching the horizon.

The Crown of Stars reached the zenith, high overhead, crowning the heavens. Below the earth, unseen, the sun reached nadir.

"Let the weaving be complete!" she cried, her voice joined to six others, resounding, triumphant.

Light flashed in her antlers and ripped through her like lightning.

"Adica!" he screamed, leaping forward, but the hounds knocked him flat or maybe it was the ground beneath his feet shaking and shuddering that threw him down before he could reach her. Light exploded before his eyes. A howl of fear rose from the throats of the Cursed Ones. Their attack faltered and they broke, running.

But it was too late.

Magic tore the world asunder.

Earthquakes ripple across the land, but what is seen on the surface is nothing compared to the devastation left in their wake underground. Caverns collapse into rubble. Tunnels slam shut like bellows snapped tight. The magnificent cities of the goblinkin, hidden from human sight and therefore unknown and disregarded, vanish in cave-ins so massive that the land above is irrevocably altered. Rivers of molten fire pour in to burn away what survives.

Fire boils up under the sea, washing a wave of destruction over the vast whorled city beneath the waves, home of the merfolk. Where once they danced and sang to rhythms born out of the tides, corpses bob on the swells and sharks feed. Survivors flee in terror, leaving everything behind, until the earth heaves again like a fish thrashing in its death throes. The sea floor rises. Water pours away into cracks riven in the earth, down and down and down, meeting molten fire and spilling steam hissing and spitting into every crevice until the backwash disgorges steam and sizzling water back into the sea.

The caves in which Horn's people have sheltered flood with steaming water. A storm of earth and debris buries Shu-Sha's palace. Massive waves obliterate a string of peaceful villages along the shores of Falling-down's island. Children scream helplessly for their parents as they flail in the surging water.

White fire spears up into the dragons which, launching into the sky in alarm, have barely gotten into the air above the fjall where Spitslast and his kinsfolk stand in the midst of their stone loom, one old wisewoman by each stone and the crippled sorcerer in the middle. Screaming rage and pain, the dragons plunge, but before they can reach the safety of the earth their hearts burst. Blood and viscera rain down on the humans desperately and uselessly taking shelter against the stones. The hail of scalding blood burns flesh into stone, melding them into one being.

A tsunami of sand buries the oasis where the desert people have camped, trees simply flattened under the blast of the wind. The lion women race ahead of the storm wave but, in the end, they, too, are buried beneath a mountain of sand. Gales scatter the tents of the Horse people, winds so strong that what is not flattened outright is flung heavenward and tossed roughly back to earth, so much fragile chaff. All the trees for leagues around Queens' Grave erupt into flame, and White Deer villagers fall, dying, where arrows and war had spared them.

"Adica!" he cried hoarsely, struggling against the jaws of Rage and Sorrow as he fought forward to throw himself down beside her crumpled body.

She was already dead.

White fire exploded from the crest of the hill, slicing open the stone loom, and swallowed him.

4

SHE moved fast, grabbing the haft of Cat Mask's spear below the point. Just as he jerked back, startled, she found the memory of fire within the wood and called flame. With a

shout of pain and surprise, he dropped the spear and jumped
backward as she rose, holding the burning spear in her hand,
thrust out to challenge them. It hissed and sparked, as bright
as though she held lightning.

"I am not your enemy!" The warriors facing her backed
away nervously as the haft of the spear burned into nothing yet
left her skin unscathed. She caught the obsidian spear point as
it fell and pricked her middle finger. Blood welled up.

"Child! Do nothing rash!" Eldest Uncle's shout came from
the pine grove behind her.

She dared not turn to see him, not with fifty armed warriors staring her down. Masks closed their expressions to her;
she saw proud hawks, fierce panthers, snarling bears, and
biting lizards. Cloaks covered their shoulders, and while most
of these short cloaks were woven of linen, a few had the look
of skin, cured and cut. Some of the warriors displayed bare
torsos but most wore short, heavily-quilted tunics marked
by sigils: a feather, a reed, a knife, a skull. All wore tattoos
along their arms or on their chins, ranging from simple lines
to more complicated hatching, diamonds or dots faded to
blue.

Cat Mask drew a flint knife and lunged toward her.

She squeezed her finger and let blood fall.

Where it struck the ground, ten serpents boiled up out of
the earth, hissing and coiling. Cat Mask leaped back. Another
drop of blood spattered, and a third and a fourth. Flowers
swayed alarmingly as serpents slithered through them.
Warriors shouted in fear and backed away. One bright-banded
snake slid right over her foot, and she sprang up in dismay.
Snakes seethed everywhere, coming to life among the flowers.

She unfurled her wings of flame and rose above the meadow,
fire streaming off her.

That was enough for Cat Mask's war band. To a man, they
broke and ran for the river.

She stuck her finger in her mouth and sucked away the
blood as she settled down at the edge of the pine wood,

beside Eldest Uncle and a young-looking woman. The two Ashioi threw up hands to protect their faces from the hot wash of her wings, so she furled them, pulling them down inside, bound tight into her soul where they had, after all, resided all along.

"So," said Eldest Uncle, looking her up and down with a charming grin. He hadn't forgotten the pleasure of admiring a young woman's body. "You walked the spheres. You have found your answers, and your power."

"I have discovered the truth," she admitted, blushing as she remembered modesty. She didn't know where to place her hands. A glance toward the meadow showed the brilliant flowers still dancing drunkenly as the tangle of serpents raised by her blood worked their way outward through the dense growth. All her clothing lay out there, surrounded by snakes.

"So," said the woman standing beside Eldest Uncle as she, too, measured Liath, "I am not surprised at the attraction."

"Who is this?" asked Liath, looking her over, although truly it was difficult to stand confidently when she wasn't wearing a stitch of clothing. The other woman, however, wore only a pale, skin skirt cut off raggedly at knee length. She had a powerful torso, with broad shoulders and full breasts. A double stripe of red paint ran from the back of either hand all the way up her arms to her shoulder, covered in one spot by a garment draped over her left forearm. A green feather stuck jauntily out of the topknot she had made of her hair, a match to her jade-green eyes. Her eyes, the cast of her face, seemed familiar.

"This one is my younger daughter, the child of my old age," said Eldest Uncle with a glint of anger in his expression as he glanced at his companion. He did not seem pleased to introduce her. "The-One-Who-Is-Impatient. Who has caused enough trouble!"

Old angers boiled below the surface as father and daughter looked at each other and, as with one thought, away. The woman shifted, and the folded garment hanging over her arm spilled open.

"That's my tunic," cried Liath, "the one I left in the saddle-bags, on Resuelto. Ai, God! It was you, standing at the river's edge and wearing my tunic, when I first walked the flower trail." She grabbed the cloth, shook it open and, without asking permission, slid into it. Properly clothed, she could speak without embarrassment. "Where did you get it?"

"From my son."

The resemblance, once noted, became obvious.

"Sanglant!" Was that the ground, shaking, or only emotion flooding her? "You're Sanglant's mother! Ai, God." The one who abandoned him when he was only an infant. She could not say those words; to face a woman who had done nothing different than she had herself left her speechless, and confused. She turned to the old sorcerer. "And you are my daughter's great grandfather, then?"

"Ssa!" Eldest Uncle leaped forward and whacked his staff hard against the ground, crushing a serpent's head. Its body writhed, shuddered, and stilled. "I hate those things! Women never think before they take action! Blood! Sex! What do they care about consequences? Their wombs protect them. Their magic gives them power!" With a hiss, he smacked another serpent, hopped to one foot to avoid a third as more churned out of the meadow. "Quick! Climb a tree."

They scrambled up branches, hanging awkwardly as a score of snakes slithered off through the ground litter, vanishing into the pine woods. The old sorcerer's white cloak brushed the ground, but because of his precarious position he dared not pull it up. Each time a snake passed under it the white shell trim clacked softly, and the serpent would hiss and strike at the fluttering cloth before snaking hurriedly on.

Liath finally began to laugh at their ridiculous situation. "Are all the snakes poisonous?"

"Serpents are the creatures of women," the old man muttered, thoroughly cross by now if only because he was hanging by knees and hands from the branches, "so of course they are poisonous, just as women are poisonous to men. That is why women rule."

"That's not so! Both women and men can rule in the lands I grew up in, although it's true that inheritance is more reliable through the mother's line."

"Tss!" He hissed at a slender brown snake passing under his cloak. It reared up, hissing, then sank down and vanished into the undergrowth. "I will not be having this argument with you as well, Bright One. I have been arguing with my daughter for three days. What use for her to risk the dangerous journey to the land below a second time, only to return here to tell me that the men of the human tribes will not listen even to a woman's counsel!"

"You have been to Earth? What of my husband?"

"Sanglant is as stubborn as his father!" The Impatient One swung down from her perch and prodded the ground around her with a stick. Satisfied that the last of the serpents had escaped from the meadow, she relaxed, if in truth a woman of her temperament knew how to relax. "Henri—" She said the name as a Salian would. "—refused to believe my tale, nor would he believe his son. He will walk blindly into the trap laid for him by the human sorcerers." She spat on the ground. "I say, let him and his people suffer at the hands of the wicked ones. You claimed all along that there could be accommodation, my father, and I listened to you and acted to build a bridge—"

"Without anyone's permission! Without thinking it through! Rash actions lead to broken bridges!"

The way her lips tightened, pressed hard together, betrayed her anger, but she went on as though he hadn't spoken. "But now I no longer believe we can make peace if they will not listen in their turn. The old stories are true. Instead of wearing the masks of animals to borrow their power, humankind acts like animals in their hearts."

"Nay! Not that argument again! The gold feather of peace

was given to me by a stranger. He was no animal. I gave it to this one in my turn, because she came to me for aid. Now she has returned, and even you must admit that she has come back to me in peace."

"Perhaps you would rather that *she* be your daughter, than that I am!"

"Silence!" cried Liath. Softly, she added, "I beg your pardon. You are welcome to argue all you like once I am gone, but I ask you to listen while I am still here. I came back, Uncle, only to tell you that I must return to Earth." She turned to regard Sanglant's mother. "I beg you, if you bear any love for your son and your granddaughter, tell me now if there is anything I should know before I walk the crossroads and return to the ones waiting for me. I do not know how long ago you came from there, or how long it has been since I left this place to walk the spheres. I do not know how many months or years have passed on Earth since I left. I do not know how long I have until the Seven Sleepers will bind their power to cast a great working. Nor do I understand how they mean to raise so much power that they can hope to create a spell strong enough to cast an entire land as vast as this one back again into the aether."

Eldest Uncle bowed his head, burdened by memory. "We only suffered. We never fully understood what magic they wove against us."

"I should have listened to Cat Mask," muttered his daughter. "The humans can never be trusted. Maybe he's the one I should be talking to now." She began to walk away but paused to face Liath. "My son is no better than an exile in his own country. He turned his back on his father when Henri would not listen either to him or to me, and walked away to find some means to fight the sorcerers on his own. That is how I left him and the child. You would know better than I if he can succeed."

"You left him to face the Seven Sleepers? Alone? Your own son?"

"You left him," echoed the other woman, "to face your enemies? Alone? With what weapon do you stab me, Sister? Surely only with the one that impales yourself. I almost died giving birth to him. Did he greet me with any warmth when I saved his life and that of his daughter? Nay, he treated me as a stranger, despite our kinship. I will not shed any more blood or tears on that field." Hoisting her staff, she walked haughtily away, heading back through the pine woods toward the old watchtower.

"She has no heart," murmured Eldest Uncle sadly when she had vanished down the trail. "She sacrificed it to the gods long ago when she walked the path of the spheres."

"Did she walk the seven spheres as I did, and return?"

"That she ascended the path cannot be doubted. That she returned alive you see by her presence. What she sacrificed on her journey none know except her. I can only guess." He sighed. "My child, you have changed. What did the fire daimones tell you?"

"I am their child," she said softly, humbled by the knowledge. Had her own mother given less than Sanglant's? She had given her life and her substance to bring a child into the world. She had given her very soul. "I am more, and less, than what I thought I was. But at least I am free of the chains that bound me and the veils that hid the truth. Tell me truly, Uncle. Do your people hate mine? Is there any hope for peace?"

"Mustn't there always be hope for peace? We must believe there is because I know that the other side of peace brings the worst kind of grief. I lost those most dear to me. I am not alone in the tears I have wept many a night remembering those who are gone before their time." He smiled, a wry twist of his mouth. His face was so old, lines and wrinkles everywhere, creases made equally by frowns and by smiles, by laughter and by tears. He extended a hand, hesitated, and touched her gently on the arm. "Hate is a fire fanned easily into a storm that burns everything in its path." Tears welled up in his eyes even as he blinked them away. It was hard to see the resemblance between him and Sanglant except for the color of his skin and the dark splendor of his hair, still glossy and thick despite his great age. "I beg you, my child. Save us. Do not let the descendants of the sorcerers of old destroy us utterly as they attempted to do when I was a youth."

"I will not," she promised him, then she leaned forward and kissed him on the cheek. He flushed mightily, hard to see on that copper complexion but easy to make out by the spark of emotion, the slight narrowing, in his sharp old eyes. "I will see you again, Uncle. Be looking for me."

"Fare you well, Daughter."

The flower meadow waited, silent, barely stirring in the soft breeze. Heat drowned her as she walked forward into sunlight, into the haze of bright color, pale bells of columbine, lush peonies, banks of poppies, and a rich cloud of lavender. She stayed on the path, careful to mark each patch of ground before she set her foot down. The thought of all those serpents made her queasy. She gathered up all her things, dressed properly, and girded on belt, sword, and quiver, pouch, knife, and cloak. The gold torque she stowed in her pouch.

The trail led her through the chestnut woods, and she crossed the river, which ran even more shallow than before. The glade where she had first seen and met the old sorcerer lay empty except for the flat stone on which he often sat to twist flax into rope. A few dried stalks lay scattered on the ground around the rock. A breeze rustled through desiccated leaves. Not even a fly buzzed. Silence drowned her like a heavy veil.

The land was dying. It would die, unless it returned to the place it belonged. Just as she had to return to the place she belonged.

She had a long way to go to get back to them, and a longer path yet to map out once she reached their side. Reaching into the heart of fire, she called the burning stone. It flared up in the center of the clearing, blue fire racing up and down its length. Grasping her bow more tightly, she stepped through into the crossroads between the worlds, where the river of fire ran as aether through the spheres, its many tributaries linking past and future, present and infinity. Through the endless twisting halls she searched for the gateway that would take her back to Earth. Infinite doorways offered glimpses into other worlds, other times, other places, present and past, half seen and swiftly vanished.

A boy sleeps with six companions, their beds made of precious trea-sure, shining baubles and golden armbands, silver vessels and ivory chests, scarlet beads and ropes made of pearls.

A winter storm swirls snow around a monastery where a large encampment of soldiers shelters, some in outbuildings, others in tents. Hanna, in the company of Lions, chops wood. Her face is taut, her body tense, but each time she strikes ax into wood and splits a log she swears, as though she's trying to chop rage and grief out of herself.

A woman clothed in the robes of a nun meets a sandy-haired, slen-der young man at the edge of a birch forest. Waves of wind ripple light through silver leaves. To him she gives the leashes of a half-dozen huge black hounds in exchange for a tiny swaddled figure, an infant girl sleeping softly as she is handed over from one grim-faced guardian to the other.

An army marches in good order through the grassy plains of the eastern frontier. Poplars line the banks of creeks and shallow rivers, giving way to hawthorn and dogwood and at last to the broad expanse of feather grass and knapweed. Spring flowers carpet the open lands with white-and-yellow blooms, as numerous as the stars. Is that Sanglant marching at the head of the army, a glorious red cape streaming back from his shoulders and a gold torque winking at his neck? Is that Blessing, grown impossibly old, looking like a well-grown girl of five or six? At the confluence of two rivers, a king waits to receive the army in peace. His banner flies the double-headed eagle of the Ungrian kingdom. Strange that the first gift Sanglant offers to him, as they meet and clasp hands and give each other the kiss of peace, is a wine barrel.

A woman, aged and arthritic, sits in her tower room, writing laboriously. A map lies open on the table beside her, a crude representation of Salia, held down by stones at each curling corner, but the figures on the wax tablet interest Liath more: a horoscope written for a day yet to come, or a day long past, when cataclysm racked the Earth. The elderly cleric lifts her head to call for an attendant. The woman who comes is the same woman who gave the hounds and took the child, although here she looks much older as she offers her mistress a soothing posset.

"What news, Clothilde?" *asks the first woman in the tone of a noblewoman born to command. Is this Biscop Tallia, Taillefer's favorite child? Her voice is already smoky from the growth in her neck that will kill her.*

"It is done, Your Grace," *says the other woman,* "just as we planned. The girl is pregnant. The child she bears will be related to the emperor through both parents."

Shadows ripped a gap through the image. Other sights shuddered into existence only to be torn away, as though at the heart of the crossroads the very worlds were becoming unstable, echoes of ancient troubles and troubles yet to come.

Hunched and misshapen creatures crawl among tunnels, hauling baskets of ore on their backs. An egg cracks where it is hidden underneath an expanse of silver sand, and a claw pokes through. A lion with the face of a woman and the wings of an eagle paces majestically along the sands; turning, she meets Liath's astonished gaze.

A centaur woman parts the reeds at the shore of a shallow lake. Her coat has the dense shimmer of the night sky, and her black hair falls past her waist. A coarse pale mane, the only contrast to her black coat, runs down her spine; it is braided, like her hair, twined with beads and the bones of mice. "Look!" *she cries.* "See what we wrought!"

She looses an arrow.

The burning course of its flight drove Liath backward through the crossroads of the worlds, far into the past, when the land was riven asunder.

A vast spell has splintered and split the land. Rivers run backward. Coastal towns along the shore of the middle sea are swallowed beneath rising waters, while skin coracles beached on the strands of the northern sea are left high and dry as the sea sucks away to leave long stretches of sea bottom exposed to sunlight and fish drowning in cold air.

Along a spine of hills far to the south, mountains smoke with fire, and liquid red rock slides downslope, burning everything in its path.

In the north, a dragon plunges to earth and in that eyeblink is ossified into a stone ridge.

Liath sees the spell now, seven stone looms woven with light drawn down from the stars. She can barely see the heavens themselves because the light of the spell obscures them, but her sight remains keen: the position of the stars in the sky this night matches the horoscope drawn by Biscop Tallia.

The spell like a coruscating knife cuts a line through the Earth itself. The power of its weaving slices along a chalk path worn into the ground to demarcate the old northern frontier of the land taken generations before by the Ashioi. It cuts right through the middle of a huge city overlooking the sea. It cuts through the waves themselves, like successive bolts of lighting tracing an impossibly vast border around the land where the Ashioi have made their home. The seven sorcerers weaving that spell in each of the seven looms die immediately as the spell's full force rebounds upon them.

The land where Eldest Uncle's people made their home is ripped right up by the roots, like a tree wrenched out of its soil by the hand of a giant, and flung into the sky. All the Ashioi walking beyond the limits of their land are dragged outward in its wake, drowned in its eddy, but they cannot follow it into the aether. They get yanked into the interstices between Earth and the Other Side, caught forever betwixt and between as shades who can neither walk fully on Earth nor yet leave it behind.

But they are not the only ones who suffer.

The cataclysm strikes innocent and guilty alike, old and young, animals and thinking creatures, guivres and mice, human children and masked warriors, Ashioi children and human soldiers armed with weapons crafted of stone. The Earth itself buckles and strains under the potency of the spell. Did the sorcerers themselves understand *what they were doing? Did they know how far the effects of their spell would reach? Did they mean to decimate their people in order to save their people?*

Impossible to know, and she can never ask them: they are long dead, never to be woken.

Blue winked within the lightning radiance of the spell. All at once, she saw Alain on his knees on a low hill, with a hound on either side of him. The hounds tugged desperately at him, trying to drag him back from the edge of a blazing circle of stones. Alain clawed helplessly at the body of the girl who lay crumpled on the ground. Wasn't it the same antlered girl who had met her in the realm of Mok? Who had seen with such keen sight into Liath's own heart before even Liath had been able to fathom those depths? The girl was so unbearably young, younger even than Liath, maybe not more than seventeen, but she was quite dead. In an instant more, when the spell's last storm-surge struck back at the looms in which it had been woven into life, Alain would be dead, too.

Liath unfurled her wings. She reached into the past, caught hold of him and his hounds, and dragged them with her back to the world they had left behind months, or even years, before.

EPILOGUE

THE *queen with the knife-edged smile, called Arrow Bright, is long dead yet strong enough still to see with the heart and eyes of the woman who at dawn leads the remnants of her people through what remains of the forest. They emerge at last from the shelter of charred and blistered trees, most of the children crying, a few horribly silent, and every surviving adult injured in some way. Standing here at the edge of the cultivated fields, they numbly survey the ruin of their village.*

"Come," says the one called Weiwara, leaning on her staff. She has a bright heart, made fierce by anger, by wisdom bought too dearly, and by the twin babies, barely more than one year old, who rest against her body, one slung at her chest and the other against her back, and the three-year-old tottering along gamely at her side. "The Cursed Ones are gone. It is safe now."

They stagger out into an oddly soft morning. Burned houses smolder in the village, although amazingly the council pole thrusts intact out of the collapsed roof of the council house. Mist wreathes the tumbled logs of the palisade. Bodies litter the ground, Cursed Ones who died in the first attacks. She recognizes Beor's form, fallen into the ditch just beyond the gates. He led the charge when they chose at last to break out of the doomed village, and he took the brunt of the Cursed Ones' retaliatory attack. It is due to his courage and boldness that anyone escaped the besieged village at all. The bronze sword he wielded lies half concealed under his hip. A fly crawls over his staring eye. A child sobs out loud to see the horrific sight.

"Come," she says sternly, herding them on: about forty children of varying ages and not more than a dozen adults, pregnant women, elders, and Agda and Pur, both of whom would have preferred to stay and fight but whose knowledge—of herbs and midwifery and of stoneknapping—is too valuable to lose.

They follow the detritus of the fight along the path that leads to the tumulus. There lies Urtan, abdomen sliced open. A blow crushed Tosti's head. Beor's sister, Etora, looks as if she were trampled by horses and expired at last after trying to drag herself back to the village. Many Cursed Ones lie dead, too, but of the injured they find no sign.

A shout reaches them. Folk pour out from behind the earthworks that guard the tumulus. Battered, bloody, limping, exhausted, they remain triumphant despite the destruction littering the ground around them and the death on every side. But Weiwara has no heart for rejoicing. She weeps when she sees her dear husband. He can't walk, but the wound that cut through the flesh of his right thigh to reveal bone looks clean and might heal well enough. Little Useti flings herself on her father, bawling, and after Weiwara has spoken with Ulfrega of Four Houses, she climbs grimly on up through the maze of earthworks.

At the top, she passes the remains of a burned shelter, mostly ash and the bones of branches now, and heads toward the small group huddled outside the stone circle: the five surviving Horse people, already outfitted for travel, and one sobbing young man.

The sight of the blasted, fallen stones stuns her. The bronze cauldron lies in a misshapen lump, actually melted by the force of the spell. She thought nothing could hurt as much as the sight of the devastated village and the bodies of her friends and kinsfolk, but one thing hurts more. Adica sprawls on the ground, arms flung out, antler headdress thrown askew. No mark mars her body, except of course for the old burn scar on her cheek. She looks so young.

The twins stir. Wrinkled-old-man, the younger, makes a fist to pound on his mother's back. Blue-bud, the little girl whose life Alain brought back from the path leading to the Other Side, wails as she wakes. She is often fussy, the kind of baby who flinches at bright light yet sobs if she wakes in the dark of night. The young man kneeling a stone's throw from Adica's body glances up at the sound.

"Mother Weiwara!" Kel has dug something out of the ground and now he leaps up to show her folded garments, a belt, knife, and pouch, and a heap of rusting metal rings. "These must be the garments that Alain brought with him when he came to us from the land of the dead. But he is gone, and so are his spirit guides. Even the staff I carved him is missing." He breaks down again, weeping helplessly. Though streaked with dried blood, he took no wound in the battle. None, that is, except the wound of grief.

The gray centaur paces forward, grave but determined. She limps on three legs, making her walk awkward. Dried blood coats her flanks. After a polite courtesy, she speaks, but the words, such as they are and intermixed with throaty whickering, mean nothing to Weiwara.

The wind changes, blowing suddenly out of the east. An owl skims down and settles on one of the stones, a bad omen in daylight. Mist spins upward from the ground within the broken stone circle. Kel gasps aloud. The twins quiet. Weiwara drops to her knees as she sees a majestic figure pacing forward, half veiled by the swirling mist. She covers her eyes.

"Holy One. Forgive me."

"Do not fear, Niece. You have given no offense. I have come for the infant, the elder twin."

"The baby?" After so much sorrow, can she accept more?

The Holy One's voice is as melodious as that of a stream heard far off, touched with the waters of melancholy. "We will raise her among our people. We will teach her, and her children, and her children's children, the secrets of our magic. This bond between your people and my people will live for as long as she has descendants, for it is in this way that I can honor Adica, who was dear to me."

Even as her mother's heart freezes within, knowing that she cannot say "no" to the Holy One, knowing that she cannot bear to say "yes," a cold whisper teases her ear. One infant will be easier to cope with than two. In such a time of desperation, with winter coming on and their food stores likely burned, feeding twins will be a terrible hardship, and there is Useti to consider as well, weaned early to make room for the younger ones. Blue-bud was never hers anyway, not really. She belonged to the spirits from the beginning.

But her lips refuse to form the words of acceptance. She has loved and succored the child for many months now. "What of my people, Holy One? We have no Hallowed One to watch over us any longer."

"Are not twins favored in the eyes of the power you call the Fat One? Let the younger twin be marked out to follow the hallowing path. I will see to his training myself, here in your own land, and when he is grown he will stand as Hallowed One to all the Deer people."

Mist twines around the stones. A cold wind rises out of the north, making her shudder. Winter is coming, and they will all struggle to survive among the ruins. The spell the Hallowed Ones wove rid the world of the Cursed Ones, so it seems, but she has only to look out over the scorched forest to see that it touched every soul here on Earth with its awful power.

The Holy One continues, as if she understands Weiwara's hesitation. "My cousins will bring the infant girl to me. They will suckle her as they would their own child. She will be safe and well cared for with them, as if she has five mothers and not just one. We treasure each of our daughters, here among the Horse people. You need have no fear that yours will suffer any neglect. Have you a name that is meant to be hers when she is older?"

"Kerayi," Weiwara whispers, not even knowing she meant to say those words, almost as if another voice speaks through her lips.

Sos'ka moves forward, holding out her arms. Strange, now that she thinks about it, that all the centaurs she has ever seen are female.

Better to be done with it quickly. Weiwara lifts the tiny girl out of the sling, kisses her gently, and hands her up to Sos'ka. The infant shrieks outrage, but another centaur moves forward and, with a deft swoop, places the screaming infant at a breast. After a moment, the baby gets hold of the nipple and suckles contentedly.

The mist fades as the centaur women make silent gestures of farewell and move away. Better that the parting be swift. The sling sags, *empty, against her chest. Her breasts ache as her milk lets down, and Wrinkled-old-man begins to hiccup little sobs, catching her mood. Sun streaks the blasted tops of tumbled stones.*

"What about Alain?" cries Kel.

Too late. The sun drives the last of the mist from among the stones. The Holy One has gone, and the owl no longer perches in those vanished shadows.

"I saw her!" Kel momentarily forgets his grief as he staggers forward into the stones. "I saw her!" His head bows, and his shoulders shake. "But they'll never know. Tosti, and Uncle, and Alain, they'll never know."

As soon as she feels strong enough and after she has nursed the baby, Weiwara leads Kel back down to where the ragged band of survivors waits. Most of the other White Deer people make ready to leave, wanting to return to their own villages to see how they have weathered the storm. As Weiwara surveys the destruction, she thinks maybe her people should leave, too. Ghosts and spirits swarm this place now. She can almost see them. Now and again she glimpses out of the corner of her eye the shades of the Cursed Ones, weeping and shouting curses because they are trapped forever on the road to the Other Side, neither dead nor living.

But the ancient queens have not done yet. Arrow Bright, Golden Sow, and Toothless have not forgotten the bonds that link them to their people. As the last echoes of the vast spell tremble in the earth, they grasp the fading threads and on those threads, as with a voice, they whisper.

When Weiwara and Agda carry Adica's body on a litter into the silence of the ancient tomb, the queens whisper into her ears. Weiwara arranges the corpse as Agda holds the torch. She lovingly braids Adica's beautiful hair a final time. She fixes the golden antlers to her brow and straightens her clothing, places her lax hands on her abdomen. The lapis lazuli ring that Alain gave her winks softly under torchlight. She stows next to Adica the things Alain brought with him but left behind. In this way a part of him will still attend Adica in death. Last, she places at her feet a bark bucket of beer brewed with honey, wheat, and cranberries.

"Let me share this last drink with you, beloved friend." She dips a hand in the mead and drinks that handful down. As the sharp beer tickles her throat, it seems to her that the ancient queens stir in their silent tombs.

"Do not abandon us, Daughter. Do not abandon the ones who made you strong and gave you life. Do not leave your beloved friend to sleep alone. That was all she asked, that she not be left to die alone."

*Weeping—will she always be weeping?—*Weiwara says the prayers over the dead as Agda sings the correct responses. Afterward, with some relief, she and Agda retreat into the light. At the threshold of the queens' grave, they purify themselves with lavender rubbed over their skin before they return to the gathered villagers, those who remain.

"What shall we do, Mother Weiwara?" they ask her. *"Where shall we go?"*

Kel comes running. She sent him back to the village, and with great excitement he announces that eight of the ten pits where they store grain against winter hardship have survived the conflagration.

"This is our home," says Weiwara, *"nor would I gladly leave the ancient queens, and my beloved friend, who gave us life. Let us stay here and build again."*

Arrow Bright, seeing that all transpires as she wished, withdraws her hands from the world. *"Come, Sister,"* she says to Adica's spirit, which is still confused and mourning. *"Here is the path leading to the Other Side, where the meadow flowers always bloom. Walk with me."*

Their memories fade.

In time, as the dead sleep and the living pass their lives on to their children and grandchildren down the generations, they, too, are forgotten.

Ivar hit the ground so hard that his knees cracked. His arms gave out, and his face and chest slammed into the dirt.

He lay stunned in darkness while the incomprehensible dream he'd been having faded away into confusion. Dirt had gotten into his mouth, coating his lips. Grit stung on his tongue. His ear hurt, the lobe bent back, but he couldn't move his head to relieve the pressure.

As he lay there, trying to remember how to move, he heard a man speaking, but he didn't recognize the voice.

"I was walking down a road, and I was weeping, for I knew it was the road that leads to the other world, and do you know, Uncle, more even than my dear mother I really did miss my Fridesuenda for you know we're to be married at midwinter. But I saw a man. He came walking along the road with a black hound on either side. He was dressed exactly like a Lion but with a terrible stain of blood on his tabard. He reached out to me, and then I knew he couldn't have been any Lion, for he wore a veil of light over his face and a crown of stars. I swear to you he looked exactly like that new Lion, the one what was once a lord, who's in Thiadbold's company."

Gerulf chuckled. "I recall that one well enough, Dedi." It took Ivar a moment to identify the liquid tone in the old Lion's voice: he was crying as he spoke. "He shamed you into returning that tunic to the lad who lost it dicing with you."

"Nay, Uncle, he never shamed me. He just told me the story of Folquin's aunt and how she wove it special for her nephew when he went away to the Lions. Then he and his comrades offered to work off the winnings by doing my chores for me. It seemed mean-hearted to say 'nay' to them."

"Ach, lad," said Gerulf on a shuddering breath. "Lay you still, now. I promised your mother I'd bring you home safely, and so I will. I've got to get light here and see what happened to the others."

Ivar grunted and got his arms to work, pushed up to his hands and knees just as he heard other voices whispering in alarm, many voices breaking into speech at once. "Quiet, I pray you," he said hoarsely. "Speak, one at a time, so that we know we're all here."

"I'm here," said Gerulf, "and so is my nephew Dedi—"

"I can speak for myself, Uncle."

"Is that you, Ivar?" asked Sigfrid. "I can't hear very well. My ears are ringing. I had the strangest vision. I saw an angel—"

"It's the nail he took from Tallia," said Hathumod, still weeping. "How did it come to be here?"

"Hush, Hathumod," said Ermanrich. "Best to be quiet so that we don't wake anything else. I had a nightmare! I was being chased by monsters, with human bodies but animal faces. . . ." He trailed off as, abruptly, everyone waited for the seventh voice.

In the silence, Ivar heard water dripping. "Baldwin?" he whispered. Again, in a louder voice: "Baldwin?" His heart pounded furiously with fear. Ghosts always wanted blood and living breath on which to feed, and Baldwin was the one who had disturbed the skeleton.

"Ivar!" The voice echoed eerily down unknown corridors, but even the distortion could not muffle that tone of triumph. "Come see this!"

Ivar swore under his breath.

Ermanrich gave a hiccuping laugh, blended out of relief and fear. "When we've eyes as pretty as yours, maybe we can see in the dark, too. Where are you?"

As out of nowhere they saw a gleam of pale golden light. Baldwin's head appeared, the soft light painting his features to an uncanny perfection. He smiled as his shoulders emerged, then his torso. It took a moment for Ivar, still on hands and knees and with his head twisted to one side, to realize that Baldwin was walking up stairs.

"You must come see!" Baldwin exclaimed as his cupped hands came into view. A ring adorned with a blue stone winked on one forefinger. He carried a bauble, all filigreed with cunning lacework and studded with pearls. The gold itself shone with a soft light, illuminating the walls of the chamber.

They were no longer in the same place. The stone slab and its ancient burial were gone. The dim alcoves built into the tomb had vanished, replaced by a smooth-walled, empty chamber carved out of rock. Ivar scrambled to his feet, wincing at the pain in his knees. He stared at the walls surrounding them, unmarked by the strange sigils that had decorated the walls of the tomb where they had taken refuge from the Quman army.

"Come see," said Baldwin without stepping fully out of the stairwell. "You can't believe it!" He began to descend.

Because he held the only light, they hastened to follow him. Sigfrid took Hathumod's hand, and Ermanrich walked after them as Gerulf helped his nephew to his feet. Ivar groped around and found the torch Gerulf had been holding before the blue fire had snuffed it out. With the light receding quickly, he scrambled to the opening and descended. Fear gripped his heart, making him breathe in ragged gasps. Had Baldwin been possessed by the spirits of the dead? Or had he stumbled upon an enchantment? Where were they?

Ai, God, his knees hurt.

Twenty steps took him, blinking, into a chamber no larger than the one he had come from but so utterly different that, like his companions, he could only gaze in wonder.

They had found a treasure cave heaped with gold and jewels and all manner of precious chests and bundles of finest linen and silk cloth. Strangest of all, the chamber's guardians lay asleep, seven young men dressed in the garb of a young lord and his attendants. They slept on heaps of coins with the restful comfort of folk sleeping on the softest of featherbeds. The young lord, marked out from his attendants by the exceptional richness of his clothing, lay half curled on his side, with one cheek resting on a palm. His eyes were closed, his lips slightly parted. His fair hair set off a complexion pink with health. A half smile trembled on his lips, as though he were having sweet dreams.

"Seven sleepers!" exclaimed Sigfrid in a hushed voice. "The church mothers wrote of them. Can it be that we've stumbled across their hiding place?"

"I can count!" retorted Baldwin indignantly.

"Didn't we read about the Seven Sleepers in Eusebē's *Church History*?" Ermanrich asked.

"Lord preserve us," swore Gerulf. "That's Margrave Villam's lad, his youngest son, the one called Berthold. I remember the day he disappeared. Lady bless us, but I swear that was two years or more ago." Fearful, but determined, he crossed to the young lord and knelt beside him. But for all his shaking and coaxing, he could not wake him, nor could any of the sleeping attendants be woken despite their best efforts to break the spell of sleep.

"It's sorcery," said Gerulf finally. He gave up last of all, long after the others had fallen back to huddle nervously by the stairs, which led up through rock toward the chamber above.

The glowing bauble made the chamber seem painted with a thin gold gauze, but shadows still lay at disconcerting and troubling angles, swathes of darkness untouched by light. "I think we should get out of here," said Ivar unsteadily.

"What about the Quman?" asked Baldwin. "I can't run from them anymore." He knelt and scooped up a handful of gold coins, letting them trickle through his fingers.

Shadows moved along the floor of the chamber like vines caught in wind, twining and seeking.

"Baldwin!" said Ivar sharply as a thread of shadow snaked out from the treasure and curled up Baldwin's leg. "Move back from there!"

Baldwin yawned. "I'm so tired."

Ivar darted forward, got hold of Baldwin's wrist, and shook him, hard, until all the gold scattered onto the floor. "Don't pick up anything!" The bauble rolled out of Baldwin's hand and spun over the floor, coming to rest with a clink against a chest of jewels. Shadows writhed at its passage.

"Don't take anything from here," said Ivar harshly, turning to stare at the others. The light from the bauble began to wane. "It's all enchanted. It's all sorcery! I've seen sorcery at work." The old hatred and jealousy rose up like a floodtide in his heart. He seemed to see Hugh leering at him from the shadows that massed beyond the treasure, and within the heart of those shadows he sensed a sullen enmity, whispering lies in his heart: *Hanna is dead. Liath hates you.* "Let's go!" He tugged Baldwin mercilessly backward and pushed him toward the opening made by the stairs.

Gerulf got a spark from his flint, but it died on the blackened torch stub. A second spark spit and caught, and the torch flared to smoky life. They scrambled up the stairs with Gerulf right behind Baldwin and Ivar at the rear. Cold tendrils washed his back, but they let him go. The pure gold light behind him gleamed with greed and ancient anger.

He stumbled over the last step into the cool, empty chamber where the others waited for him.

"There's another tunnel here," said Baldwin, who had gone ahead.

There was nowhere else to go, but quickly they discovered they had fallen into a maze. This was no simple burial tumulus, with a single straight tunnel leading to the central womb where ancient queens and princes had been laid to rest in the long-ago days, but rather a labyrinth of corridors, some low, others so high that Ivar couldn't touch the ceiling. All wound back on themselves and crossed in a bewildering pattern made more confusing when Sigfrid thought to leave a mark at each intersection so they'd know when they'd doubled back. They discovered quickly enough that they were walking in a complicated circle.

Finally, exasperated, Baldwin grabbed the torch out of Gerulf's hand. "This way!" he said with the certainty of one whose beauty has always gotten him the best portion of meat and the most flavorful wine.

Taking this turn and that without any obvious pattern, they found themselves smelling air and light and feeling a tickle of breeze on their faces. The torch flame shuddered and licked out, leaving a wisp of smoke. The tunnel sloped upward, but the ceiling lowered until they were forced to crawl, and now Ivar felt dirt under his hands, twining roots and, once, a moist crawling thing.

Baldwin, at the fore, shouted. Ivar heard the others in reply, and then it was his turn to tumble free through thick bushes and roll, blinking, into hard sunlight. He clapped his hands over his eyes, only to remember that he'd lost two of his fingers. Yet the wound no longer hurt. White scar tissue sealed the lowest knuckles where the fingers had been shorn off right at the hand, as though it had been a year or two since the wound was taken. After a while he dared lower his hands from over his eyes to discover that it was a cloudy day, although it seemed as bright as sin to eyes so long drowned in darkness. He laughed weakly into the grass.

Baldwin came and lay down beside him. "Are you all right?" he demanded in a low voice.

"How did you know the way?" Everything still seemed too bright to see, so he kept his eyes under a tent made by his hands.

"I don't know. I just wanted to get out of there."

Lying there in tall grass, swept by breeze and taking in heady lungfuls of air, Ivar had a revelation: Everything Baldwin had done, from running away to the monastery to running away from Margrave Judith, all of which had seemed so purposeful and clever and forcefully planned, had actually bubbled up out of a similar thoughtless impulse. Just to get away. It was only luck that Baldwin had succeeded when he had. Truly, God had granted him beauty and luck, but he had been filled so full of those that evidently there hadn't been room for much else.

"It's all right, Baldwin," said Ivar wearily, sitting up. His whole body ached, and he blinked away tears as he lowered his hands for his first good look at their surroundings. "I don't know how, but I think we escaped the Quman."

The clouds had the soft gleam of pearls, more light than gray. The seven companions sat scattered in an utterly unfamiliar clearing marked by a stone circle and four large overgrown mounds, ringed by tall trees of a kind that did not grow in the eastern borderlands, where grasslands lapped a thinning forest. The leaves had turned red, or yellow, or orange, a mottling of color across the surrounding forest. The air smelled clean, untouched by the carnage of battle, and it had the sharp clarity of late autumn. It had been late summer when they'd fought the battle at that old tumulus. Yet by the evidence of his eyes, weeks had passed instead of a single night.

There was a long silence in which he heard Baldwin breathing and, behind him, the voices of the others. Sigfrid was singing a hymn, and Lady Hathumod was alternately weeping and praying with frenzied passion while Ermanrich kept interjecting comments, trying to calm her down. Gerulf and Dedi were talking so excitedly to each other that he couldn't make out their words through the haze made by their peculiar way of pronouncing certain words. They moved out into the clearing, exclaiming over the trees and the sky. The two Lions had been so direly wounded, and he'd thought for sure that Dedi was as good as dead. How could they be charging around now as fresh as spring lambs?

"My lord Ivar!" cried Gerulf, hastening back to him. The old Lion was almost beside himself with excitement; his face shone as though light had been poured into it. "Do you know where we are?"

"As long as we're well away from the Quman, I don't care where we are." With a grunt, Ivar got to his feet, rubbing his backside.

"It's a miracle, my lord! God has delivered us from the Quman. This is the hill above Herford Monastery, in western Saony. We can see into the duchy of Fesse from here."

"Herford Monastery?" Ermanrich came forward. "That's impossible. We were in the marchlands—"

"It was summer!" cried Hathumod raggedly. "And *he* still walked among us."

"All of our wounds are healed," added Sigfrid diffidently, sliding up beside Ivar to examine his mutilated hand. "Look at your hand, Ivar. It looks as if you took that wound months or years ago."

"I'm thirsty," said Baldwin. "Haven't we anything to drink?"

"Hush." Ivar surveyed his six companions and then the clearing in which they stood. The low earthen mounds and the stone circle reminded him vaguely of the great tumulus with its embankments. Hadn't there been a ruined stone circle at the top of that ancient hill? Yet obviously they no longer stood there. For one thing, Ivar had never before seen a stone circle in as perfect repair as this one was, each stone upright and all the lintels intact. Somehow, in the space of one night, they had traveled from the marchlands all the way to the center of Wendar. In the space of one night, they had traveled from summer into autumn.

Sorcery.

Shivering, he grabbed hold of Sigfrid's hand and then Baldwin's. "Come, friends," he said, seeing that they had all clasped hands, clinging together in the face of so many things they could not explain. "Truly, I don't understand what has happened to us except that our friend Gerulf must be right. God has saved us from death at the hands of the Quman, so that we can continue to do Her work here on Earth. Don't forget the phoenix. Our task is just beginning."

Hathumod burst into tears again, clutching the rusted nail to her chest as if were a holy relic.

"God be praised," murmured Gerulf, and the others echoed his words, all except Baldwin, who was looking anxiously around the clearing.

"It's going to be night soon," said Baldwin, "and I don't like to think of sleeping out next to these old grave mounds. I don't like to think what might crawl out of them once night falls."

"Nay, I don't fancy sleeping near these old mounds either," said Dedi with a nervous laugh, and they all laughed, swept up with relief and the release of all those hours of fear and struggle.

"Is there a path that will lead us to the monastery, Gerulf?" Ivar asked, because he'd had the same thought. Yet shouldn't he trust in God to protect them from evil spirits and blood-sucking wights, given the miracle that had already happened? Still, it never hurt to help God's design along when you could.

"It's been a few years," said the old Lion, scratching his beard, "but I think . . ." He pointed toward a narrow gap in the dense wall of trees. "I think that's the path over there."

They all stood there, then, waiting, looking at Ivar. Somehow, over the course of the battle and through that long and bitter night trapped underground, he had become their leader.

"We've got a long road ahead of us," he said. "Come on."

Orbit titles available by post:

☐ A Cavern of Black Ice	J.V. Jones	£7.99
☐ A Shadow on the Glass	Ian Irvine	£6.99
☐ Shadow	K.J. Parker	£10.99
☐ Knight's Dawn	Kim Hunter	£9.99
☐ Transformation	Carol Berg	£9.99
☐ The One Kingdom	Sean Russell	£10.00

The prices shown above are correct at time of going to press. However, the publishers reserve the right to increase prices on covers from those previously advertised, without further notice.

orbit

ORBIT BOOKS
Cash Sales Department, P.O. Box 11, Falmouth, Cornwall, TR10 9EN
Tel: +44 (0) 1326 569777, Fax: +44 (0) 1326 569555
Email: books@barni.avel.co.uk

POST AND PACKING:
Payments can be made as follows: cheque, postal order (payable to Orbit Books) or by credit cards. Do not send cash or currency.

U.K. Orders under £10	£1.50
U.K. Orders over £10	**FREE OF CHARGE**
E.C. & Overseas	25% of order value

Name (Block letters) . . . .

Address . . . .

. . . .

Post/zip code: . . . .

☐ Please keep me in touch with future Orbit publications

☐ I enclose my remittance £ . . . .

☐ I wish to pay by Visa/Access/Mastercard/Eurocard

Card Expiry Date
